D0498425

# Lady Midnight

# Also by Cassandra Clare

## THE MORTAL INSTRUMENTS

*City of Bones*

*City of Ashes*

*City of Glass*

*City of Fallen Angels*

*City of Lost Souls*

*City of Heavenly Fire*

## THE INFERNAL DEVICES

*Clockwork Angel*

*Clockwork Prince*

*Clockwork Princess*

*The Shadowhunter's Codex*

With Joshua Lewis

*The Bane Chronicles*

With Sarah Rees Brennan

and Maureen Johnson

# Lady Midnight

## CASSANDRA CLARE

### THE DARK ARTIFICES

BOOK ONE

Margaret K. McElderry Books

NEW YORK LONDON TORONTO SYDNEY NEW DELHI

MARGARET K. McELDERRY BOOKS
An imprint of Simon & Schuster Children's Publishing Division
1230 Avenue of the Americas, New York, New York 10020
This book is a work of fiction. Any references to historical events, real people,
or real places are used fictitiously. Other names, characters, places, and events
are products of the author's imagination, and any resemblance to actual
events or places or persons, living or dead, is entirely coincidental.
Text copyright © 2016 by Cassandra Claire, LLC
Jacket photo-illustration copyright © 2016 by Cliff Nielsen
All rights reserved, including the right of reproduction in whole or in part in any form.
MARGARET K. McELDERRY BOOKS is a trademark of Simon & Schuster, Inc.
For information about special discounts for bulk purchases, please contact Simon & Schuster
Special Sales at 1-866-506-1949 or business@simonandschuster.com.
The Simon & Schuster Speakers Bureau can bring authors to your live event.
For more information or to book an event, contact the Simon & Schuster Speakers
Bureau at 1-866-248-3049 or visit our website at www.simonspeakers.com.
Jacket design by Russell Gordon
Interior design by Mike Rosamilia
The text for this book was set in Dolly.
Manufactured in the United States of America
First Edition
2 4 6 8 10 9 7 5 3 1
Cataloging-in-Publication data for this book is available from the Library of Congress.
ISBN 978-1-4424-6835-1 (hc)
ISBN 978-1-4424-6837-5 (eBook)
ISBN 978-1-4814-7889-2 (Indigo proprietary hc)

For Holly
Elven, he was

# PROLOGUE

Los Angeles, 2012

**Shadow Market nights were Kit's favorite.**

They were the nights he was allowed to leave the house and help his father at the booth. He'd been coming to the Shadow Market since he was seven years old. Eight years later he still felt the same sense of shock and wonder when he walked down Kendall Alley through Old Town Pasadena toward a blank brick wall—and stepped through it into an explosive world of color and light.

Only a few blocks away were Apple Stores selling gadgets and laptops, Cheesecake Factories and organic food markets, American Apparel shops and trendy boutiques. But here the alley opened out into a massive square, warded on each side to prevent the careless from wandering into the Shadow Market.

The Los Angeles Shadow Market came out when the night was warm, and it both existed and didn't exist. Kit knew that when he stepped in among the lines of brightly decorated stalls, he was walking in a space that would vanish when the sun rose in the morning.

But for the time he was there, he enjoyed it. It was one thing to have the Gift when no one else around you had it. The Gift was what his father called it, although Kit didn't think it was much of one. Hyacinth, the lavender-haired fortune-teller in the booth at the market's edge, called it the Sight.

That name made more sense to Kit. After all, the only thing that separated him from ordinary kids was that he could *see* things they couldn't. Harmless things sometimes, pixies rising from dry grass along the cracked sidewalks, the pale faces of vampires in gas stations late at night, a man clicking his fingers against a diner counter; when Kit looked again, he saw the fingers were werewolf claws. It had been happening to him since he was a little kid, and his dad had it too. The Sight ran in families.

Resisting the urge to react was the hardest. Walking home from school one afternoon he'd seen a pack of werewolves tearing each other apart in a deserted playground. He'd stood on the pavement and screamed until the police came, but there was nothing for them to see. After that his father kept him at home, mostly, letting him teach himself out of old books. He played video games in the basement and went out rarely, during the day, or when the Shadow Market was on.

At the Market he didn't have to worry about reacting to anything. The Market was colorful and bizarre even to its inhabitants. There were ifrits holding performing djinn on leashes, and beautiful peri girls dancing in front of booths that sold glittering, dangerous powders. A banshee manned a stall that promised to tell you when you'd die, though Kit couldn't imagine why anyone would want to know that. A cluricaun offered to find lost things, and a young witch with short, bright-green hair sold enchanted bracelets and pendants to catch romantic attention. When Kit looked over at her, she smiled.

"Hey, Romeo." Kit's father elbowed him in the ribs. "I didn't bring you here to flirt. Help put the sign up."

He kicked their bent metal footstool over to Kit and handed

him a slab of wood onto which he had burned his stall's name: JOHNNY ROOK'S.

Not the most creative title, but Kit's father had never been over-burdened with imagination. Which was strange, Kit thought as he clambered up to hang the sign, for someone whose clientele list included warlocks, werewolves, vampires, sprites, wights, ghouls, and once, a mermaid. (They'd met in secret at SeaWorld.)

Still, maybe a simple sign was the best. Kit's dad sold some potions and powders—even, under the table, some questionably legal weaponry—but none of that was what brought people to his booth. The fact was that Johnny Rook was a guy who knew things. There was nothing that happened in L.A.'s Downworld that he wasn't aware of, no one so powerful that he didn't know a secret about them or a way to get in touch with them. He was a guy who had information, and if you had the money, he'd tell it to you.

Kit jumped down off the footstool and his dad handed him two fifty-dollar bills. "Get change off someone," he said, not look-ing at Kit. He'd pulled his red ledger out from under the counter and was looking through it, probably trying to figure out who owed him money. "That's the smallest I've got."

Kit nodded and ducked out of the booth, glad to get away. Any errand was an excuse to wander. He passed a stand laden with white flowers that gave off a dark, sweet, poisonous aroma, and another where a group of people in expensive suits were passing out pamphlets in front of a sign that said PART SUPERNATURAL? YOU'RE NOT ALONE. THE FOLLOWERS OF THE GUARDIAN WANT YOU TO SIGN UP FOR THE LOTTERY OF FAVOR! LET LUCK INTO YOUR LIFE!

A red-lipped, dark-haired woman tried to thrust a pamphlet into his hands. When Kit didn't take it, she cast a sultry glance past him, toward Johnny, who grinned. Kit rolled his eyes—there were a million little cults that sprang up around worshipping some minor demon or angel. Nothing ever seemed to come of them.

Tracking down one of his favorite stands, Kit bought a cup of red-dyed shaved ice that tasted like passion fruit and raspberries and cream all mashed up together. He tried to be careful who he bought from—there were candies and drinks at the Market that could wreck your whole life—but no one was going to take any risks with Johnny Rook's son. Johnny Rook knew something about everyone. Cross him and you were liable to find your secrets weren't secret anymore.

Kit circled back around to the witch with the charmed jewelry. She didn't have a stall; she was, as usual, sitting on a printed sarong, the kind of cheap, bright cloth you could buy on Venice Beach. She looked up as he drew closer.

"Hey, Wren," he said. He doubted it was her real name, but it was what everyone at the Market called her.

"Hey, pretty boy." She moved aside to make room for him, her bracelets and anklets jingling. "What brings you to my humble abode?"

He slid down beside her on the ground. His jeans were worn, holes in the knees. He wished he could keep the cash his father had given him to buy himself a few new clothes. "Dad needed me to break two fifties."

"Shh." She waved a hand at him. "There are people here who'd cut your throat for two fifties and sell your blood as dragon fire."

"Not me," Kit said confidently. "No one here would touch me." He leaned back. "Unless I wanted them to."

"And here I thought I was all out of shameless flirting charms."

"I *am* your shameless flirting charm." He smiled at two people walking by: a tall, good-looking boy with a streak of white in his dark hair and a brunette girl whose eyes were shaded by sunglasses. They ignored him. But Wren perked up at the sight of the two Market-goers behind them: a burly man and a woman with brown hair hanging in a rope down her back.

"Protection charms?" Wren said winningly. "Guaranteed to keep you safe. I've got gold and brass too, not just silver."

The woman bought a ring with a moonstone in it and moved on, chattering to her partner. "How'd you know they were were-wolves?" Kit asked.

"The look in her eye," said Wren. "Werewolves are impulse buy-ers. And their glances skip right over anything silver." She sighed. "I'm doing a bang-up business in protection charms since those murders started up."

"What murders?"

Wren made a face. "Some kind of crazy magic thing. Dead bod-ies turning up all covered in demon languages. Burned, drowned, hands chopped off—all sorts of rumors. How have you *not* heard about it? Don't you pay attention to gossip?"

"No," Kit said. "Not really." He was watching the werewolf couple as they made their way toward the north end of the Market, where the lycanthropes tended to gather to buy whatever it was they needed—tableware made out of wood and iron, wolfsbane, tear-away pants (he hoped).

Even though the Market was meant to be a place where Downworlders mingled, they tended to group together by type. There was the area where vampires gathered to buy flavored blood or seek out new subjugates from among those who'd lost their masters. There were the vine-and-flower pavilions where faeries drifted, trading charms and whispering fortunes. They kept back from the rest of the Market, forbidden to do business like the others. Warlocks, rare and feared, occupied stalls at the very end of the Market. Every warlock bore a mark proclaiming their demonic heritage: some had tails, some wings or curling horns. Kit had once glimpsed a warlock woman who had been entirely blue-skinned, like a fish.

Then there were those with the Sight, like Kit and his father, ordinary folk gifted with the ability to see the Shadow World, to pierce through glamours. Wren was one of them: a self-taught witch who'd paid a warlock for a course of training in basic spells, but she kept a low profile. Humans weren't supposed to practice magic, but there was a thriving underground trade in teaching it. You could make good money, provided you weren't caught by the—

"Shadowhunters," Wren said.

"How did you know I was thinking about them?"

"Because they're right over there. Two of them." She jerked her chin to the right, her eyes bright with alarm.

In fact the whole Market was tensing up, people moving to casually slide their bottles and boxes of poisons and potions and death's-head charms out of sight. Leashed djinn crept behind their masters. The peris had stopped dancing and were watching the Shadowhunters, their pretty faces gone cold and hard.

There were two of them, a boy and a girl, probably seventeen or eighteen. The boy was red-haired, tall, and athletic-looking; Kit couldn't see the girl's face, just masses of blond hair, cascading to her waist. She wore a golden sword strapped across her back and walked with the kind of confidence you couldn't fake.

They both wore gear, the tough black protective clothing that marked them out as Nephilim: part-human, part-angel, the uncontested rulers over every supernatural creature on earth. They had Institutes—like massive police stations—in nearly every big city on the planet, from Rio to Baghdad to Lahore to Los Angeles. Most Shadowhunters were born what they were, but they could make humans into Shadowhunters too if they felt like it. They'd been desperate to fill out their ranks since they'd lost so many lives in the Dark War. The word was they'd kidnap anyone under nineteen who showed any sign of being decent potential Shadowhunter material.

Anyone, in other words, who had the Sight.

"They're heading to your dad's booth," Wren whispered. She

was right. Kit tensed as he saw them turn down the row of stalls and head unerringly toward the sign that read JOHNNY ROOK'S.

"Get up." Wren was on her feet, shooing Kit into a standing position. She leaned down to fold up her merch inside the cloth they'd been sitting on. Kit noticed an odd drawing on the back of her hand, a symbol like lines of water running underneath a flame. Maybe she'd been doodling on herself. "I've got to go."

"Because of the Shadowhunters?" he said in surprise, standing back to allow her to pack up.

"Shh." She hurried away, her colorful hair bouncing.

"Weird," Kit muttered, and headed back toward his dad's booth. He approached from the side, head down, hands in his pockets. He was pretty sure his dad would yell at him if he presented himself in front of the Shadowhunters—especially considering the rumors that they were press-ganging every mundane with the Sight under nineteen—but he couldn't help but want to eavesdrop.

The blond girl was leaning forward, elbows on the wooden counter. "Good to see you, Rook," she said with a winning smile.

She was pretty, Kit thought. Older than he was, and the boy she was with towered over him. And she was a Shadowhunter. So she was undateably pretty, but pretty nonetheless. Her arms were bare, and a long, pale scar ran from one elbow to her wrist. Black tattoos in the shapes of strange symbols twined up and down them, patterning her skin. One peeked from the V of her shirt. They were runes, the sorcerous Marks that gave the Shadowhunters their power. Only Shadowhunters could wear them. If you drew them on a normal person's skin, or a Downworlder's, they would go insane.

"And who's this?" Johnny Rook asked, jerking his chin toward the Shadowhunter boy. "The famous *parabatai*?"

Kit looked at the pair with renewed interest. Everyone who knew about Nephilim knew what *parabatai* were. Two Shadowhunters who swore to be platonically loyal to each other forever, always to fight by each other's sides. To live and die for each other. Jace Herondale and Clary Fairchild, the most famous Shadowhunters in the world, each had a *parabatai*. Even Kit knew that much.

"No," the girl drawled, picking up a jar of greenish liquid from a stack by the cash register. It was meant to be a love potion, though Kit knew that several of the jars held water that had been dyed with food coloring. "This isn't really Julian's kind of place." Her gaze flicked around the Market.

"I'm Cameron Ashdown." The redheaded Shadowhunter stuck out a hand and Johnny, looking bemused, shook it. Kit took the opportunity to edge behind the counter. "I'm Emma's *boyfriend*."

The blond girl—Emma—winced, barely perceptibly. Cameron Ashdown might be her boyfriend now, Kit thought, but he wouldn't lay bets on him staying that way.

"Huh," said Johnny, taking the jar out of Emma's hand. "So I assume you're here to pick up what you left." He fished what looked like a scrap of red cloth out of his pocket. Kit stared. What could possibly be interesting about a square of cotton?

Emma straightened up. She looked eager now. "Did you find out anything?"

"If you dropped it in a washing machine with a load of whites, it would definitely turn your socks pink."

Emma took the cloth back with a frown. "I'm serious. You don't know how many people I had to bribe to get this. It was in the Spiral Labyrinth. It's a piece of the shirt my mom was wearing when she was killed."

Johnny held up a hand. "I know. I was just—"

"Don't be sarcastic. *My* job is being sarcastic and quippy. Your job is getting shaken down for information."

"Or paid," said Cameron Ashdown. "Being paid for information is also fine."

"Look, I can't help you," said Kit's father. "There's no magic here.

It's just some cotton. Shredded up and full of seawater, but—cotton."

The look of disappointment that passed over the girl's face was vivid and unmistakable. She made no attempt to hide it, just tucked the cloth into her pocket. Kit couldn't help feeling a jolt of sympathy, which surprised him—he never thought he'd be sympathetic to a Shadowhunter.

Emma looked over at him, almost as if he'd spoken. "So," she said, and suddenly there was a glint in her eyes. "You've got the Sight, huh, like your dad? How old are you?"

Kit froze. His dad moved in front of him quickly, blocking him from Emma's view. "Now here I thought you were going to ask me about the murders that have been happening. Behind on your information, Carstairs?"

Apparently Wren had been right, Kit thought—everyone *did* know about these murders. He could tell by the warning note in his father's voice that he should make himself scarce, but he was trapped behind the counter with no escape route.

"I heard some rumors about dead mundanes," Emma said. Most Shadowhunters used the term for normal human beings with intense contempt. Emma just sounded tired. "We don't investigate mundanes killing each other. That's for the police."

"There were dead faeries," said Johnny. "Several of the bodies were fey."

"We *can't* investigate those," said Cameron. "You know that. The Cold Peace forbids it."

Kit heard a faint murmur from nearby booths: a noise that let him know he wasn't the only one eavesdropping.

The Cold Peace was Shadowhunter Law. It had come into being almost five years ago. He barely remembered a time before it. They called it a Law, at least. What it really was, was a punishment.

When Kit was ten years old, a war had rocked the universe of Downworlders and Shadowhunters. A Shadowhunter, Sebastian

Morgenstern, had turned against his own kind: He had gone from Institute to Institute, destroying their occupants, controlling their bodies, and forcing them to fight for him as an unspeakable army of mind-controlled slaves. Most of the Shadowhunters in the Los Angeles Institute had been taken or killed.

Kit had had nightmares about it sometimes, of blood running through hallways he'd never seen, hallways painted with the runes of the Nephilim.

Sebastian had been helped by the Fair Folk in his attempt to destroy the Shadowhunters. Kit had learned about fairies in school: cute little creatures that lived in trees and wore flower hats. The Fair Folk were nothing like that. They ranged from mermaids and goblins and shark-toothed kelpies to gentry faeries, those who held high rank in the faerie courts. Gentry faeries were tall and beautiful and terrifying. They were split into two Courts: the Seelie Court, a dangerous place ruled by a Queen no one had seen in years, and the Unseelie Court, a dark place of treachery and black magic whose King was like a monster out of legend.

Since the faeries were Downworlders, and had sworn allegiance and loyalty to the Shadowhunters, their betrayal was an unforgivable crime. The Shadowhunters had punished them viciously in a sweeping gesture that had come to be known as the Cold Peace: forcing them to pay huge sums to rebuild the Shadowhunter buildings that had been destroyed, stripping them of their armies, and instructing other Downworlders never to give them aid. The punishment for helping a faerie was severe.

Faeries were a proud, ancient, magical people, or so it was said. Kit had never known them as anything but broken. Most Downworlders and other denizens of the shadowy space between the mundane world and the Shadowhunter one didn't dislike faeries or hold much of a grudge against them. But none of them were willing to go against the Shadowhunters, either. Vampires, werewolves, and warlocks stayed away from faeries except in places like the Shadow Market, where money was more important than Laws.

"Really?" said Johnny. "What if I told you that the bodies have been found covered in writing?"

Emma's head jerked up. Her eyes were dark brown, almost black, surprising against her pale hair. "What did you say?"

"You heard me."

"What kind of writing? Is it the same language that was on my parents' bodies?"

"Don't know," said Johnny. "Just what I heard. Still, seems suspicious, doesn't it?"

"Emma," said Cameron warningly. "The Clave won't like it."

The Clave was the Shadowhunter government. In Kit's experience, they didn't like anything.

"I don't care," Emma said. She'd clearly forgotten about Kit completely; she was staring at his dad, her eyes burning. "Tell me what there is to know. I'll give you two hundred."

"Fine, but I don't know that much," said Johnny. "Someone gets grabbed, a few nights later they turn up dead."

"And the last time someone 'got grabbed'?" said Cameron.

"Two nights ago," said Johnny, clearly feeling he was earning his payoff. "Body'll probably be dumped tomorrow night. All you have to do is show up and catch the dumper."

"So why don't you tell us how to do that?" Emma said.

"Word on the street is that the next body dump will be in West Hollywood. The Sepulchre Bar."

Emma clapped her hands in excitement. Her boyfriend said her name again, warningly, but Kit could have told him he was wasting his time. He'd never seen a teenage girl this excited about anything—not famous actors, not boy bands, not jewelry. This girl was practically vibrating to pieces over the idea of a dead body.

"Why don't *you* do it, if you're so worked up about these murders?" Cameron demanded of Johnny. He had nice eyes, Kit thought. They were a ridiculously attractive couple. It was almost annoying. He wondered what the fabled Julian looked like. If he was sworn to be this girl's platonic best friend for eternity, he probably looked like the back of a bus.

"Because I don't want to," said Johnny. "Seems dangerous. But you guys love danger. Don't you, Emma?"

Emma grinned. It occurred to Kit that Johnny seemed to know Emma pretty well. Clearly she'd come around before asking questions—it was weird that this was the first time he'd seen her, but he didn't come to every Market. As she dug into her pocket now, took out a roll of bills, and handed it over to his father, he wondered if she'd ever been in his house. Whenever clients came to their home, Kit's dad made him head down to the basement and stay there, not making a sound.

"The kind of people I deal with aren't the kind of people you should meet" was all he said.

Once Kit had wandered upstairs by accident while his father was meeting with a group of robed and hooded monsters. At least Kit thought they looked like monsters: their eyes and lips were sewn shut, their heads bald and gleaming. His father had told him they were Gregori, Silent Brothers—Shadowhunters who had been scarred and magically tortured until they became something more than human; they spoke with their minds, and could read other people's. Kit had never come upstairs again while his father was having a "meeting."

Kit knew his dad was a criminal. He knew he sold secrets for a living, though not lies: Johnny prided himself on having good information. Kit knew his own life would probably follow the same pattern. It was hard to live normally when you were constantly pretending you didn't see what was going on in front of your face.

"Well, thanks for the info," Emma said, starting to turn away from the booth. The gold hilt of her sword gleamed in the light from the Market's illuminated stalls. Kit wondered what it would be like to be Nephilim. To live among people who saw the same things you did. To not ever be afraid of what lurked in the shadows. "See you around, Johnny."

She dropped a wink—at Kit. Johnny whirled around to look at him as she disappeared back into the crowd with her boyfriend.

"Did you say something to her?" Johnny demanded. "Why'd she zero in on you like that?"

Kit held his hands up defensively. "I didn't say anything," he protested. "I think she noticed me listening."

Johnny sighed. "Try to get noticed less."

The Market was starting up again now that the Shadowhunters had left. Kit could hear music and a rising bubble of chattering voices. "How well do you know that Shadowhunter girl?"

"Emma Carstairs? She's been coming to me for stuff for years. Doesn't seem to care that she's breaking Nephilim rules. I like her, as much as you can like any of them."

"She wanted you to find out who killed her parents."

Johnny yanked a drawer open. "I don't know who killed her parents, Kit. Probably faeries. It was during the Dark War." He looked self-righteous. "So I wanted to help her out. So what? Shadowhunter money spends."

"And you want the Shadowhunters paying attention to something that isn't you," said Kit. It was a guess, but, he suspected, a good one. "Have you got something going on?"

Johnny slammed the drawer shut. "Maybe."

"For someone who sells secrets, you sure keep a lot of them," said Kit, jamming his hands into his pockets.

His father put an arm around him, a rare affectionate gesture. "My biggest secret," he said, "is you."

# 1

## A Sepulchre
## in This Kingdom

"It's just not working out," Emma said. "This relationship, I mean."

Disconsolate noises came from the other end of the phone. Emma was barely able to decipher them—the reception wasn't particularly good on the roof of the Sepulchre Bar. She paced along the edge of the roofline, peering down into the central courtyard. Jacaranda trees were strung with electric lights, and sleek ultramodern tables and chairs were scattered around the garden space. Equally sleek and ultramodern young men and women thronged the place, glasses of wine glimmering in their hands like clear bubbles of red and white and pink. Someone had rented out the place for a private party: A sequined birthday banner hung between two trees, and waiters made their way through the crowd carrying pewter chargers of snacks.

There was something about the glamorous scene that made Emma want to break it up by kicking down some of the roof tiles or doing a front flip into the crowd. The Clave would lock you up for a good long time for that kind of behavior, though. Mundanes weren't supposed to *ever* glimpse Shadowhunters. Even if Emma *did* jump down into the courtyard, none of the partygoers would see her. She was covered in glamour runes, applied by Cristina, that rendered her invisible to anyone without the Sight.

Emma sighed and put the phone back to her ear. "All right, *our* relationship," she said. "*Our* relationship isn't working out."

"*Emma*," Cristina hissed loudly behind her. Emma turned, her boots balanced at the edge of the roof. Cristina was sitting on the shingled slope behind her, polishing a throwing knife with a pale blue cloth. The cloth matched the bands that held her dark hair back from her face. Everything about Cristina was neat and put together—she managed to look as professional in her black fighting gear as most people would look in a power suit. Her golden good-luck medallion glimmered at the hollow of her throat and her family ring, twined with a pattern of roses for Rosales, shone on her hand as she placed the knife, wrapped in its cloth, beside her. "Emma, remember. Use your *I* statements."

Cameron was still wittering away on the other end of the phone, something about getting together to talk, which Emma knew would be pointless. She focused on the scene below her—was that a shadow slipping through the crowd below, or was she imagining it? Maybe it was wishful thinking. Johnny Rook was usually reliable, and he'd seemed *very* sure about tonight, but Emma hated getting all geared up and full of anticipation only to discover there was going to be no fight to work off her energy.

"This is about *me*, not *you*," she said into the phone. Cristina gave her an encouraging thumbs-up. "*I* am sick of *you*." She smiled brightly as Cristina dropped her face into her hands. "So maybe we could go back to being friends?"

There was a click as Cameron hung up. Emma tucked the phone into her belt and scanned the crowd again. Nothing. Annoyed, she scrambled up the slope of the roof to flop down beside Cristina. "Well, that could have gone better," she said.

"Do you think so?" Cristina took her hands away from her face. "What happened?"

"I don't know." Emma sighed and reached for her stele, the delicate *adamas* writing instrument Shadowhunters used to ink protection runes onto their skin. It had a carved handle made of demon bone and had been a gift from Jace Herondale, Emma's first crush. Most Shadowhunters went through steles like mundanes went through pencils, but this one was special to Emma and she kept it as carefully intact as she kept her sword. "It always happens. Everything was fine, and then I woke up one morning and just the sound of his voice made me feel sick to my stomach." She looked at Cristina guiltily. "I *tried*," she added. "I waited weeks! I kept hoping it would get better. But it didn't."

Cristina patted her arm. "I know, *cuata*," she said. "You just aren't very good at having . . ."

"Tact?" Emma suggested. Cristina's English was nearly accentless, and Emma often forgot it wasn't her first language. On the other hand Cristina spoke seven languages on top of her native Spanish. Emma spoke English and some scraps of Spanish, Greek, and Latin, could read three demon languages, and swear in five.

"I was going to say relationships," Cristina said. Her dark brown eyes twinkled. "I've only been here for two months and you've forgotten three dates with Cameron, skipped his birthday, and now you've dumped him because it was a slow patrol night."

"He always wanted to play video games," said Emma. "I hate video games."

"No one is perfect, Emma."

"But some people are perfect for each other. Don't you think that has to be true?"

A strange look flashed over Cristina's face, gone so quickly Emma was sure she'd imagined it. Sometimes Emma was reminded that however much she felt close to Cristina, she didn't know her—didn't *know* her the way she did Jules, the way you knew someone whose every moment you had shared since you were children. What had happened to Cristina in Mexico—whatever had sent her running to Los Angeles and away from her family and friends—was something she'd never spoken of to Emma.

"Well," said Cristina, "at least you were wise enough to bring me along for moral support to help you through this difficult time."

Emma poked Cristina with her stele. "I wasn't *planning* on dumping Cameron. We were here, and he called, and his face came up on my phone—well, actually a llama came up on my phone because I didn't have a picture of him so I just used a llama—and the llama made me so angry I just couldn't help myself."

"Bad time to be a llama."

"Is it ever a good time, really?" Emma flipped the stele around and started to ink a Sure-Footedness rune onto her arm. She prided herself on having excellent balance without runes, but up on a roof it was probably a good idea to be safe.

She thought of Julian, far away in England, with a sting at her heart. He would have been pleased she was being careful. He would have said something funny and loving and self-deprecating about it. She missed him horribly, but she supposed that was how it was when you were *parabatai*, bound together by magic as well as friendship.

She missed all the Blackthorns. She had grown up playing among Julian and his sisters and brothers, lived with them since she was twelve—when she had lost her parents, and Julian, whose mother had already died, had lost his father. From being an only child she had been thrust into a big, loud, noisy, loving family. Not every part of it had been easy, but she adored them, from shy Drusilla to Tiberius, who loved detective stories. They had left at the beginning of the summer to visit their great-aunt in Sussex— the Blackthorn family was originally British. Marjorie, Julian had explained, was nearly a hundred years old and might die at any moment; they *had* to visit her. It was a moral requirement.

Off they'd gone for two months, all of them except their uncle, the head of the Institute. The shock to Emma's system had been severe. The Institute had gone from noisy to quiet. Worst of all, when Julian was gone, she *felt* it, like a constant unease, a low-level pain in her chest.

Dating Cameron had *not* helped, but Cristina's arrival had helped immeasurably. It was common for Shadowhunters who reached the age of eighteen to visit foreign Institutes and learn their different customs. Cristina had come to Los Angeles from Mexico City—there was nothing unusual about it, but she'd always had the air of someone running from something. Emma, meanwhile, had been running from loneliness. She and Emma had run directly into each other, and become best friends faster than Emma could have believed possible.

"Diana will be pleased about you dumping Cameron, at least," said Cristina. "I don't think she liked him."

Diana Wrayburn was the Blackthorn family's tutor. She was extremely smart, extremely stern, and extremely tired of Emma falling asleep in the middle of class because she'd been out the night before.

"Diana just thinks all relationships are a distraction from studying," Emma said. "Why date when you can learn an extra demonic language? I mean, who wouldn't want to know how to say 'Come here often?' in Purgatic?"

Cristina laughed. "You sound like Jaime. He hated studying." Emma perked her ears: Cristina rarely spoke of the friends or family in Mexico City she'd left behind. She knew Cristina's uncle had run the Mexico City Institute until he'd been killed in the Dark War and her mother had taken it over. She knew Cristina's father had died when she was a child. But not much else. "But not Diego. He loved it. He did extra work for fun."

"Diego? The perfect guy? The one your mom loves?" Emma began to trace the stele over her skin, the Farsighted rune taking shape on her forearm. The sleeves of her gear were elbow length, the skin below it marked all over with the pale white scars of runes long ago used up.

Cristina reached over and took the stele from Emma. "Here. Let me do that." She continued the Farsighted rune. Cristina had a gorgeous hand with runes, careful and precise. "I don't want to talk about Perfect Diego," Cristina said. "My mother talks about him enough. Can I ask you about something else?"

Emma nodded. The pressure of the stele against her skin was familiar, almost pleasant.

"I know you wanted to come here because Johnny Rook told you that there have been bodies found with writing on them, and he thinks one will turn up here tonight."

"Correct."

"And you are hoping the writing will be the same as it was on your parents' bodies."

Emma tensed. She couldn't help it. Any mention of her parents' murders hurt as if it had happened yesterday. Even when the person asking her about it was as gentle as Cristina. "Yes."

"The Clave says Sebastian Morgenstern murdered your parents," said Cristina. "That is what Diana told me. That's what they believe. But you don't believe it."

The Clave. Emma looked out into the Los Angeles night, at the brilliant explosion of electricity that was the skyline, at the rows and rows of billboards that lined Sunset Boulevard. It had been a harmless word, "Clave," when she had first learned it. The Clave was simply the government of the Nephilim, made up of all active Shadowhunters over the age of eighteen.

In theory every Shadowhunter had a vote and an equal voice. In point of fact, some Shadowhunters were more influential than others: Like any political party, the Clave had its corruption and prejudices. For Nephilim this meant a strict code of honor and rules that every Shadowhunter had to adhere to or face dire consequences.

The Clave had a motto: *The Law is hard, but it is the Law.* Every Shadowhunter knew what it meant. The rules of the Law of the Clave had to be obeyed, no matter how hard or painful. The Law overrode everything else—personal need, grief, loss, unfairness, treachery. When the Clave had told Emma that she was to accept the fact that her parents had been murdered as part of the Dark War, she had been required to do so.

She hadn't.

"No," Emma said slowly. "I don't think so."

Cristina sat with the stele motionless in her hand, the rune unfinished. The *adamas* gleamed in the moonlight. "Could you tell me why?"

"Sebastian Morgenstern was building an army," Emma said, still looking out at the sea of lights. "He took Shadowhunters and turned them into monsters that served him. He didn't mark them up with demon languages written on their bodies and then dump them in the ocean. When the Nephilim tried to move my parents' bodies, they dissolved. That didn't happen to any of Sebastian's victims." She moved her finger along a roof tile. "And—it's a feeling. Not a passing feeling. Something I've always believed. I believe it more every day. I believe my parents' deaths were different. And that laying them at Sebastian's door means—" She broke off with a sigh. "I'm sorry. I'm just rambling. Look, this is probably going to be nothing. You shouldn't worry about it."

"I worry about you," Cristina said, but she laid the stele back against Emma's skin and finished the rune without another word. It was something that Emma had liked about Cristina since the moment she'd met her—she never pressed or pressured.

Emma glanced down in appreciation as Cristina sat back, done with her work. The Farsighted rune gleamed clear and clean on Emma's arm. "The only person I know who draws better runes than you do is Julian," she said. "But he's an artist—"

"Julian, Julian, Julian," echoed Cristina in a teasing voice. "Julian is a painter, Julian is a genius, Julian would know how to fix this, Julian could build that. You know, for the past seven weeks I've heard so many wonderful things about Julian I'm starting to worry that when I meet him I will fall in love with him instantly."

Emma brushed her gritty hands carefully down her legs. She felt tight and itchy and tense. All wound up for a battle and no fighting, she told herself. No wonder she wanted to jump out of her skin. "I don't think he's your type," she said. "But he's my *parabatai*, so I'm not objective."

Cristina handed Emma's stele back to her. "I always wanted a *parabatai*," she said a little wistfully. "Someone who is sworn to protect you and to watch your back. A best friend forever, for your whole life."

*A best friend forever, for your whole life.* When Emma's parents had died, she'd fought to stay with the Blackthorns. Partly because she'd lost everything familiar to her and she couldn't bear the thought of starting over, and partly because she'd wanted to stay in Los Angeles so that she could investigate her parents' deaths.

It might have been awkward; she might have felt, the only Carstairs in a house of Blackthorns, out of place in the family. But she never had, because of Jules. *Parabatai* was more than friendship, more than family; it was a bond that tied you together, fiercely, in a way that every Shadowhunter respected and acknowledged the way that they respected the bond between husband and wife.

No one would separate *parabatai*. No one would dare try: *Parabatai* were stronger together. They fought together as if they could read each other's minds. A single rune given to you by your *parabatai* was more powerful than ten runes given to you by someone else. Often *parabatai* had their ashes buried in the same tomb so that they wouldn't be parted, even in death.

Not everyone had a *parabatai*; in fact, they were rare. It was a life-long, binding commitment. You were swearing to stay by the other person's side, swearing to always protect them, to go where they went, to consider their family your family. The words of the oath were from the Bible, and ancient: *Whither thou goest, I will go; thy people shall be my people; where thou diest, will I die, and there will I be buried.*

If there was a term for it in mundane English, Emma thought, it would have been "soul mate." Platonic soul mate. You weren't allowed to be romantically involved with your *parabatai*. Like so many things, it was against the Law. Emma had never known why—it didn't make any sense—but then, much of the Law didn't. It hadn't made sense for the Clave to exile and abandon Julian's half siblings, Helen and Mark, simply because their mother had been a faerie, but they'd done that too when they'd created the Cold Peace.

Emma stood up, sliding her stele into her weapons belt. "Well, the Blackthorns are coming back the day after tomorrow. You'll meet Jules then." She moved back toward the edge of the roof, and this time she heard the scrape of boots on tile that told her Cristina was behind her. "Do you see anything?"

"Maybe there's nothing going on." Cristina shrugged. "Maybe it's just a party."

"Johnny Rook was so sure," muttered Emma.

"Didn't Diana specifically forbid you to go see him?"

"She may have told me to stop seeing him," Emma acknowledged. "She may even have called him 'a criminal who commits crime,' which I have to say struck me as harsh, but she didn't say I couldn't go to the Shadow Market."

"Because everyone already knows Shadowhunters aren't meant to go to the Shadow Market."

Emma ignored this. "And if I ran into Rook, say, at the Market, and he dropped some information while we were chatting and I accidentally let drop some money, who's to call that 'paying for information'? Just two friends, one careless with his gossip and the other one careless with her finances . . ."

"That's not the spirit of the Law, Emma. Remember? *The Law is hard, but it is the Law.*"

"I thought it was 'the Law is annoying, but it is also flexible.'"

"That is not the motto. And Diana is going to kill you."

"Not if we solve the murders, she won't. The ends will justify the means. And if nothing happens, she never has to know about it. Right?"

Cristina didn't say anything.

"Right . . . ?" Emma said.

Cristina gave an intake of breath. "Do you see?" she asked, pointing.

Emma saw. She saw a tall man, handsome and smooth-haired, with pale skin and carefully tailored clothes, moving among the crowd. As he went, men and women turned to look after him, their faces slack and fascinated.

"There is a glamour on him," Cristina said. Emma quirked an eyebrow. Glamour was illusion magic, commonly used by Downworlders to hide themselves from mundane eyes. Shadowhunters also had access to Marks that had much the same effect, though Nephilim didn't consider that magic. Magic was warlock business; runes were a gift from the Angel. "The question is, vampire or fey?"

Emma hesitated. The man was approaching a young woman in towering heels, a glass of champagne in her hand. Her face went smooth and blank as he spoke to her. She nodded agreeably, reached up, and undid the chunky gold necklace she was wearing. She dropped it into his outstretched hand, a smile on her face as he slid it into his pocket.

"Fey," Emma said, reaching for her weapons belt. Faeries complicated everything. According to the Law of the Cold Peace, an underage Shadowhunter shouldn't have anything to do with faeries at all. Faeries were off-limits, the cursed and forbidden branch of Downworlders, ever since the Cold Peace, which had ripped away their rights, their armies, and their possessions. Their ancient lands were no longer considered theirs, and other Downworlders fought over who could claim them. Trying to calm such battles was a great part of the business of the Los Angeles Institute, but it was adult business. Shadowhunters Emma's age weren't meant to engage directly with faeries.

In theory.

*The Law is annoying, but it is flexible.* Emma drew a small cloth bag, tied at the top, out of a pouch attached to her belt. She began to flick it open as the fey moved from the smiling woman to a slender man in a black jacket, who willingly handed over his sparkling cuff links. The fey was now standing almost directly beneath Emma and Cristina. "Vampires don't care about gold, but the Fair Folk pay tribute to their King and Queen in gold and gems and other treasure."

"I have heard the Court of the Unseelie pays it in blood," said Cristina grimly.

"Not tonight," Emma said, flicking the bag she was holding open and upending the contents onto the faerie's head.

Cristina gasped in horror as the fey below them gave a hoarse cry, his glamour falling away from him like a snake shedding its skin.

A chorus of shrieks went up from the crowd as the fey's true appearance was revealed. Branches grew like twisted horns from his head, and his skin was the dark green of moss or mildew, cracked all over like bark. His hands were spatulate claws, three-fingered.

"Emma," Cristina warned. "We should stop this now—call the Silent Brothers—"

But Emma had already jumped.

For a moment she was weightless, falling through the air. Then she struck the ground, knees bent as she'd been taught. How she remembered those first jumps from great heights, the snapping, awkward falls, the days she'd have to wait to heal before trying again.

No longer. Emma rose to her feet, facing the faerie across the fleeing crowd. Gleaming from his weathered, barklike face, his eyes were yellow as a cat's. "*Shadowhunter,*" he hissed.

The partygoers continued to flee from the courtyard through the gates that led into the parking lot. None of them saw Emma, though their instincts kicked in anyway, making them pass around her like water around the pilings of a bridge.

Emma reached back over her shoulder and closed her hand around the hilt of her sword, Cortana. The blade made a golden blur in the air as she drew it and pointed the tip at the fey. "No," she said. "I'm a candygram. This is my costume."

The faerie looked puzzled.

Emma sighed. "It's so hard to be sassy to the Fair Folk. You people never get jokes."

"We are well known for our jests, japes, and ballads," the faerie said, clearly offended. "Some of our ballads last for weeks."

"I don't have that kind of time," Emma said. "I'm a Shadowhunter. Quip fast, die young." She wiggled Cortana's tip impatiently. "Now turn out your pockets."

"I have done nothing to break the Cold Peace," said the fey.

"*Technically* true, but we do frown on stealing from mundanes," Emma said. "Turn out your pockets or I'll rip off one of your horns and shove it where the sun doesn't shine."

The fey looked puzzled. "Where does the sun not shine? Is this a riddle?"

Emma gave a martyred sigh and raised Cortana. "Turn them out, or I'll start peeling your bark off. My boyfriend and I just broke up, and I'm not in the best mood."

The faerie began slowly to empty his pockets onto the ground, glaring at her all the while. "So you're single," he said. "I never would have guessed."

A gasp sounded from above. "Now that is simply rude," said Cristina, leaning over the edge of the roof.

"Thank you, Cristina," Emma said. "That was a low blow. And for your information, faerie guy, I broke up with him."

The faerie shrugged. It was a remarkably expressive shrug, managing to convey several different kinds of not caring at once.

"Although I don't know why," Cristina said. "He was very nice."

Emma rolled her eyes. The faerie was still dumping his loot—earrings, expensive leather wallets, diamond rings tumbled to the ground in a sparkling cacophony. Emma braced herself. She didn't really care about the jewelry or the stealing. She was looking for weapons, spell books, any sign of the kind of dark magic she associated with the markings on her parents. "The Ashdowns and the Carstairs don't get along," she said. "It's a well-known fact."

At that the faerie seemed to freeze in place. "Carstairs," he spat, his yellow eyes fixed on Emma. "You are Emma Carstairs?"

Emma blinked, thrown. She glanced up; Cristina had disappeared from the edge of the roof. "I really don't think we've met. I'd remember a talking tree."

"Would you?" Spatulate hands twitched at the faerie's side. "I would have expected more courteous treatment. Or have you and your Institute friends forgotten Mark Blackthorn so quickly?"

*"Mark?"* Emma froze, unable to control her reaction. In that moment, something glittering hurtled toward her face. The fey had whipped a diamond necklace at her. She ducked, but the edge of the chain caught her cheek. She felt a stinging pain and the warmth of blood.

She bolted upright, but the fey was gone. She swore, wiping at the blood on her face. "Emma!" It was Cristina, who had made it down from the roof and was standing by a barred door in the wall. An emergency exit. "He went through here!"

Emma dashed toward her and together they kicked open the door and burst out into the alley behind the bar. It was surprisingly dark; someone had smashed the nearby streetlights. Dumpsters shoved against the wall reeked of spoiled food and alcohol. Emma felt her Farsighted rune burn; at the very end of the alley, she saw the slight form of the fey spring toward the left.

She set off after him, Cristina by her side. She had spent so much of her life running with Julian that she had some difficulty adjusting her stride to someone else's; she pushed ahead, running flat out. Faeries were fast, notoriously so. She and Cristina rounded the next corner, where the alley narrowed. The fleeing fey had shoved two Dumpsters together to block their path. Emma flung herself up and over, using the Dumpsters to vault forward, her boots clanging against the metal.

She fell forward and landed on something soft. Fabric scratched under her fingernails. Clothes. Clothes on a human body. Wet clothes. The stench of seawater and rot was everywhere. She looked down into a dead and bloated face.

Emma bit down on a yell. A moment later there was another *clang* and Cristina dropped down beside her. Emma heard her friend breathe an astonished exclamation in Spanish. Then Cristina's arms were around her, pulling her away from the body. She landed on the asphalt, awkwardly, unable to stop staring.

The body was undeniably human. A middle-aged man, round-shouldered, his silvery hair worn like the mane of a lion. Patches of his skin were burned, black and red, bubbles rising where the burns were worst, like lather on a bar of soap.

His gray shirt was torn open, and across his chest and arms marched lines of black runes, not the runes of Shadowhunters, but a twisted demon script. They were runes Emma knew as well as she knew the scars on her own hands. She had stared obsessively at photographs of those marks for five years. They were the marks the Clave had found on the bodies of her own murdered parents.

"Are you all right?" Cristina asked. Emma was leaning back against the brick wall of the alley—which smelled very questionable and was covered in spray paint—and glaring laser beams at the dead body of the mundane and the Silent Brothers surrounding it.

The first thing Emma had done as soon as she'd been able to think clearly was summon the Brothers and Diana. Now she was second-guessing that decision. The Silent Brothers had arrived instantly and were all over the body, sometimes turning to speak to each other in their soundless voices as they searched and examined and took notes. They had put up warding runes to give themselves time to work before the mundane police arrived, but—politely, firmly, requiring only a slight use of telepathic force—they prevented Emma from coming anywhere near the body.

"I'm *furious*," Emma said. "I have to see those markings. I have to take photos of them. It's *my* parents that were killed. Not that the Silent Brothers care. I only ever knew one decent Silent Brother and he quit being one."

Cristina's eyes widened. Somehow she had managed to keep her gear clean through all of this, and she looked fresh and pink-cheeked. Emma imagined she herself, with her hair sticking out in every direction and alley dirt smeared on her clothes, looked like an eldritch horror. "I didn't think it was something you could just stop doing."

The Silent Brothers were Shadowhunters who had chosen to retreat from the world, like monks, and devote themselves to study and healing. They occupied the Silent City, the vast underground caverns where most Shadowhunters were buried when they died. Their terrible scars were the result of runes too strong for most human flesh, even that of Shadowhunters, but it was also the runes that made them nearly immortal. They served as advisers, archivists, and healers—and they could also wield the power of the Mortal Sword.

They were the ones who had performed Emma and Julian's *parabatai* ceremony. They were there for weddings, there when Nephilim children were born, and there when they died. Every important event of a Shadowhunter's life was marked with the appearance of a Silent Brother.

Emma thought of the one Silent Brother she'd ever liked. She missed him still, sometimes.

The alley suddenly lit up like daylight. Blinking, Emma turned to see that a familiar pickup truck had pulled into the alley's entrance. It came to a stop, headlights still on, and Diana Wrayburn jumped down from the driver's seat.

When Diana had come to work as the tutor to the children of the Los Angeles Institute five years ago, Emma had thought she was the most beautiful woman she'd ever seen. She was tall and spare and elegant, with the silvery tattoo of a koi fish standing out across the dark skin of one arched cheekbone. Her eyes were brown with flecks of green in them, and right now they were flashing with angry fire. She was wearing an ankle-length black dress that fell around her long body in elegant folds. She looked like the dangerous Roman goddess of the hunt she was named for.

"Emma! Cristina!" She hurried toward them. "What happened? Are you all right?"

For a moment Emma paused the glaring and let herself enjoy being hugged fiercely. Diana had always been too young for Emma to think of her as a mother, but an older sister, maybe. Someone protective. Diana let go of her and hugged Cristina too, who looked startled. Emma had long had the suspicion that there hadn't been much hugging in Cristina's home. "What happened? Why are you trying to burn a hole through Brother Enoch with your eyeballs?"

"We were patrolling—" Emma began.

"We saw a fey stealing from humans," Cristina added quickly.

"Yes, and I stopped him and told him to turn out his pockets—"

"A faerie?" A look of disquiet came over Diana's face. "Emma, you know you shouldn't confront one of the Fair Folk, even when Cristina's with you—"

"I've fought Fair Folk before," Emma said. It was true. Both she and Diana had fought in the Shadowhunter city of Alicante when Sebastian's forces had attacked. The streets had been full of faerie warriors. The adults had taken the children and walled them up in the fortresslike Hall of Accords, where they were meant to be safe. But the faeries had broken the locks. . . .

Diana had been there, laying to the right and left of her with her deadly sword, saving dozens of children. Emma had been one of those saved. She had loved Diana since then.

"I had a feeling," Emma went on, "that something bigger and worse was happening. I followed the faerie when he ran. I know I shouldn't have, but—I found that body. And it's covered in the same marks my parents' bodies were. The *same markings*, Diana."

Diana turned to Cristina. "Could you give us a moment alone, please, Tina?"

Cristina hesitated. But as a guest of the Los Angeles Institute, a young Shadowhunter on Leave, she was required to do as the senior staff of the Institute requested. With a glance at Emma, she moved away, toward the spot where the body still lay. It was surrounded by a ring of Silent Brothers, like a flock of pale birds in their parchment robes. They were sprinkling a sort of shimmering powder over the markings, or at least that's how it looked. Emma wished she were closer and could see properly.

Diana exhaled. "Emma, are you *sure*?"

Emma bit back an angry retort. She understood why Diana was

asking. Over the years there had been so many false leads—so many times Emma had thought she had found a clue or a translation for the markings or a story in a mundane newspaper—and every time she had been wrong.

"I just don't want you to get your hopes up," Diana said.

"I know," Emma said. "But I shouldn't ignore it. I can't ignore it. You believe me. You've always *believed* me, right?"

"That Sebastian Morgenstern didn't kill your parents? Oh, honey, you know I do." Diana patted Emma's shoulder lightly. "I just don't want you to get hurt, and with Julian not here . . ."

Emma waited for her to go on.

"Well, with Julian not here, you get hurt more easily. *Parabatai* buffer each other. I know you're strong, you are, but this is something that cut you so deeply when you were just a child. It's twelve-year-old Emma that reacts to anything to do with your parents, not almost-adult Emma." Diana winced and touched the side of her head. "Brother Enoch is calling me over," she said. Silent Brothers were able to communicate with Shadowhunters using telepathy only they could hear, though they were also able to project to groups if the need arose. "Can you make it back to the Institute?"

"I can, but if I could just see the body again—"

"The Silent Brothers say no," Diana said firmly. "I'll find out what I can, and I'll share it with you? Deal?"

Emma nodded reluctantly. "Deal."

Diana headed off toward the Silent Brothers, stopping to talk briefly to Cristina. By the time Emma reached the car she had parked, Cristina had joined her, and they both climbed in silently.

Emma sat where she was for a moment, drained, the car keys dangling from her hand. In the rearview mirror she could see the alleyway behind them, lit up like a baseball stadium by the truck's powerful headlights. Diana was moving among the parchment-robed Silent Brothers. The powder on the ground was white in the glare.

"Are you all right?" Cristina said.

Emma turned to her. "You have to tell me what you saw," she begged. "You were close to the body. Did you hear Diana say anything to the Brothers? Are they definitely the same markings?"

"I don't need to tell you," Cristina said.

"I—" Emma broke off. She felt wretched. She'd messed up the whole plan for the night, lost their faerie criminal, lost her chance of examining the body, probably hurt Cristina's feelings. "I know you don't. I'm really sorry, Cristina. I didn't mean to get you in trouble. It's just that—"

"I didn't say that." Cristina fumbled in the pocket of her gear. "I said I didn't need to tell you, because I meant I could *show* you. Here. Look at these." She held out her phone, and Emma's heart leaped—Cristina was scrolling through picture after picture she'd taken of the body and the Brothers, the alley, the blood. Everything.

"Cristina, I love you," Emma said. "I will marry you. *Marry you.*"

Cristina giggled. "My mother's already picked out who I'm going to marry, remember? Imagine what she'd say if I brought *you* home."

"You don't think she'd like me more than Perfect Diego?"

"I think you would be able to hear her screaming in Idris."

Idris was the home country of the Shadowhunters, where they had first been created, where the Clave held its seat. It was tucked away at the intersection of France, Germany, and Switzerland, hidden by spells from mundane eyes. The Dark War had ravaged its capital city of Alicante, which was still being rebuilt.

Emma laughed. Relief was coursing through her. They had something after all. A clue, as Tiberius would say, head stuck in a detective novel.

Missing Ty suddenly, she reached to start up the car.

"Did you really tell that faerie that you broke up with Cameron and not the other way around?" Cristina said.

"Please don't bring that up," Emma said. "I'm not proud of it."

Cristina snorted. It was remarkably unladylike.

"Can you come to my room after we get back?" Emma asked, flicking on the headlights. "I want to show you something."

Cristina frowned. "It isn't a strange birthmark or a wart, is it? My *abuela* said she wanted to show me something once, and it turned out to be a wart on her—"

"It's not a wart!" As Emma pulled the car out and merged with the rest of the traffic, she sensed anxiety fizzing through her veins. Usually she felt exhausted after a fight as the adrenaline drained out of her.

Now, though, she was about to show Cristina something that no one but Julian had ever seen. Something she herself wasn't exactly proud of. She couldn't help wondering how Cristina would take it.

# 2

## NEITHER THE ANGELS
## IN HEAVEN

**"Julian calls it my Wall of Crazy," Emma said.**

She and Cristina were standing in front of the closet in Emma's bedroom, the door of which was propped wide open.

The closet was empty of clothes. Emma's wardrobe, mostly vintage dresses and jeans she'd picked up in secondhand stores in Silver Lake and Santa Monica, was either hung in her armoire or folded in her dresser. The inside walls of the closet in her blue-painted room (the mural on the bedroom wall of swallows in flight over the towers of a castle had been done by Julian when she first moved in, a nod to the symbol of the Carstairs family) were covered in photographs, newspaper clippings, and sticky notes in Emma's cramped handwriting.

"Everything is color coded," she said, indicating the sticky notes. "Stories from mundane newspapers, research into spells, research into demonic languages, things I've managed to get out of Diana over the years . . . It's everything I've ever found that connects to my parents' deaths."

Cristina moved closer to examine the walls, then swung around suddenly to stare at Emma. "Some of these look like official Clave files."

"They are," Emma said. "I stole them from the Consul's office in Idris when I was twelve."

"You stole these from Jia Penhallow?" Cristina looked horrified. Emma supposed she couldn't blame her. The Consul was the highest elected official in the Clave—only the Inquisitor came close in terms of power and influence.

"Where else was I going to get photos of my parents' bodies?" Emma asked, shrugging off her jacket and tossing it onto her bed. She wore a tank top underneath, the breeze from the wilderness cool on her bare arms.

"So the pictures I took tonight—where do they go?"

Cristina handed them to Emma. They were still damp with toner—the first thing they'd done when they'd gotten back to the Institute was print out the two clearest photos of the alleyway body from Cristina's phone. Emma leaned in and pinned them carefully beside the Clave photos of her own parents' bodies—dimmed with time now and curling at the edges.

She leaned back and looked from one to the other. The markings were ugly, spiky, hard to concentrate on. They seemed to push back against being viewed. They weren't a demon language anyone had been able to identify to her, but they felt as if no human mind could have conceived of them.

"So now what?" Cristina said. "I mean, what is your plan for what to do next?"

"I'll see what Diana says tomorrow," Emma said. "If she found out anything. Do the Silent Brothers already know about the murders Rook was talking about? If they don't, I'll go back to the Shadow Market. I'll dig up whatever money I've got, or owe Johnny Rook a favor—I don't care. If someone's killing people now and covering their bodies with this writing, then it means—it means Sebastian Morgenstern didn't kill my parents five years ago. It means I'm right, and their deaths were something else."

"It might not mean exactly that, Emma." Cristina's voice was gentle.

"I'm one of the few people alive who saw Sebastian Morgenstern attack an Institute," said Emma. It was both one of her clearest memories and a blur: She remembered grabbing up baby Tavvy with Dru following, carrying him through the Institute as Sebastian's Dark warriors howled, remembered the sight of Sebastian himself, all white hair and dead black demonic eyes, remembered the blood and Mark, remembered Julian waiting for her. "I saw him. Saw his face, his eyes when he looked at me. It's not that I don't think he could have killed my parents. He would have killed anyone who stood in his way. It's just that I don't think he would have bothered." Her eyes stung. "I just have to get more proof. Convince the Clave. Because as long as this is laid at Sebastian's door, the real murderer, the person responsible, won't be punished. And I don't think I could stand that."

"Emma." Cristina touched Emma's arm lightly with her hand. "You know I think the Angel has a plan for us. For you. And whatever I can do to help you, I will."

Emma did know that. To many Shadowhunters, the Angel who had created the race of Nephilim was a distant figure. To Cristina, Raziel was a living presence. Around her throat she wore a medallion consecrated to the Angel. Raziel was etched on the front, and there were words written in Latin on the back: *Blessed be the Angel my strength, who teaches my hands to war, and my fingers to fight.*

Cristina touched her medallion often: for strength, before an exam, before a battle. In many ways, Emma envied Cristina her faith. Sometimes she thought the only things she had faith in were revenge and Julian.

Emma leaned back against the wall, paper and sticky notes rough against her bare shoulder. "Even if it means breaking the rules? I know you hate that."

"I am not as boring as you seem to think." Cristina hit Emma's shoulder lightly in mock offense. "Anyway, there is nothing more we can do tonight. What would take your mind off things? Bad movies? Ice cream?"

"Introducing you to the Blackthorns," Emma said, pushing off the wall of the closet.

"But they're not here." Cristina looked at Emma as if worried she'd hit her head.

"They aren't and they are." Emma held out her hand. "Come with me."

Cristina allowed herself to be led out into the corridor. It was all wood and glass, the windows giving out onto what during the daytime were vistas of sea and sand and desert. Emma had thought when she moved into the Institute that eventually the views would start to fade out of her consciousness, that she wouldn't wake up every morning still startled by the blue of the ocean, the sky. That hadn't happened. The sea still fascinated her with its ever-changing surface, and the desert with its shadows and flowers.

She could see the gleam of the moon off the sea now, through the night windows: silver and black.

Emma and Cristina made their way down the hall. Emma paused at the top of the enormous staircase that descended to the Institute's entryway. It was located exactly in the middle of the Institute, splitting the north and south wings. Emma had deliberately chosen a bedroom, years ago, that was at the other end of the Institute from where the Blackthorns slept. It was a way of declaring silently that she knew she was still a Carstairs.

She leaned on the railing now and looked down, Cristina beside her. Institutes were built to impress: They were meeting places for Shadowhunters, the heart of Conclaves—communities of local Nephilim. The massive entryway, a square room whose focal point was the enormous staircase that led up to the landing and the second floor, had a black-and-white marble floor and was decorated with uncomfortable-looking furniture that no one ever sat in. It seemed like the entrance of a museum.

From the landing you could see that the white and black tiles that patterned the floor formed the shape of the Angel Raziel, rising from the waters of Lake Lyn in Idris, holding two of the Mortal Instruments—a flashing sword and a gold-encrusted cup.

It was an image every Shadowhunter child knew. A thousand years ago the Angel Raziel had been summoned by Jonathan Shadowhunter, the father of all Nephilim, to put down a plague of demons. Raziel had gifted Jonathan with the Mortal Instruments and the Gray Book, in which all runes were inscribed. He had also mixed his blood with human blood and given it to Jonathan and his followers to drink, allowing their skin to bear runes and creating the first of the Nephilim. The image of Raziel rising was sacred to Nephilim: It was called the Triptych and was found in places where Shadowhunters met or where they had died.

The image on the floor of the Institute's entryway was a memorial. When Sebastian Morgenstern and his faerie army had stormed the Institute, the floor had been plain marble. After the Dark War, the Blackthorn children had returned to the Institute to find that the room where so many had died was already being torn up. The stones where Shadowhunters had bled were replaced, and the mural put in to commemorate those who had been lost.

Every time Emma walked on it, she was reminded of her parents and of Julian's father. She didn't mind—she didn't want to forget.

"When you said they are and they aren't, did you mean because Arthur was here?" Cristina asked. She was looking thoughtfully down on the Angel.

"Definitely not." Arthur Blackthorn was the head of the Los Angeles Institute. At least, that was his title. He was a classicist, obsessed with the mythology of Greece and Rome, constantly locked in the attic with bits of old pottery, moldering books, and endless essays and monographs. Emma didn't think she'd ever seen him take a direct interest in a Shadowhunter issue. She could count on one hand the number of times she and Cristina had seen him since Cristina's arrival at the Institute. "Although I'm impressed you remember he lives here."

Cristina rolled her eyes.

"Don't roll your eyes. It punctures my dramatic moment. I want my dramatic moment unpunctured."

"What dramatic moment?" Cristina demanded. "Why have you dragged me out here when I want to shower and change out of this gear? Besides, I need coffee."

"You always need coffee," said Emma, moving back toward the corridor and the other wing of the house. "It's a debilitating addiction."

Cristina said something uncomplimentary under her breath in Spanish, but she followed Emma nonetheless, her curiosity clearly winning out. Emma spun around so she could walk backward, like a tour guide.

"Okay, most of the family is in the south wing," she said. "First stop, Tavvy's room." The door of Octavian Blackthorn's room was already open. He wasn't that invested in privacy, being only seven. Emma leaned in, and Cristina, looking puzzled, leaned in beside her.

The room contained a small bed with a brightly striped coverlet, a playhouse nearly as tall as Emma, and a tent full of books and toys. "Tavvy has nightmares," Emma said. "Sometimes Julian comes and sleeps in the tent with him."

Cristina smiled. "Di—my mother used to do that for me when I was a little girl."

The next room was Drusilla's. Dru was thirteen and obsessed with horror movies. Books about slasher films and serial killers littered the floor. The walls were black, and vintage horror posters were pasted up over the windows. "Dru loves horror movies," said Emma. "Anything with the word 'blood' or 'terror' or 'prom' in it. Why do they call it a prom, I wonder—"

"It's short for 'promenade,'" said Cristina.

"Why do you speak English so much better than I do?"

"That wasn't English," Cristina pointed out, as Emma darted farther down the hall. "That was French."

"The twins have rooms across from each other." Emma gestured at two closed doors. "This is Livvy." She swung a door open to reveal a beautifully clean and decorated bedroom. Someone had artfully covered the headboard with whimsical fabric decorated with a pattern of teacups. Bright costume jewelry hung from screens nailed to the wall. Books about computers and programming languages were stacked in careful rows by her bed.

"Programming languages," Cristina exclaimed. "Does she like computers?"

"She and Ty," said Emma. "Ty likes computers, he likes the way they organize patterns so that he can analyze them, but he's actually not great at math. Livvy does the math and they tag team."

The next room was Ty's. "Tiberius Nero Blackthorn," said Emma. "I think his parents may have gone a little overboard with the name. It's like naming someone Magnificent Bastard."

Cristina giggled. Ty's room was neat, with books lined up not in alphabetical order but by color. Colors that Ty liked the most, like blue and gold and green, were at the front of the room and near the bed. Colors he didn't like—orange and purple—were relegated to nooks and spaces by the window. It might have looked haphazard to someone else, but Emma knew that Ty was aware of the location of every volume.

On the bedside table were his most beloved books: Arthur Conan Doyle's Sherlock Holmes stories. Beside them were a collection of small toys. Julian had made them for Ty years before when he found that having something in his hand calmed Ty down and helped him focus. There was a squiggly ball of pipe cleaners, and a black plastic cube made up of clicking parts that could be twisted into different patterns.

Cristina cast a look at Emma's wry-fond expression and said, "You've talked about Tiberius before. He's the one who loves animals."

Emma nodded. "He's always outside, bothering lizards and squirrels." She waved her arm to indicate the desert that spread out behind the Institute—unspoiled land, without houses or human occupation, that stretched to the ridge of mountains that separated the beach from the Valley. "Hopefully he's having fun in England, collecting tadpoles and frogs and toads-in-the-hole. . . ."

"That's a kind of food!"

"Can't be," Emma said, moving down the hall.

"It's pudding!" Cristina objected as Emma found the next door and opened it. The room inside was painted almost the exact same blue as the sea and sky outside. During the day it looked as if it were part of them, floating in a blue forever. Murals covered the walls— intricate patterns, and along the whole wall that faced the desert, the outline of a castle wrapped by a high wall of thorns. A prince rode toward it, his head down, his sword broken.

"*La Bella Durmiente*," said Cristina. *Sleeping Beauty*. "But I did not remember it being so sad, or the prince so defeated." She glanced at Emma. "Is he a sorrowful boy, Julian?"

"No," Emma said, only half paying attention. She hadn't come into Jules's room since he'd gone. It looked like he hadn't cleaned up before he left, and there were clothes on the floor, half-done sketches scattered over the desk, even a mug on the nightstand that probably held coffee that had long since molded. "Not depressed or anything like that."

"Depressed is not the same as sad," Cristina observed.

But Emma didn't want to think about Julian being sad, not now, not when he was so close to coming home. Now that it was past midnight, he was technically coming home tomorrow. She felt a shiver of excitement and relief.

"Come on." She went out of the room and across the hall, Cristina following. Emma put her hand against a closed door. It was wood, like the others, the surface chipped as if no one had cleaned or sanded it in a long time.

"This was Mark's room," she said.

Every Shadowhunter knew Mark Blackthorn's name. The half-faerie, half-Shadowhunter boy who had been taken during the Dark War and made a part of the Wild Hunt, the most vicious of the fey. The ones who rode through the sky once a month, preying on humans, visiting the scenes of battle, feeding on fear and death like murderous hawks.

Mark had always been gentle. Emma wondered whether he still was anymore.

"Mark Blackthorn was part of the reason I came here," Cristina said, a little shyly. "It has always been my hope that one day I might be part of brokering a better treaty than the Cold Peace. Something more fair to Downworlders and those Shadowhunters who might love them."

Emma felt her eyes widen. "I didn't know. You never told me that."

Cristina gestured around them. "You have shared something with me," she said. "You have shared the Blackthorns. I thought I should share something with you."

"I'm glad you came here," Emma said impulsively, and Cristina blushed. "Even if it was partly for Mark. And even if you won't tell me anything else about why."

Cristina shrugged. "I like Los Angeles." She gave Emma a sly sideways smile. "Are you absolutely sure you don't want bad movies and ice cream?"

Emma took a deep breath. She remembered Julian telling her

once that when things got to be too much, he imagined locking certain situations and emotions away in a box. *Shut them away,* he'd said, *and they won't bother you. They're gone.*

She imagined, now, taking her memories of the body in the alley, of Sebastian Morgenstern and the Clave, her breakup with Cameron, her need for answers, her anger at the world over her parents' deaths, and her eagerness to see Julian and the others tomorrow, and locking them up in a box. She imagined placing the box somewhere she could get to it easily, somewhere she could find it and open it again.

"Emma?" Cristina said anxiously. "Are you all right? You look a little as if you might throw up."

*Click* went the lock on the box. In her mind, Emma set it aside; back in the world, she smiled at Cristina. "Ice cream and bad movies sounds great," she said. "Let's go."


The sky above the ocean was streaked with the pink and rose of sunset. Emma slowed from a run to a jog, gasping, her heart pounding in her chest.

Usually Emma trained in the afternoon and evening and ran in the early morning, but she'd woken up late after staying up nearly all night with Cristina. She'd spent the day feverishly rearranging her evidence, calling Johnny Rook to cajole further details about the murders out of him, writing up notes for her wall, and waiting impatiently for Diana to turn up.

Unlike most tutors, Diana didn't live in the Institute with the Blackthorns—she had her own house in Santa Monica. Technically, Diana didn't need to be at the Institute at all today, but Emma'd sent her at least six texts. Maybe seven. Cristina had stopped her from sending eight, and suggested she go for a run to get rid of her anxiety.

She leaned forward, hands on her bent knees, trying to catch her breath. The beach was nearly deserted except for a few mundane couples finishing their romantic sunset walks, heading back up to the cars they'd left parked along the highway.

She wondered how many miles she'd run up and down this stretch of beach in the years she'd lived in the Institute. Five miles a day, every day. And that was after three hours at least in the training room. Half the scars Emma had on her body she'd put there herself, teaching herself to fall from the highest rafters, training herself to fight through pain by practicing barefoot—on broken glass.

The most brutal scar she had was on her forearm, and she'd given herself that, too, in a sense. It had come from Cortana, the day her parents had died. Julian had placed the blade in her arms, and she'd cradled it through the blood and the pain, weeping as it cut her skin. It had left a long white line along her arm, one that sometimes made her feel shy about wearing sleeveless dresses or tank tops. She wondered if even other Shadowhunters would stare at the scar, wonder where it came from.

Though Julian never stared.

She straightened up. From the waterline, she could see the Institute, all glass and stone, up on the hill above the beach. She could see the bump of Arthur's attic, even the dark window of her own bedroom. She'd slept restlessly there today, dreaming about the dead mundane man, the marks on his body, the marks on her parents. She'd tried to conjure up a vision of what she'd do when she found out who'd killed them. How any amount of physical pain she could inflict could ever even begin to make up for what she'd lost.

Julian had been in the dream too. She didn't know what exactly she'd dreamed, but she'd woken up with a clear picture of him in her mind—tall, slender Jules, with his dark brown curls and startling blue-green eyes. His dark lashes and pale skin, the way he bit his nails when he was under stress, his confident handling of weapons and even more confident handling of brushes and paints.

Julian, who would be home tomorrow. Julian would understand

exactly what she was feeling—how long she'd waited for a clue about her parents. How now that she'd found one, the world suddenly seemed full of a terrifyingly imminent possibility. She remembered what Jem, the ex–Silent Brother who'd helped preside over her *parabatai* ceremony, had said about what Julian was to her, that there was an expression for it in his native Chinese, *zhi yin*. "The one who understands your music."

Emma couldn't play a note on any instrument, but Julian understood her music. Even the music of revenge.

Dark clouds were rolling in from the ocean. It was about to rain. Trying to put Jules out of her mind, Emma started to run again, darting up the dirt road toward the Institute. Nearing the building, she slowed, staring. There was a man coming down the steps. He was tall and narrow, dressed in a long coat the color of crow feathers. His hair was short and graying. He usually dressed in black; she suspected that was where his last name came from. He wasn't a warlock, Johnny Rook, even if he had a name like one. He was something else.

He saw her and his eyes widened. She broke into a sprint, cutting him off before he could dart around the side of the house, away from her.

She skidded to a stop in front of him, blocking his way. "What are you doing here?"

His odd eyes darted around, seeking an escape route. "Nothing. Stopping by."

"Did you say anything about me coming to the Shadow Market to Diana? Because if you did—"

He drew himself up. There was something odd about his face, as well as his eyes; it had an almost ravaged look, as if something awful had happened to him when he was young, something that had cut lines like knife scars into his skin. "You're not the head of the Institute, Emma Carstairs," he said. "The information I gave you was good."

"You said you'd stay quiet!"

"Emma." Emma's name, spoken firmly and with precision. Emma turned with slow dread to see Diana watching her from the top of the steps, the evening wind blowing her curly hair. She was wearing another long, elegant dress that made her look tall and imposing. She also looked absolutely furious.

"I guess you got my texts," Emma said. Diana didn't react.

"Leave Mr. Rook alone. We need to talk. I want to see you in my office in precisely ten minutes," she said.

Diana turned and went back into the Institute. Emma shot Rook a venomous glare. "Deals with you are supposed to be secret," she said, stabbing her index finger into his chest. "Maybe you didn't promise you'd keep your mouth shut, but we both know that's what people want from you. What they expect."

A small smile played around his mouth. "You don't scare me, Emma."

"Maybe I should."

"That's what's funny about you Nephilim," said Rook. "You know about Downworld, but you don't live in it." He put his lips to her ear, uncomfortably close. His breath raised the hairs on her neck when he spoke. "There are far more frightening things than you in this world, Emma Carstairs."

Emma wrenched herself away from him, turned, and ran up the Institute steps.

Ten minutes later Emma was standing in front of Diana's desk, her hair, still wet from her shower, dripping onto the polished tile floor.

Though Diana didn't live at the Institute, she had an office there, a comfortable corner room overlooking the highway and the sea. Emma could see the grass stretching out in front of the Institute in the twilight, blue-shadowed at the edges with coastal sage scrub. Rain had begun to patter down, streaking the windows.

The office was sparsely decorated. On the desk was a photograph of a tall man with his arm around a small girl who resembled Diana despite her youth. They stood in front of a shop whose sign read DIANA'S ARROW.

There were flowers on the windowsill that Diana had placed there to brighten the room. She folded her arms across the top of the desk and looked at Emma levelly.

"You lied to me last night," she said.

"I didn't," Emma said, "not exactly. I—"

"Don't say you omitted, Emma," said Diana. "You know better than that."

"What did Johnny Rook tell you?" Emma said, and was immediately sorry she'd said it. Diana's expression darkened.

"Why don't you tell me?" she said. "In fact, tell me what you did and what your punishment should be. Does that seem fair?"

Emma crossed her arms defiantly over her chest. She hated being caught, and Diana was good at catching her. Diana was smart, which was often awesome, but not when she was angry.

Emma could either fill in for Diana what she thought Diana was angry about, thus possibly revealing more than Diana already knew, or she could stay silent, thus possibly annoying Diana further. After a moment's deliberation, she said, "I should have to take care of a box of kittens. You know how cruel kittens are, with their tiny little claws and terrible attitudes."

"Speaking of terrible attitudes," Diana said. She was idly playing with a pencil. "You went to the Shadow Market, against specific rules. You talked to Johnny Rook. He tipped you off that there'd be a body dump at the Sepulchre that might be connected to your parents' deaths. You didn't just happen to be there. You weren't patrolling."

"I paid Rook not to say anything," Emma muttered. "I trusted him!"

Diana threw her pencil down. "Emma, the guy is known as

Rook the Crook. In fact, he's not just a crook, he's on the Clave's watch list because he works with faeries without permission. Any Downworlder or mundane who works in secret with faeries is locked out of business with Shadowhunters and forfeits their protection; you know that."

Emma threw up her hands. "But those are some of the most useful people out there! Cutting them off isn't helping the Clave, it's punishing Shadowhunters!"

Diana shook her head. "The rules are the rules for a reason. Being a Shadowhunter, a good one, is about more than just training fourteen hours a day and knowing sixty-five ways of killing a man with salad tongs."

"Sixty-seven," Emma said automatically. "Diana, I'm sorry. I really am, especially for dragging Cristina into this. It's not her fault."

"Oh, I know that." Diana was still frowning. Emma plunged ahead.

"Last night," she said, "you told me you believed me. About Sebastian not killing my parents. About there being more to it. Their deaths weren't just—just Sebastian wiping out the Conclave. Someone wanted them dead. Their deaths meant something—"

"Everyone's death means something," Diana said in a clipped tone. She passed a hand across her eyes. "I talked to the Silent Brothers last night. I found out what they know. And God, I've been telling myself I ought to lie to you about it—I've been struggling with it all day—"

"Please," Emma whispered. "Please, don't lie."

"But I can't. I remember when I came here, and you were this little girl, you were twelve years old, and you were wrecked. You'd lost everything. All you had to hang on to was Julian and your need for revenge. For Sebastian not to have been the reason your parents died, because if he was, then how could you punish him?" She took a deep breath. "I know Johnny Rook told you there've been a rash of murders. He's right. Twelve total, counting the one last night. No trace of the murderer left behind. All of the victims unidentified. Their teeth broken, wallets missing, fingerprints sanded off."

"And the Silent Brothers didn't know about this? The Clave, the Council—?"

"They did know. And this is the part you're not going to like." Diana's fingernails tapped on the glass of her desk. "Several of the dead were Fair Folk. That makes this a matter for the Scholomance, the Centurions, and the Silent Brothers. Not for Institutes. The Silent Brothers knew. The Clave knew. They didn't tell us, deliberately, because they don't want us involved."

"The *Scholomance?*"

The Scholomance was a piece of Shadowhunter history come to life. A cold castle of towers and corridors carved into the side of a mountain in the Carpathians, it had existed for centuries as a place where the most elite of Shadowhunters were trained to deal with the double menaces of demons and Downworlders. It had been closed when the first Accords were signed: a show of faith that Downworlders and Shadowhunters were no longer at war.

Now with the advent of the Cold Peace, it had been reopened and was operational again. One had to pass a series of harsh tests to be admitted, and what was learned at the school was not to be shared with others. Those who graduated were called Centurions, scholars and legendary warriors; Emma had never met one in person.

"It might not be fair, but it's the truth."

"But the markings. They admitted they were the same markings that were on my parents' bodies?"

"They didn't admit anything," Diana said. "They said they'd handle it. They said not to get involved, that the rule had come down from the Council itself."

"The bodies?" Emma said. "Did the bodies dissolve when they tried to move them, like my parents' bodies?"

"Emma!" Diana rose to her feet. Her hair was a dark, lovely cloud around her face. "We don't interfere with what happens to the fey, not anymore. That's what the Cold Peace means. The Clave hasn't just suggested we don't do this. It's forbidden to interfere with faerie business. If you involve yourself, it could have consequences not just for you but for Julian."

It was as if Diana had picked up one of the heavy paperweights from the desk and smashed it into Emma's chest. "Julian?"

"What does he do every year? On the anniversary of the Cold Peace?"

Emma thought of Julian, sitting here, in this office. Year after year, from the time he was twelve and all scraped elbows and torn jeans. He would sit patiently with pen and ink, writing his letter to the Clave, petitioning them to let his sister Helen come home from Wrangel Island.

Wrangel Island was the seat of all the world's wards, a set of magical spells that had been set up to protect the earth from certain demons a thousand years ago. It was also a tiny ice floe thousands of miles away in the Arctic Sea. When the Cold Peace had been declared, Helen had been sent there; the Clave had said it was in order that she study the wards, but no one believed it was anything other than an exile.

She had been allowed a few trips home since then, including the one to Idris when she had married Aline Penhallow, the daughter of the Consul. But even that powerful connection couldn't free her. Every year Julian wrote. And every year he was denied.

Diana spoke in a softer voice. "Every year the Clave says no because Helen's loyalty might be to the Fair Folk. How will it look if they think we're investigating faerie killings against their orders? How would it affect the chance that they might let her go?"

"Julian would want me to—" Emma started.

"Julian would cut off his hand if you asked him to. That doesn't mean you should." Diana rubbed her temples as if they ached. "Revenge isn't family, Emma. It isn't a friend, and it's a cold bedfellow." She dropped her hand and moved toward the window, glancing back over her shoulder at Emma. "Do you know why I took this job, here at the Institute? And don't give me a sarcastic answer."

Emma looked down at the floor. It was made up of alternating blue and white tiles; inside the white tiles were drawings: a rose, a castle, a church spire, an angel wing, a flock of birds, each one different.

"Because you were there in Alicante during the Dark War," said Emma, a catch in her voice. "You were there when Julian had to—to stop his father. You saw us fight, and you thought we were brave and you wanted to help. That's what you've always said."

"I had someone when I was younger who helped me become who I really am," said Diana. Emma's ears perked. Diana rarely spoke about her life. The Wrayburns had been a famous Shadowhunter family for generations, but Diana was the last. She never talked about her childhood, her family. It was as if her life had started when she'd taken over her father's weapons shop in Alicante. "I wanted to help you become who you really are."

"Which is?"

"The best Shadowhunter of your generation," said Diana. "You train and fight like no one I've ever seen. Which is exactly why I don't want to see you throw your potential away in the pursuit of something that won't heal your wounds."

*Throw my potential away?* Diana didn't know, didn't understand. None of her family had died in the Dark War. And Emma's parents hadn't died fighting; they'd been murdered, tortured and mutilated. Crying out for her, maybe, in those moments, short or long or endless, between life and death.

There was a sharp knock on the door. It swung open to reveal Cristina. She wore jeans and a sweater and her cheeks were pink, as if she was embarrassed to be interrupting. "The Blackthorns," she said. "They've come home."

Emma completely forgot whatever she'd been about to say to Diana and spun toward the door. "What? They're not supposed to get here until tomorrow!"

Cristina shrugged helplessly. "It could be a different huge family that just Portaled into the entryway."

Emma put her hand to her chest. Cristina was right. She could feel it: That faint pain that had existed behind her ribs ever since Julian had gone had become suddenly both better and worse—less painful, more like a butterfly wildly flapping its wings under her heart.

She darted out of the office, her bare feet slapping against the polished hardwood of the corridor. She hit the stairs and took them two at a time, swinging around the landings. She could hear voices now too. She thought she heard Dru's high, soft voice raised in a question, and Livvy answering.

And then she was there, on the second-floor gallery overlooking the foyer. The space was lit up as if it were daytime by a myriad of swirling colors, remnants of a vanishing Portal. In the center of the room stood the Blackthorns: Julian towering over the fifteen-year-old twins, Livvy and Ty. Beside them was Drusilla, holding the hand of the youngest, Tavvy. He looked asleep on his feet, his curly head against Dru's arm, his eyes closed.

"You're back!" Emma cried.

They all looked up at her. The Blackthorns had always been a family with a strong resemblance to each other: They shared the same wavy dark-brown hair, the color of bitter chocolate, and the same blue-green eyes. Though Ty, with his gray eyes, skinny frame, and tousled black hair, looked as if he'd wandered in from another branch of the family.

Dru and Livvy were smiling, and there was welcome in Ty's

grave nod, but it was Julian who Emma saw. She felt the *parabatai* rune on her upper arm throb as he looked up at her.

She darted down the stairs. Julian was bending to say something to Dru. Then he turned and took several quick strides toward Emma. He filled up her vision; he was all she could see. Not just Julian as he appeared now, walking toward her across the Angel-patterned floor, but Julian handing her seraph blades he'd named, Julian always giving her the blanket when it was cold in the car, Julian standing opposite her in the Silent City, white and gold fire rising up between them as they said their *parabatai* vows.

They collided in the middle of the foyer, and she threw her arms around him. "Jules," she said, but the sound was muffled against his shoulder as he hugged her back. She could hear the *parabatai* vows in the back of her mind as she breathed in the familiar scent of him: cloves, soap, salt.

*Whither thou goest, I will go.*

For a moment his arms were so tight around her that she could barely breathe. Then he let her go and stepped back.

Emma nearly unbalanced. She hadn't expected either quite such a tight hug or such a quick shove away.

He looked different too. Her mind couldn't quite take it in.

"I thought you were coming tomorrow morning," Emma said. She tried to catch Julian's eye, to get him to return her welcoming smile. Instead, he was looking at his brothers and sisters as if counting to make sure they were all there.

"Malcolm showed up early," he said to her, over his shoulder. "Suddenly appeared in Great-Aunt Marjorie's kitchen, wearing pajamas. Said he'd forgotten the time difference. She screamed the house down."

Emma felt the tension in her chest easing. Malcolm Fade, the head of the warlocks of Los Angeles, was a family friend, and his eccentricity was an old joke between her and Jules.

"Then he accidentally Portaled us to London instead of here," Livvy announced, bounding forward to hug Emma. "And we had to hunt someone down to open another Portal—Diana!"

Livvy detached herself from Emma and went to greet her tutor. For a few moments, everything was welcoming hubbub: questions and hellos and hugs. Tavvy had woken up and was wandering around sleepily, tugging on people's sleeves. Emma ruffled his hair.

*Thy people shall be my people.* Julian's family had become Emma's when they had made themselves *parabatai*. It was almost like marriage in that way.

Emma looked over at Julian. He was watching his family, his expression intent. As if he'd forgotten she was there. And in that moment her mind suddenly seemed to wake up and present her with a catalog of the ways in which he seemed different.

He'd always kept his hair short and practical, but he must have forgotten to cut it in England: It had grown out, in thick, luscious, curly Blackthorn waves. The tips hung down past his ears. He was tanned, and it wasn't as if she didn't know the color of his eyes, but now they seemed suddenly both brighter and darker at once, the intense blue-green of the ocean a mile down from the surface. The shape of his face had changed as well, resettling into more adult lines, losing the softness of childhood, revealing the clean sweep of jawbone that peaked at his slightly sharp chin, an echo of the wing shape of his collarbone, visible just beneath the collar of his T-shirt.

She looked away. To her surprise, her heart was beating fast, as if she was nervous. Flustered, she knelt down to hug Tavvy. "You're missing teeth," she told him when he grinned at her. "Careless of you."

"Dru told me that faeries steal your teeth while you're sleeping," Tavvy said.

"That's because that's what I told her," Emma said, rising to her feet. She felt a light touch on her arm.

It was Julian. With his finger he began to trace words against her skin—it was something they had been doing their whole lives, ever since they realized they needed a way to silently communicate during boring study sessions or time with adults. A-R-E Y-O-U A-L-L R-I-G-H-T?

She nodded at him. He was looking at her with faint concern, which was a relief. It felt familiar. Did he really look so different? He was less thin, more muscular, though it was a slender sort of muscle. He looked like the swimmers she had always admired for their spare beauty. He still wore the same arrangement of leather and shell and sea-glass bracelets around his wrists, though. His hands were still spotted with paint. He was still Julian.

"You're all so tanned," Diana was saying. "How are you all so tanned? I thought it rained all the time in England!"

"I don't have a tan," said Tiberius matter-of-factly. It was true, he didn't. Ty detested the sun. When they all went to the beach he was usually to be found under a terrifyingly huge umbrella, reading a detective story.

"Great-Aunt Marjorie made us train outside all day," Livvy said. "Well, not Tavvy. She kept him inside and fed him bramble jelly."

"Tiberius hid," said Drusilla. "In the barn."

"It wasn't hiding," said Ty. "It was a strategic retreat."

"It was hiding," said Dru, a scowl spreading across her round face. Her braids stuck out on either side of her head like Pippi Longstocking's. Emma tugged on one of them affectionately.

"Don't argue with your brother," said Julian, and turned to Ty. "Don't argue with your sister. You're both tired."

"What does being tired have to do with not arguing?" asked Ty.

"Julian means you should all be asleep," Diana said.

"It's only eight o'clock," Emma protested. "They just got here!"

Diana pointed. Tavvy had curled up on the floor and was asleep in the angled beam of light from a lamp, exactly like a cat. "It's considerably later in England."

Livvy stepped forward and picked up Tavvy gently. His head lolled against her neck. "I'll put him to bed."

Julian's eyes met Diana's briefly. "Thanks, Livvy," he said. "I'll go tell Uncle Arthur we got in all right." He looked around and sighed. "We can deal with luggage in the morning. Everybody, bedtime."

Livvy grumbled something; Emma didn't hear it. She felt puzzled; more than puzzled. Even though Julian had answered her texts and calls with short, neutral missives, she hadn't been prepared for a Julian who looked different, who seemed different. She wanted him to look at her the way he always had, with the smile that seemed reserved for their interactions.

Diana was saying good night, picking up her keys and handbag. Taking advantage of the distraction, Emma reached out to trace lightly against Julian's skin with her finger.

*I N-E-E-D T-O T-A-L-K T-O Y-O-U,* she wrote.

Without looking at her, Julian dropped his own hand and wrote along her forearm. *W-H-A-T A-B-O-U-T?*

The foyer door opened and closed behind Diana, letting in a chilly gust of wind and rain. Water splashed on Emma's cheek as she turned to look at Julian. "It's important," she said. She wondered if she sounded incredulous. She'd never had to tell him something was important before. If she said she needed to talk to him, he knew she meant it. "Just—" She dropped her voice. "Come to my room after you see Arthur."

He hesitated, just for a moment; the glass and shells on his wristbands rattled as he pushed his hair out of his face. Livvy was already headed upstairs with Tavvy, the others in her wake. Emma felt her annoyance soften immediately into guilt. Jules was exhausted, obviously. That was all.

"Unless you're too tired," she said.

He shook his head, his face unreadable—and Emma had always been able to read his face. "I'll come," he said, and then he put a hand on her shoulder. Lightly, a casual gesture. As if they hadn't been separated for two months. "It's good to see you again," he said, and turned to head up the stairs after Livvy.

Of course he would have to go see Arthur, Emma thought. Someone had to tell their eccentric guardian that the Blackthorns were home. And of course he was tired. And of course he seemed different: people did, when you hadn't seen them in a while. It could take a day or two to get back to the way they used to be: Comfortable. Inseparable. Secure.

She put her hand against her chest. Though the pain she had felt while Julian was in England, the stretched-rubber-band feeling she'd hated, was gone, she now felt a new strange ache near her heart.

# 3

## THE MOON NEVER BEAMS
## WITHOUT BRINGING ME DREAMS

**The attic of the Institute was dim. Two skylights were built into** the roof, but Uncle Arthur had covered them with butcher paper when he had first moved his books and papers into this room, saying that he was worried the sunlight would damage the delicate instruments of his studies.

Arthur and his brother, Julian's father Andrew, had been brought up by parents obsessed with the classical period: with Ancient Greek and Latin, with the lays of heroes, the mythology and history of Greece and Rome.

Julian had grown up knowing the stories of the *Iliad* and the *Odyssey*, of the Argonauts and the *Aeneid*, of men and monsters, gods and heroes. But while Andrew had retained only a fondness for the classics (one that extended, admittedly, to naming his children after emperors and queens—Julian was still grateful to his mother for the fact that he was a Julian and not a Julius, which was what his father had wanted), Arthur was obsessed.

He had brought hundreds of books with him from England, and in the years since, the room had become stuffed with hundreds more. They were arranged according to a filing system only Arthur understood—Sophocles's *Antigone* tipping over onto Thucydides's *History of the Peloponnesian War*, scattered monographs, and books with their bindings ripped, the individual pages spread carefully across various surfaces. There were probably at least six desks in the room: When one became too overwhelmed with papers and bits of broken pottery and statuary, Uncle Arthur simply purchased another.

He was sitting at one near the west side of the room. Through a tear in the butcher paper covering the window beside it, Julian could see a flash of blue ocean. The sleeves of Arthur's old sweater were rolled up. Under the hems of his frayed khakis, his feet were stuffed into ratty bedroom slippers. His cane, which he rarely used, was propped against a wall.

"Achilles had a phorminx," he was muttering, "with a crossbar of silver; Hercules was taught to play the cithara. Both instruments have been translated as 'lyre,' but are they the same instrument? If they are, why the different words to describe them?"

"Hello, Uncle," Julian said. He hefted the tray he was carrying, on which he'd placed a hastily assembled dinner. "We've come back."

Arthur turned slowly, like an old dog cocking its head warily at the sound of a shout. "Andrew, good to see you," he said. "I was pondering the Greek ideals of love. Agape, of course, the highest love, the love that Gods feel. Then eros, romantic love; and philia, the love of friends; and storge, the love of family. Which would you say it is that our *parabatai* feel? Is it closer to philia or to agape— eros, of course, being forbidden? And if so, are we gifted with something, as Nephilim, that mundanes can never understand—and so how did the Greeks know of it? A paradox, Andrew . . ."

Julian exhaled. The last thing he wanted to talk about was the kind of love *parabatai* felt for each other. And he did not want to be called by his dead father's name. He wished he were somewhere, anywhere else, but he came forward anyway into where the light was stronger, where his uncle could see his face. "It's Julian. I said that we're back. All of us. Tavvy, Dru, the twins . . ."

Arthur stared at him with uncomprehending blue-green eyes, and Julian fought against the sinking of his heart. He hadn't wanted to come up here at all; he'd wanted to go with Emma. But he could tell from the last fire-message he'd gotten from Diana that a trip to the attic would be necessary the moment he got back.

It had always been his job. It always would be.

He set the tray on the desk, careful to avoid the piles of paper. There was a stack of outgoing mail and scrawled patrol notes beside Arthur's elbow. Not enormous, but not as diminished as Julian had hoped it would be. "I brought you dinner."

Arthur gazed at the tray of food as if it were a distant object barely seen through fog, his brows crinkling. It was a bowl of soup, quickly heated in the kitchen, now cooling in the chilly attic air. Julian had carefully wrapped the cutlery in napkins and placed a basket of bread on the tray, though he knew that when he returned in the morning to collect the remains, the food would be nearly untouched.

"Do you think it's a clue?" Uncle Arthur said.

"Do I think what's a clue?"

"The cithara and the phorminx. They fit into the pattern, but the pattern is so large. . . ." Uncle Arthur leaned back with a sigh, gazing up at the wall in front of him, where hundreds of pieces of paper covered in spidery handwriting had been glued or tacked. "Life is short, and wisdom long to learn," he whispered.

"Life's not that short," Julian said. "Or at least, it doesn't have to be." It had been for his parents, he supposed. It often was for Shadowhunters. But what was likely to harm Arthur, hidden away in his cloistered attic? He'd probably outlive all of them.

He thought of Emma, the risks she took, the scars on her body that he saw when they swam or practiced. She had that in her, the blood of Shadowhunters who had risked their lives down through the generations, who lived off the oxygen of adrenaline and fighting. But he pushed away the thought of her dying as her parents had; it was not a thought he could bear.

"No man under the sky lives twice," Arthur murmured, probably quoting something. He usually was. He was looking down at the desk again, and seemed lost in thought. Julian remembered years ago and the floor of the attic covered in Arthur's bloody handprints. That was the night he had first called on Malcolm Fade.

"If you have everything you need, Uncle," Julian said, starting to move away.

Arthur's head snapped up. For a moment his gaze was clear and focused. "You're a good boy," he said to Julian. "But it won't help you, in the end."

Julian froze. "What?"

But Arthur had already gone back to his papers.

Julian turned and went down the attic steps. They creaked familiarly under his weight. The Los Angeles Institute wasn't particularly old, certainly not as old as other Institutes, but something about the attic felt ancient and dusty and cut off from the rest of the place.

He reached the door at the foot of the stairs. He leaned for a moment against the wall, in the dimness and silence.

Silence was something he had rarely, unless he was going to sleep. He was usually surrounded by the constant chatter of his siblings. He had them around him always, wanting his attention, needing his help.

He thought too of the cottage in England, the quiet buzzing of the bees in the garden, the hush under the trees. Everything green and blue, so different from the desert and its dry browns and sere golds. He hadn't wanted to leave Emma, but at the same time he'd thought it would help. Like an addict getting away from the source of his addiction.

Enough. There were some things there was no point thinking about. In the dark and the shadows where secrets lived, that was where Julian survived. It was how he had managed for years.

Taking a deep breath, he went back out into the hallway.

*Emma was standing on the beach. There was no one else there; it was entirely deserted. Vast tracts of sand spread out on either side of her, dully sparkling with shards of mica underneath a clouded sun.*

*The ocean was before her. It was as beautiful and deadly as the creatures who lived inside it; the great white sharks with their rough, pale sides, the killer whales striped in black and white like an Edwardian garden chaise. Emma looked at the ocean and felt what she always felt: a mixture of yearning and terror, a desire to throw herself into the green cold that was like the desire to drive too fast, jump too high, leap into battle unarmed.*

*Thanatos, Arthur would have called it. The heart's desire for death.*

*The sea gave a great cry, like the cry of an animal, and began to draw back. It rushed away from her, leaving dying fish flopping in its wake, heaps of seaweed, the ruins of wrecked ships, the detritus of the bottom of the sea. Emma knew she should run, but she stood paralyzed as the water gathered itself up into a tower, a massive wall with clear sides—she could see helpless dolphins and flailing sharks caught in the boiling sides. She cried out and fell to her knees as she saw the bodies of her parents, prisoned in the rising water as if they were trapped in a massive coffin of glass, her mother limp and twitching, her father's hand reaching out to her through the foam and boil of the waves—*

Emma sat bolt upright, reaching for Cortana, which was laid across her bedside table. Her hand slipped, though, and the sword rattled to the floor. She reached for the bedside lamp and snapped it on.

Warm yellow light filled the room. She looked around, blinking. She had fallen asleep in her pajamas, on top of the covers.

She threw her legs over the side of the bed, rubbing at her eyes. She'd lain down on the bed to wait for Jules, her closet door open, the light on.

She'd wanted to show the new photos to Julian. She'd wanted to tell him everything, to hear his voice: soothing, familiar, loving. Hear him help her puzzle out what to do next.

But Julian hadn't come.

She stood up, grabbing up a sweater from the back of a chair. A quick glance at the clock on the bedside table told her it was nearly three in the morning. She grimaced and slipped out into the hallway.

It was dark and silent. No bars of light under the doorways showed that anyone else was awake. She moved down the hall to Julian's room, pushed the door open, and slipped inside.

She almost hadn't expected him to be there. She'd thought he might have gone to his studio—surely he'd missed painting there—but he was sprawled on his bed, asleep.

The room was lighter than the hallway outside. The window faced the moon where it hung over the mountains, and the white illumination outlined everything in the room in silver. Julian's curling hair was a dark spill against the pillow, his dark lashes entirely black. They lay against his cheekbones, fine and soft as dusted soot.

His arm was stretched behind his head, pulling his T-shirt up. She glanced away from the bare skin revealed under the hem and clambered onto the bed, reaching out for his shoulder.

"Julian," she said softly. "Jules."

He stirred, eyes opening slowly. In the moonlight they looked silvery-gray, like Ty's.

"Emma," he said, his voice sounding blurry with sleep.

*I thought you were going to come to my room*, she wanted to say, but she couldn't: He looked so tired, it melted her heart. She reached out to brush his hair out of his eyes, paused, and put her hand on his shoulder instead. He had rolled onto his side; she recognized the worn T-shirt and sweatpants he wore.

His eyes were starting to flutter closed again.

"Jules," she said impulsively. "Can I stay?"

It was their code, the short version of the longer request: *Stay and make me forget my nightmares. Stay and sleep next to me. Stay and chase the bad dreams away, the memories of blood, of dead parents, of Endarkened warriors with eyes like dead black coals.*

It was a request they'd both made, more than once. Since they were little kids, they'd crawled into each other's beds to sleep. Emma had once imagined their dreams mingling as they'd let go of consciousness together, sharing bits and pieces of each other's sleeping worlds. It was one of the things about being *parabatai* that made it a magic toward which she had yearned: In a way, it meant you were never alone. Waking and sleeping, in battle and out of it, you had someone twinned by your side, bound to your life and hopes and happiness, a near-perfect support.

He moved aside, his eyes half-open, his voice muffled. "Stay."

She crawled in under the covers beside him. He made room for her, his long body folding and unfolding, giving her space. In the depression his body had made, the sheets were warm and smelled like cloves and soap.

She was still shivering. She moved an inch closer to him, feeling the heat radiating off his body. He slept on his back, one arm folded behind his head, his other hand flat against his stomach. His bracelets gleamed in the moonlight. He looked at her—she knew he'd seen her move toward him—and then his eyes flashed as he shut them deliberately, dark lashes sweeping down over his cheeks.

His breathing began to even out almost immediately. He was asleep, but Emma lay awake, looking at him, at the way his chest rose and fell, a steady metronome.

They didn't touch. They rarely did touch, sleeping in bed

together. As kids they'd fought over the blankets, stacked books between them sometimes to settle arguments about who was encroaching on whose side of the bed. Now they'd learned to sleep in the same space, but they kept the distance of the books between them, a shared memory.

She could hear the ocean pounding in the distance; she could see the green wall of water rising behind her eyelids in her dream. But it all seemed distant, the terrifying crash of waves drowned out by the soft breathing of her *parabatai*.

One day she and Julian would both be married, to other people. There would be no crawling into each other's beds. There would be no exchanging of secrets at midnight. Their closeness wouldn't break, but it would bend and stretch into a new shape. She would have to learn to live with that.

One day. But not quite yet.

When Emma woke, Julian was gone.

She sat up groggily. It was midmorning, later than she usually rose, and the room was lit with a pinkish-gold tinge. Julian's navy-blue sheets and blanket were tangled down at the foot of the bed. When Emma put her hand against his pillow, it was still warm—he must have just left.

She pushed down her feeling of uneasiness that he'd gone without saying anything. He probably just hadn't wanted to wake her; Julian had always been an uneasy sleeper, and the time difference couldn't be helping. Telling herself it was no big deal, she went back to her room and changed into leggings and a T-shirt, and slid her feet into flip-flops.

Normally she would have checked Julian's studio first, but she could see from a glance out the window that it was a bright, brilliant summer day. The sky was filled with the light brushstrokes of white cloud. The sea glimmered, the surface dancing with flecks of

gold. In the distance Emma could see the black dots of surfers bob-
bing on the surface.

She knew he'd missed the ocean—knew it from the few brief,
infrequent texts and fire-messages he'd sent her while he was in
England. She made her way through the Institute and down the
path that led to the highway, then darted across it, dodging surfers'
vans and luxury convertibles on their way to Nobu.

He was exactly where she'd thought he'd be when she reached
the beach: facing the water and the sun, the salt air lifting his hair
and rippling the cloth of his T-shirt. She wondered how long he'd
been standing there, hands in the pockets of his jeans.

She took a hesitant step onto the damp sand. "Jules?"

He turned to look at her. For a moment he looked dazzled, as if
he were looking into the sun, though it was above them—Emma
could feel its warmth, bright and hot on her back.

He smiled. A wave of relief went through her. It was Julian's
familiar smile, the one that lit up his face. She jogged down to the
waterline: The tide was coming in, sliding up the beach to reach
the tips of Julian's shoes. "You woke up early," she said, splashing
through the shallows toward him. The water made silvery inroads
into the sand.

"It's almost noon," he said. His voice sounded ordinary, but he
still looked different to Emma, strangely different: the shape of his
face, his shoulders under his T-shirt. "What did you want to talk to
me about?"

"What?" Emma was caught temporarily off guard, both by the
difference in him and the sudden question.

"Last night," he said. "You said you wanted to talk to me. How
about now?"

"Okay." Emma looked up at the gulls wheeling overhead. "Let's
go sit down. I don't want to get washed away when the tide comes in."

They settled in farther up the beach, where the sand was warm from the sunlight. Emma kicked her shoes off to dig her toes in, exulting in the grainy feeling. Julian laughed.

She looked at him sideways. "What is it?"

"You and the beach," he said. "You love the sand, but you hate the water."

"I know," she said, widening her eyes at him. "Isn't it ironic?"

"It's not ironic. Irony is the unexpected outcome of an expected situation. This is just one of your quirks."

"You shock me," Emma said, pulling out her phone. "I am shocked."

"Sarcasm noted," he said, turning the phone over in his right hand. Cristina's photos from the previous night had loaded. As he ran his eyes over them, she explained how she'd followed the tip from Johnny Rook to the Sepulchre, the way she'd found the body, and Diana's scolding following Rook's visit to the Institute. As she spoke, she relaxed, her odd new awareness of Julian fading. This was normal, this was them the way they always were: talking, listening, working as *parabatai*. "I know these are the same markings," she finished. "I'm not out of my mind, am I?"

Julian looked up at her. "No," he said. "But Diana thinks that if you look into this, it'll compromise the Clave's willingness to let Helen come home?"

"Yeah." Emma hesitated, then reached out and took his hand. The sea-glass bracelet on his left wrist clinked musically. She felt his calluses against her fingers, as familiar to her as a map of her own bedroom. "I would never do anything to hurt Helen, or Mark, or you," she said. "If you think Diana's right, I won't—" She swallowed. "I'll leave it alone."

Julian glanced down at their entwined fingers. He was still, but a pulse had started up at the base of his throat; she could see it beating, hard. It must have been the mention of his sister.

"It's been five years," he said, and drew his hand back. He didn't yank it out of her grip or anything like that, just drew it back as he turned toward the water. A completely natural movement that nevertheless left her feeling awkward. "The Clave hasn't budged on letting Helen come home. They haven't budged on looking for Mark. And they haven't budged on considering that maybe your parents weren't killed by Sebastian either. It seems wrong to sacrifice finding out what happened to your family for a doomed hope."

"Don't say it's doomed, Jules—"

"There's another way of thinking about this too," he said, and she could practically see the gears turning in his quick brain. "If you actually solved this, if we solved this, the Clave would owe us. I believe you that whoever killed your parents, it wasn't Sebastian Morgenstern. We're looking at a demon or some other force that has the power to murder Shadowhunters and get away with it. If we defeated something like that . . ."

Emma's head was starting to ache. Her ponytail holder was twisted hard into her hair; she reached up to loosen it. "Then they'd give us special treatment, you mean? Because everyone would be watching?"

"They'd have to," Julian said. "If everyone knew what we did. And we could make sure everyone knew." He hesitated. "We do have connections."

"You don't mean Jem, do you?" asked Emma. "Because I don't know how to reach him."

"Not Jem and Tessa."

"So Jace and Clary," Emma said. Jace Herondale and Clary Fairchild ran the New York Institute. They were some of the youngest Shadowhunters ever to hold such a senior position. Emma had been friends with Clary since she was twelve, when Clary had first followed her out of the Council Hall in Idris, the only person among all the Clave, it seemed, to care that she had lost her parents.

Jace was probably one of the best Shadowhunters who had ever lived, purely in terms of fighting prowess. Clary had been born with a different talent: She could create runes. It was something no other Shadowhunter had ever been able to do. She had explained once to Emma that she couldn't force the runes that came to her—either they did or they didn't. Over the years she'd added several useful runes to the Gray Book—one for breathing underwater, another for running long distances, and a rather controversial one for birth control that had nevertheless quickly become the most often used rune in the lexicon.

Everyone knew Jace and Clary. That was how it went when you saved the world. They were heroes to most—to Emma they were people who had held her hands during the darkest part of her life.

"Yeah." Julian reached around, rubbed the back of his neck. He looked tired. There was a faint sheen to the skin under his eyes, as if it was stretched thin with exhaustion. He worried at his lip with his teeth, as he always did when he was anxious or bothered. "I mean, they were made some of the youngest heads of an Institute ever. And look at what the Clave did for Simon, and for Magnus and Alec. When you're a hero, they'll do a lot for you." Julian stood up, and Emma rose with him, pulling the band out of her ponytail. Her hair came free, tumbling in waves down her shoulders and her back. Julian looked at her quickly, and then away.

"Jules—" she began.

But he had already turned away, heading back toward the road.

She shoved her feet into her shoes and caught up with him where the sand rose up toward the pavement. "Is everything okay?"

"Of course. Here, sorry, I forgot to give you this back." He handed Emma her phone. "Look, the Clave makes their rules. And they live by their rules. But that doesn't mean that with the right pressure, the rules never change."

"You're being cryptic."

He smiled, the corners of his eyes crinkling.

"They don't like letting Shadowhunters as young as we are get involved with serious issues. Never have. But Jace and Clary and Alec and Isabelle saved the world when they were our age. They were honored for it. Results—that's what makes them change their minds."

They had reached the highway. Emma looked up, toward the hills. The Institute was perched on a low bluff over the coast road.

"Julian Blackthorn," she said as they crossed the highway. "You revolutionary, you."

"So we'll look into this, but do it quietly," Julian said. "First move, compare the photos of the body you found to the photos of the bodies of your parents. Everyone will want to help. Don't worry."

They were halfway up the Institute road. Cars were backed up even now, mundanes commuting to work downtown. Sunlight sparked off their windshields.

"And if it turns out the markings are just gibberish, and it's some random lunatic on a murder spree?"

"Couldn't be a spree. Sprees happen all at once, but in different locations. Like if you drive from place to place shooting people, that's a spree."

"So what's this? A mass murder?"

"Mass murders also all take place at the same time, but are in the same location," Julian said loftily, in the same tone he used when explaining to Tavvy why he couldn't have Cheerios for breakfast. "This is definitely a serial killer. That's when the murders are spaced out over time."

"It's disturbing that you know this," Emma said. In front of the Institute, stretching to the edge of the bluff, was a sun-dried lawn, edged with sea grass and scrub brush. The family spent little time there: too close to the highway, unshaded, and overlaid with scratchy grass.

"Dru's into true crime right now," Jules said. They'd reached the

Institute stairs. "You wouldn't believe how much she told me about how to hide a body."

Emma sprang past him, up three steps, and turned to look down. "I'm taller than you," she announced. It was a game they'd played when they were little—Emma always swearing she'd grow up taller than he was, finally giving up when he'd turned fourteen and shot up five inches.

Julian looked up at her. The sun was shining directly into his eyes, overlaying the blue-green with gold, making them look like the patina that shone on the Roman glass Arthur collected. "Em," he said. "However much we might joke about it, you know I take this seriously. It's your parents. You *deserve* to know what happened."

She felt a sudden lump in her throat. "This just feels different," she whispered. "I know how many times I've thought I found out something and it was nothing, or I've followed a false lead, but this feels like something else, Jules. This feels real."

Her phone rang. She looked away from Jules, fishing it out of her pocket. When she saw the name flash up on-screen she made a face and shoved it back. Jules raised an eyebrow, his expression neutral.

"Cameron Ashdown?" he said. "Why aren't you picking up?"

"Just not in the mood." The words came out almost to her surprise; she wondered why she wasn't telling him. *Cameron and I broke up.*

The front door banged open. "Emma! Jules!"

It was Drusilla and Tavvy, both still in pajamas. Tavvy had a lollipop in one hand and was sucking on it industriously. When he saw Emma, his eyes lit up and he ran toward her. "Emma!" he said around the candy.

She pulled him close and wrapped her arms around his round little-boy middle, squeezing until he giggled.

"Tavvy!" Julian said. "Don't run with lollipops in your mouth. You could choke."

Tavvy removed the lollipop and stared at it the way someone might stare at a loaded gun. "And die?"

"Hideously," Julian said. "Fatally, fatally die." He turned to Drusilla, who had her hands on her hips. Her black pajamas were decorated with cartoon drawings of chain saws and skeletons. "What's up, Dru?"

"It's Friday," Drusilla said. "Pancake day? You remember? You promised?"

"Oh, right, I did." Julian tugged affectionately on one of his little sister's braids. "You go wake up Livvy and Ty, and I'll—"

"They're already awake," Dru said. "They're in the kitchen. Waiting." She looked at him pointedly.

Julian smiled. "Okay. I'll be right there." He picked Tavvy up and deposited him back in the entryway. "You two scoot along to the kitchen and reassure the twins before they get desperate and start trying to do the cooking themselves."

They scampered off, giggling. Julian turned back to Emma with a sigh. "I have been lollipoped," he said, indicating where Tavvy had managed to leave a blue sugar circle at the collar of his shirt.

"Badge of honor." Emma laughed. "See you in the kitchen. I need to shower." She darted up the steps, pausing at the open front door to look down at him. Framed against the blue sea and blue sky, his eyes looked like bits of the landscape. "Jules—was there something you wanted to ask me?"

He glanced away, shaking his head. "No. Nothing at all."

Someone was shaking Cristina by the shoulder. She woke up slowly, blinking. She'd been dreaming about home, about the heat of summer, the shade of the cool gardens of the Institute, the roses her mother cultivated in a climate not always friendly to the delicate flower. Yellow roses were preferred, because they had been the favorite flower of her most beloved writer, but roses of any color were necessary to illuminate the proud name of Rosales.

Cristina had been walking in a garden, about to turn a corner, when she heard the murmur of familiar voices. She sped up, a smile spreading over her face. Jaime and Diego . . . Her oldest friend and her first love. Surely they would be happy to see her.

She swung around the corner and stared. There was no one there. Just the echo of voices, the distant sound of a mocking laugh carried on the wind.

The shade and petals faded away and Cristina looked up to find Emma leaning over her, wearing one of her crazy flowered dresses. Her hair hung down around her shoulders in strands damp from the shower.

"*¡Deja de molestarme, estoy despierta!*" protested Cristina, batting Emma's hands away. "Emma! Stop it! I'm awake!" She sat up and put her hands to her head. She prided herself on not ever mixing up her first language with English while she was in the U.S., but sometimes when she was tired or barely awake it slipped out.

"Come with me to breakfast," Emma wheedled. "Or it might be brunch. It's almost noon. But whatever—I want to introduce you to everyone. I want you to meet Julian—"

"I saw him last night from the top of the stairs," said Cristina with a yawn. "He has nice hands."

"Great, you can tell him that in person."

"No, thank you."

"Get up," Emma said. "Or I'll sit on you."

Cristina threw a pillow at her. "Go wait outside."

A few minutes later, Cristina—having dressed quickly in a pale pink sweater and pencil skirt—found herself being marched down the hall. She could hear voices, raised in chatter, coming from the kitchen. She touched the medallion at her throat, the way she always did when she needed a bit of extra bravery.

She'd heard so much about the Blackthorns, especially Julian, since she'd arrived at the Institute that they'd taken on an almost mythical status in her mind. She was dreading meeting them—not only were they the most important people in Emma's life, but they were also the ones who could make the rest of her stay either pleasant or miserable.

The kitchen was a large room with painted walls and windows looking out over the blue-green ocean in the distance. A massive farmer's table dominated the space, surrounded by bench seats and chairs. The counters and table were tiled in what looked like bright Spanish designs, but if you glanced more closely, they formed scenes from classical literature: Jason and the Argonauts, Achilles and Patroclus, Odysseus and the Sirens. Someone, once, had decorated this space with a loving hand—someone had picked out the copper cooking range, the porcelain double sinks, the exact shade of yellow on the walls.

Julian was standing over the stove, barefoot, a dish towel slung around his broad shoulders. The younger Blackthorns were crowded around the table. Emma came forward, pulling Cristina behind her. "Everyone, this is Cristina," she said. "She's saved my life about sixteen times this summer, so be nice to her. Cristina, this is Julian—"

Julian looked over and smiled. The smile made him look like sunlight in human form. It didn't hurt that the dish towel around his neck had kittens on it, and there was pancake batter on his calloused hands. "Thanks for not letting Emma get killed," he said. "Contrary to whatever she might have told you, we need her around here."

"I'm Livvy." The pretty girl who was one half of the twins came forward to shake Cristina's hand. "And that's Ty." She pointed to a boy with black hair who was curled up on a bench seat reading *The*

*Case-Book of Sherlock Holmes.* "Dru has the braids, and Tavvy is the one with the lollipop."

"Don't run with a lollipop, Cristina," said Tavvy. He looked around seven, with a thin, serious face.

"I . . . won't?" Cristina assured him, puzzled.

"Tavvy," Julian groaned. He was pouring batter from a white ceramic pitcher into the frying pan on the stove. The room filled with the smell of butter and pancakes. "Get up and set the table, you useless layabouts—not you, Cristina," he added, looking embarrassed. "You're a guest."

"I'll be here for a year. I'm not really a guest," Cristina said, and went with the rest of them to get cutlery and plates. There was a buzz of pleasant activity, and Cristina felt herself relax. If she had to admit it, she'd been dreading the Blackthorns descending, disrupting the pleasant rhythm of her life here with Emma and Diana. Now that the family was here, here and real, she felt guilty for having resented them.

"First pancakes are up," Julian announced.

Ty put down his book and picked up a plate. Cristina, reaching into the refrigerator for more butter, heard him say to Julian, "I thought you forgot it was pancake day." There was accusation in his voice, and something else besides—a slight edge of nervousness? She remembered Emma saying in passing that Ty got upset when his routine was interrupted.

"I didn't forget, Ty," Julian said gently. "I was distracted. But I didn't forget."

Ty seemed to relax. "All right."

He went back over to the table, and Tavvy bounded up after him. They were organized, the Blackthorns, in the unconscious way that only a family could be: knowing who got pancakes first (Ty), who wanted butter and syrup (Dru), who wanted just syrup (Livvy), and who wanted sugar (Emma).

Cristina ate hers plain. It was buttery and not too sweet, crisp around the edges. "These are good," she said to Julian, who had finally sat down on a bench seat beside Emma. Up close she could see lines of tiredness at the edges of his eyes, lines that seemed out of place on the face of a boy so young.

"Practice." He smiled at her. "I've been making them since I was twelve."

Livvy gave a bounce in her seat. She was wearing a black tank dress and reminded Cristina of the stylish mundane girls in Mexico City, striding purposefully around Condesa and Roma in their sheath dresses and delicate strappy heels. Her brown hair was streaked liberally with gold where the sun had bleached it. "It's so good to be back," she said, licking syrup off her finger. "It just wasn't the same at Great-Aunt Marjorie's without you two looking after us." She pointed at Emma and Julian. "I see why they say you shouldn't separate *parabatai*, you just go together, like—"

"Sherlock Holmes and Dr. Watson," said Ty, who had gone back to reading.

"Chocolate and peanut butter," said Tavvy.

"Captain Ahab and the whale," said Dru, who was dreamily drawing patterns in the syrup on her empty plate.

Emma choked on her juice. "Dru, the whale and Captain Ahab were enemies."

"True," Julian agreed. "The whale without Ahab is just a whale. A whale with no problems. A stress-free whale."

Dru looked mutinous. "I heard you guys talking," she said to Emma and Julian. "I was out on the lawn, before I went back in to get Tavvy. About Emma finding a body?"

Ty looked up immediately. "Emma found a body?"

Emma glanced a little worriedly at Tavvy, but he appeared absorbed in his food. She said, "Well, while you guys were gone, there've been a series of murders—"

"Murders? How come you didn't say anything to Julian or us about it?" Ty was bolt upright now, his book dangling from his hand. "You could have sent an e-mail or a fire-message or a postcard—"

"A murder postcard?" said Livvy, wrinkling up her nose.

"I only found out about it the night before last," Emma said, and explained quickly what had happened at the Sepulchre. "The body was covered in runes," she finished. "The same kind of markings that were on my parents' bodies when they were found."

"No one's ever been able to translate those, right?" Livvy said.

"No one." Emma shook her head. "Everyone's tried to decode them. Malcolm, Diana, even the Spiral Labyrinth," she added, naming the underground headquarters of the world's warlocks, where a great deal of arcane knowledge was hidden.

"Before, they were unique as far as we knew," Ty said. His eyes were really a very startling gray, like the back of a silver spoon. A pair of headphones hung around his neck, the cord snaking down into his shirt. "Now there's another example. If we compare them, we might learn something."

"I made a list of everything I know about the body," Emma said, producing a piece of paper and setting it on the table. Ty picked it up immediately. "Some is what I saw, some I heard from Johnny Rook and Diana. The fingertips were sanded down, teeth broken, wallet missing."

"Someone trying to hide the identity of the victim," said Ty.

"And probably not that uncommon," said Emma. "But there was also the fact that the body was soaked in seawater and showed signs of burning, and was lying in a chalked ring of symbols. And was covered in writing. That seems unusual."

"Like the sort of thing you could search for in back archives of mundane newspaper articles," said Ty. His gray eyes glowed with excitement. "I'll do it."

"Thank you," Emma said. "But—" She glanced toward Julian, and then around at the others, her brown eyes grave. "Diana can't know, okay?"

"Why not?" asked Dru, frowning. Tavvy was paying no attention at all; he'd gotten down on the floor and was playing under the table with a set of toy trucks.

Emma sighed. "Several of the dead bodies were fey. And that puts this squarely out of any territory we should be messing with." She glanced over at Cristina. "If you don't want to do any of this, that's fine. Faerie business is tricky and Diana doesn't want us involved."

"You know how I feel about the Cold Peace," said Cristina. "Absolutely I will help." There was a murmer of agreement.

"Told you not to worry," Julian said, touching Emma's shoulder lightly before standing up to start clearing the breakfast dishes. There was something about that touch—light and casual as it was, it sent a jolt through Cristina. "You've got today off from classes, Diana's gone up to Ojai, so now's a good time for us to do this. Especially since we've got Clave testing this weekend."

There was a collective groan. Clave testing was a twice-yearly chore in which students were evaluated to see if their skills were up to par or if they needed to be sent to the Academy in Idris.

But Ty ignored Julian's announcement. He was looking at Emma's paper. "How many have died, exactly? People and faeries?"

"Twelve," said Emma. "Twelve dead bodies."

Tavvy emerged from under the table. "Were they all running with lollipops?"

Ty looked baffled, Emma guilty, Tavvy slightly lip-wobbly. "Maybe that's enough for now," Julian said, scooping up his smallest brother. "Let's see what you find out, Tiberius, Livia?"

Ty murmured assent, rising to his feet. Emma said, "Cristina and I were going to practice, but we can—"

"No! Don't cancel it!" Livvy bounced upright. "I need to practice! With another girl. Who isn't reading," she said, shooting a glare at Dru. "Or watching a horror movie." She glanced over at her twin. "I'll help Ty for half an hour," she said. "Then I'll come to train."

He nodded and slipped his headphones on, making his way toward the door. Livvy went with him, chattering about how she'd missed training and her saber, and about how their great-aunt's idea of a training room was her barn, which was full of spiders.

Cristina glanced back as she left the kitchen. The room was full of bright light, and it cast an odd halo over Emma and Julian, blurring out their features. Julian was holding Tavvy, and as Emma leaned in they made up an odd family picture. "You don't have to do this for me," Emma was saying, softly but earnestly, in a voice Cristina had never heard her use before.

"I think I do," Julian said. "I think I remember making a vow to that effect."

"'Whither thou goest, I will go, whatever stupid thing you do, I shall do also'?" Emma said. "Was that the vow?"

Julian laughed. If there were more words between the two, Cristina didn't hear them spoken. She let the door close behind her without looking back again. She had once thought she would have a *parabatai* herself; though it was a dream she had long put to bed, there was something about that sort of intimacy that was painful to overhear.

# 4

## And This Was the Reason

Emma hit the training mat hard, rolling quickly so that Cortana, still strapped to her back, wouldn't be damaged—or damage her. In the early years of her training she'd inflicted more injuries on herself by accident with Cortana's sharp edges than any exercises had, thanks to her stubborn refusal to take it off.

Cortana was hers, her father's, and her father's father's. She and Cortana were what was left of the Carstairs family. She never left the blade behind when she went to fight, even if they planned to use daggers or holy water or fire. Therefore she needed to know how to fight with it strapped to her in every conceivable circumstance.

"Are you all right?" Cristina hit the mat beside her more lightly; she wasn't armed, and was wearing only her training clothes. Cristina had sense, Emma thought, sitting up and rubbing her sore shoulder.

"Fine." Emma stood up, shaking out the kinks in her muscles. "One more time."

The medal around Cristina's throat gleamed decorously as she craned her head back, watching Emma shinny back up the rope ladder. Dark gold sunlight was pouring through the windows—it was late afternoon. They'd been training for hours, and before that they'd been busy bringing the contents of Emma's Wall of Proof (Cristina refused to call it a Wall of Crazy) into the computer room so Livvy and Ty could scan it all. Livvy was still promising to come train with them, though she'd clearly been absorbed into the online search for clues. "You can stop there," Cristina called when Emma was halfway up, but Emma ignored her and kept going, until her head was nearly bumping the ceiling.

Emma looked down. Cristina was shaking her head, managing to look both composed and disapproving at the same time. "You can't jump from such a height! Emma—"

Emma let go and dropped like a stone. She hit the mat, rolled, and sprang up into a crouch, reaching back over her shoulder for Cortana.

Her hand closed on empty air. She shot upright, only to find Cristina holding the blade. She'd slipped it from Emma's scabbard as she was rising to her feet.

"There is more to fighting than jumping the highest and falling the farthest," Cristina said, and held Cortana out to her.

Emma rose and took the blade back with a grudging smile. "You sound like Jules."

"Maybe he has a point," Cristina said. "Have you always been this careless about your safety?"

"More since the Dark War." Emma slipped Cortana back into its scabbard. She drew the stiletto blades from her boots and handed one to Cristina before turning to face the target painted on the opposite wall.

Cristina moved to Emma's side and raised the blade in her hand, sighting down along the line of her arm. Emma hadn't thrown knives with Cristina before, but she was unsurprised to see that Cristina's posture and grip on the knife—her thumb parallel to the blade—were perfect. "Sometimes I regret that I knew little of the war. I was in hiding in Mexico. My uncle Tomás was convinced Idris would not be safe."

Emma thought of Idris burning, of the blood in the streets, bodies stacked like kindling in the Accords Hall. "Your uncle was right."

"He died in the war, so I suppose he was." Cristina released her blade; it flew through the air and thumped into the central ring of the target. "My mother owned a house in San Miguel de Allende. We went there, because the Institute was not safe. I always feel a coward when I think about it."

"You were a kid," Emma said. "They were right to send you where you would be safe."

"Maybe," said Cristina, looking downcast.

"Really. I'm not just saying that," Emma told her. "I mean, how does Perfect Diego feel about it? Does he feel like a coward?"

Cristina made a face. "I doubt it."

"Of course not. He's totally well-adjusted about everything. We should all be more like Perfect Diego."

"Hello!" A greeting rang through the room. It was Livvy, in practice gear, heading toward them. She paused to pet her saber, which was hanging on the wall near the door with the other fencing swords. Livvy had chosen the saber for her weapon when she was about twelve years old and had practiced tenaciously ever since. She could discourse on types of saber, wooden grips versus rubber or leather ones, tangs and pommels, and it was better not to get her started on pistol grips.

Emma admired her loyalty. She'd never felt a need to pick a weapon: Hers was always Cortana. But she liked to be at least competent in everything, so she'd sparred with Livvy more than once.

"I missed you," Livvy crooned to the saber. "I love you so much."

"That was heartfelt," Emma said. "If you'd said that to me when you got back, I would have cried."

Livvy abandoned the saber and bounced over toward them. She commandeered a mat and began to stretch her muscles. She could fold herself easily in half, tucking her fingers under her toes. "I did miss you," she said, voice muffled. "It was boring in England and there were no cute boys."

"Julian said there were no humans for miles," said Emma. "Anyway, it's not like you missed anything here."

"Well, aside from the serial killings," Livvy said, moving across the room to take up two throwing knives. Emma and Cristina moved out of the way as she lined herself up across from the target. "And I bet you dated Cameron Ashdown again, then dumped him."

"She did," said Cristina. Emma shot her a look that said *traitor*.

"Ha!" Livvy's knife went wide of the target. She turned around, her braid bouncing on her shoulders. "Emma goes out with him, like, every four months, then dumps him."

"Oh?" Cristina cut a glance toward Emma. "Why has he been singled out for this special torture?"

"Oh, for goodness' sake," Emma said. "It wasn't serious."

"Not to you," said Livvy. "Bet it was to him." She held out her second knife to Cristina. "Want a try?"

Cristina took the knife and moved into Livvy's position.

"Who's Perfect Diego?" Livvy asked.

Cristina had been frowning at the knife; now she turned around and gaped at Livvy.

"I heard you," Livvy said cheerfully. "Before I came in. Who is he? Why's he so perfect? Why is there a perfect boy in the world and no one's told me?"

"Diego is the boy Cristina's mother wants her to marry," Emma told Livvy. Now it was Cristina's turn to look betrayed. "It's not an arranged marriage, that would be gross; it's just that her mother loves him, his mother carried the Rosales name—"

"He's related to you?" Livvy asked Cristina. "Isn't that a problem? I mean, I know Clary Fairchild and Jace Herondale are a famous love story, but they weren't actually brother and sister. Otherwise I think it would probably be a . . ."

"Less famous love story," said Emma with a grin.

Cristina threw her knife. It hit close to the target's center. "His full name is Diego Rocio Rosales—Rocio is his father's last name, and Rosales his mother's, just like my mother's last name is Rosales. But that doesn't mean we're even cousins. The Rosaleses are a huge Shadowhunting family. My mother just thinks he's perfect, so handsome, so smart, such a Shadowhunter, perfect perfect perfect—"

"And now you know how he got his nickname," said Emma, going to retrieve the knives from the wall.

"Is he perfect?" Livvy asked.

"No," Cristina said. When Cristina was upset, she didn't get angry; she just stopped talking. She was doing that now, staring at the target painted on the wall. Emma spun the knives she'd retrieved in her hands.

"We'll protect you from Perfect Diego," Emma said. "If he comes here, I'll impale him." She moved toward the throwing line.

"Emma's a master of the impalement arts," Livvy said.

"You'd be better off impaling my mother," Cristina muttered. "All right, *flaquita*, impress me. Let's see you throw two at a time."

A knife in each hand, Emma took a step back from the throwing line. She had taught herself to throw two knives at once over the course of a year, throwing again and again, the sound of the blades splitting the wood a balm to shattered nerves. She was left-handed, so normally would have taken a step back and to the right, but she'd forced herself to be nearly ambidextrous. Her step back was direct, not diagonal. Her arms went back and then forward; she opened her hands and the knives flew like falcons whose jesses had been cut. They soared toward the target and thudded, one after the other, into its heart.

Cristina whistled. "I see why Cameron Ashdown keeps coming back. He's afraid not to." She went to retrieve the knives, including her own. "Now I am going to try again. I see that I am far behind where I should be."

Emma laughed. "No, I was cheating. I practiced that move for years."

"Still," Cristina said, "if you ever change your mind and decide you don't like me, I'd better be able to defend myself."

"Good throw," Livvy said in a whisper, coming up behind Emma as Cristina, several feet away, paced back and forth at the throwing line.

"Thanks," Emma whispered back. Leaning against a rack of gloves and protective gear, she glanced down into Livvy's sunny face. "Did you get anywhere with Ty? And the *parabatai* thing?" she inquired, almost dreading the answer.

Livvy's face clouded. "He still says no. It's the only thing we've ever disagreed about."

"I'm sorry." Emma knew how badly Livvy wanted to be *parabatai* with her twin. Brothers and sisters who became *parabatai* were unusual but not unheard of. Ty's stark refusal was surprising, though. He rarely said no to Livvy about anything, but he was obdurate about this.

Cristina's first blade slammed home, just at the rim of the target's inside circle. Emma cheered.

"I like her," Livvy said, still in a whisper.

"Good," Emma said. "I like her too."

"And I think Perfect Diego maybe broke her heart."

"He did something," Emma said guardedly. "That much I've guessed."

"So I think we should set her up with Julian."

Emma almost overturned the rack. "What?"

Livvy shrugged. "She's pretty, and she seems really nice, and she's going to be living with us. And Jules hasn't ever had a girlfriend—you know why." Emma just stared. Her head seemed full of white noise. "I mean, it's our fault—mine and Ty's, and Dru's and Tavvy's. Raising four kids, you don't exactly have a lot of time to date. So since we sort of took having a girlfriend away from him . . ."

"You want to set him up," Emma said blankly. "I mean, it doesn't work like that, Livvy. They'd have to like each other. . . ."

"I think they could," said Livvy. "If we gave them a chance. What do you say?"

Her blue-green eyes, so much like Julian's, were full of affectionate mischief. Emma opened her mouth to say something, she didn't know what, when Cristina let her second knife go. It slammed into the wall so hard that the wood seemed to crack.

Livvy clapped her hands. "Awesome!" She shot Emma a triumphant look, as if to say *See, she's perfect.* She glanced at her watch. "Okay, I have to go help Ty some more. Yell for me if anything awesomely exciting happens."

Emma nodded, a little stunned, as Livvy danced away to hang up her weapons and head for the library. She was nearly startled out of her skin when a voice spoke from just over her shoulder—Cristina had come up behind her and was looking worried. "What were you two talking about?" she asked. "You look like you've seen a ghost."

Emma opened her mouth to say something, but never found out what, because at that moment, a commotion burst out from downstairs. She could hear the sound of someone pounding on the front door, followed by running feet.

Catching up Cortana, Emma was out the door in a flash.

The pounding on the front door of the Institute echoed through the building. "Just a minute!" Julian yelled, zipping up his hoodie as he jogged toward the door. He was almost glad someone had shown up. Ty and Livvy had ordered him out of the computer room with the announcement that Julian was wrecking their concentration by pacing, and he'd been bored enough to consider going to check on Arthur, which he was fairly sure would put him in a bad mood for the rest of the day.

Julian swung the door open. A tall, pale-haired man lounged on the other side, wearing tight black pants and a shirt unbuttoned halfway down his chest. A plaid jacket hung from his shoulders.

"You look like a strip-o-gram," Julian said to Malcolm Fade, High Warlock of Los Angeles.

There had been a time when Julian had been so impressed by the fact that Malcolm was High Warlock—the warlock to whom all other warlocks answered, at least in Southern California—that he'd been nervous around him. That had passed after the Dark War, when visits from Malcolm had become commonplace. Malcolm was in reality what most people thought Arthur was: an absent-minded professor type. He had been forgetting important things for almost two hundred years.

All warlocks, being the offspring of human beings and demons, were immortal. They stopped aging at different points in their lives, depending on their demon parents. Malcolm looked as if he had stopped aging at about twenty-seven, but he had been (he claimed) born in 1850.

Since most of the demons Julian had ever seen had been disgusting, he didn't like to think too much about how Malcolm's parents had met. Malcolm didn't seem inclined to share, either. Julian knew he'd been born in England, and he still had traces of the accent.

"You can mail someone a stripper?" Malcolm looked bemused, then glanced down at himself. "Sorry, I forgot to button my shirt before I left the house."

He took a step inside the Institute and instantly fell over, sprawling lengthwise on the tiles. Julian moved aside and Malcolm rolled onto his back, looking disgruntled. He peered down his long body. "I seem to have also tied my shoelaces together."

Sometimes it was hard not to feel bitter, Julian reflected, that all the allies and friends in his life were either people he had to lie to, ridiculous, or both.

Emma came rushing down the staircase, Cortana in her hand. She was wearing jeans and a tank top; her damp hair was pulled back in an elastic band. The tank top was sticking to her skin, which Julian wished he hadn't noticed. She slowed down as she approached, relaxing. "Hey, Malcolm. Why are you on the floor?"

"I tied my shoelaces together," he said.

Emma had reached his side. She brought Cortana down, neatly severing Malcolm's shoelaces in half and freeing up his feet.

"There you go," she said.

Malcolm looked warily at her. "She may be dangerous," he said to Julian. "Then again, all women are dangerous."

"All people are dangerous," said Julian. "Why are you here, Malcolm? Not that I'm not pleased to see you."

Malcolm staggered to his feet, buttoning his shirt. "I brought Arthur's medicine."

Julian's heart thumped so loudly he was sure he could hear it. Emma frowned.

"Has Arthur not been feeling well?" she asked.

Malcolm, who had been reaching into his pocket, froze. Julian saw the realization dawn on his face that he'd said something he shouldn't, and he silently cursed Malcolm and his forgetfulness a thousand times.

"Arthur told me last night he's been under the weather," Julian said. "Just the usual stuff bothering him. It's chronic. Anyway, he was feeling low on energy."

"I would have looked for something at the Shadow Market if I'd known," Emma said, sitting down on the bottom step of the staircase and stretching out her long legs.

"Cayenne pepper and dragon's blood," said Malcolm, retrieving a vial from his pocket and proffering it to Julian. "Should wake him right up."

"That would wake the dead up," said Emma.

"Necromancy is illegal, Emma Carstairs," scolded Malcolm.

"She was just joking." Julian pocketed the vial, keeping his gaze fixed on Malcolm, silently begging him not to say anything.

"When did you have a chance to tell Malcolm that your uncle wasn't feeling well, Jules? I saw you last night and you didn't say anything," Emma said.

Julian was glad he was facing away from Emma; he was sure he'd gone white.

"Vampire pizza," Malcolm said.

"What?" Emma said.

"Nightshade's opened up an Italian place on Cross Creek Road," Malcolm said. "Best pizza for miles, and they deliver."

"Don't you worry about what's in the sauce?" Emma asked, clearly diverted. "Oh!" Her hand flew to her mouth. "That reminds me, Malcolm. I was wondering if there was something you'd look at."

"Is it a wart?" said Malcolm. "I can cure that, but it'll cost you."

"Why does everyone always think it's a wart?" Emma pulled her phone out and in a few seconds was showing him the photos of the body she'd found at the Sepulchre Bar. "There were these white markings, here and here," she said, pointing. "They look like graffiti, not paint but chalk or something like that. . . ."

"First, gross," Malcolm said. "Please don't show me pictures of dead bodies without a warning." He peered closer. "Second, those look like remnants of a ceremonial circle. Someone drew a protective ring on the ground. Maybe to protect themselves while they were casting whatever nasty spell killed this guy."

"He was burned," Emma said. "And drowned, I think. At least, his clothes were wet and he smelled like salt water."

She was frowning, her eyes dark. It could have been the memory of the body, or just the thought of the ocean. It was an ocean she lived across from, ran beside every day, but Julian knew how much it terrified her. She could force herself into it, sick and shaking, but he hated watching her do it, hated watching his strong Emma torn to shreds by the terror of something so primal and nameless she couldn't explain it even to herself.

It made him want to kill things, destroy things to keep her safe. Even though she could keep herself safe. Even though she was the bravest person he knew.

Julian snapped back to the present. "Forward me the photos," Malcolm was saying. "I'll look them over more closely and let you know."

"Hey!" Livvy appeared at the top of the stairs, having changed out of her training gear. "Ty found something. About the killings."

Malcolm looked puzzled.

"On the computer," Livvy elaborated. "You know, the one we're not supposed to have. Oh, hi, Malcolm." She waved vigorously. "You guys should come upstairs."

"Would you stay, Malcolm?" Emma asked, scrambling to her feet. "We could use your help."

"That depends," Malcolm said. "Does the computer play movies?"

"It can play movies," said Julian cautiously.

Malcolm looked pleased. "Can we watch *Notting Hill?*"

"We can watch anything, if you're willing to help," Emma said. She glanced at Jules. "And we can find out what Ty discovered. You're coming, right?"

Silently Julian cursed Malcolm's love of romantic movies.

He wished he could head to his studio and paint. But he couldn't exactly avoid Ty or abandon Malcolm.

"I could get snacks from the kitchen," Emma said, sounding hopeful. After all, for years it had been their habit to watch old movies on their witchlight-powered TV, eating popcorn by the flickering illumination.

Julian shook his head. "I'm not hungry."

He almost thought he could hear Emma sigh. A moment later she disappeared after Livvy, up the stairs. Julian made as if to follow them, but Malcolm stopped him with a hand on his shoulder.

"It's gotten worse, hasn't it?" he said.

"Uncle Arthur?" Jules was caught off guard. "I don't think so. I mean, it's not great that I haven't been here, but if we'd kept refusing to go to England, someone would have gotten suspicious."

"Not Arthur," said Malcolm. "You. Does she know about you?"

"Does who know what?"

"Don't be dense," Malcolm said. "Emma. Does she know?"

Julian felt his heart wrench inside his chest. He had no words for the feeling of upheaval Malcolm's words caused. It was too much like being tumbled by a wave, solid footing giving way in the slide of sand. "Stop."

"I won't," Malcolm said. "I like happy endings."

Julian spoke through his teeth. "Malcolm, *this is not a love story.*"

"Every story is a love story."

Julian drew away from him and started toward the stairs. He was rarely actually angry at Malcolm, but right now his heart was pounding. He made it to the landing before Malcolm called after him; he turned, knowing he shouldn't, and found the warlock looking up at him.

"Laws are meaningless, child," Malcolm said in a low voice that somehow still carried. "There is nothing more important than love. And no law higher."

* * *

Technically, the Institute wasn't supposed to have a computer in it.

The Clave resisted the advent of modernity but even more so any engagement with mundane culture. But that had never stopped Tiberius. He'd started asking for a computer at the age of ten so that he could keep up to date on violent mundane crimes, and when they'd come back from Idris, after the Dark War, Julian had given him one.

Ty had lost his mother and father, his brother, and his older sister, Jules had said at the time, sitting on the floor amid a tangle of wires, trying to figure out how to plug the computer into one of the few electrical outlets they had; almost everything in the Institute ran on witchlight. If he could give this to Ty, at least it would be something.

And indeed, Ty loved the computer. He named it Watson and spent hours teaching himself how to use it, since no one else had a clue. Julian told him not to do anything illegal; Arthur, locked away in his study, didn't notice.

Livvy, ever dedicated to her sibling, had also taught herself to use it, with Ty's help, once he'd familiarized himself with how it worked. Together they were a formidable team.

It looked like Ty, Dru, Livvy, and even Tavvy had been busy. Dru had spread maps all over the floor. Tavvy was standing by a whiteboard with a blue dry-erase marker, making possibly helpful notations, if they could ever be translated out of seven-year-old.

Ty was seated at the swivel chair in front of the computer, his fingers moving swiftly over the keyboard. Livvy was perched on the desk, as she often was; Ty worked around her, completely aware of where she was while at the same time focusing on the task at hand.

"So, you found something?" Julian said as they came in.

"Yes. Just a second." Ty held up his hand imperiously. "You can talk to each other if you like."

Julian grinned. "That's very kind."

Cristina came hurrying in, braiding her damp, dark hair. She'd clearly showered and re-dressed, in jeans and a flowered blouse. "Livvy told me—"

"Shh." Emma put her finger to her lips and indicated Ty, staring intently at the computer's blue screen. It lit up his delicate features. She loved the moments when Ty was playing detective; he so clearly fell into the part, into the dream of being Sherlock Holmes, who always had all the answers.

Cristina nodded and sat down on the overstuffed love seat beside Drusilla. Dru was nearly as tall as she was, despite being only thirteen. She was one of those girls whose body had grown up quickly: She had breasts and hips, was soft and curvy. It had led to some awkward moments with boys who thought she was seventeen or eighteen years old, and a few incidents where Emma had barely stopped Julian from murdering a mundane teenager.

Malcolm settled himself in a patched armchair. "Well, if we're waiting," he said, and began typing on his phone.

"What are you doing?" Emma asked.

"Ordering pizza from Nightshade's," said Malcolm. "There's an app."

"A what?" said Dru.

"Nightshade?" Livvy turned around. "The vampire?"

"He owns a pizza place. The sauce is divine," Malcolm said, kissing his fingers.

"Aren't you worried what's in it?" said Livvy.

"You Nephilim are so paranoid," said Malcolm, returning to his phone.

Ty cleared his throat, spinning his chair back around to face the room. Everyone had settled themselves on couches or chairs except Tavvy, who was sitting on the floor under the whiteboard. "I've found some stuff," he said. "There definitely have been bodies that fit Emma's description. Fingerprints sanded off, soaked in seawater, skin burned." He pulled up the front page of a newspaper on-screen. "Mundanes think it's satanic cult activity, because of the chalk markings found around the bodies."

"Mundanes think everything is satanic cult activity," said Malcolm. "Most cults are actually in service of completely different demons than Lucifer. He's quite famous and very hard to reach. Rarely does favors for anyone. Really an unrewarding demon to worship."

Emma and Julian exchanged looks of amusement. Ty clicked the computer mouse, and pictures flashed up on the screen. Faces—different ages, races, genders. All of them slack in death.

"There are only a few murders that match the profile," said Ty. He seemed pleased to be using the word "profile." "There's been one every month for the past year. Twelve counting the one Emma found, like she said."

Emma said, "But nothing before a year ago?"

Ty shook his head.

"So, there was a gap of four years since my parents were killed. Whoever it was—if it was the same person—stopped and started up again."

"Is there anything that links all these people?" Julian asked. "Diana said some of the bodies were fey."

"Well, this is all mundane news," said Livvy. "They wouldn't know, would they? They'd think the bodies were human, if they were gentry fey. As for anything linking them, none of them have been identified."

"That's weird," said Dru. "What about blood? In movies they can identify people using blood and DTR."

"DNA," corrected Ty. "Well, according to the newspapers none of the bodies were identified. It could have been that whatever spells were done on them altered their blood. Or they could have decayed fast, like Emma's parents did. That would have limited what the coroners could have found out."

"There is something else, though," Livvy said. "The stories all reported where the bodies were found, and we mapped them. They have one thing in common."

Ty had taken one of his hand toys out of his pocket, a mass of intermingled pipe cleaners, and was untangling it. Ty had one of the fastest-working minds of anyone Emma knew, and it calmed him to have a way to use his hands to diffuse some of that quickness and intensity. "The bodies have all been dumped at ley lines. All of them," he said, and Emma could hear the excitement in his voice.

"Ley lines?" Dru furrowed her brow.

"There's a network, circling the world, of ancient magical pathways," said Malcolm. "They amplify magic, so for centuries Downworlders have used them to create entrances into Faerie, that sort of thing. Alicante is built on a convergence of ley lines. They're invisible, but some can train themselves to sense them." He frowned, staring at the computer screen, where one of the images Cristina had taken of the dead body at the Sepulchre was displayed. "Can you do that thing?" he said. "You know, where you make the picture bigger?"

"You mean zoom in?" said Ty.

Before Malcolm could answer, the doorbell of the Institute rang. It was no ordinary, shrilling doorbell. It sounded like a gong being struck through the building, shivering the glass and stone and plaster.

Emma was up and on her feet in a second. "I'll get it," she said, and hurried downstairs, even as Julian half-rose from his seat to follow her.

But she wanted to be alone, just for a second. Wanted to process the fact that these killings dated back to the year of her parents' death. They had started then. Her father and mother had been the first.

These murders were connected. She could see the threads coming together, forming a pattern she could only begin to glimpse but knew was real. Someone had done these things. Someone had tortured and killed her parents, had carved evil markings on their skin and dumped them in the ocean to rot. Someone had taken Emma's childhood, torn away the roof and walls of the house of her life, leaving her cold and exposed.

And that someone would pay. *Revenge is a cold bedfellow*, Diana had said, but Emma didn't believe that. Revenge would give her the air back in her lungs. Revenge would let her think about her parents without a cold knot forming in her stomach. She would be able to dream without seeing their drowned faces and hearing their voices cry out for her help.

She reached the front door of the Institute and threw it open. The sun had just set. A glum vampire stood in the doorway, carrying several stacked boxes. He looked like a teenager with short brown hair and freckled skin, but that didn't mean much. "Pizza delivery," he said in a tone that suggested that most of his closest relatives had just died.

"Seriously?" Emma said. "Malcolm wasn't making that up? You really deliver pizza?"

He looked at her blankly. "Why wouldn't I deliver pizza?"

Emma fumbled at the small table near the door for the cash they usually kept there. "I don't know. You're a vampire. I figured you'd have something better to do with your life. Your unlife. Whatever."

The vampire looked aggrieved. "You know how hard it is to get a job when your ID says you're a hundred and fifty years old and you can only go out at night?"

"No," Emma admitted, taking the boxes. "I hadn't considered that."

"Nephilim never do." As he tucked a fifty into his jeans, Emma noticed that he was wearing a gray T-shirt that said TMI across the front. "Too much information?" she said.

He brightened. "The Mortal Instruments. They're a band. From Brooklyn. You heard of them?"

Emma had. Clary's best friend and *parabatai*, Simon, had belonged to them when he was a mundane. That was how they'd wound up named after the three most holy objects in the Shadowhunter world. Now Simon, too, was a Shadowhunter. She wondered how he felt about the band going on without him. About everything going on without him.

She made her way back up the stairs, her mind on Clary and the others in the New York Institute. Clary had found out she was a Shadowhunter when she was fifteen years old. There had been a time when she thought she'd lead a mundane life. She'd talked about it before, around Emma, the way anyone might talk about a road not taken. She'd carried a lot with her into her Shadowhunter life, including her best friend, Simon. But she could have chosen differently. She could have been a mundane.

Emma wanted to talk to her, suddenly, about what that might have meant. Simon had been Clary's best friend for her whole life, like Jules had been Emma's. Then they had been *parabatai*, once Simon was a Shadowhunter. What had changed? Emma wondered. What did it feel like to go from best friend to *parabatai* without having always known you were going to do it, how was it different?

And why didn't she know the answer to that herself?

When she arrived back in the computer room, Malcolm was standing near the desk, violet eyes snapping. "You see, it's not a protection circle at all," he was saying, then broke off as Emma came in. "It's pizza!"

"It can't be pizza," said Ty, staring perplexedly at the screen. His long fingers had nearly untangled all the pipe cleaners; when he was done, he'd tangle them back up and start again.

"All right, enough," said Jules. "We're taking a break from killings and profiles for dinner." He took the boxes from Emma, shooting her a grateful look, and set them down on the coffee table. "I don't care what you all want to talk about, it just can't involve murder or blood. Any blood."

"But it's vampire pizza," Livvy pointed out.

"Immaterial," Julian said. "Couch. Now."

"Can we watch a movie?" Malcolm piped up, sounding remarkably like Tavvy.

"We can watch a movie," Julian said. "Now, Malcolm, I don't care if you *are* the High Warlock of Los Angeles, sit your butt down."

The vampire pizza was shockingly good. Emma decided fairly quickly that she didn't care what was in the sauce. Mouse heads, stewed people parts, whatever. It was amazing. It had a crispy crust and just the right amount of fresh mozzerella. She sucked the cheese off her fingers and made faces at Jules, who had excellent table manners.

The film was much more puzzling. It appeared to be about a man who owned a bookstore and was in love with a famous woman, except Emma recognized neither of them and wasn't sure if she was supposed to. Cristina watched in large-eyed bafflement, Ty put his headphones on and closed his eyes, and Dru and Livvy sat on either side of Malcolm, patting him gently while he wept.

"Love is beautiful," he said while the man on-screen ran through traffic.

"That's not love," said Julian, leaning back against the couch. The flickering light from the screen played over his skin, making it seem unfamiliar, adding frecklings of darkness to the smooth, pale places and lighting the shadows under his cheekbones, at the hollow of his throat. "That's movies."

"I came to Los Angeles to bring back love," Malcolm said, his dark violet eyes mournful. "All great movies are about love. Love lost, found, destroyed, regained, bought, sold, dying, and being born. I love movies, but they've forgotten what they're about. Explosions, effects, that wasn't what it meant when I first got here. It was about lighting cigarette smoke so it looked like heavenly fire and lighting women so they looked like angels." Malcolm sighed. "I came here to bring true love back from the dead."

"Oh, Malcolm," said Drusilla, and burst into tears. Livvy handed her a napkin from the pizza place. "Why don't you have a boyfriend?"

"I'm straight," Malcolm said, looking surprised.

"Well, all right, then a girlfriend. You should find a nice Downworlder girl, maybe a vampire, so she'll live forever."

"Leave Malcolm's love life alone, Dru," said Livvy.

"True love is hard to find," Malcolm said, gesturing at the people kissing on-screen.

"Movie love is hard to find," said Julian. "Because it's not real."

"What do you mean?" said Cristina. "Are you saying there is no true love? I don't believe that."

"Love isn't chasing someone to the airport," said Julian. He leaned forward, and Emma could see just the edge of the *parabatai* Mark on his collarbone, escaping above the neck of his T-shirt. "Love means you see someone. That's all."

"You see them?" Ty echoed, sounding dubious. He'd turned the music down on his player, but his headphones were still on, his black hair scrunched up around them.

Julian took hold of the remote. The movie had ended; white credits scrolled down the screen. "When you love someone, they become a part of who you are. They're in everything you do. They're in the air you breathe and the water you drink and the blood in your veins. Their touch stays on your skin and their voice stays in your ears and their thoughts stay in your mind. You know their dreams because their nightmares pierce your heart and their good dreams are your dreams too. And you don't think they're perfect, but you know their flaws, the deep-down truth of them, and the shadows of all their secrets, and they don't frighten you away; in fact you love them more for it, because you don't want perfect. You want them. You want—"

He broke off then, as if realizing everyone was looking at him.

"You want what?" said Dru with enormous eyes.

"Nothing," Julian said. "I'm just talking." And he shut off the TV and picked up the pizza boxes. "I'm going to throw these away," he said, and left.

"When he falls in love," said Dru, looking after him, "it's going to be like . . . wow."

"Of course then we'll probably never see him again," said Livvy. "Lucky girl, whoever she'll be."

Ty's brows drew together. "You're joking, right?" he said. "You don't mean we'll actually never see him again?"

"Definitely not," Emma said. When Ty was much younger, he'd been puzzled by the way people talked and the way they exaggerated to make a point. Phrases like "raining cats and dogs" had caused him annoyance—and sometimes a small amount of betrayal, since he liked cats and dogs a great deal more than he liked rain.

At some point Julian had begun a series of silly drawings for him, showing the literal meaning of phrases and then the figurative ones. Ty had giggled at the illustrations of cats and dogs falling out of the sky and people having their socks knocked off, as well as the bubble pictures of animals and people explaining what the idioms really meant. After that he was often to be found in the library, looking up expressions and their meanings, committing them to memory. Ty didn't mind having things explained to him, and he never forgot what he'd been taught, but he preferred teaching himself.

He still sometimes liked to be reassured that an exaggeration was an exaggeration, even if he was 90 percent sure of it. Livvy, who knew better than anyone the anxiety that imprecise language could cause her brother, scrambled to her feet and went over to him. She put her arms around him, her chin against his shoulder. Ty leaned against her, his eyes half-lidded. Ty liked physical affection when he was in the mood for it, as long as it wasn't too intense— he liked having his hair ruffled and his back patted or scratched. Sometimes he reminded Emma a bit of their cat, Church, when Church wanted an ear rub.

Light flared. Cristina had gotten up and flicked the witchlight back on. Brightness expanded to fill the room as Julian came back in and looked around; whatever composure he'd lost was back. "It's late," he said. "Bedtime. Especially for you, Tavvy."

"Hate bedtime," said Tavvy, who was sitting in Malcolm's lap, playing with a toy the warlock had given him. It was square and purple and sent off bright sparks.

"That's the spirit of the revolution," said Jules. "Malcolm, thanks. I'm sure we'll be needing your help again."

Malcolm set Tavvy gently aside and stood up, brushing pizza dust from his rumpled clothes. Picking up his discarded jacket, he headed out into the hallway, Emma and Julian following him. "Well, you know where to find me," he said, zipping the jacket up. "I was going to talk to Diana tomorrow about—"

"Diana can't know," Emma said.

Malcolm looked puzzled. "Can't know about what?"

"That we're looking into this," Julian said, cutting Emma off. "She doesn't want us involved. Says it's dangerous."

Malcolm looked disgruntled. "You could have mentioned that before," he said. "I don't like keeping things from her."

"Sorry," Julian said. His expression was smooth, faintly apologetic. As always, Emma was both impressed and a little frightened by his ability to lie. Julian was an expert liar when he wanted to be; no shadow of what he really felt would touch his face. "We can't go much further with this without help from the Clave and the Silent Brothers anyway."

"All right." Malcolm looked at them both closely; Emma did her best to match Julian's poker face. "As long as you talk to Diana about this tomorrow." He shoved his hands into his pockets, the light gleaming off his colorless hair. "There is one thing I didn't get a chance to tell you. Those markings around the body that Emma found, they weren't for a protective spell."

"But you said—" Emma started.

"I changed my mind when I got a closer look," Malcolm said. "They're not protective runes. They're summoning runes. Someone's using the energy of the dead bodies to summon."

"To summon what?" said Jules.

Malcolm shook his head. "Something to this world. A demon, an angel, I don't know. I'll look at the photos some more, ask around the Spiral Labyrinth discreetly."

"So if it was a summoning spell," Emma said, "was it successful or unsuccessful?"

"A spell like that?" Malcolm said. "If it was successful, believe me, you'd know."

Emma was woken up by a plaintive meow.

She opened her eyes to find a Persian cat sitting on her chest. It was a blue Persian, to be precise, very round, with tucked-in ears and large yellow eyes.

With a yelp Emma leaped to her feet. The cat went flying. The next few moments were chaos as she stumbled over her nightstand while the cat yowled. Finally she succeeded in turning on the light, to find the cat sitting by the door of her room, looking smug and entitled.

"Church," she wailed. "*Seriously?* Don't you have somewhere to be?"

It was clear from Church's expression that he didn't. Church was a cat who sometimes belonged to the Institute. He'd shown up on the front step four years ago, left in a box on the doorstep with a note addressed to Emma and a line of script underneath. *Please take care of my cat. Brother Zachariah.*

At the time Emma hadn't been able to figure out why a Silent Brother, even a former Silent Brother, had wanted her to take care of his cat. She'd called Clary, who'd said that the cat had once lived at the New York Institute but did truly belong to Brother Zachariah, and if Emma and Julian wanted the cat they should keep him.

His name was Church, she said.

Church turned out to be the kind of cat who didn't stay where he was put. He was endlessly escaping out open windows and disappearing for days or even weeks. At first Emma had been frantic every time he left, but he always came back looking sleeker and more self-satisfied than ever. When Emma turned fourteen, he'd begun to come back with presents for her tied to his collar: shells and pieces of sea glass. Emma had put the shells on her windowsill. The sea glass had become Julian's good-luck bracelet.

By then, Emma knew the presents were from Jem, but she had no way of reaching him to thank him. So she did her best to take care of Church. There was always dry cat food left out for Church in the entryway, and clean drinking water. They were happy to see him when he showed up, and not worried when he didn't.

Church meowed and scraped at the door. Emma was used to this: It meant he wanted her to follow him. With a sigh she pulled on a sweater over her leggings and tank top and shoved her feet into flip-flops.

"This better be good," she told Church, grabbing up her stele. "Or I'll make you into a tennis racket."

Church didn't appear worried. He led Emma through the hall, down the stairs, and out the front door. The moon was high and bright, reflecting off the water in the distance. It made a path that Emma wandered toward, bemused, as Church kept up his trotting. She scooped him up as they crossed the highway, and deposited him on the beach when they reached the other side.

"Well, we're here," she said. "The world's biggest litter box."

Church gave her a look that suggested he wasn't impressed with her wit, and sauntered toward the shoreline. They wandered along the edge of the water together. It was a peaceful night, the surf slow and shallow, quieter than the wind. Occasionally Church would make a run for a sand crab, but he always came back, trotting just ahead of Emma, toward the northern constellations. Emma was starting to wonder if he was actually leading her anywhere at all when she realized that they'd rounded the curve of rocks that hid her and Julian's secret beach, and that the beach wasn't uninhabited.

She slowed down. The sand was lit up with moonlight, and Julian was sitting in the middle of it, well up from the shoreline. She went toward him, her feet silent on the sand. He didn't look up.

She rarely had a chance to look at Julian when he didn't know she was watching. It felt strange, even a little unnerving. The moon was bright enough that she could see the color of his T-shirt— red—and that he was wearing old blue jeans, and that his feet were bare. His bracelet of sea glass seemed to glow. She rarely wished that she could draw, but she did now, just so that she could draw the way he was all one perfect single line, from the angle of his bent leg to the curve of his back as he leaned forward.

Only a few feet from him, she stopped. "Jules?"

He looked up. He didn't seem the least bit startled. "Was that Church?"

Emma glanced around. It took her a moment before she located the cat, perched on top of a rock. He was licking his paw. "He came back," she said, sitting down on the sand next to Jules. "You know, for a visit."

"I saw you coming around the rocks." He gave her a half smile. "I thought I was dreaming."

"Couldn't sleep?"

He rubbed the back of his hand across his eyes. His knuckles were splattered with paint. "You could say that." He shook his head. "Weird nightmares. Demons, faeries—"

"Pretty standard Shadowhunter stuff," Emma pointed out. "I mean, that just sounds like a Tuesday."

"Helpful, Emma." He flopped back down on the sand, his hair making a dark halo around his head.

"I'm all about being helpful." She flopped down next to him, looking up at the sky. Light pollution from Los Angeles spilled out to the beach, too, and the stars were dim but visible. The moon moved in and out behind clouds. A strange sense of peace had fallen over Emma, a sense that she was where she belonged. She hadn't felt it since Julian and the others had left for England.

"I was thinking about what you said earlier," he said. "About all the dead ends. All the times we've thought we found something that pointed toward what happened to your parents, but it was nothing."

She looked toward him. The moonlight made his profile sharp.

"I was thinking maybe there was a meaning to it," he said. "That maybe finding out who it was had to wait until now. Until you were ready. I've watched you train, I've watched you get better. And better. Whoever it is, whatever it is, you're ready now. You can face it down. You can win."

Something fluttered under Emma's rib cage. Familiarity, she thought. This was Jules, the Jules she knew, who had more faith in her than she had in herself.

"I like to think things have a point," she said softly.

"They do." He paused for a moment, eyes on the sky. "I've been counting stars. Sometimes I think it helps to set yourself a pointless task."

"Remember, when we were younger, we used to talk about running away? Navigating by the North Star?" she said. "Before the war."

He folded his arm behind his head. Moonlight spilled down, illuminating his eyelashes. "Right. I was going to run off, join the French Foreign Legion. Rename myself Julien."

"Because no one was ever going to crack *that* code." She tipped her head to the side. "Jules. What's bothering you? I know something is."

He was silent. Emma could see his chest rising and falling slowly. The sound of his breath was drowned out by the sound of the water.

She reached over and laid her hand against his arm, her finger tracing lightly down the skin. *W-H-A-T I-S I-T?*

He turned his face away from hers; she saw him shudder, as if a chill had passed over him. "It's Mark."

Julian was still looking away from her; she could see only the curve of his throat and chin. "Mark?"

"I've been thinking about him," Julian said. "More than usual. I mean, Helen is always there for me on the other end of the phone if I need her, even if she's on Wrangel Island. But Mark might as well have died."

Emma sat up straight. "Don't say that. He's not dead."

"I know. You know *how* I know?" Jules asked, his voice tightening. "I used to look for the Wild Hunt every night. But they never come. Statistically, they should have ridden by here at least once in the past five years. But they never have. I think Mark won't let them."

"Why not?" Emma was staring at him now. Jules hardly ever talked like this. Not with this bitterness in his voice.

"Because he doesn't want to see us. Any sign of us."

"Because he loves you?"

"Or because he hates us. I don't know." Julian dug restlessly at the sand. "I'd hate us, if I was him. I hate him, sometimes."

Emma swallowed. "I hate my parents, too, for dying. Sometimes. It's not—it doesn't mean anything, Jules."

He turned his face toward her at that. His eyes were huge, black rings around the blue-green irises. "That's not the kind of hate I mean." His voice was low. "If he was here, God, everything would be different. Would have been different. I wouldn't be the one who ought to be home now in case Tavvy wakes up. I wouldn't be doing an immoral thing, walking down to the beach because I needed to get away. Tavvy, Dru, Livvy, Ty—they would have had someone to raise them. Mark was sixteen. I was *twelve*."

"Neither of you chose—"

"No, we didn't." Julian sat up. The collar of his shirt hung loose, and there was sand on his skin and in his hair. "We didn't choose. Because if I'd ever been able to choose, I would have made really different decisions."

Emma knew she shouldn't ask. Not when he was like this. But she had no experience of Julian like this; she didn't know how to react to him, how to *be*. "What would you have done differently?" she whispered.

"I don't know if I would have wanted a *parabatai*." The words came out clear and precise and brutal.

Emma flinched back. It felt like standing in knee-high water and being slapped in the face suddenly and unexpectedly by a wave. "Do you actually mean that?" she said. "You wouldn't have wanted it? This, with me?"

He got to his feet. The moon had come out entirely from behind the clouds and it shone down undimmed, bright enough that she could see the color of the paint on his hands. The light freckles across his cheekbones. The tightness of the skin around his mouth and temples. The visceral color of his eyes. "I shouldn't want it," he said. "I absolutely shouldn't."

"*Jules,*" she said, baffled and hurt and angry, but he was already walking away, down toward the shoreline. By the time she'd scrambled to her feet, he'd reached the rocks. He was a long, lean shadow, climbing over them. And then he was gone.

She could have caught up to him if she'd wanted to, she knew that. But she didn't want to. For the first time in her life, she didn't want to talk to Julian.

Something brushed against her ankles. Looking down, she saw Church. His yellow eyes seemed sympathetic, so she picked him up and held him against her, listening to him purr as the tide came in.

## Idris, 2007, The Dark War

When Julian Blackthorn was twelve years old, he killed his own father.

There were, of course, extenuating circumstances. His father wasn't his father anymore, not really. More like a monster wearing his father's face. But when the nightmares came, in the dead of night, it didn't matter. Julian saw Andrew Blackthorn's face, and his own hand holding the blade, and the blade going into his father, and he knew.

He was cursed.

That was what happened when you killed your own father. The gods cursed you. His uncle had said it, and his uncle knew quite a lot of things, especially things that had to do with the curses of gods and the price of bloodshed.

Julian had known a great deal of bloodshed, more than any twelve-year-old ought to know. It was Sebastian Morgenstern's fault. He was the Shadowhunter who had started the Dark War, who had used spells and tricks to turn ordinary Shadowhunters into mindless killing machines. An army at his disposal. An army meant to destroy all of the Nephilim who would not join him.

Julian, his brothers and sisters, and Emma had been hiding in the Hall of Accords. The greatest hall in Idris, it was meant to be able to keep out any monster. But it could not keep out Shadowhunters, even those who had lost their souls.

The huge double doors had cracked open and the Endarkened had surged into the room, and like a poison released into the air, where they went, death followed. They cut down the guards, and they cut down the children who were being guarded. They didn't care. They had no conscience.

They were pressing farther into the Hall. Julian had tried to herd the children into a group: Ty and Livvy, the solemn twins; and Dru, who was only eight; and Tavvy, the baby. He stood in front of them with his arms outstretched as if he could protect them, as if he could make a wall with his body that would hold back death.

And then death stepped out in front of him. A Dark Shadowhunter, demon runes blazing on his skin, with tangled brown hair and bloodshot blue-green eyes the same color as Julian's.

Julian's father.

Julian looked around for Emma but she was fighting a faerie warrior, fierce as fire, her sword, Cortana, flashing in her hands. Julian wanted to go to her, wanted it desperately, but he couldn't step away from the children. Someone had to protect them. His older sister was outside; his older brother taken by the Hunt. It would have to be him.

That was when Andrew Blackthorn reached them. Bloody cuts scissored across his face. His skin was slack and gray, but his grip on his sword was tight, and his eyes were fixed on his children.

"Ty," he said, his voice low and hoarse. And he looked at Tiberius, his son, and there was rapacious hunger in his eyes. "Tiberius. My Ty. Come here."

Ty's gray eyes opened wide. His twin, Livia, clutched at him, but he strained forward, toward his father. "Dad?" he said.

Andrew Blackthorn's face seemed to split with his grin, and Julian thought he could see through the split that tore it open, see the evil and darkness inside, the writhing pestilential core of horror and chaos that was all that animated the body that had once been his father's. His father's voice rose in a croon. "Come here, my boy, my Tiberius . . ."

Ty took another step forward, and Julian pulled the shortsword from his belt and threw it.

He was twelve. He was not particularly strong or particularly skilled. But the gods who would soon hate him must have smiled on that throw, because the blade flew like an arrow, like a bullet, and plunged into Andrew Blackthorn's chest, knocking him to the ground. He was dead before he hit the marble floor, his blood spreading around him in a dark red pool.

"I hate you!" Ty threw himself at Julian, and Julian threw his arms around his little brother, thanking the Angel over and over that Ty was all right, was breathing, was thrashing and pounding his chest and looking up at him with tearful, angry eyes. "You killed him, I hate you, I hate you—"

Livvy had her hands on Ty's back, trying to pull him away. Julian could feel the blood rushing through Ty's veins, the rise and fall of his chest; he felt the force of his brother's hatred and knew it meant that Ty was alive. They were all alive. Livvy with her soft words and her soothing hands, Dru with her enormous, terrified eyes, and Tavvy with his uncomprehending tears.

And Emma. His Emma.

He had committed the most ancient and worst of sins: He had killed his own father, the person who gave him life.

And he would do it again.

What kind of person was he?

# 5

## HIGHBORN KINSMEN

"Now, when were the first Accords signed?" asked Diana. "And what was their effect?"

It was a distractingly bright day. Sunlight poured in through the high windows of the schoolroom, illuminating the board in front of which Diana paced, tapping the palm of her left hand with a stele. Her lesson plan was scrawled on the board in nearly illegible handwriting: Emma could make out the words *Accords*, *Cold Peace*, and *evolution of Law*.

She looked sideways at Jules, but he had his head bent over some papers. They hadn't really spoken so far today, aside from being polite to each other at breakfast. She had woken up with her stomach feeling hollow and her hands hurting from clenching the bedclothes.

Also Church had abandoned her sometime during the night. Stupid cat.

"They were signed in 1872," said Cristina. "They were a series of agreements between the species of the Shadow World and Nephilim, meant to keep the peace among them and establishing common rules for all of them to follow."

"They also protect Downworlders," said Julian. "Before the Accords, if Downworlders harmed each other, Shadowhunters couldn't and wouldn't step in. The Accords gave Downworlders our protection." He paused. "At least until the Cold Peace."

Emma remembered the first time she had heard of the Cold Peace. She and Julian had been in the Hall of Accords when it was proposed. The punishment of the faeries for their part in Sebastian Morgenstern's Dark War. She remembered the confusion of her feelings. Her parents had died because of that war, but how did Mark and Helen, who she loved, deserve to bear the brunt of that simply because of the faerie blood in their veins?

"And where were the papers of the Cold Peace signed?" Diana asked.

"In Idris," said Livvy. "At the Hall of Accords. Everyone who usually attends the Accords was supposed to be there, but the Seelie Queen and the Unseelie King never showed up to sign the treaty, so it was altered and signed without them."

"And what does the Cold Peace mean for faeries?" Diana's look at Emma was pointed. Emma glared down at her desk.

"Faeries aren't protected under the Accords anymore," said Ty. "It's forbidden to help them, and they're forbidden from contacting Shadowhunters. Only the Scholomance and the Centurions are meant to deal with faeries—and the Consul and Inquisitor."

"A faerie who carries a weapon can be punished by death," Jules added. He looked exhausted. There were dark circles under his eyes.

Emma wished he would look at her. She and Julian didn't fight. They *never* fought. She wondered if he was as baffled as she was. She kept hearing what he'd said over and over: that he wouldn't have wanted a *parabatai*. Was it any *parabatai* he didn't want, or her specifically?

"And what is the Clave, Tavvy?" It was a question too elementary for any of the rest of them, but Tavvy looked pleased to be able to answer something.

"The government of the Shadowhunters," he said. "Active

Shadowhunters are all in the Clave. The ones who make decisions are the Council. There are three Downworlders on the Council, each one representing a different Downworlder race. Warlocks, werewolves, and vampires. There hasn't been a faerie representative since the Dark War."

"Very good," said Diana, and Tavvy beamed. "Can anyone tell me what other changes have been wrought by the Council since the end of the war?"

"Well, the Shadowhunter Academy was reopened," said Emma. This was familiar territory for her—she had been invited by the Consul to be one of the first students. She'd chosen to stay with the Blackthorns instead. "A lot of Shadowhunters are trained there now, and of course they bring in a lot of Ascendant hopefuls— mundanes who want to become Nephilim."

"The Scholomance was reestablished," said Julian. Wavy strands of his hair, dark and glossy, fell against his cheek as he lifted his head. "It existed before the first Accords were signed, and when the Council was betrayed by faeries, they insisted on opening it again. The Scholomance does research, trains Centurions . . ."

"Think of what it must have been like in the Scholomance for all those years it was closed," said Dru, her eyes gleaming with horror-movie delight. "All the way up in the mountains, totally abandoned and dark, full of spiders and ghosts and shadows . . ."

"If you want to think about somewhere scary, think about the Bone City," said Livvy. The City of Bones was where the Silent Brothers lived: It was an underground place of networked tunnels built out of the ashes of dead Shadowhunters.

"I'd like to go to the Scholomance," interrupted Ty.

"I wouldn't," said Livvy. "Centurions aren't allowed to have *parabatai*."

"I'd like to go anyway," said Ty. "You could come too if you wanted."

"I don't want to go to the Scholomance," said Livvy. "It's in the middle of the Carpathian Mountains. It's freezing there, and there are bears."

Ty's face lit up as it often did at the mention of animals. "There are bears?"

"Enough chatter," said Diana. "When was the Scholomance reopened?"

Cristina, who had the seat closest to the window, raised her hand to interrupt. "There's someone coming up the path to the front door," she said. "Several someones, in fact."

Emma glanced over at Jules again. It was rare that anyone paid an unscheduled visit to the Institute. There were only a few people who might, and even most of the members of the Conclave would have made an appointment with Arthur. Then again, maybe someone did have an appointment with Arthur. Though by the look on Julian's face, if they did, it was one he didn't know about.

Cristina, who had risen to her feet, drew her breath in. "Please," she said. "Come and see."

Everyone bolted to the one long window that ran across the main wall of the room. The window itself looked out onto the front of the Institute and the winding path that led from the doors down to the highway that divided them from the beach and the sea. The sky was high and blue and cloudless. The sunlight sparked off the silver bridles of three horses, each with a silent rider seated on its bare back.

"*Hadas*," Cristina said, the word emerging on a staccato beat of astonishment. "Faeries."

It was undeniably the case. The first horse was black, and the rider who sat on him wore black armor that looked like burned leaves. The second horse was black as well, and the rider who sat on him wore a robe the color of ivory. The third horse was brown, and its rider was wrapped head to toe in a hooded robe the color of earth. Emma couldn't tell if it was a man or a woman, a child or an adult.

"'So first let pass the horses black and then let pass the brown,'" Jules murmured, quoting an old faerie poem. "One robed in black, one brown, one white—it's an official delegation. From the Courts." Julian looked across the room at Diana. "I didn't know Arthur had a meeting with a delegation from Faerie. Do you think he told the Clave?"

She shook her head, clearly puzzled. "I don't know. He never mentioned it to me."

Julian's body was taut like a bowstring; Emma could feel the tension coming off him. A delegation from Faerie was a rare, serious thing. Permission from the Clave had to be granted before a meeting could be held. Even by the head of an Institute. "Diana, I have to go."

Frowning, Diana tapped her stele against one hand, then nodded. "Fine. Go ahead."

"I'll come with you." Emma slid down from the window seat.

Julian, already headed to the door, paused and turned. "No," he said. "It's all right. I'll take care of it."

He walked out of the room. For a moment Emma didn't move.

Normally if Julian told her he didn't need her with him, or that he had to do something alone, she wouldn't have given it a second thought. Sometimes events necessitated splitting up.

But the night before had solidified her feeling of unease. She didn't know what was going on with Jules. She didn't know if he didn't want her with him, or did but was angry with her or angry with himself or both.

She knew only that the Fair Folk were dangerous, and there was no way Julian was facing them alone.

"I'm going," she said, and headed toward the door. She stopped to take down Cortana, which was hanging beside it.

"Emma," said Diana, her voice tight with meaning. "Be careful."

The last time faeries had been in the Institute, they had helped Sebastian Morgenstern wrench the soul from the body of Julian's father. They had taken Mark.

Emma had carried Tavvy and Dru to safety. She had helped save the lives of Julian's younger brothers and sisters. They had barely escaped alive.

But Emma hadn't had years of training then. She hadn't killed a single demon herself, not when she was twelve. She hadn't spent years training to fight and kill and defend.

There was no way she was hanging back now.

Faeries.

Julian raced down the corridor and into his bedroom, his mind whirling.

Faeries at the doors of the Institute. Three steeds: two black, one brown. A contingent from a Faerie Court, though Seelie or Unseelie, Julian couldn't have said. They seemed to have been flying no banner.

They would want to talk. If there was anything faeries were good at, it was talking circles around humans. Even Shadowhunters. They could pierce the truth of a lie, and see the lie at the heart of a truth.

He grabbed up the jacket he'd been wearing the day before. There it was, in the inside pocket. The vial Malcolm had given him. He hadn't expected to need it so soon. He had hoped—

Well, never mind what he had hoped. He thought of Emma, briefly, and the chaos of broken hopes she represented. But now wasn't the time to think about that. Clutching the vial, Julian broke into a run again. He reached the end of the hallway and yanked open the door to the attic. He pounded up the steps and burst into his uncle's study.

Uncle Arthur was seated at his desk, wearing a slightly ragged

T-shirt, jeans, and loafers. His gray-brown hair hung nearly to his shoulders. He was comparing two massive books, muttering and marking down notes.

"Uncle Arthur." Julian approached the desk. "Uncle Arthur!"

Uncle Arthur made a shooing gesture at him. "I'm in the middle of something important. Something very important, Andrew."

"I'm Julian." He moved up behind his uncle and slammed both books shut. Arthur looked up at him in surprise, his faded green-blue eyes widening. "There's a delegation here. From Faerie. Did you know they were coming?"

Arthur seemed to shrink in on himself. "Yes," he said. "They sent messages—so many messages." He shook his head. "But why? It is forbidden. Faeries, they—they cannot reach us now."

Julian prayed silently for patience. "The messages, where are the messages?"

"They were written on leaves," Arthur said. "The leaves crumbled. As everything faeries touch crumbles, withers, and dies."

"But what did the messages *say?*"

"They insisted. On a meeting."

Julian took a deep breath. "Do you know what the meeting is *about*, Uncle Arthur?"

"I'm sure they mentioned it in their correspondence . . . ," Uncle Arthur said nervously. "But I don't recall it." He looked up at Julian. "Perhaps Nerissa would know."

Julian tensed. Nerissa had been Mark and Helen's mother. Julian knew little about her—a princess of the gentry, she had been beautiful, according to Helen's stories, and ruthless. She had been dead for years, and on his good days, Arthur knew that.

Arthur had different kinds of days: quiet ones, where he sat silently without responding to questions, and dark days, where he was angry, depressed, and often cruel. Mentioning the dead meant not a dark day or a quiet day, but the worst kind, a chaotic day, a day when Arthur would do nothing Julian expected—when he might lash out in anger or crumple into tears. The kind of day that brought the bitter taste of panic to the back of Julian's throat.

Julian's uncle had not always been this way. Julian remembered him as a quiet, almost silent man, a shadowy figure rarely present at family holidays. He had been an articulate enough presence in the Accords Hall when he had spoken up to say that he would accept the running of the Institute. No one who did not know him very, very well would ever know something was wrong.

Julian knew that his father and Arthur had been held prisoner in Faerie. That Andrew had fallen in love with Lady Nerissa, and had two children with her: Mark and Helen. But what had happened to Arthur during those years was cloaked in shadow. His lunacy, as the Clave would have termed it, was to Julian's mind a faerie-spun thing. If they had not destroyed his sanity, they had planted the seeds of its destruction. They had made his mind a fragile castle, so that years later, when the London Institute was attacked and Arthur injured, it shattered like glass.

Julian put his hand over Arthur's. His uncle's hand was slender and bony; it felt like the hand of a much older man. "I wish you didn't have to go to the meeting. But they'll be suspicious if you don't."

Arthur drew his glasses off his face and rubbed the bridge of his nose. "My monograph . . ."

"I know," Julian said. "It's important. But this is also important. Not just for the Cold Peace, but for us. For Helen. For Mark."

"Do you remember Mark?" Arthur said. His eyes were brighter without the glasses. "It was so long ago."

"Not that very long ago, Uncle," said Julian. "I remember him perfectly."

"It does seem like yesterday." Arthur shuddered. "I remember the Fair Folk warriors. They came into the London Institute with their armor covered in blood. So much, as if they had been in the Achaean lines when Zeus rained down blood." His hand, holding his glasses, shook. "I cannot meet with them."

"You have to," Julian said. He thought of everything unspoken: that he himself had been a child during the Dark War, that he had seen faeries slaughter children, heard the screams of the Wild Hunt. But he said none of it. "Uncle, you must."

"If I had my medication . . . ," Arthur said faintly. "But I ran out while you were gone."

"I have it." From his pocket, Julian produced the vial. "You should have asked Malcolm for more."

"I didn't remember." Arthur slid his glasses back onto his nose, watching as Julian tipped the contents of the vial into the glass of water on the desk. "How to find him . . . who to trust."

"You can trust me," Julian said, almost choking on the words, and held the glass out to his uncle. "Here. You know how the Fair Folk are. They feed on human unease and take advantage of it. This will help keep you calm, even if they try their tricks."

"Yes." Arthur looked at the glass, half with hunger and half fear. The contents of it would affect him for an hour, maybe less. Afterward he would have a blinding, crippling headache that might keep him in bed for days. Julian hardly ever gave it to him: The aftereffect was rarely worth it, but it would be worth it now. It had to be.

Uncle Arthur hesitated. Slowly he lifted the glass to his mouth, tipped the water in. Slowly he swallowed.

The effect was instant. Suddenly everything about Arthur seemed to sharpen, to become crisp, clear, precise, like a sketch that had been refined into a careful drawing. He rose to his feet and reached for the jacket that hung on a peg by his desk. "Help me find some clothes to change into, Julian," he said. "We must make a decent appearance in the Sanctuary."

* * *

Every Institute had a Sanctuary.

It had always been that way. The Institute was a mixture of city hall and residence, a place where Shadowhunters and Downworlders alike came to meet with the Institute's head. The head was the local representative of the Clave. In all of Southern California, there was no more important Shadowhunter than the head of the Los Angeles Institute. And the safest place to meet him was the Sanctuary, where vampires did not need to fear hallowed ground, and Downworlders were protected by oaths.

The Sanctuary had two sets of doors. One led outside and could be entered by anyone, who would find themselves inside the massive stone-bound room. The other set of doors connected the inside of the Institute to the Sanctuary. Like the front doors of the Institute, the inner doors of the Sanctuary yielded only to those with Shadowhunter blood.

Emma paused on the landing of the stairs to look out the window for the Fair Folk delegation. She had seen their horses, riderless, waiting near the front steps. If the Fair Folk delegation had experience with Shadowhunters, and they likely did, then they were already inside the Sanctuary.

The inner doors to the Sanctuary were at the end of a corridor that led off the Institute's main entryway. They were made of copper metal that had long since gone green with verdigris, and runes of protection and welcome wound their way around the framework of the doors like vines.

Emma could hear voices from the other side of the doors: unfamiliar voices, one clear like water, one sharp like a twig snapping underfoot. She tightened her hold on Cortana and pushed through the entrance.

The Sanctuary itself was built in the shape of a crescent moon, facing the mountains—the shadowy canyons, the silver-green brush scattered across the landscape. The mountains blocked the sun, but the room was bright, thanks to a pendant chandelier hanging from the ceiling. Light bounced off the cut glass and illuminated the checkerboard floor: alternating squares of darker and lighter wood. If you climbed to the chandelier and looked down, they revealed themselves as the shape of the Angelic Power rune.

Not that Emma would admit she'd done that. Though one did get an excellent view of the massive stone chair of the Institute's head from that angle.

In the center of the room were the faeries. There were only two of them, the one in white robes and the one in black armor. Nowhere could she see the brown rider. Neither of their faces was visible. She could see the fingertips of long, pale hands extending beyond their sleeves but couldn't tell if they were male or female.

Emma could sense a wild, unwieldy power rolling off them, the breathy edge of otherworldliness. A feeling like the cool damp of wet earth brushed her skin, carrying the scent of roots and leaves and jacaranda blossoms.

The faerie in black laughed and drew his hood down. Emma started. Skin the color of dark green leaves, clawed hands, yellow owl's eyes. He wore a cloak, woven with the pattern of a rowan tree.

It was the faerie she had seen at the Sepulchre the other night.

"We meet again, fair one," he said, and his mouth, which was like a slit in the bark of a tree, grinned. "I am Iarlath of the Unseelie Court. My companion in white is Kieran of the Hunt. Kieran, lower your hood."

The other faerie lifted two slender hands, each of them tipped by nearly translucent, square nails. He took hold of the edges of his hood and thrust it back with an imperious, almost rebellious gesture.

Emma suppressed a gasp. He was beautiful. Not like Julian was beautiful, or Cristina—in human ways—but like the cutting edge of Cortana. He looked young, no more than sixteen or seventeen, though she guessed he was older than that. Dark hair with a faint blue sheen framed a sculpted face. His light tunic and trousers were faded and worn; they had been elegant once, but now the sleeves and hems were slightly too short on a lithe and graceful body. His wide-spaced eyes were two-colored: the left black and the right a deep silver. He wore the battered white gauntlets that proclaimed him a prince of Faerie, but his eyes—his eyes said that he was part of the Wild Hunt.

"Is this because of the other night?" Emma said, looking from Iarlath to Kieran. "At the Sepulchre?"

"In part," said Iarlath. His voice sounded like boughs creaking in the wind. Like the dark depths of fairy-tale forests, where only monsters lived. Emma wondered that she hadn't noticed it at the bar.

"Is this the girl?" Kieran's voice was very different: It sounded like waves sliding up the shore. Like warm water under pale light. It was seductive, with an edge of cold. He looked at Emma as if she were a new kind of flower, one he wasn't sure he liked. "She's pretty," he said. "I didn't think she'd be pretty. You didn't mention it."

Iarlath shrugged. "You've always been partial to blondes," he said.

"Okay, seriously?" Emma snapped her fingers. "I am *right here*. And I was not aware I was being invited to a game of 'Who's the Hottest?'"

"I wasn't aware you were invited at all," said Kieran. His speech had a casual edge, as if he was used to talking to humans.

"Rude," said Emma. "This is my house. And what are you doing here, anyway? Did you show up to tell me that he"—she pointed at Iarlath—"isn't responsible for the murder at the Sepulchre? Because that seems like going way out of your way just to say you didn't do it."

"Of course I didn't do it," Iarlath snapped. "Don't be ridiculous."

Under any other circumstances, Emma would have dismissed the comment. Faeries, though, couldn't lie. Not full-blooded faeries, anyway. Half faeries, like Mark and Helen, could tell untruths, but they were rare.

Emma crossed her arms over her chest. "Repeat after me: 'I did not murder the victim you speak of, Emma Carstairs,'" she said. "So I know it's true."

Iarlath's yellow eyes fixed on Emma with dislike. "I did not murder the victim you speak of, Emma Carstairs."

"Then why are you here?" Emma demanded. "Oh, is this one of those missed-connections things? We met the other night, you felt a spark? Sorry, but I don't date trees."

"I am not a tree." Iarlath looked angry, his bark peeling slightly.

"Emma," said a warning voice from the doorway.

To Emma's surprise, it was Arthur Blackthorn. He stood at the entrance to the Sanctuary wearing a somber dark suit, his hair neatly combed back. The sight gave Emma a jolt; it was a long time since she remembered him wearing anything but a ragged robe or old, coffee-stained jeans.

Standing beside him was Julian, his brown hair rumpled. She searched his face for signs of anger but saw none—he looked like someone who'd run a marathon, actually, and was holding himself back from crumpling with exhaustion and relief.

"My apologies for the behavior of my ward," said Arthur, striding into the room. "Though it is not forbidden to squabble in the Sanctuary, it is against the spirit of the place." He sank down in the massive stone chair under the chandelier. "I am Arthur Blackthorn. This is my nephew Julian Blackthorn." Julian, who had come to stand beside Arthur's seat, inclined his head as Kieran and Iarlath introduced themselves. "Now, pray tell us why you are here."

The faerie convoy exchanged glances. "What," said Kieran, "no words about the Cold Peace or about how this visit breaks your Law?"

"My uncle does not administrate the Cold Peace," said Julian.

"And it is not what we wish to discuss. You know the rules as well as we do; if you've chosen to break them, it must be for an important reason. If you don't wish to share the information, my uncle will have to ask you to leave."

Kieran looked haughty. "Very well," he said. "We have come to ask a favor."

"A *favor*?" Emma said in amazement. The wording of the Cold Peace was clear: Shadowhunters were not to give aid to either the Seelie or the Unseelie Court. The representatives of the Courts had never appeared to sign the Nephilim's treaty; they had scorned it, and this was their punishment.

"Perhaps you are confused," Arthur said coldly. "You might have heard of my niece and nephew; you might think that because our relatives Mark and Helen have faerie blood you will find a kinder hearing here than you would at some other Institute. But my niece was sent away because of the Cold Peace, and my nephew was stolen from us."

Kieran's lip curled up at the corner. "Your niece's exile was a Shadowhunter decree, not a faerie one," he said. "As for your nephew—"

Arthur took a shaking breath. His hands were gripping the armrests of his chair. "The hand of the Consul was forced by the betrayal of the Seelie Queen. Unseelie warriors fought beside hers. No faerie hand is free of blood. We are not well disposed toward faeries here."

"The Cold Peace wasn't what took Mark away from us," said Julian, his cheeks burning with color. "That was you. The Wild Hunt. We can see by your eyes that you ride with Gwyn, don't deny it."

"Oh," said Kieran with a slight smirk on his lips. "I would not deny that."

Emma wondered if anyone else heard Julian's intake of breath. "So you know my brother."

The smirk never left Kieran's face. "Of course I do."

Julian looked as if he were barely holding himself back. "*What do you know about Mark?*"

"What is this pretense of surprise?" demanded Iarlath. "It is foolishness. We mentioned Mark of the Hunt in the letter we sent."

Emma saw the look on Julian's face, a flicker of shock. She stepped forward quickly, not wanting him to be the one to have to ask. "What letter?"

"It was written on a leaf," Arthur said. "A leaf that crumbled." He was sweating; he took the handkerchief from his breast pocket and mopped at his forehead. "There were words on it about killings. About Mark. I didn't believe it was real. I was—"

Julian stepped forward, half-blocking his uncle from view. "Killings?"

Kieran looked at Julian, and his bicolored eyes darkened. Emma felt the uncomfortable sensation that Kieran thought he knew something about her *parabatai*, something she didn't know herself. "You know of the murders," he said. "Emma Carstairs found one of the bodies. We know you are aware there have been others."

"Why do you care?" said Julian. "Faeries do not normally involve themselves in the bloodshed of the human world."

"We do if the blood being shed is faerie blood," said Kieran. He looked around at their surprised faces. "As you know, the killer has been murdering and mutilating faeries, too. That is why Iarlath was at the Sepulchre. That is why Emma Carstairs encountered him. You were hunting the same prey."

Iarlath reached into his cloak and drew out a handful of glittering mica. He tossed it into the air, where the particles hung and separated, coalescing into three-dimensional images. Images of bodies, faerie bodies—human-looking gentry faeries, all dead. All had skin carved with the spiky dark markings that had adorned the body Emma had found in the alley.

Emma found herself unconsciously leaning forward, trying to get a better view of the illusion. "What are these? Magic photographs?"

"Memories, preserved with magic," said Iarlath.

"Illusions," said Julian. "Illusions can lie."

Iarlath turned his hand to the side, and the images changed. Emma was suddenly looking at the dead man she'd found in the alley three nights ago. It was an exact image, down to the twisted look of horror on his face. "Does this lie?"

Emma stared at Iarlath. "So you saw him. You must have come across him before I did. I wondered."

Iarlath closed his hand, and the glittering pieces of mica fell to the floor like drops of rain, the illusion vanishing. "I did. He was already dead. I could not have helped him. I left him for you to find."

Emma said nothing. It was quite evident from the picture that Iarlath was telling the truth.

And faeries didn't lie.

"Shadowhunters have been killed too, we know," Kieran said.

"Shadowhunters are often killed," said Uncle Arthur. "There is no safe place."

"Not so," said Kieran. "There is protection where there are protectors."

"My parents," Emma said, ignoring Julian, who was shaking his head at her, as if to say, *Don't tell them, don't share, don't give them anything.* She knew he was likely right—it was in the nature of faeries to take your secrets and turn them against you. But if there was the chance, the smallest chance that they knew something . . . "Their bodies were found with those same markings on them, five years ago. When the Shadowhunters tried to move them, they crumbled to ashes. The only reason we know about the markings was because the Nephilim took photos first."

Kieran glanced at her with shimmering eyes. Neither looked quite human: The black eye was too dark, the silver too metallic. And yet the overall effect was haunting, inhumanly beautiful. "We know about your parents," he said. "We know of their deaths. We know of the demon language with which their bodies were inscribed."

"Mutilated," Emma said, her breath catching, and felt Julian's eyes on her, a reminder that he was there, a silent support. "Disfigured. Not *inscribed*."

Kieran's expression didn't change. "We understand as well that you have tried for years to translate or understand the markings, with no success. We can help you change that."

"What are you saying, exactly?" Julian demanded. His eyes were guarded; his whole posture was. The tension in his body kept Emma from bursting out with questions.

"The scholars of the Unseelie Court have studied the markings," said Iarlath. "It looks like a language from an ancient time of Faerie. One long before your human memory. Before there were Nephilim."

"Back when faeries were more closely tied to their demonic ancestry," said Arthur hoarsely.

Kieran's lip curled as if Arthur had said something distasteful. "Our scholars began to translate it," he said. He drew several sheets of thin, parchment-like paper from his cloak. Emma recognized on them the markings she was so familiar with. Below the markings were more words, written in a spidery script.

Emma's heart started to pound.

"They translated the first line," he said. "It does appear to perhaps be part of a spell. There our knowledge fails us—the Fair Folk do not deal in spells; that is warlock territory—"

"You translated the first line?" Emma burst out. "What is it?"

"We will tell you," said Iarlath, "and give you the work our scholars have done so far, if you will agree to our terms."

Julian looked at them with suspicion. "Why would you translate only the first line? Why not the whole thing?"

"Scarce had the scholars worked out the meaning of that first line when the Unseelie King forbade them to continue," said Kieran. "The magic of this spell is dark, demonic in origin. He did not want it awakened in Faerie."

"You could have continued the work yourself," said Emma.

"All faeries are forbidden by the King to touch these words," snapped Iarlath. "But that does not mean our involvement ends. We believe this text, these markings, may help lead you to the killer, once they are understood."

"And you want us to translate the rest of the markings?" Julian said. "Using the line you've worked out as a key?"

"More than that," said Iarlath. "The translation is but the first step. It will lead you to the murderer. Once you have found that person, you will turn them over to the Unseelie King that they might stand trial for the murder of the fey and receive justice."

"You want us to conduct an investigation on your behalf?" Julian snapped. "We're *Shadowhunters.* We're bound by the Cold Peace, just like you. It is forbidden for us to help the Fair Folk, forbidden for us to even entertain you here. You know what we'd be risking. How dare you ask?"

There was rage in Julian's voice—rage out of proportion to the suggestion, but Emma couldn't blame him. She knew what he saw when he looked at faeries, especially faeries with the broken eyes of the Wild Hunt. He saw the cold wastes of Wrangel Island. He saw the empty bedroom in the Institute where Mark no longer was.

"It isn't just their investigation," Emma said quietly. "It's mine, too. This has to do with my parents."

"I know," Julian said, and his anger was gone. There was an ache in his voice instead. "But not this way, Emma—"

"Why come here?" Arthur interrupted, looking pained, his face gray. "Why not to a warlock?"

Kieran's beautiful face twisted. "We cannot consult a warlock," he said. "None of Lilith's Children will deal with us. The Cold Peace has left us shunned by other Downworlders. But you can visit the High Warlock Malcolm Fade, or Magnus Bane himself, and demand an answer to your question. We are chained, but *you*—" He spoke the word with scorn. "You are free."

"This is the wrong family to have come to," said Arthur. "You are asking us to break the Law for you, as if we have some special regard for the Fair Folk. But the Blackthorns have not forgotten what you have taken from them."

"No," Emma said. "We need those papers, we need—"

"Emma." Arthur's look was sharp. "Enough."

Emma dropped her gaze, but her blood was singing through her veins, a determined melody of rebellion. If the faeries left and took the papers with them, she would find some way to track them down, to retrieve the information, to learn what she had to learn. Some way. Even if the Institute couldn't risk it, she could.

Iarlath looked at Arthur. "I do not think you wish to make such a hasty decision."

Arthur's jaw tightened. "Why do you second-guess me, neighbor?"

*The Good Neighbors.* An old, old term for faerie folk. It was Kieran who replied: "Because we have something that you want above all other things. And if you help us, we are willing to give it to you."

Julian paled. Emma, staring at him, was for a moment too caught up in his reaction to realize herself what they were implying. When she did, her heart gave an uneven throb inside her chest.

"What is it?" Julian whispered. "What do you have that we want?"

"Oh, come now," Kieran said. "What do you think?"

The door of the Sanctuary, the one that went to the outside of the Institute, opened, and the faerie in the brown robes came in. He moved with grace and silence, no hesitation or trepidation—without anything human about his movements at all. Entering the pattern of the angelic rune on the floor, he came to a stop. The room was completely silent as he raised his hands to his hood and—for the first time—hesitated.

His hands were human, long-fingered, tanned pale brown. Familiar.

Emma wasn't breathing. She couldn't breathe. Julian looked as if he were in a dream. Arthur's face was blank, confused.

"Take your hood down, boy," said Iarlath. "Show your face."

The familiar hands tightened on the hood and yanked it down. Pushing, then shoving the cloak off his shoulders, as if the material of it clung unpleasantly. Emma saw the flash of a long, lithe body, of pale hair, of thin hands, as the cloak was wrenched away and slid to the ground in a dark puddle.

A boy stood in the heart of the rune, panting. A boy who looked about seventeen, with fair hair that curled like acanthus vines, tangled with twigs and briars, hanging to his shoulders. His eyes showed the shattered doubling of the Wild Hunt: two colors—one gold, one Blackthorn blue. His feet were bare, black with dirt, his clothes ragged and torn.

A wave of dizziness passed through Emma along with a terrible mixture of horror and relief and amazement. Julian had stiffened, as if he'd been shocked with electricity. She saw the slight tightening of his jaw, the twitch of a muscle in his cheek. He didn't open his mouth; it was Arthur who spoke, half-rising from his chair, his voice thready and uncertain:

"*Mark?*"

\* \* \*

Mark's eyes widened in confusion. He opened his mouth to answer. Iarlath whirled on him. "Mark Blackthorn of the Wild Hunt," he snapped. "Do not speak until given permission to speak."

Mark's lips slammed together. His face was still.

"And you," said Kieran, holding up a hand as Julian started forward, "stay where you are."

"What have you done to him?" Julian's eyes flashed. *"What have you done to my brother?"*

"Mark belongs to the Wild Hunt," said Iarlath. "If we choose to release him to you, it will be at our recognizance."

Arthur had sunk back into the chair behind him. He was blinking owlishly and looking from Mark to the faerie host. The gray color was back in his face. "The dead rise and the lost return," he said. "We should fly blue banners from the tops of the towers."

Kieran seemed coldly puzzled. "Why does he say that?"

Julian looked from Arthur to Mark to the other two faeries. "He's in shock," he said. "His health is fragile; it has been since the war."

"It's from an old Shadowhunter poem," said Emma. "I'm surprised you don't know it."

"Poems contain much truth," said Iarlath, and there was humor in his voice, but a bitter sort. Emma wondered if he was laughing at them or himself.

Julian was staring at Mark, a look on his face of unmitigated shock and longing. "Mark?" he said.

Mark looked away.

Julian looked as if he had been pierced by elf-bolts, the sly faerie arrows that burrowed under the skin and released deadly poison. Any anger Emma had felt toward him about the night before evaporated. The look on his face was like knife blades in her heart. "Mark," he said again, and then in a half whisper, "Why? Why can't he speak to me?"

"He is forbidden by Gwyn to speak until our bargain is sealed," said Kieran. He glanced at Mark, and there was something cold in his expression. Hatred? Envy? Did he despise Mark for being half-human? Did they all? How had they showed their hate all these years, when Mark was at their mercy?

Emma could sense how hard Julian was holding himself back from going to his brother. She spoke for him. "So Mark is your bargaining chip."

Rage flashed across Kieran's face, sudden and startling. "Why must you state things that are obvious? Why must all humans do it? Foolish girl—"

Julian changed; his attention snapped away from Mark, his spine straightening, his voice hardening. He sounded calm, but Emma, who knew him so well, could hear the ice in his voice. "Emma is my *parabatai*," he said. "If you ever speak to her like that again, there will be blood on the floor of the Sanctuary, and I do not care if they put me to death for it."

Kieran's beautiful, alien eyes gleamed. "You Nephilim are loyal to your chosen partners, I will give you that." He waved a dismissive hand. "I suppose Mark is our bargaining chip, as you put it, but do not forget that it is the fault of the Nephilim that we need one at all. There was a time when Shadowhunters would have investigated the killings of our kind because they believed in their mandate to protect more than they believed in their hate."

"There was a time when the Fair Folk might have freely returned to us one of our own," said Arthur. "The pain of loss goes both ways, as does the loss of trust."

"Well, you will have to trust us," said Kieran. "You have no one else. Do you?"

There was a long silence. Julian's gaze went back to his brother, and in that moment Emma hated the Fair Folk, for in holding Mark, they also held Julian's human, breakable heart. "So you want us to find out who is responsible for these killings," he said. "Stop the murders of faeries and humans. And in return you will give us Mark, if we succeed?"

"The Court is prepared to be far more generous," said Kieran. "We will give you Mark now. He will assist you in your investigation. And when the investigation is over, he may choose whether he remains with you or returns to the Hunt."

"He will choose us," Julian said. "We are his family."

Kieran's eyes shone. "I would not be so sure, young Shadow-hunter. Those of the Hunt are loyal to the Hunt."

"He isn't of the Hunt," Emma said. "He's a Blackthorn."

"His mother, Lady Nerissa, was fey," said Kieran. "And he has ridden with us, reaped the dead with us, mastered the use of elf-bolt and arrow. He is a formidable warrior in the faerie fashion, but he is not like you. He will not fight like you. He is not Nephilim."

"Yes, he is," said Julian. "Shadowhunter blood breeds true. His skin can bear Marks. You know the laws."

Kieran did not reply to that, just looked at Arthur. "Only the head of the Institute can decide this. You must let your uncle speak freely."

Emma looked to Arthur; they all did. Arthur picked nervously, fretfully at the arm of his chair. "You wish the fey boy here that he might report on us to you," he said finally in a quavering voice. "He will be your spy."

*The fey boy.* Not Mark. Emma looked over at Mark, but if a flicker of hurt passed across his stony face, it was invisible.

"If we wished to spy on you, there are easier ways," said Kieran in a tone of cold reproach. "We would not need to give up Mark—he is one of the best fighters of the Hunt. Gwyn will miss him sorely. He will not be a spy."

Julian drew away from Emma, fell on his knees by his uncle's chair. He leaned in and whispered to Arthur, and Emma strained

to hear what he was saying, but could make out only a few words—
"brother" and "investigation" and "murder" and "medicine" and
"Clave."

Arthur held up a shaking hand, as if to silence his nephew, and
turned to the faeries. "We will accept your offer," he said. "On the
condition that there will be no tricks. At the end of the investigation, when the killer is caught, Mark will make his own free choice
to stay or to go."

"Of course," said Iarlath. "As long as the murderer is clearly
identified. We wish to know the one with the blood on his hands—
it will not be enough for you to say 'it was done by that one or this
one' or 'vampires were responsible.' The murderer or murderers will be placed in the custody of the Courts. We will mete out
justice."

*Not if I find the murderer first*, Emma thought. *I'll deliver his dead
body to you, and that had better be good enough.*

"First you swear," said Julian, his blue-green eyes bright and
hard. "Say, 'I swear that when the terms of the bargain are fulfilled,
Mark Blackthorn will make his own free choice whether he wishes
to be part of the Hunt or return to his life as a Nephilim.'"

Kieran's mouth tightened. "I swear that when the terms of the
bargain are fulfilled, Mark Blackthorn will make his own free choice
whether he wishes to be part of the Hunt or return to his life as a
Nephilim."

Mark was expressionless, unmoving as he had been all this
time, as if they weren't discussing him but someone else. He looked
as if he were seeing through the walls of the Sanctuary, seeing the
distant ocean perhaps, or a place even farther away than that.

"Then I think we have an arrangement," Julian said.

The two faeries looked at each other, and then Kieran walked
over to Mark. He laid his white hands on Mark's shoulders and
said something to him in a guttural language Emma didn't

understand—it was nothing Diana had taught them, not the high, fluting speech of the Court fey or any other magical speech. Mark didn't move, and Kieran stepped away, looking unsurprised.

"He is yours for now," he said. "We will leave his steed for him. They have become . . . attached."

"He won't be able to use a horse," Julian said, his voice tight. "Not in Los Angeles."

Kieran's smile was full of contempt. "I think you'll find he can use this one."

"God!" It was Arthur, crying out. He lurched forward, his hands cradling his head. "It hurts—"

Julian moved to his uncle's side, reaching to grip his arm, but Arthur threw him off, rising to his feet, his breath uneven. "I must excuse myself," he said. "My headache. It is unbearable."

He looked horribly unwell, it was true. His skin was the color of dirty chalk, his collar sticking to his throat with sweat.

Both Kieran and Iarlath said nothing. Neither did Mark, who still stood swaying blindly on his feet. The fey watched Arthur with avid curiosity burning in their eyes. Emma could read their thoughts. *The head of the Los Angeles Institute. He is weak, unwell. . . .*

The inner doors rattled, and Diana came in. She looked cool and calm as always. Her dark gaze took in the scene before her. Her glance brushed over Emma once; there was cold anger in it. "Arthur," she said. "You are needed upstairs. Do go. I will escort the convoy outside to discuss the bargain."

*How long was she out there eavesdropping?* Emma wondered as Arthur, looking desperately grateful, limped past Diana and toward the door. Diana was as quiet as a cat when she wanted to be.

"Is he dying?" Iarlath asked with some curiosity, his gaze following Arthur as he left the Sanctuary.

"We're mortal," Emma said. "We get sick, we age. We're not like you. But it's nothing that should be a surprise."

"Enough," Diana said. "I will lead you from the Sanctuary, but first—the translation." She held out a slim brown hand.

Kieran handed over the near-translucent papers with a wry look. Diana glanced down at them. "What does the first line say?" Emma said, unable to stop herself.

Diana frowned. *"Fire to water,"* she said. "What does that mean?"

Iarlath gave her a single cool look and moved to join her. "It will be the task of your people to find out."

*Fire to water?* Emma thought of the bodies of her parents, drowned and then crumbling like ashes. Of the body of the man in the alley, scorched and then soaked in seawater. She looked at Julian, wondering if his mind was following the same paths as hers—but no, he was looking at his brother, unmoving, as if frozen in place.

She itched to get her hands on the papers, but they were folded into Diana's jacket, and Diana was leading the two faerie men toward the Sanctuary exit. "You understand that we will be investigating this without the knowledge of the Clave," she said as Iarlath fell into step beside her. Kieran walked behind them, scowling.

"We understand that you fear your government, yes," said Iarlath. "We fear them too, the architects of the Cold Peace."

Diana didn't rise to the bait. "If you must contact us during the investigation, you'll need to take care in doing so."

"We will come only to the Sanctuary, and you may leave messages here for us," said Kieran. "If we hear that you have spoken of our bargain to anyone outside these walls, especially one who is not Nephilim, we will be most displeased. Mark, too, is under orders of secrecy from the Hunt. You will find he will not disobey them."

Sunlight speared into the Sanctuary as Diana opened the doors. Emma felt a flash of gratitude for her tutor as Diana and the two faeries vanished outside. Gratitude for sparing Arthur—and for sparing Julian one more second of pretending he was all right.

For Jules was looking at his brother—finally, *really* looking at him, with no one to see or judge his weakness. With no one to, at the last moment, take Mark away from him again.

Mark raised his head slowly. He was thin as a lath, so much narrower and more angular than Emma remembered him. He didn't seem to have aged so much as sharpened, as if the bones of chin and cheek and jaw had been refined with careful tools. He was gaunt but graceful, in the manner of the fey.

"Mark," Julian breathed out, and Emma thought of the nightmares Jules had woken up from over the years, screaming for his brother, for *Mark*, and how hopeless he had sounded, and how lost. He was pale now, but his eyes were shining as if he were looking at a miracle. And it was a sort of miracle, Emma thought: The faeries didn't give back what they had taken.

Or at least, they never gave it back unchanged.

A chill ran suddenly up Emma's veins, but she didn't make a sound. She didn't move as Julian took a step toward his brother, and then another one, and then spoke, his voice breaking. "Mark," he whispered. "Mark. It's me."

Mark looked Julian straight in the face. There was something about his two-colored eyes; both eyes had been blue when Emma had last seen him, and the bifurcation seemed to speak to something broken inside him, like a piece of pottery cracked along the glaze. He looked at Julian—taking in his height, his broad shoulders and lanky frame, his tousled brown hair, his Blackthorn eyes— and he spoke for the first time.

His voice sounded rough, scraped, as if he had not used it in days.

"Father?" he said, and then, as Julian drew in a startled breath, Mark's eyes rolled back in his head and he collapsed to the floor in a dead faint.

# 6

## MANY FAR WISER

**Mark's bedroom was full of dust.**

They had left it untouched for years after he disappeared. Finally, on what would have been his eighteenth birthday, Julian had thrown the door of the room open and cleared it out in a savage spree. Mark's clothes, toys, games, all had gone into storage. The room was cleaned out and stripped down, a bare, empty space waiting for decoration.

Emma moved around, pushing back dusty curtains and opening windows, letting in light, while Julian, who had carried his brother up the stairs, set Mark down on the bed.

The blankets were pulled tight, a thin layer of dust across the coverlet. It puffed up as he set Mark down; Mark coughed but didn't stir.

Emma turned away from the windows; open, they flooded the room with light and turned the dust motes in the air into dancing creatures.

"He's so thin," Julian said. "He hardly weighs anything at all."

Someone who didn't know him might have thought he was expressionless: His face betrayed only a kind of tightening of the muscles, his soft mouth compressed into a hard line. It was the way he looked when he was struck to the heart with some strong emotion and was trying to hide it, usually from his younger siblings.

Emma came over to the bed. For a moment they both stood looking down at Mark. Indeed, the curves of elbows and knees and collarbone were painfully sharp under the clothes he wore: ragged jeans and a T-shirt gone almost transparent with years and washing. Tangled blond hair half-covered his face.

"Is it true?" said a small voice from the doorway.

Emma whirled around. Ty and Livia had come into the room, only a little way. Cristina was in the doorway behind them; she looked at Emma as if to say she'd tried to hold them back. Emma shook her head. She knew how impossible it was to stop the twins when they wanted to be part of something.

It was Livvy who had spoken. She looked across the room now, past Emma, to where Mark lay on the bed. She sucked in a breath. "It *is* true."

"It can't be." Ty's hands were fluttering at his sides. He was counting on his fingers, one to ten, ten to one. The gaze he fixed on his unconscious brother was full of disbelief. "The Fair Folk don't give back what they take."

"No," Julian said, his voice gentle, and Emma wondered not for the first time how he could be so gentle when she knew he must feel like screaming and flying apart into a thousand pieces. "But sometimes they give you back what belongs to you."

Ty said nothing. His hands were still fluttering in their repetitive movements. There had been a time when Ty's father had tried to train him to immobility, had held his son's hands tightly at his sides when he was upset and said, "Still, *still*." It had panicked Ty into throwing up. Julian never did that. He just said everyone got butterflies when they were nervous; some people got them in their stomachs, and Ty showed his in his hands. Ty had been pleased by that. He loved moths, butterflies, bees—anything with wings.

"He doesn't look like I remember," said a tiny voice. It was Dru, who had edged into the room around Cristina. She was holding hands with Tavvy.

"Well," said Emma. "Mark *is* five years older now."

"He doesn't look older," said Dru. "He just looks different."

There was a silence. Dru was right. Mark didn't look older, certainly not five years older. Partly it was because he was so thin, but there was more to it than that.

"He's been in Faerie all these years," Julian said. "And time—time works differently there."

Ty stepped forward. His gaze raked the bed, examining his brother. Drusilla hung back. She'd been eight when Mark had gone; Emma couldn't imagine what her memories of him were like—cloudy and blurred, probably. And as for Tavvy—Tavvy had been two. To him the boy in the bed would be a total stranger.

But Ty. Ty would remember. Ty moved closer to the bed, and Emma could almost see the quick mind working behind his gray eyes. "That would make sense. There are all sorts of stories about people vanishing for a night with the faeries and coming back to find a hundred years have passed. Five years could have been like two years for him. He looks about the same age as you, Jules."

Julian cleared his throat. "Yeah. Yeah, he does."

Ty cocked his head to the side. "Why did they bring him back?"

Julian hesitated. Emma didn't move; she didn't know, any more than he did, how to tell the children who were looking at them with wide eyes that the lost brother who appeared to have been returned to them forever might be here only temporarily.

"He's bleeding," Dru said.

"What?" Julian tapped the witchlight lamp at the side of the bed and the glow in the room intensified to a hot brightness. Emma drew in her breath. The side of Mark's ragged white T-shirt, at his shoulder, was red with blood—a patch that was slowly spreading.

"Stele," Julian barked, holding out his hand. He was already pulling at his brother's shirt, baring his shoulder and collarbone, where a half-healed gash had opened. Blood was trickling from the wound, not fast, but Tavvy made an inarticulate sound of distress.

Emma pulled her stele from her belt and threw it. She didn't say anything; she didn't need to. Julian's hand came up and he caught it out of the air. He bent to press the tip to Mark's skin, to begin the healing rune—

Mark screamed.

His eyes flew open, bright and crazed, and he thrashed out at the air with his stained, dirty, bloody hands.

"Get it *away*," he snarled, struggling upright. "Get it away, get that thing *away from me!*"

"Mark—"

Julian reached for his brother, but Mark batted him away. He might have been thin, but he was strong; Julian stumbled, and Emma felt it like a burst of pain in the back of her head. She dashed forward, putting herself between the two brothers.

She was about to shout at Mark, to tell him to stop, when she caught sight of his face. His eyes were wide and white with fear, his hand clutched to his chest—there was something there, something that glittered at the end of a cord around his throat—and then he hurled himself off the bed, his body jerking, hands and feet scrabbling at the hardwood.

"Move *back*," Julian said to his siblings, not shouting, but his voice quick and authoritative. They scrambled away, scattering. Emma caught a glimpse of Tavvy's unhappy face as Dru lifted him off his feet and carried him out of the room.

Mark had darted into the corner of the bedroom, where he

froze, his hands wrapped around his knees, his back pressed hard to the wall. Julian started after his brother, then stopped, the stele dangling helplessly from his hand.

"Don't touch me with that," Mark said, and his voice—very recognizably Mark's voice, and very cold and precise—was shockingly at odds with the filthy scarecrow look of him. He held them at bay with his glare.

"What's wrong with him?" Livvy asked in a near whisper.

"It's the stele." It was Julian, voice soft.

"But why?" said Emma. "How can a Shadowhunter be afraid of a stele?"

"You call me afraid?" demanded Mark. "Insult me again and find your blood spilled, girl."

"Mark, this is *Emma*," Julian said. "Emma Carstairs."

Mark pressed himself farther back into the wall. "Lies," he said. "Lies and dreams."

"I'm Julian," Jules said. "Your brother Julian. And that's Tiberius—"

"*My brother Tiberius is a child!*" Mark shouted, suddenly livid, his hands clawing behind him at the wall. "He is a *little boy!*"

There was a horrified silence. "I'm not," said Ty, finally, into the quiet. His hands were fluttering at his sides, pale butterflies in the dim light. "I'm not a child."

Mark said nothing. He closed his eyes, and tears slid out from beneath his lids, tracking down his face, mixing with the dirt.

"Enough." To everyone's surprise, it was Cristina who had spoken. She looked embarrassed as everyone turned to look at her, but stood her ground, chin up, straight-backed. "Can't you see this is tormenting him? If we were to go into the hall—"

"You go," said Julian, looking at Mark. "I'll stay here."

Cristina shook her head. "No." She sounded apologetic but firm. "All of us." She paused as Julian hesitated.

"Please," she said.

She crossed the room and opened the door. Emma watched in amazement as the Blackthorns, one by one, filed out of the room; a moment later they were all standing in the corridor, and Cristina was shutting the door of Mark's room behind her.

"I don't know," Julian said immediately as the door clicked shut. "Leaving him alone in there—"

"It's his room," Cristina said. Emma stared at her in amazement; how could she be so calm?

"But he doesn't remember it," Livvy said, looking agitated. "He doesn't remember—anything."

"He does remember," Emma said, laying a hand on Livvy's shoulder. "It's just that everything he remembers has changed."

"We haven't." Livvy looked so woebegone that Emma pulled her close and kissed the top of her head, which was no mean feat since Livvy was only an inch shorter than her.

"Oh, you have," she said. "We all have. And so has Mark."

Ty looked agitated. "But the room is dusty," he said. "We threw out his things. He'll think we forgot him, that we don't care."

Julian winced. "I kept his things. They're in one of the storerooms on the ground floor."

"Good." Cristina brought her hands together sharply. "He'll need them. And more. Clothes to replace the ones he's wearing. Anything of his that was kept. Anything that'll seem familiar. Photos, or things he might remember."

"We can get those," said Livvy. "Me and Ty."

Ty looked relieved to have been given a specific task. He and Livvy headed downstairs, their voices a low murmur.

Julian, looking after them, exhaled raggedly—mingled tension and relief. "Thanks for giving them something to do."

Emma reached out to squeeze Cristina's hand. She felt oddly proud, as if she wanted to point to Cristina and say: "Look, my friend knows exactly what to do!"

"How *do* you know exactly what to do?" she asked aloud, and Cristina blinked.

"This is my field of study, remember," Cristina said. "Faerie and the results of the Cold Peace. Of course the Folk have returned him to you with demands, that is part of their cruelty. He needs time to recover, to begin to recognize this world and his life again. Instead they would thrust him back into it as if it would be easy for him to be a Shadowhunter again."

Julian leaned back against the wall beside the door. Emma could see the dark fire in his eyes, banked under his lowered eyelids. "They injured him," he said. "Why?"

"So you would do what you did," said Emma. "So you would get a stele."

He cursed, short and harsh. "So I would see what they did to him, how he hates me?"

"He doesn't hate you," said Cristina. "He hates himself. He hates that he is Nephilim, because they would have taught that to him. Hate for hate. They are an old people and that is their idea of justice."

"How is Mark?" It was Diana, emerging at the top of the stairs. She hurried toward them, her skirts whispering around her ankles. "Is someone in there with him?"

As Julian explained what had happened, Diana listened silently. She was buckling on her weapons belt. She had put on boots, and her hair was tied back. A leather satchel was slung over her shoulder.

"Hopefully he can rest," she said when Julian finished. "Kieran said the journey here took them two days through Faerie, no sleep, he's probably exhausted."

"Kieran?" said Emma. "It's weird calling gentry faeries by their first names. He is gentry, right?"

Diana nodded. "Kieran's a prince of Faerie; he didn't say so, but it's obvious. Iarlath is from the Unseelie Court, not a prince, but some sort of Court member. You can tell."

Julian glanced toward the door of his brother's room. "I should go back in there—"

"No," Diana said. "You and Emma are going to Malcolm Fade's." She fished into her satchel and came out with the faerie documents that Kieran had given to her earlier. Up close Emma could see that they were two sheets of parchment, thin as onion-skin. The ink on them looked as if it had been carved there. "Take this to him. See what he can make of it."

"Now?" Emma said. "But—"

"Now," said Diana flatly. "The Folk have given you—given us—three weeks. Three weeks with Mark to solve this. Then they take him back."

"Three *weeks*?" Julian echoed. "That's not nearly enough time."

"I could go with them," Cristina said.

"I need you here, Cristina," said Diana. "Someone has to watch over Mark, and it can't be one of the children. And it can't be me. I have to go."

"Go where?" Emma demanded.

But Diana only shook her head, unforthcoming. It was a familiar wall. Emma had crashed against it more than once. "It's important," was all Diana said. "You'll have to trust me."

Julian said nothing. Emma suspected Diana's aloofness both-ered him as much, if not more, than it bothered her, but he never showed it.

"But this changes things," Emma said, and she fought down the emotion in her voice, the spark of relief, even triumph, that she knew she shouldn't feel. "Because of Mark. Because of Mark, you're willing to let us try to find out who did this."

"Yes." For the first time since she'd come into the hallway, Diana looked directly at Emma. "You must be pleased," she said.

"You got exactly what you wanted. We've got no choice now. We'll have to investigate these killings, and we'll have to do it without the knowledge of the Clave."

"I didn't make this happen," Emma protested.

"No situation in which you have no choice is a good one, Emma," Diana said. "Which you will eventually learn. I only hope it isn't too late. You might think this is a good thing that's happened, but I can assure you it isn't." She turned away from Emma, fixing her attention on Julian. "As you well know, Julian, this is an illegal investigation. The Cold Peace forbids cooperation with the Fair Folk, and certainly forbids what amounts to working *for* them, no matter the inducement. It's to our advantage to figure this out as quickly and cleanly as we can, so the Clave has as little opportunity as possible to find out what we're doing."

"And when it's done?" Julian said. "And Mark's back? How do we explain that?"

Something in Diana's eyes shifted. "We'll worry about that when it happens."

"So we're racing the Clave and the Courts," said Julian. "Fantastic. Maybe there's someone else we can piss off. The Spiral Labyrinth? The Scholomance? Interpol?"

"No one's pissed off yet," said Diana. "Let's just keep it that way." She handed the papers to Emma. "Just to be clear: We can't cooperate with the Fair Folk and we can't harbor Mark without reporting it, except obviously we're going to, so the upshot is that no one outside the building can know. And I refuse to lie to the Clave directly, so hopefully we can get this done with before they start asking questions." She looked at them each in turn, her expression serious. "We have to work together. Emma, no more fighting me. Cristina, if you want to be reassigned to another Institute, we'll understand. We'd just ask you to keep this to yourself."

Emma gasped. "No!"

Cristina was already shaking her head. "I don't need a new assignment," she said. "I will keep your secret. I will make it my secret too."

"Good," Diana said. "Speaking of keeping things secret, don't tell Malcolm how we got our hands on these papers. Don't mention Mark, don't mention the faerie delegation. If he says anything, he'll have me to deal with."

"Malcolm's our friend," said Julian. "We can trust him."

"I'm trying to make sure he doesn't get in trouble if anyone finds out," she said. "He needs to be able to deny it." She zipped up her jacket. "Okay, I'll be back tomorrow. Good luck."

"Threatening the High Warlock," Julian muttered as Diana disappeared down the hall. "Better and better. Maybe we should head down to vampire clan headquarters and punch Anselm Nightshade in the face?"

"But think of the consequences," Emma said. "No more pizza."

Julian gave her a wry sideways-looking smile.

"I could go to Malcolm's alone," Emma said. "You could stay here, Jules, wait for Mark to—"

She didn't finish. She wasn't sure she knew what exactly they were waiting for Mark to do, that any of them knew.

"No," Julian said. "Malcolm trusts me. I know him the best. I can convince him to keep this secret." He straightened up. "We'll both go."

*As* parabatai. *As we should.*

Emma nodded and caught at Cristina's hand. "We'll make it as fast as we can," she said. "You'll be all right?"

Cristina nodded. Her hand was at her throat, her fingers resting on her necklace. "I will watch over Mark," she said. "It will be all right. *Everything* will be all right."

And Emma almost believed her.

* * *

Being a High Warlock must pay well, Emma thought, as she always did when she saw Malcolm Fade's house. It looked like a castle.

Malcolm lived up the highway from the Institute, past Kanan Dume Road. It was a spot where the bluffs rose high above, threaded with green sea grass. The house was shrouded by glamour spells, hiding it from mundanes. If you were driving—which Emma was—you had to look hard at a spot between two bluffs, and a silvery bridge that climbed up into the hills would appear.

Emma pulled over to the side of the highway. Lines of cars were parked along the sides of the PCH here, most of them surfers drawn by the wide beach to the west.

Emma exhaled, turning the car off. "Okay," she said. "We—"

"Emma," Julian said.

She paused. Julian had been almost completely silent since they'd left the Institute. She couldn't blame him. She couldn't find words herself. She'd let the distraction of driving take her, the need to concentrate on the road. She'd been aware of him beside her the whole time, though, his head back against the seat, his eyes closed, his fist clenched against the knee of his jeans.

"Mark thought I was my father," said Julian abruptly, and she could tell he was remembering that awful moment, the look of hope in his brother's eyes, a hope that had nothing to do with him. "He didn't recognize me."

"He remembers you twelve," Emma said. "He remembers all of you as so young."

"And you, too."

"I doubt he remembers me at all."

He unsnapped his seat belt. Light sparked off the bracelet of sea glass he wore on his left wrist, turning it to bright colors: flame red, fire gold, Blackthorn blue.

"He does," he said. "No one could forget you."

She blinked at him in surprise. A moment later Julian was out of the car. She scrambled to follow him, slamming the driver's side door as cars whizzed by just a lane away.

Jules was standing at the foot of Malcolm's bridge, looking up toward the house. She could see his shoulder blades under the thin cotton of his T-shirt, the nape of his neck, a shade lighter than the rest of his skin where his hair had kept it from getting tanned.

"The Fair Folk are tricksters," Julian said without turning. "They won't want to give Mark up: Faerie blood and Shadowhunter blood together, that's too valuable. There'll be some clause that'll allow them to take him back when we're done."

"Well, it's up to him," said Emma. "He gets to choose whether to stay or go."

Julian shook his head. "A choice seems simple, I know," he said. "But a lot of choices aren't simple."

They began to climb the stairs. The staircase was helical, twisting upward through the hills. It was glamoured, visible only to supernatural creatures. The first time Emma had visited, Malcolm had escorted her; she had looked down in wonder at all the mundanes speeding by below in their cars, entirely unaware that above them, a crystal staircase rose impossibly against the sky.

She was more used to it now. Once you'd seen the staircase, it would never be invisible to you again.

Julian didn't say anything else as they walked, but Emma found she didn't mind. What he'd said in the car—he'd meant it. His gaze had been level and direct as he'd spoken. It had been *Julian* talking, her Jules, the one who lived in her bones and her brain and at the base of her spine, the one who was threaded all through her like veins or nerves.

The staircase ended abruptly in a path to Malcolm's front door. You were meant to climb down, but Emma jumped, her feet landing on the hard-packed dirt. A moment later Julian had landed beside her and reached out to steady her, his fingers five warm lines across her back. She didn't need the help—of the two of them, she likely had the better balance—but, she realized, it was something he'd always done, unthinkingly. A protective reflex.

She glanced toward him, but he seemed lost in thought, barely noticing that they were touching. He moved away as the staircase behind them vanished back into its glamour.

They were standing in front of two obelisks that thrust up out of the dusty ground, forming a gateway. Each was carved with alchemical symbols: fire, earth, water, air. The path that led up to the warlock's house was lined with desert plants: cactus, sagebrush, California lilacs. Bees buzzed among the flowers. The dirt turned to crushed seashells as they neared the brushed-metal front doors.

Emma knocked and the doors slid open with a near-silent hiss. The hallways inside Malcolm's house were white, lined with pop-art reproductions, snaking off in a dozen different directions. Julian was at her side, unobtrusive; he hadn't brought his crossbow with him, but she felt the ridge of a knife strapped to his wrist when he nudged her with his arm.

"Down the hall," he said. "Voices."

They moved toward the living room. It was all steel and glass, entirely circular, giving out onto views of the sea. Emma thought it looked like the sort of place a movie star might own—everything was modern, from the sound system that piped in classical music to the infinity-edged swimming pool that hung over the cliffs.

Malcolm was sprawled on the long couch that ran the length of the room, his back to the Pacific. He wore a black suit, very plain and clearly expensive. He was nodding and smiling agreeably as two men in much the same kind of dark suits stood over him with briefcases in hand, speaking in low, urgent voices.

Malcolm, seeing them, waved. The vistors were white men in their forties with nondescript faces. Malcolm made a nonchalant gesture with his fingers, and they froze in place, eyes staring blankly.

"It always creeps me out when you do that," Emma said. She walked up to one of the frozen men and poked him thoughtfully. He tilted slightly.

"Don't break the movie producer," said Malcolm. "I'd have to hide the body in the rock garden."

"You're the one who froze him." Julian sat down on the arm of the couch. Emma slumped down onto the cushions beside him, feet on the coffee table. She wiggled her toes in their sandals.

Malcolm blinked. "But how else am I meant to talk to you without them hearing?"

"You could ask us to wait till your meeting is over," Julian said. "It probably wouldn't be a major risk to any lives."

"You're Shadowhunters. It could always be life-or-death," said Malcolm, not unreasonably. "Besides, I'm not sure I want the job. They're movie producers and they want me to cast a spell to ensure the success of their new release. But it looks terrible." He stared glumly at the poster on the sofa beside him. It showed several birds flying toward the viewer, with the caption EAGLE EXPLOSION THREE: FEATHERS FLY.

"Does anything happen in this movie that wasn't adequately covered in *Eagle Explosion One* and *Two*?" Julian asked.

"More eagles."

"Does it matter if it's terrible? Terrible movies do well all the time," Emma pointed out. She knew more about movies than she wished she did. Most Shadowhunters paid little attention to mundane culture, but you couldn't live in Los Angeles and escape it.

"It means a stronger spell. More work for me. But it does pay well. And I've been thinking of installing a train in my house. It could bring me shrimp crackers from the kitchen."

"A train?" Julian echoed. "How big a train?"

"Small. Medium. Like this." Malcolm gestured, low to the ground. "It would go 'choo-choo'—" He snapped his fingers to punctuate the noise, and the movie producers jerked into life.

"Whoops," Malcolm said as they blinked. "Didn't mean to do that."

"Mr. Fade," said the older one. "You'll consider our offer?"

Malcolm looked dispiritedly at the poster. "I'll get in touch."

The producers turned toward the front door, and the younger one jumped at the sight of Emma and Julian. Emma could hardly blame him. From his perspective, they must have appeared out of thin air.

"Sorry, gents," said Malcolm. "My niece and nephew. Family day, you know."

The mundanes looked from Malcolm to Jules and Emma and back again, clearly wondering how someone who looked twenty-seven could possibly have a niece and nephew in their teens. The older one shrugged.

"Enjoy the beach," he said, and they marched out, brushing by Emma with a whiff of expensive cologne and the rattle of briefcases.

Malcolm stood up, listing a bit to one side—he had a slightly awkward way of walking that made Emma wonder if he'd once been injured and hadn't completely healed. "Everything all right with Arthur?"

Julian tensed beside Emma, almost imperceptibly, but she felt it. "The family's fine, thanks."

Malcolm's violet eyes, his warlock's mark, darkened before clearing like a sky briefly touched by clouds. His expression as he ambled over to the bar that ran along one wall and poured himself a glass of clear liquid was amiable. "Then what can I help you with?"

Emma moved over toward the couch. They had made copies of the papers the faeries had given them. She set them down on the coffee table. "You remember what we were talking about the other night. . . ."

Malcolm put his glass aside and picked up the papers. "That demon language again," he said. "The one that was on that body you found in the alley, and on your parents' bodies . . ." He paused to whistle through his teeth. "Look at that," he said, stabbing his finger at the first page. "Someone's translated the first line. *Fire to water.*"

"It's a breakthrough, right?" Emma said.

Malcolm shook his bone-white head of hair. "Maybe, but I can't do anything with this. Not if it's a secret from Diana and Arthur. I can't get involved in something like that."

"It's fine with Diana," Emma said. Malcolm gave her a dubious look. "Seriously. Call her and ask—"

She broke off as a man ambled into the room, hands in his pockets. He looked about twenty, tall, with spiked black hair and cat's eyes. He wore a white suit that contrasted crisply with his brown skin.

"Magnus!" Emma said, jumping to her feet. Magnus Bane was the High Warlock of Brooklyn, and also held the warlock's seat on the Council of Shadowhunters. He was possibly the most famous warlock in the world, though you'd never guess it; he seemed young, and had been kind and friendly to Emma and the Blackthorns since he'd met them during the Dark War.

She'd always liked Magnus. He seemed to bring a sense of infinite possibility with him wherever he went. He looked the same as the last time she'd seen him, down to his sardonic smile and the heavy jeweled rings on his fingers. "Emma, Julian. A pleasure. What are you doing here?"

Emma darted her gaze toward Julian. They might have been fond of Magnus, but she could tell from Julian's expression—it was quickly hidden, smoothed over by a look of mild interest, but she could still see it—that he wasn't thrilled Magnus was there. This was already going to be a secret Malcolm needed to keep. Adding someone else in . . . especially someone on the Council . . .

"What are you doing in town?" Julian's tone was casual.

"Ever since the Dark War, the Clave has been tracking inci-dences of the kind of magic Sebastian Morgenstern used," said

Magnus. "Energy raised from evil sources, Hell dimensions and the like, to draw power and extend life. *Necyomanteis*, the Greeks called it."

"Necromancy," Emma translated.

Magnus nodded. "We built a map," he said, "with help from the Spiral Labyrinth, from the Silent Brothers—even Zachariah—that reveals where necromantic magic is being used. We caught a flare of it here in Los Angeles, out by the desert, so I thought I'd stop by, see if Malcolm knew about it."

"It was a rogue necromancer," said Malcolm. "Diana said she took care of him."

"God, I hate rogue necromancers," said Magnus. "Why can't they just follow the rules?"

"Probably because the biggest rule is 'no necromancy'?" Emma suggested.

Magnus grinned at her, sideways. "Anyway. It was no big deal for me to stop by here on my way to Buenos Aires."

"What's in Buenos Aires?" said Julian.

"Alec," Magnus said. Alexander Lightwood was Magnus's boyfriend of half a decade. They could have gotten married under the new laws that allowed Shadowhunters to marry Downworlders (other than faeries), but they hadn't. Emma didn't know why. "Routine check on a vampire-worshipping cult, but he ran into some trouble there."

"Nothing serious?" said Julian. He'd known Alec Lightwood longer than Emma had; the Blackthorns and the Lightwoods had been friends for years.

"Complicated, but not serious," said Magnus, just as Malcolm pushed himself away from the wall.

"I'm going to go call Diana. Be right back," he said, and vanished down the hallway.

"So." Magnus sat down on the couch, in the place Malcolm had just vacated. "What brings you to the High Warlock of the City of Angels?"

Emma exchanged a worried look with Julian, but short of diving across the table and whacking Magnus over the head—inadvisable for so many reasons—she couldn't think of anything to do.

"Something you're not supposed to tell me, I take it." Magnus templed his hands under his chin. "About the killings?" At their surprised looks, he added, "I have friends at the Scholomance. Catarina Loss, for one. Anything about rogue magic or the Fair Folk interests me. Is Malcolm helping out?"

Julian shook his head, a minute gesture.

"Some of the bodies were fey," said Emma. "We're not meant to get involved. The Cold Peace—"

"The Cold Peace is despicable," Magnus said, and the humor had gone out of his voice. "Punishing a whole species for the actions of a few. Denying them rights. Exiling your sister," he added, looking at Julian. "I've spoken to her. She helped make the map I spoke of; any magic that global involves the wards. How often do you talk to her?"

"Every week," said Jules.

"She said you always told her that everything was fine," said Magnus. "I think she was worried you weren't telling her the truth."

Julian said nothing. It was true that he talked to Helen every week; they all did, passing the phone or computer back and forth. And it was also true that Julian never told her anything except that everything was fine, they were all fine, there was no need for her to worry.

"I remember her wedding," Magnus said, and there was gentleness in his eyes. "How young you both were. Though it wasn't the last wedding I saw you at, was it?"

Emma and Julian exchanged puzzled glances. "I'm pretty sure it was," said Julian. "What other wedding would it have been?"

"Hm," said Magnus. "Perhaps my memory is going in my old

age." He didn't sound as if he thought that was likely, though. He leaned back instead, sliding his long legs under the coffee table. "As for Helen, I'm sure it's just an older sibling's anxiety. Certainly Alec worries about Isabelle, whether it's warranted or not."

"What do you think about ley lines?" Emma asked abruptly.

Magnus's eyebrows flew up. "What about them? Spells done at ley lines are amplified."

"Does it matter what kind of magic? Dark magic, warlock magic, faerie magic?"

Magnus frowned. "It depends. But it's unusual to use a ley line to amplify dark magic. Usually they're used to move power. Like a delivery system for magic—"

"Well, how about that." Malcolm, returning to the living room, darted an amused look at Emma. "Diana corroborates your story. Color me astonished." His gaze moved to Magnus. "What's going on?"

A light flashed in his eyes, whether amusement or something else, Emma couldn't quite tell. Sometimes Malcolm seemed completely childlike, going on about trains and shrimp crackers and eagle movies. At other times he seemed as sharp and focused as anyone she knew.

Magnus stretched his arms along the back of the sofa. "We were talking about ley lines. I was saying they amplify magic, but only certain kinds of magic. Magic that has to do with energy transferrals. Didn't you and Catarina Loss run into some kind of trouble with ley lines back when you lived in Cornwall, Malcolm?"

A vague expression passed over Malcolm's face. "I can't remember precisely. Magnus, stop bothering Emma and Julian," he said, and there was a tinge of something like annoyance in his voice. Professional jealousy, Emma guessed. "This is *my* domain. You've got your own hopeless humans in New York."

"One of those hopeless humans is the father of my child," Magnus pointed out.

Magnus had not ever been pregnant, though that would have been interesting, Emma thought. He and Alec Lightwood had an adopted warlock child, named Max, who was a scintillating shade of navy blue.

"And," Magnus added, "the rest of them have all saved the world, at least once."

Malcolm gestured toward Julian and Emma. "I have high hopes for these."

Magnus's face broke into a grin. "I'm sure you're right," he said. "Anyway, I should go. Long trip ahead of me and Alec doesn't like me to be late."

There was a flurry of good-byes. Magnus clapped Malcolm on the arm and paused to hug Julian, and then Emma. His shoulder bumped her forehead as he bent his head, and she heard his voice in her ear, whispering. She looked at him in surprise, but he only let her go and marched toward the door, whistling. Halfway to the door there was the familiar shimmer and burned-sugar smell of Portal magic, and Magnus disappeared.

"Did you tell him about the investigation?" Malcolm looked anxious. "He mentioned ley lines."

"I asked him about them," Emma admitted. "But I didn't say why I wanted to know. And I didn't mention anything about translating the markings."

Malcolm circled around to look at the paper again. "I don't suppose you'll tell me who untangled the first line? *Fire to water.* It would help to know what it means."

"We can't," Julian said. "But I don't think the translator knew what it meant either. You can use it, though, right? To get the rest of the spell or message or whatever it is?"

"Probably, though it would help if I knew the language."

"It's a very old language," Emma said carefully. "Older than Nephilim."

Malcolm sighed. "You're not giving me much. Okay, old demony language, very ancient. I'll check with the Spiral Labyrinth."

"Be careful what you tell them," Julian said. "Like we said—the Clave can't know we're investigating this."

"Which means faerie involvement," said Malcolm, amusement flickering across his face as he saw their horrified expressions. "Don't worry, I won't tell. I don't like the Cold Peace any more than any other Downworlder does."

Julian was expressionless. He ought to take up a career playing poker, Emma thought. "How long do you think you'll need?" he asked. "To translate?"

"Give me a few days."

A few days. Emma tried to conceal her disappointment.

"Sorry I can't do it any faster." Malcolm sounded genuinely sorry. "Come on. I'll walk you outside. I need some air."

The sun had come out from behind the clouds and was blazing down on Malcolm's front garden. The desert flowers shivered, silver-edged, in the wind from the canyons. A lizard darted out from behind a piece of shrubbery and stared at them. Emma stuck her tongue out at it.

"I'm worried," Malcolm said abruptly. "I don't like this. Necromantic magic, demon languages, a series of killings no one understands. Working without the Clave's knowledge. It seems, dare I say it, dangerous."

Julian stared off toward the distant hills, silent. It was Emma who answered.

"Malcolm, last year we fought off a battalion of Forneus demons with tentacles and no faces," Emma said. "Don't try to freak us out about this."

"I'm just saying. Danger. You know, that thing most people avoid."

"Not us," Emma said cheerfully. "Tentacles, Malcolm. No *faces*."

"Stubborn." Malcolm sighed. "Just promise to call me if you need me or if you find out anything else."

"Definitely," said Julian. Emma wondered if the cold knot of guilt that she felt at hiding things from Malcolm also sat in his chest. The wind off the ocean had picked up. It caught the dust in the garden and blew it into swirls. Julian pushed his hair out of his eyes. "Thanks for helping," he added. "We know we can depend on you." He headed down the path, toward the steps to the bridge, which shimmered alive as he approached it.

Malcolm's face had turned somber, despite the bright noon light reflecting off the ocean. "Don't depend on me too much," he said, so softly she wondered if he knew she would hear him.

"Why not?" She turned her face up to him in the sunlight, blinking. His eyes were the color of jacaranda blossoms.

"Because I'll let you down. Everyone does," Malcolm said, and went back inside his house.

# 7

## THE SOUNDING SEA

**Cristina sat on the floor outside Mark Blackthorn's bedroom.**
There had been no sound from inside for what felt like hours.
The door was cracked open and she could see him, curled into a ball
in a corner of the room like a trapped wild animal.

Faeries had been her area of study at home. She had always been
fascinated by tales of the *hadas*, from the noble warriors of the Courts
to the *duendes* who teased and bothered mundanes. She had not been
in Idris for the declaration of the Cold Peace, but her father had, and
the story sent a shiver through her. She had always wanted to meet
Mark and Helen Blackthorn, to tell them—

Tiberius appeared in the hall, carrying a cardboard box. His
twin sister was beside him, a patchwork quilt in her hand. "My
mother made this for Mark when he was left with us," she said,
catching Cristina eyeing it. "I thought he might remember."

"We couldn't get into the storeroom, so we brought Mark some
gifts. So he'd know we want him here," said Ty. His gaze moved
restlessly around the hall. "Can we go in?"

Cristina glanced into the bedroom. Mark was unmoving. "I
don't see why not. Just try to be quiet and not wake him."

Livvy went in first, laying the quilt on the bed. Ty set the cardboard box on the floor, then wandered over to where Mark was lying. He picked up the quilt that Livvy had set down and knelt beside his brother. A little awkwardly, he laid the quilt on top of Mark.

Mark jerked upright. His blue-gold eyes flew open and he caught hold of Ty, who gave a sharp frightened cry like the cry of a seabird. Mark moved with incredible speed, flinging Ty to the ground. Livvy screamed and darted from the room, just as Cristina hurtled inside.

Mark was kneeling over Tiberius, pinning him to the ground with his knees. "Who are you?" Mark was saying. "What were you doing?"

"I'm your brother! I'm Tiberius!" Ty was wriggling madly, his headphones sliding off to hit the floor. "I was giving you a blanket!"

"Liar!" Mark was breathing hard. "My brother Ty is a little boy! He's a child, my baby brother, my—"

The door rattled behind Cristina. Livvy burst back into the room, her brown hair flying. "Let him go!" A seraph blade appeared in her hand, already beginning to glow. She spoke to Mark through gritted teeth, as if she'd never met him. As if she hadn't been carrying a patchwork quilt for him through the Institute only moments before. "If you hurt Tiberius, I'll kill you. I don't care if you're Mark, I'll kill you."

Mark stilled. Ty was still writhing and twisting, but Mark had stopped moving entirely. Slowly, he turned his head toward his sister. "Livia?"

Livvy gasped and began to sob. Julian would be proud, though, Cristina thought: She was weeping without moving, the blade still steady in her hand.

Ty took advantage of Mark's distraction to hit at him, connecting solidly with Mark's shoulder. Mark winced and rolled away without striking back. Ty leaped to his feet and darted across the room to join Livvy; they stood shoulder to shoulder staring at their brother with wide eyes.

"Both of you, go," Cristina said to them. She could feel the panic and worry rolling off them in waves; Mark could clearly feel it too. He was wincing, opening and closing his hands as if in pain. She bent down to whisper to the twins. "He's frightened. He didn't mean it."

Livvy nodded and sheathed her blade. She took Ty's hand and said something to him in the quiet, private language they had. He followed her out of the room, pausing only briefly to look back at Mark, his expression hurt and bewildered.

Mark was sitting up, panting, his body bent over his knees. He was bleeding from the reopened cut on his shoulder, staining his shirt. Cristina began to back slowly out of the bedroom.

Mark's body tensed. "Please don't go," he said.

Cristina stared. As far as she knew, this was the first coherent thing he'd said since arriving at the Institute.

He lifted his chin, and for a brief moment she saw beneath the dirt, the bruises, and the scratches, the Mark Blackthorn she had seen pictures of, the Mark Blackthorn who could be related to Livvy and Julian and Ty. "I'm thirsty," he said. There was something rusty, almost disused, about his voice, like an old motor starting up again. "Is there water?"

"Of course." Cristina fumbled a glass off the dresser and went into the small attached bathroom. When she emerged and handed the full glass to Mark, he was sitting up, his back against the footboard of the bed. He looked at the glass wryly. "Water from taps," he said. "I'd almost forgotten." He took a long swallow and wiped his mouth with the back of his hand. "Do you know who I am?"

"You're Mark," she said. "Mark Blackthorn."

There was a long pause before he nodded, almost imperceptibly. "No one has called me that in a long time."

"It's still your name."

"Who are you?" he said. "I should remember, probably, but—"

"I'm Cristina Mendoza Rosales," she said. "There is no reason you should remember me, since we have never met before."

"That's a relief."

Cristina was surprised. "Is it?"

"If you don't know me and I don't know you, then you won't have any—expectations." He looked suddenly exhausted. "Of who I am or what I'm like. I could be anyone to you."

"Earlier," Cristina said. "On the bed. Were you sleeping or pretending?"

"Does it matter?" he said, and Cristina couldn't help thinking that it was a most faerielike reply, a reply that didn't actually answer her question. He shifted against the footboard. "Why are you in the Institute?"

Cristina knelt down, putting her head on a level with Mark's. She smoothed her skirt over her knees—even when she didn't want them to, her mother's words about how an off-duty Shadowhunter must always be neat and presentable echoed in her head.

"I am eighteen," she said. "I was assigned to study the ways of the Los Angeles Institute as part of my travel year. How old are you?"

This time Mark's hesitation went on for so long, Cristina wondered if he was going to speak at all. "I don't know," he said finally. "I was gone—I thought I was gone—a long time. Julian was twelve. The others were babies. Ten and eight and two. Tavvy was two."

"For them it has been five years," Cristina said. "Five years without you."

"Helen," Mark said. "Julian. Tiberius. Livia. Drusilla. Octavian. Every night I counted out their names among the stars, so I would not forget. Are they all living?"

"Yes, all of them, though Helen is not here—she is married and lives with her wife."

"Then they are living, and happy together? I am glad. I had heard the news of her wedding in Faerie, though it seems long ago now."

"Yes." Cristina studied Mark's face. Angles, planes, sharpness, that curve at the top of his ear that spoke of faerie blood. "You have missed a great deal."

"You think I don't know that?" Heat boiled up in his voice, mixed with bewilderment. "I don't know how old I am. I don't recognize my own sisters and brothers. I don't know why I'm here."

"You do," said Cristina. "You were there when the faerie convoy was speaking to Arthur in the Sanctuary."

He tilted his face toward hers. There was a scar across the side of his neck, not the mark of a vanished rune, but a raised welt. His hair was untidy and looked as if it had been uncut for months, years even. The curling white tips touched his shoulders. "Do you trust them? The faeries?"

Cristina shook her head.

"Good." He looked away from her. "You shouldn't." He reached for the cardboard box that Ty had left on the floor and pulled it toward him. "What is this?"

"Things they thought you might want," Cristina said. "Your brothers and sisters."

"Gifts of welcome," said Mark in a puzzled tone, and knelt down by the box, removing a hodgepodge of odd items—some T-shirts and jeans that were probably Julian's, a microscope, bread and butter, a handful of desert wildflowers from the garden behind the Institute.

Mark raised his head to look at Cristina. His eyes glittered with unshed tears. His shirt was thin and ragged; she could see through the material, see other welts and scars on his skin. "What do I say to them?"

"To who?"

"My family. My brothers and sisters. My uncle." He shook his head. "I remember them, and yet I don't. I feel as if I have lived here all my life, and yet I have also always been with the Wild Hunt. I hear the roar of it in my ears, the call of the horns, the sound of the wind. It overpowers their voices. How do I explain that?"

"Don't explain it," said Cristina softly. "Just say you love them and you missed them every day. Tell them you hated the Wild Hunt. Tell them you're glad to be back."

"But why would I do that? Won't they know I'm lying?"

"Didn't you miss them? Aren't you glad to be back?"

"I don't know," he said. "I cannot hear my heart or what it tells me. I can only hear the wind."

Before Cristina could reply, a sharp tap came at the window. It rattled again, a pattern of taps that sounded almost like a code.

Mark sprang to his feet. He crossed the room to the window and flung it open, leaning out. When he ducked back in, there was something in his hand.

An acorn. Cristina's eyes widened. Acorns were one of the ways faeries sent messages to each other. Hidden in leaves, flowers, and other wild things.

"Already?" she said, unable to help it. They couldn't leave him even for this long, alone with his family, in his home?

Looking pale and strained, Mark crushed the acorn in his fist. A twist of pale parchment fell out. He caught it and read the message silently.

His hand opened. He slid to the floor, pulling his knees up against his chest, dropping his head in his hands. His long pale hair fell forward as the parchment fluttered to the ground. A low sound issued from his throat, halfway between a groan and a wail of pain.

Cristina picked up the parchment. On it was written, in a delicate script, *Remember your promises. Remember that none of it is real.*

"*Fire to water,*" said Emma as they sped down the highway toward the Institute. "After all these years, I finally know what some of those markings mean."

Julian was driving. Emma had her feet propped on the dashboard, her window down, the sea-softened air filling the car and lifting the light hair around her temples. This was how she'd always ridden in cars with Julian, with her feet up and the wind in her hair.

It was something Julian loved, Emma beside him in the car, driving with the blue sky overhead and the blue sea to the west. It was an image that felt full of infinite possibility, as if they could simply keep driving forever, the horizon their only destination.

It was a fantasy that played out sometimes when he was falling asleep. That he and Emma packed their things into the trunk of a car and left the Institute, in a world where he had no children and there was no Law and no Cameron Ashdown, where nothing held them back but the limits of their love and imagination.

And if there were two things he believed were limitless, it was love and imagination.

"It does sound like a spell," Julian said, wrenching his mind back to the present moment. He revved the engine, the wind rushing in through Emma's window as they gathered speed. Her hair lifted, pale corn silk spilling out from the neatness of her braids, making her look young and vulnerable.

"But why would the spell be recorded on the bodies?" Emma asked. The thought of anything hurting her made an ache form inside his chest.

And yet he was hurting her. He knew it. Knew it and hated it. He'd believed he'd had such a brilliant idea when he'd thought of taking the children to England for eight weeks. Knowing Cristina Rosales was coming, knowing Emma wouldn't be alone or unhappy. It had seemed perfect.

He'd thought things would be different when he came back. That he would be different.

But he wasn't.

"What did Magnus say to you?" he asked as she looked out the window, her scarred fingers drumming an arrhythmic tattoo on her bent knee. "He whispered something."

A furrow appeared between her brows. "He said that there are places where ley lines converge. I assume he means that since they bend and curve, there are locations where more than one of them meet. Maybe all of them."

"And that's important because . . . ?"

She shook her head. "I don't know. We do know all the bodies have been dumped at ley lines, and that's a specific kind of magic. Maybe the convergences have some quality we need to understand. We should find a map of ley lines. I bet Arthur would know where to look in the library. If not, we can find it ourselves."

"Good."

"Good?" She sounded surprised.

"It's going to take a few days for Malcolm to translate those papers, and I don't want to spend those days sitting around the Institute, staring at Mark, waiting for him to—waiting. It's better if we keep working, have something to do." His voice sounded stretched thin to his own ears. He hated it, hated any visible or audible sign of weakness.

Though at least it was only with Emma, who he could show these things to. Emma, alone in his life, did not need his caretaking. Did not need him to be perfect or perfectly strong.

Before Julian could say anything else, Emma's phone went off with a loud buzz. She pulled it out of her pocket.

Cameron Ashdown. She frowned at the llama on the screen. "Not now," she told it, and shoved the phone back into her jeans.

"Are you going to tell him?" Julian asked, and heard the stiffness in his own voice, and hated it. "About all of this?"

"About Mark? I would never tell. Never."

He kept his grip on the wheel tight, his jaw set.

"You're my *parabatai*," she said, and now there was anger in her voice. "You know I wouldn't."

Julian slammed on the brakes. The car lurched forward, the wheel slewing out of his hands. Emma yelped as they skidded off the road and bumped down into a ditch by the side of the highway, in between the road and the dunes over the sea.

Dust was rising up around the car in plumes. Julian whirled toward Emma. She was white around the mouth. "Jules."

"I didn't mean it," he said.

She stared. "What?"

"You being my *parabatai* is the best thing in my life," Julian said. The words were steady and simple, spoken without a trace of anything held back. He'd been holding back so tightly that the relief of it was almost unbearable.

Impulsively she undid her safety belt, rising up in her seat to look down on him solemnly. The sun was high overhead. Up close he could see the gold lines inside the brown of her eyes, the faint spatter of light freckles across her nose, the bits of lighter, sun-bleached hair mixed with the darker hair at her nape. Raw umber and Naples yellow, mixed with white. He could smell rose water on her, and laundry detergent.

She leaned into him, and his body chased the feeling of closeness, of having her back and near. Her knees bumped against his. "But you said—"

"I know what I said." He turned toward her, slewing his body around in the driver's seat. "While I was away, I realized some things. Hard things. Maybe I even realized them before I left."

"You can tell me what they are." She touched his cheek lightly. He felt his whole body lock into tension. "I remember what you said about Mark last night," she went on. "You were never the oldest brother. He always was. If he hadn't been taken, if Helen had been able to stay, you would have made different choices because you would have had someone to take care of you."

He breathed out. "Emma." Raw pain. "Emma, I said what I said because—because sometimes I think I asked you to be my *parabatai* because I wanted you to be tied to me. The Consul wanted you to go to the Academy and I couldn't stand the thought. I'd lost so many people. I didn't want to lose you, too."

She was so close to him he could feel the heat from her sun-warmed skin. For a moment she said nothing, and he felt as if he were on the gallows, having the hangman's noose fastened around his throat. Waiting only for the drop.

Then she put her hand over his on the console between them.

Their hands. Hers were delicate-looking, but more scarred than his own, more calloused, her skin rough against his. His sea-glass bracelet glowed like jewels in the sunlight.

"People do complicated things because people are compli-cated," she said. "All that stuff about how you're supposed to make the *parabatai* decision only for totally pure reasons, that's a crock."

"I wanted to tie you to me," he said. "Because I was tied here. Maybe you should have gone to the Academy. Maybe it would have been the right place for you. Maybe I took something away from you."

Emma looked at him. Her face was open and completely trust-ing. He almost thought he could feel his convictions shatter, the convictions he'd built up before he'd left at the beginning of the summer, the convictions he'd carried with him all the way back home until the moment he'd seen her again. He could feel them breaking inside him, like driftwood shattered against rocks.

"Jules," she said. "You gave me a family. You gave me *everything*."

A phone shrilled again. Emma's. Julian sat back, heart pound-ing, as she thumbed it out of her pocket. He watched as her face set.

"Livvy's texting," she said. "She says Mark woke up. And he's screaming."

Julian floored the car on the way home, Emma keeping her hands clasped around her knees as the speedometer crept up past eighty.

They careened into the parking lot behind the Institute and slammed on the brakes. Julian threw himself out of the car and Emma raced after him.

They reached the second floor to find the younger Blackthorns seated on the floor outside Mark's door. Dru was curled up with Tavvy against Livvy's side; Ty sat alone, his long hands dangling between his knees. They were all staring; the door was cracked partway open and through it Emma could hear Mark's voice, raised and angry, and then another voice, lower and more soothing—Cristina.

"Sorry I texted," said Livvy in a small voice. "It's just that he was screaming and screaming. He finally stopped, but— Cristina's in there with him. If any of the rest of us go in, he howls and yells."

"Oh my God." Emma moved toward the door, but Julian caught her, swinging her around to face him. She looked over and saw that Ty had begun to rock back and forth, his eyes closed. It was something he did when things were too much: too loud, too harsh or hard or fast or painful.

The world was extra intense for Ty, Julian had always said. It was as if his ears could hear more clearly, his eyes see more, and sometimes it was too much for him. He needed to cover noise, to feel something in his hand to distract him. He needed to rock back and forth to soothe himself. Everyone processed stress in a different way, Julian said. This was Ty's, and it hurt nobody.

"Em," Julian said. His face was taut. "I need to go in alone."

She nodded. He let go of her almost reluctantly. "Guys," he said, looking at his siblings—at Dru's round, worried face, Tavvy's uncomprehending one, Livvy's unhappy eyes, and Ty's hunched shoulders. "It's going to be hard for Mark. We can't expect him to be okay all at once. He's been away a long time. He has to get used to being here."

"But we're his family," said Livvy. "Why would you have to get used to your own family?"

"You might," Julian said, in that patient soft voice that amazed Emma sometimes, "if you'd been away from them a long time and you'd been somewhere where your mind plays tricks on you."

"Like Faerie," said Ty. He had stopped rocking and was leaning back against the wall, dark hair damp and in his face.

"Right," Julian said. "So we're going to have to give him time. Maybe leave him alone a little." He looked over at Emma.

She pasted a smile onto her face—God, she was so much worse at this than Jules—and said, "Malcolm's working on the investigation. The murders. I thought we could head to the library and look into ley lines."

"Me too?" Drusilla piped up.

Emma said, "You can help us plot a map. Okay?"

Dru nodded. "Okay." She rose to her feet and the others followed. As Emma led them away down the hall, a quietly subdued group, she looked back only once. Julian was standing by the door to Mark's room, watching them go. His eyes met hers for a split second before he looked away, as if he hadn't seen her glance at all.

If only Emma was with him, Julian thought as he pushed open the door, this would be easier. It would have to be easier. When Emma was with him it was like he was breathing twice as much oxygen, had twice as much blood, had two hearts to drive the motion of his body. He put it down to the doubling magic of *parabatai*: She made him twice what he would be otherwise.

But he'd had to send her away with the kids; he didn't trust anyone else with them, and definitely not Arthur. Arthur, he thought bitterly, who was hiding in his attic while one of his nephews desperately tried to hold his family together and another one—

"Mark?" Julian said.

The bedroom was dim, the curtains closed. He could just see that Cristina was sitting on the floor, her back to the wall. She had one hand pressed to the pendant at her throat, and the other at her hip, where something gleamed between her fingers.

Mark was pacing back and forth at the foot of the bed, his hair hanging in his face. You could see how painfully thin he was; there was sinewy muscle on him, but it was the kind you got from starving sometimes and driving yourself anyway. His head jerked up when Julian said his name.

Their eyes met and for a brief moment Julian saw a flicker of recognition in his brother's eyes.

"Mark," he said again, and moved forward, his hand out. "It's me. It's Jules."

"Don't—" Cristina started up, but it was too late. Mark had bared his teeth in an angry hiss.

"Lies," he snarled. "Hallucinations—I know you—Gwyn sent you to trick me—"

"I'm your brother," Julian said again. The look on Mark's face was wild.

"You know the wishes of my heart," said Mark. "And you turn them against me, like knives."

Julian looked across the room at Cristina. She was rising to her feet slowly, as if preparing to throw herself between the two brothers if needed.

Mark whirled on Jules. His eyes were blind, unseeing. "You bring the twins in front of me and you kill them over and over. My Ty, he doesn't understand why I can't save him. You bring me Dru and when she laughs and asks to see the fairy-tale castle, all ringed round with hedges, you throw her against the thorns until they pierce her small body. And you bid me wash in Octavian's blood, for the blood of an innocent child is magic under the hill."

Julian came no closer. He was remembering what Jace Herondale and Clary Fairchild had told him and his sister, their meeting with Mark years ago under the faerie hills, his broken eyes and the whip marks on his body.

Mark was strong, he had told himself in the dead darkness of the thousand nights afterward. He could endure it. Julian had thought about only torture of the body. He had not thought about torture of the mind.

"And Julian," Mark said. "He is too strong to break. You try to break him on the wheel, and tear him with thorns and blades, but even then he won't give up. So you bring to him Emma, for the wishes of our hearts are knives to you."

That was too much for Julian. He lurched forward, grabbing hold of one of the posts of the bed to steady himself.

"Mark," he said. "Mark Antony Blackthorn. Please. It's not a dream. You're really here. You're home."

He reached for Mark's hand. Mark whipped it back, away from him. "You are lying smoke."

"I'm your brother."

"I have no brothers and sisters, no family. I am alone. I ride with the Wild Hunt. I am loyal to Gwyn the Hunter." Mark recited the words as if by rote.

"I'm not Gwyn," said Julian. "I'm a Blackthorn. I have Blackthorn blood in me, just like you."

"You are a phantom and a shadow. You are the cruelty of hope." Mark turned his face away. "Why do you punish me? I have done nothing to displease the Hunt."

"There's no punishment here." Julian took a step closer to Mark. Mark didn't move, but his body trembled. "This is home. I can prove it to you."

He glanced back over his shoulder. Cristina was standing very still against the wall, and he could see that the gleam in her hand was a knife. Clearly she was waiting to see if Mark would attack him. Julian wondered why she had been willing to stay in the room with Mark alone; hadn't she been afraid?

"There is no proof," Mark whispered. "Not when you can weave any illusion before my eyes."

"I'm your brother," Julian repeated. "And to prove it to you, I'll tell you something only your brother would know."

At that Mark raised his eyes. Something flickered in them, like a light shining on distant water.

"I remember the day you were taken," Julian said.

Mark recoiled. "Any of the Folk would know about that—"

"We were up in the training room. We heard noises, and you went downstairs. But before you went you said something to me. Do you remember?"

Mark stood very still.

"You said, 'Stay with Emma,'" Julian said. "You said to stay with her, and I have. We're *parabatai* now. I've looked after her for years and I always will, because you asked me to, because it was the last thing you ever said to me, because—"

He remembered, then, that Cristina was there, and cut himself off abruptly. Mark was staring at him, silent. Julian felt despair well up inside him. Maybe this was a trick of the faeries; maybe they had given Mark back, but so broken and hollowed out that he wasn't Mark anymore. Maybe—

Mark nearly fell forward, and threw his arms around Julian.

Julian barely managed to catch himself before almost falling over. Mark was whipcord thin, but strong, his hands fisting in Julian's shirt. Julian could feel Mark's heart hammering, feel the sharp bones under his skin. He smelled like earth and mildew and grass and nighttime air.

"Julian," Mark said, muffled, his body shaking. "Julian, my brother, my brother."

Somewhere in the distance, Julian heard the click of the

bedroom door as it shut; Cristina had left them alone together.

Julian sighed. He wanted to relax into his older brother, let Mark hold him up the way he once had. But Mark was slighter than he was, fragile under his hands. He would be holding Mark up from now on. It was not what he had imagined, dreamed of, but it was the reality. It was his brother. He tightened his hands on Mark and adjusted his heart to bear the new burden.

The library in the Los Angeles Institute was small—nothing like the famous libraries of New York and London, but well-known regardless for its surprisingly large collection of books in Greek and Latin. They had more books on the magic and occultism of the classical period than the Institute in Vatican City.

Once the library had been terra-cotta tile and Mission windows; now it was a starkly modern room. The old library had been destroyed in Sebastian Morgenstern's attack on the Institute, the books scattered among bricks and desert. Rebuilt, it was glass and steel. The floor was polished mountain ash, smooth and shining with applications of protective spells.

A spiral ramp began at the north side of the first floor and climbed the walls; the outer side of the ramp was lined with books and windows, while the inner, facing the library's interior, was a shoulder-high railing. At the very top was an oculus—a skylight held closed with a large copper lock, made of foot-thick glass decorated all over with protective runes.

Maps were kept in a massive chest decorated with the crest of the Blackthorn family—a ring of thorns—with their family motto beneath it: *Lex malla, lex nulla.*

*A bad law is no law.*

Emma suspected that the Blackthorns hadn't exactly always gotten along with the Council.

Drusilla was rummaging around in the map chest. Livvy and Ty were at the table with more maps, and Tavvy was playing under it with a set of plastic soldiers.

"Can you tell if Julian's all right?" Livvy asked, propping her chin on her hand to look at Emma anxiously. "You know, how he's feeling . . ."

Emma shook her head. "*Parabatai* stuff isn't really like that. I mean, I can feel if he's hurt, physically, but not his emotions so much."

Livvy sighed. "It would be so great to have a *parabatai*."

"I don't really see why," Ty said.

"Someone who always has your back," said Livvy. "Someone who will always protect you."

"I would do that for you anyway," Ty said, pulling a map toward himself. This was an argument they'd had before; Emma had heard some variation of it half a dozen times.

"Not everyone's cut out to have one," she said. She wished for a moment that she had the words to explain it properly: how loving someone more than you loved yourself gave you strength and courage; how seeing yourself in your *parabatai*'s eyes meant seeing the best version of yourself; how, at its best, fighting alongside your *parabatai* was like playing instruments in harmony with one another, each piece of the music improving the other.

"Having someone who's sworn to shield you from danger," said Livvy, her eyes shining. "Someone who would put their hands in a fire for you."

Briefly Emma remembered that Jem had once told her that his *parabatai*, Will, had thrust his hands into a fire to retrieve a packet of medicine that would save Jem's life. Maybe she shouldn't have repeated the story to Livvy.

"In the movies Watson throws himself in front of Sherlock when there's gunfire," Ty said, looking thoughtful. "That's like *parabatai*."

Livvy looked mildly outfoxed, and Emma felt for her. If Livvy said it wasn't like *parabatai*, Ty would argue. If she agreed it was, he would point out you didn't need to be *parabatai* to jump in front of someone when there was danger. He wasn't wrong, but she sympathized with Livvy's desire to be *parabatai* with Ty. To make sure her brother was always by her side.

"Got it!" Drusilla announced suddenly. She stood up from rummaging around in the map chest with a long piece of parchment in her hands. Livvy, abandoning the *parabatai* discussion, hurried over to help her carry it to the table.

In a clear bowl on the table's center was a heap of sea glass the Blackthorns had collected over the years—lumps of milky blue, green, copper, and red. Emma and Ty used the blue glass to weigh down the edges of the ley line map.

Tavvy, now sitting on the edge of the table, had begun sorting the rest of the sea glass into piles by color. Emma let him; she didn't know how else to keep him distracted just now.

"Ley lines," Emma said, running her index finger over the long black lines on the map. It was a map of Los Angeles that probably dated back to the forties. Landmarks were visible under the ley lines: the Crossroads of the World in Hollywood, the Bullocks building on Wilshire, the Angels Flight railroad in Bunker Hill, the Santa Monica Pier, the never-changing curve of the coast and the ocean. "All the bodies were left under the span of a ley line. But what Magnus said is that there are places where all the ley lines converge."

"What does that have to do with anything?" Livvy asked, practical as always.

"I don't know, but I don't think he would have said it if it didn't matter. I imagine the place of convergence has some pretty powerful magic."

As Ty applied himself to the map with renewed vigor, Cristina came into the library and gestured for Emma to come talk to her.

Emma slid off the table and followed Cristina to the coffeemaker by the window. It was witchlight powered, which meant there was always coffee, although the coffee wasn't always very good.

"Is Julian all right?" Emma asked. "And Mark?"

"They were talking when I left." Cristina filled two cups with black coffee and dumped in sugar from a small enamel pot on the windowsill. "Julian calmed him down."

"Julian could calm anyone down." Emma picked up the second cup of coffee, enjoying the warmth against her skin, though she didn't really like coffee and didn't tend to drink it. Besides, her stomach was tied in so many knots she didn't think she could force anything down.

She walked back toward the table where the Blackthorns were arguing about the ley line map. "Well, I can't help it if it doesn't make sense," Ty was saying peevishly. "That's where it says the convergence is."

"Where?" Emma asked, coming up behind him.

"Here." Dru pointed at a circle Ty had sketched on the map in pencil. It was over the ocean, farther out from Los Angeles than Catalina Island. "So much for anyone doing magic there."

"Guess Magnus was just making conversation," said Livvy.

"He probably didn't know—" Emma began, and broke off as the library door opened.

It was Julian. He stepped into the room and then moved to the side, diffidently, like a conjuror presenting the result of a trick.

Mark moved into the doorway after him. Julian must have gotten Mark's old things out of the storeroom. He was wearing jeans that were slightly short on him—probably a pair of his old ones—and one of Julian's T-shirts, heather gray and washed to a soft fadedness. In contrast, his hair looked very blond, almost silvery. It hit his shoulders, looking slightly less tangled, as if he'd brushed the twigs out of it at least.

"Hello," he said.

His siblings looked at him in silent, wide-eyed astonishment.

"Mark wanted to see you," Julian said. He reached around to ruffle the hair on the back of his neck, looking bemused, as if he had no idea what to do next.

"Thank you," Mark said. "For the gifts of welcome you gave me."

The Blackthorns continued to stare. Nobody moved except Tavvy, who slowly laid his sea glass down on the table.

"The box," Mark clarified. "In my room."

Emma felt the coffee cup she was holding plucked out of her hand. She made an indignant noise, but Cristina was already holding it, crossing the room, past the table, and walking up to Mark, her back straight. She held out the mug.

"Do you want some?" she said.

Looking relieved, he took it. He lifted it to his mouth and swallowed, his whole family watching him in amazed fascination as if he were doing something no one had ever done before.

He grimaced. Moving away from Cristina, he coughed and spit. "What is that?"

"Coffee." Cristina looked startled.

"It tastes of the most bitter poison," Mark said indignantly.

Livvy suddenly giggled. The sound cut through the stillness of the rest of the room, the frozen tableau of the others.

"You used to love coffee," she said. "I remember that about you!"

"I can't imagine why I would have. I've never tasted something so disgusting." Mark made a face.

Ty's eyes flicked between Julian and Livvy; he looked eager and excited, his long fingers tapping at the table in front of him. "He isn't used to coffee anymore," he said to Cristina. "They don't have it in Faerie."

"Here." Livvy stood up, scooping an apple from the table. "Have this instead." She went forward and held out the apple to her brother. Emma thought she looked like a latter-day Snow White, with her long dark hair and the apple in her pale hand. "You don't mind apples, do you?"

"My thanks, gracious sister." Mark bowed and took the apple, while Livvy looked at him with her mouth partly open.

"You never call me 'gracious sister,'" she said, turning to Julian with an accusing look.

He grinned. "I know you too well, runt."

Mark reached up and drew the chain from around his throat. Dangling from the end of it was what looked like the head of an arrow. It was clear, as if made of glass, and Emma recalled having seen something like it in pictures Diana had showed them.

Mark began to use the edge of it to peel his apple, matter-of-factly. Tavvy, who had crawled under the table again and was looking out, made an interested noise. Mark glanced at him and winked. Tavvy ducked back under the table, but Emma could see that he was smiling.

She couldn't stop looking at Jules. She thought of the way he'd cleaned out Mark's room, hurling his brother's things savagely into a pile as if he could shatter the memories of him. It had lasted only a day, but there had been shadows in his eyes since. She wondered, if Mark stayed, would the shadows disappear?

"Did you like the presents?" Dru demanded, swiveling around on the table, her round face anxious. "I put bread and butter in for you in case you were hungry."

"I did not know what all of them were," Mark said candidly. "The clothes were very useful. The black metal object—"

"That was my microscope," Ty said, looking at Julian for approval. "I thought you might like it."

Julian leaned against the table. He didn't ask Ty why Mark would want a microscope, just smiled his sideways, gentle smile. "That was nice of you, Ty."

"Tiberius wants to be a detective," Livvy explained to Mark. "Like Sherlock Holmes."

Mark looked puzzled. "Is that someone we know? Like a warlock?"

"He's a book character," Dru said, laughing.

"I've got all the Sherlock Holmes books," said Ty. "I know all the stories. There are fifty-six short stories and four novels. I can tell them to you. And I'll show you how to use the microscope."

"I think I buttered it," Mark admitted, looking shamefaced. "I did not remember it was a scientific tool."

Emma looked worriedly at Ty—he was meticulous about his things and could be deeply upset by anyone touching them or moving them. But he didn't look angry. Something about Mark's candidness seemed to delight him, the way he sometimes was delighted by an unusual kind of demonic ichor or the life cycle of bees.

Mark had cut his apple into careful pieces and was eating them slowly, in the manner of someone who was used to making what food they had last. He was quite thin, thinner than a Shadowhunter his age would usually be—Shadowhunters were encouraged to eat and train, eat and train, build their muscle and stamina. Most Shadowhunters, due to the constant brutal physical training, ranged from wiry to muscular, though Drusilla was round-bodied, something that bothered her more the older she got. Emma always felt pained to see the blush that colored Dru's cheeks when the gear designated for girls in her age group didn't fit.

"I heard you speak of convergences," Mark said, moving toward the others—carefully, as if unsure of his welcome. His eyes lifted, and to Emma's surprise, he looked at Cristina. "The convergence of ley lines is a place where dark magic can be done undetected. The Fair Folk know much of ley lines, and use them often." He had slung his arrowhead back around his neck; it glimmered as he bent his head to look at the map on the table.

"This is a map of ley lines in Los Angeles," said Cristina. "All of the bodies have been found along them."

"Wrong," Mark said, leaning forward.

"No, she's right," Ty said with a frown. "It is a map of ley lines, and the bodies have been dumped along them."

"But the map is incorrect," Mark said. "The lines are not accurate, nor are the points of convergence." His long-fingered right hand brushed over the pencil circle Ty had made. "This is not right at all. Who made this map?"

Julian moved closer and for a moment he and his brother were shoulder to shoulder, their pale hair and dark hair a startling contrast. "It's the Institute's map, I assume."

"We took it from the trunk," Emma said, leaning over it from the opposite side of the table. "With all the other maps."

"Well, it has been tampered with," said Mark. "We will need a correct one."

"Maybe Diana could get us one," Julian said, reaching for a pad of paper and a pencil. "Or we could ask Malcolm."

"Or check out what's at the Shadow Market," said Emma, and grinned unrepentantly at Julian's look. "Just a suggestion."

Mark glanced at his brother, and then the others, clearly worried. "Was that helpful?" he said. "Was it a thing I should not have said?"

"Are you sure?" said Ty, looking from the map to his brother, and something in his face was open as a door. "That the map is incorrect?"

Mark nodded.

"Then it was helpful," said Ty. "We could have wasted days on a map that was wrong. Maybe longer."

Mark exhaled in relief. Julian put his hand on Mark's back. Livvy and Dru beamed. Tavvy was looking out from under the table, clearly curious. Emma glanced at Cristina. The Blackthorns seemed to be wound together by a sort of invisible force; in that moment they were completely a family, and Emma could not even mind that she and Cristina were on the outside.

"I could attempt to correct it," said Mark. "But I do not know if I have the skill. Helen—Helen could do it." He glanced at Julian. "She is married, and away—but I assume she will return for this? And to see me?"

It was like watching glass shatter in slow motion. None of the Blackthorns moved, not even Tavvy, but blankness spread over their features as they realized exactly how much it was that Mark did not know.

Mark paled and slowly set the core of his apple down on the table. "What is it?"

"Mark," Julian said, looking toward the door, "come and talk to me in your room, not here—"

"No," Mark interrupted, his voice rising with fear. "You will tell me now. Where is my full-blood sister, the daughter of Lady Nerissa? Where is Helen?"

There was an achingly awkward silence. Mark was looking at Julian; they were no longer standing beside each other. Mark had moved away, so quietly and quickly Emma had not seen it happen. "You said she was alive," he said, and in his voice there was fear and accusation.

"She is," Emma hastened to say. "She's fine."

Mark made an impatient noise. "Then I would know where my sister is. Julian?"

But it wasn't Julian who answered. "She was sent away when the Cold Peace was decided," Ty said, to Emma's surprise. He sounded matter-of-fact. "She was exiled."

"There was a vote," said Livvy. "Some of the Clave wanted to kill her, because of her faerie blood, but Magnus Bane defended the rights of Downworlders. Helen was sent to Wrangel Island to study the wards."

Mark leaned against the table, his palm flat against it, as if he were trying to catch his breath after being punched. "Wrangel Island," he whispered. "It is a cold place, ice and snow. I have ridden over those lands with the Hunt. I never knew my sister was down there, in among the frozen wastes."

"They would never have let you see her, even if you had known," Julian said.

"But you let her be sent away." Mark's two-colored eyes were flashing. "You let them exile her."

"We were children. I was twelve years old." Julian didn't raise his voice; his blue eyes were flat and cold. "We had no choice. We talk to Helen every week, we petition the Clave every year for her return."

"Speech and petitions," Mark spat. "Might as well do nothing. I knew—I knew they had chosen not to come for me. I knew they had abandoned me to the Wild Hunt." He swallowed painfully. "I thought it was because they feared Gwyn and the vengeance of the Hunt. Not because they hated and despised me."

"It wasn't hate," said Julian. "It was fear."

"They said that we couldn't look for you," said Ty. He had taken one of his toys out of his pocket: a length of cord that he often ran through and under his fingers, bending and shaping it into figure eights. "That it was forbidden. It's forbidden to visit Helen, too."

Mark looked toward Julian, and his eyes were dark with anger, black and bronze. "Did you ever even try?"

"I won't fight with you, Mark," Julian said. The side of his mouth was twitching; it was something that happened only when he was deeply upset, and something, Emma guessed, that only she would notice.

"You won't fight *for* me either," Mark said. "That much is clear." He glanced around the room. "I have come back to a world where I am not wanted, it seems," he said, and slammed his way out of the library.

There was an awful silence.

"I will go after him," Cristina said, and darted from the room. In the soundlessness left by her departure, the Blackthorns looked at Jules, and Emma fought the urge to run to put herself between him and his siblings' pleading eyes—they looked at him as if he could fix it, fix everything, as he always had.

But Julian was standing very still, his eyes half-closed, his hands twisted into fists. She remembered the way he had looked in the car, the desperation in his expression. There were few things in life that could undo Julian's calm, but Mark was, and had always been, one of them.

"It's going to be all right," Emma said, reaching out to pat Dru's soft arm. "Of course he's angry—he has every right to be angry—but he's not angry at any of *you*." Emma stared over Drusilla's head at Julian, trying to catch his gaze, to steady him. "It's going to be fine."

The door opened again, and Cristina came back into the room. Julian turned his gaze toward her sharply.

Cristina's dark, glossy braids were coiled around her head; they shone as she shook her head. "He is all right," she said, "but he has closed himself in his room, and I think it is best if we leave him alone. I can wait in the corridor, if you like."

Julian shook his head. "Thanks," he said. "But no one needs to keep a watch on him. He's free to come and go."

"But what if he hurts himself?" It was Tavvy. His voice was small and thin.

Julian bent down and lifted his brother up, arms around Tavvy, hugging him tightly, once, before setting him down again. Tavvy kept his hand fixed on Jules's shirt. "He won't," Julian said.

"I want to go up to the studio," Tavvy said. "I don't want to be here."

Julian hesitated, then nodded. The studio where he painted was somewhere that he often brought Tavvy when his little brother was frightened: Tavvy found the paints, the papers, even the brushes soothing. "I'll bring you up," he said. "There's leftover pizza in the kitchen if anyone wants it, and sandwiches, and—"

"It's okay, Jules," Livvy said. She had seated herself on the table, by her twin; she was above Ty as he looked down at the ley line map, his mouth set. "We can handle dinner. We'll be fine."

"I'll bring you up something to eat," Emma said. "And for Tavvy, too."

*Thank you*, Julian mouthed to her before he turned toward the door. Before he reached it, Ty, who had been quiet since Mark had left, spoke. "You won't punish him," he said, his cord wrapped tightly around the fingers of his left hand, "will you?"

Julian turned around, clearly surprised. "Punish Mark? For what?"

"For all the things he said." Ty was flushed, unwinding the cord slowly as it slid through his fingers. Over years of watching his brother, and trying to learn, Julian had come to understand that where sounds and light were concerned, Ty was far more sensitive to them than most people. But where touch was concerned, it fascinated him. It was the way Julian had learned to create Ty's distractions and hand tools, by watching him spend hours investigating the texture of silk or sandpaper, the corrugations of shells and the roughness of rocks. "They were true—they were the truth. He told us the truth and he helped with the investigation. He shouldn't be punished for that."

"Of course not," said Julian. "None of us would punish him."

"It's not his fault if he doesn't understand everything," Ty said. "Or if things are too much for him. It's not his fault."

"Ty-Ty," said Livvy. It had been Emma's nickname for Tiberius when he was a baby. Since then, the whole family had adopted it. She reached to rub his shoulder. "It'll be all right."

"I don't want Mark to leave again," Ty said. "Do you understand, Julian?"

Emma watched as the weight of that, the responsibility of it, settled over Julian.

"I understand, Ty," he said.

# 8

## OUT OF THE CLOUD
## BY NIGHT

**Emma shouldered open the door to Julian's studio, trying hard** not to spill any liquid out of the two overflowing mugs of soup she was carrying.

There were two rooms in Julian's studio: the one Julian let people see, and the one he didn't. His mother, Eleanor, had used the larger room as a studio and the smaller one as a darkroom to develop photographs. Ty had often voiced the question of whether the developing chemicals and setup were still intact, and whether he could use them.

But the second studio room was the only issue on which Julian didn't bend to the will of his younger siblings or offer to give up what was his for them. The black-painted door stayed closed and locked, and even Emma wasn't allowed inside.

Nor did she ask. Julian had so little privacy, she didn't want to begrudge him the bit he could claim.

The main studio was beautiful. Two of the walls were glass, one facing the ocean and one the desert. The other two walls were painted creamy taupe, and Julian's mother's canvases—abstracts in bright colors—still adorned them.

Jules was standing by the central island, a massive block of granite whose surface was covered with sheafs of paper, boxes of watercolors, and piled tubes of paint with lyrical names: alazarin red, cardinal purple, cadmium orange, ultramarine blue.

He raised one hand and put a finger to his lips, glancing to the side. Seated at a small easel was Tavvy, armed with a box of open nontoxic paints. He was smearing them over a long sheet of butcher paper, seeming pleased with his multicolored creation. There was orange paint in his brown curls.

"I just got him calmed down," Julian said as Emma approached and set the mugs on the island. "What's going on? Has anyone talked to Mark?"

"His door's still locked," Emma said. "The others are in the library." She pushed one of the mugs toward him. "Eat," she said. "Cristina made it. Tortilla soup. Although she says we have the wrong chiles."

Julian picked up a mug and knelt down to place it next to Tavvy. His little brother looked up and blinked at Emma as if he'd just noticed she was there. "Did Jules show you the pictures?" he demanded. Blue had joined the orange and yellow in his hair. He looked like a sunset.

"Which pictures?" Emma asked as Julian straightened up.

"The ones of us. The card ones."

She raised an eyebrow at Jules. "The card what?"

He flushed. "Portraits," he said. "I did them in the Rider-Waite style, like the tarot."

"The mundane tarot?" Emma said as Jules reached for a port-folio book. Shadowhunters tended to eschew the objects of mundane superstition: palmistry, astrology, crystal balls, tarot cards. They weren't forbidden to own or touch, but they were associated with unsavory dwellers on the fringes of magic, like Johnny Rook.

"I made some changes to it," Julian said, opening the book to show a flutter of papers, each sporting a colorful, distinctive illustration. There was Livvy with her saber, hair flying, but instead of her name beneath, it read THE PROTECTOR. As always, Julian's paintings seemed to reach out, a direct line to her heart, making her feel as if she understood what Julian had felt while he was painting. Looking at the picture of Livvy, Emma felt a flash of admiration, love, a fear of loss, even—Julian would never speak of it, but she suspected he was watching Livvy and Ty become adults with more than a little terror.

Then there was Tiberius, a death's-head moth fluttering on his hand, his pretty face turned down and away from the viewer. The painting gave Emma a sense of fierce love, intelligence, and vulnerability mixed together. Beneath him it said THE GENIUS.

Then there was THE DREAMER—Dru with her head in a book—and THE INNOCENT, Tavvy in his pajamas, sleepy head cradled in his hand. The colors were warm, affectionate, caressing.

And then there was Mark. Arms crossed over his chest, hair as blond as straw, he wore a shirt that bore the design of spread wings. Each wing sported an eye: one gold, one blue. A rope circled his ankle, trailing out of the frame.

THE PRISONER, it said.

Jules's shoulder brushed against Emma's as she leaned in to study the image. Like all Julian's drawings, it seemed to whisper to her in a silent language: loss, it said, and sorrow, and years that you could not recapture.

"Is this what you were working on in England?" she asked.

"Yes. I was hoping to do the whole set." He reached back and scrubbed at his tangled brown curls. "I might have to change the title of Mark's card," said Julian. "Now that he's free."

"If he stays free." Emma brushed the drawing of Mark aside and saw that the next portrait was of Helen, standing among ice floes, her pale hair covered by a knitted cap. THE SEPARATED, it said. There was another card, THE DEVOTED, for her wife, Aline, whose dark hair made a cloud around her. She wore the Blackthorn ring on her hand. And the last was of Arthur, sitting at his desk. A red ribbon ran along the floor beneath him, the color of blood. There was no title.

Julian reached out and shuffled them back into the notebook. "They're not finished yet."

"Am I going to get a card?" Emma teased. "Or is it just Blackthorns and Blackthorns-by-marriage?"

"Why don't you draw Emma?" Tavvy asked, looking at his brother. "You never draw Emma."

Emma saw Julian tense. It was true. Julian rarely drew people, but even when he did, he'd stopped sketching Emma years ago. The last time she remembered him drawing her was the family portrait at Aline and Helen's wedding.

"Are you all right?" she said, her voice low enough that she hoped Tavvy couldn't hear.

He exhaled, hard, and opened his eyes, his muscles unclench-ing. His eyes met hers and the curl of anger that had begun unfurl-ing in her stomach vanished. His gaze was open, vulnerable. "I'm sorry," he said. "It's just, I always thought when he got back—when Mark got back—he'd help. That he'd take over, take care of every-thing. I never thought he'd be something else I had to deal with."

Emma was carried back in that moment to all the weeks, the months, after Mark had first been taken and Helen sent away, when Julian had woken up screaming for the older brother and sister who weren't there, who would never be there again. She remembered the panic that sent him stumbling to the bathroom to throw up, the nights she'd held him on the cold tiled floor while he shook as if he had a fever.

*I can't,* he'd said. *I can't do this alone. I can't bring them up. I can't raise four children.*

Emma felt the anger uncurl in her stomach again, but this time it was directed at Mark.

"Jules?" Tavvy asked, sounding nervous, and Julian passed a hand over his face. It was a nervous habit, as if he were wiping an easel free of paint; when he dropped his hand, the fear and emotion had gone from his eyes.

"I'm here," he said, and went over to pick up Tavvy. Tavvy put his head down on Jules's shoulder, looking sleepy, and getting paint all over Jules's T-shirt. But Jules didn't seem to care. He put his chin down in his younger brother's curls and smiled at Emma.

"Forget it," he said. "I'm going to take this one off to bed. You should probably get some sleep too."

But Emma's veins were buzzing with a sharp elixir of anger and protectiveness. No one hurt Julian. No one. Not even his much-missed, much-loved brother.

"I will," she said. "I've got something to do first."

Julian looked alarmed. "Emma, don't try to—"

But she was already gone.

Emma stood in front of Mark's door, her hands on her hips. "Mark!" She rapped with her knuckles for the fifth time. "Mark Blackthorn, I know you're in there. Open the door."

Silence. Emma's curiosity and anger warred with her respect for Mark's privacy, and won. Opening runes didn't work on doors inside their Institute, so she drew a thin knife from her belt and slid it into the gap between the door and the doorjamb. The latch popped, and the door swung wide.

Emma stuck her head in. The lights were on, curtains drawn against the darkness outside. The bedcovers were rumpled, the bed empty.

In fact, the whole room was empty. Mark wasn't there.

Emma pulled the door shut and turned around with an exasperated sigh—and almost screamed. Dru was standing behind her with wide, dark eyes. She was clutching a book to her chest.

"Dru! You know, usually when people sneak up on me from behind, I stab them." Emma exhaled shakily.

Dru looked glum. "You're looking for Mark."

Emma saw no point in denying it. "True."

"He's not in there," Dru said.

"Also true. This is a big night for stating the obvious, huh?" Emma smiled at Dru, feeling a pang. The twins were so close, and Tavvy so young and dependent on Jules, it was hard, she thought, for Dru to find the place she fit. "He'll be okay, you know."

"He's on the roof," Dru said.

Emma raised an eyebrow. "What makes you say that?"

"He always used to go up there when he was upset," said Dru. She glanced toward the window at the far end of the hall. "And up there, he'd be under the sky. He could see the Hunt if they rode by."

Emma felt chilled. "They won't," she said. "They won't ride by. They won't take him away again."

"Even if he wants to go?"

"Dru—"

"Go up there and bring him back down," Drusilla said. "Please, Emma."

Emma wondered if she looked bewildered; she *felt* bewildered. "Why me?"

"Because you're a pretty girl," said Dru, a little wistfully, looking down at her own round body. "And boys do what pretty girls want. Great-Aunt Marjorie said so. She said if I wasn't such a butterball, I'd be a pretty girl and boys would do what I wanted."

Emma was appalled. "That old bi—that old *bat*, sorry, said what?"

Dru hugged the book more tightly to her. "You know, it doesn't sound so bad, does it? Butterball? Like you could be something cute, like a squirrel, or a chipmunk."

"You're much cuter than a chipmunk," Emma said. "Weird teeth, and I have it on good authority that they speak in high, squeaky voices." She ruffled Dru's soft hair. "You're gorgeous," she said. "You always will be gorgeous. Now, I'll go see what I can do about your brother."

The hinges on the trapdoor that led to the roof hadn't been oiled in months; they squeaked loudly as Emma, bracing herself on the top rung of the ladder, shoved upward. The trapdoor gave way and she crawled out onto the roof.

She straightened up, shivering. The wind off the ocean was cold, and she had only thrown a cardigan on over her tank top and jeans. The shingle of the roof was rough under her bare feet.

She'd been up here too many times to count. The roof was flat, easy to walk on, only a slight slant at the edges where the shingles gave way to copper rain gutters. There was even a folding metal chair up here, where Julian sat sometimes when he painted. He'd gone through a whole phase of painting the sunset over the ocean— he'd given it up when he'd kept chasing the changing colors of the sky, convinced each stage of the setting sun was better than the one before, until every canvas ended up black.

There was very little cover up here; it took only a moment to spot Mark, sitting at the edge of the roof with his legs dangling over the edge, staring out toward the ocean.

Emma made her way over to him, the wind whipping her pale braids across her face. She pushed them away impatiently, wondering if Mark was ignoring her or if he was actually unaware of her approach. She stopped a few feet from him, remembering the way he'd hit out at Julian.

"Mark," she said.

He turned his head slowly. In the moonlight he was black and white; it was impossible to tell that his eyes were different colors. "Emma Carstairs."

Her full name. That wasn't very auspicious. She crossed her

arms over her chest. "I came up here to bring you back down," she said. "You're freaking out your family and you're upsetting Jules."

"Jules," he said carefully.

"Julian. Your *brother*."

"I want to talk to my sister," he said. "I want to talk to Helen."

"Fine," said Emma. "You can talk to her whenever. You can borrow an extra cell phone and call her, or we can have her call you, or we can freaking *Skype*, if that's what you want. We would have told you that before if you hadn't started yelling."

"Skype?" Mark looked as if she'd sprouted several heads.

"It's a computer thing. Ty knows about it. You'll be able to look at her when you talk to her."

"Like the scrying glass of the fey?"

"Sort of like that." Emma edged a little closer to him, as if she were sidling up to a wild animal that might spook at her approach. "Come back downstairs?"

"I prefer it here. I was choking inside on all that dead air, crushed under the weight of all that *building*—roof and timbers and glass and stone. How do you live like that?"

"You did just fine for sixteen years."

"I barely remember," he said. "It seems like a dream." He glanced back toward the ocean. "So much water," he said. "I can see it and through it. I can see the demons down under the sea. I look at it and it doesn't seem real."

That was something Emma could understand. The sea was what had taken her parents' bodies and then returned them, broken and empty. She knew from the reports that they'd been dead when they'd been cast into the water, but it didn't help. She remembered the lines of a poem Arthur had recited once, about the ocean: *water washes, and tall ships founder, and deep death waits.*

That was what the sea beyond the waves was, to her. Deep death waiting.

"Surely there's water in Faerie?" she said.

"Not any sea. And never enough water. The Wild Hunt would often ride for days without water. Only if we were fainting would Gwyn let us stop to drink. And there are fountains in the Wild of Faerie, but they run with blood."

"'For all the blood that's shed on earth, runs through the springs of that country,'" said Emma. "I didn't realize that was literal."

"I didn't realize you knew the old rhymes," said Mark, glancing over with the first real interest he'd shown in her since his return.

"The whole family has always tried to learn everything they can about Faerie," said Emma, sitting down beside him. "Ever since we came back from the Dark War, Diana has taught us, and even the little ones wanted to know about the Fair Folk. Because of you."

"That must be a rather unpopular part of the Shadowhunter curriculum," said Mark, "considering recent history."

"It isn't your fault, what the Clave thinks of faeries," said Emma. "You're a Shadowhunter, and you were never part of the betrayal."

"I am a Shadowhunter," Mark agreed. "But I am part Fair Folk, too, like my sister. My mother was the Lady Nerissa. She died after I was born, and with no one to raise us, Helen and I were given back to our father. My mother was gentry, though, one of the highest rank of the fey."

"Did they treat you better in the Hunt because of her?"

Mark shook his head once. "I believe they think of my father as responsible for her death. For breaking her heart by leaving her. That did not dispose them well toward me." He tucked a lock of pale hair behind his ear. "Nothing the Fair Folk did to my body or mind was as cruel as the moment I was told that the Clave would not be coming to find me. That they would send no rescue parties. Jace told me, when he saw me in Faerie, 'show them what a Shadowhunter is made of.' But what are Shadowhunters made of, if they desert their own?"

"The Council isn't all Shadowhunters in the world," said Emma. "A lot of Nephilim thought what was done to you was wrong. And Julian never stopped trying to get the Clave to change their minds." She considered reaching to pat his arm, then thought better of it. There was still something a little feral about him; it would have been like reaching to pat a leopard. "You'll see, now that you're home."

"Am I home?" asked Mark. He shook his head, like a dog shaking off water. "Perhaps I was unfair to my brother," he said. "Perhaps I should not have lashed out. I feel like—like I am in a dream. It seems weeks ago they came to me at the Hunt and told me I was to go back to the world."

"Did they tell you that you'd be coming home?"

"No," he said. "They told me I had no choice but to leave the Hunt. That the King of the Unseelie Court had commanded it. They pulled me down from my horse and bound my hands. We rode for days. They gave me something to drink, something that made me hallucinate and imagine things that were not there." He looked down at his hands. "It was so I would not be able to find my way back, but I wish they had not done it," he said. "I wish I could have arrived here as I have been for years, a capable member of the Hunt. I would have liked my brothers and sisters to see me standing tall and proud, not fearful and crawling."

"You do seem very different now," Emma said. It was true. He seemed like someone who had woken up after a hundred years of sleep, shaking the dust of a century's dreams from his feet. He had been terrified; now his hands were steady, his expression somber.

Suddenly he smiled wryly.

"When they ordered me to reveal myself in the Sanctuary, I thought it was another dream."

"A good dream?" Emma said.

He hesitated, then shook his head. "In the early days of the

Hunt, when I disobeyed, I was made to see dreams, horrors, visions of my family dying. I thought that was what I was meant to be seeing again. I was terrified—not for myself, but for Julian."

"But now you know it's not a dream. Seeing your family, your home—"

"Emma. Stop." He squeezed his eyes shut as if in pain. "I can say this to you because you are not a Blackthorn. You do not have Blackthorn blood running through your veins. I have been in the land of Faerie for years and it is a place where mortal blood is turned to fire. It is a place of beauty and terror beyond what can be imagined here. I have ridden with the Wild Hunt. I have carved a clear path of freedom among the stars and outrun the wind. And now I am asked to walk upon the earth again."

"You belong where you're loved," Emma said. It was something her father had said, something she had always believed. She belonged here because Jules loved her and the children loved her. "Were you loved in Faerie?"

A shadow seemed to come down over Mark's eyes, like curtains closing in a dark room. "I meant to tell you. I am sorry about your parents."

Emma waited for the familiar burn of sickening rage that the mention of her parents by anyone but Jules always brought on, but it didn't come. There was something in the way he said it—something about the strange mixture of formal, faerie speech and sincere regret—that was oddly calming.

"And I'm sorry about your father," she told him.

"I saw him Turned," Mark said. "Though I did not see him die in the Dark War. I hope he did not suffer."

Emma felt a ripple of shock pass up her spine. Did he not know how his father had died? Had no one told him? "He—" she began. "It was in the middle of battle. It was very quick."

"You saw it?"

Emma scrambled to her feet. "It's late," she said. "We should get to sleep."

He looked up at her with his eerie eyes. "You do not want to sleep," he said, and he looked wild to her suddenly, wild as the stars or the desert, wild as all natural, untamed things. "You have always been one for adventure, Emma, and I do not think that has died in you, has it? Tied though you might be to my unadventurous little brother?"

"Julian isn't unadventurous," Emma said angrily. "He's responsible."

"You would have me believe there is a difference?"

Emma looked up at the moon, and then back at Mark. "What are you suggesting?"

"It occurred to me, as I looked out at the ocean," he said, "I may be able to find the place where the ley lines converge. I have seen such places before, with the Hunt. They give off a certain energy that fey folk can feel."

"*What?* But how—"

"I'll show you. Come with me to look for the place. Why wait? The investigation is urgent, isn't it? We must find the killer?"

Excitement rose up in Emma, and sharp desire; she tried to keep it off her face, how badly she wanted, needed to know, to take the next step, to throw herself into searching, fighting, finding. "Jules," she said, rising to her feet. "We have to get Jules and bring him."

Mark looked grim. "I do not wish to see him."

Emma stood her ground. "Then we don't go," she said. "He's my *parabatai*—where I go, he goes."

Something flashed in Mark's eyes. "If you won't go without him, we will not go at all," he said. "You cannot force me to give up the information."

"Force you? Mark—" Emma broke off, exasperated. "Fine. Fine. We can go. Just us."

"Just us," he repeated. He stood up. His movements were impossibly light and fast. "But first you must prove yourself."

He stepped off the roof.

Emma skidded to the edge of the shingle and leaned out. There was Mark, clinging to the wall of the Institute, an arm's length below her. He looked up with a fierce grin. A grin that spoke of empty air and cold wind, the torn surface of the ocean, the ragged edge of clouds. A grin that beckoned to the wild, unbound side of Emma, the side that dreamed of fire and battle and blood and vengeance.

"Climb down with me," he said, and now there was an edge of mockery in his voice.

"You're crazy," she hissed, but he had already begun to move down the wall, using handholds and footholds that Emma couldn't even see. The ground swung under her. Real heights: If she fell from the roof of the Institute, she might well die; there was no assurance an *iratze* could save her.

She got down on her knees and turned her back to the ocean. She slid down, her nails scraping shingle, and then she was clinging to the gutter with her hands, her legs dangling out into the air.

She scrabbled at the wall with her bare feet. Thank the Angel she wasn't wearing boots. Her feet were calloused from walking and fighting; they slipped along the wall until they found a crack in the surface. She jammed her toes into it, relieving the weight on her arms.

*Don't look down.*

For as long as Emma could remember, the voice in her head that calmed her panic had been Jules's. She heard it now, bringing her hands down, her fingers jamming into the space between two stones. She lowered herself down, an inch at first, then farther as she found another foothold. She heard Jules: *You're climbing over the rocks at Leo Carrillo. It's only a few feet down to soft sand. Everything's safe.*

The wind blew her hair across her face. She turned her head to shake it out of her eyes and realized she was passing a window. Pale light burned behind the curtains. Cristina's room, maybe?

*Have you always been this careless?*

*More since the Dark War . . .*

She was halfway down now, she guessed from looking up, the roof receding. She had started to speed up, her fingertips and toes swiftly discovering new handholds and footholds. The plaster in between the stones helped, kept her sweaty hands from slipping as she gripped and released, gripped and released, pressing her body hard against the wall until suddenly she was reaching down with her foot and struck solid ground.

She let go and fell, landing with a soft puff of sand. They were on the east side of the house, facing the garden, the small parking area, and the desert beyond.

Mark was already there, of course, bleached by moonlight and looking like part of the desert, a curious carving of pale new stone. Emma was breathing hard as she stepped away from the wall, but it was with exhilaration. Her heart was hammering, her blood drumming; she could taste salt on the wind, in her mouth.

Mark rocked backward, hands in his pockets. "Come with me," he whispered, and turned away from the building, toward the sand and scrub of the desert.

"Wait," Emma said. Mark stopped and looked over his shoulder at her. "Weapons," she said. "And shoes." She went to the car. A quick Open rune unlocked the trunk, revealing piles of weapons and gear. She hunted until she found a belt and a spare pair of boots. She buckled the belt on quickly, slammed some blades and daggers into it, grabbed up some spares, and kicked her feet into the boots.

Luckily, in the rush back from Malcolm's she'd left Cortana strapped to the inside of the trunk. She freed the blade and slung it over her back before hurrying over to Mark, who silently accepted her offer of a seraph blade and a set of knives before gesturing for her to follow him.

Behind the low wall bordering the parking lot was the rock garden, usually peaceful, planted with cacti and dotted here and there with plaster statues of classical heroes, placed there by Arthur. He'd had them shipped from England when he'd first moved to the Institute and they stuck out among the cacti, anomalous.

There was something else there now, a dark, hulking shadow, covered by a cloth. Mark moved toward it, again with that odd smile; Emma stepped aside to let him go ahead of her, and he plucked the long black cloth away.

Beneath it was a motorcycle.

Emma gave a little gasp. It wasn't any make of motorcycle that she knew: It was silvery-white, as if it had been carved out of bone. It glimmered under the moonlight, and Emma almost thought for a moment she could see through it, the way she sometimes saw through glamours, to a shape beneath, with a tossing mane and wide eyes. . . .

"When you take a steed from Faerie, whose substance is magic, its nature can change to suit the mundane world," said Mark, smiling at her stunned expression.

"You mean this was once a horse? This is a pony-cycle?" Emma demanded, forgetting to whisper.

His smile broadened. "There are many sorts of steeds who ride with the Wild Hunt."

Emma was already beside the motorcycle, running her hands over it. The metal felt smooth like glass, cool under her fingers, milk white and glowing. She had wanted to ride a motorcycle all her life. Jace and Clary had ridden a flying motorcycle. There were paintings of it. "Does it fly?"

Mark nodded, and she was lost.

"I want to drive it," she said. "I want to drive it myself."

He swept an elaborate bow. It was a graceful, alien gesture, the kind that might have existed in the court of a king, hundreds of years ago. "Then you are welcome to do so."

"Julian would kill me," Emma said reflexively, still stroking the machine. Beautiful as it was, she felt a thrill of trepidation at the thought of riding it—it didn't have an exhaust pipe, a speedometer, any of the normal gear she associated with a cycle.

"You don't strike me as that easy to kill," Mark said, and now he wasn't smiling, and the way he looked at her was direct and challenging.

Without another word Emma swung her leg over the bike. She reached to grip the handlebars, and they seemed to bend inward to fit her hands. She looked at Mark. "Get on behind me," she said, "if you want to ride."

She felt the cycle rock under her as he climbed on behind her; his hands clasped her sides lightly. Emma exhaled, her shoulders tensing. "It's alive," Mark whispered. "It will respond to you, if you will it."

Her hands tightened on the handlebars. *Fly.*

The cycle shot up into the air and Emma screamed, half in shock and half in delight. Mark's hands tightened on her waist as they hurtled up, the ground receding below them. The wind poured around them. Untrammeled by gravity, the cycle shot forward as Emma urged it on, leaning forward to communicate with her body what she wanted it to do.

They whipped past the Institute, the road that led down toward the highway opening up under them. They raced along above it, desert wind giving way to salt on Emma's tongue as they reached the Pacific Coast Highway, cars darting past below them in blaring lines of pale gold headlights. She cried out in delight, willing the cycle onward: *Faster, go faster.*

The beach flew by beneath them, pale gold sand turned white by starlight, and then they were out over the ocean. The moon lit a silvery path for them; Emma could hear Mark yelling something in her ear, but for the moment there was nothing but the ocean and the cycle under her, the wind whipping her hair back and making her eyes water.

And then she looked down.

On either side of the moonlit path was the water, navy blue in the darkness. Land was a distant line of brilliant lights, the etched shadow of mountains against the sky. And below was ocean, miles of ocean, and Emma felt the familiar cold of fear, like a block of ice applied suddenly to the back of her neck and spreading through her veins.

*Miles of ocean, and oh, the vastness of it, shadows and salt, fierce dark water filled with alien emptiness and the monsters that lived there. Imagine falling into that water and knowing it was below you, even as you treaded water, desperately trying to remain on the surface; the terror of the realization of what was under you—miles and miles of nothingness and monsters, blackness stretching away everywhere and the sea floor so far below—would tear your mind apart.*

The cycle jerked under her hands, rebelling. She bit down hard on her lip, summoning blood to the surface, focusing her mind.

The cycle slewed around under her hands and shot back toward the beach. *Faster*, Emma urged it, suddenly desperate to have dry land under them. She thought she could see shadows moving under the skin of the sea. She thought of old stories of sailors whose boats were lifted out of the water on the backs of whales and sea monsters. Of small craft torn apart by sea demons, their crews fed to the sharks—

She caught her breath, the cycle jumping under her, momentarily losing her grip on the handlebars. They plunged downward.

Mark cried out as they shot past the crashing waves and toward the beach. Emma's fingers scrabbled and seized on the handlebars again, her grip tight as the front wheel grazed the sand, and then the bike was rising again, skimming over the beach, lifting to pass over the highway below them.

She heard Mark laugh. It was a wild sound; she could hear the echo of the Hunt in it, the roar of the horn and the pounding of hooves. She breathed in cool, clear air; her hair whipped behind her; there were no rules. She was free.

"You have proved yourself, Emma," he said. "You could ride with Gwyn, if you chose."

"The Wild Hunt doesn't allow women," she pointed out, the words torn from her mouth by the wind.

"The more fool they," he said. "Women are fiercer by far than men." He pointed at the shore, toward the ridges of the mountains that ran along the coast. "Go that way. I will take you to the convergence."

# 9

## KINGDOM BY THE SEA

**No wonder Jace Herondale had once jumped at the chance to** fly a motorcycle, Emma thought. It was a completely different vantage point on the world. She and Mark followed the line of the highway north, flying over mansions with massive swimming pools that hung out over the ocean, castles tucked up into canyons and bluffs, dipping down low enough once to see a party going on in someone's backyard, complete with glowing multicolored lanterns.

Mark guided her from behind with taps on her wrists; the wind had risen too high for her to hear his voice. They passed over a late-night seafood shack, music and light pouring out of the windows. Emma had been there before and remembered sitting on the big wooden picnic tables with Jules, dunking fried oysters in tartar sauce. Dozens of Harley-Davidsons were parked outside the restaurant, though Emma doubted any of them could fly.

She grinned to herself, unable to help it, feeling drunk on the height and the cold air.

Mark tapped her right wrist. A smooth stretch of sand spilled from the beach, reaching halfway up high bluffs. Emma tilted the cycle so that they were nearly vertical, hurtling up the side of a cliff. They cleared the lip of the bluff with a foot of space and shot forward, the wheels scraping the tips of the California thistle that grew among the long grass.

A granite rise loomed in front of them, a dome-like hill atop the bluffs. Emma leaned back, preparing to gun the cycle, but Mark reached around her, his voice in her ear: "Stop! *Stop!*"

The cycle skidded to a halt just as they passed the tangle of weeds that bordered the bluffs. Inside the border of coastal shrubs was a stretch of grass that reached to the low granite hill. The grass looked trampled in places, as if it had been walked on, and in the distance, to the right of the grassy stretch, Emma could see a faint dirt road winding down the bluffs toward the highway.

Emma swung herself off the cycle. Mark followed, and they stood for a moment, the sea a gleam in the distance, the hill rising dark in front of them.

"You drive too fast," said Mark.

Emma snorted and checked the strap of Cortana where it fastened across her chest. "You sound like Julian."

"It brought me joy," Mark said, moving to stand beside her. "It was as if I flew with the Hunt again, and tasted the blood of the sky."

"Okay, you sound like Julian on drugs," Emma muttered. She glanced around. "Where are we? Is this the ley line convergence?"

"There." Mark pointed at a dark opening in the rock of the hill. As they moved toward it, Emma reached back to touch the hilt of Cortana. Something about the place was giving her shivers—maybe it was simply the power of the convergence, but as they neared the cave, and the hair rose on the back of her neck, she doubted it.

"The grass is flat," she said, indicating the area around the cave with a sweep of her hand. "Trampled. Someone's been walking here. A lot of someones. But there are no fresh tire tracks on the road."

Mark glanced around, head tilted back, like a wolf scenting the air. His feet were still bare, but he seemed to have no problem walking on the rough ground, despite the thistles and sharp rocks visible between the grasses.

There was a sharp, bright trill—Emma's phone ringing. *Jules*, she thought, and snatched it out of her pocket.

"Emma?" It was Cristina, her low, sweet voice oddly startling— a sharp reminder of reality after the unreal flight through the sky. "Where are you? Did you find Mark?"

"I found him," Emma said, glancing over toward Mark. He appeared to be examining the plants growing around the mouth of the cave. "We're at the convergence."

"*What?* Where is it? Is it dangerous?"

"Not yet," Emma said as Mark ducked into the cave. "Mark!" she called. "Mark, don't—Mark!"

The phone connection dropped. Swearing, Emma stuck the phone back into her pocket and took out her witchlight. It came on, soft and bright, raying out through her fingers. It illuminated the mouth of the cave. She headed toward it, cursing Mark under her breath.

He was just inside the cave, looking down at more of the same plants, clustering around the dry, soft stone. "*Atropa belladonna*," he said. "It means 'beautiful lady.' It's poisonous."

Emma made a face. "Does it grow around here normally?"

"Not in this quantity." He reached down to touch it. Emma caught his wrist.

"Don't," she said. "You said it was poisonous."

"Only if swallowed," he said. "Hasn't Uncle Arthur taught you anything about the death of Augustus?"

"Nothing I haven't worked hard to forget."

Mark straightened up, and she let go of him. She flexed her fingers. There was wiry strength in his arms.

As he moved forward into the cave, which began to narrow into a tunnel, she couldn't help but remember Mark the last time she had seen him, before he had been taken by Sebastian Morgenstern. Smiling, blue-eyed, short pale hair curling over the tips of his pointed ears. Broad-shouldered—or at least she, at twelve, had thought so. Certainly he had been bigger than Julian, taller and broader than all of them. Grown up.

Now, prowling ahead of her, he seemed a feral child, hair gleaming in the witchlight. He moved like a cloud across the sky, vapor at the mercy of wind that could tear it to shreds.

He vanished around a bend of rock, and Emma almost closed her eyes against the image of a vanished Mark. He belonged to the past that contained her parents, and you could drown in the past if you let it have you while you were working.

And she was a Shadowhunter. She was always working.

"Emma!" Mark called, his voice echoing off the walls. "Come and see this."

She hurried after him down the tunnel. It opened out into a circular chamber lined with metal. Emma turned on her heel in a slow circle, staring. She wasn't sure what she had expected, but not something that looked like the inside of an occult ocean liner. The walls were bronze, covered in strange symbols, a scrawled mixture of languages: some demonic, some ancient but human—she recognized demotic Greek and Latin, a few passages from the Bible. . . .

Two massive glass doors like portholes were set into the walls, shut and bolted with rivets. A strange metal ornament had been fixed in the wall between them. Through the glass, Emma could see only surging darkness, as if they were underwater.

There was no furniture in the room, but a circle of symbols, done in chalk, was drawn onto the smooth black stone floor. Emma brought out her phone and began to take pictures. The flash going off seemed eerie in the dimness.

Mark moved toward the circle. "Don't—" Emma lowered her phone. "Go in there," she sighed.

He was already inside the circle, looking around curiously. Emma couldn't see anything in there with him besides bare floor.

"Please come out," she said wheedlingly. "If there's some magic spell in there and it kills you, explaining to Jules is going to be *so awkward*."

There was a faint shimmer of light as Mark stepped out of the circle. "'Awkward' seems like an understatement," he said.

"That's the point," Emma said. "That's why it's funny." He looked blank. "Never mind."

"I read once that explaining a joke is like dissecting a frog," Mark said. "You find out how it works, but the frog dies in the process."

"Maybe we should get out of here before *we* die in the process. I took some pictures with my phone, so—"

"I found this," Mark said, and showed her a square leather object. "It was inside the circle along with some clothes and what looked like"—he frowned—"broken teeth."

Emma snatched the object out of his hand. It was a wallet—a man's wallet, semi-scorched by fire. "I didn't see anything," she said. "The circle looked empty."

"Glamour spell. I felt it when I passed through."

She flipped the wallet open, and her heart leaped. Pressed behind plastic was a driver's license with a familiar picture. The man whose body she'd found in the alley.

There was money in the wallet and credit cards, but her eyes were fixed on the license and his name—Stanley Albert Wells. The same longish, graying hair and round face she remembered, only this time his features weren't twisted up and stained with blood. The address under the name had been burned to illegibility, but the birth date and other information were clear.

"Mark. Mark!" She waved the wallet over her head. "This is a clue. An actual *clue*. I think I love you."

Mark's eyebrows went up. "In Faerie, if you said that, we would have to pledge our troth, and you might put a *geas* upon me that I would not stray from you or I would die."

Emma shoved the wallet in her pocket. "Well, here it's just an expression that means 'I like you very much' or even 'Thanks for the bloodstained wallet.'"

"How specific you humans are."

"You're human, Mark Blackthorn."

A sound echoed through the room. Mark jerked his gaze from hers and raised his head. Emma almost imagined his pointed ears twitching toward the sound and suppressed a smile.

"Outside," he said. "There's something outside."

Her incipient smile disappeared. She slipped into the tunnel, sliding her witchlight into her pocket to douse the illumination. Mark fell into step behind her as she drew out her stele with her left hand, scrawling a number of quick runes onto her arms—Sure-Strike, Swift-Footedness, Battle-Rage, Soundless. She turned to Mark as they neared the entrance, her stele out, but he shook his head. *No. No runes.*

She flipped the stele back into her belt. They had reached the mouth of the cave. The air was cooler here, and she could see the sky, dotted with stars, and the grass, silvery in the moonlight. The field in front of the cave looked bare and empty. Emma could see nothing but grass and thistles, pounded flat as if by the tread of boots, reaching all the way to the edge of the bluff. There was a sharp musical sound in the air, like the buzz of insects.

She heard Mark's sharp intake of breath behind her. Light flared as he spoke. "*Remiel.*"

His seraph blade blazed to life. As if the light had ripped away a glamour, suddenly, she could see them. Whistling and chittering among the long grass.

Demons.

She whipped Cortana free so quickly it was as if it had leaped into her hand. There were dozens of them, spread between the cave and the bluff. They looked like enormous insects: praying mantises, to be precise. Triangular heads, elongated bodies, massive grasping arms ridged with blades of chitin, sharp as razors. Their eyes were pallid, flat, and milky.

They were between her and Mark and the motorcycle.

"Mantid demons," Emma whispered. "We can't fight all of them." She looked up at Mark, his face illuminated by Remiel. "We have to get to the cycle."

Mark nodded. "Go," he said.

Emma sprang forward. It came down like a cage the moment her boots hit the grass: a wave of cold that seemed to slow time. She saw one of the Mantids turn toward her, lashing out with grasping, spiked forelegs. She bent her knees and sprang, rising into the air as she slashed downward, severing the Mantid's head from its body.

Green ichor sprayed. She landed on soaked ground as the demon's body folded up and vanished, sucked back to its home dimension. A flicker rose in her peripheral vision. She spun and struck out again, jamming the point of Cortana into another Mantid's thorax. She jerked her sword back, struck again, watched the demon crumble around the blade.

Her heart was beating in her ears. This was the sharp point of the blade, the moments when all the training, all the hours and the passion and the rage narrowed down to a single point of focus and determination. Killing demons. That was what mattered.

Mark was easily visible, his seraph blade lighting up the grass around him. He slashed out at a Mantid, severing its forelegs. It wobbled, chittering, still alive. Mark's face twisted with disgust. Emma ran toward a heap of rocks, darted up the side, and sailed down, slicing the crippled Mantid in half. It vanished as she landed in front of Mark.

"That was mine to dispatch," he said with a cold look.

"Trust me," Emma said, "there's plenty." She grabbed him with her free hand and spun him around. Five Mantids were lurching toward them from cracks in the granite hill. "Kill those," she said. "I'll get the cycle."

Mark leaped forward with a cry like a hunting horn. He cut at the Mantids' legs and forelegs, crippling them; they fell around him, spraying green-black ichor. It stank like burning gasoline.

Emma began to run for the bluff. Demons surged up at her as she went. She slashed at where they were weakest, the connective tissue where the chitin was thin, severing heads from thoraxes, legs from bodies. Her jeans and cardigan were wet with demon blood. She skidded around a dying Mantid, slid toward the edge of the bluff—

And froze. A Mantid was lifting the cycle in its forelegs. She could swear it was grinning at her, its triangular head splitting open to reveal rows of needle teeth, as it clamped razored forelegs around the cycle, crushing it to pieces. Metal screamed and rent, tires popped, and the Mantid chittered in joy as the machine came apart, the pieces hurtling down the side of the bluff, taking with it Emma's hope of an easy escape.

She glared at the Mantid. "That," she said, "was a *really sweet ride*," and catching up a knife from her belt, she threw it.

It jammed into the Mantid's body, severing thorax from pro-thorax. Ichor sprayed from the demon's mouth as it tipped backward, spasming, its body following the cycle down the cliffside.

"Jerk," Emma muttered, whirling back toward the field. She hated using throwing knives to kill an enemy, mostly because you were unlikely to get them back. She had three more in her belt, a seraph blade, and Cortana.

She knew it wasn't nearly enough to take on the two dozen Mantids still prowling the grass. But it was what she had. It would have to do.

She could see Mark, who had climbed the face of the granite hill and was perched on an outcropping, stabbing downward with his blade. She began to run toward him. She dodged a lashing foreleg, arcing Cortana up to sever the limb as she ran. She heard the Mantid shriek in pain.

One of the taller Mantids was reaching up toward Mark, jagged forelegs grasping. He brought Remiel down, hard, severing its head—and as it collapsed, a second Mantid appeared, its jaws biting down on the blade. It fell back, shrieking its high insect shriek. It was dying, but it had taken Remiel with it. They subsided together into a sizzling puddle of ichor and *adamas*.

Mark had used all the weapons Emma had given him. He pressed his back against the granite as another Mantid reached out. Emma's heart lurched into her throat. She raced forward, flinging herself at the wall, scrambling toward Mark. A massive Mantid loomed up in front of him. He reached for his throat as the Mantid leaned in, jaws gaping, and Emma wanted to scream at him to back down, back away.

Something shone between his fingers. A silver chain, gleaming arrowhead dangling. He whipped it forward toward the head of the Mantid, slashing open its bulging white eyes. Milky fluid burst forth. It reared back, screaming, just as Emma leaped to the ridge beside Mark and slashed Cortana forward to cut it in half.

Mark dropped the chain back over his head as Emma swore and pressed her only seraph blade into his hand. Ichor was running down the blade of Cortana, burning her skin. She gritted her teeth and ignored the pain as Mark raised his new blade.

"Name it," she said, breathing hard, pulling a knife from her belt. She clutched it in her right hand, Cortana in her left.

Mark nodded. *"Raguel,"* he said, and the blade exploded with light. The Mantids screeched, crouching down, wincing away from the glow, and Emma leaped from the rock.

She fell, whipping Cortana and the dagger around herself like the blades of a helicopter. The air was filled with insectile screeches as her weapons connected with chitin and flesh.

The world had slowed. She was still falling. She had all the time in the world. She reached out, left hand and right, severing head from thorax, mesothorax from metathorax, hacking through the jaws of two Mantids to leave them drowning in their own blood. A foreleg reached for her. She slashed through it with an angled twist of Cortana. When she hit the ground six Mantid bodies tumbled after her, each landing with a dull thud and vanishing.

Only the foreleg remained, sticking into the ground like a strange cactus plant. The remaining Mantids were circling, hissing and clicking, but not yet attacking. They seemed wary, as if even their tiny bug brains had noted the fact that she was a danger to them.

One of them was missing its foreleg.

She glanced toward Mark. He was still balanced on the rock outcropping—she couldn't blame him; it made an excellent fixed position to fight from. As she watched, a Mantid lunged toward him, swiping a razored limb across his chest; he brought Raguel down, stabbing into its abdomen. It roared, staggering back.

In the bright light of the seraph blade, Emma saw blood bloom across Mark's shirt, red-black.

"Mark," she whispered.

He spun gracefully. His seraph blade cut the Mantid apart. It fell into two pieces, vanishing just as the night exploded with light.

A car burst from the road and hurtled into the center of the clearing. A familiar red Toyota. The headlights burned through the darkness, sweeping across the field, illuminating the Mantids.

A figure knelt on the car's roof, a light crossbow raised to its shoulder.

Julian.

The car shot forward, and Julian rose to his feet, lifting the crossbow. It was an intricate weapon, Julian's crossbow, capable of firing multiple bolts fast. He pivoted toward the demons, firing off a bolt, then another, all the while riding the roof of the car like a surfboard, his feet firmly planted as the Toyota bumped and hurtled over the rough ground.

Pride swelled in Emma. People often acted as if Julian couldn't be a warrior because he was gentle in his life, gentle to his friends and family.

People were wrong.

Each bolt connected, each sank home into the body of a demon. The bolts were runed: As they struck, the Mantids exploded with silent screams.

The car screeched through the clearing. Emma saw Cristina at the wheel, her jaw set. The Mantid demons were scattering, vanishing back into the shadows. Cristina gunned the engine, and the car rammed into several of them, mashing them flat. Mark leaped off the rock, landing in a crouch, and dispatched a twitching, spasming demon, grinding his blade into its anvil-shaped head and smearing it across the grass. The front of his shirt was dark with blood. As the demon vanished with a wet, sticky sound, Mark collapsed to his knees, his seraph blade tumbling into the grass beside him.

The car jerked to a halt. Cristina had just flung the driver's door open when one of the Mantids slithered out from under the wheels of the car. It bounded toward Mark.

Julian shouted aloud, leaping down from the car. The Mantid reared up over Mark, who shoved himself up on his knees, reaching for the chain around his neck—

Energy poured through Emma, like a jolt of caffeine. Julian's presence, making her stronger. She jerked the severed foreleg out of the ground in front of her and flung it. It whipped through the air, spinning like a propellor, and punched into the body of the

Mantid with a thick smack. The demon shrieked in agony and disappeared in a cloud of ichor.

Mark sank back into the grass. Julian was bending over him, Emma already running. Jules had his stele out. "Mark," he said as Emma reached them. "Mark, please—"

"No," Mark said thickly. He batted away his brother's hands. "No runes." He dragged himself to his knees, then his feet, and stood swaying. "No runes, Julian." He glanced toward Emma. "Are you all right?"

"I'm fine," Emma said, sheathing Cortana. The coldness of battle had faded away, leaving her feeling light-headed. In the moonlight Julian's eyes were a coldly burning blue. He was in gear, his dark hair a mess from the wind, his right hand clasping the stock of his crossbow.

He put his other hand up to her face. Her gaze felt dragged up to his. She could see the night sky in his pupils. "Fine?" he echoed, and his voice was rough. "You're bleeding."

He lowered his arm. His fingers were red. Her free hand sprang to her cheek; she felt the ragged cut, the blood. The sting. "I didn't realize," she said, and then, the words spilling out: "How did you find us? Jules, how did you know where to go?"

Before Julian could answer, the Toyota backed up with a roar, spun around, and drove back toward them. Cristina leaned out the driver's side window, her medallion gleaming at her throat. "Let's go," she said. "It's dangerous here."

"The demons have not gone," Mark agreed. "They have only retreated."

He wasn't wrong. The night around them was alive with moving shadows. They clambered hastily into the car: Emma beside Cristina, Julian and Mark in the backseat. As the car sped away from the cave, Emma reached into her cardigan pocket, feeling for the hard square of leather.

The wallet. It was still there. She felt a burst of relief. She was here, in the car, with Julian beside her, and evidence in her hand. Everything was all right.

"You need an *iratze*," said Julian. "Mark—"

"Stay away from me with that thing," said his brother in a low, intent voice, glaring at Julian and the stele in his hand. "Or I will leap from the window of this moving vehicle."

"Oh, no you won't," said Cristina in her calm, sweet voice, reaching to depress the button that locked all the car doors with a firm click.

"You're *bleeding*," Julian said. "All over the car."

Emma craned around in her seat to look back at them. Mark's shirt was bloody, but he didn't seem to be in much pain. His eyes flickered with annoyance. "I am still protected by the magic of the Wild Hunt," he said. "My wounds heal quickly. You need not trouble yourself." He picked up the edge of his shirt and mopped at the blood on his chest; Emma caught a quick glimpse of pale skin stretched tightly over a hard stomach, and the edges of old scars.

"It's a good thing you showed up when you did," Emma said, turning to look at Cristina and then Julian. "I don't know how you figured out what was going on, but—"

"We didn't," Julian said shortly. "After you hung up on Cristina, we checked your phone's GPS and realized you were out here. It seemed weird enough to follow up."

"But you didn't know we were in trouble," Emma realized. "Just that we were at the convergence."

Cristina gave her an expressive look. Julian didn't say anything.

Emma unzipped her cardigan and shrugged out of it, transferring Wells's wallet to the pocket of her jeans. Battle brought on a sort of numbness, a lack of awareness of injury that let her go forward. The aches and pains were coming now, and she winced as she peeled her sleeve away from her forearm. A long burn reached from her elbow to her wrist, red-black at the edges.

She glanced up at the rearview mirror and saw Jules registering the injury. He leaned forward. "Can you pull over here, Cristina?"

Unfailingly polite Jules. Emma tried to smile at him in the mirror, but he wasn't looking at her. Cristina pulled off the highway and into the parking lot of the seafood shack Emma and Mark had flown over earlier. A massive neon sign reading POSEIDON'S TRIDENT hung over the ramshackle building.

The four of them piled out of the car. The shack was nearly deserted except for a few tables of long-distance truckers and campers from the sites down the road, huddling over coffee and plates of fried oysters.

Cristina insisted on going inside to order them some food and drinks; after a moment's argument, they let her. Julian threw his jacket on a table, claiming it. "There's an outdoor shower around the back," he said. "And some privacy. Come on."

"How do you know that?" Emma asked, joining him as he stalked around the building. He didn't answer. She could feel his anger, not just in the way he looked at her, but in a tight knot under her rib cage.

The dirt path that circled the shack opened out into an area ringed by Dumpsters. There was a massive steel double sink, and— as Jules had promised—a large open shower with surfing equipment stacked next to it.

Mark crossed the sand to the shower and flipped the spigot.

"Wait," Julian began. "You'll get—"

Water poured down, soaking Mark instantly. He lifted his face up to it as calmly as if he were bathing in tropical rainfall and not unheated shower water on a chilly night.

"—Wet." Julian raked his fingers through his tangled hair. Chocolate-colored hair, Emma had thought when she was younger.

People thought brown hair was boring, but it wasn't: Julian's had bits of gold in it and hints of russet and coffee.

Emma went to the sink and ran water over the cut on her arm, then splashed it up over her face and neck, rinsing off the ichor. Demon blood was toxic: It could burn your skin, and it was a bad idea to get it into your mouth and eyes.

Mark flipped the shower off and stepped away, water streaming off him. She wondered if he was uncomfortable—his jeans stuck to him, as did his shirt. His hair was plastered to his neck.

His eyes met hers. Cold burning blue and colder gold. In them Emma saw the wildness of the Hunt: the emptiness and freedom of the skies. It made her shiver.

She saw Julian look at her sharply. He said something to Mark, who nodded and vanished around the side of the building.

Emma reached to turn the sink water off, wincing: There was a burn on her palm. She reached for her stele.

"Don't," said Jules's voice, and there was a warm presence behind her suddenly. She gripped the edge of the sink and closed her eyes, feeling momentarily dizzy. The heat of Jules's body was palpable up and down her back. "Let me."

Healing runes—any runes—given to you by your *parabatai* worked better, amplified by the magic of the bonding spell. Emma turned around, her back against the sink. Julian was so close to her that she had to turn carefully so as not to bump into him. He smelled of fire and cloves and paint. Goose bumps exploded across her skin as he took her arm, cupping her wrist, drawing his stele with his free hand.

She could feel the path each of his fingers traced on the sensitive skin of her forearm. His skin was hard with calluses, roughened with turpentine.

"Jules," she said. "I'm sorry."

"Sorry for what?"

"Going to the convergence without you," she said. "I wasn't trying to—"

"Why did you?" he asked, and the stele began its journey over her skin, forming the lincs of the healing rune. "Why go off with just Mark?"

"The motorcycle," Emma said. "It could only take two. The *motorcycle*," she said again, at Julian's blank look, and then remembered the Mantid demon crushing it in its jagged, razored arms.

"Right," she said. "Mark's steed? The one the faerie convoy was talking about in the Sanctuary? It was a motorcycle. One of the Mantids crushed it, so I guess it's an ex-motorcycle."

The *iratze* was finished. Emma drew her hand back, watching as the cut began to heal itself, closing up like a seam.

"You're not even wearing gear," Julian said. He sounded quiet, intent, but his fingers were trembling as he put his stele away. "You're still human, Emma."

"I was fine—"

"You can't do this to me." The words sounded as if they had bcen dredged up from the bottom of the ocean.

She froze. "Do what?"

"I'm your *parabatai*," he said as if the words were final, and in a way, they were. "You were facing down what, two dozen Mantid demons before we got there? If Cristina hadn't called you—"

"I would have fought them off," Emma said heatedly. "I'm glad you showed up, thank you, but I would have gotten us out of there—"

"Maybe!" His voice rose. "Maybe you would have, maybe you could have done it, but what if you didn't? What if you *died*? It would kill me, Emma, it would *kill me*. You know what happens . . ."

He didn't finish the sentence. *You know what happens to someone when their* parabatai *dies.*

They stood, staring at each other, breathing hard. "When you were away, I felt it here," Emma said finally, touching her upper arm, where the *parabatai* rune was etched. "Did you feel it?" She splayed her hand over the front of his T-shirt, warm from his body. Julian's rune was at the outside edge of his collarbone, about five inches above his heart.

"Yeah," he said, eyelashes lowering as his gaze traced the movement of her fingers. "It hurt me being away from you. It feels like there's a hook dug in under my ribs, and there's something pulling at the other end. Like I'm tethered to you, no matter the distance."

Emma inhaled sharply. She was remembering Julian, fourteen years old, in the overlapping circles of fire in the Silent City, where the *parabatai* ritual was performed. The look on his face as they each stepped into the central circle and the fire rose up around them, and he unbuttoned his shirt to let her touch the stele to his skin and carve the rune that would bind them together for their whole lives. She knew if she just moved her hand now, she could touch the rune cut into his chest, the rune she had put there. . . .

She reached out and touched his collarbone. She could feel the warmth of his skin through his shirt. He half-closed his eyes, as if her touch hurt. *Please don't be angry, Jules,* she thought. *Please.*

"I'm not a Blackthorn," she said, her voice ragged.

"What?"

"I'm not a Blackthorn," she said again. The words hurt to say: They came from a deep place of truth, one she hesitated to look at too closely. "I don't belong in the Institute. I'm there because of you, because I'm your *parabatai*, so they had to let me stay. The rest of you don't have to prove you're giving back. I do. Everything I do is a—is a test."

Julian's face had changed; he was looking down at her in the moonlight, the cupid's bow of his lips parted. His hands came up and gently looped her upper arms. Sometimes, she thought, it was as if she were a kite, and Julian the flier: She soared above the ground, and he kept her tethered to the earth. Without him she would be lost among the clouds.

She lifted her head. She could feel his breath on her face. There was something in his eyes, something breaking open, not like a crack in a wall but like a door swinging wide, and she could see the light.

"I'm not testing you, Emma," he said. "You've proved everything to me already."

There was a wild feeling in Emma's blood, the desire to seize Julian, to do something, *something*, crush his hands in hers, put her arms around him, cause them both pain, make them both taste the same seeking desperation. She couldn't understand it, and it terrified her.

She moved aside, gently breaking Julian's hold on her. "We should get back to Mark and Cristina," she murmured. "It's been a while."

She turned away from him, but not before she saw the expression on his face shut, a slamming door. She felt it like a hollow in her stomach, the intractable certainly that no matter how many demons she had killed that night, her nerve had failed her when she needed it most.

When they got back to the front of the restaurant, they found Mark and Cristina seated on top of a picnic table, surrounded by cardboard boxes of french fries, buttered rolls, fried clams, and fish tacos. Cristina was holding a bottle of lime soda and smiling at something Mark had said.

The wind off the ocean had dried Mark's hair. It blew around his face, highlighting how much he looked like a faerie and how little he seemed like Nephilim.

"Mark was telling me about the fight at the convergence point," said Cristina as Emma clambered onto the table and reached for a fry. Julian climbed up after her and snagged a soda.

Emma launched into her own version of events, from their

discovery of the cave and the wallet to the appearance of the Mantid demons. "They crushed Mark's motorcycle so we couldn't get away," she said.

Mark looked glum.

"Thy steed is no more, methinks," Emma said to him. "Will they get you another one?"

"Unlikely," said Mark. "The Fair Folk are not generous."

Julian looked at Emma with his eyebrows raised. "Methinks?" he echoed.

"I can't help it." She shrugged. "It's catching."

Cristina held out a hand. "Let's see what you found," she said. "Since you sacrificed so much to get it."

Emma pulled the square leather object from her pocket and let them all pass it around. Next she retrieved her phone and held it out while she flipped through the photos of the inside of the cave with the odd languages scrawled on the walls.

"We can translate the Greek and Latin," said Emma. "But we'll need to hit the library for the other languages."

"Stanley Wells," said Julian, looking through the half-burned wallet. "Name sounds familiar."

"When we get back, Ty and Livvy can find out who he is," Emma said. "And we can figure out his address, see if there's anything to find at his house. See if there's a reason he might have been targeted for sacrifice."

"They could be randomly chosen," said Julian.

"They are not," said Mark.

They all paused, Julian with a bottle halfway to his mouth. "What?" Emma said.

"Not everyone makes a fit subject to be sacrificed for a summoning spell," said Mark. "It cannot be completely random."

"They teach you much about dark magic in the Wild Hunt?" Julian asked.

"The Wild Hunt *is* dark magic," said Mark. "I recognized the circle in the cave." He tapped Emma's phone. "This is a sacrificial circle. This is necromancy. The power of death harnessed to some purpose."

They were all quiet for a moment. The cold wind off the ocean ruffled Emma's damp hair. "The Mantids were guards," she said finally. "Whoever the necromancer is doesn't want anyone finding the secret ceremonial chamber."

"Because he needs it," said Jules.

"It could be a she," said Emma. "It isn't just men who get to be psycho magic serial killers."

"Granted," said Julian. "Either way, there's nowhere else near the city with a ley line convergence like this. Necromancy that was done at a ley line extension would probably show up on Magnus's map—but what if it was done at a *convergence*?"

"Then it might well be hidden from the Nephilim," said Mark. "The killer could be doing the ceremonial killings at the convergence point—"

"And then dumping the bodies at the ley line extensions?" finished Cristina. "But why? Why not leave them in the cave?"

"Perhaps they want the bodies to be found," said Mark. "After all, the marks on them are writing. It could be a message. A message they want to communicate."

"Then they should have written the message in a language we know," Emma muttered.

"Maybe the message isn't for us," said Mark.

"The convergence will have to be watched," said Cristina. "Someone will have to monitor it. There is no other convergence point; the murderer will have to come back at some point."

"Agreed," Julian said. "We'll need to set up something at the convergence. Something that'll warn us."

"Tomorrow, during the day," Emma said. "The Mantid demons ought to be inactive—"

Julian laughed. "You know what we have tomorrow? Testing," he said. Twice a year Diana was required to test them on certain basics, from rune drawing to training to languages, and report back to the Clave on their progress.

There was a chorus of protest. Julian held his hands up. "I'll text Diana about it," he said. "But if we don't do it, the Clave will get suspicious."

Mark said something unprintable about what the Clave could do with its suspicions.

"I don't think I know that word," Cristina said, looking amused.

"I'm not sure I do either," Emma said. "And I know a lot of bad words."

Mark leaned back with the beginning of a smile, then sucked in his breath. He pulled his bloody shirt collar away from his neck and glanced down gingerly at his injured chest.

Julian set his bottle down. "Let me see."

Mark let go of his collar. "There is nothing you can do. It will heal."

"It's a demon injury," said Julian. "Let me see it."

Mark looked at him, startled. The waves made a soft soughing sound around them. There was no one left outside the restaurant except them; the other tables had emptied. Mark hadn't heard that voice of Julian's before, Emma thought, the one that brooked no argument, the one that sounded like a grown man's. The kind of man you listened to.

Mark lifted the front of his shirt. The cut ran jaggedly across his chest. It was no longer bleeding, but the sight of the ragged pale flesh made Emma grit her teeth.

"Let me—" Julian began.

Mark sprang off the table. "I am *fine*," he said. "I do not need your healing magic. I do not need your runes of safety." He touched his shoulder, where a black Mark bloomed like a butterfly: a permanent rune of protection. "I have had this since I was ten," he said. "I had this when they took me, and this when they broke me and made me one of them. Never has it helped me. The runes of the Angel are lies cast into the teeth of Heaven."

Hurt bloomed and faded in Julian's eyes. "They're not perfect," he said. "Nothing is perfect. But they do help. I just don't want to see you hurt."

"Mark," Cristina said in a soft voice. But Mark had gone somewhere else, somewhere where none of their voices could reach him. He stood with his eyes blazing, his hands opening and closing into fists.

Slowly, his hand came up, caught the hem of his shirt. Pulled it up and over his head. He shrugged the shirt off, dropping it to the sand. Emma saw pale skin, much paler than hers, a hard chest and a narrow waist cut with the fine lines of old scars. Then he turned around.

His back was covered in runes, from nape to waist. But not like a normal Shadowhunter's, where the black Marks faded eventually to a thin white line against the skin. These were raised and thick and livid.

Julian had gone white around the mouth. "What . . . ?"

"When I first came to Faerie, they mocked me for my Nephilim blood," Mark said. "The Folk of the Unseelie Court took my stele and broke it, they said it was nothing but a dirty stick. And when I fought back for it, they used knives to cut the Angel's runes into my skin. After that I stopped fighting with them about Shadowhunters. And I swore no other rune would touch my skin."

He bent down and picked up his bloody, wet shirt, and stood facing them, his rage gone, vulnerable again.

"Maybe they could still be healed," Emma said. "The Silent Brothers—"

"I don't need them healed," said Mark. "They serve as a reminder."

Julian slid off the table. "A reminder of what?"

"Not to trust," said Mark.

Cristina looked at Emma across the boys' heads. There was a terrible sadness on her face.

"I am sorry your protection rune failed you," Julian said, and his voice was low and careful, and Emma had never wanted to put her arms around him so much as she did then, as he faced his brother in the ocean-washed moonlight, his heart in his eyes. His hair was a tangle, his soft curls like question marks against his forehead. "But there are other kinds of protection. Your family protects you. We will always protect you, Mark. We won't let them make you go back."

Mark smiled, the oddest, sad smile. "I know," he said. "My gentle little brother. I know."

# 10

## And She Was a Child

"It's done," Diana said, tossing her duffel bag onto the kitchen island with a clanking sound.

Emma looked up. She'd been over by the window with Cristina, testing the bandages on her hands. Julian's healing runes had taken care of most of her injuries, but there were some ichor burns that were still sore.

Livvy, Dru, and Tavvy were crowded around the kitchen table, fighting over who got the chocolate milk. Ty had his headphones on and was reading, calm in his own world. Julian was at the stove, making bacon and toast and eggs—with burned bits in them, the way Dru liked.

Diana went over to the sink and rinsed off her hands. She was in jeans and a T-shirt, dirt on her clothes and streaking her face. Her hair was pulled back in a tightly knotted bun.

"You set it up?" Emma asked. "The monitor on the convergence?"

Diana nodded, reaching for a dish towel to dry her hands. "Julian texted me about it. Did you think I was about to let you get out of the Clave testing?"

There were groans.

"Thought, no," said Emma. "Hoped, maybe."

"Anyway, I did it myself," Diana said. "If anyone goes in and out of that cave, we'll get a call on the Institute's phone."

"And if we're not home?" Julian asked.

"Texts," Diana said, turning around so that her back was to the sink. "Texts go to Julian, Emma, and myself."

"Why not Arthur?" Cristina said. "Does he not have a cell phone?"

He didn't, as far as Emma knew, but Diana didn't answer that. "Now here's the other thing," she said. "Mantid demons guard the convergence during the night, but as you know, demons are inactive outside during the day. They can't stand sunlight."

"I wondered," said Emma. "It didn't make sense that whoever's doing this would leave the convergence unguarded for half the day."

"You were right to wonder," Diana said. Her voice was neutral; Emma searched her face in vain for a clue to whether she was still angry. "During the day the door to the cave seals itself closed. I watched the entrance disappear when the sun rose. It didn't interfere with setting up the monitoring runes and wards—I did that outside the cave—but no one's going into that convergence while the sun's up."

"All the murders, the body dumping, all of them *have* happened at night," Livvy said. "Maybe there's a demon behind this after all?"

Diana sighed. "We just don't know. By the Angel, I need coffee."

Cristina hurried to get her a mug, while Diana brushed at the dirt on her clothes, frowning.

"Did Malcolm help set it up?" Julian asked.

Diana took the coffee gratefully from Cristina and smiled. "All you need to know is that it's taken care of," she said. "Now, you've got testing today, so I'll see you in the classroom after breakfast."

She left, taking her bag and her coffee with her. Dru looked glum. "I can't believe we have class," she said. She was wearing jeans and a T-shirt that had a picture of a screaming face and the words DR. TERROR'S HOUSE OF HORRORS across the front.

"We're in the middle of an investigation," Livvy said. "We shouldn't have to take tests."

"It's an affront," said Ty. "I am affronted." He had pushed his headphones down, but his hand was under the table. She could hear him clicking a retractable pen—it was something he had done often before Julian had built him better focus tools, but it was still something he did when anxious.

Against a background of grumbling from everyone, Emma's phone trilled. She glanced down and saw the screen flash. CAMERON ASHDOWN.

Julian looked over for a moment, then went briskly back to stirring the eggs. He was in a combination of gear, apron, and torn T-shirt that at another time would have had Emma teasing him. Now she just edged toward the window and picked up the call.

"Cam?" Emma said. "Is something going on?"

Livvy looked over and rolled her eyes, then got up to start ferrying plates back and forth between the stove and the table. The rest of the kids were still arguing, though Tavvy had wound up with the chocolate milk.

"I didn't call to ask you to get back together, if that's what you're thinking," Cameron said. She pictured him as his voice came down the phone: frowning, his red hair messy and askew as it always was in the morning.

"Wow," said Emma. "Good morning to you, too."

"Milk thief," Dru said to Tavvy, and put a piece of toast on his head. Emma stifled a smile.

"I was at the Shadow Market," said Cam. "Yesterday."

"Gasp! Shame on you."

"I heard some gossip around Johnny Rook's table," he said. "It was about you. He said he'd argued with you a few days ago."

His voice lowered. "You shouldn't be seeing him outside the Market, Em."

Emma leaned back against the wall. Cristina gave her a pointed look, then sat down with the others; soon everyone was buttering toast and forking up eggs. "I know, I know. Johnny Rook is a criminal who does crime. I got the lecture already."

Cam sounded put out. "Someone else said you were poking your nose into something that wasn't any of your business. And that if you kept doing it, they'd hurt you. Not the guy who said it—I shook him down a little, and he said he meant someone else. That he'd heard things. What are you poking around in, Emma?"

Julian was still at the stove; Emma could tell by the set of his shoulders that he was listening. "It could be so many things."

Cameron sighed. "Fine, be flip about it. I was worried about you. Be careful."

"Always am," she said, and hung up.

Silently, Julian handed her a plate of eggs. Emma accepted it, conscious that everyone was looking at her. She put the eggs down on the kitchen island and perched herself on one of the stools, poking at her breakfast with a spoon.

"Okay," Livvy said. "If no one else asks, I will. What was that about?"

Emma looked up, about to give an annoyed answer, when the words died in her throat.

Mark was standing in the doorway. The tension of last night's altercation in the library seemed to reappear, dropping a heavy silence over the kitchen. The Blackthorns looked at their brother, wide-eyed; Cristina stared down at her coffee.

Mark looked—normal. He wore a clean blue henley shirt and dark jeans that actually fit, along with a weapons belt around his waist, though there were no weapons in it. Still, it was unmistakably a Shadowhunter belt, runes of angelic power and precision punched into the leather. There were gauntlets on his wrists.

They all stared at him, Julian with his spatula in midair. Mark put his shoulders back and for a moment Emma thought he was going to sweep another bow, the way he had last night. Instead he spoke.

"I apologize for yesterday evening," he said. "I should not have blamed you, my family. The politics of the Clave are complex and often dark, and not your fault. I would like to, with your permission, start over and introduce myself to you."

"But we know who you are," Ty said. Livvy leaned over and whispered in his ear, her hand brushing his shoulder. Ty looked back at Mark, clearly still puzzled, but also expectant.

Mark took a step forward. "I am Mark Antony Blackthorn," he said. "I come from a long line of proud Shadowhunters. I have served with the Wild Hunt for years I cannot count. I have ridden through the air on a white horse made of smoke, and gathered up the bodies of the dead, and brought them to Faerie, where their bones and skin have fed the savage land. I have never felt guilty, but perhaps I should." He let his hands, which had been clasped behind his back, fall to his sides. "I don't know where I belong," he said. "But if you let me, I will try to belong here."

There was a moment of silence. The kids at the table stared; Emma sat with her spoon poised, holding her breath. Mark looked toward Jules.

Julian reached up to rub the back of his neck. "Why don't you sit down, Mark," he said a little hoarsely. "I'll make you some eggs."

Mark was quiet all through breakfast, as Julian, Emma, and Cristina filled in the others on what they'd discovered the previous night. Emma kept the details of the Mantid attack minimal; she didn't want to give Tavvy nightmares.

Stanley Wells's wallet was passed over to Ty, who looked thrilled to be handling a clue. He promised a full investigation of the unfortunate Stanley after the testing. Since Mark had no need to participate in the testing, Julian asked him if he would look after Tavvy in the library.

"I will not feed him to a tree, as is done in the Unseelie Court with unruly children," Mark promised.

"That's a relief," Julian said dryly.

Mark bent down toward Tavvy, whose eyes were sparkling. "Come with me, little one," Mark said. "There are books in the library, that I remember, that I loved as a child. I could show them to you."

Tavvy nodded and placed his hand in Mark's with total trust. Something went through Mark's eyes then, a lightning flash of emotion. He went out of the room with Tavvy without another word.

Cameron's warning stayed with Emma through the rest of the meal, as they cleaned up, and after they all filed to the classroom to find Diana there, holding a heavy stack of testing papers. She couldn't get his words off her mind, and as a result scored dismally on languages and memorization of the classes of various demons and Downworlders. She mixed up Azazel and Asmodeus, Purgatic and Cthonian, and nixies and pixies. Diana glared at her as she marked the paper with Emma's name on it with a fat red pen.

Everyone else scored high, and the few that Julian missed were ones Emma suspected he had gotten wrong on purpose to make her feel better.

Emma was grateful when they finished up the written and oral parts of the test. They took a break for lunch before moving down the hall to the training room. Diana had already set up the space. There were targets for knife throwing, swords of various sizes, and, in the middle of the room, a large training dummy. It had a wooden trunk, several arms that could be positioned and repositioned, and a stuffed cloth head like a scarecrow.

A circle of black-and-white powder surrounded the dummy—rock salt mixed with ash. "Attacking from a distance, with care and precision," Diana said. "Disrupt the ash circle and you fail." She moved toward the black box on the floor and flipped a switch. It was a radio. Noise exploded into the room, harsh and discordant. It sounded as if someone had recorded a mob in action, shouting and yelling and smashing windows.

Livvy looked horrified. Ty winced and reached for his headphones, dropping them over his ears.

"Distraction," said Diana loudly. "You have to work past it—"

Before she could finish, there was a knock at the door: It was Mark, looking diffident. "Tavvy is busy with his books," he said to Diana, who had reached to turn the noise down slightly, "and you had asked if I could join this part of the testing. I thought it best to oblige."

"But Mark doesn't need to be tested," objected Julian. "It's not as if his scores can be reported to the Clave."

"Cristina doesn't need her scores reported either," Diana said. "But she's joining in. I want to see how you all do. If you're going to work together, it would be best if you all knew each other's skill levels."

"I can fight," Mark said. He didn't add anything about the night before, the fact that he'd held off Mantid demons on his own, without new runes. "The Wild Hunt are warriors."

"Yes, but they fight differently than Shadowhunters," Diana said, gesturing around the training room, at the runed blades, the *adamas* swords. "These are the weapons of your people." She turned back to the others. "Each of you must choose one."

Mark's expression flattened at that, but he said nothing. Nor did he move as the rest of them scattered—Emma went for Cortana,

Cristina for her butterfly knives, Livvy for her saber, and Dru for a long, thin misericord. Julian chose a pair of *chakhrams*, circular razored throwing stars.

Ty hung back. Emma couldn't help but wonder if Diana noticed that it was Livvy who picked up a dagger for Ty and pressed it into his palm. Emma had seen Ty throw knives before: He was good at it, sometimes excellent, but only when he felt like it. When he didn't, there was no moving him.

"Julian," Diana said, turning the music back up. "You first."

Julian stepped back and threw, the *chakhrams* spinning from his hands like circles of light. One sheared off the training dummy's right arm, the other its left, before they buried themselves in the wall.

"Your target isn't dead," Diana pointed out. "Just armless."

"Exactly," said Julian. "So I can question him. Or *it*, you know, if it's a demon."

"Very strategic." Diana tried to hide a smile as she made a note in her book. She picked up the dummy's arms and fastened them back on. "Livvy?"

Livvy dispatched the dummy with a swing of her saber without passing the ash barrier. Dru acquitted herself decently with a thrown misericord, and Cristina flipped open her balisongs and hurled them so that one point of each blade stuck into the dummy's head exactly where its eyes would have been.

"Gross," said Livvy admiringly. "I like it."

Cristina retrieved her knives and winked at Emma, who had climbed partway up the rope ladder, Cortana in her free hand.

"Emma?" Diana said, craning her head up. "What are you doing?"

Emma flung herself from the ladder. It wasn't the cold fury of battle, but there was a moment of falling freedom that was pure pleasure, that drove the annoyance of Cameron's warning out of her mind. She landed on the dummy, feet planted on its shoulders, and slashed down, driving Cortana's hilt deep into its trunk. Then she flipped herself backward, over and down, landing on her feet inches outside the circle of ash.

"That was showing off," Diana said, but she was smiling as she made another note. She glanced up. "Tiberius? It's your turn."

Ty took a step toward the circle. The white band of his headphones was stark against his black hair. He was as tall as the dummy, Emma realized with a jolt. She often thought of Ty as the child he had been. But he wasn't—he was fifteen years old, older than she'd been when she and Julian had undergone the *parabatai* ceremony. His face wasn't a little boy's face anymore. Sharpness had replaced the softness.

Ty lifted his knife.

"Tiberius," said a voice from the doorway. "Take the headphones off."

It was Uncle Arthur. They all looked up in surprise: Arthur rarely ventured downstairs, and when he did, he avoided conversation, meals—all contact. It was strange to see him hovering in the doorway like a gray ghost: gray robe, gray stubble, worn gray pants.

"The pollution of mundane technology is everywhere," said Arthur. "In those phones you carry. Cars—at the London Institute we didn't own them. That computer you think I don't know about." An odd anger flashed across his face. "You're not going to be able to go into battle wearing *headphones*."

He said the word as if it were poisonous.

Diana closed her eyes.

"Ty," she said. "Take them off."

Ty slid the headphones down so that they hung around the back of his neck. He winced as the chatter of noise and voices from the radio struck his ears. "I won't be able to do it, then."

"Then you'll fail," said Arthur. "This has to be fair."

"If you don't let him use them, it won't be fair," said Emma.

"This is the test. Everyone has to do it," Diana said. "Battle doesn't always happen under optimum conditions. There's noise, blood, distractions—"

"I won't be in battle," Ty said. "I don't want to be that kind of Shadowhunter."

"*Tiberius*," Arthur said sharply. "Do as you're asked."

Ty's face set. He lifted the knife and threw it, with deliberate awkwardness but great force. It slammed into the black plastic radio, which shattered into a hundred pieces.

There was silence.

Ty looked down at his right hand; it was bleeding. A piece of the shattered radio had gone wide and nicked his skin. Scowling, he went to stand by one of the pillars. Livvy watched him with miserable eyes; Julian made as if to start after him, when Emma caught him by the wrist.

"Don't," she said. "Give him a minute."

"My turn," said Mark. Diana turned toward him in surprise. He was already stalking toward the training dummy. He strode directly up to it, his boots scuffing the ash and salt on the ground.

"Mark," Diana said, "you're not supposed to—"

He caught hold of the dummy and yanked it toward himself, ripping the stuffed head from its body. Straw rained down around him. He tossed the head aside, seized hold of the attached arms, and bent them back until they snapped. He took a step back, planted his foot in the middle of the thing's trunk, and shoved. It went over with a crash.

It would almost have been funny, Emma thought, if not for the look on his face.

"These are the weapons of my people," he said, holding out his hands. A cut on the right one had opened and was bleeding.

"You weren't supposed to touch the circle," said Diana. "Those are the rules, and I don't make them. The Clave—"

"*Lex malla, lex nulla*," Mark said coldly, and walked away from the dummy. Emma heard Arthur draw in his breath at the words of the Blackthorn family motto. He turned without a word and stalked out of the room.

Julian's eyes tracked his brother as Mark went toward Ty and leaned against the pillar beside him.

Ty, who had been holding his right hand with his left, his jaw set, looked up in surprise. "Mark?"

Mark touched his younger brother's hand, gently, and Ty did not pull away. They both had the Blackthorn fingers, long and delicate, with sharp, articulated bones.

Slowly, the angry look faded from Ty's face. Instead he looked sideways up at his brother, as if the answer to a question Emma couldn't guess at could be read in Mark's face.

She remembered what Ty had said about his brother in the library.

*It's not his fault if he doesn't understand everything. Or if things are too much for him. It's not his fault.*

"Now we both have hurt hands," Mark said.

"Julian," Diana said. "We need to talk about Ty."

Julian stood motionless in front of her desk. He could see past Diana, past the huge glass windows behind her, down to the highway and the beach below, and the ocean beyond that.

He held a very clear memory in his mind, though he no longer remembered how old he had been when it happened. He had been on the beach, sketching the sun going down and the surfers out in the water. A loose sketch, more about the joy of movement than about getting the picture right. Ty had been there too, playing: He had been building a row of small, perfect squares of damp sand, each exactly the same size and shape.

Julian had looked at his own inexact, messy work and Ty's

methodical rows, and thought: *We both see the same world, but in a different way. Ty feels the same joy I do, the joy of creation. We feel all the same things, only the shapes of our feelings are different.*

"This was Arthur's fault," said Julian. "I—I don't know why he did that." He knew he sounded troubled. He couldn't help it. Usually on Arthur's bad days, his hate and anger were turned inward, toward himself. He wouldn't have thought his uncle even knew of Ty's headphones: He didn't think Arthur paid attention to any of them enough to notice such things, and to Ty least of all. "I don't know why he treated Ty that way."

"We can be cruelest to those who remind us of ourselves."

"Ty is not like Arthur." Julian's voice sharpened. "And he shouldn't have to pay for what Arthur does. You should let him do the test again, with the headphones."

"Not necessary," Diana said. "I know what Ty can do; I'll amend his test scores to reflect that. You don't have to worry about the Clave."

Julian looked at her, puzzled. "If this isn't about Ty's scores, why did you want to see me?"

"You heard what Ty said in there," Diana said. "He doesn't want to be *that kind of Shadowhunter*. He wants to go to the Scholomance. It's why he refuses to be *parabatai* with Livvy. And you know he'd do almost anything for her."

Ty and Livvy were in the computer room now, searching for whatever they could find on Stanley Wells. Ty seemed to have put his anger at the testing aside, had even smiled after Mark had come to talk to him.

Julian wondered if it was wrong to feel irrationally jealous that Mark, who had reappeared in their life only yesterday, was able to talk to his younger brother when he was not. Julian loved Ty more than he loved his own life, and yet he hadn't thought of anything as elegantly simple to say to his brother as *now we both have hurt hands.*

"He can't go," Julian said. "He's only fifteen. The other students are eighteen at least. It's meant for Academy graduates."

"He's as smart as any Academy graduate," Diana said. "He knows as much."

She leaned forward, elbows on her glass desk. Behind her the ocean stretched to the horizon. It was creeping toward late afternoon, and the water was a dark silver-blue. Julian thought about what would happen if he brought his hand down hard on the desk; did he have the strength to shatter the glass?

"It's not about what he knows," Julian said, and stopped himself. He was getting dangerously close to exactly what they never talked about: the way in which Ty was different.

Julian often thought the Clave was a black shadow over his life. They had stolen his older brother and sister from him just as much as the Fair Folk had. Down through the centuries, the exact way Shadowhunters could and should behave had been strictly regimented. Tell a mundane about the Shadow World and be disciplined, even exiled. Fall in love with a mundane, or your *parabatai*, and have your Marks ripped off—an agonizing process not everyone survived.

Julian's art, his father's interest in the classics: all had been regarded with deep suspicion. Shadowhunters weren't meant to have outside interests. Shadowhunters weren't artists. They were warriors, born and bred, like Spartans. And individuality was not something they valued.

Ty's thoughts, his beautiful, curious mind, were not like everyone else's. Julian had heard stories—whispers, really—of other Shadowhunter children who thought or felt differently. Who had trouble focusing. Who claimed letters rearranged themselves on the page when they tried to read them. Who fell prey to dark sadnesses that seemed to have no reason, or fits of energy they couldn't control.

Whispers were all there were, though, because the Clave hated to admit that Nephilim like that existed. They were disappeared into the "dregs" portion of the Academy, trained to stay out of the way of other Shadowhunters. Sent to far corners of the globe like shameful secrets to be hidden. There were no words to describe Shadowhunters whose minds were shaped differently, no real words to describe differences at all.

Because if there were words, Julian thought, there would have to be acknowledgment. And there were things the Clave refused to acknowledge.

"They'll make him feel like there's something wrong with him," Julian said. *"There's nothing wrong with him."*

"I know that." Diana sounded sorrowful. Tired. Julian wondered where she had gone the day before, when they'd been at Malcolm's. Who had helped her ward the convergence.

"They'll try to force him into their mold of what a Shadowhunter ought to be like. He doesn't know what they'll do—"

"Because you haven't told him," Diana said. "If he has a rosy picture in his mind of what the Scholomance is like, it's because you've never corrected him. Yeah, it's harsh there. It's brutal. Tell him so."

"You want me to tell him he's different," Julian said coldly. "He's not stupid, Diana. He knows that."

"No," said Diana, standing up. "I want you to tell him how the Clave feels about people who are different. *Shadowhunters* who are different. Because how can he make up his mind if he doesn't have all the information?"

"He's my *little* brother," Julian snapped. The day outside was hazy; parts of the windows seemed mirrored, and he could see bits of himself—an edge of cheekbone, a set jaw, tangled hair. The look in his own eyes frightened him. "He's three years from graduation—"

Diana's brown eyes were fierce. "I know you've basically brought him up since he was ten, Julian. I know you feel like all of them are your children. And they are yours, but Livvy and Ty at least aren't children anymore. You're going to have to let go—"

"*You're* telling me to be more forthcoming?" Julian demanded. "Really?"

Her jaw tightened. "You're walking the edge of a razor blade, Julian, with everything you hide. Believe me. I've walked that razor blade half my life. You get used to it, so used to it sometimes you forget that you're bleeding."

"I don't suppose you want to be any more specific about that?"

"You have your secrets. I have mine."

"I can't believe this." Julian wanted to yell, punch a wall. "Keeping secrets is all you ever do. Remember when I asked you if you wanted to run the Institute? Remember when you said no and told me not to ask why?"

Diana sighed and ran one finger along the back of her chair. "Being angry at me won't help anything, Jules."

"You might be right," he said. "But that's the one thing you could have done that would probably really have helped me. And you didn't. So forgive me if I feel like I'm in this totally alone. I love Ty, God, believe me, I want him to have what he wants. But say I told Ty how harsh the Scholomance was, and he wanted to go anyway. Could you *promise* me that he'd be fine there? Could you swear he and Livvy would be all right separated when they've never spent a day apart in their whole lives? Can you guarantee it?"

She shook her head. She looked defeated, and Julian felt no sense of triumph. "I could tell you there are no guarantees in life, Julian Blackthorn, but I can already see you don't want to hear anything I say about Ty," she said. "So I'll tell you something else instead. You may be the most determined person I've ever known. For five years, you have kept everything and everyone in this house together in a way I wouldn't have thought was possible." She looked directly at him. "But this situation can't hold. It's like a fault line in the earth.

It will break apart under pressure, and then what? What will you lose—what will *we* lose—when that happens?"

"What is this?" Mark asked, picking up Tavvy's stuffed lemur, Mr. Limpet, and holding it gingerly by one foot. Mark was sitting on the floor of the computer room with Emma, Tavvy, and Dru. Dru had a book called *Danse Macabre* in one hand and was ignoring them. Tavvy was trying to get Mark, wet-haired and barefoot, to play with him.

Cristina hadn't yet returned from changing out of training clothes. Ty and Livvy, meanwhile, were manning the desk—Ty was typing, and Livvy was sitting on the desk beside the keyboard, issuing orders and suggestions. Stanley Wells had turned out to have an unlisted address, and Emma strongly suspected that whatever they were doing to try to track it down was probably illegal.

"Here," Emma said, reaching out to Mark. "Give me Mr. Limpet." She was feeling anxious and unsettled. Diana had wrapped up the testing shortly after Arthur had left, and had called Julian to her office. The way he'd thrown his testing gear into a corner of the training room before following her had made Emma think it wasn't an interview he was looking forward to.

Cristina came into the room, running her fingers through her long, wet black hair. Mark, holding out Mr. Limpet to Emma, looked up—and there was a tearing sound. The lemur's leg came away and its body thumped to the ground, scattering stuffing.

Mark said something in an unrecognizable language.

"You killed Mr. Limpet," said Tavvy.

"I think he died of old age, Tavs," said Emma, picking up the stuffed lemur's body. "You've had him since you were born."

"Or gangrene," Drusilla said, looking up from her book. "It could have been gangrene."

"Oh no!" Cristina's eyes were wide. "Wait here—I'll be right back."

"Don't—" Mark began, but Cristina had already hurried from

the room. "I am a clodpole," he said mournfully. He reached to ruffle Tavvy's hair. "I am sorry, little one."

"Did you get an address for Wells?" It was Julian, striding into the room.

Livvy held up her arms in triumph. "Yep. It's in the Hollywood Hills."

"No surprise there," Emma said. Rich people often lived in the Hills. She was fond of the area herself, despite the expensiveness of the neighborhood. She liked the twisty roads, the massive sprays of flowers climbing over walls and down the sides of houses, and the views out over the electric, lit-up city. At night the air that blew through the Hills smelled like white flowers: oleander and honeysuckle, and a dry promise of the desert, miles away.

"There are sixteen people named Stanley Wells in the greater Los Angeles area," said Ty, swinging his chair around. "We narrowed the possibilities down."

"Good work," Julian said as Tavvy sprang up and came over to him.

"Mr. Limpet died," Tavvy said, tugging on Julian's jeans. Jules reached down and lifted him up in his arms.

"Sorry, kiddo," Julian said, putting his chin down on Tavvy's curls. "We'll get you something else."

"I am a murderer," said Mark gloomily.

"Don't be dramatic," Emma whispered, kicking his bare ankle.

Mark looked cross. "Faeries are dramatic. It's what we do."

"I loved Mr. Limpet," said Tavvy. "He was a good lemur."

"There are lots of other good animals." Tiberius spoke earnestly; animals were one of his favorite subjects, along with detectives and crime. Tavvy smiled at him, his face full of trust and love. "Foxes are smarter than dogs. You can hear lions roar from forty kilometers away. Penguins—"

"And bears," Cristina said, reappearing breathlessly in the doorway. She handed Tavvy a stuffed gray bear. He looked at it dubiously. "That was mine when I was a little girl," she explained.

"What's its name?" Tavvy inquired.

"Oso," said Cristina, and shrugged. "It means 'bear' in Spanish. I was not very creative."

"Oso." Tavvy took the bear and smiled a gap-toothed smile. Julian looked at Cristina as if she'd brought him water in the desert. Emma thought of what Livvy had said about Jules and Cristina in the training room, and felt a small, inexplicable sting at her heart.

Livvy was chattering away to Jules, swinging her legs cheerfully. "So we should all go," she said. "Ty and I can go in the car with Emma and Mark, and you can go with Cristina, and Diana can stay here—"

Julian set his little brother down. "Nice try," he said. "But this is really a two-person job. Emma and I will be in and out fast, see if there's anything unusual about the house, that's it."

"We never get to do anything fun," protested Livvy.

"I should be allowed to examine the house," Ty said. "You'll miss everything important. All the clues."

"Thanks for the vote of confidence," Julian said dryly. "Look, Livs, Ty-Ty, we really need you here to go over the photos from the convergence cave. See if you can identify the languages, translate them—"

"More translating," Livvy said. "Sounds thrilling."

"It will be fun," Cristina said. "We can make hot chocolate and work in the library." She smiled, and Julian shot her a second grateful look.

"It's not busywork," Julian promised. "It's because you guys can genuinely do things we can't." He nodded toward the computer. Livvy flushed, and Ty looked pleased.

Mark, however, didn't. "I should go with you," he said to Jules. "The Courts wished me to be part of the investigation. To accompany you."

Julian shook his head. "Not tonight. We need to figure out what to do about not being able to use runes on you."

"I don't need them—" Mark began.

"You do." There was steel in Julian's voice. "You need glamour runes, if you want to blend in. And you're still injured from last night. Even if you do heal quickly, I saw you reopened your wound in the training room—you were bleeding—"

"My blood is not your concern," Mark said.

"It is," said Julian. "That's what it means to be family."

"*Family*," Mark began bitterly, and then seemed to realize that his younger siblings were there and were looking at him, silent and still. Cristina, too, was quiet, gazing at Emma across the room, her gaze dark and worried.

Mark seemed to swallow back whatever he had been about to say. "If I had wanted to take orders, I would have stayed with the Hunt," he said instead, in a low voice, and walked out the door.

# 11

## A MAIDEN THERE LIVED

"I think Ty's doubled up on his detective reading," Julian said with a smile. He had his window cranked down, and the air blowing into the car lifted his curling hair off his forehead. "He asked me if I thought the killings were an inside job."

"Inside what?" Emma smiled.

She was leaning back in the passenger seat of the car, her booted feet up on the dashboard. The windows were open to the night, and Emma could hear the sounds of the city rising all around them as they idled at a red light.

They had turned up Sunset off the Coast Highway. At first as they wound through the canyons and into Beverly Hills and Bel Air, the suburbs were quiet, but they had moved into the heart of Hollywood now, the Sunset Strip, lined with expensive restaurants and massive, hundred-foot-high billboards plastered with ads for movies and TV shows. The streets were crowded and noisy: tourists posing for photos with celebrity imitators, street musicians collecting change, pedestrians hurrying back and forth from work.

Julian seemed more at ease than he had in the past few days, leaning back in his seat, his hands casual on the wheel. Emma knew exactly how he felt. Here, in gear jacket and jeans, with Julian beside her and Cortana in the trunk, she felt like she belonged.

Emma had tried to bring up Mark, briefly, when they had first settled into the car. Julian had only shaken his head and said, "He's getting adjusted," and that was all. She sensed he didn't want to talk about Mark, and that was fine: She didn't know that she had any solutions to offer. And it was easy, so easy, to slip back into their normal joking banter.

"I think he was asking if I thought the killer was a Shadowhunter." Traffic was gathering as they reached the intersection of Sunset and Vine, and the car rolled slowly under the palm trees and neon. "I said no—it was obviously someone who knew magic, and I didn't think a Shadowhunter would hire a warlock to murder for them. Mostly we do our own murdering."

Emma giggled. "You told him Shadowhunters are DIY about their killing?"

"We're DIY about *everything*."

The traffic started up again; Emma glanced down, watching the play of muscle and tendon in Jules's hand as he shifted gears. The car slid forward, and Emma glanced out the window at the people in line at Grauman's Chinese Theatre. She wondered idly what they would think if they knew the two teenagers in the Toyota were actually demon hunters with a trunk full of crossbows, polearms, daggers, *katanas*, and throwing knives.

"Everything all right with Diana?" Emma asked.

"She wanted to talk about Ty." Julian's voice was even, but Emma saw him swallow. "He wants so badly to go to the Scholomance and study. They have access to the libraries of the Spiral Labyrinth, the Silent Brothers' archives—I mean, think of everything we don't know about runes and rituals, the mysteries and puzzles he could solve. But at the same time . . ."

"He'd be the youngest person there," said Emma. "That would

be hard on anyone. Ty's only ever been with us." She touched Julian's wrist, lightly. "I'm glad I never went to the Academy. And the Scholomance is supposed to be much harder. And lonelier. Some of the students have wound up failing out with—well, Clary called it nervous breakdowns. I think it's a mundane term."

Julian glanced down at the GPS and made a left turn, heading up toward the hills. "How often do you talk to Clary these days?"

"About once a month." Clary had been calling her to check on her ever since they'd first met in Idris when Emma was twelve. It was one of the few things Emma didn't talk about much with Jules: The conversations with Clary felt like something that belonged just to her.

"Is she still with Jace?"

Emma laughed, feeling her tension drain. Clary and Jace were an institution, a legend. They belonged together. "Who'd break up with *him*?"

"I might, if he was insufficiently attentive to my needs."

"Well, she doesn't talk about her love life to me. But yeah, they're still together. If they broke up I might have to stop believing in love entirely."

"I didn't know you *did* believe in love," said Jules, and paused, as if he realized what he'd said. "That came out wrong."

Emma was indignant. "Just because I wasn't in love with Cameron—"

"You weren't?" Traffic sped up; the car lurched forward. Julian struck the wheel with the heel of his palm. "Look, none of this is my business. Forget it. Forget I asked about Jace and Clary, or Simon and Isabelle—"

"You didn't ask about Simon and Isabelle."

"I didn't?" The side of his mouth quirked up. "Isabelle was my first crush, you know."

"Of course I know." She threw the cap of her water bottle at him. "It was so obvious! You were staring at her at the party after Aline and Helen's wedding."

He ducked the bottle cap. "I was not."

"You so were," she said. "Do we need to talk about what we're looking for at Wells's place?"

"I think we should play it by ear."

"'The quality of decision is like the well-timed swoop of a falcon, which enables it to strike and destroy its victim,'" said Emma.

Julian looked at her incredulously. "Was that a quote from *The Art of War?*"

"Maybe." Emma felt a happiness so intense it was almost sorrow: She was with Jules, they were joking, everything was the way it should be between *parabatai*. They had turned onto a series of residential streets: wide mansions twined with flowers rose above high hedges, cocooned behind sweeping driveways.

"Are you being pithy? You know how I feel about pithiness in my car," Julian said.

"It's not your car."

"Either way, we're here," Jules said, pulling the car up to the curb and killing the engine. It was twilight now, not quite full dark, and Emma could see Wells's house, looking like it had in the satellite photos on the computer: the peaks of the roof just rising over the massive wall that surrounded it, covered with draped trellises of bougainvillea.

Julian hit the button that raised the car windows. Emma looked over at him. "Just about dark. We worried about demonic activity?"

He checked the glove compartment. "Nothing on the Sensor, but just to be sure, let's rune up."

"Okay." Emma pushed up her sleeves, holding out her bare arms as Julian drew the pale-white, glimmering stele from his pocket. In the dark of the car, he leaned over, put the tip of the stele to her skin, and began to draw. Emma could feel his hair brush against her cheek and neck, and smell the faint scent of cloves that hung around him.

She looked down, and as the black lines of runes spread across her skin, Emma remembered what Cristina had said about Jules: *He has nice hands.* She wondered if she'd ever really looked at them before. Were they nice? They were Julian's hands. They were hands that painted and fought; they had never failed him. In that way they were beautiful.

"All right." Jules sat back, admiring his handiwork. Neat runes of precision and stealth, soundlessness and balance decorated her forearms. Emma drew down her sleeves and reached for her own stele.

He shivered when the stele touched his skin. It must be cold. "Sorry," Emma whispered, bracing her hand on his shoulder. She could feel the edge of his collarbone under her thumb, the ribbed cotton of his T-shirt soft beneath her touch; she tightened her grip, her fingertips sliding against the bare skin at the edge of his collar. He drew in a sharp breath.

She stopped. "Did I hurt you?"

He shook his head. She couldn't see his face. "I'm fine." He reached behind himself and unlocked the driver's side door; a second later he was out of the car and shrugging on his jacket.

Emma followed him. "But I didn't finish the Sure-Strike rune—"

He had moved around to the trunk and opened it. He took out his runed crossbow and handed her Cortana and its sheath.

"It's fine." He closed the trunk. He didn't seem bothered: same Julian, same calm smile. "Besides, I don't need it."

He raised the crossbow casually and shot. The bolt flew through the air and plunged directly into the security camera over the gate. It blew apart with a whine of shattered metal and a wisp of smoke.

"Show-off," Emma said, sheathing her sword.

"I'm *your* parabatai. I have to show off occasionally. Otherwise no one would understand why you keep me around." An elderly couple appeared from a driveway near them, walking an Alsatian. Emma had to fight the urge to conceal Cortana, though she knew the weapon was glamoured. To the mundanes walking by, she and Julian would look like ordinary teenagers, long sleeves concealing their runes. They passed around the corner of the road and out of sight.

"I keep you around because I need an audience for my witty remarks," she said as they reached the gates and Jules took out his stele to draw an Open rune.

The gate popped open. Julian turned sideways to slide through the opening. "What witty remarks?"

"Oh, you are going to pay for that," Emma muttered, following him. "I am incredibly witty."

Julian chuckled. They had come to a lined pathway that led up to a large stucco house with enormous arched front doors, two huge panes of glass on either side. The lights lining the path were on, but the house was dark and silent.

Emma sprang up the steps and peered in through one of the windows; she could see nothing but dark, smudged shapes. "No one home—oh!" She jumped back a step as something flung itself against the window: a lumpy, hair-covered ball. Slime slicked the glass. Emma was already crouching, about to pull a stiletto from her boot. "What is it?" She straightened. "A Raum demon? A—"

"I think it's a minipoodle," said Julian, the corner of his mouth twitching. "And I don't think it's armed," he added as she glanced down to stare accusingly at what was, yes, definitely a small dog, its face pressed to the glass. "I'm *almost* positive, in fact."

Emma hit him on the shoulder, then drew an Open rune on the door. There was the snapping click of the lock, and the door swung open.

The dog left off licking the window and rushed out, barking. It darted around them in a circle, then lunged toward a fenced area at the far end of the yard. Julian darted off after the canine.

Emma followed him through ankle-high grass. It was a nice garden, but nobody had taken real care of it. The plants were running wild, the flowered hedges overgrown. There was a pool, bordered by a waist-high ironwork fence, the gate hanging open. As Emma neared it, she could see that Julian was standing by the side of it, very still. It was the kind of pool that had LED lights in it, cycling through a rainbow of garish colors. Rows of pool chairs surrounded it, made of white metal with white cushions, dusted with fallen pine needles and blown jacaranda blossoms.

Emma slowed as she reached the water. The dog was crouched by the pool ladder, not barking but whimpering. At first Emma thought she was looking at a shadow on the water; then she realized it was a body. A dead woman in a white bikini, floating on the surface of the pool. She was facedown, long black hair drifting around her head, arms dangling at her sides. The purple glow from the pool lights made her skin look bruised.

"By the Angel, Jules . . . ," Emma breathed.

It wasn't as if Emma hadn't seen dead bodies before. She'd seen plenty. Mundanes, Shadowhunters, murdered children in the Hall of Accords. Still, there was something plaintive about this body: the woman was tiny, so skinny you could see the lines of her spinal column.

There was a splash of red against one of the pool chairs. Emma moved toward it, thinking it was blood, then realized it was a Valentino handbag made of bright red intaglio leather, slightly unzipped. A gold wallet had spilled out of it, and a pink phone.

She glanced at the phone, then picked up the wallet and flicked through it. "Her name's Ava Leigh," she said. "She is—she was—twenty-two. Home address listed as here. Must have been his girlfriend."

The dog whimpered again and lay down, his paws by the pool's edge. "He thinks she's drowning," Julian said. "He wants us to save her."

"We couldn't have," Emma said softly. "Look at her phone. None of the calls have been answered in two days. I think she's been dead at least that long. We couldn't have done anything, Jules."

She put the wallet back into the bag. She was reaching for the handles when she heard it: the click of a crossbow loading.

Without looking or thinking, she threw herself at Jules, knocking him down. They hit the Spanish tile hard as a bolt whistled by them and vanished into the hedges.

Julian kicked off against the ground and spun them over, rolling between two of the chairs. The phone Emma had been carrying flew out of her hand; she heard it hit the pool water with a splash and cursed silently to herself. Julian levered himself up, his hands gripping her shoulders; his eyes were wild, his body pressing hers into the ground. "Are you all right? Were you hit?"

"I wasn't—I'm fine—" she gasped. The dog was huddled by the fence, howling, as another bolt whistled down and struck the corpse in the pool. Ava's body flipped over, baring her swollen, drowning-blackened face to the night sky. One of her arms floated up, as if she were raising it to protect herself. With a brief flash of horror, Emma saw that her right hand was missing; not just missing, but looked as if it had been hacked away, the skin around her wrist ragged and bloodless in the chlorinated water.

Emma rolled out from under Julian and sprang to her feet. There was a figure standing on the roof of the house; she could see it only in outline. Tall, most likely masculine, dressed all in black, crossbow in hand. He raised it and took aim. Another bolt whistled by.

Rage settled over Emma, cold and hard. How dare he shoot at them, how dare he shoot at *Jules*? She took a running jump and cleared the pool. She hurtled over the gate and ran at the house, leaping up to seize hold of the wrought-iron bars covering the lower windows. She levered herself higher, aware that Julian was shouting at her to get down, ignoring where the metal bit into her palms. She swung herself up, then up again, pushing off from the wall to flip herself onto the roof.

The shingles crunched under her feet as she landed in a crouch. She looked up and caught a quick glimpse of the black-clad figure on the rooftop; he was backing away from her. His face was covered with a mask.

Emma unsheathed Cortana. The blade glittered long and wicked in the dusk light.

"What are you?" she demanded. "A vampire? Downworlder? Did you kill Ava Leigh?" She took a step forward; the strange figure backed away. He moved without alarm, very deliberately, which only angered Emma more. There was a dead girl in the pool below them, and Emma had arrived too late to save her. Her body was thrumming with the desire to do *something* to fix it.

Emma narrowed her eyes. "Listen up. I'm a Shadowhunter. You can either surrender to the authority of the Clave, or I'll bury this blade in your heart. Your choice."

He took a step toward her and for a moment Emma thought it had worked; he was actually giving up. Then he dived suddenly to the side. She lunged forward as he tumbled backward off the roof. He fell silently as a star.

Emma cursed and ran to the edge of the roof. There was nothing. Silence, darkness; no sign of anything or anyone. She could see the glimmer of the pool. She moved around the side and saw Julian bending down, one of his hands on the dog's head.

Trust Jules to try to comfort a puppy at a time like this. She braced herself and jumped—the image of the training room flashed behind her eyelids—landing in the overgrown grass with only a slight sting.

"Jules?" she said, coming closer. With a whimper the dog darted away, into the shadows. "He got away."

"Yeah?" He straightened up, sounding preoccupied. "What do you think he was doing here?"

"I don't know; I guessed vampire, but Nightshade keeps a pretty tight leash on them and—Jules?" She heard her voice skip upward an octave as she drew close enough to see that he had one hand pressed against his side. His black gear jacket was torn. "*Jules?* Are you okay?"

He drew his hand away from his side. His palm was a welter of blood, black under the blue LED lighting of the pool. "I'm fine," he said. He rose to his feet and took a step toward her—and stumbled. "It's fine."

Her heart flipped over. He was holding something in his bloody hand, and her insides went cold as she saw what it was. A short metal crossbow bolt, with a wide triangular head like an arrow, wet with blood. He must have pulled it from his side.

You were never, never supposed to pull an arrow out of your skin: It did more damage coming out than going in. Julian knew that.

"What did you do?" Emma whispered. Her mouth had gone dry.

Blood was leaking steadily from the tear in his jacket. "It was burning," he said. "Not like a normal arrow. Emma—"

He dropped to his knees. His expression was dazed, though he was clearly fighting it. "We need to get out of here," he said hoarsely. "The shooter might come back, alone or with more—"

His voice choked off and he fell backward, sprawling in the grass. Emma moved faster than she ever had in her life, leaping across the pool, but she still wasn't there in time to catch him before he hit the ground.

Clouds were gathering out over the ocean. The wind up on the roof was cool, the ocean acting like a giant air conditioner. Cristina could hear the roar and crash of the surf in the distance as she moved gingerly across the shingles. What was it about the Blackthorns and Emma that meant that ever since she'd come to Los Angeles she'd spent half her time on top of buildings?

Mark was sitting near one of the copper gutters, his legs dangling over the side. The wind blew his fair hair around his face. His hands were long and white and bare, bracing him against the roof tiles behind him.

He was holding one of the Institute's spare cell phones in his hand. It seemed incongruous—it *was* incongruous, the faerie boy with the long, tangled hair, the tapestry of stars behind him, and the phone in his hand. "I am so sorry, Helen," she heard him say, and the word echoed with such a depth of love and loneliness that she nearly turned away.

Leaving silently didn't seem to be an option, though. Mark had heard her approach: He turned slightly, and gestured for Cristina to remain.

She hovered uncertainly. It was Dru who had told her that she would find Mark on the roof, and the others had urged her to go up and see if he was all right. She had wondered if it was really her place, but Ty and Livvy had been absorbed in their translation job, and she'd sensed Dru was afraid of Mark's harsh words. And it wasn't as if Tavvy could be sent to fetch his brother down. So with some reluctance, Cristina had climbed the ladder to the roof.

Now that she was here, though, she felt an aching sympathy for the boy perched at the roof's edge. The look on his face as he spoke to Helen—she couldn't imagine what it must be like for him, to know there was only one other person in his family quite like him, who shared his blood and heritage, and to know she was separated from him by a cruel and unbreakable Law.

"And I, you, my sister," Mark said, and let the phone fall from his hand. It was an old-fashioned one, with a screen that flickered and went dark as the call disconnected.

He slid it into a pocket and looked over at Cristina, the clouds casting shadows on his face.

"If you have come to tell me I behaved ill, I already know it," he said.

"That's not why I came," she said, moving closer to him but not sitting down.

"But you agree," he said. "I behaved ill. I should not have spoken as I did to Julian, especially in front of the little ones."

Cristina spoke carefully. "I don't know Julian well. But I do believe he was worried about you, and that's why he didn't want you to go with them."

"I know that," Mark said, surprising her. "But do *you* know what it's like, to have your little brother worry about you as if you were the child?" He raked his fingers through his hair. "I thought, while I was gone, that Helen would be raising them. I never thought it would fall so much upon Julian's shoulders. I cannot tell if that is why he seems unknowable to me."

Cristina thought of Julian, of his quiet competence and careful smiles. She remembered saying to Emma in a joking way that perhaps she would fall in love with Julian when she met him. And he had been much more beautiful than she'd thought, than Emma's blurry photos or vague descriptions had led her to believe. But though she liked him, she doubted she could love him. Too much of him was hidden for that.

"A great deal of him is, I think, locked away," she said. "Have you seen the mural on the wall of his room? The one of the fairy tale? He is like that castle, I think, surrounded by thorns that he has grown to protect himself. But with time, you can cut those thorns away. I believe you will know your brother again."

"I don't know how much time I have," he said. "If we do not solve their puzzle, the Wild Hunt will reclaim me."

"Do you want them to?" Cristina asked softly.

He said nothing, only glanced up at the sky.

"Is that why you come up to the roof? Because from here you can see the Hunt if they go by?"

Mark was silent for a long time. Then he said, "I imagine sometimes I can hear them. That I can hear the sound of their hooves against the clouds."

She smiled. "I like the way you talk," she said. "It always sounds like poetry."

"I speak the way I was taught by the Folk. So many years under their tutelage." He turned his hands over and placed them on his knees. The insides of his wrists were marked by odd, long scars.

"How many years? Do you know?"

He shrugged. "Time is not measured there as it is measured here. I could not say."

"The years do not show on your face," she said quietly. "Sometimes you look as young as Julian and sometimes you look as the fey do—ageless."

Now he looked at her sideways. "You don't think I look like a Shadowhunter?"

"Do you want to?"

"I want to look like my family," he said. "I cannot have the Blackthorn coloring, but I can look as much like Nephilim as possible. Julian was right—if I wish to be part of the investigation, I cannot stand out."

Cristina held back from telling Mark that there was no world in which he didn't stand out. "I can make you look like a Shadowhunter. If you come downstairs with me."

He moved as noiselessly on the shingled roof as if he had the padded feet of a cat or as if he were wearing a Soundless rune. He stepped aside to let her lead the way downstairs. Even that was hushed, and when she brushed by him, his skin was cool as night air.

She led the way to his room; he had left the lights off, so she illuminated her witchlight and set it down by the bed. "That chair," she said, pointing. "Bring it into the middle of the room and sit down. I'll be right back."

He looked after her quizzically as she left the room. When she returned, carrying a damp comb, a towel, and a pair of scissors, he was seated in the chair, still with the same quizzical look. He didn't sit the way other teenage boys did, all sprawl and legs and arms. He sat the way kings did in drawings, upright but deliberate, as if the crown rested uneasily on his head.

"Are you going to cut my throat?" he asked as she came toward him with the towel and the sharp scissors gleaming.

"I'm going to cut your *hair*." She looped the towel around his neck and moved to stand behind him. His head tipped back to follow her movements as she took hold of his hair, running her fingers through it. It was the kind of hair that should have been curly but was weighed down by its own length and tangles.

"Hold still," she said.

"As my lady requests."

She ran the comb through his hair and began to cut, careful to keep the length even. As she snipped away the weight of his silvery-blond mane, it sprang free in adorable curls like Julian's. They twined up against the back of his neck as if they wanted to be close to him.

She remembered touching Diego's hair; it had been thick under her fingers, dark and textured. Mark's was fine, like corn silk. It fell like gleaming chaff, catching the witchlight.

"Tell me about the faerie Court," she said. "I've always heard stories. My mother told me some, and my uncle."

"We didn't see it much," he said, sounding very ordinary for a moment. "Gwyn and the Hunters aren't part of any Court. He keeps himself to himself. We joined the Courts and the gentry only on nights when there were revels. But those were—"

He was silent for so long she wondered if he had fallen asleep or was perhaps simply deathly bored.

"If you had been to one you would not forget it," he said. "Great sparkling caves or deserted copses in woodlands full of will-o'-the-wisp lights. There are still some parts of this world that are undiscovered by all but the Folk. There was dancing to wear your feet down, and there were beautiful boys and girls, and kisses were cheaper than wine but the wine was sweet and the fruit sweeter. And you would wake up in the morning and it would all be gone, but you could still hear the music in your head."

"I think I would find it very frightening." She moved around to stand in front of him. He looked up at her with his curious two-colored eyes and she felt a tremor run through her hand, one she'd never felt when she cut Diego's hair or his brother Jaime's or any of her little cousins'. Of course, they'd been twelve when she'd clipped their hair, showing off what her mother had taught her, so maybe it was different when you were older. "Everything so glamorous and beautiful. How can a human compare?"

He looked surprised. "But you would be lovely in the Court," he said. "They would turn leaves and flowers into jeweled crowns and sandals for you. You would sparkle and be admired. The Folk love nothing more than mortal beauty."

"Because it fades," she said.

"Yes," he admitted. "It is true that eventually you will become gray and bent and withered, and it is possible that hair will sprout from your chin. And there is also the issue of warts." He caught her glare. "But that time is a long time away," he added hastily.

Cristina snorted. "I thought faeries were meant to be charming." She slid a hand under his chin to steady his head as she snipped away the last unruly strands. That was different too; his skin was as smooth as hers, no hint of stubble or roughness. His eyes narrowed, their color thinning to a gleam as she set the scissors aside and cleared her throat. "There," she said. "Would you like to see?"

He straightened up in the chair. Cristina was bending down; their heads were on a level. "Lean closer," he said. "For years I have had no mirror; I have learned to make do. The eyes of another can be a mirror more effective than water. If you will look at me, I can see my reflection in yours."

*I have had to make do.* Whose eyes had he been looking into, all those years? Cristina wondered as she leaned forward. She didn't know why she did it, exactly; maybe it was the way his eyes stayed fixed on hers, as if he couldn't imagine anything more fascinating than looking at her. His gaze didn't stray, either, not to the V of her shirt or her bare legs or even her hands, as she opened her eyes wide and looked directly back at him.

"Beautiful," he said finally.

"Do you mean your haircut?" she asked, trying for a teasing voice, but it wobbled in the middle. Maybe she shouldn't have offered to so intimately touch a complete stranger, even if he did seem harmless, even if she hadn't meant anything by it—had she?

"No," he said on a soft exhale. She felt his breath warm on her neck, and his hand slid over hers. His was rough and calloused, scarred along the palm. Her heart gave an uneven leap in her chest just as Mark's bedroom door opened.

She nearly jumped away from him as Ty and Livvy appeared in the doorway. Livvy was holding her phone, and her eyes were wide and worried. "It's Emma," she said, lifting the phone. "She texted nine-one-one. We need to go meet them right away."

# 12

## STRONGER BY FAR

**Emma made a screeching right turn off Fairfax into a parking** lot down the street from Canter's Delicatessen. It belonged to a paint store that was closed now. She wheeled around to the back, where the lot was totally empty, and pulled the car to a jerking stop, making Jules swear.

She looked back at him, unbuckling her belt. He was pale, clutching his side. She couldn't see much, given the darkness inside the car and the black clothes he was wearing, but blood was leaking through his fingers in slow pulses. Her stomach went cold.

When he'd fallen at Wells's house, the first thing she'd done was sketch a healing rune on his skin. The second was get him to his feet and half-drag him, the weapons, and Ava's purse into the backseat of the car.

It was only after they'd driven a few blocks that he'd moaned and she'd looked back to realize he was still bleeding. She'd pulled over and put on another healing rune, and then another. That would work. It had to.

There were very few kinds of wounds that healing runes couldn't help. Those made by demon poisons, and those bad enough to kill you. She'd felt her brain hitch and freeze up at the thought of either of those possibilities and had gone immediately for her phone. She'd texted Livvy the first location she could think of that was familiar—they all knew and loved Canter's—and then driven straight for it as fast as she could.

She turned the car off with a jerk of her wrist and climbed into the backseat beside Jules. He was wedged into the corner, pale and sweating with obvious pain. "Okay," she said in a shaking voice. "You have to let me look at you."

He was biting his lip. The streetlights from Fairfax illuminated the backseat, but not enough for Emma to see him well. He reached down for the hem of his shirt—and hesitated.

She took her witchlight out of her pocket and lit it, filling the car with bright light. Jules's shirt was soaked with blood, and worse, the healing runes she'd drawn had vanished from his skin.

They weren't working.

"Jules," she said. "I have to call the Silent Brothers. They can help you. I *have* to."

His eyes screwed shut with pain. "You can't," he said. "You know we can't call the Silent Brothers. They report directly to the Clave."

"So we'll lie to them. Say it was a routine demon patrol. I'm calling," she said, and reached for her phone.

"No!" Julian said, forcefully enough to stop her. "Silent Brothers know when you're lying! They have the Mortal Sword, Emma. They'll find out about the investigation. About Mark—"

"You're not going to bleed to death in a car for Mark!"

"No," he said, looking at her. His eyes were eerily blue-green, the only deep color in the witch-lit interior of the car. "You're going to fix me."

Emma could feel it when Jules was hurt, like a splinter lodged under her skin. The physical pain didn't bother her—it was the terror, the only terror worse than her fear of the ocean. The fear of

Jules being hurt, of him dying. She would give up anything, sustain any wound, to prevent that from happening.

"Okay," she said. Her voice sounded dry and thin to her own ears. "Okay." She took a deep breath. "Hang on."

She unzipped her jacket, threw it aside. Leaned over the console between the seats to put her witchlight on the floorboard. Then she reached for Jules. The next few seconds were a blur of Jules's blood on her hands and his harsh breathing as she pulled him partly upright, wedging him against the back door. He didn't make a sound as she moved him, but she could see him biting his lip and the blood on his mouth and chin, and she felt as if her bones were popping inside her skin.

"Your jacket," she said through gritted teeth. "I have to cut it off."

He nodded, letting his head fall back. She reached for Cortana.

Despite the toughness of the material, the blade went through the gear jacket like a knife through paper. It fell away in pieces. Emma sliced down the front of his T-shirt and pulled it apart as if she were peeling open a fruit.

Emma had seen blood before, often, but this felt different. It was Julian's, and there seemed to be a lot of it. It was smeared up and down his chest and rib cage; she could see where the arrow had gone in and where the skin had torn when he'd yanked it out.

"Why did you pull the arrow out?" she demanded, pulling her sweater over her head. She had a tank top on under it. She patted his chest and side with the sweater, absorbing as much of the blood as she could.

Jules's breath was coming in harsh pants. "Because when someone—shoots you with an arrow—" he gasped, "your immediate response is not—'Thanks for the arrow, I think I'll keep it for a while.'"

"Good to know your sense of humor is intact."

"Like I said, it was burning," Julian said. "Not like a normal wound. Like there was something on the arrowhead, acid or something."

Emma had mopped away as much of the blood as she could. It was still welling from the puncture wound, running in thin streams down his stomach, gathering in the lines between his abdominal muscles. He had deep gaps above his hip bones, too, and his sides were hard and smooth to the touch.

She took a deep breath. "You're too skinny," she said as brightly as she could. "Too much coffee, not enough pancakes."

"I hope they put that on my tombstone." He gasped as she shifted forward, and she realized abruptly that she was squarely in Julian's lap, her knees around his hips. It was a bizarrely intimate position.

"I— Am I hurting you?" she asked.

He swallowed visibly. "Try with the *iratze* again."

"Fine," she said. "Grab the panic bar."

"The what?" He opened his eyes and peered at her.

"The plastic handle! Up there, above the window!" She pointed. "It's for grabbing on to when the car is going around curves."

"Are you sure? I always thought it was for hanging things on," he said. "Like dry cleaning."

"Julian, *now is not the time to be pedantic*. Grab the bar or I swear—"

"All right!" He reached up, grabbed hold of it, and winced. "I'm ready."

She nodded and set Cortana aside, reaching for her stele. Maybe her previous *iratzes* had been too fast, too sloppy. She'd always focused on the physical aspects of Shadowhunting, not the more mental and artistic ones: seeing through glamours, drawing runes.

She set the tip of it to his shoulder and drew, carefully and slowly. She had to brace herself with her hand against his body. She tried to press as lightly as she could, but she could feel him tense under her fingers. The skin on his shoulder was smooth under her touch, and she wanted to get closer to him, put her hand over the wound on his side and heal it with the sheer force of her will—

*Stop.* She had finished the *iratze.* She sat back, her hand clamped around the stele. Julian straightened, the ragged remnants of his shirt hanging off his shoulders. He took a deep breath, glancing down at himself—and the *iratze* faded back into his skin, like black ice melting, spreading, being absorbed by the sea.

He looked up at Emma. She could see her own reflection in his eyes: She looked wrecked, panicked, blood on her neck and her white tank top. "It hurts less," he whispered.

The wound pulsed again; blood slid down the side of his rib cage, staining his leather belt and the waistband of his jeans. She put her hands on his bare skin, panic rising up inside her. His skin felt hot, too hot. Fever hot.

"You're lying," she said. "Jules. Enough. I'm going to get help—"

She moved to climb off him, but his hand shot out and clamped over her wrist. "Em," he said. "Emma, look at me."

She looked. There was a little blood on his cheek and his hair hung in sweaty dark curls, but otherwise he just looked like Jules, like he always did. His left hand was pressed to his side, but his right came up, his fingers curling around the back of her neck. "Em," he said again, his eyes wide and dark blue in the dim light. "Did you kiss Mark the other night?"

"What?" Emma stared. "Okay, you've *definitely* lost too much blood."

He shifted minutely under her, keeping his hand where it was, gentle, tickling the fine hairs at the nape of her neck. "I saw the way you looked at him," he said. "Outside Poseidon's."

"If you're worried about Mark's well-being, you shouldn't be. He's a mess. I know that. I don't think he needs to be more confused."

"It wasn't that. I wasn't worried about Mark." He closed his eyes, as if he were counting silently inside his head. When he opened them again his pupils were wide black circles sketched onto his irises. "Maybe it should have been that. But it wasn't."

Was he actually hallucinating? Emma thought in a panic. It wasn't like him to ramble like this, to make no sense at all. "I have to call the Silent Brothers," she said. "I don't care if you hate me forever or the investigation gets canceled—"

"Please," he said, desperation clear in his voice. "Just—just one more try."

"One more?" she echoed.

"You'll fix this. You'll fix *me*, because we're *parabatai*. We're forever. I said that to you once, do you remember?"

She nodded warily, hand on the phone.

"And the strength of a rune your *parabatai* gives you is special. Whatever was on that arrowhead was meant to prevent healing magic, but Emma, you can do it. You can heal me. We're *parabatai* and that means the things we can do together are . . . extraordinary."

There was blood on her jeans now, blood on her hands and her tank top, and he was still bleeding, the wound still open, an incongruous tear in the smooth skin all around it.

"Try," Jules said in a dry whisper. "For me, try?"

His voice went up on the question, and in it she heard the voice of the boy he had been once, remembered him smaller, skinnier, younger, standing upright before his siblings in the Great Hall in Alicante as his father advanced on him with his blade unsheathed.

And she remembered what Julian had done then. Done to protect her, to protect all of them, because he always would do everything to protect them.

She took her hand off the phone and gripped the stele, so tightly she felt it dig into her damp palm. "Look at me, Jules," she said, and he met her eyes with his. She placed the stele against his skin, and for a moment she held still, just breathing, breathing and remembering.

*Julian.* A presence in her life for as long as she could recall, splashing water at each other in the ocean, digging in the sand together, him putting his hand over hers and them marveling at the difference in the shape and length of their fingers. Julian singing, terribly and off-key, while he drove, his fingers in her hair carefully freeing a trapped leaf, his hands catching her in the training room when she fell, and fell, and fell. The first time after their *parabatai* ceremony when she'd smashed her hand into a wall in rage at not being able to get a sword maneuver right, and he'd come up to her, taken her still-shaking body in his arms, and said, "Emma, Emma, don't hurt yourself. When you do, I feel it too."

Something in her chest seemed to split and crack; she marveled that it wasn't audible. Energy raced along her veins and the stele moved in her hand, tracing the graceful outline of a healing rune across Julian's chest. She heard him gasp, his eyes flying open. His hand slid down her back and he pressed her against him, his teeth gritted.

"Don't *stop*," he said.

Emma couldn't have stopped if she'd wanted to. The stele seemed to be moving of its own accord; she was blinded with memories, a kaleidoscope of them, all of Julian. Sun in her eyes and Julian asleep on the beach in an old T-shirt and her not wanting to wake him, but he'd woken anyway when the sun went down and looked for her, immediately, not smiling till his eyes found her and he knew she was there. Falling asleep talking and waking up with their hands interlocked; they'd been children in the dark together once but now they were something else, something intimate and powerful, something Emma felt she was touching only the very edge of as she finished the rune and the stele fell from her fingers.

"Oh," she said softly. The rune seemed lit from within by a soft glow. Julian was breathing hard, his stomach muscles rising and falling quickly, but the bleeding had stopped. The wound was closing, sealing itself up like an envelope. "Does it—does it hurt?"

A smile was spreading across Julian's face. His hand was still on Emma's hip, gripping hard; he must have forgotten. "No," he said. His voice was hushed, soft, as if he were speaking inside a church. "You did it; you fixed it." He was looking at her like she was a rare miracle. "Emma, my God, Emma."

Emma slumped against his shoulder as the tension drained out of her. She let her head rest there as his arms circled her body.

"It's all right." He slid his hands down her back, clearly able to tell that she was shaking. "Everything's fine, I'm fine."

"Jules," she whispered. His face was close to hers; she could see the light freckles across his cheekbones, under the smears of blood. Could feel his body against hers, vividly alive, the slamming of his heart in his rib cage, the heat of his skin, as if on fire from the power of the *iratze*. Her own heart was beating hard as her hands found his shoulders—

The front door of the car flew open. Light streamed in and Emma jerked away from Julian as Livvy clambered into the front seat.

Livvy was holding a witchlight in her right hand, and its irregular beams illuminated the strange scene in the back of the Toyota: Emma in her bloody clothes; Julian, shirtless, jammed against the rear door. His hands fell away from Emma.

"Is everything okay?" Livvy demanded. She was gripping her phone in one hand; she must have been waiting for more messages, Emma thought guiltily. "You texted nine-one-one—"

"Everything's fine." Emma slid across the bench seat, away from Jules.

He struggled upright, looking down dubiously at his shredded shirt. "Someone shot me with a crossbow bolt. The *iratzes* weren't working."

"Well, you look fine now." Livvy eyed him, puzzled. "Bloody, but . . ."

"A little *parabatai* magic," said Jules. "They weren't working, then they were. Sorry to scare you."

"It looks like a mad science lab back here." There was relief on Livvy's face. "Who shot you, anyway?"

"It's a long story," said Jules. "How did you get here? *You* didn't drive, did you?"

Another head suddenly appeared beside Livvy's. Mark, his blond hair haloed in the witchlight. "I drove," he announced. "Upon a faerie steed."

"What? But—but your faerie steed was shredded by demons!"

"There are as many faerie steeds as there are riders," Mark said, looking pleased to be mysterious. "I did not say it was *my* faerie steed. Just *a* faerie steed." Mark disappeared from his side of the car. Before Emma could determine where he'd gone, the door behind Julian flew open. Mark leaned in, picked up his younger brother bodily, and lifted him out of the car.

"What—?" Emma seized up her stele and scrambled out after them.

There were two more figures standing on the asphalt of the parking lot—Cristina and Ty, illuminated by the lights of a motorcycle. In fact, the whole motorcycle was glowing. It wasn't Mark's: It was black, with a painted design of horns on the chassis.

"Jules?" Ty looked blanched and frightened as Julian pulled free of Mark's grip, yanking down the tattered remains of his shirt.

Cristina hurried over to Emma as Julian turned to his younger brother. "Ty, everything's all right," he said. "I'm fine."

"But you're covered in blood," said Ty. He wasn't looking directly at Julian, but Emma couldn't help wondering if he was remembering—remembering the Dark War, and the blood and the dying all around him. "People have only so much blood they can lose before—"

"I'll get some blood-replacement runes," said Julian. "Remember, Ty, we're Shadowhunters. We can handle a lot."

"You're covered in blood too," Cristina murmured to Emma, shrugging off her own jacket. She slung it around Emma's shoulders, covering her bloody tank. She brushed her hands through Emma's hair, looking at her worriedly. "You sure you're not hurt?"

"Julian's blood," Emma whispered, and Cristina made a murmuring noise and pulled Emma into a hug. She patted Emma's back and Emma hung on to her for dear life and decided there and then that if anyone ever tried to hurt Cristina she would grind them to a pulp and make amusing sand castles out of the remains.

Livvy had moved to stand next to Ty and was holding his hand, murmuring to him that the blood was just blood, Julian wasn't hurt, everything was fine. Ty was breathing quickly, his hand opening and closing over Livvy's.

"Here." Mark shrugged out of his blue T-shirt. He was wearing another T-shirt under it, this one gray. Julian blinked at him. "Proper vestments." He offered it to his brother.

"Why are you wearing a T-shirt under your other T-shirt?" Livvy asked, temporarily diverted.

"In case one of them is stolen," Mark said, as if this were entirely normal. Everyone paused to stare at him, even Julian, who had stripped off the rags of his shirt and covered himself with Mark's.

"Thanks," Julian said, pulling Mark's shirt down over his belt. He tossed the scraps of his old shirt on top of a Dumpster. Mark seemed pleased—and, Emma realized belatedly, looked different. His hair was no longer hanging past his shoulders, but was cut short—or shorter, curling around his ears. It made him look both younger and more modern, less incongruous in his jeans and boots.

More like a Shadowhunter.

Mark looked back. She could still see the wind in his eyes, and the stars, and vast fields of empty clouds. Wildness and freedom. She wondered how deep his transformation back into a Shadowhunter ran. How deep it would ever run.

She put a hand to her head. "I feel dizzy."

"You need food." It was Livvy, grabbing her hand. "We all do. Nobody's eaten tonight, and Jules, you're forbidden from cooking. Let's go to Canter's, grab some dinner, and figure out what to do next."

Everything inside Canter's was yellow. The walls were yellow, the booths were yellow, and most of the food was a shade of yellow. Not that Emma minded; she'd been coming to Canter's since she was four years old with her parents to eat their chocolate-chip pancakes and challah French toast.

They piled into a corner booth and for a few minutes everything was absolutely ordinary: The waitress, a tall woman with gray hair, came by to dump a pile of laminated menus on their table; Livvy and Ty shared one, and Cristina asked Emma in a whisper what *matzo brei* was. They were scrunched together in the booth, and Emma found herself pressed up against Julian's side. He still felt hot against her, as if the *iratze* hadn't worked its way out of his system yet.

Her skin still felt supersensitized too, as if she would jump or scream the moment someone touched her. She nearly did scream when the waitress returned to get their orders. She just stared until Julian ordered waffles and hot chocolate for her and handed the menu back hastily, looking at her worriedly.

*A-R-E Y-O-U A-L-L R-I-G-H-T?* he scribbled on her back.

She nodded, reaching for her plastic glass of ice water, just as Mark smiled at the waitress and ordered a plate of strawberries.

The waitress, whose name tag said JEAN, blinked. "We don't have that on the menu."

"But you do have strawberries on the menu," said Mark. "And I have seen plates being carried to and fro. So it stands to reason that the strawberries could be placed upon a plate and brought to me."

Jean stared.

"He has a point," said Ty. "Strawberries are offered as a topping on several dishes. Surely you could separate them out."

"A plate of strawberries," Jean repeated.

"I would take them in a bowl," said Mark with a winning gaze. "It has been many years since I have eaten freely at my choice, fair one, and a plate of strawberries is all that I desire."

Jean looked dazed. "Right," she said, and disappeared with the menus.

"Mark," said Julian. "Was that necessary?"

"Was what necessary?"

"You don't *have* to sound like a medieval faerie poem," Julian said. "You sound perfectly normal half the time. Maybe we should discuss keeping a low profile."

"I cannot help it," Mark said with a small smile. "It's something about mundanes. . . ."

"You need to act more like a normal human being," said Jules. "When we're out in public."

"He doesn't need to act normal," said Ty sharply.

"He bumped into a pay phone and said, 'Excuse me, miss,' on our way in," said Julian.

"It's polite to apologize," said Mark with the same small smile.

"Not to inanimate objects."

"All right, enough," said Emma. She filled them in quickly on the events at Stanley Wells's house, including Ava's body and the mysterious figure on the roof.

"So she was dead, but it was nothing like the other murders?" Livvy asked with a frown. "It seems unrelated—no markings, body dumped in a pool outside her own house, not at a ley line. . . ."

"What about the guy on the roof?" Cristina said. "Do you think he's the killer?"

"Doubt it," said Emma. "He had a crossbow, and none of them

have been killed with crossbows. But he hurt Jules, so when we track him down, I'm going to chop him up and feed him to my fish."

"You don't have fish," Julian said.

"Well, I'm going to buy some," said Emma. "I'm going to buy goldfish and feed them blood until they acquire a taste for human flesh."

"That's disgusting," said Livvy. "Does this mean we still need to return to Wells's house and search it?"

"As long as we check the roof first," said Emma.

"We can't," Ty said. He held up his phone. "I was looking at the news. Someone called in the body. The mundane police are crawling all over the place. We won't be able to get anywhere near it for a few days at least."

Emma blew out an exasperated breath. "Well," she said, "at least we have this," and she reached behind her to grab Ava's bag. She upended it on the table and the contents rattled out: wallet, makeup case, lip balm, mirror, hairbrush, and something flat, golden, and shiny.

"No phone," Ty observed, a line of annoyance gathering between his brows. Emma didn't blame him. He could have done a lot with the phone. Too bad; it was at the bottom of Wells's pool.

"What's this?" Livvy picked up the shining square. It was blank.

"Not sure." Emma flicked through the wallet. Credit cards, driver's license, about eleven dollars in cash that made her feel a little queasy. Taking evidence was one thing; taking cash was another. Not that they could have returned it to Ava.

"No photos or anything?" Julian asked, looking over her shoulder.

"I don't think people keep photos in their wallets except in movies," Emma said. "Not since iPhones."

"Speaking of movies." Livvy furrowed her brow, looking

briefly—as she did sometimes—like Ty. "This thing looks like the Golden Ticket. You know, from *Charlie and the Chocolate Factory*." She waved the shining piece of laminated paper.

"Let me see it." Cristina held out her hand. Livvy gave it to her as the waitress returned with their food: grilled cheese for Ty, a turkey sandwich for Cristina, a BLT for Julian, waffles for Emma and Livvy, and Mark's plate of strawberries.

Cristina took out her stele and scribbled, humming, on a corner of the gold paper. Mark, looking beatific, took the dispenser of maple syrup off the table and upended it over his strawberries. He picked one up and put it in his mouth, stem and all. Julian stared at him.

"What?" Mark said. "This is a perfectly normal thing to eat."

"Sure it is," said Julian. "If you're a hummingbird."

Mark raised an eyebrow. "Look," Cristina said, and pushed the golden paper toward the middle of the table. It was no longer blank. Instead it featured the shimmering photo of a building, and beside it words in block letters.

*THE FOLLOWERS OF THE GUARDIAN*

*INVITE YOU TO THE LOTTERY*

*THIS MONTH'S PERFORMANCE: AUGUST 11, 7 P.M.*

*THE MIDNIGHT THEATER*

*This ticket admits one group. Semiformal attire.*

"*The Lottery?*" Julian echoed. "That's the name of a famous horror story. Did they make it into a play or something?"

"It doesn't sound like a play," said Livvy. "It sounds creepy."

"It could be a creepy play," said Ty.

"It was a creepy story." Julian picked up the ticket. There was paint under his fingernails, shimmering small crescents of blue.

"And the creepiest thing about this is that this theater is shut down. I know the place; it's up past Highland Park. It's been been shut down for years."

"Sixteen years," said Ty. He had mastered the art of using his phone one-handed and was squinting at the screen. "Shut down after a fire and never rebuilt."

"I've driven past it," Emma said. "It's all boarded up, isn't it?"

Julian nodded. "I painted it once. I was painting abandoned buildings, places like the Murphy Ranch, closed businesses. I remember that one. It had a ghostly feel."

"It's interesting," Mark said. "But does it have anything to do with the investigation? The murders?"

Everyone looked mildly surprised that Mark had asked something so practical. "I think it might," Emma said. "I was at the Shadow Market last week—"

"I wish you'd quit going to the Shadow Market," Julian muttered. "It's dangerous there—"

"Oh, NO," Emma said. "Not *danger*, Mr. I-Just-Almost-Bled-Out-in-My-Car."

Julian sighed and reached for his soda. "I can't believe I ever complained about 'Jules' as a nickname."

"Maybe we should talk about the Shadow Market," said Cristina hastily. "It is where Emma first heard information about the murders."

"Well, you can imagine how happy the Marketers were to see me and Cameron—"

"You went with *Cameron*?" Julian said.

Livvy held up a hand. "In Emma's defense, Cameron's annoying, but he's hot." Julian gave her a look. "I mean, if you like guys who look like a redheaded Captain America, which I . . . don't?"

"Captain America is definitely the most handsome Avenger," said Cristina. "But I like the Hulk. I would like to heal his broken heart."

"We're *Nephilim*," said Julian. "We're not even supposed to know about the Avengers. Besides," he added, "Iron Man is obviously the best-looking."

"Can I finish my story?" Emma demanded. "I was at the Market with Cameron, and I remember now, I saw a booth that had a placard up that said something like 'Sign Up for the Lottery.' So I think it's something supernatural, not experimental theater or whatever."

"I have no idea who the Avengers are," observed Mark, who had finished his strawberries and was eating sugar out of a packet. Ty looked gratified—he had no time for superheroes. "But I agree with you. This is a lead. Someone murdered Stanley Wells, and now his girlfriend is dead too. Even if it is in a completely different way."

"I think we can all agree it can't be a coincidence," said Emma. "Them both dying."

"I don't think it is," said Mark. "But she could have been killed because she knew something, not because she was a sacrifice like he was or part of the same ritual. Death breeds death, after all." He looked thoughtful. "She was invited to this Lottery performance. She thought it was important enough to carry the ticket around with her. I think it could be a thread to follow."

"Or it could be nothing," said Jules.

"We don't have much else to investigate," pointed out Emma.

"We do, actually," said Jules. "We've still got your photos from the inside of the cave at the convergence. And now we have whoever was at Wells's house and shot at me—we've still got my gear jacket with whatever poison he used on it. Maybe Malcolm could look into that, find out if it's associated with a particular demon or warlock who might sell it."

"Great," Emma said. "We can do both. August eleventh is tomorrow night." She frowned at the ticket. "Oh God, semiformal. Fancy. I don't think I have any dresses that fancy, and Mark will need a suit. . . ."

"Mark doesn't have to go," Julian said quickly. "He can stay at the Institute."

"No," Mark said. His voice was calm, but his eyes sparked. "I will not. I was brought here to help you investigate these murders, and that is what I will do."

Julian sat back. "Not if we can't rune you. It's not safe."

"I have protected myself without runes for many years. If I do not go with you, then those in Faerie who sent me here will learn of it, and they will not be pleased. The punishment will be severe."

"Oh, let him go," Livvy said, looking anxious. "Jules—"

Julian touched the edge of his shirt, the gesture half-unconscious. "How will they know to punish you," he said, "if you don't tell them?"

"You think it is easy to lie when you have grown up around people who do not lie?" Mark said, cheeks flushing with anger. "And do you think they do not have their own ways to ferret out lies when humans tell them?"

"You're human," Julian said hotly. "You're not one of them, you don't act like one of them—"

Mark flung himself up from the table and stalked across the room.

"What's he doing?" Emma stared. Mark had made his way to a neighboring table of pierced and tattooed mundane girls who looked like they'd just come from a nightclub and were giggling madly as he talked to them.

"By the Angel." Julian threw down some money on the table and scrambled to his feet, ducking out of the booth. Emma scraped everything back into Ava's handbag and hastily followed Julian, the others at her heels.

"Might I make free with your lettuce, my lady?" Mark was saying to a girl with bright pink hair and a pile of salad on her plate. She pushed it toward him, grinning.

"You're gorgeous," she said. "Even with the fake elf ears. Forget the lettuce, you can make free with my—"

"All right, you've made your point, enough." Julian took Mark—who was cheerfully eating a baby carrot—by the wrist and tried to draw him toward the door. "Sorry, ladies," he said as a chorus of protests rose.

The girl with pink hair stood up. "If he wants to stay, he can stay," she said. "Who are you, anyway?"

"I'm his brother," Julian said.

"Boy, do you two not look alike," she said in a way that made Emma bristle. She'd called Mark gorgeous—Julian was just as gorgeous, just in a quieter, less flashy way. He didn't have Mark's sharp cheekbones or faerie charm, but he had luminous eyes and a beautiful mouth that—

She goggled at herself. What was *wrong* with her? What was wrong with her *thoughts*?

Livvy made an exasperated noise, stomped forward, and seized Mark by the back of the shirt. "You don't want him," she said to the pink-haired girl. "He has syphilis."

The girl stared. "*Syphilis?*"

"Five percent of people in America have it," said Ty helpfully.

"I do not have syphilis," Mark said angrily. "There are no sexually transmitted diseases in Faerieland!"

The mundane girls fell instantly silent.

"Sorry," Jules said. "You know how syphilis is. Attacks the brain." The table of girls were open-mouthed as Livvy hauled Mark by his shirt through the restaurant and into the parking lot, the rest of them following.

The moment they were outside and the door had closed behind them, Emma burst out laughing. She leaned against Cristina, who was also giggling, as Livvy let go of Mark and smoothed down her skirt, looking unruffled. "Sorry," Emma said. "It's just—*syphilis?*"

"Ty was reading about it today," said Livvy.

Julian, who had been trying to hide a smile, looked over at Ty. "Why have you been reading about syphilis?"

Ty shrugged. "Research."

"Was that really necessary?" Mark demanded. "I was merely making conversation. I thought I would practice my gentry speech on them."

"You were being ridiculous on purpose," said Emma. "I'm beginning to get the feeling you think faeries sound silly."

"I did at first," said Mark candidly. "Then you get used to it. Now . . . Now I don't know what to think." He sounded a little lost.

"We're not supposed to talk to mundanes," Julian said, his smile vanishing. "It's—it's basic, Mark. One of the first things we learn. *Especially* not about things like Faerieland."

"I spoke to those mundanes, and no one exploded or caught on fire," said Mark. "No doom came down upon us. They thought I was wearing a costume." He ducked his head, then looked up at Julian. "You are right that I will stand out, but people see what they want to see."

"Maybe the rules about not going out in battle without runes are stupid rules," said Ty, and Emma thought of the way Mark had spoken to Ty in the training room. *Now we both have hurt hands.*

"Maybe a lot of the rules are stupid rules," said Julian, and there was an edge of bitterness to his voice that surprised Emma. "Maybe we just have to follow them anyway. Maybe that's what makes us Shadowhunters."

Livvy looked puzzled. "Having to follow stupid rules makes us Shadowhunters?"

"Not the rules," said Julian. "The penalty for breaking them."

"The penalty for breaking the rules of Faerie are just as severe, if not more so," said Mark. "You must trust me on this, Julian. If they think I am not part of the investigation, they will punish not just me, but also all of you. They do not require me to tell them. They will *know*." His eyes burned. "You understand me?"

"I understand, Mark. And I trust you." Julian smiled at his brother, then, unexpectedly, that smile that was all the more bright for its unpredictability. "Anyway. Everyone into the car, okay? We're heading back."

"I must return with the steed," said Mark. "I cannot leave him— it—here. If it were lost, the Wild Hunt would take it amiss."

"Fine," said Julian. "Take it back alone. Ty and Livvy aren't get- ting onto it again, understood? Too dangerous."

Livvy looked disappointed, Ty relieved. Mark nodded almost imperceptibly.

"I'll go with Mark," Cristina said suddenly. Emma saw Mark's face light up in a way that surprised her.

"I shall fetch the steed," Mark said. "I find I desire to fly."

"And go the speed limit!" Julian yelled as Mark disappeared around the side of the building.

"It's the sky, Julian," said Emma. "There isn't really a speed limit."

"I know," he said, and smiled. It was the smile Emma loved, the one she felt like was just for her, the one that said that although life often forced him to be serious, Julian wasn't actually serious by nature. She wanted to hug him suddenly or touch his shoulder, so badly that she forced her hands down and clasped them together. She looked down at her fingers; for some reason she had inter- twined them, as if they made a cage that would hold her feelings in.

The moon was high and full in the sky when Mark brought the motorcycle to a gentle stop in the sand behind the Institute.

The trip into the city had been all panic, Livvy gripping on to Cristina's belt with small, worried hands, Ty telling Mark not to go too fast, the freeway disappearing under their feet. They'd nearly crashed into the Dumpster in the parking lot.

The way back was quiet, Cristina holding Mark lightly around the waist, thinking about how close they seemed to be flying to the clouds. The city below them was an interlocking pattern of colored lights. Cristina had always hated amusement park rides and airplane flights, but this was like neither of those: She felt a part of the air, buoyed up by it like a small craft on the water.

Mark slid off the cycle and held out his hand to help her down after him. She took it, her eyes still full of the sight of the Santa Monica Pier below them, the bright lights of the turning Ferris wheel. She'd never felt so far away from her mother, from the Institute in Mexico City, from the Rosaleses.

She liked it.

"My lady," he said as her feet touched the sand.

She felt her lips curl up. "That seems so formal."

"The Courts are nothing if not formal," he agreed. "Thank you for coming back with me. You didn't have to."

"You seemed like maybe you didn't want to be alone," Cristina said. The soft wind was blowing off the desert, moving the sand, lifting his newly cut hair away from his face. Short now, it looked like a halo, so pale blond as to be almost silver.

"You see a great deal." His eyes studied her face. She wondered what he had looked like when both of his eyes had been Blackthorn eyes, blue-green as the sea. She wondered if the strangeness of his eyes, now, added to his beauty.

"When no one you know tells the truth, you learn to see under the surface," she said, and thought of her mother and the yellow petals of roses.

"Yes," he said. "But then, I come from a place where everyone tells the truth, no matter how dreadful."

"Is that something you miss about Faerie?" Cristina asked. "That there were no lies there?"

"How did you know I miss Faerie?"

"Your heart is not settled here," said Cristina. "And I think it is more than just familiarity that draws you back. You spoke of feeling free there—but then you also said that they cut runes into your back. I am trying to understand how that can be something you could miss."

"That was the Unseelie Court, not the Hunt," said Mark. "And I cannot speak of what I miss. I cannot speak of the Hunt, not truly. It is forbidden."

"That is terrible. How can you choose if you cannot speak of your choice?"

"The world is terrible," said Mark tonelessly. "And some are drawn down into it and drown there, and some rise above and carry others with them. But not very many. Not everyone can be Julian."

"Julian?" Cristina was startled. "But I thought perhaps you didn't even like him. I thought—"

"You thought?" He arched his silvery eyebrows.

"I thought you didn't like any of us," she said sheepishly. It seemed a foolish thing to say, but his face softened. He reached to take her hand, brushing his own fingers along her palm. A shiver raced up her arm—the touch of his hand was like an electric current.

"I like you," he said. "Cristina Mendoza Rosales. I like you very much."

He leaned down toward her. His eyes filled her vision, blue and gold—

"Mark Blackthorn." The voice that spoke his name was sharp, clipped. Both Cristina and Mark whirled around.

The tall faerie warrior who had brought Mark to the Institute stood in front of them, as if he had simply evolved out of the black-and-white sand and sky. He looked black and white himself, his hair the color of ink, curling darkly against his temples. His silver eye glowed in the moonlight; his black eye looked pupil-less. He wore a gray tunic and trousers, and daggers at his belt. He was as inhumanly lovely as a statue.

"Kieran," said Mark, a sort of half-shocked exhale. "But I—"

"Should have expected me." Kieran stalked forward. "You asked to borrow my steed; I lent it. The longer I go without it, the more chary Gwyn will grow. Did you hope to raise his suspicions?"

"I intended to return it," Mark said, his voice low.

"Did you?" Kieran crossed his arms over his chest.

"Cristina, go inside," said Mark. He had dropped his hand and was looking at Kieran, not at her, his expression fixed.

"Mark—"

"Please," he said. "This is—if you respect my privacy, please, go inside."

She hesitated. But his expression was clear. He knew what he was asking. She turned and went in through the Institute's back door, letting it bang loudly shut behind her.

The stairs loomed up in front of her, but she couldn't climb them. She barely knew Mark Blackthorn. But as she went to put her foot on the first step, she thought of the scars on his back. Of the way he had curled into a ball in his bedroom that first day, the way he had accused Julian of being a dream or a nightmare sent to haunt him by the Wild Hunt.

She didn't believe in the Cold Peace, had never believed in it, but Mark's pain had torn away at her beliefs. Perhaps the faeries truly were that cruel. Perhaps there really was no good in them, no honor. And if that was the case, how could she leave Mark out there, alone, with one of them?

She whirled around and pushed the door open—and froze.

It took a moment for her gaze to find them, but when it did, Mark and Kieran seemed to leap out at her like the images from a lighted screen. They stood in a patch of moonlight at the edge of the lot, Mark's back against one of the scrub oak trees. Kieran was leaning against him, pinning him to the tree, and they were kissing.

Cristina hesitated a moment, blood rising into her face, but it was clear Mark wasn't being touched against his will. Mark's hands were tangled in Kieran's hair, and he was kissing him as fiercely as if he were starving. Their bodies were pressed together tightly; nevertheless, Kieran clutched at Mark's waist, his hands moving restlessly, desperately, as if he could pull Mark closer still. They slid up, pushing Mark's jacket off his shoulders, stroking the skin at the edge of his collar. He made a low keening sound, like a cry of grief, deep in his throat, and broke away.

He was staring at Mark, his gaze as hungry as it was hopeless. Never had a faerie looked so human to Cristina as Kieran did then. Mark looked back at him, eyes wide, shining in the moonlight. A shared look of love and longing and terrible sadness. It was too much. It had already been too much: Cristina knew she shouldn't have been watching them but she hadn't been able to stop, mingled shock and fascination rooting her to the spot.

And desire. There was desire, too. Whether for Mark, or for both of them, or just for the idea of wanting someone so much, she wasn't sure. She moved back, her heart pounding, about to pull the door shut after her—

And the whole parking lot lit up like a stadium as a car rounded the corner and turned into it. Music blared out the windows; Cristina could hear Emma's and Julian's voices.

Her gaze darted back toward Mark and Kieran, but Kieran had vanished, a shadow into shadows. Mark was bending down to pick up his jacket as Emma and the others piled out of the car.

Cristina pulled the door shut. Through it she heard Emma ask Mark where she was, and Mark say that she had gone inside. He sounded casual, calm, as if nothing had happened.

But everything had happened.

She had wondered, when he'd looked in her eyes and said that he'd had to make do without mirrors in the Wild Hunt, whose eyes he'd been looking into for all those years.

Now she knew.

# The Wild Hunt, Some Years Ago

*Mark Blackthorn came to the Wild Hunt when he was sixteen years old, and not because he wanted to.*

*He remembered only darkness after he had been taken from the Institute that was his home, before he woke in underground caverns, amid lichen and dripping moss. A massive man with eyes of two different colors was standing over him, carrying a horned helmet.*

*Mark recognized him, of course. You couldn't be a Shadowhunter and not know about the Wild Hunt. You couldn't be half-faerie and not have read about Gwyn the Hunter, who had led the hunt for centuries. He wore a long blade of hammered metal at his waist, blackened and twisted as if it had been through many fires. "Mark Blackthorn," he said, "you are with the Hunt now, for your family is dead. We are your blood kin now." And drawing the sword, he sliced across his palm until he drew blood, and dripped it into water for Mark to drink.*

*In the years to come Mark would see others come to the Hunt, and Gwyn say the same thing to them, and watch them drink his blood. And he would watch their eyes change, splintering into two different colors as if to symbolize the division of their souls.*

Gwyn believed a new recruit had to be broken down to be built back up again as a Hunter, someone who could ride through the night without sleep, someone who could suffer hunger that was close to starvation and endure pain that would break a mundane. And he believed their loyalty must be unswerving. They could choose no one over the Hunt.

Mark gave his loyalty to Gwyn, and his service, but he did not make friends among the Wild Hunt. They were not Shadowhunters, and he was a Shadowhunter. The others were all of the faerie Courts, pressed into service with the Hunt as punishment. They did not like the fact that he was Nephilim, and he felt their scorn and scorned them in turn.

He rode through the nights alone, on a silver mare given to him by Gwyn. Gwyn seemed, perversely, to like him, perhaps to spite the others of the Hunt. He taught Mark to navigate by the stars and to listen for the sounds of a battle that might echo through hundreds, even thousands of miles: cries of anger and the shouts of the dying. They would ride to the field of battle and, invisible to mundane eyes, divest the dead bodies of precious things. Most of them were paid in tribute to the Seelie and Unseelie Courts, but some Gwyn kept for himself.

Mark slept alone, every night, on the cold ground, wrapped in a blanket, a stone for his pillow. When it was cold, he shivered, and dreamed of runes that would warm him, of the hot blaze of seraph blades. In his pocket he kept the witchlight rune-stone Jace Herondale had given him, though he dared not light it except when he was alone.

Each night as he fell asleep he recited the names of his sisters and brothers, in order of age. Each word was weighted like an anchor, cleaving him to the earth. Keeping him alive.

Helen. Julian. Tiberius. Livia. Drusilla. Octavian.

The days blurred into months. Time was not like it was in the mundane world. Mark had given up counting days—there was no way to mark them down, and Gwyn hated such things. Therefore he had no idea how long he had been with the Hunt when Kieran came.

He had known they were getting a new Hunter; gossip spread

quickly, and besides, Gwyn always Turned the newest of them in the same place: a cavern near to the entrance of the Unseelie Court, where the walls were thickly carpeted in emerald lichen and a small natural pool welled among the rocks.

They found him there when they arrived, left for Gwyn to discover. At first all Mark could see was the outline of a boy with a tangle of black hair and a slender body, the chains binding his wrists and ankles pulling it into a strange torsion. He appeared to be all bones and angles.

"Prince Kieran," said Gwyn as he approached the boy, and a murmur ran through the Hunt. If the newcomer was a prince, he was more exalted than faerie gentry. And what could a prince have done to get himself so brutally exiled from the Court, cut off from family and name, kith and kin?

The boy lifted his head when Gwyn came to him, revealing his face. He was certainly gentry. He had their strange, luminous, almost inhumanly beautiful features, high-cheekboned and black-eyed. His hair had a sheen to it of blue and green among the black, the color of the ocean at night. He turned his face away when Gwyn tried to press the water on him, mixed with blood, but Gwyn forced it down his throat. Mark watched in fascination as Kieran's right eye turned from black to silver, and the chains fell away from lacerated wrists and ankles.

"You are of the Hunt now," said Gwyn with a grimness that was unusual. "Rise and join us."

Kieran was a strange addition to the group. Though his rank as prince had been stripped from him when he was exiled to the Hunt, he still carried an indefinable air of arrogance and royalty with him, which did not sit well with the others. They mocked him, called him "princeling," and would have done worse if Gwyn had not stayed their hands. It seemed there was someone in the Courts looking out for Kieran, despite his exile.

Mark could not help but watch him. Something about Kieran fascinated him. He soon learned that the prince's hair changed color depending on his mood, from night black (when he was despairing) to pale blue (when he laughed, which was not often)—always colors of the sea. It was thick and curling and sometimes Mark wanted to touch it and see if it felt like hair or something else, shot silk, a fabric that changed color in the light. Kieran rode his horse—given to him by Gwyn; it was the fiercest Mark had ever seen, black and skeletal, a mount of the dead—as if he were born to it. Like Mark, he seemed determined to ride out the pain of exile and friendlessness alone, rarely speaking to the others of the Hunt, rarely even glancing at them.

Only he looked at Mark sometimes, when the others called him Nephilim and Shadow-spawn and angel-boy and other names much worse. A day came when news spread that the Clave had hanged a group of faeries in Idris for treason. The faeries had had friends among the Hunt, and in a rage, Mark's fellows demanded that Mark kneel and say the words "I am not a Shadowhunter."

When he would not, they stripped Mark's shirt from his body and whipped him bloody. They left him crumpled under a tree in a snowy field, his blood turning the white flakes to red.

When he woke there was firelight and warmth, and he was lying in someone's lap. Only groggily did he come to enough consciousness to realize that it was Kieran's. Kieran lifted him in his arms and gave him water and folded a blanket around his shoulders. His touch was gentle and light. "I believe among your people," he said, "there are healing runes."

"Yes," Mark said in a croak, moving only very slightly. Pain from his lacerated skin jolted through him. "They're called iratzes. One would mend these injuries for me. But they cannot be made without a stele, and my stele was broken years past."

"That is a pity," said Kieran. "I believe your skin will be scarred forevermore."

"What care I?" said Mark, listless. "It is not as if it matters much, here in the Hunt, whether I am beautiful."

Kieran gave a secret half smile at that and touched Mark's hair lightly. Mark closed his eyes. It had been years since anyone had touched him, and the feeling sent shivers down through his body despite the pain of the cuts.

*After that, when they rode out, they rode out together. Kieran made of the Hunt an adventure for the two of them. He showed Mark wonders that only the Fair Folk knew of: sheets of ice lying silent and silver under moonlight, and hidden glens, blooming with night flowers. They rode among the spray of waterfalls and amid the towers of clouds. And Mark was, if not happy, no longer tortured by loneliness.*

*At night they slept curled together under Kieran's blanket, made of a thickly woven material that was always warm. One night they stopped on a hilltop, in a place green and north. There was a cairn of stones crowning the hill, something built by mundanes a thousand years back. Mark leaned against the side of it and looked out over the green country, silvering in the dark, to the distant sea. The sea, everywhere, he thought, was the same, the same sea that broke against the shores in the place he still thought of as home.*

*"Your scars have healed," Kieran said, touching one of his light, slender fingers to a torn place in Mark's shirt where the skin showed through.*

*"But they are still ugly," Mark said. He was waiting for the first stars to come out, so he could name his family on them. He didn't see Kieran draw closer until the other boy was opposite him, his face elegantly shadowed in the twilight.*

*"Nothing about you is ugly," Kieran said. He leaned in to kiss Mark and Mark, after a moment of surprise, turned his face up and met Kieran's lips with his.*

*It was the first time he had ever been kissed, and he had never thought it would be by a boy, but he was glad it was Kieran. He had never expected a kiss to be so agonizing and pleasurable at the same time. He had wanted to touch Kieran's hair for months, and now he did, burying his fingers in the strands, which were turning from black to blue edged with gold. They felt like licks of flame against his skin.*

*They curled up under the blanket together that night, but they got little sleep, and Mark forgot to number the names of his family on the stars—for that night and most nights after. Soon Mark grew used to* waking with his arm thrown over Kieran's body or his hand tangled in blue-white curls.

He learned that kisses and touches and professions of love could make you forget, and that the more he was with Kieran, the more he wanted to be with him and not with anyone else. He lived for the time they were alone together, usually at night, whispering so no one could overhear them. "Tell me of the Unseelie Court," Mark would say, and Kieran would murmur tales of the dark Court and the pale King, his father, who ruled over it. And "Tell me of the Nephilim," Kieran would say, and Mark would speak of the Angel, and of the Dark War and what had happened to him, and of his brothers and sisters.

"You don't hate me?" Mark said, lying in Kieran's arms, somewhere in a high Alpine meadow. His unkempt blond hair brushed against Kieran's shoulder as he turned his head. "For being Nephilim? The others do."

"You need not be Nephilim anymore. You could choose to be of the Wild Hunt. Embrace your faerie nature."

Mark shook his head. "When they beat me for saying I was a Shadowhunter, it only made me more sure. I know what I am even if I cannot say it."

"You can say it only to me," said Kieran, his long fingers ghosting across Mark's cheek. "Here in this space between us. It is safe."

So Mark pressed up against his lover and only friend and whispered into the space between them, where his cold body pressed against Kieran's warm one. "I am a Shadowhunter. I am a Shadowhunter. I am a Shadowhunter."

# 13
## WITH NO OTHER THOUGHT

**Emma stood in front of the mirror in her bathroom, slowly** peeling off her tank top.

Twenty minutes with a bottle of bleach had removed the blood from the inside of the Toyota. That had been fine. She was used to bloodstains. But there was something more visceral about this, about Julian's blood dried on her skin, red-brown patches over her ribs and shoulder. As she unzipped her jeans and wriggled out of them, she could see splatters of dried blood along the waistband, the telltale pinpricks of it up and down the seams.

She balled up the jeans and top and threw them in the trash.

In the shower, the water scalding hot, she scrubbed away the blood and dirt and sweat. She watched the water run pinkish down the drain. She couldn't count how many times that had happened, how often she'd made herself bleed during training and battles. Scars slashed across her midriff and shoulders, along her arms, at the backs of her knees.

But Julian's blood was different.

When she saw it she thought of him, shot and crumpling, the way his blood had run like water through her fingers. It was the first time in years that she'd actually thought he might die, that she might lose him. She knew what people said about *parabatai*, knew that it was meant to be a loss as profound as that of a spouse or a sibling. Emma had lost her parents; she had thought she knew what loss was, was prepared for it.

But nothing had prepared her for the feeling that the idea of losing Jules wrenched out of her: that the sky would go dark forever, that there would never be solid ground again. Even stranger had been the feeling that had rushed through her when she realized he was going to be all right. She had become aware of his physical presence in a way that almost hurt. She had wanted to put her arms around him, to grab on to him with her fingers digging in as if she could press them together hard enough to seal their skin, interlock their bones. She knew it didn't make sense, but she couldn't explain it another way.

She just knew it was intense, and painful, and a thing she hadn't felt about Julian before. And that it scared her.

The water had gone cold. She spun the shower off with a savage twist of her wrist, stepped out, and toweled her hair dry. She found a clean camisole and boxer shorts folded on her laundry basket and, dressed, stepped out into her bedroom.

Cristina was sitting on her bed.

"Whoa," Emma said. "I didn't know you were in here! I could have come out of the bathroom stark naked or something."

"I doubt you have anything I don't have." Cristina looked distracted; her dark hair was down in braids, and she was interweaving her fingers the way she did when she was preoccupied.

"Is everything all right?" Emma asked, sitting down on the edge of the bed. "You look—bothered."

"Do you think Mark had friends in the Wild Hunt?" Cristina asked abruptly.

"No." Emma was taken aback. "At least he's never mentioned any. And you'd think he would have, if there was someone he missed." She frowned. "Why?"

Cristina hesitated. "Well, he borrowed that motorcycle tonight from someone. I just hope he hasn't gotten himself in any trouble."

"Mark's clever," said Emma. "I doubt he bartered his soul for the temporary use of a motorbike or anything."

"I'm sure you're right," Cristina murmured, and glanced toward Emma's wardrobe. "Can I borrow a dress?"

"Right now?" Emma said. "Have you got a midnight date?"

"No, for tomorrow night." Cristina got to her feet to peer into the wardrobe. Several badly folded rayon dresses fell out. "It is meant to be formal. I didn't bring any formal dresses with me from home."

"You won't fit into anything of mine," Emma said as Cristina held up a black dress with a design of rockets and frowned at it. "We're different shapes. You're way more—boom-chicka-boom."

"Is that even English?" Cristina frowned, tossing the rocket dress onto a shelf and shutting the wardrobe door. "I don't think that's English."

Emma smiled at her. "I'll take you shopping tomorrow," she said. "Deal?"

"That seems so normal." Cristina smoothed her braids back. "After tonight . . ."

"Cameron called me," Emma said.

"I know," Cristina said. "I was in the kitchen. Why are you telling me now? Are you back together?"

Emma rocked backward on the bed. "No! He was warning me. He told me that there were people who didn't want me investigating these murders."

"Emma." Cristina sighed. "And you didn't say anything to us?"

"He said it about *me*," Emma said. "I figured any danger would be my danger."

"But Julian got hurt," said Cristina, knowing what Emma was going to say before she said it. "So you are worrying it was your fault."

Emma picked at the fringe on the edge of her blanket. "Isn't it? I mean, Cameron warned me, he said he heard it at the Shadow Market, so I don't know if it was mundanes talking or faeries or warlocks or what, but the fact is, he warned me and I ignored it."

"It was *not* your fault. We already know there's someone, a necromancer most likely, killing and sacrificing mundanes and Downworlders. We already know he has an army of Mantid demons at his beck and call. It isn't as if Julian wasn't expecting and prepared for danger."

"He almost died on me," Emma said. "There was so much blood."

"And you fixed him. He's fine. You saved his life." Cristina waved a hand—her nails were perfect, shining ovals, where Emma's were ragged from sparring and training. "Why are you second-guessing yourself, Emma? Is it because Julian was hurt and that frightened you? Because you have taken risks since the first time I ever met you. It is part of who you are. And Julian knows that. He doesn't just know it, he likes it."

"Does he? He's always telling me not to risk myself—"

"He has to," said Cristina. "You are the two halves of a whole. You must be different, like light and shadow—he brings you caution to temper your recklessness, and you bring him recklessness to temper his caution. Without each other you would not function as well as you do. That is what *parabatai* means." She tugged lightly on the ends of Emma's wet hair. "I do not think it is Cameron that is bothering you. That is just an excuse to berate yourself. I think it is that Julian was hurt."

"Maybe," Emma said in a tight voice.

"Are you sure you're all right?" Cristina's dark brown eyes were worried.

"I'm fine." Emma sat back against the pillows. She collected kitschy California pillows: some looked like postcards, some were shaped like the state or said I LOVE CALI.

"You don't look fine," Cristina said. "You look like—my mother used to say there was a look people got when they realized something. You look like someone who has realized something."

Emma wanted to close her eyes, to hide her thoughts from Cristina. Thoughts that were treacherous, dangerous, wrong to have.

"Just shock," she said. "I came close to losing Julian and—it threw me off. I'll be fine tomorrow." She forced a smile.

"If you say so, *manita*." Cristina sighed. "If you say so."

After Julian cleaned himself up, washed the blood off, and arranged to send the shreds of his poison-burned gear jacket to Malcolm, he walked down the hall to Emma's room.

And stopped halfway. He'd wanted to lie down on the bed beside her, and for them to talk over the night's events, and to close their eyes together, with the sound of her breathing like the sound of the ocean, measuring out the steps toward sleep.

But. When he thought of that night in the back of the car, of Emma hovering over him, panic on her face and blood on her hands, he didn't feel what he knew he should feel: fear, the memory of pain, relief that he'd healed.

Instead he felt a tightening in his body that sent an ache down to the center of his bones. When he closed his eyes, he saw Emma in the witchlight, her hair tumbling out of its fastening, the light of the streetlamps shining through the strands and turning them to a sheet of pale summer-frozen ice.

Emma's hair. Maybe because she took it down so rarely, maybe because Emma with her hair down was one of the first things he'd ever wanted to paint, but the long, looping pale strands of it had always been like cords that connected directly to his nerves.

His head hurt, and his body ached unreasonably, wanting to be back in that car with her. It made no sense, so he forced his steps away from her door, down the hall, to the library. It was dark in there and cold and smelled of old paper. Still, Julian didn't need a light; he knew exactly what section of the room he was headed toward.

*Law.*

Julian was pulling down a red-bound book from a high shelf when a reedy cry drifted down the hall. He grabbed hold of the tome and was out of the room in an instant, rushing down the corridor. He rounded the corner and saw Drusilla's door open. She was leaning out of it, witchlight in hand, her round face illuminated. Her pajamas were covered in a pattern of frightening masks.

"Tavvy's been crying," she said. "He stopped for a while, but then he started again."

"Thanks for telling me." He dropped a kiss on her forehead. "Go back to bed, I'll deal with it."

Drusilla withdrew, and Julian slipped into Tavvy's room, closing the door behind him.

Tavvy was a curled-up ball under the covers of his bed. He was asleep, his body curved around one of his pillows, his mouth open on a gasp. Tears ran down his face.

Julian sat down on the bed and put a hand on Tavvy's shoulder. "Octavian," he said. "Wake up; you're having a nightmare, wake up."

Tavvy shot upright, his brown hair in wild disarray. When he saw Julian, he hiccuped and flung himself at his older brother, arms wrapping around his neck.

Jules held Tavvy and rubbed his back, gently patting the sharp knobs of his spine. Too small, too skinny, his mind said. It had been a battle to get Tavvy to eat and sleep ever since the Dark War.

He remembered running through the streets of Alicante with Tavvy in his arms, stumbling on the cracked paving, trying to keep his little brother's face mashed against his shoulder so that he wouldn't see the blood and the death all around him. Thinking that if they could just get through everything without Tavvy seeing what was happening, it would be all right. He wouldn't remember. He wouldn't know.

And still Tavvy woke up with nightmares every week, shaking and sweating and crying. And every time it happened, the dull realization that he hadn't really saved his baby brother at all went through Julian like spikes.

Tavvy's breaths evened out slowly as Julian sat there, arms around him. He wanted to lie down, wanted to curl up around his youngest brother and sleep. He needed rest so badly it was dragging at him, like a wave pulling him under and down.

But he couldn't sleep. His body felt restless, unsettled. The arrow going into him had been agony; pulling it out had been worse. He'd felt his skin tear and a moment of pure, animalistic panic, the surety that he was going to die, and then what would happen to them, *livvyandtyanddrusillaandtavvyandmark?*

And then Emma's voice in his ear, and her hands on him, and he'd known he was going to live. He looked at himself now, the mark on his ribs entirely gone—well, there was something there, a faint line of white against his tanned skin, but that was nothing. Shadowhunters lived through scars. Sometimes he thought they lived for them.

Unbidden, in his mind rose the image he'd been trying to crush down since he'd returned to the Institute: Emma, in his lap, her hands on his shoulders. Her hair like drifts of pale gold around her face.

He remembered thinking that if he died, at least he would die with her as close to him as she could possibly be. As would ever be allowed by the Law.

As Tavvy slept, Julian reached for the law book he'd taken from the library. It was a book he'd looked at so many times that it now always fell open to the same well-worn page. *On Parabatai*, it said.

*It is decreed that those who have undergone the ceremony of parabatai and are forever bound by the terms of the oaths of Saul and David, of Ruth and Naomi, shall not enter into marriage, shall not bear children together, and shall not love each other in the manner of eros, but only the manner of philia or agape.*

*The punishment for the contravention of this law shall be, at the discretion of the Clave: the separation of the parabatai in question from each other, exile from their families, and should the criminal behavior continue, the stripping of their Marks and their expulsion from the Nephilim. Never again shall they be Shadowhunters.*

*So it is decreed by Raziel.*

*Sed lex, dura lex. The Law is hard, but it is the Law.*

When Emma came into the kitchen, Julian was by the sink, cleaning up the remains of breakfast. Mark was leaning against the kitchen island in dark jeans and a black shirt. With his new short hair, in the daylight, he looked astonishingly different from the ragged feral boy who'd pushed back his hood in the Sanctuary.

She'd gone for a deliberately long run on the beach that morning, missing the family meal on purpose, trying to clear her head. She grabbed a bottled smoothie out of the refrigerator instead. When she turned around, Mark was grinning.

"As I understand it, what I am currently wearing is not semiformal enough for the performance tonight?" he inquired.

Emma glanced from him to Julian. "So Mr. Rules unbent and decided you could come tonight?"

Julian gave a fluid shrug. "I'm a reasonable man."

"Ty and Livvy have promised to help me find something to wear," said Mark, heading for the kitchen door.

"Don't trust them," Julian called after him. "Don't—" He shook his head as the door closed. "Guess he'll have to learn on his own."

"That reminds me," Emma said, leaning on the counter. "We have an emergency situation."

"An emergency?" With a concerned look, he thumbed off the water and turned to face her.

Emma set her bottled drink down. Soap suds were clinging to Jules's forearms, and his T-shirt was damp from the hot water. She couldn't help a flash of memory: Jules in the back of the car, looking up at her with gritted teeth. The way his skin had felt, under her hands, the slipperiness of his blood.

"Is it Diana?" he said, reaching for paper towels.

"What?" That snapped her out of her reverie. "Is Diana all right?"

"Presumably," he said. "She left a note saying she was going to be gone today. Back to Ojai to see her warlock friend."

"She doesn't know about tonight." Emma leaned on the counter. "Does she?"

Jules shook his head. A damp curl stuck to his cheekbone. "Didn't exactly get a chance to tell her."

"You could text," Emma pointed out. "Or call."

"I could," he said neutrally. "But then I'd feel like I needed to tell her about me getting hurt last night."

"Maybe you should."

"I'm fine," he said. "I mean, really, fine. Like nothing ever happened." He shook his head. "I don't want her insisting I stay back from tonight. The theater could be nothing, but if it's something, I want to be there." He dropped the paper towels in the trash. "If *you're* there, I want to be there."

"I like it when you're deceptive." Emma stretched up on her toes, arms behind her head, trying to work out the kinks in her back muscles. Cool air touched the bare skin of her stomach as her tank pulled up. "If you're totally fine, though, maybe you don't ever have to tell Diana? Just a suggestion."

When Julian didn't answer, she glanced up at him.

He was arrested midmotion, looking at her. Each of his lashes was a perfect dark line; he was expressionless, his gaze shuttered, as if caught in a peculiar stillness.

He was beautiful. The most beautiful thing she'd ever seen. She wanted to crawl inside his skin, live where he breathed. She *wanted*.

She was terrified. She had never *wanted* like this around Julian before. It was because he'd almost died, she told herself. Her whole system was wired to monitor his survival. She needed him to live. He'd nearly died, and everything inside her was short-circuiting.

He would be horrified, she told herself. If he knew how she was feeling—he'd be disgusted. Things would go back to the way they were when he'd first come back from England, when she'd thought that he was angry at her. That maybe he hated her.

*He knew even then*, said a small voice at the back of her mind. *He knew about your feelings. He knew what you didn't know.*

She pressed her hands hard against the counter, the marble digging into her palms, the pain clearing her head. *Shut up*, she told the voice in her head. *Shut up.*

"An emergency." His voice was low. "You said there was an emergency?"

"A fashion emergency—Cristina needs a dress to blend in tonight, and there's literally nothing in the house." She glanced at her watch. "It should take us thirty minutes, tops."

He relaxed, clearly relieved. "Hidden Treasures?" he asked. It was a good guess: Emma's favorite vintage store was well known to the family. Every time she went she picked things up for them: a bow tie for Tavvy, a flowered headband for Livvy, an old horror movie poster for Dru.

"Yep. Do you want anything?"

"I've always kind of wanted a Batman clock that says 'WAKE UP, BOY WONDER' when it goes off," he said. "It would liven up my room."

"We've got it!" Livvy said, bounding into the kitchen. "Well, some of it, anyway. But it's weird."

Emma turned to her with relief. "Got what?"

"In English, Livvy," said Julian. "What's weird?"

"We translated some of the lines in the cave," said Ty, trailing in on Livvy's heels. He was wearing an oversize gray hooded sweater that swallowed up his hands. His dark hair spilled over the edge of the hood. "But they don't make sense."

"Are they a message?" Emma said.

Livvy shook her head. "Lines from a poem," she said, unfolding the paper she held.

> But our love it was stronger by far than the love
> Of those who were older than we—
> Of many far wiser than we—
> And neither the angels in Heaven above
> Nor the demons down under the sea
> Can ever dissever my soul from the soul
> Of the beautiful Annabel Lee. . . .

"'Annabel Lee,'" said Julian. "Edgar Allan Poe."

"I know the poem," Livvy said, scrunching up her eyebrows. "I just don't know why it was written on the walls of the cave."

"I thought maybe it was a book cipher," said Ty. "But that would mean there was a second half of it. Something in another location, maybe. Might be worth checking with Malcolm."

"I'll add it to the list," said Julian.

Cristina stuck her head in through the kitchen door. "Emma?" she said. "Are you ready to go?"

"You look worried," said Livvy. "Is Emma taking you some-where to kill you?"

"Worse," Emma said, heading over to join Cristina at the door. "Shopping."

"For tonight? First, I am so jealous, and second, don't let her take you to that place in Topanga Canyon—"

"That's enough!" Emma clapped her hands over Cristina's ears. "Don't listen to her. She's lost her mind from all that code breaking."

"Pick me up some cuff links," Jules called, heading back toward the sink.

"What color?" Emma paused halfway out the door with Cristina.

"I don't care as long as they hold my cuffs together. Otherwise they'll be sad and unlinked," Jules said. "And get back as quick as you can." The sound of the water running in the sink was drowned out by Livvy, who had already begun reciting more of the poem.

It was many and many a year ago,
In a kingdom by the sea . . .

"This is where you want to buy clothes?" Cristina asked, her eye-brows arched, as Emma pulled the Toyota into a dirt parking lot surrounded by trees.

"It's the closest place," Emma said, turning off the car. In front of them was a single freestanding building with a sign boast-ing foot-high letters in glitter that spelled out the words HIDDEN TREASURES. A massive red-and-white popcorn machine stood next to the store, along with a painted model of a curtained caravan, advertising the services of Gargantua the Great. "And besides, it's awesome."

"This does not look like a place you buy glamorous dresses," Cristina said, wrinkling up her nose. "This looks like a place where you are kidnapped and sold to the circus."

Emma grabbed her by the wrist. "Don't you trust me?" she wheedled.

"Of course not," Cristina said. "You're crazy."

But she let Emma drag her into the store, which was filled with kitschy knickknacks: Fiestaware platters, old china dolls, and, up by the register, racks of vintage jewelry and watches. A second room opened off the first. It was full of clothes—amazing clothes. Secondhand vintage Levi's, fifties pencil skirts in tweed and bombazine, and tops in silk and lace and crushed velvet.

And in a smaller second room off the main one, the dresses. They looked like hanging butterflies: sheets of red organza, watercolor-printed charmeuse, the hem of a Balmain gown, the froth of a tulle petticoat, like foam on water.

"Didn't Julian say he needed cuff links?" Cristina said, pulling Emma to a stop by the counter. The salesgirl behind it, wearing a pair of cat's-eye glasses and a name tag that said SARAH, studiously ignored them.

Emma ran her eyes over the display of men's cuff links—most were joke items, shaped like dice or guns or cats, but there was a section of nicer ones: consignment Paul Smith and Burberry and Lanvin.

As she ran her gaze over them, she felt suddenly shy. Picking out cuff links seemed like something a girlfriend would do. Not that she'd ever done it for Cameron, or anyone else she'd dated even briefly, but she'd never cared enough to want to. When Julian had a girlfriend, Emma knew, she would absolutely be the sort of girl who would pick out cuff links for him. Who would remember his birthday and call him every day. She would adore him. How could she not?

Emma picked up a pair of gold-plated cuff links with black stones set in them, almost blindly. The thought of Julian with a girlfriend sent a pain through her that she couldn't comprehend.

Setting the cuff links down on the counter, she walked into the small room full of dresses. Cristina followed her, looking worried.

*I used to come here with my mom*, Emma thought, running the back of her hand across the rack of satins and silks and bright rayons. *She loved crazy vintage things, old Chanel jackets, beaded flapper dresses.* But out loud all she said was "We have to hurry—we shouldn't be spending so much time away from the Institute while the investigation's happening."

Cristina grabbed up a shimmering cocktail dress in pink brocade sprinkled with tiny gold flowers. "I'm going to try this on."

She disappeared into a changing booth with a curtain made from a Star Wars bedsheet. Emma pulled another dress from the rack: pale silk with beaded silver straps. Looking at it made her feel the way she did when she looked at a gorgeous sunset or one of Julian's paintings or his hands moving over the brushes and bottles of paint.

She went into the dressing room to change. When she came out, Cristina was standing in the middle of the room, scowling down at her pink dress. It clung like Saran Wrap to her every curve. "I think it's too tight," she said.

"I think it's supposed to be that tight," said Emma. "It makes your boobs look great."

"Emma!" Cristina looked up, scandalized, then gasped. "Oh, you look so lovely!"

Emma touched the ivory-and-silver material of the dress with uncertain hands. White meant death and mourning to Shadowhunters; they rarely wore it casually, though the fact that it was ivory meant she could get away with it. "You think?"

Cristina was smiling at her. "You know, sometimes you are just like I thought you would be, and sometimes you are so different."

Emma moved to look in the mirror. "What do you mean, what you thought I would be like?"

Cristina picked up a snow globe and frowned at it. "You know, it wasn't just Mark I heard about before I came here. I heard about you. Everyone said you would be the next Jace Herondale. The next great Shadowhunter warrior."

"I'm not going to be that," said Emma. Her own voice sounded calm and small and distant in her ears. She couldn't believe she was saying what she was saying. The words seemed to be coming out without her thoughts forming them first, as if they were creating their own reality by being spoken. "I'm not special, Cristina. I don't have extra Angel blood or special powers. I'm an ordinary Shadowhunter."

"You are not ordinary."

"I am. I don't have magic powers, I'm not cursed or blessed. I can do exactly what everyone else can do. The only reason I'm good is because I train."

The salesgirl, Sarah, stuck her head back around the door, her eyes saucer wide. Emma had forgotten she was there. "Do you need any help?"

"I need so much help, you have no idea," Emma said. Alarmed, Sarah retreated to her counter.

"This is embarrassing," Cristina said in a whispered hiss. "She probably thinks we are lunatics. We should go."

Emma sighed. "I'm sorry, Tina," she said. "I'll pay for everything."

"But I don't even know if I want this dress!" Cristina called as Emma vanished back into the changing cubicle.

Emma whirled around and pointed at her. "Yes, you do. I was serious about your boobs. They look amazing. I don't even think I've ever seen that much of your boobs before. If I had boobs like that, you better believe I'd show them off."

"Please stop saying 'boobs,'" Cristina wailed. "It's a terrible word. It sounds ridiculous."

"Maybe," said Emma, yanking the dressing room door shut. "But they look great."

Ten minutes later, dresses in shopping bags, they were driving back down the canyon road toward the ocean. Cristina, in the seat next to Emma, sat with her legs crossed demurely at the ankles, not propped up on the dashboard like Emma's would have been.

All around them the familiar scenery of the canyon rose up: gray rock, green scrub, and chaparral. Oak trees and Queen Anne's lace. Once, Emma had climbed up into these mountains with Jules and found an eagle's nest, a tiny cache of the bones of mice and bats inside it.

"You are wrong about why you are good at what you do," Cristina said. "It is not just training. Everyone trains, Emma."

"Yeah, but I kill myself training," Emma said. "It's just about all I do. I get up and train, and run, and I split my hands on the punching bag, and I train for hours into the night, and I have to, because there is nothing else special about me and nothing else that matters. All there is, is training and finding out who killed my parents. Because they were the ones who thought I was special, and whoever took them away from me—"

"Other people think you are special, Emma," said Cristina, sounding more like an older sister than ever.

"What I have is *trying*," said Emma, her voice tinged with bitterness. She was thinking of the tiny bones in the nest, how fragile they'd been, how easily snapped between a pair of fingers. "I can try harder than anyone else in the world. I can make revenge the only thing I have in my life. I can do that, because I have to. But it means it's all I have."

"It's not all you have," Cristina said. "What you haven't had is your moment. Your chance to be great. Jace Herondale and Clary Fairchild weren't heroes in a vacuum—there was a war. They were forced to make choices. Those moments come for all of us. They will come for you, too." She laced her fingers together. "The Angel has a plan for you. I promise it. You are more prepared than you think. You have stayed strong not just through training but through the people around you—loving them and being loved. Julian and the others, they have not let you isolate yourself, alone with your revenge and your bitter thoughts. The sea wears down cliffs, Emma, and turns them into sand; so love wears us down and breaks our defenses. You only do not know how much it means, to have people who will fight for you when it goes wrong—"

Her voice cracked, and she looked toward the window. They had reached the highway; Emma almost drove into traffic in alarm. "Cristina? What is it? What happened?"

Cristina shook her head.

"I know something happened to you in Mexico," Emma said. "I know someone hurt you. Just please tell me what it was and what they did. I promise I won't try to hunt them down and feed them to my imaginary fish. I just—" She sighed. "I want to help."

"You cannot." Cristina glanced down at her interlaced fingers. "Some betrayals cannot be forgiven."

"Was it Perfect Diego?"

"Let it go, Emma," Cristina said, and so Emma did, and the rest of the way back to the Institute they talked about their dresses and how best to conceal weapons in items of clothing that were not meant to hide an armory. But Emma had noticed the way Cristina had flinched when she'd said Diego's name. Maybe not now, maybe not today, she thought, but she *would* find out what had happened.

Julian flew downstairs at the loud, repetitive pounding on the front door of the Institute. He was still barefoot; he hadn't had a chance to put shoes on yet. Once he'd finished cleaning up after breakfast, he'd spent an hour trying to convince Uncle Arthur that no one had stolen his bust of Hermes (it was under his desk), found out that Drusilla had locked herself in Tavvy's playhouse in a sulk because she hadn't been invited to the diner the night before. Tavvy discovered Ty had been hiding a skunk in his room and started screaming. Livvy was busy convincing Ty to release the skunk back into the wild; Ty thought that the fact that he and Livvy had translated the Poe lines meant he'd earned the right to keep the skunk.

Mark, the only sibling who hadn't given Julian any trouble that day, was hiding somewhere.

Julian swung the door open. Malcolm Fade stood on the other side, wearing jeans and the kind of sweatshirt you could tell was expensive because it appeared to be filthy and torn, but artfully so. Someone had spent time and money ripping that sweatshirt.

"You know, it's not a good idea to whack on the door like that," said Julian. "We keep a lot of weapons down here in case someone tries to break in."

"Huh," said Malcolm. "I'm not sure what that first statement has to do with the second statement."

"Don't you? I thought it was obvious."

Malcolm's eyes were a brilliant purple, which usually meant he was in a peculiar mood. "Aren't you going to let me in?"

"No," Julian said. His mind was whirling with thoughts of Mark. Mark was upstairs, and Malcolm couldn't see Mark. Mark's return was too much of a secret to ask him to keep—and too much of a clue as to the reason for their investigation.

Julian schooled his features into a look of pleasant blandness, but didn't move from his place blocking the door. "Ty brought a skunk inside," he said. "Believe me, you don't want to come in."

Malcolm looked alarmed. "A skunk?"

"A skunk," Julian said. Julian believed that all the best lies were based on truth. "Did you translate any of the markings?"

"Not yet," Malcolm said. He moved his hand—not much, a small gesture, but the copies of the partially translated markings they'd given him appeared, held delicately between his fingers. Sometimes, Julian thought, it was easy to forget that Malcolm was a powerful user of magic. "But I did discover their origins."

"Really?" Julian tried to look shocked. They already knew the language was an ancient one of Faerie, though they hadn't been able to tell Malcolm that.

On the other hand, this was a chance to check and see if the Fair Folk had been telling them the truth. Julian eyed Malcolm with renewed interest.

"Wait, maybe this isn't the markings." Malcolm eyed the papers. "It seems to be a recipe for orange cake."

Julian crossed his arms over his chest. "No, it isn't."

Malcolm frowned. "I definitely remember looking at a recipe for orange cake recently."

Julian rolled his eyes silently. Sometimes with Malcolm you just had to be patient.

"Never mind," Malcolm said. "That was in a copy of *O* magazine. This—" He tapped the paper. "An ancient language of Faerie—you were right; it predates Shadowhunters. Anyway, that's the language origin. I can probably get more done in the next few days. But that's not why I came by."

Julian brightened.

"I did some examining of the poison on that fabric you sent me last night. I checked it against different toxins. It was a cataplasm—a concentrate of a rare type of the belladonna plant with demon poisons. It should have killed you."

"But Emma healed me," said Julian. "With an *iratze*. So are you saying we should be looking for—"

"I wasn't saying anything about looking," Malcolm interrupted. "I'm just telling you. No *iratze* should have been able to fix you. Even accounting for the strength of *parabatai* runes, you absolutely shouldn't have survived." His odd violet eyes fixed on Julian. "I don't know if it's something you did, or something Emma did, but whatever it was—was impossible. You shouldn't be breathing right now."

Julian trailed up the stairs slowly. He could hear yelling from above him, but not the sort that sounded as if anyone was in actual trouble. Telling the difference between play yelling and actual yelling was an absolute necessity when you were in charge of four kids.

His mind was still on what Malcolm had told him, about the cataplasm. It was unnerving to be told that you should be dead. There was always the possibility that Malcolm was wrong, but somehow Julian doubted it. Hadn't Emma said something about finding belladonna plants near the convergence?

Thoughts of poison and convergences vanished from his mind as he turned down the corridor from the stairs. The room they kept Tiberius's computer in was filled with light and noise. Julian moved into the doorway and stared.

There was a video game alive and flickering on the computer screen. Mark was sitting in front of it, mashing rather desperately at the buttons on a controller as a truck sped toward him on-screen. It crushed his character with a splat, and he tossed the controller aside. "The box serves the Lord of Lies!" he announced indignantly.

Ty laughed, and Julian felt something tug at his heart. The sound of his brother laughing was one of Julian's favorite noises, in part because Ty did it so sincerely, without any attempt to cover up his laughter or any sense he should hide it. Wordplay and irony often weren't funny to Ty, but people acting silly was, and he had an absolute and sincere amusement at the behavior of animals—Church falling off a table and trying to regain his dignity—that was beautiful to Julian.

In the dead of night, lying in bed staring at his murals of thorns, Julian sometimes wished he could put down the role that required him to always be the one telling Ty he couldn't have skunks in his room or reminding him it was time to study or coming in to shut his lights off when he was reading instead of sleeping. What if, like a normal brother, he could watch Sherlock Holmes movies with Ty and help him collect lizards without worrying that they were going to escape and run through the Institute? *What if?*

Julian's mother had always stressed the difference between doing something for someone and giving them the tools to do it themselves. It was how she had taught Julian to paint. Julian had always tried to do that for Ty, too, though it had often seemed like he was feeling his way in the dark: making books, toys, lessons that seemed tailored to the special way Ty thought—was it the right thing to do? He thought it had helped. He hoped. Sometimes hope was all you had.

Hope, and watching Ty. There was a pleasure in seeing Ty become more himself, need help and guidance less and less. Yet there was a sadness, too, for the day his brother wouldn't need him anymore. Sometimes, in the depths of his heart, Julian wondered if Ty would want to spend time with him at all, once that day had come—with the brother who was always making him do things and was no fun at all.

"It's not a box," Ty said. "It's a controller."

"Well, it lies," said Mark, turning around in his chair. He saw Julian, leaning in the doorway, and nodded. "Well met, Jules."

Julian knew this was a faerie greeting and struggled internally not to point out to Mark that they'd already met that morning in the kitchen, not to mention several thousand times before that. He won over his baser impulses, but just barely. "Hi, Mark."

"Is everything all right?"

Julian nodded. "Could I talk to Ty for a second?"

Tiberius stood up. His black hair was messy, getting too long. Julian reminded himself to schedule a haircut for both twins. Another thing to add to the calendar.

Ty came out into the corridor, pulling the computer room door shut behind him. His expression was wary. "Is this about the skunk? Because Livvy took it back outside."

Julian shook his head. "It's not about the skunk."

Ty lifted his face. He'd always had delicate features, more elfin than Helen or Mark's. His father had said he was a throwback to earlier generations of Blackthorns, and he looked not unlike some of the family portraits in the dining room they rarely used, slender Victorian men in tailored clothes with porcelain faces and black, curling hair. "Then what is it?"

Julian hesitated. The whole house was still. He could hear the faint crackle of the computer on the other side of the door.

He had thought about asking Ty to look into the poison that he had been shot with. But that would require him to say, *I was dying. I should be dead.* The words wouldn't come. They were like a dam, and behind them were so many other words: *I'm not sure about anything. I hate being in charge. I hate making the decisions. I'm terrified you'll all learn to hate me. I'm terrified of losing you. I'm terrified of losing Mark. I'm terrified of losing Emma. I want someone to take over. I'm not as strong as you think. The things I want are wrong and broken things to want.*

He knew he could say none of this. The facade he showed them, his children, had to be perfect: A crack in him would be like a crack in the world to them.

"You know I love you," he said, instead, and Ty looked up at him, startled, meeting his gaze for a flicker of a moment. Over the years, Julian had come to understand why Ty didn't like looking into other people's eyes. It was too much movement, color, expression, like looking into a blaring television set. He *could* do it—he knew it was something people liked, and that it mattered to them—but he didn't see what the fuss was about.

Ty was searching now, though, seeking in Julian's face the answer to his odd hesitancy. "I do know," Ty said, finally.

Julian couldn't help the ghost of a smile. It was what you wanted to hear, wasn't it, from your children? That they knew they were loved? He remembered when he had been carrying Tavvy upstairs, once, when he'd been thirteen; he'd tripped and fallen, twisting his body around so that he would land on his back and head, not caring if he was hurt as long as Tavvy was all right. He'd cracked himself pretty hard on the head, too, but he'd sat upright fast, his mind racing: *Tavvy, my baby, is he okay?*

It was the first time he'd thought "my baby" and not "the baby."

"I don't understand why you wanted to talk to me, though," Ty said, his dark brows drawn together in puzzlement. "Was there a reason?"

Julian shook his head. In the distance, he could hear the front door open, the faint sound of Emma and Cristina's laughter carrying. They were back. "No reason at all," he said.

# 14

## BRIGHT EYES

**Standing in the marble entryway, Julian chanced one last look** in the mirror.

He had made Livvy look up "semiformal" for him and had his grim suspicions confirmed: It meant a dark suit. The only one he had was a black Sy Devore vintage one Emma had fished out of a bin at Hidden Treasures. It had a charcoal silk lining and mother-of-pearl buttons on the vest. When he'd put it on she'd clapped her hands and told him he looked like a movie star, so of course he'd bought it.

"You look very handsome, Andrew."

Julian spun around. It was Uncle Arthur. His stained gray robe was loosely belted around sagging jeans and a torn T-shirt. Gray stubble spiked along his jaw.

Julian didn't bother to correct his uncle. He knew how much he looked like his father had when he was young. Maybe it comforted Arthur to imagine that his brother was still alive. Maybe seeing Julian in formal clothes reminded Arthur of years past, when he and his brother had been young and gone to parties and dances. Before everything had fallen apart.

Julian knew that Arthur grieved for his brother, in his own way.

It was hidden under the layers of faerie enchantment and trauma that had shattered his mind. If it were not for the fact that Arthur was so retiring and so studious, Julian could only assume his condition would have been discovered before, when he lived at the London Institute. He also guessed that his uncle had gotten worse since the trauma of the Dark War. Still, sometimes, when Arthur had taken the medicine Malcolm provided, Julian could catch glimpses of the Shadowhunter he had been long ago: brave, sharp, and with a sense of honor like Achilles or Aeneas.

"Hello, Arthur," he said.

Arthur nodded decidedly. He placed his open palm against Julian's chest. "I have a meeting with Anselm Nightshade," he said in a deep voice.

"Good to know," Julian said. It *was* good to know. Arthur and Anselm were friends, sharing a love of the classics. Anything that kept Arthur busy was an asset.

Arthur turned with almost military precision and marched across the foyer and through the doors of the Sanctuary. They clanged shut behind him.

Laughter floated down into the entryway. Julian turned away from the mirror just in time to see Cristina coming down the steps. Her brown skin glowed against the old-fashioned pink brocade of her dress. Gold chandelier earrings swung from her ears.

After her came Emma. He registered her dress, but barely— that it was pale ivory, that it floated around her like angel wings. The hem brushed her ankles, and he could see the tips of white boots underneath, knew there were knives tucked into the tops, their handles pressed against her calves.

Her hair was loose, and it rippled down her back in dark gold waves. There was a movement, a softness to it that he knew he could never capture in paint. Gold leaf, maybe, if he painted like Klimt, but even then it would be a pale comparison to the real thing.

She reached the bottom of the stairs and he realized that the material of her dress was just fine enough that he could see the shape and suggestion of her body through it. His pulse started a hard beat against the inside of his cuffs. His suit felt too tight, his skin hot and scratchy.

She smiled at him. Her brown eyes were outlined with gold; it picked up the lighter flecks in her irises, those circles of copper he had spent his childhood counting, memorizing.

"I brought them," she said, and for a moment he forgot what she was talking about. Then he remembered and held out his wrists.

Emma unfurled her fingers. Gold cuff links set with black stones glimmered in her palm. Her touch was gentle as she took each of his hands in hers, turned it over, and carefully fastened the French cuffs of his shirt. She was quick, efficient, but he felt each glide and movement of her fingertips against the skin of his inner wrist like the touch of hot wires.

She dropped his hands, stepped back, and pretended to survey him thoughtfully.

"I guess you'll do," she said.

Cristina gave a gasp. She was looking up, toward the top of the stairs; Julian followed her gaze.

Mark was descending the staircase. Julian blinked, not quite believing his eyes. His older brother seemed to be wearing a long, slightly ratty fake-fur coat—and nothing else.

"Mark," he said. "What are you *wearing?*"

Mark paused halfway down the stairs. His legs were bare. His feet were bare. Julian was 99 percent sure all of him was bare except for the coat, which was fairly loose. It was more of Mark than Julian had seen since they'd shared a bedroom when he was two.

Mark looked puzzled. "Ty and Livvy told me this was semi-formal."

It was then that Julian became aware of the pealing laughter from above. Ty and Livvy were seated along the upstairs railing of the staircase, giggling. "And I told you not to trust them!"

Emma's lips were twitching. "Mark, just—" She held out a hand. Cristina was standing looking up at Mark with both her cheeks bright red, her hands clapped over her mouth. "Go back up to the landing, okay?" She turned to Jules and dropped her voice. "You have to find him something else to wear!"

"You think?"

Emma raised her eyes in exasperation. "Jules. Go into my room, okay? Trunk at the foot of the bed, there's some of my parents' old clothes. My dad wore a tux at his wedding. There were rune bands around the cuffs but we can rip those off."

"But your dad's tux—"

She looked up at him, sideways. "Don't worry about it."

A dozen flecks of gold in her left eye, only seven in her right. Each one like a tiny starburst.

"I'll be right back," Julian said, and jogged up the stairs toward his brother. Mark was on the landing, his arms held out in front of him as if he were examining the sleeves of his fur coat and deciding that they, in fact, were the problem.

Dru, holding Tavvy's hand, had joined the twins. They were all giggling. The glow on Ty's face when he looked at Mark made Julian warm and cold all at once.

What if Mark decided not to stay? What if they couldn't find the killer and he was taken back to the Wild Hunt? *What if?*

"Would you say I'm overdressed or underdressed?" Mark inquired, arching his eyebrows.

Emma burst out laughing. She collapsed onto the bottom step of the staircase. A moment later Cristina had joined her. They clutched each other, helpless with laughter.

Julian wanted to laugh too. He wished he could. He wished he could forget the darkness that flickered at the edge of his vision. He wished he could close his eyes and fall, forgetting for one moment that there was no net stretched out below to catch him.

"Are you ready yet?" Julian asked the closed door of the bathroom. He'd retrieved John Carstairs's suit from Emma's trunk and dragged Mark back to his own bedroom to change. The thought of his brother being naked in Emma's room didn't sit well with him, even if Emma wasn't there.

The door to the bathroom opened and Mark stepped out. The tux was black, simple. It was impossible to see where the runed bands of fabric had been snipped away. The elegant lines of it seemed to sweep upward, making Mark appear taller, more polished. For the first time since his return, every bit of the feral faerie child in him appeared to have been brushed away like cobwebs. He looked human. Like someone who'd always been human.

"Why do you bite your nails?" he said.

Julian, who hadn't even been conscious that he was gnawing on the side of his thumb—*the satisfying pain of skin between his teeth, the metal of the blood in his mouth*—dropped his hands into his lap. "Bad habit."

"It's something people do when they're stressed," said Mark. "Even I know that." His fingers scrabbled uselessly at his tie. He frowned down at it.

Julian got to his feet and went over to his brother, taking the loops of the tie in his hands. He couldn't remember who had taught him how to knot a tie. Malcolm, he thought. It had almost certainly been Malcolm.

"But what do you have to be stressed about, little brother?" Mark said. "You weren't carried away by the faeries. You've spent your life here. Not that the life of a Shadowhunter isn't stressful, but why are you the one with the bloody hands?"

Julian's fingers faltered for a moment. "You don't know

everything about me, Mark. Just like I'm willing to bet I don't know everything about you."

Mark's blue-and-gold eyes were wide and guileless. "Ask me."

"I'd rather learn in my own time." Julian gave the tie a final tug and stepped back to examine his handiwork. Mark looked as if he might have stepped out of a catalog advertising tuxedoes—if male catalog models had pointed ears.

"I wouldn't," said Mark. "Tell me one thing I don't know about you that makes you bite your fingers."

Julian turned toward the door, then paused, hand on the knob. "Our father," he said. "You know what happened to him?"

"He was Turned into one of the Endarkened by Sebastian Morgenstern," said Mark. "How could I forget?"

"And then?"

"And then?" Mark sounded puzzled. "And then he died during the Dark War."

"Yes, he died," said Julian. "Because I killed him."

Mark drew in his breath. There was shock in that gasp, and pity. Julian tensed. He couldn't bear being pitied.

"He was coming for Ty," said Julian. "I did what I had to do."

"It wasn't him," Mark said swiftly.

"That's what everyone says." Julian was still facing the door. He felt a light tap on his shoulder and turned to see Mark looking at him.

"But everyone didn't see it happen, Julian, our father being Turned. I did," Mark said, and suddenly in his voice there was the sound of the older brother he had been, the one who knew more, had lived more. "The light in his eyes went out like a candle guttering in the dark. He was already dead inside. All you did was bury the body."

There was sadness in Mark's eyes, and knowledge, the knowledge of dark things. Mark had blood on his hands too, Julian thought, and for a moment the idea was such a relief that he felt the weight on his shoulders lift incrementally.

"Thank you for the assistance," Mark said formally. "With my manner of dress. I will not trust the twins again with important matters of human tradition."

Julian felt his lip twitch up at the corner. "Yeah, I wouldn't."

Mark looked down at himself. "I am presentable?"

"You look like James Bond."

Mark smiled and Julian felt a small swell of absurd gladness rise up in his chest, that his brother had gotten the reference, that he was pleased.

They made their way back toward the entryway in silence, a silence pierced as they reached the landing by the sound of someone shouting. Together, they were brought up short at the top of the stairs.

"Does your vision match mine, brother?" Mark asked.

"If you mean am I seeing what you're seeing . . . ?" Julian hazarded. "Then yes, if you mean that the foyer is full of Chihuahuas."

"It's not just Chihuahuas," said Ty, who was sitting on the top step, enjoying the spectacle. "It's a number of different small dogs of various breeds."

Julian snorted. The foyer was, indeed, full of small dogs. They yipped and barked and surged. "Don't worry about the dogs," he said. "Nightshade likes to stash them in the entryway when he meets with Uncle Arthur."

"Nightshade?" Mark's eyebrows went up. "*Anselm* Nightshade? The head of the Los Angeles vampire clan?"

"Yep," Julian said. "He comes around sometimes. He and Arthur get along surprisingly well."

"And the dogs . . . ?"

"He likes dogs," said Ty. One of the Chihuahuas had fallen asleep by the front door, all four paws in the air. "That dog looks dead."

"It isn't dead. It's relaxing." Ty seemed amused; Julian ruffled his brother's hair. Ty leaned into it, catlike. "Where are Emma and Cristina?"

"They went to bring the car around," said Ty. "And Livvy went back to her room. Why can't I come with you?"

"Too many of us will look suspicious," Julian said. "You'll have to stay here—guard the Institute."

Ty looked unconvinced. He frowned after them as Mark and Julian hurried out the front doors. The car was pulled up in front of the Institute, the engine idling.

Emma pushed the passenger-side door open and whistled. "Mark. You look amazing."

Mark glanced down at himself, surprised. A surge of prickly heat ran up the insides of Julian's wrists. Cristina was in the back-seat, also looking at Mark. Julian couldn't read her expression.

Emma patted the seat beside her. In the dimness of the car, she was a shadow: white dress, golden hair, like a faded illustration in a children's picture book. "Hop in, Jules. You're mine—my navigator."

*You're mine.* He slid into the seat beside hers.

"Right turn here," Julian said, pointing.

"You'd think the Institute could afford to have reliable GPS installed in this stupid car," Emma muttered, slewing the wheel to the right. She'd tried to program it when they'd gotten into the Toyota, but it had refused to turn on. Once, the GPS had only spoken in a heavy German accent for weeks. Julian had decided it was possessed.

Cristina squeaked and subsided. Emma could see her in the rearview mirror. She was subtly leaning away from Mark; it wasn't anything that someone who didn't know her well could have spotted. Mark didn't seem to have noticed. He was staring out his open window, blond hair ruffled, humming tunelessly.

"Slow down, speed racer," Julian said as someone behind Emma honked.

"We're late," she said. "The show is supposed to start in ten minutes. If *some people* hadn't decided that 'semiformal' meant 'seminaked'—"

"Why are you calling me 'some people'?" Mark inquired. "I am only one person."

"This is weird," Julian observed, turning back to look straight ahead. "There's nobody around on this street."

"There are houses," Cristina pointed out.

"They're all dark." Julian's gaze scanned the road. "A little early, don't you think, for everyone to have gone to bed?" He pointed. "There's the theater."

He was right. Emma could see lights, hot neon and electricity, up ahead, the arrow shape of a sign: THE MIDNIGHT THEATER. The Hollywood Hills glittered in the distance as if they'd been dusted with starlight. Everything else was dark, even the streetlights.

As they neared the theater, the sides of the street became more thickly packed with parked cars. Expensive ones—BMWs, Porsches, Italian sports cars whose names Emma couldn't remember. She pulled into a spot across from the theater and killed the engine.

"Are we ready?" She swung around to look into the backseat. Cristina winked at her. Mark nodded. "Then let's go."

Julian was already out of the car, opening the trunk. He rummaged through the weapons and steles, reaching out to Cristina with a pair of slim throwing knives. "Need these?"

Cristina slipped the strap of her dress aside. Clipped to her bra was one of her butterfly knives, the etched rose gleaming on the handle. "I came prepared."

"I didn't." Mark reached out to take the two sheathed knives, and unbuttoned his jacket to slide them into his belt. He reached up to his throat, touching the arrowhead that hung around his neck.

Arrested, Julian watched him. His blue-green eyes were dark, uncertain. Emma could read the look on his face: He didn't know if his brother was ready to go into potential danger. Didn't like it. Didn't see another way.

"Okay," Julian said. "Weapons hidden, any runes you want to put on now, put them in places no one will see them. Permanent runes, check to make sure they're covered up. We can't risk running into a situation where we'll be recognized by anyone with the Sight."

Emma nodded. They'd already put concealing makeup on her Voyance and *parabatai* runes back at the Institute. She'd even done what she could to cover up the small scars that showed where runes had been and then vanished.

Some runes were permanent and some temporary. Voyance, which looked like an open eye and helped you see through glamours, was permanent. So were wedding and *parabatai* runes. Temporary runes disappeared slowly as they were used up—healing *iratzes*, for instance, vanished with varying speed depending on the seriousness of the wound. A Sure-Footedness rune might last the duration of a climb up a mountain. To get the absolute best results, when going into battle, a rune ought to be as new as possible.

Jules rolled his sleeve up and held his arm out to Emma. "The honors?" he said.

She took a stele from the trunk and ran it over his bare forearm. Sure-Strike, Swiftness, and Courage. When she was done, she lifted her hair and turned, offering her bare back to Julian. "If you put the runes between my shoulder blades, my hair should cover them," she said.

Julian didn't say anything. She felt him hesitate, and then the lightest touch of his hand on her back, steadying her. He was breathing quickly. Nerves, she thought. It was a strange situation they were walking into, and he was worried for Mark.

He started on the second rune, and Emma felt a slight biting sting as the stele moved. She frowned. Usually, though runes could sting or burn when applied, runes placed on you by your *parabatai* didn't hurt. In fact they were almost pleasant—it was like being wrapped in the protection of friendship, the sense that someone else had sealed their dedication to you onto your skin.

Strange for it to hurt.

Julian finished, stepping back, and Emma let her hair fall. She turned and drew a quick Agility rune on Cristina's shoulder, under the strap of her dress. Then she looked at Mark.

He shook his head, just as he had every time a rune had been offered to him before. "No runes," he said tightly.

"It's fine," Julian said before anyone else could speak. "He doesn't have Marks on him, besides the Voyance, and that's covered in makeup. He looks normal."

"Normal-ish," said Emma. "His ears and his eyes—"

Cristina stepped forward and reached up to muss Mark's hair, spilling the curls down to cover his pointed ears. "There's nothing we can do about the eyes, but—"

"Mundanes have heterochromia too," said Jules. "The main thing is, Mark, try to *act* normal."

Mark looked affronted. "Do I ever not?"

No one answered that, not even Cristina. After sliding a pair of daggers into the shoulder harness under his shirt, Julian slammed the trunk closed, and they headed across the street.

The doors of the theater were thrown open. Light spilled out onto the dark pavement. Emma could hear laughter and music, smell the mingled scents of perfume and wine and smoke.

At the door a young woman in a slinky red dress was taking tickets and stamping hands. Her hair was done up in forties-style Victory roll curls, and her lips were blood red. She wore ivory satin gloves that reached her elbows.

Emma recognized her immediately. She'd seen her at the Shadow Market, winking at Johnny Rook. "I've seen her before," she whispered to Jules. "Shadow Market." He nodded and tucked his hand around Emma's. She jolted slightly, both at the sudden heat around her palm and in surprise.

She glanced over at him, saw the look on his face as he smiled at the familiar-looking ticket girl. A little bored, a little arrogant, a lot entitled. Someone who wasn't worried about getting inside at all. He was playing a role, and taking her hand was part of it, that was all there was to it.

He held out their ticket. "Mr. Smith, plus three guests," he said.

There was a slight commotion behind them as Mark opened his mouth, doubtless to ask who Mr. Smith was, and Cristina stomped on his foot.

The ticket girl smiled, her red lips curving up into a bow, and slowly tore the ticket in half. If she recognized Emma, she didn't show it. "*Mr.* Smith," she said. "Hold out your hand."

Julian offered his free hand, and the ticket girl stamped it with red-black ink. The stamp was an odd little symbol, lines of water underneath a flame. "The performance is running a bit late tonight. You'll find your row and seat numbers have appeared on your ticket. Please don't sit in anyone else's seat." Her gaze went to Mark—a sharp, intent, assessing gaze. "And welcome," she said. "I believe you will find the Followers a . . . sympathetic group."

Mark looked baffled.

Hands stamped and ticket torn, the four of them trailed into the theater. The moment they crossed the threshold, the music rose to deafening levels, and Emma recognized it as the kind of big-band jazz ensemble her father had loved. *Just because I play the violin doesn't mean I don't like dancing*, she remembered him saying, swinging her mother into an impromptu fox-trot in the kitchen.

Julian turned to her. "What is it?" he asked gently.

Emma wished he couldn't read her moods quite so perfectly. She glanced away to hide her expression. Mark and Cristina were behind them, looking around. There was a concession stand, selling popcorn and candy. A sign reading DANCE HALL/THEATER hung over the stand, pointing left. People in fancy dress were moving excitedly down the hallway.

"Nothing. We should go that way," Emma said, and tugged on Julian's hand. "Follow the crowd."

"Hell of a crowd," he muttered. He wasn't wrong. Emma didn't think she'd seen so many expensively dressed people in one place before. "It's like walking into a noir film."

Everywhere were beautiful people, the kind of Hollywood beautiful Emma was used to seeing around Los Angeles: people who had access to gyms and tanning salons and expensive hairdressers and the best clothes. Here they looked as if they'd dressed as extras for a Rat Pack movie. Silk dresses and seamed stockings, fedoras and skinny ties and peaked lapels. Apparently Julian's Sy Devore suit had been a presciently smart choice.

The room was elegant, with a pressed copper ceiling, arched windows, and closed doors marked THEATER LEFT and THEATER RIGHT. A rug had been rolled back for dancing, and couples were swirling together to the sound of a band playing on a raised stage at the end of the room. Thanks to her father's tutelage, she recognized trombones and trumpets, drums and piano, an upright bass and—no special knowledge needed there—a piano. There was a clarinet player too, who took his lips away from the instrument long enough to grin at Emma as she came into the room. He had auburn curls, and there was something odd about his eyes.

"He is faerie," Mark said, his voice suddenly tight. "At least in part."

*Oh.* Emma shot a second look around the room, gaze sweeping over the dancers. She had dismissed them as mundanes, but . . .

glancing through the crowd, she saw a pointed ear there, a flash of orange eyes or taloned fingernails here.

*W-H-A-T I-S I-T?* Jules wrote on her back, his fingertips warm through the thin material of her dress.

"They're all something," Emma said. She remembered the sign at the Shadow Market. PART SUPERNATURAL? YOU'RE NOT ALONE. "Good thing we covered our runes. They've all got the Sight, they've all got some kind of magic."

"The musicians are half-gentry Fair Folk," said Mark, "which is not surprising, for there is nothing the shining ones value more than music. But there are others here whose blood is mixed with those of merfolk, and some who are weres."

"Come on, newbies!" the auburn-haired clarinetist shouted, and a sudden spotlight shone down on the Shadowhunters. "Get into the swing of things!"

When Emma looked at him blankly, he wiggled his eyebrows, and she realized what was strange about his eyes. They were like a goat's, with square black pupils. *"Dance!"* he shouted, and the others in the room whooped and clapped.

The glare of the moving spotlight rendered Julian's face a white blur as he reached for Cristina and pulled her into the crowd. Emma's heart gave a slow, heavy thump.

She pushed the feeling down, turned to Mark, and held her hands out to him. "Dance?"

"I don't know how." There was something in his expression, half puzzlement and half anxiety, that sent a twinge of sympathy through Emma's heart. He took her hands uncertainly. "Faerie dances are—not like this."

Emma drew him toward the crowd. His fingers in hers were slim and cold, not like Jules's warm clasp. "It's all right. I'll lead."

They moved in among the dancers. Emma led, trying to remember what she'd seen in movies where there was dancing like this.

Despite her promise to lead, she wondered if she'd be better off leaving Mark in charge. He had incredible grace, while all her years of fight training made her want to lunge and spin kick more than twirl and shuffle.

Emma glanced over at a girl with short, bright green hair. "Can you tell what everyone is?" she asked Mark.

He blinked, his pale lashes scattering light. "She's part dryad," he said. "Wood faerie. Probably not as much as half. Faerie blood can show up generations later. Most humans who have the Sight have faerie blood years back."

"What about the musicians?"

Mark swung Emma in a turn. He'd started to lead, instinctively. There was something forlorn about the music, Emma thought, as if it were drifting down from a high, distant place. "The clarinetist is part satyr. The bassist with the pale blue skin, some kind of mer-folk. Kieran's mother was a nixie, a water faerie, and—"

He broke off. Emma could see Jules and Cristina, her hot pink dress startling against the black of his suit. He twirled her. Emma bit the inside of her lip. "Kieran? That gentry prince who came with you to the Institute?"

Mark was sharp-boned light and shadows in the moving illumination. The air smelled like incense—like the cheap sweet stuff they burned on the Venice boardwalks. "We were friends in the Wild Hunt."

"Well, he could have been less of a jerk to you, then," Emma muttered.

"I don't think he could have, actually." Mark smiled, and Emma could see where the human in him mixed with the fey—faeries, in her experience, never smiled with such openness.

She made a face. "Was there anything about the Hunt that wasn't awful? Was any of it, I don't know, fun?"

"Parts." He laughed and spun her. There was that edge of fey again, the wildness of it. She paced back, slowing the dance.

"What parts?"

He whirled her in a circle. "I'm not supposed to talk about it. It's a *geas*."

Emma exhaled. "Like if you told me, then you'd have to kill me?"

"Why would I kill you?" Mark sounded honestly bewildered.

She tipped her head back and smiled at him. Sometimes talking to him was like talking to Ty, she thought. She found herself making jokes she thought were obvious and then realizing they weren't obvious at all unless you understood the subtle codes of social interaction. She didn't know how she'd learned them, just that she had, and Ty still struggled with them, and so, it seemed, did Mark.

Trying to look at the world through Ty's eyes, Julian had said once, was like looking into a kaleidoscope, shaking it up, and then looking again. You saw all the same glimmering crystals, just in a different formation.

"The Wild Hunt was freedom," Mark said. "And freedom is necessary."

In Mark's eyes Emma could see a wilderness of stars and treetops, the fierce shine of glaciers, all the glittering detritus of the roof of the world.

It made her think of riding that motorcycle over the ocean. Of the freedom to be wild and untrammeled. Of the ache she felt in her soul sometimes to be connected to nothing, answerable to nothing, bound by nothing.

"Mark—" she began.

Mark's expression changed; he was looking past her suddenly, his hand tightening on hers. Emma glanced where he was looking but saw only the cloakroom. A bored-looking coat-check girl perched on the counter, smoking a cigarette out of a silver holder.

"Mark?" Emma turned back to him, but he was already moving away from her, vaulting over the counter of the coat-check station—much to the bored girl's amusement—and vanishing. Emma was about to follow him when Cristina and Julian swung into her line of sight, blocking her.

"Mark ran off," Emma announced.

"Yeah, he's not exactly a team player yet," said Julian. He was ruffled from dancing, his cheeks flushed. Cristina didn't have a hair out of place. "Look, I'll go after him, and you two dance—"

"If I might cut in?" A tall young man appeared in front of them. He looked like he was probably about twenty-five, nattily dressed in a herringbone suit and matching fedora. His hair was bleached blond and he wore expensive-looking shoes with red soles that flashed fire as he walked. A gaudy pink cocktail ring glittered on his middle finger. His gaze was fixed on Cristina. "Would you like to dance?"

"If you don't mind," Julian said, his voice easy, polite, reaching to put a hand on Cristina's arm. "My girlfriend and I, we're . . ."

The man's friendly expression changed—infinitesimally, but Emma could see it, a tautness behind his eyes that made Julian's words trail off. "And if *you* don't mind," he said, "I think you may have failed to notice I'm a Blue." He tapped his pocket, where an invitation that matched the one they'd found in Ava's purse was folded—matched it, except for being a pale shade of blue. He rolled his eyes at their puzzled expressions. "Newbies," he muttered, and there was an undercurrent of something unpleasant—almost scornful—in his dark eyes.

"Of course." Cristina shot a quick look at Julian and Emma, and then turned back to the stranger with a smile. "We're so sorry to have misunderstood."

Julian's face was grim as Cristina headed onto the dance floor with the man who'd called himself a Blue. Emma sympathized. She comforted herself with the knowledge that if he tried anything on the dance floor, Cristina would fillet him with her butterfly knife.

"We'd better dance too," said Julian. "Looks like it's the only way not to be noticed."

*We've already been noticed*, Emma thought. It was true: Though no fuss had been made over their arrival, plenty of people in the crowd were casting them sideways glances. There were quite a few of the Followers who looked entirely human—and indeed, Emma wasn't totally clear on their policy regarding mundanes—but as newcomers, she imagined they were still objects of attention. Certainly the behavior of the clarinetist had indicated as much.

She took Julian's hand and they moved into the outside of the crowd, toward the end of the room, where the shadows were deeper. "Half faeries, ifrits, weres," Emma murmured, taking Julian's other hand so that they faced each other. He looked more ruffled than he had before, his cheeks flushed. She couldn't blame him for being unsettled. In most crowds, their runes, if discovered, would mean nothing. She had the feeling this crowd was different. "Why are they all here?"

"It isn't easy, having the Sight, if you don't know others who do," Julian said in a low voice. "You see things nobody else sees. You can't talk about it because no one will understand. You have to keep secrets, and secrets—they break you apart. Cut you open. Make you vulnerable."

The low timbre of his voice shuddered down through Emma's bones. There was something in it that frightened her. Something that reminded her of the glaciers in Mark's eyes, distant and lonely.

"Jules," she said.

Muttering something like "never mind," he spun her away, then pulled her back toward him. Years of practicing fighting together made them an almost perfect dancing team, she realized with surprise. They could predict each other's movements, glide with each other's bodies. She could tell which way Julian would step by the cadence of his breath and the faint tightening of his fingers around hers.

Julian's dark curls were wildly tousled, and when he drew her near him, she could smell the clove spice of his cologne, the faint scent of paint underneath.

The song ended. Emma looked up and over at the band; the clarinetist was watching her and Julian. Unexpectedly, he winked. The band struck up again, this time a slower, softer number. Couples moved together as if magnetized, arms wrapping around necks, hands resting on hips, heads leaning together.

Julian had frozen. Emma, her hands still in his, stood stock-still, not moving, not breathing.

The moment stretched out, interminable. Julian's eyes searched hers; whatever he saw there seemed to decide him. His arms came up around her and he pulled her close. Her chin hit his shoulder, awkwardly. It was the first awkward thing they'd done together.

She felt him inhale, a hitching breath against her. His hands splayed, warm, under her shoulder blades. She turned her head. She could hear his heartbeat, swift and furious, under her ear, feel the hardness of his chest.

She reached up to loop her arms around his neck. There was enough of a height difference between them that when she locked her fingers, they tangled in the hair at his nape.

A shiver went through her. She'd touched Julian's hair before, of course, but it was so soft there, there at the vulnerable space just under the fall of loose curls. And the skin was soft too. She stroked downward with her fingers, reflexively, and felt at the same time the top bump of his spine and his swiftly inhaled breath.

She looked up at him. His face was white, eyes cast down, dark lashes feathered against his cheekbones. He was biting his bottom lip, the way he always did when he was nervous. She could see the dents his teeth made in the soft skin.

If she kissed him, would he taste like blood or cloves or a mixture of the two? Sweet and spicy? Bitter and hot?

She made herself shove the thought down. He was her *parabatai*. He wasn't for kissing. He was—

His left hand moved down over her back to her waist, sliding around to lightly cup her hip. Her body jolted. She'd heard of people having butterflies in their stomachs, and she knew what they meant: that flapping, uneasy feeling deep in your gut. But she had it now *everywhere*. Butterflies under all of her skin, fluttering, sending shivers that moved in waves up and down her body. She began to trace her finger over his wrist, meaning to write on him: *J-U-L-I-A-N, W-H-A-T A-R-E Y-O-U D-O-I-N-G?*

But he didn't seem to notice. For the first time, he wasn't hearing their secret language. She stopped, stared up at him; his eyes when they met hers were unfocused, dreamy. His right hand was in her hair, winding it through his fingers. She felt the sensations as if each individual hair were a live wire connected to one of her nerve endings.

"When you came down the stairs tonight," he said, his voice thick and low, "I was thinking about painting you. Painting your hair. That I'd have to use titanium white to get the color right, the way it catches light and almost glows. But that wouldn't work, would it? It's not all one color, your hair, it's not just gold: It's amber and tawny and caramel and wheat and honey."

Normal Emma would have made a joke. *You make it sound like a breakfast cereal.* Normal Emma and Normal Julian would have laughed. But this wasn't Normal Julian; this was a Julian she'd never seen, a Julian with his expression stripped down to the elegant bones of his face. She felt a wave of desperate wanting, lost in the way his eyes looked, in the curves of his cheekbones and jaw, the unexpected softness of his mouth.

"But you never paint me," she whispered.

He didn't answer. He looked agonized. His pulse was pounding triple time. She could see it in his throat. His arms were locked in place; she sensed he needed to hold her where she was, not let her come an inch closer. The space between them was heated, electric. His fingers curled around her hip. His other hand slid down her back, slowly, gliding along her hair until he reached bare skin where the back of the dress dipped down.

He closed his eyes.

They had stopped dancing. They were standing still, Emma barely breathing, Julian's hands moving over her. Julian had touched her a thousand times: while they trained, while they fought or tended each other's wounds.

He had never touched her like this.

He seemed like someone under a spell. Someone who knew he was under a spell, and was fighting against the pull of it with every nerve and fiber, the percussion of a terrible internal struggle pounding through his veins. She could feel his pulse through his hands, against the bare skin of her back.

She moved toward him, just a little, barely an inch. He gasped. His chest expanded against hers, brushing the swell of her breasts through the thin material of her dress. The sensation whipped through her like electricity. She couldn't think.

"Emma," he said in a choked voice. His hands contracted, sharply, as if he'd been stabbed. He was pulling her. Toward him. Her body slammed up against his. The crowd was a blur of light and color around them. His head lowered toward hers. They breathed the same breath.

There was a clash of cymbals: shattering, deafening. They broke apart as the doors of the theater were thrown open, the room flooding with bright light. The music stopped.

A loudspeaker crackled to life. "Will the audience please enter the theater," said a sultry female voice. "The performance of the Lottery is about to begin."

Cristina had broken away from the man in the herringbone suit and was making her way toward them, face flushed. Emma's heart was pounding. She chanced a look up at Julian. For the briefest of moments he looked like someone who'd been staggering through the Mojave Desert, half-dead from sun, and had seen a glimmer of water up ahead only to have it turn out to be a mirage.

"Still no Mark?" Emma said hastily as Cristina reached them. Not that there was a real reason Cristina would know where Mark was; Emma just didn't want her looking at Julian. Not when he looked like that.

Cristina shook her head.

"We'd better go in, then," Julian said. His voice was normal, his expression smoothing itself into normalcy. "Mark'll catch up."

Emma couldn't help but look at him in surprise. She'd always known Julian was a decent actor—Shadowhunters had to lie and play parts all the time—but it was as if she'd imagined the expression she'd seen on his face a second ago. As if she'd imagined the last ten minutes.

As if none of it had happened at all.

# 15

## THE ANGELS
## NOT HALF SO HAPPY

**"What are you doing here?" Mark hissed into the darkness.**

He was standing in the coat closet, surrounded by racks of expensive clothes. The temperature dropped in Los Angeles at night, even in the summer, but the coats were light: linen and seersucker men's jackets, silk and gossamer women's wraps. There was very little light, but Mark didn't fight it when a pale hand reached out from behind a leather trenchcoat and yanked him through a coatrack.

Kieran. His hair was the darkest of dark blues today, almost black, the color of waves during a roiling storm. Which meant he was in a vile mood. His silver-black eyes glowed in the darkness.

"How else am I supposed to see you?" he demanded, shoving Mark up against the wall. There was little space behind the coats; it was close and hot. Mark felt himself gasp, and not just from the force of the wall hitting his back. Rage was rolling off Kieran in waves that he could feel; they twisted inside him, deep down in a place where the cold waters of Faerie had once chilled his heart. "I cannot enter the Institute, save the Sanctuary, and I would be killed if I was found there. Am I meant to spend every night waiting in the desert shadows in the hopes that you might deign to visit me?"

"No," Mark said, even as Kieran pressed him farther back, his knee wedging itself between Mark's legs. His words were furious but his hands on Mark's body were familiar: thin, cool fingers working the buttons of his shirt, slipping between them to brush his skin. "We're supposed to stay away from each other until this is over."

Kieran's eyes blazed. "And then what? You will come back to the Hunt voluntarily, for me? You think me such a fool. You have always hated it."

"But I did not hate you," Mark said. The coatroom smelled like a million perfumes mixed together: colognes that clung to coats and jackets tickling his nose. They were synthetic smells, not real: false tuberose, false jasmine, false lavender. Nothing in the mundane world was real. But then, was anything in Faerie any realer?

"*Did not hate me?*" Kieran said in a cold voice. "What an honor. How complimented I am. Do you even miss me?"

"I miss you," said Mark.

"And am I meant to believe that? Remember, half blood, I know well that you can lie."

Mark flicked his eyes up to Kieran's. He saw the storm in those eyes, but behind the storm he saw two boys as small as stars in a distant sky, locked together under a blanket. They were the same height; he had only to reach across slightly and press his mouth to Kieran's.

The faerie prince stiffened against him. He didn't move, hesitant rather than unresponsive. Mark's hands came up to cradle Kieran's face, and then Kieran did move, pressing forward to kiss Mark with an intensity that sent Mark's head flying back against the wall.

Kieran tasted of blood and cold night sky and for a moment Mark was flying free with the Hunt. The night sky was his road to conquer. He rode a silver-white horse made of moonlight down a path of stars. Surrounded by shouts and laughter and cries, he cut a path through the night that opened the world to his searching eyes; he saw places no human gaze had seen, hidden waterfalls and secret valleys. He stopped to rest on the peaks of icebergs and galloped his horse down the foam of waterfalls, the white arms of water nymphs reaching up to catch at him. He lay with Kieran in the grass of a high Alpine meadow, hand in hand, and counted a thousand billion stars.

Kieran was the first to break away.

Mark's breath was coming hard. "Was there a lie in that kiss?"

"No. But—" Kieran looked wondering. "Are those stars in your eyes for me or for the Hunt?"

"The Hunt was pain and glory," said Mark. "But you were what made me able to see the glory and not only the pain."

"That girl," Kieran said. "You came back with her the other night, on my steed." Mark realized with a jolt that he meant Cristina. "I thought perhaps you loved her."

His eyes were lowered. His hair had lightened to a silvery blue, the ocean after a storm. Mark remembered that Kieran was no older than he was; though an ageless faerie, he had lived less than twenty years. And he knew even less than Mark did about humans. "I don't think one falls in love that quickly," said Mark. "I like her."

"You cannot give her your heart," said Kieran, "though you may do whatever else you like with her."

Mark had to stifle a laugh. Kieran, showing his own sort of kindness. Faeries believed in promises over fidelity of body or heart. One made a promise to one's beloved, and one abided by that promise.

Demanding a promise of physical fidelity was rare, but one could absolutely demand fidelity of the heart, and faeries usually did. The punishment for breaking a promise of love was severe.

"She is the daughter of an old family," he said. "A sort of princess. I don't think she would look at me twice."

"She looked at you several times while you were dancing with the blond girl."

Mark blinked. Partly in surprise that he had so quickly forgotten how literal faeries were. And partly in surprise that he himself had remembered such a human expression and used it so unconsciously.

It was pointless to try to explain to Kieran all the ways that Cristina would never want him. She was too kind to show her revulsion at his faerie blood, but revolted he was sure she must be, under the surface. Instead he tucked his hands into the waistband of Kieran's breeches and pulled the other boy toward him to take another kiss, and with it memories of the Hunt like sweet wine.

Their kisses were hot, tangled. Two boys under a blanket, trying not to make noise, not to wake the others. Kissing to blot out the memories, kissing away the blood and dirt, kissing away the tears. Mark's hands made their way under Kieran's shirt, tracing the lines of scars on his back. There, they were matched in pain, though at least those who had whipped Mark were not his own family.

Kieran's hands slipped ineffectually on Mark's pearl buttons. "These mundane clothes," he said between his teeth. "I hate them."

"Then take them off me," Mark murmured, forgetful and dazed and lost in the Hunt. His hands were on Kieran but in his mind he was spinning through the northern lights, the sky painted blue and green like the heart of the ocean. Like Blackthorn eyes.

"No." Kieran smiled and stepped back. He was rumpled, his shirt gaping open at the front. Wanting beat through Mark's blood, to lose himself in Kieran and forget. "You told me once humans want what they cannot have. And you are half-human."

"We want what we cannot have," Mark said. "But we love what shows us kindness."

"I will take wanting, for now," said Kieran, and placed his hand over the necklace at Mark's throat. "And the memory of my gift to you."

Elf-bolts took a great deal of magic to make and were very valuable. Kieran had given it to him not long after he joined the Wild Hunt, and had strung the point on a chain so Mark could wear it near his heart.

"Shoot straight and true," said Kieran. "Find the killer, and then come back to me."

"But my family," Mark said, his hand closing reflexively over Kieran's. "Kier, you must—"

"Come back to me," Kieran repeated. He kissed Mark's closed hand, once, and ducked out through the dangling coats. Though Mark scrambled after him immediately, he was already gone.

The interior of the theater was gorgeous, a romantic ode to the glory days of cinema's golden age. A curved ceiling split into eights by gold-painted beams, each segment painted with a scene from a classic film, done in baroque jewel tones: Emma recognized *Gone with the Wind* and *Casablanca*, but not others—a man carrying another man across burning golden sands, a girl kneeling at the feet of a boy holding a gun across his shoulders, a woman whose white dress blew up around her like the petals of an orchid.

A heavy sweet scent hung in the air as people hurried to take their seats in the semicircular space. The seats were upholstered in purple velvet, each with a gold *M* embroidered across the back. As the ticket girl had promised, their ticket now had their row and seat numbers printed on it. They found them and filed in, Cristina first, then Emma, then Julian. He sat down beside Emma.

"*M* for *Midnight*?" she said, pointing at the seat backs.

"Probably," he said, and went back to looking at the stage. The curtains were drawn back and a massive painting of an ocean view covered the back wall. The stage itself was bare, the floor gleaming polished boards.

Emma felt flushed. Julian's voice had been calm, neutral. But the expression on his face only a few minutes ago flashed across her vision anyway: the way he'd looked when he held her on the dance floor, that naked look in his eyes, all pretense stripped away.

That glimpse had shown her an intent and agonized Julian she'd never known. A hidden face she'd never seen, that she didn't think anyone had ever seen.

She felt Cristina shift beside her and turned with quick guilt: She'd been so caught up in her own bewilderment that she'd forgotten to ask Cristina why she'd looked so flustered.

Cristina was glaring across the theater. Her eyes were glued to the man in the herringbone suit. He was seating himself next to an elegant blond woman in a silver dress and high heels.

"Ugh," Cristina said. "I practically had to peel him off me. What a pervert. My mother would just have stabbed him."

"Do you want us to kill him?" Emma suggested, only half-joking. "We could kill him, after the show."

"That would be a waste of our energy," Cristina said dismissively. "I'll tell you what I found out: He is a half werewolf. And he's been a member of the Followers, that's what he called them, for six months now. That's what he meant by being a Blue."

"The fact that he's been a Follower for a long time, or the fact that he's part lycanthrope?" Julian asked.

"Both, I think," Cristina said. "He went to great pains to tell me all about what it meant to be part werewolf. How he's stronger and faster than a human. He says he could kick through a brick wall." She rolled her eyes.

"I don't even get it," said Emma. "How do you wind up being half-werewolf?"

"It means you have the werewolf virus, but it's dormant," said Jules. "You can pass it on, but you can't Turn yourself. You'll never change into a wolf, but you do have increased speed and strength."

"He said they all have increased speed and strength," said Cristina. "Every time they hold a Lottery, he said, the Followers all get stronger."

"Sympathetic magic," Julian said. Suddenly there was a commotion in their row.

"Am I late?" It was Mark, seeming flustered, tumbling into the seat beside Julian. His fair hair looked as if he'd been standing in front of a wind machine. "Sorry, I got distracted."

Julian looked at him for a long moment. "Don't tell me," he said finally. "I don't want to know."

Mark looked surprised. "You don't?" he said. "I would."

"I *do*," chimed in Emma, but before Mark could say anything, the lights in the theater dimmed. Silence fell instantly—not the slow hushing of voices Emma would have expected, but an abrupt, unnatural cessation of noise.

A shiver passed up the back of her neck just as a single spotlight lit up the stage.

The band had gathered in the orchestra pit. They began to play a quiet melody, almost mournful, as a black-velvet-draped object was wheeled out onto the stage by two uniformed men. The music faded, and there was the tap-tap of high heels; a moment later the woman who had been taking tickets at the door appeared. She had changed and was wearing a gorgeous full-length dress of black and dark blue lace that looked like foam on the ocean. Even at a distance Emma could see the dark kohl liner ringing her eyes.

The woman reached out a hand, the nails painted viper red, and seized hold of the black velvet, tearing it aside and hurling it dramatically to the floor.

Revealed underneath was a machine. A large transparent drum sat atop a metal plinth; inside the glass were hundreds of colored, numbered balls. A metal chute stuck out from the machine, and in front of the chute was a tray.

"Ladies and gentlemen," said the woman onstage. "I'm Belinda Belle."

"'Belinda Belle'?" Julian whispered. "Made-up name."

"You're a genius detective," Emma whispered back. "Genius."

He made a face at her, and Emma felt a wave of relief. This was her and Julian, making faces at each other, making each other laugh. That was normal.

The woman on the stage continued, "Welcome to the Lottery."

The room was silent. Belinda smiled, resting her hand on the device, perfectly still.

"A lottery machine," murmured Julian. "*That's* literal."

"The Guardian could not be with us tonight," said Belinda. "Security has required tightening. The last hunt was interrupted by Nephilim, and the value of the sacrifice was endangered."

There was a low hum. A jolt went through Emma. *Nephilim.* The woman had said "Nephilim." These people knew about Shadowhunters. It wasn't a surprise so much as a confirmation of what Emma had suspected all along. There was something going on here, something that reached its threaded tendrils into Downworld and clawed at the roots of everything they knew.

"The sacrifice?" Emma whispered. "Does she mean *human* sacrifice?"

*S-H-H-H,* Julian wrote on her arm. She saw with a pang as his fingers touched her skin that his nails were bitten down to the quick.

The music picked up. Onstage, Belinda pressed a button on the side of the machine. The metal arms whirred to life. The balls spun around inside the globe, becoming a blur of color like the inside of a kaleidoscope.

*Turn, and turn, and turn. Emma on the beach, her dad's arm around her. Kaleidoscopes are like magic, Emma. No two people who look into them ever see the same thing.*

Emma's heart ached with memory. The machine whirred more quickly, then more quickly still, and spit out a red ball. It shot down the chute and fell into the tray.

Belinda picked it up delicately. A tense stillness had fallen over the crowd. It was the stillness of cats poised to spring.

"Blue," she said, her voice ringing in the silence. "Blue 304."

The moment hung, frozen and suspended. It was broken by a man rising to his feet. He moved warily, like a statue brought to sudden and reluctant life.

It was the man Cristina had danced with, the one in the herringbone suit. He was very pale now, and the woman in the silver dress was edging away from him.

"Mr. Sterling," said Belinda, and let the ball fall back into the tray with a clink. "The Lottery has chosen you."

Emma couldn't help but look around, trying not to seem as if she was staring. The audience sat stonily, most expressionless. Some wore looks of relief. The man in the herringbone suit—Sterling—seemed dazed, as if he'd been punched in the solar plexus and was about to gasp in air.

"You know the rules," Belinda said. "Mr. Sterling has two days of freedom before the hunt begins. No one may help him. No one may interfere with the hunt." Her eyes searched the audience. "May Those Who Are Older grant us all good fortune."

The music started up again. Everyone began to rise to their feet, the room filling with the buzz of low conversation. Emma was on her feet like a shot, but Julian's hand closed around her arm before she could bolt out of the room. He was smiling; it looked clearly fake to her but would probably convince anyone who didn't know him.

"They're going to kill him," Emma whispered urgently. "Everything she said—the *hunt*—"

"We don't know that," Julian said without moving his lips.

"Emma is right," Mark said. They were hurrying forward, pushed toward the exits by the mass of the crowd. The band was playing "As Time Goes By" from *Casablanca*, the sweet melody completely incongruous with the sense of anxiety whipping through the room. "A hunt means death."

"We have to offer him help," Cristina said. Her tone was flat.

"Even if he is a pervert," Emma confirmed. "It's what we do—"

"You heard the rules," Jules said. "No interfering."

Emma spun around, stopping dead. Her eyes met Julian's. "Those rules," she said, and took his hand, her fingers moving over his skin. *T-H-E-Y D-O-N-T A-P-P-L-Y T-O U-S.*

Darkness blossomed in the blue-green irises she knew so well: an admission of defeat. "Go," he said. "Take Cristina." Emma caught Cristina's hand and the two of them were shoving through the crowd, Emma using her elbows and boots—stomping viciously on several feet—to push past the other theatergoers. They reached the central aisle. She was aware of Cristina asking her in a hissed whisper how they were going to find Mark and Julian again.

"At the car," said Emma. She saw Cristina's puzzled look but didn't bother saying that she knew the plan the way she always knew Julian's plans. She knew them because she knew him.

"There he is." Cristina pointed with her free hand. They had made it to the lobby. Emma followed her indication and saw a flash of the red soles of shoes. Mr. Sterling, slipping out the door. The woman he'd come with was nowhere to be seen.

They bolted after him, darting around the crowd. Emma crashed into a girl with rainbow-dyed hair who made a surprised "Oof!" sound.

"Sorry!" Emma yelled just as she and Cristina escaped through the small circle of people standing around the theater entrance.

The Hollywood sign twinkled, brilliant, above them. Where the street curved, Emma could see Sterling disappearing around a corner. Emma broke into a flat-out run, Cristina on her heels.

This was why she ran every day on the beach. So she could fly over pavement without feeling it, so that her breath didn't catch and running felt like flying. Cristina was just behind her. Her dark hair had come down out of its careful bun and flew behind her like a dark flag.

They turned the corner. They were on a side street; bungalow houses lined the road, most of their windows dark. Sterling was standing just beside a massive, expensive-looking silver Jeep, his hand still on the remote key. He stared at them in total astonishment as they skidded to a halt in front of him.

"What—?" he sputtered. Up close it was possible to see how shaken he looked. He was pale and sweating, his throat working convulsively. "What are you doing?"

His eyes flashed yellow-green in the light from the streetlamps. Half-werewolf he might be, Emma thought, but he looked like a scared mundane.

"We can help you," she said.

His throat worked again. "What are you talking about?" he demanded, so savagely that Emma heard a snicking sound to her left and realized Cristina had flipped open her butterfly knife. She hadn't moved, but it shone in her hand, a silent threat should Sterling take one step toward Emma.

"The Lottery," Emma said. "You got picked."

"Yeah, I know. You think I don't know?" Sterling snarled. "You shouldn't even be talking to me." He ran his hands through his hair distractedly. His key ring fell from his grip and rattled to the ground. Emma took a step forward, reaching for it. She held it out to him. "No!" he shouted hoarsely and skittered backward, like a crab. "Don't touch me! Don't come near me!"

Emma tossed the keys at his feet and held her hands up, palms open. She was aware of where all her own weapons were, the daggers in her boots, under the hem of her dress.

She missed Cortana, though.

"We don't want to hurt you," she said. "We want to help, that's all."

He bent down and warily grabbed his keys. "You can't help me. No one can help me."

"Your lack of trust is very hurtful," said Emma.

"You have no idea what's going on here." He laughed a sharp, unnatural laugh. "Don't you get it? *No one can help me*, especially not some stupid kids—" He paused then, looking at Emma. At her arm, specifically. She glanced down and cursed under her breath. The makeup that covered her *parabatai* rune was smeared—probably from when she had bumped into that girl in the lobby—and the Mark was clearly visible.

Sterling looked the opposite of thrilled. "Nephilim," he snarled. "Jesus, just what I need."

"We know Belinda said not to interfere," Emma began hastily. "But since we *are* Nephilim—"

"That's not even her name." He spat into the gutter. "You don't know anything, do you? Goddamn Shadowhunters, thinking they're the kings of Downworld, messing everything up. Belinda should never have allowed you in."

"You could be a little more polite." Emma felt an edge creep into her voice. "Considering we're trying to help you. And that you felt Cristina up."

"I didn't," he said, his eyes flicking between them.

"You did," Cristina said. "It was very disgusting."

"Then why are you trying to help me?" Sterling asked.

"Because nobody deserves to die," Emma said. "And to be honest, there're things we want to know. What's the point of the Lottery? How does it make you all stronger?"

He stared at them, shaking his head. "You're insane." He slammed his thumb down on his key remote; the Jeep's headlights flashed as it unlocked. "Stay away from me. Like Belinda said. No interfering."

He jerked the door open and hurled himself into the car. A second later the Jeep was screeching away down the street, leaving black tire marks on the asphalt.

Emma expelled a breath. "Kind of hard to stay desperately concerned about his well-being, isn't it?"

Cristina looked after the Jeep. "It is a test," she said. Her knife had disappeared, slipped back under her collar. "The Angel would say we were put here to save not only those we like but also the unpleasant and disagreeable."

"You said your mother would have stabbed him."

"Yes, well," said Cristina. "We don't always agree about everything."

Before Emma could reply, the Institute's Toyota pulled up in front of them. Mark leaned out the back window. Even with everything that was happening, Emma felt a spark of happiness that Jules had saved the seat next to him for her. "Your chariot, fair ones," Mark said. "Enter and hie we away before we are followed."

"Was that English?" Cristina demanded, climbing in beside him. Emma darted to the car to slide into the front seat.

Julian looked over at her. "That looked like a pretty dramatic conversation." The car slid forward, away from the odd street, the peculiar theater. They passed over the tire tracks the Jeep had made on the road.

"He didn't want our help," said Emma.

"But he's getting it anyway," Julian said. "Isn't he?"

"If we can track him down," said Emma. "They could all have been using assumed names." She put her feet up on the dashboard. "It might be worth asking Johnny Rook. Since they were advertising at the Shadow Market and he knows everything that happens there."

"Didn't Diana tell you to stay away from Johnny Rook?" said Julian.

"Isn't Diana kind of far away right now?" Emma said sweetly.

Julian looked resigned but also amused. "Fine. I trust you. If you think there's a reason, we'll go ask Rook."

They were turning onto La Cienega. The lights and clamor and traffic of Los Angeles exploded all around them. Emma clapped her hands. "And that's why I love you."

The words slipped out without her thinking. Neither Cristina nor Mark seemed to notice—they were arguing about whether "hie" was a word—but Julian's cheeks turned a dull brick red and his hands tightened on the wheel.

When they reached the Institute, a storm was building out over the ocean—a roil of blue-black clouds spiked with lightning. Lights were on inside the building. Cristina began mounting the steps wearily. She was used to late nights of hunting, but something about the experience at the theater had tired her soul.

"Cristina."

It was Mark, on the step below her. One of the first things Cristina had noticed about the Institute was that depending on which direction the wind was blowing from, it smelled either of ocean water or of the desert. Of sea salt or of sage. Tonight it was sage. The wind blew through Mark's hair: Blackthorn curls bleached of all their color, silvery as the moon on the water.

"You dropped these outside the theater," he said, and held out his hand. She looked down and past him for a moment, to where Julian and Emma were standing by the foot of the steps. Julian had pulled the car up and was lifting Cortana out of the trunk. It caught the light and shimmered like Emma's hair. She reached for it, glancing down to run her hand along the scabbarded blade, and Cristina saw Julian glance involuntarily at the curve of her neck. As if he couldn't help it.

Cold fear weighted down Cristina's stomach; she felt as if she were watching trains hurtling toward each other on the same track, with no way of stopping either one.

"Cristina?" Mark said again, a question rising in his voice. Something glittered in his open palm. Two somethings. The gold earrings that had fallen out while she was running, that she had assumed were lost somewhere on a Los Angeles square of pavement.

"Oh!" She took them from him, slipping them into the pocket of her coat. He watched her, his mismatched eyes curious. "They were a gift," she said. "From someone—from an old friend."

She remembered Diego putting them into her hand, and there had been nervousness in his dark eyes, a wondering if she would like them. But she had, because he had given them to her.

"They're pretty," Mark said. "Especially against your hair. It looks like black silk."

Cristina exhaled. Emma was looking up at Julian, smiling. There was uncertainty on her face, uncertainty that cut at Cristina's heart. Emma reminded her of herself, she thought, just before she turned that corner in the garden where she'd heard Jaime and Diego talking. Before everything had fallen apart.

"You shouldn't say those sort of things to me," she said to Mark.

The wind blew his hair across his face; he pushed it back. "I thought mortal women liked compliments." He sounded honestly puzzled.

"Do faerie women like them?"

"I don't know many," he said. "The Seelie Queen does enjoy a compliment. But there were no women in the Hunt."

"But there was Kieran," she said. "And what would he say if he knew you were telling me I was pretty? Because the way he looks at you . . ."

A look of shock passed over Mark's face. He glanced down quickly at Julian, but his brother was absorbed in Emma. "How do you—?"

"I saw you," she said. "In the parking lot. And when you disappeared today at the theater, I would guess that was because of him as well?"

"Please tell no one, Cristina." The look of fear on his face broke her heart. "They would punish him, and me as well. We both swore we would not reveal our relationship to any Shadowhunters, lest they think I would be too loyal to Faerie and too likely to return to it, and not agree to our bargain. Also, Kieran is forbidden to see me now that I am out of the Hunt."

"I will tell no one," said Cristina. "I have not mentioned it, not to Emma, not to anyone."

"You are as kind as you are lovely," he said, but the words sounded rehearsed.

"I know you think you can't trust mortals. But I will not betray you."

There was nothing rehearsed about the look he gave her then. "I meant it when I said you were beautiful. I want you, and Kieran would not mind—"

"You *want* me?"

"Yes," Mark said simply, and Cristina looked away, suddenly very aware of how close his body was to hers. Of the shape of his shoulders under his jacket. He was lovely as faeries were lovely, with a sort of unearthliness, as quicksilver as moonlight on water. He didn't seem quite touchable, but she had seen him kiss Kieran and knew better. "You do not want to be wanted?"

In another time, the time before, Cristina would have blushed. "It is not the sort of compliment mortal women enjoy."

"But why not?" said Mark.

"Because it makes it sound like I am a thing you want to use. And when you say Kieran would not mind, you make it sound as if he would not mind because I do not matter."

"That is very human," he said. "To be jealous of a body but not a heart."

Cristina had studied faeries closely. It was true that unmarried faerie folk, regardless of sexual orientation, placed a very low value on physical fidelity, though a much greater value than humans did on emotional loyalty. There were few if any vows that had to do with sex, but many that had to do with true love. "You see, I do not want a body without a heart," she said.

He did not reply, but she could read the look in his eyes. If she said the word, she could have Mark Blackthorn, for some value of having him. It was a strange thing to know, even if she did not want what he offered. But if he were offering *more*—well, there had been a time she had thought she would never want anyone again.

It was good to know that wasn't true.

"Is Kieran the reason?" she said. "That you might return to Faerie, even if the killer is caught?"

"Kieran saved my life," said Mark. "I was nothing in the Wild Hunt."

"You are not nothing. You are the son of the Lady Nerissa."

"And Kieran is the son of the King of the Unseelie Court," said Mark flatly. "He did everything for me in the Wild Hunt. Protected me and kept me alive. And he has only me. Julian and the others, they have each other. They do not need me."

But he didn't sound convinced. He spoke as if the words were dead leaves, blowing across some hollow and aching space inside him. And in that moment Cristina yearned toward him more than she ever had, for she knew that feeling, to be so hollowed out by loss that you felt as if the wind could blow through you.

"That is not love," Cristina said. "That is debt."

Mark set his jaw. He had never looked more like a Blackthorn. "If there is one thing I have learned in my life, and I grant I have not learned much, it is this: Neither Fair Folk nor mortals know what love is or is not. No one does."

# 16
## By the Side

"So, basically, you kind of solved the investigation," said Livvy. She was lying on the rug in Julian's room. They were all sprawled around his bedroom: Cristina perched neatly on a chair, Ty sitting against a wall with his headphones on, Julian cross-legged on his bed. He'd taken off his jacket and rolled up his sleeves. The cuff links Emma had given him gleamed on the nightstand. Mark lay on his stomach across the foot of the bed, eye to eye with Church, who'd decided to pay them a visit, probably because of the weather. "I mean, now we know who did it. The murders."

"Not exactly," said Emma. She was sitting on the floor, leaning her back against the nightstand. "I mean, here's what we do know. This group, these Followers or whatever they call themselves, they're responsible for Stanley Wells's murder. The Followers are mostly people who've had some brush with the supernatural. They have the Sight, they're part faerie—Sterling's sort of a werewolf. Every month they hold a Lottery. Someone gets picked, and that someone becomes a sacrifice."

"Wells was a sacrifice," said Julian. "So it stands to reason that the other eleven murders have been because of this cult too."

"It also explains the fey bodies," said Cristina. "Since so many of them are half-fey, it makes sense that they've been picked for the sacrifices."

Julian glanced at Mark. "Do you think the Courts know if the bodies were half-fey or full-blooded?"

"Hard to say," said Mark, still staring at the cat. "They often cannot tell just by looking, and some of the Followers are full-blood faeries."

"It seems like full-blood faeries would have better things to do." It was Ty, having pulled the headphones from his ears. Emma could faintly hear classical music drifting from them. "Why would they join something like this?"

"It is a place for lost souls," said Mark. "And since the Cold Peace, many of the Fair Folk are lost. It makes sense."

"I saw them advertising at the Shadow Market," said Emma. "I saw Belinda there too. They seemed to be specifically looking for anyone with the Sight, anyone who seemed frightened or alone. Having a group to belong to, being promised good luck and wealth, getting strength from the sacrifices—you can see how it would be appealing."

"They do seem very confident," Cristina said. "How much do they know about the existence of Nephilim, I wonder?"

"Sterling seemed afraid of us," said Emma. "It's weird. He got picked, so that means they're going to sacrifice him. You'd think he'd want any help he could get, even from Shadowhunters."

"But getting help is forbidden, right?" said Livvy. "If they caught him accepting it, they could torture him. Do worse than kill him."

Cristina shuddered. "Or he could be a true believer. Maybe he thinks it would be a sin to accept help."

"Men have gone to their deaths for less," said Mark.

"How many of them do you think there were? The Followers?"

"About three hundred," said Julian.

"Well, if we can't go to the faeries yet, we've got two options," said Emma. "One, we track down every one of those three hundred losers and beat them up until they tell us who did the actual killing."

"That seems impractical," said Ty. "And time-consuming."

"Or we could go straight to finding out who the leader is," Emma said. "If anyone knows, it's that Belinda girl."

Julian ran a hand through his hair. "Belinda's not her real name—"

"I'm telling you, Johnny Rook knows her," Emma said. "In fact, he probably knows a lot, given that information about the Shadow World is his business. We're asking him."

"Yes, you agreed to this already in the car," Mark said, and frowned. "This cat is looking at me with judgment."

"He's not," said Jules. "That's just his face."

"You look at me the same way," Mark said, glancing at Julian. "Judgy face."

"This is still progress," Livvy said stubbornly. She glanced at Mark sideways, and Emma saw anxiety in her gaze. It was so rare for Livvy to show the worry she felt that Emma sat up straight. "We should go to the faerie convoy, tell them the Followers are responsible—"

"We can't," said Diana, appearing in the doorway. "The fey were very specific. 'The one with blood on his hands.' You might think they want progress reports, but I don't think they do. They want results, and that's all."

"How long have you been eavesdropping?" Julian asked, though there was no hostility in the question. He glanced at his watch. "It's awfully late for you to be here."

Diana sighed. She did look bone weary. Her hair was untidy and she was uncharacteristically dressed down in a sweatshirt and jeans. There was a long scrape across one of her cheeks.

"I went by the convergence on my way back from Ojai," she said. "I got in and out fast. Only had to kill one Mantid." She sighed again. "It doesn't look like anyone's been back there since the night you went. I'm worried our necromancer's found a new place."

"Well, if he doesn't use a convergence, the next time he uses dark magic, he'll show up on Magnus's map," said Ty.

"Did you find anything useful in Ojai?" Emma asked. "What warlock is up there? It's not anyone we know, is it?"

"No." Diana leaned against the doorjamb, clearly not planning on saying anything else. "I did hear about the Followers; I suppose I shouldn't be surprised you were tracking them down here. I wish you'd told me, but—"

"You'd already left," said Jules. He leaned back on his hands. His dress shirt stretched across his chest. Knowing what his body looked like under the cotton was not helping Emma's concentration. She looked away, hating her uncontrolled thoughts. "But I can give you the summary."

As he started to talk, Emma quietly turned and walked out of the room. She could hear Julian's voice behind her, recounting the events of the evening. She knew he'd tell the story exactly right; she knew she didn't have to worry. But right now there were two people she urgently needed to talk to, and she needed to do it alone.

"Mom," Emma whispered. "Dad. I need your help."

She had taken off her dress and boots and stashed them in a corner with her weapons. The weather had worsened: Gusts tore around the Institute, rattling the copper gutters, streaking the panes of glass with feathery patterns of silver. In the distance, lightning flashed over the water, illuminating it like a sheet of glass. In her pajamas, Emma sat cross-legged, facing her open closet.

To a stranger the closet might look like a jumble of photos and string and scribbled notes, but to her it was a love letter. A love letter to her parents, whose photograph was at the center of the compilation. A photo of them smiling at each other, her dad caught in the middle of laughing, his blond hair shining in the sun.

"I feel lost," she said. "I started this because I thought there was some connection between these murders and what happened to you. But if there is, I think I'm losing it. Nothing connects to the attack on the Institute. I feel like I'm wandering through fog and I can't see anything clearly."

It felt like there was something stuck in her throat, something hard and painful. Part of her wanted nothing more than to run out into the rain, feel it spill down over her. Walk or run down to the beach, where the sea and the sky would be melding into one, and let her screams be drowned out by thunder.

"There's more," she whispered. "I think I'm messing up. As—as a Shadowhunter. Ever since the night Jules got hurt, when I healed him, ever since then when I look at him, I feel—things I shouldn't. I think about him the way you aren't supposed to think about your *parabatai*. I'm sure he doesn't feel the same way, but just for a few minutes tonight, when we were dancing, I was . . . happy." She closed her eyes. "Love's supposed to make you happy, isn't it? It's not supposed to hurt?"

There was a knock on her door.

*Jules*, she thought. She scrambled up just as the door opened.

It was Mark.

He was still in his formal clothes. They were very dark against his blond hair. Anyone else would have seemed awkward, she thought as he moved into the room and glanced at her closet, then at her. Anyone else would have asked if they were barging in or interrupting, considering she was in pajamas. But Mark behaved as if he'd arrived for an appointment.

"The day I was taken," he said. "It was the same day your parents were killed."

She nodded, glancing at the closet. Having it open made her feel strangely exposed.

"I told you I was sorry about what happened to them," he said. "But that isn't enough. I didn't realize that this investigation would become about me. About my family trying to keep me here. That my presence would be stealing from you the meaning of what you were doing."

Emma sat down on the foot of the bed. "Mark . . . It's not like that."

"It is like that," he said. His eyes were luminous in the strange light—her window was open, and the illumination that streamed in was touched by the glow of lightning-infused clouds. "They should not be working on this only to keep me, when I might not stay."

"You wouldn't go back to Faerie. You wouldn't."

"All that was promised was that I would choose," he said. "I have not—I cannot—" His hands balled into fists at his sides, the frustration clear on his face. "I thought you would understand. You are not a Blackthorn."

"I am Julian's *parabatai*," she said. "And Julian needs you to stay."

"Julian is strong," he said.

"Julian *is* strong," she agreed. "But you are his brother. And if you go—I don't know if I can pick up those pieces."

His eyes flicked back to her closet. "We survive losses," he whispered.

"We do," Emma said. "But my parents didn't leave me on purpose. I don't know what would have happened to me if they had."

Thunder cracked, snapping through the room. Mark's hand crept to his throat. "When I hear thunder, see lightning, I think I should be riding through it," he said. "My blood calls out for the sky."

"Who gave you that pendant?" she asked. "It's an elf-bolt, isn't it?"

"In the Hunt, I had skill with them," he said. "I could strike at an enemy while riding, and hit the target nine times out of ten. He called me 'elf-shot' because—" Mark broke off, turning to look at Emma where she perched on the bed. "We are alike, you and I," he said. "The storm calls you as it calls me, doesn't it? I saw in your eyes earlier—you wanted to be out in it. To run on the beach, perhaps, as the lightning comes down."

Emma took a shaking breath. "Mark, I don't—"

"What's going on?" It was Julian. He had changed out of his suit and was standing in the doorway. The look on his face as he glanced from Mark to Emma—Emma couldn't describe it. She'd never seen Jules look like that before.

"If you two are busy," he said, and his voice was like the edge of a knife, "with each other, I can come back some other time."

Mark looked puzzled. Emma stared. "Mark and I were talking," Emma said. "That's it."

"We are done now." Mark rose to his feet, one of his hands resting on the elf-bolt.

Julian looked at them both levelly. "Tomorrow afternoon, Diana's taking Cristina to Malcolm's," he said. "Something about Cristina needing to interview the High Warlock about how we do things here as opposed to Mexico City. Probably Diana just wants to check up on how Malcolm's translation is coming and she needs an excuse."

"Okay, then we can head to Rook's," said Emma. "Or I could go on my own if you want—he's used to me. Not that our last interaction was so friendly." She frowned.

"No, I'll come with you," Julian said. "Rook needs to understand it's serious."

"And I?" said Mark. "Am I to be a part of this expedition?"

"No," Julian said. "Johnny Rook can't know you're back. The Clave doesn't know, and Rook is someone who doesn't keep secrets, he sells them."

Mark looked up at his brother through his hair, his strange, odd-colored eyes gleaming. "Then I suppose I will sleep in," he said. He gave one last glance at Emma's closet—there was something in his expression, something disquieted—and left, closing the door behind him.

"Jules," Emma said, "what's wrong with you? What was that about, 'if you two are busy with each other'? Do you think Mark and I were making out on the floor before you came in?"

"It wouldn't have been my business if you had been," Julian said. "I was giving you privacy."

"You were being a jerk." Emma slid off the bed and went over to her dresser to take off her earrings, looking at Julian in the mirror as she did so. "And I know why."

She saw his expression change and tighten, surprise giving way to unreadability. "Why?"

"Because you're worried," she said. "You don't like breaking the rules and you don't think going to Rook's is a good idea."

He moved restlessly into the room and sat down on her bed. "Is that how you think of me?" he said. "Emma, if we need to go to Rook's, then I'm part of the plan. I'm in it, a hundred percent."

She looked at herself in the mirror. Long hair didn't hide the Marks on her shoulders; her arms had muscles; her wrists were strong and sturdy. She was a map of scars: the old white scars from used-up runes, wending trails of cuts, and the splotches of burns from acidic demon blood.

She felt suddenly old, not just seventeen instead of twelve, but *old*. Old in her heart, and too late. Surely if she were going to find her parents' murderer she would have done so by now.

"I'm sorry," she said.

He leaned back against her headboard. He was wearing an old T-shirt and pajama bottoms. "What for?"

*For the way I feel.* She shoved the words back. If she was having strange feelings about Jules, it wasn't fair to tell him about them. She was the one in the wrong.

And he was hurting. She could see it in the set of his mouth, the darkness behind his light eyes.

"Doubting you," she said.

"Back at you." He flopped back onto her pillows. His shirt, untucked, rode up, giving Emma a clear view of his stomach, the corrugation of muscles, the smatter of golden freckles over his hip. . . .

"I don't think I'm ever going to find out what happened to my parents," she said.

At that he sat up, which was a relief. "Emma," he said, and then paused. He didn't say *Why would you say that?* Or *What do you mean?* Or any of the other things people said to fill up space. Instead, he said, "You will. You're the most determined person that I've ever known."

"I feel farther away now than I've ever felt. Even though we actually have a connection, even though we're following up on it. I don't see how their deaths could be connected to the Midnight Theater or the Lottery. I don't see—"

"You're afraid," Jules said.

Emma leaned against the dresser. "Afraid of what?"

"Afraid we'll find out something about them you don't want to know," he said. "In your mind, your parents are perfect. Now that we're actually closing in on answers, you're worried you'll find out they were—"

"Not perfect?" Emma fought to keep the edge of tension out of her voice. "Bad people?"

"Human," he said. "We all find out the people who are supposed to take care of us are human eventually. That they make mistakes." He pushed his hair back out of his eyes. "I live in dread of the day the kids all figure that out about me."

"Julian," Emma said. "I hate to tell you this, but I think they've already figured that out."

He smiled and slid off the bed. "Insults," he said. "I guess that means you're fine." He moved to the door.

"We can't tell Diana we're going to Rook's," she said. "She thinks he's a crook."

"She's not wrong." The dim light in the room sparked off Julian's bracelet. "Emma, do you want me to—"

He hesitated, but Emma heard the unspoken words. *Stay with you?*

*Stay with me,* she wanted to say. *Stay and make me forget my nightmares. Stay and sleep next to me. Stay and chase the bad dreams away, the memories of blood.*

But she only forced a smile. "I should get to sleep, Jules."

She couldn't see his expression as he turned to leave the room. "Good night, Emma."

Emma woke late the next day: sometime overnight, the storm had washed the sky clean of clouds, and the afternoon sun was bright. Her head aching, she clambered out of bed, showered and changed, and nearly collided with Cristina outside her bedroom door.

"You slept so long, I was worried," Cristina scolded. "Are you okay?"

"I will be once I have breakfast. Maybe something chocolate."

"It's much too late for breakfast. It's past lunchtime. Julian sent me up to get you—he says he has drinks and sandwiches in the car but you have to get going now."

"Do you think they're chocolate sandwiches?" Emma inquired, falling into step beside Cristina as they both headed for the stairs.

"What's a chocolate sandwich?"

"You know: bread, chocolate bar, butter."

"That is disgusting." Cristina shook her head; the pearls in her earlobes gleamed.

"Not as disgusting as coffee. You off to Malcolm's?"

Cristina flashed a smile. "I shall ask a million questions of your purply-eyed warlock so that Diana doesn't think about you and Julian or whether you might be at Mr. Rook's."

"I'm not sure he's a mister," Emma said, stifling a yawn. "I've never heard anyone call him anything but 'hey, Rook' or sometimes 'that bastard.'"

"That is very rude," said Cristina. There was something playful in her dark eyes. "I think Mark is nervous about being alone with the younger ones. This should be very amusing." She tugged one of Emma's damp braids. "Julian is waiting for you downstairs."

"Good luck distracting Malcolm," Emma called as Cristina strode off down the hallway toward the kitchen where Diana was, presumably, waiting.

Cristina winked. "Good luck getting information, *cuata*."

Shaking her head, Emma headed down to the parking lot, where she found Julian standing beside the Toyota, examining the contents of the trunk. Beside him was Mark.

"I thought Cristina was going to be here," Mark was saying as Emma approached. "I did not realize she was going to Malcolm's. I did not think that I would be left alone with the children."

"They're not children," Julian said, nodding a greeting at Emma. "Ty and Livvy are fifteen; they've looked after the others before."

"Tiberius is angry that you are not allowing him to come with you to Rook's," said Mark. "He said he was going to lock himself in his room."

"Terrific," said Julian. His voice was rough; he looked as if he hadn't slept. Emma wondered what could have kept him up. Research? "I guess you'll know where he is. Look, the only one who needs looking after is Tavvy."

Mark looked ill with horror. "I know."

"He's a kid, not a bomb," said Emma, buckling on a weapons belt. There were several seraph blades and a stele thrust through it. She wasn't in gear, just jeans and a jacket that would hide the sword on her back. Not that she expected trouble, but she hated going out without Cortana, currently napping in the trunk. "It'll be okay. Dru and Livvy can help."

"Maybe this mission of yours is too dangerous," Mark said, as Julian slammed the trunk shut. "A faerie would tell you that a rook is a black crow—a bird of ill omen."

"I know," Julian said, sliding a final, thin dagger into the holder strapped around his wrist. "It also means to cheat or to swindle. It was my word of the day last year from Diana."

"Johnny Rook is a swindler, all right," Emma agreed. "He swindles *mundanes*. We'll be fine."

"The children could set themselves on fire," Mark said. He didn't sound like he was joking.

"Ty and Livvy are *fifteen*," said Emma. "They're nearly the same age you were when you joined the Hunt. And you were—"

"What?" Mark turned his odd eyes on her. "I was fine?"

Emma felt herself flush. "An afternoon in their own home is not exactly the same as being kidnapped by cannibalistic faerie predators."

"We didn't eat people," Mark said indignantly. "At least not to my knowledge."

Julian unlocked the driver's side door and slid inside. Emma climbed into the passenger seat as he leaned out the window and looked sympathetically at his brother. "Mark, we have to go. If anything happens, have Livvy text us, but right now Rook is the best chance we have. Okay?"

Mark straightened up as if readying for battle. "Okay."

"And if they do manage to set themselves on fire?"

"Yes?" Mark said.

"You'd better find a way to put them out."

Johnny Rook lived in Victor Heights, in a small craftsman bungalow with dusty windows sandwiched between two ranch houses. It had a disused air that Emma assumed was carefully cultivated. It looked like the sort of place neighborhood children would skip over when searching for candy on Halloween.

Otherwise it was a nice street. There were kids playing hopscotch a few houses down, and an old man reading a newspaper in his gazebo, surrounded by lawn gnomes. When Julian pictured mundane life, it looked a lot like this. Sometimes he thought it wouldn't be so bad.

Emma was strapping Cortana on. They were already glamoured, so there was no worry about the children down the street seeing her as she pulled the strap tight, a small frown line appearing between her eyebrows as she got the fit right. Her hair shone in the California sunlight, brighter than the gold of Cortana's hilt. The white scars on her hands gleamed, too, diffuse, a lacelike patchwork.

No. Mundane life was not an option.

Emma lifted her head and smiled at him. A familiar smile, easy. It was like last night—the dancing and the music that still seemed to him like a fever dream—hadn't happened. "Ready to go?" she said.

The paved path that led to the front door was cracked where the roots of trees had grown up, their inexorable force snapping the pavement. The persistence of growing things, Julian thought, and wished he had a canvas and paints. He was reaching for his phone to snap a picture when it went off with the dull ring that signaled a text message.

He glanced at the screen. It was from Mark.

CAN'T FIND TY.

Julian frowned and thumbed a reply while jogging up the steps after Emma. DID YOU LOOK IN HIS BEDROOM?

There was an ornate knocker on the front door in the shape of a wild-haired, wild-eyed Green Man. Emma lifted it and let it fall as Julian's phone beeped again.

DO YOU TAKE ME FOR A BUFFOON? OF COURSE I DID.

"Jules?" Emma said. "Is everything all right?"

"Buffoon?" he muttered, his fingers flying over the touch pad. WHAT DOES LIVVY SAY?

"Did you just mutter 'buffoon'?" Emma demanded. Julian could hear footsteps approaching from the other side of the door. "Julian, *try* to act not weird, okay?"

The door flew open. The man standing on the other side was tall and rangy, dressed in jeans and a leather jacket. His hair was so close-cropped it was hard to tell its color, and tinted glasses hid his eyes.

He slumped against the doorjamb the moment he saw Emma. "Carstairs," he said. It was a sound between a prayer and a groan.

Julian's phone pinged. LIVVY SAYS SHE DOESN'T KNOW.

The man raised an eyebrow. "Busy?" he said sardonically. He turned to Emma. "Your other boyfriend was politer."

Emma flushed. "This isn't my boyfriend. This is Jules."

"Of course. I should have recognized the Blackthorn eyes." Rook's voice turned silky. "You look just like your father, Julian."

Julian didn't much like the man's smirk. Then again, he'd never liked anything about Emma associating with Rook. Mundanes who dabbled in magic, even ones with the Sight, were a gray area to the Clave—there wasn't a Law, but neither were you supposed to deal with them. If you needed magic done, you hired a nice, Clave-approved warlock.

Not that Emma had ever cared much about the approval of the Clave.

LIVVY'S LYING. SHE ALWAYS KNOWS WHERE TY IS. MAKE HER TELL YOU. Jules shoved the phone back into his pocket. It wasn't unusual for Ty to vanish, into corners of the library or places in the hill where he could coax lizards out from under their rocks. And he was angry, which made it more likely he'd hide.

The man swung the door open. "Come in," he said in a resigned tone. "You know the rules. No taking out weapons, Carstairs. And no back talk."

"Define 'back talk,'" Emma said, stepping inside. Julian followed her. A wave of magic as thick as smoke in a burning building hit him. It hung in the air of the small living room, almost visible in the dim light that filtered through the yellowing curtains. Tall craftsman bookshelves held spell books and grimoires, copies of *The Malleus Maleficarum*, the *Pseudomonarchia Daemonum*, *The Lesser Key of Solomon*, and a blood-red volume with the words *Dragon Rouge* lettered on the spine. A yellowish rag rug that matched the curtains lay crookedly on the floor; Rook kicked it aside with an unpleasant grin.

Under it was revealed a spell circle chalked onto the hardwood planks. It was the kind of circle warlocks stood inside when they summoned demons; the circle created a protective wall. It was actually two circles, one inside the other, making a sort of frame, and inside the frame were scrawled the sigils of the seventy Lords of Hell. Julian frowned as Rook stepped neatly into the circle and crossed his arms.

"A protection circle," Rook said unnecessarily. "You can't get in."

"And you can't get out," Julian observed. "Not easily, anyway."

Rook shrugged. "Why would I want to?"

"Because that's some powerful magic you're playing with."

"Don't judge," Rook said. "We who cannot wield the magic of Heaven must use what comes to hand."

"The sigils of Hell?" Julian said. "There's some middle ground between Hell and Heaven, surely."

Rook flashed a grin. "There's all the world," he said. "It's a messy place, Shadowhunter, and we don't all get to keep our hands clean."

"There's a difference between dirt and blood," Julian said. Emma shot him a quelling look, one that said: *We're here because we need something.* She didn't always have to write on his skin for him to know what she was thinking.

The curtains rustled, though there was no breeze. "Look, we're not here to bother you," Emma said. "We just want some information, and we'll go."

"Information isn't free," said Rook.

"I've got something good for you this time. Better than cash," Emma said. Avoiding Julian's eyes, she took a pale column of silvery-white stone from the inside of her jacket pocket. She flushed slightly, aware of Julian's eyes on her as he realized what she was holding: an unnamed seraph blade.

"What is he going to do with *adamas?*" Julian demanded.

"*Adamas* that has been treated by the Iron Sisters goes for a high price at the Shadow Market," said Rook, not taking his eyes off Emma's prize. "But it still depends on what you want to know about."

"The Midnight Theater and the Followers," Emma said. "We want to know about them."

Rook narrowed his eyes. "What do you want to know?"

Emma gave him a brief rundown of the events of the night before, leaving out Mark and how they'd found out about the Lottery in the first place. When she was done, Rook whistled.

"Casper Sterling," he said. "I always thought that guy was a scumbag. Yakking on about how he was better than werewolves, better than humans, too. Can't say I'm sorry his number came up."

"Johnny," Emma said severely. "They're going to *kill* him."

An odd expression flickered across Rook's face, but it vanished quickly. "And you want me to do what about it? They're a whole organization, Carstairs."

"We need to know who their leader is," said Julian. "Belinda called him the Guardian. He's the one we need to find."

"I don't know," said Rook. "I'm not sure pissing off the Followers is worth even *adamas*." But his eyes clung to the silvery-white stuff longingly. Emma pressed the advantage.

"They'll never know you had anything to do with it," she said. "But I saw you flirting with Belinda at the Shadow Market. She's got to know."

Rook shook his head. "She doesn't."

"Huh," Emma said. "Okay, which of them does?"

"None of them. The leader's identity is totally secret. I don't even know if it's a man or a woman. The Guardian could be either, you know?"

"If I find out you're hiding something you know from me, Johnny," Emma said in a cold voice, "there will be consequences. Diana knows I'm here. You won't be able to get me in trouble with the Clave. But I could get you in trouble. Serious trouble."

"Emma, forget it," Julian said in a bored voice. "He doesn't know anything. Let's take the *adamas* and go."

"They get two days," Rook said in a thin, angry voice. "When their numbers get picked. They get two days before the kill has to happen." He glared at them both, as if somehow this was their fault. "It's sympathetic magic. The energy of the death of a supernatural creature powers the spell that makes them all stronger. And the leader—he shows up for the kill. That much I know. If you're there for the death, you'll see him. Or her. Whoever it is."

"The Guardian shows up at the murder?" Emma said. "To harvest the energy?"

"So if we shadow Sterling, if we wait for someone to attack him, we'll see the Guardian?" Julian said.

"Yeah. That should work. I mean, you're crazy to want to be there at some big dark-magic party, but I guess it's your business."

"I guess it is," Julian said. His phone buzzed again. LIVVY WON'T TELL ME ANYTHING. SHE'S LOCKED HERSELF IN HER ROOM. HELP.

A tendril of worry uncurled in Julian's stomach. He told himself he was being stupid. He knew he worried about his siblings too much. Ty had probably wandered off after an animal, was petting a squirrel or cuddling a stray cat. Or he might have shut himself away with a book, not wanting to socialize.

Julian thumbed out a response: GO OUTSIDE AND LOOK FOR HIM IN THE BACK GARDEN.

"Still texting?" said Rook, a mocking tone to his voice. "I'm guessing you have a pretty rich social life."

"I wouldn't worry," said Julian. "My phone's almost out of battery."

The phone whirred again. HEADED OUTSIDE, it said, and then the screen went black. He shoved it into his pocket as an enormous crash sounded from downstairs, and after it, the sound of a bitten-off cry.

"What the hell?" said Rook.

The shock in his voice was real; Emma must have heard it too, because she was already moving toward the steps that led downstairs. Rook shouted after them, but Julian knew it would take him a moment to free himself from his protection circle. Without another glance at Rook, he darted after Emma.


Kit Rook pressed himself into the shadow of the stairwell. Voices filtered down from upstairs, along with dim sunlight. His father always sent him down into the cellar when they had visitors. Especially the kind of visitors that had him running for his chalk so he could draw a protection circle.

Kit could only see shadows moving upstairs, but he could hear two voices. Young voices, to his surprise. A boy's and a girl's.

He had a pretty good idea what they were, and it wasn't

Downworlders. He'd seen the look on his father's face when they'd knocked on the door. Rook hadn't said anything, but he wore that expression for only one thing: Shadowhunters.

*Nephilim.* Kit felt the slow burn of anger start in his stomach. He'd been sitting on the sofa watching TV and now he was crouched in the basement like a thief in his own home because Shadowhunters thought they had the right to legislate magic. To tell everyone what to do. To—

A figure hurtled at him out of the shadows. It hit him hard in the chest and he staggered back and slammed into the wall behind him, breath knocked out of his body. He gasped as light flared up around him—pale white light, held in the cup of a human hand.

Something sharp kissed the base of Kit's throat. He sucked in air and raised his eyes.

He was staring right at a boy his own age. Ink-black hair and eyes the color of the edge of a knife, eyes that darted away from his as the boy scowled. He had a long, thin, black-clad body and pale skin Marked all over with the runes of the Nephilim.

Kit had never been this close to a Shadowhunter. The boy had one hand on his glowing light—it wasn't a flashlight or anything electronic; Kit knew magic when he saw it—and the other gripped a dagger whose point rested against Kit's throat.

Kit had imagined before what he'd do if a Nephilim ever grabbed him. How he'd stomp on their feet, break their bones, snap their wrists, spit in their faces. He did none of those things, thought of none of those things. He looked at the boy with the knife to his throat, the boy whose black eyelashes feathered down against his cheekbones as he glanced away from Kit, and he felt something like a shock of recognition pass through him.

He thought, *How beautiful.*

Kit blinked. Though the other boy wasn't looking directly at him, he seemed to note the movement. In a harsh whisper, he demanded, "Who are you? What are you doing here? You're too young to be Johnny Rook."

His voice was lovely. Clear and low, with a rasp to it that made him sound older than he was. A rich boy's voice.

"No," said Kit. He felt dazed and puzzled, as if a bright camera flash had gone off in his eyes. "I'm not."

The boy still wasn't looking directly at Kit. As if Kit weren't worth looking at. Kit's dazed feeling was starting to fade, to be replaced by anger.

"Go on," Kit said, challenging. "Figure it out."

The boy's expression clouded, then cleared. "You're his son," he said. "Johnny Rook's son."

And then his lip did curl, just the slightest curl of contempt, and anger boiled up in Kit. He jerked aside fast, away from the dagger, and kicked out. The other boy spun, but Kit caught him with a glancing blow. He heard a cry of pain. The light tumbled from the boy's hand, winking out, and then Kit was being shoved up against the wall again, a hand scrabbling to fist itself in his shirt, and the dagger was back at his throat, and the other boy was whispering, "Be quiet, be quiet, be *quiet*," and then the room was full of light.

The other boy froze. Kit looked up to see two other Shadow-hunters standing on the cellar steps: a boy with blazing blue-green eyes and the blond girl he had seen at the Shadow Market the week before. They were both staring—not at him, but at the boy gripping his shirt.

The boy winced but held his ground, defiance chasing alarm across his face. *Aha*, Kit thought with dawning realization. *You're not supposed to be down here, are you?*

"Tiberius Blackthorn," said the boy with blue-green eyes. "What on earth are you doing?"

* * *

Emma stood and gawked at Ty, completely brought up short. It was as if the Institute had suddenly appeared in the middle of Johnny Rook's cellar: The sight of Ty was familiar, and yet totally incongruous.

Ty looked rumpled and more frazzled than she'd seen him in years, though his grip on his dagger was steady. Diana would have been pleased. She would probably not have been pleased that he was pointing it at the throat of a mundane boy—he looked about fifteen, and oddly familiar. She'd seen him before, Emma realized, at the Shadow Market. His hair was a mass of blond tangles; his shirt was clean but ragged, his jeans worn to a faded pallor. And he looked ready to punch Ty in the face, which was unusual for a mundane in his position. Most of them were much more unsettled by a knife to the throat.

"Ty," Julian said again. He looked furious—fury with an edge of panic. "Ty, let go of Johnny Rook's son."

The blond boy's eyes widened. "How did you—how do you know who I am?" he demanded.

Julian shrugged. "Who else would you be?" He tilted his head to the side. "Maybe you know something about the Lottery at the Midnight Theater?"

"Jules," Emma said. "He's just a kid."

"I'm not a kid!" the boy protested. "And my name is Kit."

"We're trying to help," Julian said. The blond boy—Kit—scowled. Julian softened his voice. "We're trying to save lives."

"My father told me that's what Shadowhunters always say."

"Do you believe everything he says?"

"He was right this time, wasn't he?" Kit pointed out. His gaze slid to Emma; she remembered noticing that he had the Sight. She'd thought he was Rook's assistant, though, not his son. They looked nothing alike. "You said it."

"I meant—" Julian began.

"I don't know anything about a lottery," Kit snapped. He glanced at Tiberius. What was odder, perhaps, was that Ty was looking at him. Emma remembered Ty, years ago, saying, *Why do people say "look at me" when they mean "look at my eyes"? You could be looking at any part of a person and you're still looking at them.* But he was looking curiously at Kit's eyes as if they reminded him of something.

"Kit!" The voice was a roar. Emma heard skidding footsteps on the stairs, and Johnny Rook appeared. One of his sleeves was singed. Emma had never seen him look so furious. "Leave my son *alone!*"

Ty steadied his grip on the knife, straightening his spine. He faced Johnny Rook without a speck of fear. "Tell us about the Lottery," he said.

Kit winced. Emma could see it, even in the gloom. Ty didn't seem frightening to her, but then, she'd cuddled him when he was three years old. But fear was clear in Johnny Rook's face: As far as he was concerned, Nephilim had snuck a Shadowhunter into his basement to murder his son.

"I'll give you Casper Sterling's address," he said as Kit stared at him, looking bewildered. Clearly he had rarely seen his father so shaken. "I've got it, okay? He's got a bunch of identities, he isn't easy to find, but I know where he lives. All right? Good enough? Let my son *go!*"

Ty lowered the knife and stepped back. He kept it in his hand, his eyes on Kit as the other boy rubbed ruefully at the dent in his throat. "Dad, I—" Kit started.

"Be quiet, Kit," Johnny Rook snapped. "I've told you. Don't say anything in front of Nephilim."

"We're on the same side," Julian said in his calmest voice.

Johnny Rook whirled on him. His face was red, his throat working. "Don't you dare tell me what side I'm on, you know nothing, *nothing*—"

*"Enough!"* Emma shouted. "By the Angel, what are you so frightened of?"

Johnny slammed his mouth shut. "I'm not frightened," he said through his teeth. "Just get out," he said. "Get out, and don't ever come here again. I'll text you the address but after that, don't call, don't ask me for favors. We're done, Nephilim."

"Fine," Emma said, gesturing for Ty to come toward her and Julian. "We'll go. Ty—"

Ty slid the knife he'd been holding into his belt and darted up the steps. Julian turned and went after him. The boy at the bottom of the stairs didn't watch them go; his eyes were fixed on his father.

He wasn't much younger than Emma—maybe by a year or two— but she felt a sudden inexplicable surge of protectiveness toward Johnny Rook's son. If he had the Sight, then all of Downworld was open to him: terrifying and inexplicable. In his own way he was like Tiberius, living in a world he saw differently than everyone else.

"Fine, Johnny," Emma said again, loudly. "But if you change your mind, you have my number in your phone. Under Carstairs."

Johnny Rook glared at her.

"Call me," Emma said again, and this time she looked directly at Kit. "If you ever need anything."

*"Get OUT."* Rook looked as if he were going to explode or have a heart attack, so with a last look over her shoulder, Emma went.

Emma found Ty out by the car. Clouds had gathered, scudding in quick bursts across the sky. Ty was leaning against the trunk, the wind ruffling his black hair. "Where's Jules?" she asked as she got close.

"Over there." He pointed. "I got into the house with an Open rune. I broke the lock on the basement door. He's fixing it."

Emma glanced over toward Johnny Rook's and saw Jules's lean, long figure outlined by the stuccoed wall. She opened the trunk of the car, unbuckling her weapons belt. "How did you get here, anyway?"

"I hid in the backseat. Under that blanket." Ty pointed. Emma could see the edge of a pair of headphones peeking out from under the quilt's fuzzy edge. "You think Julian's mad at me?" With the knife put away, he looked very young, his gray eyes clear and open, fixed on the clouds overhead.

"Ty." Emma sighed. "He's going to murderate you."

Julian was heading back toward them. Ty said, "That's a neologism."

Emma blinked. "It's a what?"

"A word you made up. Shakespeare made up words all the time."

Emma smiled at him, oddly touched. "Well, 'murderate' isn't exactly Shakespeare."

Ty braced himself as Julian walked directly up to him, not breaking stride, his jaw set, his blue-green eyes as dark as the deep part of the ocean.

He reached Ty and caught hold of him, pulling him into a fierce hug. He pressed his face down into his little brother's black hair as Ty stood, frozen and astonished at Julian's lack of anger.

"Jules?" he said. "Are you all right?"

Julian's shoulders shook. He held his little brother tighter, as if he could crush Ty into himself, into a place where he'd always be safe. He put his cheek against Ty's curls, squeezing his eyes shut, his voice muffled. "I thought something happened to you," he said. "I thought Johnny Rook might—"

He didn't finish his sentence. Ty put his arms carefully around Julian. He patted his back, gently, with his slender hands. It was the first time Emma had seen Ty comfort his older brother—almost the first time she'd ever actually seen Julian let someone else take care of him.

* * *

They were silent on the long highway drive back to the Institute; silent as the clouds cleared away, blown inland by the ocean air. The sun was low on the water as they drove up the Pacific Coast Highway. They were silent as they got out of the car and Julian finally really spoke.

"You shouldn't have done that," he said, looking at Tiberius. He'd stopped shaking—thankfully, since he'd been driving—and his voice was steady and soft. "It was too dangerous for you to come with us."

Ty put his hands in his pockets. "I know what you think. But this is my investigation too."

"Mark texted me to tell me you were missing," Julian said, and Emma started; she should have guessed that was what all the business with Jules's phone had been about. "I almost walked right out of Rook's house. I don't think he would have let us back in."

"I'm sorry you were worried," said Ty. "That's why I hugged you outside Rook's house, because I was sorry you were worried. But I'm not Tavvy. I'm not a child. I don't need to always be there so that you or Mark can find me."

"You shouldn't have come into Rook's house either." Julian's voice rose. "It wasn't safe."

"I wasn't planning to come inside. Just to look at the house. Observe it." Ty's soft mouth hardened. "Then I saw you go in, and I saw someone moving around downstairs. I thought they might come up and attack you when you didn't expect it. I knew you didn't realize anyone was down there."

"Jules," Emma said. "You would have done the same thing."

Jules shot her an exasperated look. "Ty's only fifteen."

"Don't say it's dangerous because I'm fifteen," Ty said. "You did things just as dangerous when you were fifteen. And Rook wouldn't have told you Sterling's address if I hadn't been holding a knife on his son."

"That's true," said Emma. "He got into that protection circle too fast."

"You couldn't have known he had a son hidden down there," Julian said. "You couldn't have predicted what would happen, Ty. It was luck."

"Prediction is magic," Ty said. "It wasn't that, and it wasn't luck, either. I've heard Emma talk about Rook. Diana too. He sounded like someone who would hide things. Who you couldn't trust. And I was right." He looked hard at Jules; he wasn't looking him in the eye, but his gaze was direct. "You always want to protect me," he said. "But you won't ever tell me when I'm right. If you let me make decisions on my own, maybe you'd worry about me less."

Julian looked stunned.

"It could help that we know Rook has a son," said Ty. He spoke with a clear confidence. "You can't be sure it won't. And I got you Sterling's address. I helped, even if you didn't want me there."

In the dim light spilling down from the Institute, Julian looked as vulnerable as Emma had ever seen him. "I'm sorry," he said, almost formally. "I didn't mean to make it sound like you didn't help."

"I know the Law," said Ty. "I know fifteen isn't grown up. I know we need Uncle Arthur, and we need you." He frowned. "I mean, I can't cook at all, and neither can Livvy. And I wouldn't know how to put Tavvy to bed. I'm not saying you need to put me in charge or let me do whatever I want. I know there are rules. But some things—maybe Mark could do them?"

"But Mark—" Julian began, and Emma knew his fear. *Mark might not stay. He might not want to.*

"Mark's just getting to know you all again and know what it's like being here," Julian said. "I don't know if we could ask him to do too much."

"He wouldn't mind," said Ty. "He likes me. He likes *us.*"

"He loves you," said Julian. "And I love you too. But Ty, Mark might not— If we don't find the killer, Mark might not be able to stay here."

"That's why I want to help solve the mystery," said Ty. "So Mark can stay. He could take care of us, and you could rest." He pulled his jacket closed, shivering; the wind off the ocean was intensely cool. "I'm going to go inside and find Livvy. Mark too. He was probably worried."

Julian stared after Ty as he went into the house. The look on his face—it was as if Emma were looking at one of his paintings, but crumpled and torn, the colors and lines jumbled. "They all think that, don't they?" he said slowly. "They all think Mark is going to stay."

Emma hesitated. A few days before, she would have told Julian not to be ridiculous. That Mark would stay with his family, no matter what. But she had seen the night sky in Mark's eyes when he talked of the Hunt, heard the cold freedom in his voice. There were two Marks, she thought sometimes: the human and the faerie. Human Mark would stay. Faerie Mark could not be predicted.

"How could they *not?*" Emma said. "If I got one of my parents back somehow—and then thought they were going to leave again, voluntarily—"

Julian looked ashen. "We live in a world of demons and monsters, and the thing that scares me the most is the idea that Mark might decide he belongs with the Wild Hunt and leave. Even if we solve the mystery and satisfy the Fair Folk. He might still go. And he'll smash their hearts to pieces. They'll never recover."

Emma moved closer to Julian, laying a hand against his shoulder.

"You can't protect the kids against everything," she said. "They have to live in the world and deal with what happens in the world. And that means loss sometimes. If Mark chooses to leave, it'll be awful. But they're strong kids. They'll live through it."

There was a long silence. Finally Julian spoke. "Sometimes I almost wish Mark hadn't come back," he said in a dry, tense voice. "What does that make me?"

*H-U-M-A-N*, Emma traced on his back, and for a moment he leaned into her, seeming to draw comfort from her, the way *parabatai* were supposed to. The noises of the desert dimmed around them—it was something *parabatai* could do, create a quiet space where there was nothing but themselves and the live connection of magic that bound them.

A loud crash broke through the silence. Julian drew away from Emma with a start. There was another crash, clearly coming from inside the Institute. Julian spun around; a moment later he was racing up the back steps of the house.

Emma followed him. There was more noise: She could hear it even on the staircase, the clanging of dishware, the sound of laughing voices. They hurried upstairs, side by side. Emma reached the kitchen first and swung the door open.

She gasped.

# 17

## THE DEMONS DOWN
## UNDER THE SEA

**It looked as if the kitchen had exploded.**

The refrigerator had been emptied out. Ketchup decorated its once-white surface in scarlet swirls. One of the pantry doors was hanging off its hinges. The Costco tub of maple syrup had been dragged out, and syrup covered almost every available surface. A massive bag of powdered sugar had been torn open and Tavvy was sitting inside it, completely covered in white powder. He looked like a tiny abominable snowman.

Mark seemed to have tried cooking, since there were pans on the stove, filled with burned substances that were pouring smoke into the air. The flames were still on. Julian darted to turn them off while Emma stared.

Julian's kitchen, which he'd stocked with food for five years, kept clean and cooked in, made pancakes in—was destroyed. Bags of candy had been ripped open and littered the floor. Dru was sitting on the counter, poking at a glass of something foul-looking and humming happily to herself. Livvy was curled up on one of the bench seats, giggling, a stick of licorice in her hand. Ty was beside her, licking a speck of sugar from the back of his wrist.

Mark emerged from the pantry wearing a white apron with red hearts on it and carrying two pieces of singed bread. "Toast!" he announced happily, before catching sight of Julian and Emma.

There was a silence. Julian appeared to be struggling for words; Emma found herself backing toward the door. She had suddenly remembered the fights Mark and Julian used to have when they were children. They had been vicious and bloody in scope, and Julian had given as good as he got.

In fact, sometimes he had given *before* he got.

Mark raised his eyebrows. "Toast?"

"That's *my* toast," Ty pointed out.

"Right." Mark crossed the room, side-eyeing Julian as he went. Julian was still wordless, slumped against the stove. "And what do you want on your toast?"

"Pudding," Ty said promptly.

"Pudding?" Julian echoed. Emma had to admit that when she'd imagined the first word Julian was going to say out loud in this situation, it hadn't been "pudding."

"Why not pudding?" Livvy said equably, locating a container of tapioca pudding and handing it to her twin, who began to spoon it onto the bread in measured doses.

Julian turned to Mark. "I thought you said she was locked in her room."

"She came out when you guys texted that you found Ty," said Mark.

"There didn't seem to be any reason not to," said Livvy.

"And why is the toaster in the pantry?" Julian said.

"I couldn't find any other . . ." Mark seemed to be searching for words. "Electrical outlets."

"And why is Tavvy in a bag of sugar?"

Mark shrugged. "He wanted to be in a bag of sugar."

"That doesn't mean you should *put* him in a bag of sugar."

Julian's voice rose. "Or practically destroy the stove. Or let Drusilla drink—what *is* in that glass, Dru?"

"Chocolate milk," Dru said promptly. "With sour cream and Pepsi."

Julian sighed. "She shouldn't be drinking that."

"Why not?" Mark untied the apron around his waist and flung it aside. "I do not understand the source of your anger, brother. They're all alive, aren't they?"

"That's a pretty low bar," Julian said. "If I'd realized all you thought you had to do was keep them alive—"

"That's what you said," Mark said, half angry and half bewildered. "You joked about it, said they could take care of themselves—"

"They can!" Julian had risen to his full height; he seemed suddenly to tower over Mark, bigger and broader and altogether more adult than his brother. "You're the one causing the chaos! You're their older brother, do you even know what that means? You're meant to take better care of them than this!"

"Jules, it's fine," Livvy said. "We're *fine*."

"Fine?" Julian echoed. "Ty sneaked out—and I'll talk to you about that later, Livia—got into Johnny Rook's house, and held his son at knifepoint; Livvy locked herself in her room, and Tavvy is possibly permanently coated in sugar. As for Dru, we've got about five minutes until she throws up."

"I won't," Dru said, scowling.

"I'll clean it," Mark said.

"You don't know how!" Julian was white-faced and furious. Emma had rarely seen him so angry. "You," he said, still looking at Mark, "you used to look after them, but I guess you've forgotten that. I guess you've forgotten how to do anything normal."

Mark flinched. Tiberius stood up; his gray eyes burned in his pale face. His hands were moving at his sides, fluttering. Moth's wings—wings that could hold a knife, could cut a throat. "Stop," he said.

Emma didn't know whether he was talking to Julian, to Mark, or to the room in general, but she saw Julian freeze. She felt her heart contract as he looked around the room at his brothers and sisters. Dru sat unmoving; Tavvy had climbed out of the sugar and was gazing at Julian with wide blue-green eyes.

Mark was unmoving: his face pale, color striping the high cheekbones that marked out his faerie heritage.

There was love in his family's eyes as they looked at Julian, and worry and fear, but Emma wondered if Jules could see any of it. If all he saw was the children he had given up so much of his life for, happy with someone else. If, like her, he looked at the kitchen and remembered how he had taught himself to clean it when he was twelve years old. Taught himself to cook: simple things at first, spaghetti and butter, toast and cheese. A million cheese sandwiches, a million burns on Julian's hands and wrists from the stove and the spatter. The way he'd walked down the path to the highway every few days to accept the grocery delivery, before he could drive. The way he'd dragged and carried all their food back up the hill.

Julian on his knees, skinny in jeans and sweatshirt, scrubbing the floor. The kitchen had been designed by his mother, it was a piece of her, but it was also a piece of everything he'd given over the years to his family.

And he would do it again, Emma thought. Of course he would: He loved them that fiercely. The only thing that made Julian angry was fear, fear for his sisters and brothers.

He was afraid now, though Emma wasn't sure why. She saw only the look on his face as he registered their resentment of him, their disappointment. The fire seemed to go out of him. He slid down the front of the stove until he was sitting on the floor.

"Jules?" It was Tavvy, white granules coating his hair. He shuffled close and put his arms around Julian's neck.

Jules made an odd sound, and then he pulled his brother in and hugged him fiercely. Sugar sifted down onto his black gear, dusting it with white powder.

The kitchen door opened and Emma heard a gasp of surprise. She turned and saw Cristina gaping at the mess. "¡Qué desastre!"

It didn't exactly require a translation. Mark cleared his throat and began stacking dirty dishes in the sink. Not so much stacking them as flinging them, really. Livvy went over to help him while Cristina stared.

"Where's Diana?" Emma asked.

"She's home. Malcolm Portaled us there and back," said Cristina, not taking her eyes off the charred pots on the stove. "She said she needed to catch up on sleep."

Still holding Tavvy, Julian stood up. There was powdered sugar on his shirt, in his hair, but his face was calm, expressionless. "Sorry about the mess, Cristina."

"It's fine," she said, looking around the room. "It is not my kitchen. Though," she added hastily, "I can help you clean up."

"Mark will clean up," Julian said, without looking at his brother. "Did you and Diana find anything out from Malcolm?"

"He had gone to see some warlocks he thought might be able to help," said Cristina. "We talked about Catarina Loss. I've heard of her—she teaches at the Academy sometimes, Downworlder studies. Apparently both Malcolm and Diana are good friends with her, so they exchanged a lot of stories I didn't really understand."

"Well, here's what we learned from Rook," said Emma, and launched into the story, leaving out the part where Ty had almost sliced off Kit Rook's head.

"So someone needs to tail Sterling," said Livvy eagerly when Emma was done. "Ty and I could do it."

"You can't drive," Emma pointed out. "And we need you here for research."

Livvy made a face. "So we get stuck here reading 'it was many and many a year ago' nine thousand times?"

"There's no reason we can't learn how to drive," said Ty, looking mulish. "Mark was saying, it's not like it matters that we're not sixteen, it's not as if we have to obey mundane laws anyway—"

"Did Mark say that?" Julian said quietly. "Fine. Mark can teach you how to drive."

Mark dropped a plate into the sink with a crash. "Julian—"

"What is it, Mark?" said Jules. "Oh, right, you don't actually know how to drive, either. And of course teaching someone to drive takes time, but you might not actually be here. Because there's no guarantee you're staying."

"That's not true," Livvy said. "We've practically solved the case—"

"But Mark has a choice." Julian was looking at his older brother over his baby brother's head. His blue-green gaze was a steady fire. "Tell them, Mark. Tell them you're sure you'll choose us."

*Promise them*, his gaze said. *Promise them you won't hurt them.*

Mark said nothing.

*Oh*, Emma thought. She remembered what Julian had said to her outside. This was what he was afraid of: that they loved Mark too much already. He would give up the children he loved to Mark without a murmur, if it was what they wanted—if, as Ty had said, they wanted Mark to take care of them. He would give them up because he loved them, because their happiness was his, because they were his breath and blood.

But Mark was his brother too, and he loved him as well. What did you do, what could you do, when what threatened the ones you loved was something else you loved just as much?

"Julian." To everyone's surprise, it was Uncle Arthur, standing in the doorway. He cast a brief, uninterested look over the mess in the kitchen, before zeroing in on his nephew. "Julian, I need to talk to you about something. Privately."

Faint worry flickered in the back of Julian's eyes. He nodded to his uncle just as something buzzed in Emma's pocket. Her phone.

Her stomach clenched. It was only two words, not from a number but from a series of zeroes. THE CONVERGENCE.

Something had tripped the monitor at the convergence site. Her mind raced. It was nearly sunset. The convergence door would be opening—but the Mantids would be stirring as well. She needed to leave immediately to get there at the safest time.

"Did someone call you?" Julian asked, glancing over at her. He was setting down Tavvy, ruffling his hair, gently pushing him toward Dru, who was looking distinctly green.

Emma stifled a frown—wouldn't the message have gone to him, too? Or not—she remembered him saying that his phone was nearly dead, back at Johnny Rook's. And Diana was asleep. Emma realized she might well be the only person here who had received the convergence message.

"Just Cameron," she said, grabbing for the first available name she could think of. Jules's eyes shuttered; maybe he was still worried she was going to tell Cameron about Mark. He looked pale. His expression was calm, but she could feel a tense misery coming off him in waves. She thought of the way he had clung to Ty in front of Johnny Rook's house, the way he had looked at Mark. At Arthur.

Her training said she should bring Julian with her to the convergence. He was her *parabatai*. But she couldn't tear him away from his family right now. She just couldn't. Her mind rebelled against the thought in a way she couldn't bring herself to examine too closely.

"Cristina." Emma turned to her friend. "Can I talk to you in the hallway?"

With a worried look, Cristina followed Emma out into the corridor.

"Is this about Cameron?" Cristina said as soon as the kitchen door shut behind them. "I do not think I am up to giving any romantic advice right now—"

"I do have to go see Cameron," said Emma, her mind working quickly. She could bring Cristina with her to the convergence. Cristina was trustworthy; she wouldn't mention to anyone what they were doing. But Julian had been so clearly hurt—not just hurt, gutted—by her going to the cave alone with Mark and not telling him. And so much had strained and troubled their *parabatai* relationship—she couldn't do it to him again by bringing someone else with her. "But it's not that. Look, someone needs to tail Sterling. I don't think anything's going to happen with him—we're still within the window of two days—but just in case."

Cristina nodded. "I can do it. Diana left the truck; I'll take it. I need the address, though."

"Julian has it. And I'll give you a note for him."

"Good, because he'll ask," said Cristina dryly. There was a sudden terrible noise from the kitchen: the sound of Dru running across the kitchen floor and throwing up noisily into the sink.

"Oh, poor girl," said Emma. "But I mean, that thing she drank was really disgusting. . . ."

"Emma, I know that you're not telling me the truth. I know you are not going to see Cameron Ashdown." Cristina held up a hand, stifling Emma's protest. "And it is all right. You would not lie to me without good reason. It's just—"

"Yes?" Emma said. She tried to keep her eyes guileless. It was better, she told herself. If Diana caught her, if she got in trouble, she'd be the only one who did: Cristina and Julian didn't deserve that. She could weather it on her own.

"Be careful," Cristina said. "Don't make me regret lying for you, Emma Carstairs."

\* \* \*

The sun was a brilliant ball of flame out over the ocean as Emma steered the Toyota up the dirt road that led to the convergence. The sky was darkening fast. The Toyota bumped the last few yards over the field, nearly rolling into a shallow ditch before she braked and cut the engine.

She got out, reaching back inside to pull out weapons. She had left Cortana back at the Institute. It had caused her a pang, but walking out with it strapped to her back would have invited questions. At least there were seraph blades. She tucked one into her belt and thumbed her witchlight stone out of her pocket, glancing around as she did—it was oddly quiet here, with no sound of insects, small animals, or birdsong. Only the wind in the grass.

*The Mantid demons.* At night they probably came out and ate everything living. She shuddered and strode toward the cave. The convergence entrance was opening, a thick black line against the granite.

She glanced back once, worriedly—the sun was lower than she would have liked, dying the ocean water bloody. She'd parked as close as she could to the cave entrance so that if it was dark when she emerged, she could get to the car quickly. It was looking more and more likely that she'd have to kill some Mantids on the way, though.

As she strode toward the sheer wall of rock, the black line widened a little more, as if welcoming her. She leaned against the rock with one hand, peering into the gap. It smelled oddly of seawater.

She thought of her parents. *Please let me find something*, she prayed. *Please let me find a clue, discover how this connects to what was done to you. Please let me avenge you.*

*So I can sleep at night.*

Inside the gap, Emma could see the dim gleam of the rock corridor leading into the cave's heart.

Gripping her witchlight, Emma plunged into the convergence.

\* \* \*

Night had nearly fallen—the sky was shading from blue to indigo, the first stars twinkling out above the distant mountains. Cristina sat with her legs up on the dashboard of the truck, her eyes fixed on the two-story ranch house that belonged to Casper Sterling.

The Jeep she recognized was parked in the court in front of the house, under an old-growth olive tree. A low wall ran around the property; the neighborhood, just beside Hancock Park, was full of expensive but not particularly showy houses. Sterling's was closed, shuttered and dark. The only evidence she had that he was home was the car in the driveway.

She thought of Mark, then wished she hadn't. She was doing that a lot these days—thinking of Mark and then regretting it. She had worked hard to return her life to normal after she left Mexico. No more romances with brooding and troubled men, no matter how handsome.

Mark Blackthorn wasn't brooding or troubled exactly. But Mark Blackthorn belonged to Kieran and the Wild Hunt. Mark Blackthorn had a divided heart.

He also had a soft, husky voice, startling eyes, and a habit of saying things that turned her world backward. And he was an excellent dancer, from what she'd seen. Cristina rated dancing highly. Boys who could dance well, kissed well—that was what her mother always said.

A dark shadow ran across the roof of Sterling's house.

Cristina was up and out of the car in seconds, her seraph blade in her hand. *"Miguel,"* she whispered, and it blazed up. She was heavily glamoured enough that she knew no mundane could see her, but the blade provided precious light.

She moved forward carefully, her heart pounding. She remembered what Emma had told her about the night Julian had been shot: the shadow on the roof, the man in black. She eased up to the house itself. The windows were dark, the curtains motionless. Everything was still and silent.

She moved toward the Jeep. She slipped her stele out of her pocket just as a shape dropped to the ground beside her with an *oomph*. Cristina leaped out of the way as the shadow unfolded; it was Sterling, dressed in what Cristina imagined mundanes thought gear looked like. Black pants, black boots, a tailored black jacket.

He stared at her, and his face turned slowly purple. "*You*," he snarled.

"I can help you," Cristina said, keeping her voice and her blade steady. "Please let me help you."

The hatred in his eyes startled her. "Get *away*," he hissed, and yanked something out of his pocket.

A gun. A handgun, small caliber, but enough to make Cristina step back. Guns were something that rarely entered Shadowhunter life; they belonged to mundanes, to their world of ordinary human crime.

But they could still spill Shadowhunter blood and split Shadowhunter bones. He backed away, pointing the gun at her, until he reached the end of his driveway. Then he turned and ran.

Cristina bolted after him, but by the time she'd reached the end of the driveway, he was disappearing around the corner of the street. Apparently he hadn't exaggerated—weres really were faster than humans. Faster, even, than Shadowhunters.

Cristina muttered a mild curse and trudged back to the Jeep. She drew her stele from her belt with her free hand and, crouching down, carefully marked a small tracking rune into the side of the vehicle, just above the wheel.

It wasn't a total disaster, she thought, trudging back to the truck. As Emma had said, they were still within the two-day window before the "hunt" began. And having put a tracking rune on Sterling's car was sure to help. If they just stayed away from his house, let him think they'd given up, hopefully he'd get careless and start driving.

Only when she climbed into the truck and slammed the door behind her did she see that her phone was flashing. She'd missed a call. She picked it up and her heart fell into her stomach.

*Diego Rocio Rosales.*

She dropped the phone as if it had turned into a scorpion. Why, why, *why* would Diego call her? She'd told him never to speak to her again.

Her hand stole to the charm at her throat and she clutched it, her lips moving in a silent prayer. *Give me the strength not to call him back.*

"Are you feeling better, Uncle?" Julian said.

Arthur, slumped behind the desk in his office, looked up with faded, distant eyes.

"Julian," he said. "I need to talk to you."

"I know. You said." Julian leaned back against a wall. "Do you remember what it was about?"

He felt exhausted, scraped out, hollow as a dry bone. He knew he should regret what he'd said in the kitchen about Mark. He knew he should be sympathetic to his uncle. But he couldn't dredge up the emotion.

He didn't really remember leaving the kitchen: He recalled handing Tavvy off, as much as you could hand off a sugarcoated seven-year-old; he recalled them all promising they would clean up their dinner of cheese and chocolate and brownies and burned things. Even Dru, once she'd stopped throwing up into the sink, had sworn she'd scrub the floor *and* get the ketchup off the windows.

Not that Julian had realized until that moment that there was ketchup on the windows.

He'd nodded and gone to leave the room, and then stopped to look around for Emma. But at some point Emma had left with Cristina. Presumably they were somewhere talking about Cameron

Ashdown. And there was nothing Julian wanted less than to join in on that.

He didn't know when that had happened, that the thought of Cameron made him not want to see Emma. *His* Emma. You always wanted to see your *parabatai*. They were the most welcome face in the world to you. There was a wrongness about not wanting it, as if the earth had suddenly started spinning in the other direction.

"I don't think I do," Arthur said after a moment. "There was something I wanted to help with. Something about the investigation. You are still investigating, aren't you?"

"The murders? The ones the faerie convoy came to us about? Yes."

"I think it was about the poem," Arthur said. "The one Livia was reciting in the kitchen." He rubbed at his eyes, obviously tired. "I was passing by and I heard it."

"The poem?" Julian echoed, confused. "'Annabel Lee'?"

Arthur spoke in his deep, rumbling voice, sounding out the lines of poetry as if they were the lines of a spell.

"But our love it was stronger by far than the love
Of those who were older than we—
Of many far wiser than we—
And neither the angels in Heaven above
Nor the demons down under the sea
Can ever dissever my soul from the soul
Of the beautiful Annabel Lee—"

"I know the poem," Julian interrupted. "But I don't—"

"'Those who were older,'" Arthur said. "'I've heard the phrase before. In London. I can't remember what it was in connection with." He picked up a pen from the desk, tapped it against the wood. "I'm sorry. I just—I can't remember."

"Those Who Are Older," murmured Julian. He remembered Belinda, back at the theater, smiling with her blood-red lips. *May Those Who Are Older grant us all good fortune*, she'd said.

An idea bloomed in the back of Julian's mind, but, elusive, disappeared when he tried to chase it.

He needed to go to his studio. He wanted to be alone, and painting would unlock his thoughts. He turned to go and only paused when Uncle Arthur's voice cut through the dusty air.

"Did I help you, boy?" he said.

"Yes," said Julian. "You helped."

When Cristina returned to the Institute, it was dark and silent. The entryway lights were off, and only a few windows glowed—Julian's studio, the bright spot of the attic, the square that was the kitchen.

Frowning, Cristina went directly there, wondering if Emma had returned yet from her mysterious errand. If the others had managed to clean up the mess they'd made.

At first glance the kitchen seemed deserted, only a single light on. Dishes were piled in the sink, and though someone had clearly scrubbed the walls and counters, there was still food crusted onto the stove, and two large trash bags, stuffed full and half-spilling their contents, propped against the wall.

"Cristina?"

She blinked into the dimness, though there was no mistaking the voice.

Mark.

He was sitting on the floor, his legs crossed. Tavvy was asleep beside him—on him, really, his head resting in the crook of Mark's arm, his small legs and arms curled up like a potato bug's. Mark's T-shirt and jeans were covered with powdered sugar.

Cristina slowly unwound her scarf and placed it on the table. "Has Emma returned yet?"

"I don't know," Mark said, his hand carefully stroking Tavvy's hair. "But if she has, she's probably gone to sleep."

Cristina sighed. She'd probably have to wait until tomorrow to see Emma, find out what she'd been doing. Tell her about Diego's phone call, if she could get up the nerve.

"Could you—if you don't mind—get me a glass of water?" Mark asked. He looked down half-apologetically at the boy in his lap. "I don't want to wake him."

"Of course." Cristina went to the sink, filled a glass, and returned, sitting down cross-legged opposite Mark. He took the glass with a grateful expression. "I'm sure Julian isn't that angry with you," she said.

Mark made an inelegant noise, finishing the water and setting the glass down.

"You could pick up Tavvy," Cristina suggested. "You could carry him to bed. If you want him to sleep."

"I like him here," Mark said, looking down at his own long, pale fingers tangled in the little boy's brown curls. "He just— They all left, and he fell asleep on me." He sounded amazed, wondering.

"Of course he did," Cristina said. "He's your brother. He trusts you."

"Nobody trusts a Hunter," Mark said.

"You are not a Hunter in this house. You are a Blackthorn."

"I wish Julian agreed with you. I thought I was keeping the children happy. I thought that's what Julian would have wanted."

Tavvy shifted in Mark's arms and Mark moved too, so that the edge of his boot was touching the tip of Cristina's. She felt the contact like a small shock.

"You have to understand," she said. "Julian does everything for these children. Everything. I have never seen a brother who is so much like a parent. He cannot only tell them yes, he has to tell them no. He must deal in discipline and punishment and denial. Whereas you, you can give them anything. You can have fun with them."

"Julian can have fun with them," Mark said a little sulkily.

"He can't," said Cristina. "He is envious because he loves them but he cannot be their brother. He must be their father. In his mind, they dread him and adore you."

"Julian's jealous?" Mark looked astonished. "Of me?"

"I think so." Cristina met his eyes. At some point, in knowing him, the mismatch between his blue and his golden one had stopped seeming strange to her. The same way it had stopped seeming strange to be in the Blackthorns' kitchen, speaking English, instead of at home, where things were warm and familiar. "Be kind to him. He has a gentle soul. He is terrified you will leave and break the hearts of all these children he loves so very much."

Mark looked down at Tavvy. "I don't know what I will do," he said. "I did not realize how it would tear at my heart to be back among them. It was thinking of them, of my family, that helped me live through the first years I was in the Hunt. Every day we would ride, and steal from the dead. It was cold, a cold life. And at night I would lie down and conjure their faces to lull me to sleep. They were all I had until—"

He broke off. Tavvy sat up, scrubbing his small hands through his tangled hair. "Jules?" He yawned.

"No," said his brother quietly. "It's Mark."

"Oh, right." Tavvy gave him a blink-eyed smile. "Think I crashed from all the sugar."

"Well, you were inside a bag of it," Mark said. "That could have an effect on anyone."

Tavvy got to his feet and stretched, a full little-boy stretch with his arms outraised. Mark watched him, a look of wistfulness in his eyes. Cristina wondered if he was thinking about all the years and milestones he'd missed in Tavvy's life. Of all his siblings, his youngest had changed the most.

"Bed," Tavvy said, and wandered out of the kitchen, pausing at the door to say, "Night, Cristina!" shyly before scampering off.

Cristina turned back to Mark. He was still sitting with his back against the refrigerator. He looked exhausted, not just physically, but as if his soul were tired.

She could get up and go to bed, Cristina thought. She probably should. There was no reason for her to stay here and sit on the floor with a boy she barely knew, who would most likely disappear out of her life in months, and who was probably in love with someone else.

Which, she thought, might be exactly what drew her to him. She knew what it was like to leave someone you loved behind.

"Until?" she prompted.

Mark's eyelids lifted slowly, showing her the banked fire in gold and blue eyes. "What?"

"You said your family, the memory of your family, was all you had until something. Until Kieran?"

"Yes," Mark said.

"Was he the only one who was kind to you?"

"In the Hunt?" said Mark. "There is not kindness in the Hunt. There is respect, and a sort of camaraderie of brothers. They feared Kieran, of course. Kieran is gentry, a Prince of Faerie. His father, the King, gave him to the Hunt as a sign of goodwill to Gwyn, but he also demanded his good treatment. That good treatment was extended to me, but even before Kieran, they came slowly to respect me." His shoulders hunched. "It was worst when we attended the revels. Faeries from all over would come to those, and they did not appreciate a Shadowhunter's attendance. They would do their best to draw me aside, to taunt and torment me."

"Did no one intervene?"

Mark laughed shortly. "The ways of Faerie are brutal," he said. "Even for the greatest among them. The Queen of the Seelie Court can be deprived of her powers if her crown is stolen. Even Gwyn, who leads the Wild Hunt, must yield authority to any who steals his cloak. You cannot imagine they would show mercy to a half-Shadowhunter boy." His lip curled. "They even had a rhyme they would mock me with."

"A rhyme?" Cristina held up a hand. "Never mind, you do not need to tell it to me, not if you don't wish to."

"I no longer care," Mark said. "It was an odd bit of doggerel. *First the flame and then the flood, in the end it's Blackthorn blood.*"

Cristina sat up straight. "What?"

"They claimed it meant Blackthorn blood was destructive, like flood or fire. That whoever made up the rhyme was saying Blackthorns were bad luck. Not that it matters. It's just a bit of nonsense."

"That isn't nonsense," Cristina exclaimed. "It means something. The words written on the bodies . . ." She frowned in concentration. "They are the same."

"What do you mean?"

"'Fire to water,'" she said. "It is the same—they are simply different translations. When English is not your first language, you understand the sense of the words differently. Believe me, 'Fire to water' and 'First the flame and then the flood,' they could be the same thing."

"But what does that mean?"

"I'm not sure." Cristina pushed her hands into her hair in frustration. "Please, promise me you'll mention it to Emma and Jules as soon as you can. I could be wrong, but . . ."

Mark looked baffled. "Yes, of course—"

"Promise."

"Tomorrow, I promise." His smile was bemused. "It occurs to me that you know a great deal about me, Cristina, and I know very little about you. I know your name, Mendoza Rosales. I know you left something behind in Mexico. What was it?"

"Not a something," she said. "Someone."

"Perfect Diego?"

"And his brother, Jaime." She waved away Mark's raised eyebrow. "One of them I was in love with, and the other was my best friend. They both broke my heart." She was almost astonished to hear the words come out of her mouth.

"For your heart twice broken, I am sorry," said Mark. "But is it wrong that I am glad that it brought you into my life? If you had not been here when I arrived—I do not know that I could have borne it. When I first saw Julian, I thought he was my father. I did not know my brother so grown. I left them children, and now they are no longer that. When I knew what I had lost, even with Emma, those years of their lives . . . You are the only one I have not lost something with, but rather gained a new friendship."

"Friendship," Cristina agreed.

He extended his hand, and she looked at him, bemused.

"It is traditional," he said, "among the fey, for a declaration of friendship to be accompanied by a clasp of hands."

She put her hand in his. His fingers closed about her own; they were rough where they were calloused, but lithe and strong. And not cool, as she had imagined they would be, but warm. She tried to hold back the shiver that threatened to spread up her arm, realizing how long it had been since she had held someone's hand like this.

"Cristina," he said, and her name sounded like music when he spoke it.

Neither of them noticed the movement at the window, the flash of a pale face looking in, or the sound of an acorn being viciously crushed between narrow fingers.

The large chamber inside the cave hadn't changed since the last time Emma had been in it. The same bronze walls, the same chalked circle on the floor. The same large glass doors fixed into the walls and wavering darkness behind them.

Energy crackled against her skin as she walked into the circle. The magic of the glamour. From inside the circle, the room looked different—the walls seemed faded and flowing, as if they were in an old photograph. The porthole doors were dark.

The circle itself was empty, though there was a strange smell inside it, a mixture of sulfur and burned sugar. Making a face, Emma stepped out of the circle and approached the leftmost porthole door.

Up close it no longer looked dark. There was light behind it. It was illuminated from within, like a museum display. She stepped closer still and stared through the glass.

Beyond the glass door was a small, square space, like a closet.

Inside it was a large brass candelabra, though there were no candles fastened to the holders. It would have made a wicked weapon, Emma thought, with its long spikes, meant to be jammed into soft wax. There was also a small pile of what looked to Emma like ceremonial clothes—a dark red velvet robe, a pair of long earrings that flashed with rubies. Delicate gold sandals.

Was the necromancer a woman?

Emma stepped quickly to the second door. With her nose to the glass, she could see what looked like water. It surged and moved, and dark shapes slipped through it—one bumped against the glass, and she jumped back with a shout before realizing that it was only a small, striped fish with orange eyes. It gazed at her for a moment before disappearing back into the dark water.

She lifted her witchlight close to the glass, and now the water was truly visible—it was radiant, a deep blue-green, the color of Blackthorn eyes. She could see fish and drifting seaweed and strange lights and colors beyond the glass. Apparently they were dealing with a necromancer who liked aquariums and fish. Maybe even turtles. Shaking her head, Emma stepped back.

Her eyes lit on the metal object fixed between the doors. At first she had thought it looked like a carved knife sticking out of the wall, but now she realized it was a lever. She reached out and closed her hand around it. It was cold under her fingers.

She yanked it down.

For a moment nothing happened. Then both of the porthole doors swung wide.

An unearthly howl tore through the room. Emma turned and stared in horror. The second porthole was wide open and glowing bright blue, and Emma could see that it wasn't an aquarium at all—it was a door into the ocean. A great, deep universe of water opened on the other side of the door, of whipping seaweed and surging currents and the dark, shadowy shapes of things much bigger than fish.

The stench of salt water was everywhere. *Flood*, Emma thought, and then she found herself lifted off her feet and dragged toward the ocean as if she were being sucked down a drain. She only had time to scream once before she was hauled through the doorway and the water closed over her head.

*Cameron Ashdown.*

Julian was painting. Cristina had given him Emma's note after he'd left the attic: a terse note, to the point, just saying she was going to Cameron's and not to wait up.

He'd crumpled it up in his hand and muttered something to Cristina. A second later he was sprinting toward the stairs and his studio. Ripping open his supply cabinet, tumbling out the paints. Unzipping his gear jacket, throwing it down, yanking the caps off the tubes of oil paint and squeezing the colors onto the palette until the sharp smell of the paint filled the room and cut through the fog in his head.

He attacked the canvas, holding the brush like a weapon, and the paint seemed to spill out of him like blood.

He was painting in black and red and gold, letting the events of the past days drain out of him as if they were poisonous venom. The brush slashed across the blank canvas and there was Mark on the beach, the moonlight shining across the vicious scars on his back. There was Ty with his knife to Kit Rook's throat. Tavvy screaming with his nightmares. Mark cringing away from Julian's stele.

He was aware he was sweating, his hair sticking to his forehead. He tasted salt and paint in his mouth. He knew he shouldn't be here; he should be doing what he always did: minding Tavvy, finding new books to feed Ty's curiosity, putting healing runes on Livvy when she cut herself fencing, sitting with Dru while she watched bad horror films.

He should be with Emma. But Emma wasn't here; she was off having her own life, and that was as it should be, as *parabatai* were meant to be. It wasn't a marriage, the *parabatai* bond. It was something there were no words for in mundane English. He was meant to want Emma's happiness more than he wanted his own, and he did. He *did.*

So why did he feel like he was being stabbed to death from the inside?

He fumbled for the gold paint, because the longing was rising up in him, beating in his veins, and only painting her would take it away. And he couldn't paint her without gold. He caught up the tube and—

Choked. The brush rattled from his hand onto the ground, and he crumpled to his knees. He was gasping, his chest spasming. He couldn't drag air into his lungs. His eyes burned and the back of his throat burned too.

Salt. He was choking on salt. Not the salt of blood, but the salt of the ocean. He tasted the sea in his mouth and coughed, his body clenching as he spat up seawater onto the floor.

*Seawater?* He wiped the back of his hand across his mouth, his heart pounding. He'd gone nowhere near the ocean today. And yet he could hear it in his ears, as if he were listening to a seashell. His body ached, and his *parabatai* rune throbbed.

Shocked and dizzy, he placed his hand over the rune. And he *knew*. He knew without knowing how he knew, knew it down in his soul where his connection to Emma had been forged in blood and fire. He knew in the way that she was a part of him, the way her breathing was his breathing, and her dreams were his dreams, and her blood was his blood, and when her heart stopped he knew that his would too, and he would be glad, because he wouldn't want to live one second in a world that didn't have her in it.

He closed his eyes and saw the ocean rise up behind his eyelids, blue-black and depthless, charged with the force of the first wave that had ever crashed on the first lonely beach. And he knew.

*Whither thou goest, I will go.*

"Emma," he whispered, and took off at a run.

Emma was not sure what terrified her most about the ocean. There was the rage of the waves—dark blue and tipped with white like lace, they were deceptively beautiful, but as they neared the shore, they closed in like fists. She had been trapped by a breaking wave once and she remembered the feeling of falling, as if she were plunging down an elevator shaft, and then the force of the water pinning her to the sand. She had choked and struggled, trying to free herself, to push her way back up to the air.

There was also the depth of it. She had read, before, about people who had been abandoned out to sea, how they had gone insane thinking about what was below them: the miles and miles of water and the dark and toothy and slippery things that lived in it.

As she was slammed through the porthole door and into the ocean, salt water swallowed Emma, filled her eyes and ears. She was surrounded by water, blackness opening up below her like a pit.

She could see the pale square of the porthole door, receding in the distance, but try as she might, she couldn't kick her way toward it. The current was too strong.

Hopelessly, she looked up. Her witchlight stone was gone, sinking through the water below her. The light from the ever-receding porthole lit the area around her, but she could see nothing but darkness above. Her ears were popping. Raziel only knew how deep down she was. The water near the porthole was pale green, the color of jade, but everywhere else it was black as death.

She reached for a stele. Her lungs were already aching. Floating in the water, kicking out against the current, she jammed the tip of the stele against her arm and scrawled a Breathing rune.

The ache in her lungs eased. With the pain gone, the fear came crashing in, blinding in its intensity. The Breathing rune kept her from struggling for air, but the horror of what might be around her was nearly as intense. She reached for the seraph blade in her belt and pulled it free.

*Manukel*, she thought.

The blade came to life in her hand, spilling out light, and the water around her turned to murky gold. For a moment Emma was dazzled; then her vision cleared, and she saw them.

Demons.

She screamed, and the bubbles rose up around her, silent. They were below her, like nightmares rising: lumpy, slippery creatures. Waving tentacles crowned with jagged teeth flailed toward her. She swung Manukel and severed the spiked limb reaching for her leg. Black blood exploded into the water, billowing up in clouds.

A scarlet, snakelike thing shot toward her through the water. She kicked out, collided with something fleshy and soft. She gagged on revulsion and stabbed downward; more blood spilled. The sea around her was turning to charcoal.

She kicked up toward the surface, carried on a billow of demon blood. As she rose, she could see the white moon, a blurred pearl on the surface of the water. The Breathing rune had burned off her skin; her lungs felt as if they were collapsing. She could feel the churn of water under her feet, didn't dare to look down. She reached up, up toward where the water ended, felt her hand break the surface, the chill of air on her fingers.

Something caught at her wrist. Her seraph blade fell from her hand, a glowing point of light that tumbled away from her as she was hauled to the surface of the water. She gasped in air, but it was too soon. Water filled her lungs, her chest, and darkness slammed into her with the force of a truck.

## Idris, 2009

*It was at Emma and Julian's* parabatai *ceremony that she learned two important things. The first was that she wasn't the only Carstairs left in the world.*

*Their* parabatai *ceremony was performed in Idris, because they had fought in the Dark War, and their valor was recognized. At least, Julian said, it was recognized sometimes—not when they really wanted anything important, like his sister back from Wrangel Island, but when the Nephilim felt like throwing a party about how awesome Nephilim were, it was always a feature.*

*When they arrived, they looked around the streets of Alicante, astonished. The last time they had been in the capital city of Idris, it had been wrecked by the Dark War. The streets torn up, nails hammered into walls to keep out faeries, the doors of the Accords Hall torn away. Now it was pristine again, the cobblestones back in place, the canals winding by the houses, and the demon towers glimmering over it all.*

*"It seems smaller," Julian said, looking around from the Accords Hall steps.*

*"It's not that it's smaller." The voice belonged to a young man with*

dark hair and dark eyes, smiling down at them. "It's that you've grown."

They stared at him.

"Don't you remember me?" he said. He lowered his voice as if he were quoting. "Emma Cordelia Carstairs. Stay with your parabatai. Sometimes it's braver not to fight. Protect them, and save your vengeance for another day."

"Brother Zachariah?" Emma was astonished. "You helped us during the Dark War—"

"I am no longer a Silent Brother," he said. "Only an ordinary man. My name is James. James Carstairs. But everyone calls me Jem."

There was astonishment, and there was chatter, and Julian gave Emma space to be shocked and to pepper former Brother Zachariah with questions. Jem explained that he had become a Silent Brother in 1878, but he had shed the role now so that he could marry the woman he loved, the warlock Tessa Gray. Julian asked if that meant he was a hundred and fifty years old and Jem admitted that he nearly was, though he didn't look it. He looked about twenty-three.

"Why didn't you tell me back then?" Emma demanded as they wended their way into the Silent City, down long stone staircases. "That you were a Carstairs?"

"I thought I might die," he said candidly. "It was a battle. It seemed a cruel thing to tell you if I wasn't going to live through the day. And after that Tessa cautioned me that I should give you time, to grieve for your parents, to adjust to your new life." He turned and looked at her, and his expression was both sorrowful and affectionate. "You're a Shadowhunter, Emma. And neither Tessa nor I are Nephilim, not anymore. To come and live with me, though you would be welcome, you'd have to give up being a Shadowhunter. And that was too cruel a choice to place in front of you."

"Come and live with you?" It was Julian, a warning sharp in his tone. "Why would she do that? She has a home. She has a family."

"Exactly," Jem said. "And there is more. Can you give me a moment alone with Emma?"

Julian checked in with Emma with his eyes, and she nodded. He turned and made his way down the stairs, glancing back several times to make sure she was all right.

Jem touched her arm with light fingers. She was wearing ceremonial gear, ready for the ritual, but she could feel the scar she had given herself with Cortana flare when he touched her, as if recognizing their shared blood. "I wanted to be here for you, for this," he said. "For I had a para-batai myself once, and the bond of it is precious to me."

Emma didn't ask what had happened to Jem's parabatai. Silent Brothers were forbidden from having parabatai, and besides, a hundred and thirty years was a long, long time.

"But I don't know when I can be with you again," he said. "Tessa and I, we have to find something. Something important." He hesitated. "It will be dangerous looking for it, but once it's found I'd like to be part of your life once more. Like a sort of uncle." He gave a half smile. "You might not guess it, but I have a lot of experience in being an uncle."

His gaze was steady on hers, and though there was no physical resemblance between them, for that moment Emma was reminded of her father—of his level gaze and kind face.

"I'd like that," she said. "Can I ask you one more thing?"

He nodded, his expression serious. It was easy to imagine him as an uncle: He looked so young, but there was a calm certainty underneath that made him seem ageless, like a faerie or a warlock. "Yes?"

"Did you send me your cat?"

"Church?" He started to laugh. "Yes. Has he been taking care of you? Did he bring you the gifts I gave?"

"The shells and sea glass?" She nodded. "The bracelet Julian's wearing is made out of sea glass Church brought me."

His laughter softened into a smile that was a little bit sad. "As it should be," he said. "What belongs to one parabatai, belongs to the other. For you are one heart now. And one soul."

Jem stayed with Emma through the ceremony, which was witnessed by Simon and Clary, whom she suspected would become parabatai them-selves one day.

After the ceremony, Julian and Emma were led through the streets to the Accords Hall, where there was a special dinner in their honor. Tessa—a pretty, brown-haired girl who looked about Clary's age—had joined them, hugging Emma tightly and exclaiming over Cortana, which she said she had seen before a long time ago. Other parabatai got up and spoke about their bond and their experiences. Waves of radiant happiness seemed to come off the pairs of best friends as they talked. Jace and Alec spoke about nearly dying in the demon realms together, grinning, and Emma felt a sense of joy at the thought that one day she and Jules would be up there, smiling dopily at each other and talking about how their bond had gotten them through times when they'd thought they were going to die.

At some point during the speeches, Jem had slipped quietly from his chair and disappeared through the doors to Angel Square. Tessa had dropped her napkin and hurried after him; as the doors closed, Emma could see them on the dimly lit steps. Jem had his head down on Tessa's shoulder.

She wanted to go after them, but she was already being swept up to the front of the Hall by Clary and made to give some sort of speech, and Julian was with her, smiling that calm smile that hid a million thoughts. And Emma had been happy. She'd been wearing one of her first great thrift store finds, a real gown, not like the ragged jeans she usually wore until they fell to pieces. Instead she'd put on a brown Paraphernalia dress scat-tered with pale gold blossoms like sunflowers growing out of a field and let her hair, which reached her waist, out of its usual ponytail. She'd shot up like a weed in the past year, and she nearly reached Jace's shoulder when he came over to congratulate her and Julian.

She'd had the worst crush of all time on Jace when she was twelve and she still felt a little awkward around him. He was nearly nineteen years old now, and even better-looking than he had been—taller, broader, tanned, and with his hair bleached from sunlight, but more than anything else, happier-looking. She remembered a tense-looking, beautiful boy who burned with revenge and heavenly fire, and now he looked at ease with himself.

Which was nice. She was happy for him, and for Clary, who smiled and waved at her across the room. But she no longer got butterflies in her stomach when he smiled at her, or wanted to crawl under something and die when he hugged her and told her she looked pretty in her new dress. "You've got a lot of responsibility now," he said to Julian. "You'll have to make sure she winds up with a guy who deserves her."

Julian was strangely white-faced. Maybe he was feeling the effects of the ceremony, Emma thought. It had been strong magic, and she still felt it sizzling through her blood like champagne bubbles. But Jules looked as if he were getting sick.

"What about me?" Emma said quickly. "Don't I have to make sure Jules winds up with someone who deserves him?"

"Absolutely. I did it for Alec, Alec did it for me—well, actually, he hated Clary at first, but he came around."

"I bet you didn't like Magnus much, either," said Julian, still with the same odd, stiff look on his face.

"Maybe not," said Jace, "but I never would have said so."

"Because it would have hurt Alec's feelings?" Emma asked.

"No," said Jace, "because Magnus would have turned me into a hat rack," and he wandered back toward Clary, who was laughing with Alec, both of them looking happy.

Which was as it should be, Emma thought. One's parabatai should be friends with the person you loved, your spouse or boyfriend or girlfriend, because that was how it worked. Though when she tried to imagine the person she'd be with, someone she might marry and stay with forever, there was only a sort of blurry space. She couldn't picture the person at all.

"I have to go," Julian said. "I need some air." He brushed the back of his hand across Emma's cheek before making for the double doors of the Hall. It was a ragged touch: His nails were bitten down to the edges.

Later that night Emma woke up from a dream of fiery circles, her skin burning hot, the sheets tangled around her legs. They had been put up in the old Blackthorn manor house, and Julian was far away, down corridors she didn't know like she knew the hallways of the Institute. She went to the window. It was a short drop down to the garden path. She kicked her feet into slippers and climbed outside.

The path curved around the gardens. Emma made her way along it, breathing in the cool, clean air of Idris, untouched by smog. The sky above was brilliant with a million stars, totally free of light pollution, and she wished Julian was with her so she could show it to him, and then she heard voices.

The Blackthorn manor had burned down quite a long time ago and been rebuilt near to the Herondale manor. Emma wandered down a number of pretty paths until she found a wall.

There was a gate set into the wall. As Emma approached it, she could hear the murmured voices more clearly. She crept to the side of the gate and peered through the bars.

On the other side, a green lawn sloped down to the Herondale manor, a pile of white and tawny stone. The grass was sparkling with dew under the starlight and starred with the white flowers that grew only in Idris.

"And that constellation right there, that's the Rabbit. See how it has ears?" It was Jace's voice. He and Clary were sitting in the grass, shoulder to shoulder. He was wearing jeans and a T-shirt, and Clary was in her nightgown, Jace's jacket around her shoulders. Jace was pointing at the sky.

"I'm pretty sure there's no Rabbit constellation," Clary said. She hadn't changed as much as Jace had in the past years—she was still slight, her red hair bright as Christmas, her small face freckled and thoughtful. She had her head against Jace's shoulder.

"Sure there is," he said, and as the starlight touched his pale curls, Emma felt a faint flutter of her old crush. "And that one there, that's the Hubcap. And there's the Great Pancake."

"I'm going back inside," Clary said. "I was promised an astronomy lesson."

"What? Sailors used to navigate by the Great Pancake," said Jace, and Clary shook her head and started to stand up. Jace grabbed her ankle and she laughed and tumbled over on top of him, and then they were kissing and Emma froze, because what had been a casual moment, one she could have interrupted with a friendly hello, had suddenly become something else.

Jace rolled over on top of Clary in the grass. She had her arms wrapped around him, her hands in his hair. His jacket had fallen off her shoulders and the straps of her nightgown were sliding down her pale arms.

Clary was laughing and saying his name, saying maybe they should go back inside, and Jace kissed her neck. Clary gasped and Emma heard him say, "Remember the Wayland manor? Remember that time outside?"

"I remember." Her voice was low and throaty.

"I didn't think I could have you," Jace said. He was propped over Clary on his elbows, tracing the line of her cheek with his finger. "It was like being in Hell. I would have done anything for you. I still would."

Clary flattened her hand against his chest, over his heart, and said, "I love you."

He made a noise, a very un-Jace-like noise, and Emma jerked herself away from the gate and ran back toward the Blackthorn house.

She reached her window and climbed up inside, gasping. The moon shone down like a floodlight, illuminating her room. She kicked off her slippers and sat down on the bed. Her heart was hammering inside her chest.

The way Jace had looked down at Clary, the way she'd touched his face. She wondered if anyone would ever look at her like that. It didn't seem possible. She couldn't imagine loving anyone that much.

Anyone but Jules.

But that was different. Wasn't it? She couldn't imagine Julian lying on top of her, kissing her like that. They were different, they were something else, weren't they?

She lay back down on the bed, looking across the room at the door. Some part of her expected Jules to come through it, to come to her because she was unhappy the way he often did, seeming to know without being told. But why would he think she was unhappy? Today had been her parabatai ceremony; it should have been one of the happiest days of her life except for maybe her wedding day. Instead she felt flushed and strange and full of the strangest urge to cry.

Jules, she thought, but the door didn't open, and he didn't come. Instead she curled up around her pillow and lay awake until dawn.

# 18

## ALL THE NIGHT-TIDE

After the darkness, there was light. Bright white and silver—starlight on water and sand. And Emma was flying. Over the surface of the water, now shallow—she could see the sand of the beach underneath, and a pool of fire where the moon reflected.

There was a pain in her chest. She twisted to get away from it and realized she wasn't flying; she was being carried. She was being held against a hard chest and arms were around her. She saw the glimmer of blue-green eyes.

Julian. *Julian* was carrying her. Wet, dark curls crowned his head.

She tried to draw in a breath to speak, and choked. Her chest spasmed; water filled her mouth, bitter and salty like blood. She saw Julian's face twist with panic, and then he was half-running up the beach, finally crashing to his knees, depositing her in the sand. She was still coughing, choking, looking up at him with frightened eyes. She saw the same fear mirrored on his face; she wanted to tell him it would be all right, everything was going to be fine, but she couldn't speak past the water in her throat.

He fumbled a stele from his belt and she felt the tip burn against her skin. Her head fell back as the rune formed. She saw the moon over her, behind Julian's head like a halo. She wanted to tell him he had a halo. Maybe he'd think it was funny. But the words were drowning in her chest. She was drowning. Dying on land.

The rune was finished. Julian pulled the stele back and Emma's chest seemed to cave in. She cried out, and water exploded from her lungs. She curled up, racked with deep coughs. It hurt as her body expelled the seawater, as if she were being turned inside out. She felt Julian's hand on her back, his fingers between her shoulder blades, holding her steady.

At last the coughing slowed. She rolled onto her back and stared up at Julian and the sky behind him. She could see a million stars, and he still had his halo, but there was no longer anything funny about it. He was shivering, his black shirt and jeans plastered to his body, his face whiter than the moon.

"Emma?" he whispered.

"Jules," she said. Her voice sounded weak and rough to her own ears. "I—I'm all right."

"What the hell happened? What were you doing in the water?"

"I went to the convergence," she whispered. "There was some kind of spell—it sucked me out into the ocean—"

"You went to the convergence by yourself?" His voice rose. "How could you be so reckless?"

"I had to try—"

"*You didn't have to try alone!*" His voice seemed to echo off the water. His fists were clenched at his sides. She realized he wasn't shaking from cold after all—it was rage. "What the hell is the point of being *parabatai* if you go off and risk yourself without me?"

"I didn't want to put you in danger—"

"I almost drowned inside the Institute! I coughed up water! Water *you* breathed!"

Emma stared at him in shock. She started to prop herself up on her elbows. Her hair, heavy and soaked, hung down her back like a weight. "How is that possible?"

"Of course it's possible!" His voice seemed to explode out of his body. "We are bound together, Emma, bound together—I breathe when you breathe, I bleed when you bleed, I'm yours and you're mine, you've always been mine, and I have always, *always* belonged to you!"

She had never heard him say anything like this, never heard him talk this way, never seen him so close to losing control.

"I didn't mean to hurt you," she said. She started to sit up, reaching for him. He caught her wrist.

"Are you joking?" Even in the darkness, his blue-green eyes had color. "Is this a joke to you, Emma? Don't you understand?" His voice dropped to a whisper. *"I don't live if you die!"*

Her eyes searched his face. "Jules, I'm so sorry, Jules—"

The wall that usually hid the truth deep in his eyes had crumbled; she could see the panic there, the desperation, the relief that had punched through his defenses.

He was still holding her wrist. She didn't know if she leaned into him first or if he pulled her toward him. Maybe both. They crashed together like stars colliding, and then he was kissing her.

Jules. *Julian.* Kissing *her.*

His mouth moved against hers, hot and restless, turning her body to liquid fire. She clawed at his back, pulling him closer. His clothes were wet, but his skin under them was hot wherever she could touch it. When she placed her hands at his waist, he gasped into her mouth, a gasp that was half incredulity and half desire.

"Emma," he said, a word halfway between a prayer and a groan. His mouth was wild on hers; they were kissing as if they were trying to tear down the bars that held them inside a prison. As if they were both drowning and they could breathe only through each other.

Her bones felt as if they had turned to glass. They seemed to be shattering all through her body; she crumpled backward, pulling Julian with her, letting the weight of his body push them both down into the sand. She clutched at his shoulders, thought of the disoriented moment when he'd pulled her out of the water, the moment she hadn't quite known who he was. He was stronger, bigger than she remembered. More grown-up than she had let herself know, though every kiss was burning away her memories of the boy he had been.

When he leaned closer into her, she jumped in surprise at the wet coldness of his shirt. He reached down and grasped the collar, tearing it over his head. When he leaned back down over her, the expanse of his bare skin stunned her, and her hands slid up his sides, over the wings of his shoulder blades, as if she were articulating the shape of him, creating him with the touch of her palms and fingers. The light scars of his old Marks; the heat of his skin, filmed with salty ocean water; the feel of his smooth sea-glass bracelet—he took her breath away with the *Julian*-ness of him. There was no one else he could be. She knew him by touch, by the way he breathed, by the beat of his heart against hers.

The touch of her hands was undoing him. She could see him unraveling, piece by piece. Her knees came up to clasp his hips; her hand cupped the bare skin above the waistband of his jeans, gently as the ocean at low tide, and he shuddered against her as if he were dying. She had never seen him like this, not even when he was painting.

Gasping, he tore his mouth away from hers, forcing himself still, forcing his body to stop moving. She could see what it cost him in his eyes, black with hunger and impatience. In the way that when he drew his hands away, they dug into the sand on either side of her, fingers clawing into the ground. "Emma," he whispered. "You're sure?"

She nodded and reached for him. He made a sound of desperate relief and gratitude and caught her against him, and this time there was no hesitation. Her arms were open; he went into them and gathered her up against him, shivering down to his bones as she locked her ankles behind his calves, pinning him against her. As she opened herself, making her body a cradle for him to lie against.

He found her mouth with his again, and as if her lips were connected to every nerve ending in her body, her whole self seemed to spark and dance. So this was what it was supposed to be like, what kissing was supposed to be like, what *all* of it was supposed to be like. *This.*

He leaned in to outline her mouth, her cheek, the sandy curve of her jaw with kisses. He kissed his way down her throat, his breath warm on her skin. Tangling her hands in his wet curls, she stared up in wonder at the sky above them, wheeling with stars, shimmering and cold, and thought that this couldn't be happening, people didn't get things they wanted like this.

"Jules," she whispered. "My Julian."

"Always," he whispered, returning to her mouth, "always," and they fell into each other with the inevitability of a wave crashing against the beach. Fire raced up and down Emma's veins as the barriers between them vanished; she tried to press each moment, each gesture into her memory—the feel of his hands closing on her shoulders, the drowning gasp he made, the way he dissolved into her as he lost himself. To the last moment of her life, she thought, she would recall the way he buried his face against her neck and said her name over and over as if every other word had been forgotten forever in the depths of the ocean. To the last hour.

When the stars stopped spinning, Emma was lying in the curve of Julian's arm, looking up. His dry flannel jacket was spread over them. He was gazing at her, head propped up on one hand. He looked dazed, his eyes half-lidded. His fingers traced slow circles on her bare shoulder. His heart was still racing, slamming against hers. She loved him so much it felt like her chest was cracking open.

She wanted to tell him so, but the words stuck in her throat. "Was that—" she began. "Was that your first kiss?"

"No, I've been practicing on random strangers." He grinned, wild and beautiful in the moonlight. "Yes. That was my first kiss."

A shiver went through Emma. She thought, *I love you, Julian Blackthorn. I love you more than starlight.*

"It really wasn't that bad," she said, and smiled at him.

He laughed and pulled her closer against him. She relaxed into the curve of his body. The air was cold, but she was warm here, in this small circle with Julian, hidden by the outcroppings of rock, wrapped in the flannel jacket that smelled like him. His hand was gentle in her hair. "Shh, Emma. Go to sleep."

She closed her eyes.

Emma slept, by the side of the ocean. And she had no nightmares.

"Emma." There was a hand on her shoulder, shaking her. "Emma, wake up."

She rolled over and blinked, then froze in surprise. There was no ceiling over her, only bright blue sky. She felt stiff and sore, her skin abraded by sand.

Julian was hovering over her. He was fully dressed, his face gray-white like scattered ash. His hands fluttered around her, not quite touching her, like Ty's butterflies. "Someone was here."

At that she did sit up. She was sitting on the beach—a small, bare half circle of a beach, hemmed in on either side by fingers of stone reaching into the ocean. The sand around her was thoroughly churned up, and she blushed, memory crashing into her like a wave. It looked like it was at least midday, though thankfully the beach was deserted. It was familiar, too. They were close to the Institute, closer than she'd thought. Not that she'd thought much.

She dragged air into her lungs. "Oh," she said. "Oh my God."

Julian didn't say anything. His clothes were wet, crusted with sand where they folded. Her own clothes were on, Emma realized belatedly. Julian must have dressed her. Only her feet were bare.

The tide was low, seaweed lying exposed at the waterline. Their footsteps from the night before had long been washed away, but there were other footsteps embedded in the sand. It looked as if someone had climbed over one of the rock walls, walked up to them, and then doubled back and walked away. Two lines of footsteps. Emma stared at them in horror.

"Someone saw us?" she said.

"While we were sleeping," said Julian. "I didn't wake up either." His hands knotted at his sides. "Some mundane, I hope, just figuring we were a dumb teenage couple." He let out a breath. "I hope," he said again.

Flashes of memory of the night before shot through Emma's mind—the cold water, the demons, Julian carrying her, Julian kissing her. Julian and her, lying entwined on the sand.

Julian. She didn't think she could think of him as *Jules* again. Jules was her childhood name for him. And they had left their childhood behind.

He turned to look at her, and she saw the anguish in his sea-colored eyes. "I am so sorry," he whispered. "Emma, I am so, so sorry."

"Why are you sorry?" she asked.

"I didn't think." He was pacing, his feet kicking up sand. "About—being safe. Protection. I didn't think about it."

"I'm protected," she said.

He whirled to face her. "What?"

"I have the rune," she said. "And I don't have any diseases, and neither do you, do you?"

"I—no." The relief on his face was palpable and for some reason made her stomach ache. "That was my first time, Emma."

"I know," she said in a whisper. "Anyway, you don't need to apologize."

"I do," he said. "I mean, this is good. We're lucky. But I should have thought of it. I don't have an excuse. I was out of my mind."

She opened her mouth, then closed it again.

"I must have been, to do that," he said.

"To do what?" She was impressed by how clearly and calmly each word came out. Anxiety beat through her like a drum.

"What we did." He exhaled. "You know what I mean."

"You're saying what we did was wrong."

"I meant—" He looked as if he were trying to contain something that wanted to tear its way out of him. "There's nothing wrong with it morally," he said. "It's a stupid Law. But it is a Law. And we can't break it. It's one of the oldest Laws there is."

"But it doesn't make *sense*."

He looked at her without seeing her, blindly. "The Law is hard, but it is the Law."

Emma got to her feet. "No," she said. "No Law can control our feelings."

"I didn't say anything about feelings," said Julian.

Her throat felt dry. "What do you mean?"

"We shouldn't have slept together," he said. "I know it meant something to me, I'd be lying if I said it didn't, but the Law doesn't forbid sex, it forbids *love*. Being *in love*."

"I'm pretty sure sleeping together is against the rules too."

"Yeah, but it's not what they exile you for! It's not what they strip your Marks for!" He raked a hand through his snarled hair. "It's against the rules because—being intimate like that, physically intimate, it opens you up to be emotionally intimate and *that's* what they care about."

"We *are* emotionally intimate."

"You know what I mean. Don't pretend you don't." There are

different kinds of closeness, intimacy. They *want* us to be close. But they don't want *this*." He gestured around at the beach as if to encompass all of the night before.

Emma was shaking. *"Eros,"* she said. "Instead of *philia* or *agape*."

He looked relieved, as if her explanation meant she understood, she agreed. As if they had made some decision together. Emma wanted to scream. *"Philia,"* he said. "That's what we have—friendship love—and I'm sorry if I did anything to screw that up—"

"I was there too," Emma said, and her voice was as cold as the water.

He looked at her levelly.

"We love each other," he said. "We're *parabatai*, love is part of the bond. And I'm attracted to you. How could I not be? You're beautiful. And it's not like—"

He broke off, but Emma filled the rest in for him, the words so painful they almost seemed to cut at the inside of her head. *It's not like I can meet other girls, not like I can date, you're what there is, you're what's around, Cristina's probably still in love with someone in Mexico, there isn't anyone for me. There's just you.*

"It's not like I'm blind," he said. "I can see you, and I want you, but—we can't. If we do, we'll end up falling in love, and that would be a disaster."

"Falling in love," Emma echoed. How could he not see she was already fallen, in every way you could be? "Didn't I tell you I loved you? Last night?"

He shook his head. "We never said we loved each other," he said. "Not once."

That couldn't be true. Emma searched her memories, as if she were rummaging desperately through her pockets for a lost key. She'd *thought* it. *Julian Blackthorn, I love you more than starlight.* She'd thought it but she hadn't said it. And neither had he. *We're bound together*, he'd said. But not: *I love you.*

She waited for him to say, *I was out of my mind because you risked your life* or *You almost died and it made me crazy* or any variety of *It was your fault*. She thought that if he did, she would blow up like an activated land mine.

But he didn't. He stood looking at her, his flannel jacket shoved up to his elbows, his exposed bare skin red from cold water and scratched with sand.

She had never seen him look so sad.

She lifted her chin. "You're right. It's better if we forget it."

He winced at that. "I do love you, Emma."

She rubbed her hands together for warmth, thought of the way the ocean wore down even stone walls over the years, wringing fragments out of what had once been impregnable. "I know," she said. "Just not like that."

The first thing Emma saw when they returned to the Institute—having told Julian the story of her experience at the convergence on their way back from the beach—was that the car she'd left at the cave entrance the night before was parked at the foot of the front steps. The second was that Diana was sitting on the car's hood, looking madder than a hornet.

"*What* were you thinking?" she demanded as Emma and Julian stopped dead in their tracks. "Seriously, Emma, have you lost your mind?"

For a moment Emma felt actually dizzy—Diana couldn't be talking about her and Julian, could she? She wasn't the one who'd found them on the beach? She glanced sideways at Julian, but he was as white-faced with shock as she felt.

Diana's dark eyes bored into her. "I'm waiting for an explanation," she said. "What made you think it was a good idea to go to the convergence by yourselves?"

Emma was too surprised to formulate a comeback. "What?"

Diana's eyes flicked from Julian to Emma and back again. "I didn't get the message about the convergence until this morning," she said. "I raced over there and found the car, empty. Abandoned. I thought—you don't know what I thought, but . . ." Emma felt a stab of guilt. Diana had been worried about her. And about Julian, who had never even gone to the convergence.

"I'm sorry," Emma said, meaning it. Her conviction of the night before, her resolve that she was doing the right thing in going to the convergence, had evaporated. She felt weary now, and no closer to an answer. "I got the message and just went—I didn't want to wait. And please don't be angry at Julian. He wasn't with me. He found me later."

"Found you?" Diana looked puzzled. "Found you where?"

"On the beach," said Emma. "There are doorways in the cave— sort of Portals—and one of them empties right out into the ocean."

Now Diana's expression was truly concerned. "Emma, you ended up in the water? But you hate the ocean. How did you—"

"Julian came and pulled me out," said Emma. "He felt me panicking in the water. *Parabatai* thing." She glanced sideways at Julian, whose gaze was clear and open. Trustworthy. Not hiding anything. "It took us a long time to walk back."

"Well, finding the seawater is interesting," said Diana, sliding off the car's hood. "I assume it's the same water found with the bodies."

"How did you get the car back?" Emma asked as they started up the stairs.

"What you mean, of course, is 'thank you, Diana, for bringing the car back,'" Diana said as they came inside the Institute. She glanced critically up and down Julian's and Emma's wet, sandy clothes, scraped skin, and matted hair. "How about I gather everyone in the library. It's past time for an information exchange."

Julian cleared his throat. "Why didn't you?"

Diana and Emma both looked at him in puzzlement. "Why didn't who, what?" Diana asked finally.

"Why didn't you get the message about the convergence until this morning? My phone was dead, which was stupid of me, but—what about you?"

"Nothing you need concern yourself with," Diana said shortly. "Anyway, go shower. I get that you have important information, but until you clean off the sand, I don't think I could concentrate on anything but how badly you two must itch."

Emma meant to change when she got back to her room. She genuinely did. But despite her hours of sleep on the beach, she was exhausted enough that the moment she sat down on the bed, she collapsed.

Hours later, after a fast shower, she threw on clean jeans and a tank top and raced out into the hallway, feeling like a mundane teenager late for class. She flew down the hall to the library to find everyone else already there; in fact, they looked as if they'd been there for a while. Ty was sitting at one end of the longest library table in a pool of afternoon sunshine, a pile of papers in front of him. Mark was by his side; Livvy was balanced on top of the table, barefoot, dancing back and forth with her saber. Diana and Dru were amusing Tavvy with a book.

"Diana said you went to the convergence," said Livvy, waving her saber as Emma came in. Cristina, who had been standing by a shelf of books, gave her an uncharacteristically cool look.

"Fighting Mantids without me," Mark said, and smiled. "Hardly fair."

"There weren't any Mantids," said Emma. She hopped up onto the table across from Ty, who was still scribbling, and launched into the story of what she had found in the cave. Halfway through her recitation, Julian came in, his hair as damp as Emma's. He was wearing a jade-colored T-shirt that turned his eyes dark green. Their eyes met, and Emma forgot what she was saying.

"Emma?" Cristina prompted after a long pause. "You were saying? You found a dress?"

"This doesn't sound very likely," said Livvy. "Who keeps a dress in a cave?"

"It might have been a ceremonial outfit," Emma said. "It was an elaborate robe—and very elaborate jewels."

"So maybe the necromancer is a woman," said Cristina. "Maybe it really is Belinda."

"She didn't strike me as that powerful," said Mark.

"You can sense power?" asked Emma. "Is that a faerie thing?"

Mark shook his head, but the half smile he gave felt to Emma like a sliver of Faerie. "Just a feeling."

"But speaking of faerie things, Mark did give us the key to translate more of the markings," said Livvy.

"Really?" said Emma. "What do they say?"

Ty looked up from the papers. "He gave us the second line, and after that it was easier. Livvy and I worked out most of the third. From looking at the patterns of the markings, it seems to be about five or six lines, repeated."

"Is it a spell?" Emma said. "Malcolm said it was probably a summoning spell."

Ty rubbed at his face, leaving a smear of ink across one cheekbone. "It doesn't look like a summoning spell. Maybe Malcolm made a mistake. We've done a lot better than him on the translation," he added proudly as Livvy put her saber away and crouched down on the table beside him. She reached out to rub the ink from his cheek with her sleeve.

"Malcolm doesn't have Mark," said Julian, and Mark gave Julian a quick, surprised smile of gratitude.

"Or Cristina," said Mark. "I would never have figured out the connection if Cristina had not realized it was an issue of translation."

Cristina blushed. "So how does the third line go, Tiberius?"

Ty batted Livvy's hand away and recited:

First the flame and then the flood,
In the end, it's Blackthorn blood.
Seek thou to forget what's past—

"That's it," he finished. "That's what we have so far."

"Blackthorn blood?" echoed Diana. She had climbed up onto a library ladder to hand a book down to Tavvy.

Emma frowned. "I don't really love the sound of that."

"There's no indication of traditional blood magic," said Julian. "None of the bodies had those kinds of cuts or wounds."

"I wonder about the mention of the past," said Mark. "These kind of rhymes, in Faerie, often encode a spell—like the ballad of 'Thomas the Rhymer.' It is both a story and instructions on how to break someone free of Faerie."

For a moment Diana's face was arrested midexpression, as if she had either suddenly realized or suddenly remembered something.

"Diana?" Julian said. "Are you okay?"

"Fine." She climbed down from the ladder and dusted off her clothes. "I need to make a call."

"Who are you calling?" Julian asked, but Diana only shook her head, her hair brushing her shoulders.

"I'll be back," she said, and slipped out the library door.

"But what does it mean?" Emma said to the room at large. "In the end, Blackthorn blood what?"

"And if it's a faerie rhyme, then shouldn't they know if there's more of it?" Dru spoke up from the corner where she was busy distracting Tavvy. "The Fair Folk, I mean. They're meant to be on our side for this."

"I have sent a message," Mark said guardedly. "But I will tell you, I only ever heard those two lines of it."

"The most significant thing it means is that somehow this situation—the murders, the bodies, the Followers—is tied to this family." Julian looked around. "Somehow, it's connected to us. To the Blackthorns."

"That would explain why all this is happening in Los Angeles," said Mark. "It is our home."

Emma saw Julian's expression flicker slightly, and knew what he was thinking: that Mark had spoken of Los Angeles as a place they all lived, not a place where everyone lived but him. That he had spoken of it as home.

There was a loud buzzing sound. The map of Los Angeles on the table had started to vibrate. What looked like a small red dot was moving across it. "Sterling's left his house," Cristina said, reaching for the map.

"Belinda Belle said he had two days," said Julian. "That could mean the hunt starts tomorrow, or it could mean tonight, depending on how they're counting. Anyway, we can't assume."

"Cristina and I will follow him," Emma said. She was desperate to get out of the house suddenly, desperate to clear her head, desperate even to get away from Julian.

Mark frowned. "We should go with you—"

"No!" Emma said, hopping down from the table. Everyone turned to look at her in surprise; she had spoken with more force than she meant to—the truth was, she wanted to talk to Cristina alone. "We're going to have to take it in shifts," she said. "We're going to have to tail Sterling twenty-four/seven until something happens, and if we all go every time, we'll just end up with everyone exhausted. Cristina and I will go for a while, and then we can switch off with Julian and Mark, or Diana."

"Or me and Ty," suggested Livvy sweetly.

Julian's eyes were troubled. "Emma, are you sure—"

"Emma is right," Cristina said, unexpectedly. "Taking shifts is the cautious thing to do."

*Cautious.* Emma couldn't remember that word being applied to her in recent history. Julian glanced away, hiding his expression. At last, he said, "Fine. You win. You two go. But if you need any backup, swear that you'll call right away."

His gaze locked with Emma's as he spoke. The others were talking, discussing how they should search the library, look back through books detailing different kinds of spells, how long it would take to finish the rest of the translation, whether Malcolm might come to help them, whether they should order vampire pizza.

"Come on, Emma," said Cristina, rising to her feet and folding the map into her jacket pocket. "We should get going. We need to change into gear and catch up to Sterling—he's heading toward the freeway."

Emma nodded and turned to follow Cristina. She could feel Julian's gaze on her, like a sharp point between her shoulder blades. *Don't turn back to look at him,* she told herself, but she couldn't help it; at the door, she turned, and the look on his face almost undid her.

He looked like she felt. Hollow and bled dry. It wasn't that she was walking away from the boy she loved with a thousand words unsaid between them, Emma thought, though it was true that she was doing that. It was that she was terrified that a rift had opened between her and the person who had been her best friend as long as she could remember. And from the look of it, Julian was afraid of the same thing.

"Sorry," Emma said, as the car righted itself. They'd been driving around for several hours as Sterling hurtled all over the city, and her hands were starting to ache from gripping the wheel.

Cristina sighed. "Are you going to tell me what's bothering you?"

Emma shifted. She was wearing her gear jacket, and it was hot in the car. She felt as if all her skin was itching. "I'm really, really sorry, Tina," she said. "I didn't think—I shouldn't have asked you to cover up for me when I went to the convergence. It wasn't fair."

Cristina was silent for a moment. "I would have done it," she said. "If you'd told me what it was about."

Emma's throat felt tight. "I'm not used to trusting people. But I should have trusted you. When you leave, I don't know what I'm going to do. I'm going to miss you so much."

Cristina smiled at her. "Come to the D.F.," she said. "See how we do things there. You can take your travel year in my city." She paused. "I forgive you, by the way."

A small weight lifted from Emma's chest. "I'd love to go to Mexico," she said. "And Julian would—"

She broke off. Of course most people with *parabatai* accompanied them on their travel year. But the thought of Julian hurt, a sharp quick pain like a needle stick.

"Are you going to tell me what's bothering you?" Cristina asked.

"No," Emma said.

"Fine. Then turn left onto Entrada," Cristina said.

"It's like having supernatural GPS," Emma observed. She could see Cristina scowling at the map across her knees in the passenger seat.

"We head toward Santa Monica," Cristina said, tracing a finger along the map. "Go down Seventh."

"Sterling's an idiot," Emma said. "He knows someone's trying to kill him. He shouldn't be wandering around the city."

"He probably thinks his own house isn't that safe," Cristina pointed out reasonably. "I mean, I ambushed him there."

"Right," Emma said. She couldn't stop worrying a rip in the knee of her gear. The memory of Julian on the beach, the things he had said to her, pressed against the backs of her eyes. She let the thoughts pass through her. When it came time, she'd have to let them all go and concentrate on the fight.

"And, of course, there are the enormous bunny rabbits," Cristina said.

"What?" Emma snapped back to the present.

"I've been talking at you for the last three minutes! Where is your mind, Emma?"

"I slept with Julian," Emma said.

Cristina shrieked. Then she clapped her hands over her mouth and stared at Emma as if Emma had just announced there was a grenade strapped to the roof of the car and about to explode.

"Did you hear what I said?" Emma asked.

"Yes," Cristina said, taking her hands away from her mouth. "You slept with Julian Blackthorn."

Emma's breath whooshed out of her in a rush. There was something about hearing it said back to her that made her feel as if she'd been gut punched.

"I thought you weren't going to tell me what was wrong!" Cristina said.

"I changed my mind."

"Why?" They were whipping around corners lined with palm trees, stucco houses set back from the streets. Emma knew she was driving too fast; she didn't care.

"I mean—I was in the ocean, and he pulled me out, and things got out of hand—"

"No," Cristina said. "Not why did you do it. Why did you change your mind about telling me?"

"Because I'm a horrible liar," Emma said. "You would have guessed."

"Maybe. Maybe not." Cristina took a deep breath. "I suppose I should ask the real question. Do you love him?"

Emma didn't say anything. She kept her eyes on the broken yellow line in the middle of the road. The sun was a fiery orange ball lowering in the west.

Cristina exhaled slowly. "You do love him."

"I didn't say that."

"It's all over your face," Cristina said. "I know what that looks like." She sounded sad.

"Don't pity me, Tina," Emma said. "Please don't."

"I'm just frightened for you. The Law is very clear, and the punishments are so severe."

"Well, it doesn't matter," said Emma, her voice tinged with bitterness. "He doesn't love me. And being unrequitedly in love with your *parabatai* isn't illegal, so don't worry."

"He what?" Cristina said, sounding shocked.

"He doesn't love me," said Emma. "He was very clear about that."

Cristina opened her mouth, and then closed it again.

"I guess it's flattering that you're surprised," Emma said.

"I don't know what to say." Cristina put her hand over her heart. "There are the things you would normally say in this situation. If it was anyone else but Julian I'd be telling you how lucky he was to have someone as brave and smart as you are in love with him. I would be scheming with you about how we could make such a silly boy realize such an obvious thing. But it is Julian, and it is illegal, and you *must* not do anything more, Emma. Promise me."

"He doesn't want me that way," Emma said. "So it doesn't matter. I just—" She broke off. She didn't know what else to say or how to say it. There was never going to be another Julian for her.

*Don't think that way. Just because you can't imagine loving anyone else doesn't mean that you won't.* But the soft inner voice of her father didn't reassure her this time.

"I just don't know why it's illegal," she finished, though that had not been what she had meant to say. "It doesn't make any sense.

Julian and I have done everything together, for years, we've lived and nearly died for each other, how could there be anyone else better for me than him? Anyone else better—" She broke off again.

"Emma, please don't think like this. It doesn't matter why it's illegal. It just matters that it is. The Law is hard, but it is the Law."

"A bad law is no law," Emma countered, swinging a hard right onto Pico Boulevard. Pico ran almost the full length of metropolitan Los Angeles—it was swanky, gritty, dangerous, abandoned, and industrial by turns. Here between the freeway and the ocean it was full of small businesses and restaurants.

"That motto has not served the Blackthorns well," Cristina murmured, and Emma was about to ask her what she meant when Cristina sat up straight. "Here," she said, pointing. "Sterling's here. I just saw him go into that building."

On the south side of the road was a low, sloping brown-painted building, windowless, with a single door and a sign proclaiming NO ONE UNDER 21 ALLOWED.

"Looks friendly," Emma muttered, and pulled over to park.

They got out of the car and went to collect their weapons. They already bore glamour runes, and the few pedestrians passing by— hardly anyone walked in L.A., and while there were plenty of cars around, there were very few people—looked through them as if they weren't there. A girl with bright green hair glanced at Emma as she passed by, but didn't stop.

"You're right," Emma said as they buckled on their seraph blades. Each blade had a small hook that allowed it to be affixed to a weapons belt and removed with a quick downward jerk of the hand. "About Julian. I know you are."

Cristina gave her a quick, one-armed hug. "And you will do the right thing. I know you will."

Emma was already scanning the building, looking for entrances. There were no windows that she could see, but a narrow alley snaked around the back of the bar, partially blocked by an over-grown patch of needle grass. She gestured toward it, and she and Cristina slipped silently through the low, dusty vegetation that grew—barely—in the polluted air.

The sun was setting, and it was dark in the alley behind the bar. A row of chained-together trash cans were propped under a barred and boarded-up window.

"I can get the bars off, if I climb up there," Emma whispered, indicating the trash cans.

"Okay, wait." Cristina pulled out her stele. "Runes."

Cristina's runes were careful, precise, and beautiful. Emma could feel the power of a strength rune jolt through her like a kick of caffeine. It wasn't like having Julian put runes on her—that felt as if his strength were flowing into her, doubling her own.

Cristina turned around, shrugging her jacket down, present-ing the line of her bare shoulder to Emma. She handed the stele to Emma, who began to draw—two overlapping Soundless runes, Sure-Strike, Flexibility.

"Please don't think I'm angry," Cristina said, facing the oppo-site wall. "I worry for you, is all. You are so strong, Emma. You are strong down to your bones. People live through heartbreak, and you are strong enough to live through it many times. But Julian is not someone who can just touch your heart. He can touch your soul. And there is a difference between having your heart break and having your soul shatter."

The stele faltered in Emma's hand. "I thought the Angel had a plan."

"He does. But please don't love him, Emma." Cristina's voice broke. "Please."

There was a catch in Emma's throat when she spoke. "Who broke your heart?"

Cristina turned around, shrugging her jacket back on. Her brown eyes were serious. "You told me a secret, so I will tell you a secret. I was in love with Diego, and I thought he was in love with me. But it was all a lie. I thought his brother was my best friend, but that was a lie too. That is why I ran away. Why I came here." She looked away. "I lost them both. My best friend and my best love, on the same day. It was hard for me to believe that Raziel had a plan then."

*My best friend and my best love.*

Cristina took the stele and slid it back into her belt.

"I'm not the one who's strong, Tina. That's you."

Cristina gave her a quick smile and held out her hand. "Go."

Grabbing Cristina's hand, Emma pushed off to propel herself upward. Her boots hit the top of the trash cans, making the chain rattle. She grabbed the bars of the window and pulled, liking the bite of the metal into her palms.

The bars pulled free of the soft stucco with a shower of tiny pebbles. Emma handed the metal grid down, and Cristina tossed it into the grass. Emma reached a hand down, and a second later Cristina was beside her and they were both peering into a smudged window at a dirty back kitchen. Water was running in a massive metal sink full of glasses.

Emma drew her foot back, ready to smash the glass with the steel tip of her boot. Cristina caught her shoulder. "Wait." She bent down and grabbed the window by its frame. The Strength rune on her neck buckled and glowed as she wrenched the rotted frame free and dropped it onto the plastic trash cans below. "Quieter that way," she said.

Emma grinned and swung in through the window, landing on top of a crate full of vodka bottles. She sprang down and Cristina followed her. Cristina's boots hit the floor just as the kitchen door swung open and a short man in a bartender's apron with spiked black hair came into the room. The moment he caught sight of Emma and Cristina he let out a startled yelp.

Great, Emma thought. He had the Sight.

"Hello there," she said. "We're from the Department of Health. Did you know that there is no antibacterial hand gel left in these dispensers?"

This did not seem to impress the bartender. His gaze went from Emma to Cristina to the open window. "What the hell are you bitches doing, breaking in here? I'm gonna call the—"

Emma picked up a wooden spoon from the draining board and threw it. It thunked into the side of the bartender's head. He went down in a heap. She strolled over and checked his pulse; it was regular. She glanced up at Cristina. "I hate being called a bitch."

Cristina moved past her and pushed the door open, peeking out, while Emma dragged the bartender into the corner of the room and pushed him gently behind the stacked crates of bottles.

Cristina wrinkled up her nose. "Yuck."

Emma let go of the bartender's feet. They thumped to the ground. "What? Is something horrible happening out there?"

"No, it's just a really disgusting bar," said Cristina. "Why would anyone want to drink here?"

Emma joined her at the door and they both peered out.

"Bars in the D.F. are much nicer," Cristina said. "I think someone has thrown up in that corner."

She pointed. Emma didn't look, but she believed it. The bar wasn't just dimly lit, it was barely lit. The floor was concrete, strewn with cigarette butts. There was a zinc-countered bar, and a mirror behind it on which drink prices had been scrawled in marker. Men in flannel shirts and jeans crowded around a ragged-felt pool table. Others stood silently drinking at the bar. The place smelled like sour, old beer and cigarette smoke.

Hunched at the far end of the bar was a man in a familiar herringbone jacket. Sterling.

"There he is," said Emma.

"The Tracking rune doesn't lie." Cristina ducked under Emma's arm and stepped into the room. Emma followed. She felt the slight pressure on her skin that came with the gaze of many mundane eyes, but her glamour runes held. The single bartender looked up as the kitchen door swung shut, probably searching for his coworker, but turned back to polishing glasses when he didn't see anything.

As Emma and Cristina approached, an extraordinary expression crossed Sterling's face. A mixture of shock, followed by despair, followed by a sort of hilarity. There was a glass on the bar in front of him, half-full of golden liquid; he grabbed it up and tossed back the drink. When he slammed the glass back down on the bar, his eyes were gleaming.

"Nephilim," he snarled.

The bartender looked over at him in surprise. Several of the other customers shifted on their stools.

"That's right," Sterling said. "*They* think I'm crazy." He whipped his arm out to indicate the other bar patrons. "I'm talking to no one. Empty air. But *you*. You don't care. You're here to torture me."

He staggered to his feet.

"Whoa," Emma said. "You are *drunk*."

Sterling popped off two finger guns in her direction. "Very observant, blondie."

"Dude!" The bartender slammed a glass down on the counter-top. "If you're going to talk to yourself, do it outside. You're ruining the ambiance."

"This place has ambiance?" said Emma.

"Emma, focus," said Cristina. She turned to Sterling. "We're not here to torture you. We're here to help you. We keep telling you that."

"Keep telling yourselves that," he hissed, and yanked a clump of bills from his pocket. He tossed them onto the bar. "Bye, Jimmy," he said to the bartender. "See you again never."

He stalked to the door and stiff-armed it open. Emma and Cristina dashed after him.

Emma was only too pleased to be back outside. Sterling was already hurrying down the street, his head down. The sun had fully set, and the streetlights were on, filling the air with a yellow sodium glow. Cars rushed by on Pico.

Sterling was moving *fast*. Cristina called out to him, but he didn't turn around, just hunched down inside his suit jacket and moved more quickly. Suddenly he veered to the left, between two buildings, and disappeared.

Emma cursed under her breath and broke into a run. Excitement prickled up her veins. She loved running, the way it blanked her mind, the way it made her forget everything but the breath rushing in and out of her lungs.

The mouth of an alley loomed up to her left. Not a garbage alley—this one was nearly as wide as a street and ran along the back of a long line of apartment buildings with cheap stucco balconies that faced out over the backstreet. A gray concrete drain ran down the center.

Partway down the alley Sterling's gray Jeep was parked. He was leaning against the driver's side door, trying to jerk it open. Emma sprang onto his back, yanking him away from the car. He spun around, stumbled, and hit the ground.

"Dammit!" he yelped, pulling himself up onto his knees. "I thought you said you were here to help me!"

"In a larger sense, yes," said Emma. "Because it's our job. But nobody calls me 'blondie' and keeps their kneecaps."

"Emma," Cristina said warningly.

"Get up," Emma said, reaching out a hand to Sterling. "Come with us. But if you call me 'blondie' again, I'll rip your knees off and turn them into tiny hubcaps, 'kay?"

"Stop yelling at him, Emma," said Cristina. "Casper—Mr.

Sterling—we need to stay with you, all right? We know you're in danger and we want to help you."

"If you want to help me, you'll get away from me," Sterling shouted. "I need to be left *alone!*"

"So you can end up drowned and burned, covered in markings, with your fingerprints sanded off?" Emma said. "That's what you want?"

Sterling gaped at her. "What?"

"Emma!" Emma realized Cristina was looking up. A shape was slipping along the roof—a man in dark clothes, a dangerous, familiar shadow. Emma's heart thumped in her chest.

"Get *up!*" She grabbed Sterling's hand, yanking him to his feet. He struggled, then sagged against her, his mouth open, as the dark shape on the roof leaped down, landing on a jutting balcony. Emma could see him more clearly now: a man in black, a dark hood pulled up to hide his face.

There was a crossbow in his right hand. He raised it. Emma gave Sterling a shove that almost knocked him off his feet.

"*Run!*" she shouted.

Sterling didn't move. He was gaping at the figure in black, a look of total disbelief on his face.

Something whizzed by Emma's ear—a crossbow bolt. Senses heightened, she heard the loud *snick* as Cristina's butterfly knife snapped open, and the whir as it flew through the air. She heard the man in black yell, and the crossbow fell from his hand. It crashed into the alley, and a moment later the man in black followed, landing with a harsh thud on Sterling's back.

Sterling went sprawling. The man in black, crouched over him, raised his hand; something silvery flashed between his fingers. A knife. He brought it down—

And Cristina careened into him, knocking him sideways. He went sprawling, and Sterling staggered to his feet and ran for his car. He half-fell into it, gasping. Emma raced after him, but the car was already gathering speed, hurtling down the alley.

She spun back around just as the man in black sprang up. Emma was on him in seconds, flinging him up against the stained wall of the apartment building.

He tried to pull away, but Emma had her fist knotted in the front of his sweatshirt. "You shot Julian," she said. "I should kill you right here."

"Emma." Cristina was on her feet. Her gaze was fixed on the man in black. "Find out who he is first."

Emma grabbed his hood with her free hand and yanked it down, revealing—

A boy. Not a man, she thought, jolted, definitely a boy—maybe a year older than her—with tangled dark hair. His jaw was set and his black eyes snapped with anger.

Cristina gasped. *"Dios mío, ¡no puedo creer que seas tú!"*

"What?" Emma demanded, looking from the boy to Cristina and back again. "What's going on?"

"Emma." Cristina looked stunned, as if she'd had the breath knocked out of her. "This is Diego. Diego Rocio Rosales, meet Emma Carstairs."

The air outside the Institute was strong and bracing, smelling of sage and salt. Julian could hear the low hum of cicadas filling the air, softening the noise of Diana slamming the truck door shut. She came around the side of the truck and paused when she saw Julian standing on the front steps.

"Jules," she said. "What are you doing out here?"

"I could ask you that," he said. "Are you leaving? Again?"

She tucked her hair behind her ears, but several curls escaped, caught by the escalating wind. She wore dark clothes, not gear but black jeans and gloves and boots. "I have to go."

He took a step down. "How long will you be gone for?"

"I don't know."

"So we shouldn't depend on you." The heaviness in Julian's chest felt like more than he could bear. He wanted to lash out, kick something. He wanted Emma, to talk to, to reassure him. But he couldn't think about Emma.

"Believe it or not," Diana said, "I'm doing my best for you."

Julian looked down at his hands. His sea-glass bracelet glowed on his wrist. He remembered the gleam of it under the water the night before, as he swam down toward Emma. "What do you expect me to tell them?" he said. "If they ask me where you are."

"Make something up," Diana said. "You're good at that."

Anger surged up in him—if he was a liar, and a good one, it was because he had never had a choice.

"I know things about you," Julian said. "I know you left for your travel year, went to Thailand, and didn't come back until after your father died."

Diana paused, one hand on the truck door. "Have you been *investigating* me, Julian?"

"I know things because I have to know them," Julian said. "I need to be careful."

Diana yanked the door open. "I came here," she said, softly, "knowing it was a bad idea. Knowing that caring about you children was tying myself to a fate I couldn't control. I did it because I saw how much you cared about each other, you and your brothers and sisters, and it meant something to me. Try to believe that, Julian."

"I know you understand about brothers and sisters," said Julian. "You *had* a brother. He died in Thailand. You never talk about him."

She got into the truck, slammed the door shut after her, the window still open. "I don't owe you answers, Julian," she said. "I'll be back as soon as I can."

"It's all right," he said. He suddenly felt enormously tired.

"They won't ask where you are, anyway. They don't really expect you to be around."

He saw Diana cover her face with her hands. A moment later, the truck started up. Lights illuminated the front of the Institute, sweeping over the sandy grass as the truck rumbled down the hill.

Julian stood where he was for a long time. He wasn't sure how long. Long enough for the sun to go down entirely, for the glow to fade from the hills. Long enough for him to turn to go back inside, straightening his shoulders, preparing himself.

That was when he heard the noise. He spun around and saw them: a vast crowd, coming up the road toward the Institute.

# 19

## CHILLING AND KILLING

"Cristina," Diego breathed, staring past Emma. *"Pensé que eras tú, pero no estaba seguro. ¿Qué haces aquí? ¿Por qué estabas tratando de proteger a este hombre?"*

"Diego?" Not understanding a word of what he'd said, Emma examined the boy again, noting the Marks that decorated his neck, disappearing down into the collar of his shirt. He was a Shadowhunter, all right. "*This* is Perfect Diego?"

"*Emma,*" Cristina said, her cheeks flushing. "Let him go."

"I'm not letting him go." Emma glared at Perfect Diego, who glared right back, his black eyes flaring. "He shot Julian."

"I didn't know you were Nephilim," Perfect Diego snapped. "You were wearing long sleeves and jackets. I couldn't see your runes." His English was perfect, perhaps unsurprisingly, considering his nickname.

"Weren't they in gear?" Cristina demanded. She was still looking at Perfect Diego incredulously.

"Just the jackets." Emma shoved Perfect Diego hard against the wall; he winced. "I guess they look like regular jackets from a distance. Not that that's an excuse."

"You were wearing jeans. I'd never seen you before. You were going through the dead girl's purse. Why wouldn't I think you were one of the killers?"

Emma, not wanting to acknowledge that he had a point, shoved him harder against the wall. "Do you know who I am now?"

The corner of his mouth quirked up. "Oh, indeed, Emma Carstairs."

"So you know I could rip all your internal organs out at once, thread some string through them, and turn them into Christmas tree decorations without batting an eyelash?"

His eyes flashed. "You could try."

"Stop it, both of you," said Cristina. "We don't have time for this. We have to find Sterling."

"She's right," said Diego. "Now either let go of me or kill me, because we are wasting time. I know where Sterling will be. He has a meeting with a witch from the Shadow Market. We must get there soon—he is fast, as half wolves are."

"Is the witch going to kill him?" Emma let go of Diego, who went to gather up his crossbow. Cristina's butterfly knife had stuck point-down into the side of it. Diego snorted and pulled it free. He handed it to her. She took it silently.

Diego whirled around and began striding down the alley. "If that is a joke, it's not funny."

"It's not a joke," said Cristina. "We have been trying to protect him."

"*What?*" Diego turned the corner into a blind alley, where a chain-link fence closed them off from the street beyond. He climbed it expertly, dropping lightly to the ground on the other side. Emma scrambled up after, and Cristina next. Diego appeared to be fiddling with his weapons belt, but Emma could tell he was watching Cristina out of the corner of his eye, making sure she landed safely. "Why would you protect a murderer?"

"He's not a murderer," Cristina said. "He is a victim. And he's very unpleasant, but this is our job."

They had turned onto a dead-end street lined with houses. Crabgrass and cactus grew on overgrown lawns. Diego moved with purpose toward the end of the street.

"Didn't you understand?" Diego shook his head, his dark hair flying. "Why everyone must stay away from him? I can't believe this. I can't believe—everything you've done—you saw him get the number? At the Lottery? You saw him chosen?"

"Yes," said Emma, a cold feeling beginning to spread through her veins. "Yes, that's how we knew we needed to protect him—"

A sudden, blinding flare of light shot like fireworks from the far end of the street. A swirl of green-and-blue fire, edged with red. Cristina's eyes were wide, the flaring sparks touching her hair with scarlet.

Diego swore and took off running. After a split second, Emma and Cristina followed.

Emma had never met a Shadowhunter she couldn't keep up with, but Diego was fast. *Really* fast. She was breathing hard by the time they skidded to a stop at the end of the street.

The cul-de-sac ended in a row of abandoned houses. Sterling's car had slammed into a dead streetlamp, the hood crumpled, the driver's side door hanging open. One of the air bags had exploded, but Sterling was unharmed.

He was in the middle of the road, struggling with someone—the girl with green hair Emma had seen earlier, on the street in front of the bar. She was pulling to get away from him; he had a hand fisted in the back of her coat, and the look on his face was half-maniacal.

"Let her go!" Diego shouted. The three of them began to run, Emma reaching for Cortana. Sterling, seeing them, began to drag the girl around to the other side of his car. Emma, hurtling toward the Jeep, leaped onto the hood, scrambled over the roof, and dropped down on the other side.

To be met with a sheet of blue-green fire. Sterling was standing behind it, still clasping the green-haired girl. Her eyes met Emma's. She had a slight, elfin face—a recollection of seeing her at the Midnight Theater touched the edge of Emma's memory.

Emma leaped forward. The blue-green fire blasted upward, knocking her back several steps. Sterling raised his hand. Something glittered in his grasp—a knife.

"Stop him!" Diego shouted. He and Cristina had appeared on the other side of the wall of blue fire. Emma pushed forward—though it was like walking against a typhoon—just as Sterling brought the knife down, plunging it into the girl's chest.

Cristina screamed.

*No,* Emma thought, shocked through with horror. *No, no, no.* It was a Shadowhunter's job to save people, to protect them. Sterling couldn't harm the girl, he couldn't—

For a moment she saw a darkness within the fire—caught a glimpse of the inside of the convergence cave, carved all over with poetry and symbols—and then hands reached from the darkness and snatched the girl from Sterling's grip. Emma glimpsed them only briefly, amid the flame and confusion, but they seemed to be long white hands—oddly crooked, as if they had been stripped to bones—

Choking on blood, limp and dying, the girl was dragged into the darkness. Sterling turned and grinned at Emma. His shirt was marked with bloody handprints, and the blade of his knife was scarlet.

"You're too late!" he shouted. "Too late, Nephilim! She was the thirteenth—the last!"

Diego cursed and threw himself forward, but the wall of fire flared up, and he staggered back, knocked to his knees. Gritting his teeth, he rose again to his feet and advanced.

Sterling had stopped grinning. Fear flashed in his sallow eyes. He flung out an arm, and the skeletal hand reached from the fire to clasp his and drag him after the girl.

"No!" Emma sprang and rolled under the wave of fire, as if she were ducking under a wave at the beach. She caught at Sterling's leg, digging her hands into his calf.

"Let me go!" he yelled. "Let me go, let me go. *Guardian, take me, take me away from here—*"

The skeletal hand pulled at Sterling's. Emma felt herself losing her grip. She looked up, her eyes stinging and burning, just in time to see Cristina fling her butterfly knife. It struck the clawlike hand; the bones cracked and the hand withdrew hastily, releasing Sterling, who fell heavily to the ground.

"No!" Sterling rose to his knees, his arms held out, as the fire faded and disappeared. "Please! Take me with you—"

The three Shadowhunters descended on him, Diego grabbing hold of Sterling unceremoniously and hauling him to his feet. Sterling laughed painfully. "You couldn't stop me," he said. "You stupid girls, following me around, *protecting* me—"

Diego shoved him, hard, but Emma was shaking her head. "When you were picked in the Lottery," she said to Sterling through a dry throat, asking the question though she already knew the answer, "you weren't being picked to be killed. You were being picked to *do the killing?*"

"Oh, Raziel," Cristina whispered. Her hand was at her throat, clutching her pendant; she looked at a loss.

Sterling spat on the ground. "That's right," he said. "You get your number picked, you kill or be killed. Just like you, Wren didn't know how it worked. She agreed to meet me here. Stupid bitch." His eyes were half-wild. "I killed her, and the Guardian took her, and now I'll live forever. As soon as the Guardian finds me again. I'll get riches, immortality, anything I want."

"You killed for that?" Cristina demanded. "You made yourself a murderer?"

"I was a murderer from the second they picked my name in the Lottery," said Sterling. "I had no choice."

The sound of police sirens started up in the distance.

"We need to get out of here," said Cristina, glancing toward Sterling's wrecked car, the blood on the street. Emma raised Cortana, and was rewarded with a look of quivering fear on Sterling's face.

"No," he whimpered. "Don't—"

"We can't kill him," Diego protested. "We need him. I've never caught one of them alive before. We must question him."

"Relax, Perfect Diego," Emma said, and slammed the handle of Cortana into Sterling's temple. He dropped like a rock, out cold.

Carrying Sterling back to the car was awkward, since he wasn't glamoured; they slung one of his arms over Diego's shoulder, and he did his best to look as if he was helping a drunk friend home. Once they reached the Toyota, they tied Sterling's wrists and ankles with electrum wire before bundling him into the back of the car, his head lolling, his body limp.

They'd discussed whether to race straight to the convergence, but decided to head to the Institute first to pick up more weapons and consult with the others. Emma especially was eager to talk to Julian—she'd called several times, but he hadn't picked up. She told herself he was probably busy with the kids, but faint worry rankled at the back of her mind as she slid into the driver's seat, Cristina beside her. Perfect Diego clambered in beside Sterling, his dagger out, pressed to Sterling's throat.

Emma took off with a vicious screech of tires. She was filled with rage, at least half of it directed at herself. How could she not have figured out that Sterling wasn't a victim, but a killer? How could they all not have known?

"It's not your fault," Perfect Diego said from the back of the car, as if he'd read her mind. "It made sense to assume that the Lottery was choosing victims, not killers."

"And Johnny Rook lied to us," Emma snarled. "Or at least—he *let* us believe it. That we were protecting someone."

"We were protecting a killer," said Cristina. She looked miserable, her hand clamped around her pendant.

"Don't blame yourself," said Perfect Diego, being perfect. "You've been investigating with no information. No help from the Silent Brothers or—anyone else."

Cristina looked over her shoulder at him and glared. "How do you know all this?"

"What makes you think we've been investigating?" Emma demanded. "Just because you saw me and Julian at Wells's place?"

"That was my first clue," Perfect Diego said. "After that I asked around. Talked to a guy at the Shadow Market—"

"Johnny Rook again," Emma said in disgust. "Is there anyone that guy won't blab to?"

"He told me everything," Perfect Diego said. "That you were looking into the murders without the Clave knowing. That it was a secret. I was scared for you, Cristina."

Cristina snorted without turning around.

"Tina," Perfect Diego said, and his voice was filled with longing. "Tina, please."

Emma looked awkwardly out the windshield. They were almost in view of the ocean. She tried to concentrate on that and not the tension between the two other conscious occupants of the car.

Cristina clenched her medallion tighter, but said nothing.

"Rook said you were investigating because you believed the murders were tied to your parents' death," Perfect Diego said to Emma. "For what it is worth, I am sorry for your loss."

"That was a long time ago." Emma could see Perfect Diego in the rearview mirror. He had a delicate chain of runes that circled his neck, like a torque. His hair curled, not Julian's waves but ringlets that fell over the tops of his ears.

He *was* hot. And he seemed nice. And he had some serious badass moves. He really was Perfect Diego, she thought wryly. No wonder Cristina had been so hurt.

"What are *you* doing here?" Cristina demanded. "Emma has a reason to be investigating the murders, but you?"

"You know I was at the Scholomance," Perfect Diego said. "And you know Centurions are often sent to investigate matters that don't fall strictly under Shadowhunter mandate—"

There was a hoarse yell. Sterling had jerked awake and was flailing in the backseat. Perfect Diego's knife flashed in the darkness. Cars honked as Emma jerked the wheel to the right and they careened onto Ocean Avenue.

"Let me go!" Sterling jerked and flailed against the wire wrapping his wrists. "Let me go!"

He yelped in pain as Perfect Diego flung him hard against the backseat of the car, pressing the knife against his jugular. "Get off me," Sterling yelled. "Goddammit, get off me—"

Sterling shrieked as Perfect Diego dug his knee into his thigh. "Settle," Diego said in a flat, deadly voice, "down."

They were still hurtling down Ocean. Palm trees fringed either side of the street like eyelashes. Emma cut wildly in front of the left-hand turn lane and shot down the ramp to the coast highway amid a furious chorus of blaring horns.

"Jesus Christ!" Sterling shouted. "Where'd you learn to drive?"

"Nobody asked you for commentary!" Emma yelled back as they hurtled into the moving traffic. Luckily it was late and the lanes were mostly empty.

"I don't want to die on the Pacific Coast Highway!" Sterling wailed.

"Oh, I'm sorry." Emma's voice dripped acid. "Is there a *different* highway you'd like to die on? BECAUSE WE CAN ARRANGE THAT."

"Bitch," Sterling hissed.

Cristina whirled around in her seat. There was a cracking sound like a gunshot; a second later, as they hurtled past a group of surfers walking along the highway's edge, Emma realized she'd slapped Sterling across the face.

"Don't you call my friend a bitch," Cristina said. "You understand?"

Sterling rubbed his jaw. His eyes were slits. "You've got no right to touch me." There was a whine in his voice. "Nephilim only deal with issues that break the Accords."

"Wrong," Perfect Diego said. "We deal with any issues we feel like."

"But Belinda told us—"

"Yeah, about that," Cristina said. "How did you end up joining that cult or whatever it is at the Midnight Theater?"

Sterling exhaled a shaky breath. "We're sworn to secrecy," he said finally. "If I tell you everything I know, are you going to protect me?"

"Maybe," said Emma. "But you're tied up and we're all heavily armed. You really fancy your chances if you *don't* tell?"

Sterling glanced at Perfect Diego, who was holding the dagger idly, as if it were a pen. Nevertheless, there was a sense of coiled power about him, as if he could explode into action in under a second. If Sterling had any brains he'd be terrified. "I got into it through a producer friend of mine. He said he'd found a way to guarantee that everything you touched turned to gold. Not literally," Sterling hastened to add.

"No one thought you meant literally, idiot," said Emma.

Sterling made an angry noise, cut off quickly by Diego pressing the knife tighter against his throat.

"Who's the Guardian?" Cristina demanded. "Who leads the Followers at the theater?"

"I've got no idea," Sterling said sulkily. "Nobody knows. Not even Belinda."

"I saw Belinda at the Shadow Market, shilling for your little cult," Emma said. "I'm guessing they promised money and luck if you came to their meetings. You just had to risk the lotteries. Am I right?"

"They didn't seem like that big a risk," said Sterling. "They were only once in a while. If you got picked, no one could touch you. No one could interfere until you took a life."

Cristina's face twisted in disgust. "And those who took lives? What happened to them?"

"They got whatever they wanted," Sterling said. "To be rich. Beautiful. After a sacrifice, everyone gets stronger, but the one who performs the sacrifice gets stronger than the rest."

"How do you know?" said Cristina. "Had any of the people at the theater been picked in the Lottery before?"

"Belinda," said Sterling promptly. "She was the first. Most of the others didn't stick around. They're probably off somewhere, living it up. Well, except Ava."

"Ava Leigh was a Lottery winner?" asked Emma. "The one who lived with Stanley Wells?"

Perfect Diego jammed his knife harder against Sterling's throat. "What did you know about Ava?"

Sterling winced away from the knife. "Yeah, she was a Lottery winner. Look, it didn't matter who winners picked to kill—no Downworlders except faeries, that was the only rule. Some of the Lottery winners chose people they knew. Ava decided to kill her sugar-daddy boyfriend. She was tired of him. But it freaked her out. She killed herself after. Drowned herself in his pool. It was stupid of her. She could have had anything she wanted."

"She didn't commit suicide," Emma said. "She was murdered."

He shrugged. "Nah, she offed herself. That's what everyone said."

Cristina looked as if she was struggling to stay calm. "You knew her," she said. "Don't you care? Do you feel anything? What about guilt over the girl you killed?"

"Some girl from the Shadow Market," said Sterling with a shrug. "Used to sell jewelry there. I told her I could get her designs into department stores. Make her rich, if she'd just meet me." He snorted. "Everyone's greedy."

They had passed the initial highway clutter and reached a stretch of beach, dotted with blue lifeguard towers.

"That blue fire," Emma said, thinking out loud. "The Guardian was in it. They took the body to the convergence. You stabbed her, but the Guardian grabbed her before she died. So the deaths happen at the convergence, and everything else too—the burning, submerging the body in seawater, carving the runes, the whole ritual?"

"Yeah. And I was supposed to be taken to the convergence too," Sterling said, resentment coloring his voice. "It's where the Guardian would have thanked me—given me anything I wanted. I could have seen the ritual. One death strengthens us all."

Emma and Cristina exchanged looks. Sterling wasn't clearing things up; he was making them more confusing.

"You said she was the last," said Diego. "What happens after this? What's the payoff?"

Sterling grunted. "No idea. I didn't get where I am in life by asking questions I don't need the answers to."

"Get where you are in life?" Emma snorted. "You mean tied up in the back of a car?"

Emma could see the lights of the Malibu Pier up ahead. They shone against the dark water. "None of that matters. The Guardian will find me," Sterling said.

"I wouldn't count on it," said Perfect Diego in his low voice.

Emma turned off the highway onto their familiar road. She could see the lights of the Institute in the distance, illuminating the rutted track under her wheels. "And when he does find you?" she said. "The Guardian? What do you think he'll do, just welcome you back after you told us all this? You don't think he'll make you pay?"

"There's one more thing I have to give him," Sterling said. "Belinda did. And even Ava did. One last, last thing. And then—"

Sterling broke off with a yowl of terror. The Institute loomed up in front of them. Perfect Diego swore.

"Emma!" Cristina gasped. "Emma, *stop!*"

Emma saw the familiar shape of the Institute, the drive ahead of them, the canyon and hills rising behind. There were shadows everywhere, a ring of them around the Institute, but only when the car crested the last rise and the headlights swept the building did Emma feel the shock of what she was seeing.

The Institute was surrounded.

Figures—dark, human-shaped—contained the Institute in a loose square. They stood shoulder to shoulder, absolutely silent and unmoving, like old drawings Emma had seen of Greek warriors.

Sterling yelled something incomprehensible. Emma slammed on the brakes as the headlights skittered across the trampled brush in front of the building. The figures were illuminated, lit up like daylight. Some were familiar. She recognized the curly-haired boy from the band at the Midnight Theater, his face set in a stony snarl. Beside him was a woman—dark hair, red lips—who raised a hand with a gun in it—

"Belinda!" Sterling sounded stupidly terrified. "She—"

Belinda's hand rocked back with the ricochet of the gun. An explosion of noise seared Emma's ears as the right front tire of the car exploded, torn in two by a bullet. The car slewed violently to the side and skidded into a ditch.

Darkness and the sound of shattering glass. The steering wheel slammed into Emma's chest, knocking the breath out of her; the headlights went out. She heard Cristina scream, and scrambling noises from the backseat. She wrenched at her seat belt, ripping it free, turning to reach for Cristina.

She was gone. The backseat was also empty. Emma bashed the door open and half-fell out onto the packed dirt. She struggled to her feet and whirled around.

The car was mashed nose down into a ditch, smoke rising from the burst tire. Diego was coming around from the passenger-side door, boots crunching on the dry earth. He was carrying Cristina, his left arm slung under her knees; one of her legs hung at an odd angle. She had a hand on his shoulder, her fingers bunched in the sleeve of his sweatshirt.

He looked very heroic in the moonlight. A bit like Superman. Perfect Diego. Emma kind of wanted to throw something at him but she was afraid of hitting Cristina. He jerked his manly chin toward the Institute. *"Emma!"*

Emma whirled. The figures surrounding the Institute had turned—they were facing toward her now, toward her and Diego and the wreckage of the car.

In the moonlight they looked eerie. Stark figures in black and gray, a blur of faces. Weres, half faeries, vampire darklings, and ifrits: the Followers.

"Emma!" Perfect Diego called again. He had his stele out and was inking a healing rune on Cristina's arm. "Sterling's on the move—he has your sword—"

Emma whirled as Sterling shot past her, moving with inhuman speed. He'd freed his wrists and ankles, but blood stained the hems of his trousers. "Belinda!" he shouted. "I'm here! Help me!" He held something up as he ran, something that glowed gold in the darkness.

Cortana.

Rage exploded inside Emma's chest. It shot through her veins like lit gunpowder and then she was running, slamming across the grass and dirt after Sterling. She leaped over rocks, shot past blurred figures. Sterling was fast, but she was just that much faster. She caught up to him nearly at the Institute steps. He had almost reached Belinda.

She crashed into him, grabbed his jacket, and swung him around. His face was dirty, blood-streaked, pale with terror. She seized the wrist that held Cortana. Her sword. Her father's sword. Her only connection to a family that seemed to have dissolved away into the past like powder in rain.

She heard a crack. Sterling shrieked and fell to his knees, Cortana dropping to the ground. She reached down to seize it up; by the time she straightened she was surrounded by a small group of Followers, led by Belinda.

"What have you told her, Sterling?" Belinda demanded, showing small white teeth behind her red lips.

"N-nothing." Sterling was clutching his wrist. It looked badly broken. "I took the sword to give to you—proof of good faith—"

"What would I want with a sword? Idiot." She turned to Emma. "We're here for him," she said, pointing at Sterling. "Let us take him and we'll go." She grinned at Emma. "If you're wondering how we knew to come here, the Guardian has eyes everywhere."

"Emma!" It was Cristina's voice; Emma whirled and saw Cristina on the outside of the circle, Perfect Diego beside her. To Emma's relief, Cristina was only limping a little bit.

"Let them in," Belinda said, and the crowd parted so that Perfect Diego and Cristina took their places on either side of Emma. The circle closed back up around them.

"What's going on?" Perfect Diego demanded. His gaze lit on Belinda. "Are you the Guardian?"

She burst out laughing. After a moment several of the other Followers, including the curly-haired boy, started to laugh alongside her. "Me? What a hoot you are, handsome." She winked at Perfect

Diego as if acknowledging his perfectness. "I'm not the Guardian, but I know what the Guardian wants. I know what's necessary. Right now the Guardian needs Sterling. The Followers need him."

Sterling whimpered, his cry lost among the laughter of the crowd. Emma was looking around, gauging the distance to the front doors of the Institute; if they could get inside, the Followers couldn't come after them. But then they'd be trapped—and they couldn't call the Conclave for help.

Sterling curled a hand around Perfect Diego's ankle. Apparently he had decided Perfect Diego was his best bet for mercy in the circumstances. "Don't let them take me," he begged. "They'll kill me. I screwed up. They'll kill me."

"We can't let you have him," said Perfect Diego. Emma was mostly sure she was imagining the regret in his voice. "Our mandate is to protect mundanes unless they are posing a danger to our lives."

"I don't know," Emma said, thinking of the green-haired girl bleeding out her life. "This one seems killable."

Belinda gave them a red-lipped smile. "He's not a mundane. None of us are."

"Our mandate is to protect, either way," Perfect Diego said. Emma exchanged a glance with Cristina, but could tell Cristina agreed with Perfect Diego. Mercy was a quality the Angel expected Shadowhunters to have. Mercy was the Law. Sometimes Emma worried her capacity for mercy had been burned away in the Dark War.

"We need him for information," Cristina said quietly, but Belinda heard it, and her lips tightened.

"We need him more," she said. "Now hand him over and we'll go. There's three of you and three hundred of us. Think about it."

Emma threw Cortana.

It whipped out of her hand so quickly that Belinda had no chance to react; it spun around the circle of Followers like a needle around a compass, flickering and golden. She heard shouts, cries, half-pain and half-astonishment, and then the sword was back in her hand, thunking solidly into her palm.

Belinda looked around in genuine astonishment. The tip of Cortana had just grazed the shirtfronts of the circle of Followers; some were bleeding, some just had rips in their clothes. All were clutching at themselves, looking stunned and frightened.

Cristina seemed delighted. Perfect Diego just seemed thoughtful.

"Outnumbered isn't necessarily overmatched," said Emma.

"Kill her," Belinda said, raised her gun, and pulled the trigger.

Emma barely had time to brace herself before something flew across her field of vision—something bright and silver—and she heard a loud crack. A dagger dropped to the ground at her feet, a bullet lodged in the handle.

Perfect Diego was looking at her, his hand still open. He'd thrown the dagger, averted the bullet. Maybe not saved her life—gear repelled bullets—but definitely prevented her from being knocked to the ground, maybe killed with a second shot to the head.

She didn't have time to mouth a thanks. The other Followers lunged toward her, and this time the cold of battle shot through her veins. The world slowed down around her. The half-fey boy with the curly hair launched himself into the air, hurtling toward her. Emma speared him before he could hit the ground, her blade shearing through his chest. Blood sprayed around her as she jerked the sword back, a slow, hot rain of red droplets.

The curly-haired boy crumpled to the ground. There was blood on Cortana's blade as Emma swung it again, and again, and the sword became a golden blur around her. She could hear screams. Sterling was cowering on the ground, his arms over his head.

She cut at legs and arms; she chopped guns out of hands. Diego and Cristina were doing the same, slicing out with their weapons. Cristina flung her butterfly knife; it slammed into Belinda's shoulder, knocking her backward. She swore and pulled the knife free, tossing it aside. Though there was a hole torn in her white sweater, there was no blood.

Emma backed up until she was standing in front of Sterling. "Get to the Institute!" she shouted at Cristina. "Get the others!"

Cristina nodded and darted toward the steps. She was halfway there when a gray-skinned, red-eyed darkling lunged toward her, sinking its teeth into her already injured leg.

Cristina screamed. Emma and Diego both turned as Cristina stabbed down with a dagger and the darkling fell away, choking on blood. There was a rip in the leg of Cristina's gear.

Diego tore across the grass toward her. The moment had cost Emma her concentration; she saw a flicker of movement out of the corner of her eye and found Belinda hurtling toward her, her left hand outstretched. It fastened around Emma's throat.

She choked, grasping at Belinda's other arm. She yanked hard, and as Belinda staggered away from her, her glove slipped off.

Her right arm ended in a bare stump. Belinda's face contorted, and Emma heard Cristina exclaim. She had her dagger out, though the leg of her gear was soaked with blood. Diego stood beside her, a massive shadow against the shape of the Institute.

"Your hand's missing," Emma gasped, raising Cortana between her and Belinda. "Just like Ava's—"

The Institute doors slammed open. Light so bright it was blinding blazed up and Emma froze, bloody sword in hand. She looked up to see Julian in the doorway.

He stood with a seraph blade raised over his head and it burned with light like a star. It bleached the sky, the moon. The Followers actually fell back from it, as if it were the light of a crashing aircraft.

In that still moment, Emma looked directly at Jules and saw him look back at her. A fierce pride rose inside her. This was her Julian. A gentle boy with a gentle soul, but every soul contains its own opposite, and the opposite of gentleness was ruthlessness—the beautiful wreckage of mercy.

She could see it on his face. To save her he would kill everyone else in the vicinity. He wouldn't think twice until it was over, when he'd wash the blood down the drain of the sink like scarlet paint. And he would not regret it.

"Stop," Julian said, and though he didn't shout, didn't yell, the Followers who were still moving froze in place, as if they could read his expression just like Emma could. As if they were afraid.

Emma grabbed Sterling by the back of his shirt, yanking him to his feet. "Come on," she said, and began pushing through the crowd, dragging him toward the Institute. If she could just get him inside—

But Belinda was suddenly pushing herself forward, shoving among the other Followers to get close to the Institute steps. There was still no blood around the rip in her sweater. Her glove was back on her hand. Her dark hair was coming out of its elaborately crafted Victory rolls, and she looked furious.

She bounded forward, placing herself between Emma and the stairs. Cristina and Diego were just behind them; Cristina was wincing, her face pale.

"Julian Blackthorn!" Belinda shouted. "I demand that you let us take this man"—she pointed at Sterling—"away from here! And that you cease interfering in our business! The Followers of the Guardian have nothing to do with you or your Laws!"

Julian descended a single step. The glow of his seraph blade lit his eyes to an eerie undersea green. "How dare you come here," he said flatly. "How dare you invade the space of the Nephilim; how dare you make demands. Your idiot cult wasn't our business, no, until you started murdering. Now it's our business to make you stop. And we will."

Belinda gave a harsh laugh. "There are three hundred of us—there are barely any of you—and you're *children*—"

"Not all of us are children," said another voice, and Malcolm Fade stepped out onto the stairs beside Julian.

The Followers gaped. Clearly, most of them had no idea who he was. But the fact that he was surrounded by a halo of crackling violet fire was obviously making quite a few of them nervous.

"I'm Malcolm Fade," he said. "High Warlock of Los Angeles. You do know what warlocks are, don't you?"

Emma couldn't suppress a wild giggle. Perfect Diego was staring. Sterling was pallid with terror.

"One of us," said Malcolm, "is worth five hundred of you. I can burn you to the ground in six seconds flat and use the ashes to stuff a teddy bear for my girlfriend. Not that I have a girlfriend at the moment," he added, "but one lives in hope."

"You're a warlock, and you serve Nephilim?" Belinda demanded. "After all they've done to Downworlders?"

"Don't try to use your feeble knowledge of a thousand years of politics on me, child. It won't work." Malcolm looked at his watch. "I'm giving you one minute," he said. "Anyone who's still here after that gets set on fire."

Nobody moved.

With a sigh, Malcolm pointed at a shrub of California sage clustered by the bottom of the stairs. It burst into flames. A choking, sage-smelling smoke rose up. Flames danced along his fingers.

The Followers turned and ran for the road. Emma stood as they hurtled around her, as if she were planted in the middle of an avalanche. In a moment all of them were gone but Belinda.

There was a terrible rage on her face, and an even more terrible despair. It was a look that froze them all in place.

She raised her dark eyes to Julian. "You," she said. "You may think you've defeated us now, with your pet warlock, but the things we know about you—oh, the things we could tell the Clave. The truth about your uncle. The truth about who runs this Institute. The truth—"

Julian had gone white, but before he could speak or move, an agonized shriek tore the air. It was Sterling. He clutched at his chest, and as all of them, even Belinda, turned to stare, he crumpled to the grass. A gout of blood spilled from his mouth, staining the ground. His eyes bugged out with fear as his knees gave way; he clawed at the ground, his pink scarab ring sparking on his finger, and was still.

"He's dead," said Cristina in disbelief. She turned on Belinda. "What did you do?"

Briefly Belinda looked blank, as if she were just as shocked as the others. Then she said, "Wouldn't you like to know," and sashayed up to the body. She bent as if to examine it.

A moment later a knife flashed in the fingers of her left hand. There were two grotesque thick chopping noises and Sterling's hands came away from his wrists. Belinda caught them up, grinning.

"Thanks," she said. "The Guardian will be pleased to know he's dead."

Emma flashed back to Ava in the pool, the ragged skin around her severed hand. Did the Guardian always insist on this specific grisly proof that those he wanted dead were dead? But what about Belinda? She was still alive. Was it meant to be a tribute?

Belinda grinned, cutting into Emma's thoughts.

"Later, little Shadowhunters," she said. And she stalked off toward the road, her bloody trophies held high.

Emma took a step forward, meaning to climb the Institute steps, but Malcolm held up a hand to stop her.

"Emma, stay where you are," he said. "Cristina, step back from the body."

Cristina did as he asked, her hand at her throat, touching her medallion. Sterling's body lay crumpled at her feet, curled in on itself. Blood no longer pumped from his severed wrists, but the ground around him was wet with it.

As Cristina stepped back with alacrity, she bumped into Perfect Diego. He raised his hands as if to steady her, and to Emma's surprise, she allowed it. She was wincing, clearly in pain. Blood had spattered onto her shoe.

Malcolm lowered his hand, curling his fingers under. Sterling's body burst into flame. Mage-fire, burning hard and quick and clean. The body seemed to glow intensely for a moment before sifting away to ash. The fire vanished and there was only a charred and bloodstained patch on the ground to show where it had been.

Emma realized she was still holding Cortana. She knelt, mechanically wiped off the blade on the dry grass, and sheathed it. As she rose to her feet, her gaze sought out Julian. He was leaning against one of the pillars by the front doors, the seraph blade, now dark, dangling in his hand. He met her gaze for only a moment; his was bleak.

The front door of the Institute opened and Mark came out. "Is it over?" Mark asked.

"It's over," Julian said wearily. "For now, anyway."

Mark's gaze scanned over the others—Emma, then Cristina—and lit on Diego. Diego looked puzzled at the intensity of his gaze. "Who's that?"

"That's Diego," said Emma. "Diego Rocio Rosales."

"Perfect Diego?" said Mark, sounding incredulous.

Diego looked even more puzzled. Before he could say anything, Cristina dropped to the ground, clutching at her leg. "I need," she said, a little breathlessly, "another *iratze*—"

Diego lifted her up into his arms and ran up the stairs, ignoring her protests that she could walk. "I must get her inside," he said, pushing past Julian and then Mark. "You have an infirmary?"

"Of course," Julian said. "Second floor—"

"Cristina!" Emma called, running up the stairs after them, but they had already disappeared inside.

"She'll be fine," Malcolm said. "Better not to chase after them and frighten the kids."

"How are the kids?" Emma asked anxiously. "Ty, Dru—"

"They're all fine," Mark said. "I was looking after them."

"And Arthur?"

"Didn't even seem to notice anything was happening," said Mark with a quizzical look. "It was odd—"

Emma turned to Julian. "It *is* odd," she said. "Julian, what did Belinda mean? When she said she knew who really ran the Institute?"

Julian shook his head. "I don't know."

Malcolm exhaled an exasperated breath. "Jules," he said. "Tell her."

Julian looked exhausted—more than exhausted. Emma had read somewhere that people drowned when they became too tired to keep themselves afloat any longer. They gave up and let the sea take them. Julian looked that tired now. "Malcolm, don't," he whispered.

"Can you even remember all the lies you've told?" Malcolm asked, and there was none of his usual insouciance in his look. His eyes were hard as amethyst. "You didn't tell me about your brother's return—"

"Oh—Mark!" Emma exclaimed, realizing suddenly that of course Malcolm hadn't known before tonight that he was in the Institute. Quickly, she put her hand over her mouth. Mark raised an eyebrow at her. He seemed remarkably calm.

"You concealed it," Malcolm went on, "knowing that I would realize it meant faerie involvement in these murders, and that I would know I might be breaking the Cold Peace by helping you."

"You couldn't break it if you didn't know," Julian said. "I was protecting you, too."

"Maybe," said Malcolm. "But I've had enough. Tell them the truth. Or that will be the end of my help."

Julian nodded. "I'll tell Emma and Mark," he said. "It's not fair on the others."

"Your uncle would probably be able to tell you who said this," Malcolm said. "'Do nothing secretly; for Time sees and hears all things, and discloses all.'"

"I can tell you who said it." Julian's eyes burned with a low fire. "Sophocles."

"Clever boy," said Malcolm. There was affection in his voice, but weariness, too.

He turned and marched down the steps. He paused when he reached the bottom, staring off past Emma, his eyes too dark for her to read. He seemed to be seeing something in the distance she couldn't, either something too far in the future to imagine or too far in the past to remember.

"You'll help us, still?" Julian called after him. "Malcolm, you won't . . ." He trailed off; Malcolm had vanished into the shadows of the night. "Abandon us?" he said, speaking as if he knew no one was listening.

Julian was still leaning against the pillar as if it was the only thing holding him up, and Emma couldn't keep her mind from flashing to the pillars in the Hall of Accords, to Julian when he was twelve, crumpled against one and sobbing into his hands.

He'd cried since then, but not often. There wasn't much, she supposed, that measured up to having killed your father.

The seraph blade in his hand had burned out. He flung it aside just as Emma came close to him. She slid her hand into his now-empty one. There was no passion in the gesture, nothing that recalled that night on the beach. Only the absolute solidity of the friendship they had shared for more than a decade.

He looked over at her then, and she saw the gratitude in his eyes. For a moment there was nothing in the world but the two of them, breathing, his fingertip dancing across her bare wrist. *T-H-A-N-K Y-O-U.*

"Malcolm said there was something you needed to tell us," said Mark. "You seemed to agree. What is it? If we keep the kids waiting much longer, they'll riot."

Julian nodded, straightening up, drawing away from the pillar. He was the calm older brother again, the good soldier, the boy with a plan.

"I'll go tell them what's going on. You two, wait for me in the dining room," he said. "Malcolm was right. We need to talk."

## Los Angeles, 2008

*Julian would always remember the day his uncle Arthur first arrived at the Los Angeles Institute.*

*It was only the third time he'd ever been there, even though his brother, Andrew, Julian's father, had headed up the biggest Institute on the West Coast for almost fifteen years. Relations had been strained between Andrew and the rest of the Blackthorns ever since a faerie woman had arrived on his doorstep carrying two tiny sleeping children, declared them to be Andrew's son and daughter with the Lady Nerissa of the Seelie Court, and deposited them there to be taken into his care.*

*Even the fact that his wife had adopted them quickly, adored them, and treated them just as she treated her other children with Andrew hadn't entirely repaired the breach. Julian always thought there was more to it than his father was admitting. Arthur seemed to think so too, but neither of them spoke of what they knew, and now that Andrew was dead, Julian suspected the story had died with him.*

*Julian stood at the top of the Institute steps, watching his uncle get out of the car Diana had picked him up in from the airport. Arthur could have Portaled, but he'd chosen to travel like a mundane. He looked* crumpled and travel worn as he headed up the steps, Diana behind him. Julian could see that her mouth was set in a hard line, and wondered if Arthur had done something to annoy her. He hoped not; Diana had been at the Los Angeles Institute for only a month and already Julian liked her enormously. It would be better for everyone if she and Arthur got along.

Arthur entered the Institute foyer, blinking as his sun-dazzled eyes adjusted to the dimness inside. The other Blackthorns were there, dressed in their best clothes—Dru was wearing velvet, and Tiberius had a tie knotted around his throat. Livvy held Tavvy in her arms, beaming hopefully. Emma stood warily at the foot of the steps, clearly very aware of her status as part of the family, but still not one of them.

She'd had her braids pinned up, loops of pale hair swinging like coiled rope on either side of her head. Julian still remembered that.

Diana made the introductions. Julian shook hands with his uncle, who, up close, still didn't look much like Julian's father. Maybe that was a good thing. Julian's last memory of his father was not a pleasant one.

Julian stared at his uncle as Arthur clasped his hand in a firm grip. Arthur had the Blackthorn brown hair, though it was almost entirely gray, and blue-green eyes behind glasses. His features were broad and rough and he still limped slightly from the injury he'd incurred during the Dark War.

Arthur turned to greet the rest of the children and Julian felt something jolt through his veins. He saw Dru's hopeful face turned up, Ty's shy sideways glance, and thought: Love them. Love them. For the Angel's sake, love them.

It didn't matter if anyone loved him. He was twelve. He was old enough. He had Marks, he was a Shadowhunter. He had Emma. But the others still needed someone to kiss them good night, ward off the nightmares, bandage scraped knees, and soothe hurt feelings. Someone to teach them how to grow up.

Arthur moved to Drusilla and shook her hand awkwardly. The smile faded off her face as he went to Livvy next, ignoring Tavvy, and then bent to Tiberius, his hand outstretched.

*Ty didn't reach back.*

*"Look at me, Tiberius," Arthur said, his voice slightly hoarse. He cleared his throat. "Tiberius!" He straightened up and turned to Julian. "Why won't he look at me?"*

*"He doesn't always like to make eye contact," Julian said.*

*"Why?" Arthur asked. "What's wrong with him?"*

*Julian saw Livvy slip her free hand into Ty's. It was the only thing that stopped him from knocking his uncle down to get to his younger brother himself. "Nothing. It's just how he is."*

*"Odd," Arthur said, and turned away from Ty, dismissing him forever. He looked at Diana. "Where's my office?"*

*Diana's lips thinned further. Julian felt as if he were choking. "Diana doesn't live here or work for us," he said. "She's a tutor; she works for the Clave. I can help you find your office."*

*"Good." Uncle Arthur picked up his suitcase. "I have a lot of work to do."*

*Julian went up the stairs feeling as if his head were full of tiny explosions, drowning out Uncle Arthur's lecture about the important monograph on the Iliad that he was working on. Apparently the Dark War had interrupted his work, some of which had been destroyed in the attack on the London Institute.*

*"Very inconvenient, war," said Arthur, stepping into the office that had been Julian's father's. The walls were light wood; dozens of windows looked out onto the sea and the sky.*

*Particularly for the people who died in it, Julian thought, but his uncle was shaking his head, his knuckles whitening around the handle of his briefcase. "Oh no, no," Arthur said. "This won't do at all." When he turned away from the windows, Julian saw that he was white and sweating. "Too much glass," he said, his voice lowering to a mumble. "Light— too bright. Too much." He coughed. "Is there an attic?"*

*Julian hadn't been in the attic of the Institute for years, but he remembered where it was, up a narrow flight of stairs from the fourth floor. He* trudged up there with his uncle, coughing on dust. The room itself had floorboards blackened with mold, stacks of old trunks, and a massive desk with a broken leg propped in one corner.

Uncle Arthur set his case down. "Perfect," he said.

Julian didn't see him again until the next night, when hunger must have driven him downstairs. Arthur sat at the dinner table in silence, eating furtively. Emma tried to talk to him that night, and then the next. Eventually even she gave up.

"I don't like him," Drusilla said one day, frowning as he retreated down the hall. "Can't the Clave send us another uncle?"

Julian put his arms around her. "I'm afraid not. He's what we've got."

Arthur became more withdrawn. Sometimes he would speak in snatches of poetry or a few words of Latin; once he asked Julian to pass the salt in Ancient Greek. One night Diana stayed for dinner; after Arthur retired for the night, she took Julian aside.

"Maybe it would be better if he didn't eat with the family," she said quietly. "You could bring him up a tray at night."

Julian nodded. The anger and fear that had been like explosions going off in his head had quieted to the dull throb of disappointment. Uncle Arthur was not going to love his brothers and sisters. He was not going to tuck them into bed and kiss their scraped knees. He was not going to be any help at all.

Julian determined that he would love them twice as fiercely as any adult could. He would do everything for them, he thought, as he went up to the attic one night after his uncle had lived in the Institute for some months. He would make sure they had everything they wanted. He would make sure they never missed what they didn't have; he would love them enough to make up for everything they'd lost.

He shouldered open the door to the attic. For a moment, blinking in disorientation, he thought that the room was empty. That his uncle had gone, or was downstairs, sleeping, as he sometimes did at odd hours.

"Andrew?" The voice came from the floor. There was Uncle Arthur, hunched over, his back against the massive desk. It looked as if he were sitting in a pool of darkness. It took Julian a moment to realize that it was blood—black in the dim light, sticky pools of it everywhere, drying on the floor, gumming together loose pages of paper. Arthur's shirtsleeves were rolled up, his shirt itself liberally splattered with blood. He held a dull knife in his right hand. "Andrew," he said in a slurred voice, rolling his head toward Julian. "Forgive me. I had to do it. I had—too many thoughts. Dreams. Their voices are carried to me on blood, you see. When I spill the blood, I stop hearing them."

Somehow Julian found his voice. "Whose voices?"

"The angels in Heaven above," said Arthur. "And the demons down under the sea." He pressed the pad of a finger to the tip of the knife and watched the blood bead there.

But Julian barely heard him. He was staring down the barrel of the years and the Clave and the Law.

"Lunacy" was what they called it when a Shadowhunter heard voices speak to them that no one else could hear, when they saw things that no one else could see. There were other words, uglier ones, but there was no understanding, no sympathy, and no tolerance. Lunacy was a taint, a sign that your brain had rejected the perfection of the Angel's blood. Those who were considered lunatics were closed up in the Basilias and never allowed out again.

They certainly were not allowed to run Institutes.

It seemed that the matter of not being loved enough was not the ugliest possibility the Blackthorn children had to face after all.

# 20

## LONG AGO

The formal dining room at the Institute was rarely used—the family ate in the kitchen except for the rare instances when Uncle Arthur was with them. The room was hung with framed portraits of Blackthorns, brought from England, their names etched under their images. *Rupert. John. Tristan. Adelaide. Jesse. Tatiana.* They gazed down blankly on a long oak table surrounded by high-backed chairs.

Mark settled himself on the table, glancing around the walls. "I like them," he said. "The portraits. I always have."

"They seem friendly to you?" Emma was leaning against the doorway. The door was cracked partly open, and through it she could see the foyer and Julian talking to his brothers and sisters.

Livvy was gripping her saber and looked furious. Ty, beside her, was blank-faced, but his hands were busy at work, tangling and untangling.

"Tavvy's awake playing upstairs," Drusilla was saying. She was in pajamas, her brown hair mussed. "Hopefully he'll pass out. Usually he can sleep through a war. I mean—"

"That wasn't a war," Julian said. "Though there were some bad moments before Malcolm showed up."

"Julian called Malcolm, huh?" Emma said, turning back into the dining room. "Even though you were here, and Malcolm didn't know you're back?"

"He had to," Mark said, and Emma was struck by how human he sounded. He looked human too, in his jeans and sweater, perched casually on the table. "There were three hundred Followers surrounding the place, and we couldn't call the Conclave."

"He could have asked you to hide," said Emma. There was blood and dirt on her jacket. She flung it over the back of a nearby chair.

"He did," Mark said. "I refused."

"What? Why did you do that?"

Mark said nothing, only looked at her. "Your hand," he said. "It's bleeding."

Emma glanced down. He was right; there was a cut across her knuckles. "It's nothing."

He reached out to take her hand in his, gazing critically at the blood. "I could draw you an *iratze*," he said. "Just because I don't want them on my skin doesn't mean I won't draw them on anyone else."

Emma retracted her hand. "Don't worry about it," she said, returning to peeking into the entryway.

"What about next time?" Ty was asking. "We're going to have to call the Conclave. We can't do this on our own or expect Malcolm always to be there."

"The Conclave can't know," Julian said.

"Jules," Livvy said. "I mean, we all get it, but isn't there some way— I mean, the Conclave would have to understand about Mark—he's our *brother*—"

"I'll handle it," Julian said.

"What if they come back?" Dru said in a small voice.

"Do you trust me?" Julian asked gently. She nodded. "Then don't worry about it. They won't be back."

Emma sighed to herself as Julian sent his siblings upstairs. He stood, watching them go, and then turned toward the dining room. Emma drew away from the door and sat down in one of the high-backed chairs just as Julian came into the room.

The witchlight chandelier above glared down brightly: an unfor-givingly harsh interrogation white. Julian shut the door behind him and leaned against it. His blue-green eyes blazed in his color-less face. When he reached up to push his hair off his forehead, Emma saw that his fingers were bleeding where he had bitten his nails down to the quick.

The quick. She'd learned the term from Diana, watching Julian bite his hands bloody while Ty and Livvy practiced in the training room. "Biting his nails down to the quick won't help him learn to hold a sword," Diana had said, and Emma had gone and looked the term up.

*The quick: the soft, tender flesh underneath the fingernail.*

*Also means "living," as in "the quick and the dead."*

She couldn't help thinking of it as life after that, as if Julian were trying to bite into the bloody matter of his life, to cauterize the messiness somehow. She knew he did it when he was upset and anxious: when Ty was unhappy, when Uncle Arthur had a meeting with the Clave, when Helen called and he told her everything was fine, she and Aline shouldn't worry, and yes, he understood why they couldn't come back from Wrangel Island.

And he was doing it now.

"Julian," said Emma. "You don't have to do this if you don't want to. You don't have to tell us anything—"

"I do, actually," he said. "I need to talk for a little while without being interrupted. After that, I'll answer any questions you have. All right?"

Mark and Emma nodded.

"After the Dark War, it was only because of Uncle Arthur that they let us come back here, to our home," he said. "It was only because we had a guardian that we were allowed to stay together. A guardian who was related to us, not too young or too old, someone willing to promise to look after six children, make sure they were tutored and trained. No one else would have done it except Helen, and she was exiled—"

"And I was gone," Mark said bitterly.

"It wasn't your fault—" Julian stopped, took a deep breath, and shook his head minutely. "If you talk," he said, "if you say anything, I won't be able to get through this."

Mark ducked his chin. "My apologies."

"Even if you hadn't been taken, Mark, you'd have been too young. Only someone over eighteen can run an Institute and be the guardian of children." Julian glanced down at his hands, as if struggling internally, and then looked back up. "The Clave thought Uncle Arthur would be that guardian. So did we. I thought it when he came here, and even for weeks afterward. Maybe months. I don't remember. I know that he never really bothered to try to get to know any of us, but I told myself it didn't matter. I told myself we didn't need a guardian who would love us. Just someone who would keep us together."

His eyes locked with Emma's, and the next words he spoke seemed to be directly to her.

"We loved each other enough, I thought. For it not to matter. Maybe he couldn't show affection, but he could still be a good custodian of the Institute. Then as he came downstairs less and less, and the letters from other Institutes and calls from the Clave went unanswered, I started to realize there was more that was seriously wrong. It was soon after the Cold Peace, and territorial disputes were ripping the city apart, vamps and werewolves and warlocks going after what used to belong to faeries. We were besieged with calls, visits, demands we handle the problem. I'd go up to the attic, bring Arthur his food, beg him to deal with what needed to be done to keep the Clave from stepping in. Because I knew what would happen if they did. We'd no longer have a guardian, and then we'd no longer have a home. And then—"

He took a deep breath.

"They would have sent Emma to the new Academy in Idris. It was what they wanted to do in the first place. They would have sent the rest of us to London, probably. Tavvy was just a baby. They would have placed him with another family. Drusilla too. As for Ty—imagine what they would have done with Ty. The moment he didn't act the way they thought he should, they would have shoved him into the 'dregs' program at the Academy. Separated him from Livvy. It would have killed them both."

Julian paced restlessly up to the portrait of Jesse Blackthorn and stared into his ancestor's green eyes. "So I begged Arthur to respond to the Clave, to do anything that would show that he was the head of the Institute. Letters were piling up. Urgent messages. We didn't have weapons and he wouldn't requisition them. We were running out of seraph blades. I came upstairs one night to ask him—" His voice cracked. "To ask him if he'd sign letters if I wrote them, about the territorial disputes, and I found him on the floor with a knife. He was cutting his skin open, he said, to let the evil out."

He stared steadfastly at the portrait.

"I bandaged him up. But after that I talked to him, and I realized. Uncle Arthur's reality is not our reality. He lives in a dreamworld where sometimes I'm Julian and sometimes I'm my father. He talks to people who aren't there. Oh, there are times when he's clear about who he is and where he is. But they come and go. There are bad periods where he doesn't know any of us for weeks. Then times of clarity where you might imagine he was getting better. But he'll never get better."

"You're saying he's mad," said Mark. "Madness" was the faerie word for it; it was a faerie punishment, in fact, the bringing down of madness, the shattering of someone's mind. "Lunacy" was what Shadowhunters called it. Emma had a sense there were different words for it among mundanes—a faint sense she had from bits and pieces of movies she had seen, books she had read. That there was a less cruel and absolute way to think about those whose minds ran differently than most—whose thoughts gave them pain and fear. But the Clave was cruel and absolute. It was there in the words that described the code by which they lived. *The Law is hard, but it is the Law.*

"Lunatic, I guess the Clave would say," said Julian with a bitter twist to his mouth. "It's amazing that you're still a Shadowhunter if you have a sickness of the body, but apparently not if you have a sickness of the mind. I knew even when I was twelve that if the Clave found out what kind of state Arthur was really in, they'd take the Institute. They'd break up our family and scatter us. And I *would not let that happen.*"

He looked from Mark to Emma, his eyes blazing.

"I had enough of my family taken from me during the war," he said. "We all did. We'd lost so much. Mother, Father, Helen, Mark. They would have torn us apart until we were adults and by then we wouldn't be a family anymore. They were *my* children. Livvy. Ty. Dru. Tavvy. *I* raised them. I became Uncle Arthur. I took the correspondence, I answered it. I did the requisitioning. I drew up the patrol schedules. I never let anyone know Arthur was sick. I said he was eccentric, a genius, hard at work in his attic. The truth was—" He looked away. "When I was younger I hated him. I never wanted him to come out of his attic, but sometimes he had to. The disputes over territory had to be handled in person. There were face-to-face meetings that couldn't be avoided, and no one was going to hold their important summit with a twelve-year-old boy. So I went to Malcolm. He was able to create a drug that I could give to Uncle Arthur. It forced periods of clarity. They only lasted a few hours, and afterward Arthur would have headaches."

Emma thought of the way Arthur had clutched his head after the meeting with the faerie representatives in the Sanctuary. The memory of the agony on his face—she couldn't push it away, though she wanted to.

"Sometimes I'd try to keep him out of the way with other methods," Julian said, his voice full of self-loathing. "Like tonight, Malcolm gave him a sleeping draught. I know it's wrong. Believe me, I've felt like I might go to Hell for it. If there is a Hell. I knew I shouldn't do what I was doing. Malcolm kept quiet, he never told anyone, but I could tell he didn't exactly approve. He wanted me to tell the truth. But the truth would have destroyed our family."

Mark leaned forward. His expression was unreadable. "What about Diana?"

"I never exactly told her," said Julian. "But I think she's guessed at least some of it."

"Why couldn't she have been asked to run the Institute? Instead of it being in the hands of a twelve-year-old boy?"

"I asked her. She said no. She said it was impossible. She was genuinely sorry, and she said she'd help however she could. Diana has—her own secrets." He turned away from the portrait of Jesse. "One last thing. I said I hated Arthur. But that was a long time ago. I don't hate him now. I hate the Clave for what they would do to him, to us, if they knew."

He bent his head. The extraordinarily bright witchlight turned the edges of his hair to gold and the scars on his skin to silver.

"So now you know," he said. His hands tightened on the back of the chair. "If you hate me, I understand. I can't think of anything else I could have done. But I'd understand."

Emma stood up from her chair. "I think we knew," she said. "We didn't know . . . but we knew." She looked at Julian. "We did, didn't we? We knew someone was taking care of everything and that it wasn't Arthur. If we let ourselves believe he ran the Institute, it was because it was easier. It was what we wanted to be true."

Julian closed his eyes. When he opened them again, they were fixed on his brother. "Mark?" he said, and the question was implicit in the single word: *Mark, do you hate me?*

Mark slid off the table. The witchlight turned his pale hair to white. "I have no right to pass judgment upon you, brother. Once I was the elder, but now you are elder than I. When I was in the faerie country, each night I would think of each of you—of you and Helen, of Livvy and Ty and Dru and Tavvy. I gave the stars your names, so that when I saw them wink to light in the sky I felt as if you were with me. It was all I could do to still the fear that you were hurt or dying and that I would never know. But I have come back to a family not just alive and healthy, but whose bonds have not been severed, and that is because of what you have done. There is love here, among you. Such love as takes my breath out of my body. There has even been enough love left for me."

Julian was looking at Mark with hesitant astonishment. Emma tasted tears in the back of her throat. She wanted to go to Julian and put her arms around him, but a thousand things held her back.

"If you want me to tell the others," Julian said hoarsely, "I will."

"Now is not the time to decide," Mark said, and in that single sentence, in the way he looked at Julian now, for the first time since Mark had returned Emma could see a world in which Mark and Julian had been together, had raised their siblings together and come to agreements about what to do together. For the first time, she could see the harmony they had lost. "Not when there are enemies circling us and the Institute, not when our lives and blood are on the line."

"It's a heavy burden to bear, this secret," said Julian, and there was a warning in his tone, but hopefulness as well. Emma's heart ached for the wrongness of all of it: for the painful and desperate choices made by a twelve-year-old boy to keep his family with him. For the darkness that surrounded Arthur Blackthorn, which was not of his making but which if revealed would only find him punished by his own government. For the weight of a thousand lies, told in good faith, because lies told in good faith were still lies. "And if the Followers go through with their threat—"

"But how did they know?" Emma said. "How did they know about Arthur?"

Julian shook his head. "I don't know," he said. "But I think we're going to need to find out."

Cristina watched as Diego, having laid her down on one of the infirmary beds, realized that he couldn't sit beside her with a sword and crossbow attached to him and began awkwardly to remove them.

Diego was rarely awkward. In her memory he was graceful, the more graceful of the two Rocio Rosales brothers, though Jaime was more warlike and more fierce. He hung his crossbow and sword up, then unzipped his dark hoodie and flung it over one of the pegs near the door.

He was facing away from her; through his white T-shirt she could see that he had dozens of new scars, and even more Marks, some of them permanent. A great black rune for Courage in Battle spread down his right shoulder blade, a tendril of it rising above his collar. He looked as if he'd grown broader, his waist, shoulders, and back hard with a new layer of muscle. His hair had grown out, long enough to touch his collar. It brushed against his cheek as he turned to look at her.

She'd been able to fight off her shock at seeing Diego in the whirl of events since she'd seen his face in the alley. But now it was only the two of them, alone in the infirmary, and she was looking at him and seeing the past. The past she'd run away from and tried to forget. It was there in the way he pulled out the chair beside her bed and leaned over to carefully unlace her boots, pull them away, and roll up the left leg of her pants. It was there in the way his lashes brushed his cheeks when he concentrated, running the point of his stele over her leg beside the wound, circling it in healing runes. It was there in the freckle at the corner of his mouth and the way he frowned as he sat back and surveyed his rune work critically. "Cristina," he said. "Is it better?"

The pain had eased. She nodded, and he sat back, his stele in his hand. He was gripping it tightly enough that the old scar across the back of his hand stood out whitely, and she remembered the same scar and his fingers unbuttoning his shirt in her bedroom in San Miguel de Allende, while the bells of the *parroquia* rang out through the windows.

"It's better," she said.

"Good." He put the stele away. *"Tenemos que hablar."*

"In English, please," she said. "I am trying to keep up my practice."

An irritated look passed across his face. "You don't need the practice. Your English is perfect, as mine is."

"Modest as always."

His smile flashed out. "I've missed you giving me a hard time."

"Diego . . ." She shook her head. "You shouldn't be here. And you shouldn't say you miss me."

His face was all sharp lines: pronounced cheekbones and jaw and temples. Only his mouth was soft, the corners turned down now in unhappiness. She remembered the first time she had ever kissed him, in the Institute garden, then pushed the recollection away viciously.

"But it is the truth," he said. "Cristina, why did you run away like that? Why didn't you answer any of my messages or calls?"

She held up a hand. "You first," she said. "What are you doing in Los Angeles?"

He rested his chin on his folded arms. "After you left, I couldn't stay. Everything reminded me of you. I was on leave from the Scholomance. We were going to spend the summer together. Then you were gone. One minute you were in my life, and then you were ripped out of it. I was lost. I went back to study but I thought only of you."

"You had Jaime," she said in a hard voice.

"No one *has* Jaime," he said. "You think he didn't panic when you left? The two of you were supposed to be *parabatai*."

"I think he'll live." Cristina could hear her own voice, cold and small; it seemed to have frozen down to a tiny sliver of ice.

He was silent for a moment. "Reports were coming through to the Scholomance from L.A.," he said. "Flares of necromantic magic. Your friend Emma's efforts to investigate the deaths of her parents. The Clave thought she was making a fuss about nothing, that it was clear Sebastian had killed her parents but she wouldn't accept it. I thought she might be right, though. I came out here to look into it, and my first day, I went to the Shadow Market. Look, it's a long story—I found my way to Wells's house—"

"Where you decided it was a good idea to shoot a fellow Nephilim with a crossbow?"

"I didn't know they were Shadowhunters! I thought they were murderers— I wasn't shooting to kill—"

"*No manches*," Cristina said bluntly. "You should have stayed and told them you were Nephilim. Those arrows were poisoned. Julian nearly died."

"I gathered that." Diego looked rueful. "The arrows weren't poisoned by me. If I'd had any idea, I would have stayed. The weapons I bought at the Shadow Market must have been tainted without my knowing."

"Well, what were you doing buying weapons there anyway? Why didn't you come to the Institute?" Cristina demanded.

"I did," Diego said, flattening her with surprise. "I came looking for Arthur Blackthorn. I found him in the Sanctuary. I tried to tell him who I was, why I was here. He told me the damnation of the Blackthorns was their own private business, that they didn't want any interference, and that if I knew what was good for me I'd get out of town before everything burned."

"He said that?" Cristina sat up in astonishment.

"I realized I wasn't welcome here. I thought, even, that the Blackthorns might be involved in the necromancy somehow."

"They would never—!"

"Well, you can say that. You know them. I didn't know them. All I knew was that the head of the Institute had told me to go away, but I couldn't because *you* were here. Maybe in danger, maybe even in danger from the Blackthorns. I had to get weapons at the Market because I was afraid that if I went to any of the usual weapons caches it would be found out that I was still here. Look, Cristina, I am not a liar—"

"You don't *lie?*" Cristina demanded. "You want to know why I left home, Diego? In May we were in San Miguel de Allende. I'd gone to the Jardín, and when I came back, you and Jaime were sitting up on the terrace. I was coming through the courtyard; I could hear your voices very clearly. You didn't know I was there."

Diego looked puzzled. "I don't . . ."

"I heard him talking to you about how the wrong branch of the Rosales family was in power. It should have been you. He was talking about the plan he had. Surely you remember. The one where you would marry me, and he would become my *parabatai*, and together you would use your influence over me and my mother to eject her from her position as head of the D.F. Institute, and then you would take over. He said you had the easy job, marrying me, because you could leave me someday. Becoming *parabatai* means you're stuck with them forever. I remember him saying that."

"Cristina . . ." Diego had gone pale. "That's why you left that night. It wasn't because your mother was sick and needed you at the Institute in the city."

"I was the one who was sick," Cristina spat. "You broke my heart, Diego, you and your brother. I don't know what's worse, losing your best friend or losing the boy you're in love with, but I can tell you that it was like you both died for me that day. That's why I don't pick up your calls or messages. You don't take calls from a dead boy."

"And what about Jaime?" Something flared in his eyes. "What about his calls?"

"He never has called," said Cristina, and almost took pleasure in the look of shock on his face. "Maybe he has better sense than you."

"Jaime? *Jaime?*" Diego was on his feet now. A vein in his temple throbbed. "I remember that day, Cristina. Jaime was drunk and he was babbling. Did you hear me say anything or did you only hear him?"

Cristina forced herself to think back. In memory it seemed like a cacophony of voices. But . . . "I only heard Jaime," she said. "I didn't hear you say a word. Not to defend me. Not to say anything."

"There was no point talking to Jaime when he was like that," Diego said bitterly. "I let him talk. I shouldn't have. I had no interest in his plan. I loved you. I wanted to go far away with you. He is my brother, but he is— He was born with something missing, I think, some piece of his heart where compassion lives."

"He was going to be my *parabatai*," said Cristina. "I was going to be tied to him forever. And you weren't going to say anything to me? Do anything to stop it?"

"I was," Diego protested. "Jaime had planned to go to Idris. I was waiting for him to leave. I needed to speak to you when he wasn't there."

She shook her head. "You shouldn't have waited."

"Cristina." He came toward her, his hands outstretched. "Please, if you don't believe anything else, believe me that I have always loved you. Do you really think I have lied to you since we were children? Since the first time I ever kissed you and you ran away laughing? I was ten years old—do you really think that was some kind of plan?"

She didn't reach for his hands. "But Jaime," she said. "I've known him just as long. He was always my friend. But he wasn't, was he? He said things no friend would say, and you knew he was using me, and you said not a word."

"I was going to tell you—"

"Intentions are nothing," Cristina said. She had thought she would feel some relief, finally telling Diego why she hated him, finally unburdening the knowledge of what she had heard. Finally severing the thread. But it didn't feel severed. She could feel the bond connecting them, as she had when she'd blacked out in the crashing car outside the Institute and woken up with Diego holding her. He'd been whispering in her ear that she would be all right, that she was his Cristina, she was strong. And it had felt for a moment as if the past months had been a dream, and she was home.

"I must stay here," Diego said. "These killings, the Followers, they are too important. I am a Centurion; I cannot abandon a mission. But I do not need to remain at the Institute. If you want me to go away, I will."

Cristina opened her mouth. But before she could speak, her phone buzzed. It was a message from Emma. STOP MAKING OUT WITH PERFECT DIEGO AND GET TO THE COMPUTER ROOM, WE NEED YOU.

Cristina rolled her eyes and shoved the phone back in her pocket. "We'd better go."

# 21

## A WIND BLEW

The sky outside the Institute had turned the color of what was very late night or very early morning, depending on your point of view. It had always reminded Julian of blue cellophane or watercolor: the intense blue of evening turned translucent by the imminent arrival of the sun.

The inhabitants of the Institute—all but Arthur, who slept on soundly in his attic—had gathered in the computer room. Ty had brought papers and books from the library, and the others were going through them. Tavvy was curled up asleep in the corner. Piles of empty pizza boxes from Nightshade's were stacked on the table. Emma didn't even remember them being delivered, but most of them had been eaten. Mark was busy glaring at Cristina and Diego, though Diego didn't seem to notice. He didn't seem to notice Drusilla staring at him with saucer eyes either. He didn't notice much, Julian thought uncharitably. Maybe being ridiculously good-looking was more time-consuming than it seemed.

Emma had finished telling the story of the way she and Cristina had tracked down Sterling and the things he had told them on the car ride home. Ty had been taking notes with a pencil, a second pencil stuck behind his ear. His black hair was ruffled up like a cat's fur. Julian remembered when Ty had been young enough that he could reach out and smooth down his younger brother's hair when it got too messy. Something in him ached at the recollection.

"So," Ty said now, turning to Diego and Cristina, who was sitting beside Diego. She was barefoot, one of her pant legs rolled up and her calf bound with bandages. Every once in a while she would shoot Diego a look out of the corner of her eye that was half suspicion, half relief—that he'd helped her? That he was there at all? Julian wasn't sure. "You're a Centurion?"

"I studied at the Scholomance," said Diego. "I was the youngest aspirant ever to become a Centurion."

Everyone looked impressed except Mark. Even Ty. "That's like being a detective, isn't it?" he said. "You investigate for the Clave?"

"That is one of the things we do," said Diego. "We stand outside the Law that precludes Shadowhunters from involving themselves in issues that relate to faeries."

"The Clave can make that exception for any Shadowhunter, though, in exigent cases," said Julian. "Why was Diana told we couldn't investigate? Why did they send you?"

"It was judged that your family, with your connection to the Fair Folk, would not be able to objectively investigate a series of murders where some of the victims were faeries."

"That is entirely unreasonable," Mark said, his eyes flashing.

"Is it?" Diego glanced around. "From all I have heard and seen, you appear to have mounted a secret investigation into this issue, telling the Clave nothing about it. You have compiled evidence that you have not shared. You have discovered a murderous cult operating in secret. . . ."

"You make it sound so shady," Emma said. "So far all you've done is show up in L.A. and shoot another Shadowhunter."

Diego glanced over at Julian. "It's mostly healed," Julian said. "Mostly."

"I bet you didn't report that to the Scholomance," said Emma. "Did you, Perfect Diego?"

"I have reported nothing to the Scholomance," Diego said. "Not since I found out Cristina was involved in this as well. I would never hurt her."

Cristina blushed furiously.

"You're a Centurion," Ty said. "You have vows—"

"Vows of friendship and love are stronger," said Diego.

Drusilla looked at him with cartoon hearts in her eyes. "That's beautiful."

Mark rolled his eyes. He was clearly not a member of the Perfect Diego Appreciation Society.

"That's very touching," said Emma. "Now talk. What do you know?"

Julian glanced at her. She seemed like Emma, ordinary Emma, sharp and encouraging and tough and normal. She even smiled at him quickly before turning her attention back to Diego. Julian listened, half his brain recording Diego's story. The other half was in chaos.

For the past five years he had walked a narrow rockway above the ocean, falling away sheer on either side to a boiling cauldron. He had kept his balance by keeping his secrets.

Mark had forgiven him. But it wasn't just Mark he'd lied to. Lying to your *parabatai* . . . It wasn't forbidden, but most *parabatai* didn't. They didn't need or want to conceal things. That he'd concealed so much from Emma must have shocked her. He gazed at her face covertly, trying to read the signs of shock or anger. But he could tell nothing; her face was maddeningly unreadable as Diego launched into his story.

When Diego explained that he had come to the Institute when he arrived in Los Angeles, and that Uncle Arthur had chased him off, telling him he didn't want non-Blackthorns interfering in Blackthorn problems, Livvy raised a questioning hand. "Why would he do that?" she said. "Uncle Arthur doesn't like strangers, but he's not a liar."

Emma glanced away from her. Julian felt his stomach tighten. His secrets, still a burden.

"A lot of Shadowhunters of the older generation don't trust Centurions," he said. "The Scholomance was closed in 1872, and Centurions no longer trained. You know how adults are about things they didn't grow up with."

Livvy shrugged, looking mildly placated. Ty was scribbling in his notebook. "Where did you go after that, Diego?"

"He met Johnny Rook," said Cristina. "And Rook tipped him off about the Sepulchre, just like he did with Emma."

"I went there immediately," Diego said. "I'd been waiting days in the alleys behind the bar." His eyes flicked to Cristina. Julian wondered with a sort of distant cynicism if it was as obvious to everyone else as it was to him that Diego had done everything he did because of Cristina—that if he hadn't been in a panic over her welfare, it was unlikely he would have rushed to the Sepulchre and spent days watching the place to see what would happen. "Then I heard a girl screaming."

Emma sat up straight. "We didn't hear that."

"I think it was before you arrived," said Diego. "I followed the sound and saw a group of Followers, including Belinda—though I didn't know who they were then—attacking a girl. Slapping her, spitting on her. There were chalk protective circles drawn on the ground. I saw that symbol—the lines of water under the sign for fire. I had seen it at the Market. An old, old sign for resurgence."

"Resurgence," echoed Ty. "Necromancy?"

Diego nodded. "I fought off the Followers, but the girl got away. Ran to her car."

"That was Ava?" Emma guessed.

"Yes. She saw me and raced off. I followed her to her house, managed to convince her to tell me everything she knew about the Midnight Theater, the Followers, the Lottery. It wasn't much, but I learned that she had been chosen by the Lottery. That she had been the one who killed Stanley Wells, knowing that if she didn't, she would be tortured and killed herself."

"She told you everything?" Livvy said in amazement. "But they're sworn to secrecy."

He shrugged. "I don't know why she took me into her confidence—"

"Seriously, dude?" Emma said. "Do you not own any mirrors?"

"Emma!" hissed Cristina.

"She'd murdered him a few days before. She was already torn apart by guilt. She'd shown up in the alley because she wanted to see his body. She said an odd thing about the chalk circles—that they were useless, there to mislead. Very little she was saying made sense." He frowned. "I told her I would protect her. I slept on her porch. The next day she demanded I leave. She said she wished to be with the Guardian and the other Followers. That it was her place. She insisted I go, so I went. I returned to the Market, bought weaponry from Johnny Rook. When I came back to Ava's that night, she was dead. She had been choked and drowned in the pool, her hand sliced off."

"I don't understand what's going on with the hands," said Emma. "Ava was missing one hand and was killed; Belinda was missing a hand but they let her live, and she cut off both Sterling's hands after he died."

"Maybe they're proof to the Guardian that someone's dead," said Livvy. "Like the Huntsman bringing back Snow White's heart in a box."

"Or maybe they're part of the spell," said Diego, with a frown. "Ava and Belinda were missing their dominant hands—perhaps

Belinda didn't know which was Sterling's, so she took both."

"A piece of the killer to go with the sacrifice?" Julian said. "We're going to need to dig more deeply into the necromancy section of the library."

"Yes," said Diego. "I wished I had access to your library after I found Ava Leigh dead. I had failed in my duty to protect a mundane who needed my help. I swore I would find out who had done it. I waited on her roof—"

"Yeah, we know what happened," Julian said. "I'll remember it every time I have a twinge in my side during cold weather."

Diego inclined his head. "I'm very sorry about that."

"I want to know what happened next," Ty said, still scribbling away in his elegant, incomprehensible handwriting. Julian had always thought it looked like cat footprints dancing across a page. His slim, long fingers already had pencil lead on them. "You found out Sterling was the next one chosen and followed him?"

"Yes," Diego said. "And I saw you were trying to protect him. I didn't understand why. I am sorry, but after what Arthur said to me, I suspected you all. I knew I should turn you in to the Clave, but I couldn't do it." He looked at Cristina, and then away. "I was outside the bar tonight hoping to stop Sterling, but I admit I also wanted your side of the story. Now I have it. I am glad I was wrong about your involvement."

"You should be," muttered Mark.

Diego sat back. "So maybe now you tell me what you know. It would only be fair."

Julian was relieved when Mark took point on the summary. He was scrupulous about the details, even the bargain with the faeries over his own fate, and the results of his presence at the Institute.

"Blackthorn blood," Diego said thoughtfully when Mark was done. "That is interesting. I would have guessed the Carstairs had more relevance to these spells, given the deaths five years ago."

"Emma's parents, you mean," said Julian. He remembered them, their laughing eyes and their love for Emma. They could never be just "the deaths" to him.

Out of the corner of his eye, he saw Tavvy slide off the armchair where he'd been curled up. Quietly he went to the door and slipped out. He must be exhausted; he'd probably been waiting for Julian to put him to bed. Julian felt a pang for his smallest brother, so often trapped in rooms full of older people talking about blood and death.

"Yes," said Diego. "One of the questions I have had has been the fact that they were killed five years ago, and then there were no more killings until this last year. Why such a gap in time?"

"We thought maybe the spell required it," Livvy said, and yawned. She looked exhausted, dark shadows under her eyes. They all did.

"That is another thing: In the car, Sterling said it didn't matter what kind of creature they killed, human or faerie—even Nephilim, if we count the Carstairs murders."

Cristina said, "He said they couldn't murder werewolves or warlocks—"

"I imagine they were staying away from creatures protected by the Accords," said Julian. "It would have drawn attention. Our attention."

"Yes," said Diego. "But otherwise, for it not to matter what kind of victim they chose? Human or faerie, male or female, old or young? Sacrificial magic requires commonalities among the victims—all those with the Sight, all virgins, or all with a certain type of blood. Here it seems random."

Ty was looking at Diego with open admiration. "The Scholomance sounds so cool," he said. "I had no idea they let you learn so much about spells and magic."

Diego smiled. Drusilla looked as if she might fall over. Livvy looked as if she'd be impressed if she wasn't so tired. And Mark looked even more annoyed.

"Can I see the photos of the convergence?" said Diego. "It sounds very significant. I am impressed you found it."

"It was surrounded by Mantid demons when we went, so we have pictures of the inside but not the outside," Mark said as Ty went to get the photos. "As for the demons, Emma and I took care of them."

He winked at Emma. She smiled, and Julian felt that short, sharp jab of jealousy that came whenever Mark flirted with Emma. He knew it didn't mean anything. Mark flirted in that way that faeries did, with a sort of courtly humor that had no real weight behind it.

But Mark could flirt with Emma if he wanted. He had a choice, and faeries were notoriously fickle . . . and if Mark was interested, then he, Julian, had no right or reason to object. He should support his brother—wouldn't he be lucky, after all, if his brother and *parabatai* fell in love? Didn't people dream about the people who they loved loving one another?

Diego raised an eyebrow at Mark but said nothing as Tiberius spread the pictures out on the coffee table.

"It's energy magic," said Ty. "We know that much."

"Yes," said Diego. "Energy can be stored, especially death energy, and used later in necromancy. But we don't know what someone would need all that energy for."

"For a summoning spell," said Livvy, and yawned again. "That's what Malcolm said, anyway."

A small crease appeared between Diego's brows. "It is unlikely to be a summoning spell," he said. "Death energy allows you to do death magic. This magician is trying to bring back someone from the dead."

"But who?" said Ty, after a pause. "Someone powerful?"

"No," said Drusilla. "He's trying to bring back Annabel. Annabel Lee."

Everyone looked surprised that Dru had spoken—so surprised that she seemed to shrink back into herself a little. Diego, though, gave her an encouraging smile.

"The—the poem's written on the inside of the convergence cave, right?" she went on, looking around worriedly. "And everyone was trying to figure out if it was a code or a spell, but what if it's just a reminder? This person—the magician—they lost someone they loved, and they're trying to bring her back."

"Someone so mad to get back their lost love that they founded a cult, killed more than a dozen people, created that cave at the convergence, etched that poem on the wall, created a Portal to the ocean . . . ?" Livvy sounded dubious.

"I would do it," Dru said, "if it was someone I really loved. It might not even have been a girlfriend—maybe a mother or a sister or whatever. I mean, you'd do it for Emma, right, Jules? If she died?"

The black horror that was the thought of Emma dying rose against the backs of Julian's eyes. He said, "Don't be morbid, Dru," in a voice that sounded very distant to his own ears.

"Julian?" Emma said. "Are you all right?"

Thankfully he didn't need to answer. A solemn voice spoke from the doorway. "Dru is right," Tavvy said.

He hadn't gone to sleep after all. He stood by the door, wide-eyed, brown hair tousled. He had always been small for his age, and his eyes were big blue-green saucers in his pale face. He was holding something behind his back.

"Tavvy," Julian said. "Tavs, what have you got there?"

Tavvy drew his hand from behind his back. He was carrying a book—a child's book, oversize, with an illustrated cover. The title was printed in gold foil. *A Treasury of Tales for Nephilim.*

A Shadowhunter children's book. There were such things,

though not many of them. The printing presses in Idris were small.

"Where did you get that?" Emma asked, honestly curious. She'd had something like it as a child, but it had been lost with many of her parents' things in the chaos after the war.

"Great-Aunt Marjorie gave it to me," Tavvy said. "I like most of the stories. The one about the first *parabatai* is good, but some of them are sad and scary, like the one about Tobias Herondale. And the one about Lady Midnight is the saddest."

"Lady what?" said Cristina, leaning forward.

"Midnight," said Tavvy. "Like the theater you went to. I heard Mark say the rhyme and I just remembered I read it before."

"You read it before?" Mark echoed incredulously. "When did you see that faerie rhyme, Octavian?"

Tavvy opened the book. "There was a Shadowhunter lady," he said. "She fell in love with someone she wasn't supposed to be in love with. Her parents trapped her in an iron castle, and he couldn't get in. She died of sadness, so the man who loved her went to the King of the faeries and asked if there was a way to bring her back. He said there was a rhyme.

'First the flame and then the flood:
In the end, it's Blackthorn blood.
Seek thou to forget what's past
First thirteen and then the last.
Search not the book of angels gray,
Red or white will lead you far astray.
To regain what you have lost,
Find the black book at any cost.'"

"So what happened?" said Emma. "To the man who went to Faerie?"

"He ate and drank faerie food," said Tavvy. "He was trapped

there. The legend is that the sound of the waves crashing on the beach is his cries for her to return."

Julian exhaled. "How did we not find this?"

"Because it's a children's book," said Emma. "It wouldn't have been in the library."

"That's dumb," said Tavvy serenely. "It's a good book."

"But why?" Julian said. "Why Blackthorn blood?"

"Because she was a Blackthorn," said Tavvy. "Lady Midnight. They called her that because she had long black hair, but she had the same eyes as the rest of us. Look."

He turned the book around to show a haunting illustration. A woman whose jet-black hair spilled over her shoulders reached out for the retreating figure of a man, her eyes wide—and blue-green as the sea.

Livvy gave a little gasp, reaching for the book. Hesitantly, Tavvy let her have it.

"Don't tear the pages," he warned.

"So this is the full rhyme," she said. "*This* is what's written on the bodies."

"It's instructions," Mark said. "If the rhyme is a true faerie rhyme, then for the right person, it is a clear list of instructions. How to bring back the dead—not just any dead, but her. This Blackthorn woman."

"Thirteen," said Emma. Despite her exhaustion, her heart was racing with excitement. She met Cristina's eyes across the room.

"Yes," Cristina breathed. "What Sterling said—after we caught him, after he'd killed the girl. He said she was the thirteenth."

Emma said, "'First thirteen and then the last.' He's killed thirteen. He's got one last one to go and then he's done. He'll have enough magic to bring back Lady Midnight."

"So there'll be one more," said Julian. "One that might be different from the last."

"There must be more instructions than this," said Ty. "No one could figure out exactly how to complete this spell just from this rhyme." He looked around, a flicker of uncertainty in his gray eyes. The look he got very rarely, but sometimes, when he thought that there was something in the world that everyone understood but him. "Could they?"

"No," Mark said. "But the rhyme tells you where to look for the rest of the instructions. 'Search not the book of angels gray'—the answer is not in the Gray Book. Nor is it in the Book of the White or in the Red Texts."

"It is in the Black Volume of the Dead," said Diego. "I have heard of that book, in the Scholomance."

"What is it?" said Emma. "Are there copies? Is it something we could get hold of?"

Diego shook his head. "It is a book of very dark magic. Almost legendary. Even warlocks are forbidden to own it. If there are copies, I do not know where. But we should set ourselves to find out, tomorrow."

"Yeah," Livvy said, her voice blurry with sleep. "Tomorrow."

"Do you need to go to bed, Livvy?" Julian asked. It was a rhetorical question: Livvy was drooping like a wilted dandelion. At his words, though, she forced herself bolt upright.

"No, I'm fine, I could stay up—"

Ty's face changed subtly as he looked at his twin sister. "I'm exhausted," he said. "I think we should all go to sleep. In the morning we'll be able to concentrate better."

Julian doubted Ty was actually tired at all: When he was engaged in a puzzle, he could stay up for days at a time. But Livvy nodded gratefully at the words.

"You're right," she said. She slid off the chair she was sitting on and picked up Tavvy, handing him back his book. "Come on," she said. "You should definitely be in bed."

"I helped, though, didn't I?" Tavvy asked as his sister carried him toward the door. He was looking over at Julian as he said it, and Julian remembered himself as a child, looking toward Andrew Blackthorn that way. A boy looking to his father, seeking approval.

"You didn't *just* help," said Julian. "I think you may have solved it, Tavs."

"Yay," said Tavvy sleepily, and put his head down on Livvy's shoulder.

The others soon followed Ty and Livvy to bed, but Emma found she couldn't sleep. She found herself, instead, sitting on the front steps of the Institute before the sun rose.

She was in flip-flops, a tank top, and pajama bottoms. The air coming off the ocean was chilly, but she didn't feel it. She was staring at the water.

From every angle of the steps you could see the ocean: blue-black in the rising morning now, like ink, raked with swells of white foam where the waves broke far out to sea. The moon had shrunk and cast an angular shadow across the water. A blue-and-silver dawn.

She remembered the spilling cold of that blue ocean all around her. The taste of salt water and demon blood. The feeling that the water was pressing her down, crushing her bones.

And the worst part, the fear that once her parents had felt the same pain, the same panic.

She thought of Julian then. The way he had looked in the dining room. The strain in his voice as he'd stood there telling her and Mark everything he'd done for the past five years.

"Emma?"

Emma half-turned and saw Perfect Diego coming down the steps. He looked immaculate, despite the night they'd had, even his boots polished. His dark brown hair was thick and fell charmingly over one of his eyes. He looked a bit like a prince in a fairy-tale book.

She thought of Julian again. His untidy hair, his bitten nails, his dusty boots, the paint on his hands.

"Hey, Perfect Diego," she said.

"I wish you wouldn't call me that."

"You wish in vain," Emma said. "Where are you going? Is Cristina all right?"

"She's asleep." Perfect Diego looked out at the ocean. "It's very beautiful here. You must find it peaceful."

"And *you* must be kidding."

He flashed a fairly perfect smile. "You know, when there aren't murders happening and small armies surrounding the place."

"Where are you going?" Emma asked again. "It's practically dawn."

"I know the cave will not be open, but I am going to the convergence site to see it for myself. The demons should have disbanded by now. I want to take another look around the area, see if there is anything you missed."

"You are just bursting with tact, aren't you?" Emma said. "Fine. Go ahead. See what we all missed while we were nearly being cut to pieces by giant grasshopper demons."

"Mantids aren't technically grasshoppers—"

Emma glared. Diego shrugged and jogged to the foot of the steps. He paused there and looked back over his shoulder at her.

"Does anyone else in the Clave know about your investigation?" he said. "Anyone but your family?"

"Just Diana," said Emma.

"Diana is your tutor?" When Emma nodded, he frowned. "Weren't Jace Herondale and the Lightwoods betrayed by their own tutor?"

"She'd never betray us," Emma said, outraged. "Not to the Clave or to anyone else. Hodge Starkweather was different."

"Different how?"

"Starkweather wasn't Diana. He was a minion of Valentine's. Diana is a good person."

"So where is she now?" Diego asked. "I'd like to meet her."

Emma hesitated. "She . . ."

"She's in Thailand," said a voice from behind them. It was Julian. He'd shrugged on a hooded army jacket over his jeans and T-shirt. "There was a witch there she wanted to question about energy spells. Someone she knew when she was younger." He paused. "We can trust her."

Diego inclined his head. "I didn't mean to imply otherwise."

Julian leaned against one of the pillars, and he and Emma watched as Diego strode away across the trampled grass and headed down the road. The moon had disappeared entirely and the eastern sky was beginning to turn pink.

"What are you doing out here?" Julian said finally in a quiet voice.

"I couldn't sleep," said Emma.

Julian had his head tipped back, as if he were bathing in the dim illumination of the dawn. The strange light made him into something else, someone made out of marble and silver, someone whose inky curls clung to his temples and neck like the acanthus leaves in Greek art.

He wasn't perfect, like Diego, but to Emma, there had never been anyone more beautiful.

"We're going to have to talk about this eventually," she said. "What you told me and Mark."

"I know." He looked down at his long legs, the frayed hems of his jeans, his boots. "I had hoped—I suppose I'd hoped it would never happen, or that at least we'd be adults when it did."

"So let's be adults about it. Why didn't you tell me before?"

"Do you think I liked keeping secrets from you? Do you think I didn't want to tell you?"

"If you'd wanted to, you could have."

"No, I couldn't." He spoke with a quiet despair.

"Did you not trust me? Did you think I'd tell on you?"

Julian shook his head. "That wasn't it." Enough light had spread over the landscape for the color of his eyes to be visible despite the darkness. They looked like artificially illuminated water.

Emma thought of the night Julian's mother had died. She had been ill, attended by Silent Brothers to the end. There were some diseases even Nephilim magic couldn't cure: She had cancer of the bone, and it had killed her.

Andrew Blackthorn, newly widowed, had been too devastated to be the one to go to Tavvy when the baby cried in the night. Helen had been efficient: heating Tavvy's bottles, changing him, dressing him. But Julian had been the one who stayed with him during the day. While Mark and Helen trained, Julian sat in Tavvy's room and sketched or painted. Emma would sit with him there sometimes, and they would play the way they normally did, with the baby gurgling in his crib a few feet away.

At the time Emma hadn't thought much of it. She, like Julian, had been only ten years old. But she recalled it now.

"I remember when your mother died," she said. "And you took care of Tavvy during the days. I asked you why, and I remember what you said. Do you?"

"I said it was because no one else could," said Julian, looking at her quizzically. "Mark and Helen had to train. . . . My father was . . . well, you know how he was."

"Everything you've done is because no one else would or could do it. If you hadn't covered up for Arthur, no one else would even have thought of it. If you hadn't been so determined to hold everything together, no one else would have. Maybe it started back then, when you took care of Tavvy. Maybe it gave you the idea."

He exhaled. "Maybe. I don't entirely know myself."

"I still wish you'd told me. I know you thought you were being unselfish—"

"I didn't," he said.

She looked at him in surprise.

"I did it for entirely selfish reasons," he said. "You were my escape, Emma. You were my way away from everything terrible. When I was with you, I was happy."

Emma stood up. "But that can't have been the only time you were happy—"

"Of course I'm happy with my family," he said. "But I'm responsible for them—I was never responsible for you—we're responsible for each other; that's what *parabatai* means, don't you understand, Emma, you're the only one, the only one who was ever meant to look after *me*."

"Then I failed you," she said, feeling a bone-deep sense of disappointment with herself. "I should have known what you were going through, and I didn't—"

"Don't ever say that again!" He shoved himself away from the pillar, the rising sun, behind him, turning the edges of his hair to copper. Emma couldn't see his expression, but she knew it was furious.

Emma got to her feet. "What, that I should have known? I should have—"

"That you failed me," he said hotly. "If you knew—you've been all that's kept me going, for weeks sometimes, months. Even when I was in England, thinking of you kept me going. It's why I had to be *parabatai* with you—it was completely selfish—I wanted to tie you to me, no matter what, even though I knew it was a bad idea, even though I knew I—"

He broke off, a look of horror flashing across his face.

"Even though what?" Emma demanded. Her heart was pounding. "Even though what, Julian?"

He shook his head. Her hair had escaped from its ponytail and the wind was whipping it around her face, bright pale strands on the wind. He reached up to tuck one behind her ear: He looked like someone caught in a dream, trying to wake up. "It doesn't matter," he said.

"Do you love me?" Her voice was a whisper.

He wound a piece of her hair around his finger, a silver-gold ring. "What's the difference?" he asked. "It won't change anything if I do."

"It changes things," she whispered. "It changes everything for me."

"Emma," he said. "You'd better go back inside. Go to sleep. We both should. . . ."

She gritted her teeth. "If you're going to walk away from me now, you'll have to do it yourself."

He hesitated. She saw the tension in him, in his body, rise like a wave about to break.

"Walk away from me," she said harshly. "*Walk away.*"

His tension crested and fell; something in him seemed to collapse, water breaking against rocks. "I can't," he said, his voice low and broken, "God, I can't," and he half-closed his eyes, bringing up his other hand to cradle her face. His hands slid into her hair, and he drew her toward him. She inhaled a breath of cold air and then his mouth was on hers and her senses exploded.

She had wondered, in the back of her mind, if what had happened on the beach between them had been a fluke born of their shared adrenaline. Surely kisses weren't meant to be like that, so all-encompassing that they ripped through you like lightning, tore down your defenses and decimated your self-control.

Apparently not.

Her hands fisted in the material of Julian's jacket, dragging him toward her, closer, closer. There was sugar and caffeine on his lips.

He tasted like energy. Her hands slid up under his shirt, touching the bare skin of his back, and he broke away from her to suck in his breath. His eyes were closed, his lips parted.

"Emma," he breathed, and the desire in his voice tore a scorching path through her. When he reached for her, she almost fell against him. He swiveled her body around, pushing her back against a pillar, his body a strong, hot line against hers—

A sound cut through the fog in her mind.

Emma and Julian tore apart, staring.

Both of them had been in the Hall of Accords in Idris when the Wild Hunt had come, howling around the walls, tearing at the ceiling. Emma remembered the sound of Gwyn's horn, blasting through the air. Vibrating every nerve in her body. A high, hollow, lonesome sound.

It came again now, echoing through the morning.

The sun had risen while Emma had been wrapped up in Julian, and the road that led down to the highway was illuminated by sunlight. There were three figures coming up it, on horseback: one black horse, one white, and one gray.

Emma recognized two of the riders immediately: Kieran, sitting his horse like a dancer, his hair nearly black in the sunlight, and next to him, Iarlath, wrapped in dark robes.

The third rider was familiar to Emma from a hundred illustrations in books. He was a big, broad man, bearded, wearing dark armor that looked like the overlapping bark of a tree. He had tucked his horn under his arm; it was a massive object, etched all over with a pattern of deer.

Gwyn the Hunter, the leader of the Wild Hunt, had come to the Institute. And he did not look pleased.

# 22

## THOSE WHO WERE OLDER

**Mark stood at an upstairs window and looked out at the sun** rising over the desert. The mountains seemed cut out of dark paper, sharp and distinct against the sky. For a moment he imagined he could reach out and touch them, that he could fly from this window and reach the top of the highest peak.

The moment passed, and once again he saw the distance between himself and the mountains. Ever since he had returned to the Institute, he had felt as if he were struggling to see everything through a thin layer of glamour. Sometimes he saw the Institute as it was, sometimes it faded from view and instead he saw a bare landscape and the fires of the Wild Hunt burning in small encampments.

Sometimes he turned to say something to Kieran only to discover that he wasn't there. Kieran had been there every morning that Mark had woken up for years of Faerie time.

Kieran had been meant to come and see him the night Mark had watched the children in the kitchen. But he'd never come. There'd been no communication from him, either, and Mark was worried now. He told himself that the faerie prince was probably just being cautious, but he found his hand straying to the arrowhead at his throat more often than usual.

It was a gesture that reminded him of Cristina, the way she touched the medallion at her throat when she was nervous. Cristina. He wondered what had passed between her and Diego.

Mark turned away from the window just as the sound came. His hearing had been sharpened by years in the Hunt; he doubted anyone else in the Institute would have heard it or been awakened.

It was a single note, the sound of Gwyn the Hunter's horn: sharp and harsh, as lonely as mountains. Mark's blood went cold. It was not a greeting or even a call to the Hunt. It was the note Gwyn blew when they were searching out a deserter. It was the sound of betrayal.

Julian had straightened up, raking his hands through his tangled curls, his jaw set. "Emma," he said. "Go back inside."

Emma turned and strode back into the Institute—only long enough to seize up Cortana from where it hung beside the door. She stalked back outside to find that the faerie convoy had dismounted their horses, who remained unnaturally still, as if tied in place. Their eyes were blood red, their manes wound with red flowers. *Faerie steeds.*

Gwyn had approached the foot of the steps. He had a strange face, slightly alien: wide eyes, broad cheekbones, wicked eyebrows. One black eye, and one that was pale blue.

Beside him came Iarlath, his yellow eyes unblinking. And at his other side, Kieran. He was as beautiful as Emma had remembered him, and looked as cold. His pale face was as severely cut as white marble, his black and silver eyes uncanny in the daylight.

"What's going on?" Emma demanded. "Has something happened?"

Gwyn glanced at her dismissively. "This is none of your affair, Carstairs girl," he said. "This matter concerns Mark Blackthorn. None of the rest of you."

Julian crossed his arms over his chest. "Anything that concerns my brother concerns me. In fact, it concerns all of us."

Kieran's mouth set into a hard, uncompromising line. "We are Gwyn and Kieran of the Wild Hunt, and Iarlath of the Unseelie Court, here on a matter of justice. And you *will* fetch your brother."

Emma moved to stand in the center of the top step, unsheathing Cortana, which sent bright sparks skittering into the air. "Don't tell him what to do," she said. "Not here. Not on the steps of the Institute."

Gwyn gave an unexpected, rumbling laugh. "Don't be a fool, Carstairs girl," he said. "No single Shadowhunter can hold off three of the Fair Folk, not even armed with one of the Great Swords."

"I wouldn't underestimate Emma," said Julian in a voice like razor wire. "Or you'll find your head lying on the ground next to your still-twitching body."

"How graphic," said Iarlath, amused.

"I'm here," said a breathless voice behind them, and Emma half-closed her eyes, fear going through her like pain.

Mark.

It looked as if he had thrown on jeans and a sweater in a hurry, and jammed his feet into sneakers. His blond hair was ruffled and he looked younger than he usually did, his eyes wide with surprise and undefended astonishment.

"But my time isn't up," Mark said. He was speaking to Gwyn but looking at Kieran. There was an expression on his face—one Emma couldn't interpret or describe, one that seemed to mix pleading and pain and gladness. "We're still trying to find out what's going on. We're nearly there. But the deadline—"

"*Deadline?*" Kieran echoed. "Listen to you. You sound like one of them."

Mark looked surprised. "But, Kieran—"

"Mark Blackthorn," said Iarlath. "You stand accused of sharing one of the secrets of Faerie with a Shadowhunter, despite being expressly forbidden to do so."

Mark let the door of the Institute fall shut behind him. He took several steps forward, until he was standing beside Julian. He clasped his hands behind his back; they were shaking. "I—I don't know what you mean," he said. "I haven't told my family anything forbidden."

"Not your family," said Kieran, an ugly twist to his voice. "*Her.*"

"Her?" Julian said, looking at Emma, but she shook her head.

"Not me," she said. "He means Cristina."

"You didn't expect us to leave you unobserved, did you, Mark?" Kieran said. His black and silver eyes were like etched daggers. "I was outside the window when I heard you speaking with her. You told her how Gwyn could be deprived of his powers. A secret known only to the Hunt, and forbidden to repeat."

Mark had turned the color of ashes. "I didn't—"

"There is no point lying," said Iarlath. "Kieran is a prince of Faerie and cannot speak untruths. If he says he overheard this, then he did."

Mark shifted his gaze to Kieran. The sunlight no longer seemed beautiful to Emma, but merciless, beating down on Mark's gold hair and skin. Hurt spread across his face like the stain of red from a slap. "It would never mean anything to Cristina. She would never tell anyone. She would never hurt me or the Hunt."

Kieran turned his face away, his beautiful mouth twisting at the corner. "Enough."

Mark took a step forward. "Kieran," he said. "How can you do this? To me?"

Kieran's face was bleak with pain. "Mine is not the betrayal," he said. "Speak to your Shadowhunter princess of promises broken."

"Gwyn." Mark turned to plead with the Hunt's leader. "What is between myself and Kieran is not a matter for the law of the Courts or the Hunt. Since when did they interfere in matters of the heart?"

*Matters of the heart.* Emma could see it on both their faces, Mark's and Kieran's, in the way they looked at each other and the way they didn't. She wondered how she had missed it before, in the Sanctuary, that these were two people who loved each other. Two people who had hurt each other the way only two people in love could.

Kieran looked at Mark as if Mark had taken something irreplaceably precious from him. And Mark looked—

Mark looked crushed. Emma thought of herself on the beach, in the morning, with Julian, and the lonely screech of the gulls circling overhead.

"Child," said Gwyn, and to Emma's surprise, there was gentleness in his voice. "I regret the necessity of this visit more than I can say. And believe me, the Hunt does not interfere, as you say, in matters of the heart. But you broke one of the oldest laws of the Hunt, and put every member of it into danger."

"Exactly," said Kieran. "Mark has broken the law of Faerie, and for that, he must return to Faerie with us and tarry no longer in the human world."

"No," said Iarlath. "That is not the punishment."

"What?" Kieran turned to him, puzzled. His hair flared at the edges with blue and white like hoarfrost. "But you said—"

"I said nothing to you of punishments, princeling," said Iarlath, stepping forward. "You told me of Mark Blackthorn's actions and I said they would be duly dealt with. If you believed that meant he would be dragged back to Faerie to be your companion, then perhaps you should remember that the security of the gentry of Faerie is more paramount than the fancies of a son of the Unseelie King." He looked hard at Mark, his eyes eerie in the bright sunlight. "The King has given me leave to choose your punishment," he said. "It will be twenty whip-lashes across the back, and count yourself lucky it is not more."

"*NO!*" The word was like an explosion. To Emma's surprise it was Julian—Julian, who never raised his voice. Julian, who never shouted. He started down the steps; Emma followed him, Cortana ready in her hand.

Kieran and Mark were silent, looking at each other. The rest of the blood had left Kieran's face and he looked sick. He didn't move as Julian stepped forward, blocking Kieran's view of Mark.

"If any of you touch my brother to harm him," Julian said, "I will kill you."

Gwyn shook his head. "Do not think I do not admire your spirit, Blackthorn," he said. "But I would think twice before moving to harm a convoy of Faerie."

"Move to prevent this, and our agreement will be at an end," said Iarlath. "The investigation will stop, and we will take Mark back with us to Faerie. And he will be whipped there, and worse than any whipping he could receive here. You will win nothing and lose much."

Julian's hands tightened into fists. "You think you alone understand honor? You who cannot understand what we might lose by standing here and letting you humiliate and torture Mark? This is why faeries are despised—this senseless cruelty."

"Careful, boy," rumbled Gwyn. "You have your Laws and we have ours. The difference is only that we do not pretend ours are not cruel."

"The Law is hard," said Iarlath with amusement, "but it is the Law."

Mark spoke for the first time since Iarlath had pronounced his sentence. "A bad law is no law," he said. He looked dazed. Emma thought of the boy who had collapsed in the Sanctuary, who had screamed when he was touched and spoken of beatings that still clearly terrified him. She felt as if her heart was being ripped out— to whip Mark, of all people? Mark, whose body might heal but whose soul would never recover?

"You came to us," Julian said. There was desperation in his voice. "You came to us—you made a bargain with us. You needed our help. We have put everything on the line, risked everything, to solve this. Fine, Mark made a mistake, but this loyalty test is misplaced."

"It is not about loyalty," said Iarlath. "It is about setting an example. These are the laws. This is how it works. If we let Mark betray us, others will learn we are weak." His look was pleased. Greedy. "The bargain is important. But this is more important."

Mark moved forward then, catching at Julian's shoulder. "You can't change it, little brother," he said. "Let it happen." He looked at Iarlath, and then at Gwyn. He didn't look at Kieran. "I will take the punishment."

Emma heard Iarlath laugh. It was a cold, sharp sound like cracking icicles. He reached into his cloak and pulled out a handful of blood-red stones. He threw them to the ground. Mark, clearly familiar with what Iarlath was doing, blanched.

At the spot on the ground where Iarlath had thrown his stones, something had begun to grow. A tree, bent and gnarled and twisted, its bark and leaves the color of blood. Mark watched it in horrified fascination. Kieran looked as if he was going to throw up.

"Jules," Emma whispered. It was the first time she had called him that since the night on the beach.

Julian stared blindly at Emma for a moment before turning and lurching the rest of the way down the steps. After a frozen moment Emma followed him. Iarlath moved immediately to block her way.

"Put your sword away," he snarled. "No weapons in the presence of the Fair Folk. We know well you cannot be trusted with them."

Emma whipped Cortana up so fast that the blade was a blur. The tip of it sailed beneath Iarlath's chin, a millimeter from his skin, describing the arc of a deadly smile. He made a noise in his throat even as she slammed the sword into the sheath on her back with enough force to be audible. She stared at him, eyes blazing with rage.

Gwyn chuckled. "And here I thought all the Carstairs were good for was music."

Iarlath gave Emma a filthy look before whirling away and stalking toward Mark. He had begun unwinding a coil of rope from where it was tied at his waist. "Put your hands on the trunk of the quickbeam," he said. Emma assumed he meant the dark, twisted tree with its sharp branches and blood-colored leaves.

"No." Kieran, sounding desperate, whirled fluidly toward Iarlath. He dropped to the ground, kneeling, his hands outstretched. "I beg you," he said. "As a prince of the Unseelie Court, I beg you. Do not hurt Mark. Do what you will with me, instead."

Iarlath snorted. "Whipping you would incur your father's wrath. This will not. Get to your feet, child-prince. Do not shame yourself further."

Kieran staggered upright. "Please," he said, looking not at Iarlath, but at Mark.

Mark gave him a look full of so much searing hate Emma nearly recoiled. Kieran looked, if possible, even sicker.

"You should have forseen this, whelp," said Iarlath, but his gaze wasn't on Kieran—it was on Mark, hungry, full of appetite, as if the thought of a whipping drew him like the thought of food. Mark reached out toward the tree—

Julian stepped forward. "Whip me instead," he said.

For a moment everyone froze. Emma felt as if a baseball bat had slammed into her chest. "No," she tried to say, but the word wouldn't come.

Mark whirled around to face his brother. "You can't," he said. "Mine is the crime. Mine must be the punishment."

Julian stepped past Mark, almost pushing him aside in his

determination to present himself in front of Gwyn. He stood with his back straight and chin up. "In a faerie battle, one can pick a champion to represent them," he said. "If I could stand in for my brother in a fight, why not now?"

"Because I'm the one who broke the law!" Mark looked desperate.

"My brother was taken at the beginning of the Dark War," Julian said. "He never fought in the battle. His hands are clean of faerie blood. Whereas I was in Alicante. I killed Fair Folk."

"He's goading you," Mark said. "He doesn't mean it—"

"I do mean it," said Julian. "It is the truth."

"If someone volunteers to take the place of a condemned man, we cannot gainsay it." Gwyn's look was troubled. "Are you sure, Julian Blackthorn? This is not your punishment to take."

Julian inclined his head. "I'm sure."

"Let him take the whipping," Kieran said. "He wants it. Let him have it."

After that, things happened very quickly. Mark threw himself at Kieran, his expression murderous. He was shouting as he dug his fingers into the front of Kieran's shirt. Emma moved forward and was knocked back by Gwyn, who moved to pull Kieran and Mark apart, pushing Mark brutally aside.

"Bastard," Mark said. His mouth was bleeding. He spit at Kieran's feet. "You arrogant—"

"Enough, Mark," snapped Gwyn. "Kieran is a prince of the Unseelie Court."

"He is my enemy," said Mark. "Now and forevermore, my enemy." He raised a hand as if to strike Kieran; Kieran didn't move, just looked at him with shattered eyes. Mark lowered his hand and turned away, as if he couldn't bear to look at Kieran any longer. "Jules," he said instead. "Julian, please, don't do this. Let me."

Julian gave his brother a slow, sweet smile. In that smile was all the love and wonder of the little boy who'd lost his brother and against all odds, gotten him back. "It can't be you, Mark—"

"Take him," Iarlath said to Gwyn, and Gwyn, reluctance written all over his face, stepped forward and caught hold of Mark, pulling him away from Julian. Mark struggled, but Gwyn was a massive man with enormous arms. He held tightly to Mark, his expression impassive, as Julian reached down and pulled off his jacket, and then his shirt.

In the bright daylight his skin, lightly tanned but paler over his back and chest, looked vulnerable and exposed. His hair was ruffled all over from the collar of the shirt, and as he dropped it on the ground he looked at Emma.

His look broke through the icy vise of shock that gripped her. "Julian." Her voice shook. "You can't do this." She moved forward and found Iarlath blocking her way.

"Stay," Iarlath hissed. He stepped away from Emma, who went to go after him and found her legs pinned in place. She couldn't move. The buzz of enchantment prickled along her legs and spine, holding her as firmly in place as a bear trap. She tried to wrench herself forward and had to bite back a shriek of pain as the faerie magic clamped and tore at her skin.

Julian took a step forward and put his hands against the tree, bending his head. The long line of his spine was incongruously beautiful to Emma. It looked like the arch of a wave, just before it crashed. White scars and black Marks patterned his back like a child's illustration drawn in skin and blood.

"Let me go!" Mark shouted, twisting in Gwyn's grasp.

It was like a nightmare, Emma thought, one of those dreams where you were running and running and never getting anywhere, except now it was real. She was struggling to move her arms and legs against the invisible force that kept her pinned like a butterfly to a board.

Iarlath strode toward Julian. Something flashed in his hand, something long and thin and silver. As it flicked forward, tasting the air, Emma saw he was clutching the black handle of a silver whip. He drew his arm back.

"Foolish Shadowhunters," he said. "Too naive to even know who you can trust."

The whip came down. Emma saw it bite into Julian's skin, saw the blood, saw him arch back, his body bowing.

Pain exploded inside her. It was as if a bar of fire had been laid across her back. She flinched, tasting blood inside her mouth.

"Stop it!" Mark yelled. "Can't you see you're hurting them both? *That's not the punishment!* Let me go, I don't have a *parabatai*, let me go, whip me instead—"

His words ran together inside Emma's head. Pain was still throbbing through her body.

Gwyn, Iarlath, and Kieran were looking from her to Julian. There was a long, bloody welt along Julian's back, and he was clutching the trunk of the tree. Sweat darkened his hairline.

Emma's heart cracked. If what she had felt had been agony, what had *he* felt? Twice, four times as much?

"Send her away," she heard Iarlath say irritably. "This wailing is ridiculous."

"This is not hysterics, Iarlath," said Kieran. "It's because she's his *parabatai*. His warrior partner—they're bonded—"

"By the Lady, such fuss," Iarlath hissed, and brought the whip down again.

This time Julian made noise. A choked sound, barely audible. He slid to his knees, still clutching at the tree. Pain lanced through Emma again, but now she was braced, prepared. She screamed—not just any scream, but an echoing sound of horror and betrayal, a shriek of rage and pain and fury.

Gwyn threw his arm out toward Iarlath, but he was looking at Emma. "Stop," he said.

Emma felt the weight of his gaze, and then a lightness as the enchantment that had pinned her in place snapped asunder.

She dashed toward Julian and dropped down beside him, yanking her stele from her belt. She could hear Iarlath protest, and Gwyn telling him gruffly to leave it be. She paid no attention. All she could see was Julian—Julian on his knees, his arms around the trunk of the tree, his forehead pressed to it. Blood ran down his naked back. The muscles in his shoulders flexed as she reached for him, as if he were bracing himself for a third blow.

*Jules*, she thought, and as if he heard her, he half-turned his face. He had bitten through his lower lip. Blood dripped off his chin. He looked at her blindly, like a man staring at a mirage.

"Em?" he gasped.

"Shush," she said, putting her hand against his cheek, her fingers in his hair. He was wet with blood and sweat, his pupils blown wide open. She could see herself in them, see her pale, strained face.

She laid her stele against his skin. "I need to heal him," she said. "Let me heal him."

"This is ridiculous," Iarlath protested. "The boy should take the whipping—"

"Leave it, Iarlath," said Gwyn. His arms were tight around Mark.

Iarlath subsided, muttering—Mark was struggling and gasping—the stele was cold in Emma's hand—colder still as she brought it down against Julian's skin—

She drew the rune.

"Sleep, my love," she whispered, so low that only Julian could hear her. For a moment his eyes fluttered wide, clear and astonished. Then they shut, and he slumped to the ground.

"*Emma!*" Mark's voice was a shout. "What have you done?"

Emma rose to her feet, turning to see Iarlath's face, blazing with rage. Gwyn, though—she thought she caught a flash of amusement in his eyes.

"I knocked him out," she said. "He's unconscious. Nothing you can do will wake him."

Iarlath's lip curled. "You think to deprive us of our punishment by depriving him of his ability to feel it? Are you such a fool?" He turned toward Gwyn. "Bring Mark forward," he snarled. "We will whip him instead, and then we will have whipped two Blackthorns."

"No!" Kieran cried. "No! I forbid it—I cannot bear it—"

"No one cares what you can bear, princeling, least of all I," said Iarlath. His smile was twisted. "Yes, we will whip both brothers," he said. "Mark will not escape. And I doubt your *parabatai* will soon forgive you for it," he added, turning back to Emma.

"Instead of whipping two Blackthorns," she said, "you can whip a Carstairs. Wouldn't that be better?"

Gwyn hadn't moved at Iarlath's order; now his eyes widened. Kieran drew in his breath.

"Julian told you he killed faeries during the Dark War," she said. "But I have killed many more. I cut their throats; I wet my fingers with their blood. I'd do it again."

"Silence!" Rage filled Iarlath's voice. "How dare you brag of such things?"

She reached down and yanked up her shirt. Mark's eyes widened as she dropped it to the ground. She was standing in front of all of them in just her bra and jeans. She didn't care. She didn't feel naked—she felt clothed in rage and fury, like a warrior from one of Arthur's tales.

"Whip me," she said. "Agree to it and this will end here. Otherwise I swear I will hunt you through the lands of Faerie unto eternity. Mark can't, but I can."

Iarlath said something exasperated in a language Emma didn't know, turning to look at the ocean. Kieran moved forward as he did so, toward Julian's crumpled form.

"Don't you touch him!" Mark yelled, but Kieran didn't look at him, just slid his hands under Julian's arms and drew him away from the tree. He laid him down a few feet away, removing his own long tunic to wrap it around Jules's unconscious, bleeding body.

Emma expelled a breath of relief. The sun felt hot on her naked back. "Do it," she said. "Unless you are too cowardly to whip a girl."

"Emma, stop," said Mark. His voice was full of a terrible ache. "Let it be me."

Iarlath's eyes had brightened with a cruel light. "Very well, Carstairs," he said. "Do as your *parabatai* did. Ready yourself for the whip."

Emma saw Gwyn's expression turn to one of sadness as she moved toward the tree. The bark, up close, was smooth and dark red-brown. It felt cool to the touch as she slid her arms around it. She could see the individual cracks in the bark.

She gripped the wood with her hands. She heard Mark call her name again, but it seemed to be coming from very far away. Iarlath moved to stand behind her.

The whip whistled as he raised it. She closed her eyes. In the darkness behind her eyelids, she saw Julian, and fire around him. Fire in the chambers of the Silent City. She heard his voice whisper the words, those old words from the Bible, taken and remade by Shadowhunters to form the *parabatai* oath.

*Whither thou goest, I will go—*

The whip came down. If she had thought she felt pain before, it was agony now. Her back felt as if it were being opened up by fire. She ground her teeth together to silence her scream.

*Entreat me not to leave thee—*

Again. The pain was worse this time. Her fingers bit into the wood of the tree.

*Or to return from following after thee—*

Again. She slid to her knees.

*The Angel do so to me, and more also, if aught but death part thee and me.*

Again. The pain rose up like a wave, blotting out the sun. She screamed, but she couldn't hear herself—her ears were stoppered, the world crumpling, folding in on itself. The whip came down a fifth time, a sixth, a seventh, but now she barely felt it as the darkness swallowed her.

# 23

## TO LOVE AND BE LOVED

**Cristina came out of Emma's bedroom looking somber.**

Mark caught a glimpse of the room before the door closed behind her: He saw Emma's still form, looking small beneath a pile of heavy covers, and Julian sitting on the bed beside her. His brother's head was bent, his dark hair falling to cover his face.

Mark had never seen him so miserable.

"Is she all right?" he asked Cristina. They were alone in the corridor. Most of the kids were still asleep.

Mark didn't want to remember his brother's face when Julian had woken up near the quickbeam and seen Mark kneeling over Emma's body, her stele in his hand, drawing healing runes on her lacerated skin with the shaking, unpracticed hand of someone long unused to the language of angels.

He didn't want to remember the way Julian had looked when they'd come inside, Mark carrying Cortana and Julian with Emma in his arms, her blood all over his shirt, her hair matted with it. He didn't want to remember the way Emma had screamed when the whip came down, and the way she'd stopped screaming when she collapsed.

He didn't want to remember Kieran's face as Mark and Julian

had raced back toward the Institute. Kieran had tried to stop Mark, had put his hand on his arm. His face had been bleached and pleading, his hair a riot of black and despairing blue.

Mark had shaken off his grip. "Touch me again with your hand and you will see it parted from your wrist forever," he had snarled, and Gwyn had pulled Kieran away from him, speaking to him in a voice that was equal parts sternness and regret.

"Let him be, Kieran," he said. "Enough has been done here this day."

They'd carried Emma into her bedroom, and Julian had helped lay her down on the bed while Mark had gone to get Cristina.

Cristina hadn't screamed when he'd awoken her, or even when she'd seen Emma in her torn and blood-soaked clothes. She had gone to work helping them: She'd put Emma into clean, dry clothes, had retrieved bandages for Jules, had washed the blood from Emma's hair.

"She will be all right," Cristina said now. "She will heal."

Mark didn't want to remember the way Emma's skin had opened as the whip had come down, or the sound the whip made. The smell of blood mixing with the salt of the ocean air.

"Mark." Cristina touched his face. He turned his cheek into her palm, involuntarily. She smelled like coffee and bandages. He wondered if Julian had told her everything—of Kieran's suspicions of her, of Mark's inability to protect his brother or Emma.

Her skin was soft against his; her eyes, upturned, were wide and dark. Mark thought of Kieran's eyes, like fragments of the glass inside a kaleidoscope, shattered and polychromatic. Cristina's were steady. Singular.

She brought her hand down the side of his jaw, her expression thoughtful. Mark felt as if his whole body were tightening into a knot.

"Mark?" It was Julian's voice, low, from the other side of the door.

"You should go in to your brother." Cristina lowered her hand, brushing his shoulder once, reassuringly. "This is not your fault," she said. "It is not. You understand?"

Mark nodded, unable to speak.

"I will wake the children and tell them," she said, and set off down the hall, her stride as purposeful as if she were in gear, though she was wearing a T-shirt and pajama bottoms.

Mark took a deep breath and pushed open the door to Emma's bedroom.

Emma lay unmoving, her pale hair spread out over the pillow, her chest rising and falling with steady breaths. They had used sleep runes on her, as well as runes to kill pain, stop blood loss, and heal.

Julian was still sitting beside her. Her hand was limp on the blanket; Julian had moved his own hand close to hers, their fingers interlocking but not touching. His head was turned away from Mark's; Mark could only see the hunched set of his shoulders, the way the vulnerable curve of the nape of his neck looked like the curve of Emma's back as the whip came down.

He seemed very young.

"I tried," Mark said. "I tried to take the lashes. Gwyn wouldn't allow it."

"I know. I saw you try," Julian said in a flat voice. "But Emma's killed faeries. You haven't. They wouldn't have wanted to whip you, once they had the chance to whip her. It didn't matter what you did."

Mark cursed himself silently. He had no idea what the human words were with which he could comfort his brother.

"If she died," Julian went on in the same flat voice, "I would want to die. I know that's not healthy. But it's the truth."

"She won't die," Mark said. "She's going to be fine. She just needs to recover. I have seen what men—what people—look like when they're going to die. There is a look that comes over them. This is not it."

"I can't help wondering," said Julian. "This whole business. Someone's trying to bring back the person they loved, a person who died. It feels almost wrong. As if maybe we should let them."

"Jules," Mark said. He could feel the jagged edges of his little brother's emotions, like the touch of a razor on skin long covered by bandages. This was what it meant to be family, he thought. To hurt when someone else hurt. To want to protect them. "They're taking lives. You can't pay for tragedy with more tragedy, or draw life from death."

"I just know that if it were her, if it were Emma, I would do the same thing." Julian's eyes were haunted. "I would do whatever I had to."

"You wouldn't." Mark put his hand on Julian's shoulder, pulling him around. Julian moved reluctantly to face his brother. "You would do the right thing. All your life, you've done the right thing."

"I'm sorry," Julian said.

"*You're* sorry? All of this, Jules, the convoy— If I hadn't told Cristina about Gwyn's cloak—"

"They would have found something else to punish you with," said Julian. "Kieran wanted to hurt you. You hurt him, so he wanted to hurt you. I'm sorry—sorry about Kieran, because I can see you cared about him. I'm sorry I didn't know you'd left anyone you cared about behind. I'm sorry that for years I thought you were the one who had freedom, that you were enjoying yourself in Faerie while I killed myself here trying to raise four kids and run the Institute and keep Arthur's secrets. I wanted to believe you were okay—I wanted to believe one of us was okay. So much."

"You wanted to believe I was happy, just as I wanted to believe the same about you," Mark said. "I had thought about whether you were happy, thriving, living. I had never stopped to wonder what kind of man you might have grown up to be." He paused. "I am proud of you. I have had little hand in the shaping of you, but I am proud nonetheless to call you my brother—to call all of you my brothers and sisters. And I will not leave you again."

Julian's eyes widened, their color Blackthorn bright in the gloom. "You won't go back to Faerie?"

"No matter what happens," Mark said, "I will stay here. I will always, always stay here."

He put his arms around Julian and held him tightly. Julian exhaled, as if he were letting go of something heavy that he had carried for a long time, and leaning on Mark's shoulder, he let his older brother bear just a little of his weight.

Emma dreamed about her parents.

They were in the small white-painted Venice house they had lived in when she was a child. She could see the faint glimmer of the canals from the window. Her mother sat at the kitchen island, a cloth spread out in front of her. On the cloth lay an array of knives, sorted from smallest to largest. The largest was Cortana, and Emma gazed at it hungrily, drinking in the smooth goldness, the sharp glow of the blade.

Compared to the brilliance of the weapon, her mother seemed a shadow. Her hair glowed, and her hands, as she worked, but the edges of her were indistinct, and Emma was terrified that if she reached for her mother she would disappear.

Music rose around them. Emma's father, John, came into the kitchen, his violin tucked against his shoulder. Usually he played with a shoulder rest but not now. The violin poured forth music like water and—

*The sharp crack of a whip, pain like fire.*

Emma gasped. Her mother lifted her head.

"Is something wrong, Emma?"

"I—no, nothing." She turned toward her father. "Keep playing, Dad."

Her father gave his gentle smile. "You sure you don't want to try?"

Emma shook her head. Whenever she touched bow to strings, it made the sound of a strangled cat.

"Music is in the blood of the Carstairs," he said. "This violin once belonged to Jem Carstairs."

Jem, Emma thought. Jem, who had helped her through her *parabatai* ceremony with gentle hands and a thoughtful smile. Jem, who had given her his cat to watch over her.

*Pain that went through skin like a blade. Cristina's voice saying, "Emma, oh, Emma, why did they hurt you so much?"*

Her mother lifted Cortana. "Emma, I'm sure you're a thousand miles away."

"Maybe not quite that far." Her father lowered his bow.

*"Emma." It was Mark's voice. "Emma, come back. For Julian, please. Come back."*

"Trust him," said John Carstairs. "He will come to you, and he will need your help. Trust James Carstairs."

"But he said he had to go, Papa." Emma had not called her father Papa since she was very small. "He said there was something he was looking for."

"He is about to find it," said John Carstairs. "And then there will be yet more for you to do."

*"Jules, come have something to eat—"*

*"Not now, Livvy. I need to stay with her."*

"But, Papa," Emma whispered. "Papa, you're dead."

John Carstairs smiled sadly. "As long as there is love and memory, there is no true death," he said.

He put bow to strings and began to play again. Music rose up, swirling around the kitchen like smoke.

Emma stood up from the kitchen chair. The sky was darkening outside, the setting sun reflected in the canal water. "I have to go."

"Oh, Em." Her mother came around the kitchen island toward her. She was carrying Cortana. "I know."

*Shadows moved across the inside of her mind. Someone was holding her hand so tightly it hurt.* "Emma, please," *said the voice she loved the most in the world.* "Emma, come back."

Emma's mother placed the sword in her hands. "Steel and temper, daughter," she said. "And remember that a blade made by Wayland the Smith can cut anything."

"Go back." Her father kissed her on the forehead. "Go back, Emma, to where you are needed."

"Mama," she whispered. "Papa."

She tightened her grip on the sword. The kitchen whirled away from her, folding up like an envelope. Her mother and father disappeared into it, like words written long ago.

*"Cortana,"* Emma gasped.

She thrashed upward and cried out in pain. Sheets were tangled around her waist. She was in bed, in her room. The lamps were on but dimly lit, the window cracked open slightly. The table next to the bed was piled with bandages and folded towels. The room smelled of blood and burning.

"Emma?" An incredulous voice. Cristina was sitting at the foot of the bed, a roll of bandages and some scissors in her hand. She dropped them to the floor as she saw that Emma's eyes were open, and flung herself onto the bed. "Oh, Emma!"

She threw her arms around Emma's shoulders, and for a moment, Emma clung to her. She wondered if this was what it was like to have an older sister, someone who could be your friend and also take care of you.

"Ouch," Emma said meekly. "It hurts."

Cristina pulled back. Her eyes were red-rimmed. "Emma, are you all right? Do you remember everything that happened?"

Emma put a hand to her head. Her throat hurt. She wondered if it was from screaming. She hoped not. She hadn't wanted to give Iarlath the satisfaction. "I . . . how long have I been passed out?"

"Out? Oh, asleep. Since this morning. All day, really. Julian has been in here with you the whole time. I finally convinced him to eat something. He'll be horrified that you woke up and he wasn't here." Cristina pushed Emma's tangled hair back.

"I should get up. . . . I should see . . . Is everyone all right? Did anything happen?" Her mind suddenly full of awful images of the faeries, done with her, going after Mark or Julian or somehow, even, the children, Emma tried to swing her legs over the side of the bed.

"Nothing has happened." Cristina pushed her back gently. "You are tired and weak; you need food and runes. A whipping like that . . . You can whip someone to *death*, you know that, Emma?"

"Yes," Emma whispered. "Will my back be scarred forever?"

"Probably," Cristina said. "But it won't be bad—the *iratzes* closed the wounds quickly. They couldn't quite heal them all. There will be marks, but they will be light." Her eyes were red. "Emma, why did you do it? Why? You really think your body is so much stronger than Mark's or Julian's?"

"No," Emma said. "I think everyone is strong and weak in different ways. There are things I'm terrified of that Mark isn't. Like the ocean. But he's been tortured enough—what it would have done to him, I don't even know. And Julian . . . I felt it when they whipped him. In my body, in my heart. It was the worst feeling I've ever felt, Cristina. I would have done anything to stop it. It was selfish."

"It was *not* selfish." Cristina caught Emma's hand and squeezed it. "I have thought now for a while that I would never want a *parabatai*," she said. "But I would feel differently, I think, if that *parabatai* could have been you."

*I wish you were my* parabatai, *too,* Emma thought, but she couldn't say it—it felt disloyal to Julian, despite everything.

Instead she said, "I love you, Cristina," and squeezed the other girl's hand back. "But the investigation—I should go with you—"

"To where? The library? Everyone has been reading and searching all day for more information about Lady Midnight. We will find something, but we have plenty of people to look at pages."

"There are other things to do besides look at pages—"

The door opened, and Julian was on the threshold. His eyes widened and for a moment they were all Emma could see, like blue-green doors to another world.

"Emma." His voice sounded rough and cracked. He was wearing jeans and a loose white shirt and beneath it the outline of a bandage, wrapping around his chest, was visible. His eyes were red, his hair tousled, and there was a faint sprinkling of stubble along his chin and cheeks. Julian never went without shaving, ever since the first time he'd shown up with stubble and Ty had told him, without preamble, "I don't like it."

"Julian," Emma said, "are you all ri—"

But Julian had thrown himself across the room. Without seeming to see anything but Emma, he dropped to his knees and flung his arms around her, burying his face against her stomach.

She reached down with a shaking hand and stroked his curls, raising her eyes in alarm to meet Cristina's. But Cristina was already rising to her feet, murmuring that she would tell the others that Julian was looking after Emma. Emma heard the lock click as she closed the bedroom door behind her.

"Julian," Emma murmured, her hand tangling in his hair. He wasn't moving; he was entirely still. He breathed in shakily before lifting his head.

"By the Angel, Emma," he said in a cracked whisper. "Why did you do it?"

She winced, and he was suddenly on his feet. "You need more healing runes," he said. "Of course, I'm so stupid, of course you need them." It was true: She did hurt. Some places ached dully, others with a sharper pain. Emma breathed in as Diana had taught her—slowly, steadily—as he retrieved his stele.

He dropped down on the bed beside her. "Hold still," he said, and put the instrument to her skin. She felt the pain ebb until it was a dull ache.

"How long—when did you wake up?" Emma asked.

He was in the act of putting his stele back on the table. "If you mean did I see them whip you, no," he said grimly. "What do you remember?"

"I remember Gwyn and the others came . . . Iarlath . . . Kieran." She thought of blazing-hot sun, a tree with bark the color of blood. Black and silver eyes. "Kieran and Mark love each other."

"They did," Julian said. "I'm not sure how Mark feels about him now."

She drew in a ragged breath. "I dropped Cortana—"

"Mark brought it inside," he said in a voice that indicated that Cortana was the last thing on his mind. "God, Emma, when I came back to consciousness the convoy was gone and you were on the ground, bleeding, and Mark was trying to lift you up and I thought you were *dead*," he said, and there was not a trace of remoteness in his voice, just a fierce wildness she had never really associated with Julian before. "They whipped *you*, Emma, *you* took the whipping meant for Mark and for me. I hate that you did that, you understand, I hate it—" Emotion crackled and burned in his voice, like a fire raging out of control. "How could you?"

"Mark couldn't have stood the whipping," she said. "It would have broken him. And I couldn't have borne watching them whip you. It would have broken me."

"You think I don't feel the same way?" he demanded. "You think

I haven't been sitting here all day totally shattered and ripped apart? I'd rather cut my arm off than have you lose a fingernail, Emma."

"It wasn't just about you," she said. "The kids— Look, they expect me to fight, to get hurt. They think: There's Emma, scratched up again, cut up and bandaged. But you, they look to you in a way they don't look to me. If you were seriously hurt, it would scare them so badly. And I couldn't stand thinking of them so scared."

Julian's fingers tightened into a hard spiral. She could see the pulse running under his skin. She thought, randomly, of some graffiti she had seen on the side of the Malibu Pier: *Your heart is a weapon the size of your fist.*

"God, Emma," he said. "What I've done to you."

"They're my family too," she said. Emotion was threatening to choke her. She bit it back.

"Sometimes I wish—I've wished—that we were married and they were our kids," he said rapidly. His head was bowed.

"Married?" Emma echoed, shocked.

His head came up. His eyes were burning. "Why do you think that I—"

"Love me less than I love you?" she said. He flinched visibly at the words. "Because you said so. I as much as told you on the beach how I felt, and you said 'not that way, Emma.'"

"I didn't—"

"I'm tired of lying to each other," said Emma. "Do you understand? I'm sick of it, Julian."

He scrubbed his hands through his hair. "I can't see any way for this to be all right," he said. "I can't see anything but a nightmare where everything falls apart, and where I don't have you."

"You don't have me now," she said. "Not in the way that matters. The truthful way." She tried to kneel up on the bed. Her back ached, and her arms and legs felt tired, as if she had run and climbed for miles.

Julian's eyes darkened. "Does it still hurt?" He fumbled among the items on the nightstand, came up with a vial. "Malcolm made me this a while ago. Drink it."

The vial was full of a chartreuse-gold liquid. It tasted a little like flat champagne. The moment Emma swallowed it, she felt a numbness sweep over her. The ache in her limbs receded, and a cool, flowing energy replaced it.

Julian took the vial from her and dropped it onto the bed. He slid one arm under her knees, the other under her shoulders, and lifted her bodily off the bed. For a moment she clung to him in surprise. She could feel his heart beating, smell his soap and paint and cloves scent. His hair was soft against her cheek.

"What are you doing?" she said.

"I need you to come with me." His voice was tight, as if he were screwing his courage up to do something horrible. "I need you to see something."

"You make it sound like you're a serial killer with a freezer full of arms," Emma muttered as he shouldered open the door.

"The Clave would probably be happier about that."

Emma wanted to rub her cheek against his, feel the roughness of his stubble. He was entirely a mess, actually, his shirt on inside out and his feet bare. She felt a rush of affection and wanting so intense that her whole body tightened.

"You can put me down," she said. "I'm fine. I don't need to be princess-carried."

He laughed, a short, choked laugh. "I didn't know that was a verb," he said, but he set her on her feet. Carefully and slowly, and they leaned into each other, as if neither of them could stand the fact that in a moment, they would no longer be touching.

Emma's heart began to pound. It pounded as she followed Julian down the empty corridor, and it pounded as they started up the back staircase and went into his studio. It pounded as she leaned against the paint-covered island, and Julian went to take a key from a drawer by the window.

She saw him breathe in, his shoulders rising. He looked the way he had when he was steeling himself to be whipped.

Having gathered his courage, he went to the door of the locked room, the one that no one but him ever entered. He turned the key in the lock with a decisive click and the door sprang open.

He stood aside. "Go in," he said.

Years of ingrained habit and respect for Julian's privacy held Emma back. "Are you sure?"

He nodded. He was pale. She drew away from the island and crossed the room with a sense of apprehension. Maybe he did have bodies in there. Whatever it was, it had to be something awful. She'd never seen him look like he did now.

She stepped inside the room. For a moment she thought she'd stepped into a funhouse of mirrors. Reflections of herself stared back from every surface. The walls were covered with tacked-up sketches and paintings, and there was an easel as well, set up in one corner near the single window, with a half-finished drawing on it. Two countertops ran the length of the east and west walls, and those, too, were covered in art.

Every image was of her.

There she was training, holding Cortana, playing with Tavvy, reading to Dru. In one watercolor, she was sleeping on the beach, her head pillowed on her hand. The details of the slope of her shoulder, the individual grains of sand stuck to her skin like sugar, had been rendered so lovingly that she felt almost dizzy. In another, she rose above the city of Los Angeles. She was naked, but her body was transparent—one could see only the outlines of it, and the stars of the night sky shone through her. Her hair tumbled down like brilliant light, illuminating the world.

She remembered what he'd said to her when they were dancing.

*I was thinking about painting you. Painting your hair. That I'd have to use titanium white to get the color right, the way it catches light and almost glows. But that wouldn't work, would it? It's not all one color, your hair, it's not just gold: It's amber and tawny and caramel and wheat and honey.*

She reached up to touch her hair, which she'd never thought of as anything but ordinary blond, and then stared at the painting clipped to the easel. It was half-finished, an image of Emma striding out of the ocean, Cortana strapped to her hip. Her hair was down, as it was in most of the pictures, and he had made it look like the spray of the ocean at sunset, when the last rays of daylight turned the water to a brutal gold. She looked beautiful, fierce, as terrible as a goddess.

She bit her lip. "You like my hair down," she said.

Julian gave a short laugh. "Is that all you have to say?"

She turned to look at him directly. They were standing close together. "These are beautiful," she said. "Why didn't you ever show them to me? To anyone?"

He exhaled, gave her a slow, sad smile. "Ems, no one could look at these and not know how I feel about you."

She put her hand on the counter. It suddenly seemed important to have something to keep her steady on her feet. "How long have you been drawing me?"

He sighed. A moment later his hand came to rest in her hair. His fingers twined in the strands. "My whole life."

"I remember you used to, but then you stopped."

"I never stopped. I just learned to hide it." His smile vanished. "My last secret."

"I very much doubt that," Emma said.

"I have lied and lied and lied." Julian spoke slowly. "I've made myself an expert at lying. I stopped thinking lies could be destructive. Even evil. Until I stood on that beach and told you I didn't feel that way about you."

She was gripping the counter so hard her hand ached. "Feel what way?"

"You know," he said, drawing away from her.

Suddenly, she thought she'd done too much, pushed him too far, but the desperation to know inside her overrode that. "I need to hear it. Spell it out for me, Julian."

He went toward the door. Took hold of the knob—for a moment she thought he was going to leave the room—and he swung the door of the small room closed. Locked it, closing them inside. Turned to her. His eyes were luminous in the dim light.

"I tried to stop," he said. "That's why I went to England. I thought if I was away from you, maybe I'd stop feeling what I was feeling. But as soon as I got back, the first second that I saw you, I knew it hadn't made any difference." He looked around the room, his expression almost resigned. "Why all these paintings of you? Because I'm an artist, Emma. These pictures are my heart. And if my heart was a canvas, every square inch of it would be painted over with you."

Her gaze locked with his. "You mean it," she said. "You really mean it."

"I know I lied to you on the beach. But I swear on our *parabatai* oaths, I'm telling you the truth now." He spoke clearly, deliberately, as if he couldn't bear a single word he was telling her to be misunderstood or lost. "I love everything about you, Emma. I love the way I can recognize your footsteps in the hallway outside my room even when I didn't know you were coming. No one else walks or breathes or moves like you do. I love the way you gasp when you're asleep, like your dreams have surprised you. I love the way when we stand together on the beach our shadows blend into one person. I love the way you can write on my skin with your fingers and I can understand it better than I could understand someone else shouting in my ear. I didn't want to love you like this. It's the worst idea in the world that I love you like this. But I can't stop. Believe me, I've tried."

It was the pain in his voice that convinced her. It was the same pain that had beaten in her own heart for so long that she'd stopped knowing it for what it was. She let go of the counter. She took a step toward Julian, and then another one. "Are you— Are you *in* love with me?"

His smile was soft and sad. "So much."

A moment later she was in his arms and kissing him. She couldn't have said how it happened exactly, just that it seemed inevitable. And that for all that Julian's voice had been quiet when he'd spoken, his mouth on hers was eager and his body was wanting and desperate. He clutched her to him, his lips tracing the outline of her mouth. Her hands were fierce in his hair—she'd always loved his hair, and now that she could touch it freely, she buried her hands in the thick waves, winding them around her fingers.

His hands slid to the backs of her thighs and he lifted her up as if she weighed nothing. She locked her hands around his neck, clinging on as he held her against him with one arm. She was aware of him grabbing at the papers covering the counter, knocking them to the floor along with tubes of paint, until he'd cleared a space where he could set her down.

She pulled him in, keeping her legs wrapped around his waist. There was nothing closed about him now, nothing diffident or remote or reticent as their kisses grew deeper, wilder, hotter.

"Tell me I didn't screw this up forever," Julian gasped between kisses. "I was such an ass on the beach—and when I saw you with Mark in your room—"

Emma slid her hands down to his shoulders, broad and strong under her grip. She felt drunk on kissing. This was what people fought wars over, she thought, and killed each other over, and destroyed their lives for: this nerve-shredding mixture of longing and pleasure. "Nothing was happening—"

His hands stroked her hair. "I know it's ridiculous. But when you had a crush on Mark, when you were twelve, it was the first time I remember ever being jealous. It doesn't make any sense, I know that, but the things we're most frightened of, we can't make ourselves dismiss them. If you and Mark ever . . . I don't think I could come back from that."

Something about the raw honesty in his voice touched her. "Everyone has things they're afraid of," she whispered, moving closer into his arms. She slid her fingers under the hem of his shirt. "It's part of being human."

His eyes slipped half-closed. His fingers raked down through her hair; his hands caressed her back lightly, then found her waist, pulling her harder into him. Her head fell back, almost banging into one of the cabinets; his lips burned on her collarbone. His skin was hot under her touch. She could understand suddenly why people talked about passion as fire: She felt as if they had caught aflame and were burning like the dry Malibu hills, about to become ashes that would mix together forever.

"Tell me you love me, Emma," he said against her throat. "Even if you don't mean it."

She gasped; how could he think, how could he not realize—?

There was the sound of footsteps in the studio. "Julian?" Livvy's voice echoed through the door. "Hey, Jules, where are you?"

Emma and Julian ripped themselves away from each other in a panic. They were both disheveled, their hair mussed, their lips kiss-swollen. Nor could Emma imagine how they'd explain why they'd locked themselves into Julian's private room.

"Juuules!" Livvy was yelling now, good-naturedly. "We're in the library and Ty sent me to get you. . . ." Livvy paused, most likely looking around the room. "Seriously, Julian, where are you?"

The knob of the door turned.

Julian stood frozen. The knob jiggled again, the door rattling against its lock.

Emma tensed.

There was the sound of a sigh. The knob stopped jiggling. Footsteps moved away from them, and then the studio door banged closed.

Emma looked at Julian. She felt as if her blood had frozen and then unthawed suddenly; it was pounding through her veins like a spring torrent. "It's okay," she breathed.

Julian caught her and hugged her fiercely, his bitten-nailed hands digging into her shoulders. He gripped her so tightly she could barely breathe.

Then he let go. He did it as if he was forcing himself, as if he were starving and he was putting aside the last piece of food he had. But he did it.

"We'd better go," he said.

Back in her bedroom, Emma showered and changed as quickly as she could. She slid on jeans and couldn't help a wince as her T-shirt came down over her head, scraping against the bandages on her back. She was going to need new ones soon, and probably another *iratze*.

She headed out, only to discover that the hallway was already occupied.

"Emma," Mark said, unhitching himself from the wall. His voice sounded tired. "Julian said you were all right. I—I'm so sorry."

"It's not your fault, Mark," she said.

"It is," he said. "I trusted Kieran."

"You trusted him because you loved him."

He glanced at her, surprised. He looked off-kilter, and not just because of his eyes: It was as if someone had reached inside him and shaken the roots of his beliefs. She could still hear him screaming as Iarlath whipped first Julian and then her. "It was that clear?"

"You looked at him like—" *Like I look at Julian.* "Like you look at someone you love," she said. "I'm sorry I didn't realize it before. I thought you . . ." *Liked Cristina, maybe? Kieran sure seemed jealous of her.* "Liked girls," she finished. "Teach me to make assumptions."

"I do," he said quizzically. "Like girls."

"Oh," she said. "You're bisexual?"

"Last time I checked, that's what you call it," he said with a brief look of amusement. "There are no real words for these things in Faerie, so . . ."

She winced. "Double sorry on the assumptions."

"It's all right," he said. "You are correct about Kieran. He was all I had for a long time."

"If it makes any difference, he does love you," said Emma. "I could see it on his face. I don't think he expected any of us to be hurt. I think he thought they'd bring you back to Faerie, where you could be with him. He would never have thought—"

But at that, at the memory of the whip coming down not just on her back but on Julian's, her throat closed.

"Emma," Mark said. "The day that I was taken by the Hunt—the last thing I said to Julian was that he should stay with you. I thought of you, even when I was gone, as this delicate girl, this little thing with blond braids. I knew if anything happened to you, even then, Julian would be heartbroken."

Emma felt her own heart skip a beat, but if Mark meant anything out of the ordinary by "heartbroken," it wasn't evident.

"Today, you protected him," Mark said. "You took the whipping that was meant for him. It was not easy to watch what they did to you. I wish it had been me. I wish it a thousand times. But I know why my brother wanted to protect me. And I am grateful to you for protecting him in turn."

Emma breathed past the tightness in her throat. "I had to do it."

"I will always owe you," Mark said, and his voice was the voice of a prince of Faerie, whose promises were more than promises. "Anything you want, I will give it to you."

"That's quite a promise. You don't have to—"

"I want to," he said with finality.

After a moment Emma nodded, and the strangeness was broken. Mark the faerie lapsed back into being Mark Blackthorn, filling her in on the progress of the investigation as they headed down to join the others. In order to keep Uncle Arthur from finding out about what had happened with Emma and the faerie convoy, Julian had arranged for Arthur to attend a meeting with Anselm Nightshade at the pizza place on Cross Creek Road. Nightshade had sent a car for Arthur earlier, promising they both would return when night fell.

The rest of the family had been in the library. They had torn through piles of books in search of information about Lady Midnight.

"Did they learn anything?" she asked.

"I'm not sure. I was just on my way to the library when Mr. Hot and Sexy showed up and said he had information."

"Whoa." Emma held up her hand. "Mr. Hot and Sexy?"

"Perfect Diego," Mark grumbled.

"Okay, look, I know you haven't been back from Faerie all that long, but here in the human world, Mr. Hot and Sexy is *not* an effective insult."

Mark didn't get a chance to reply; they had reached the library. The moment they went inside, Emma was nearly knocked off her feet by a rushing figure with a determined hug—it was Livvy, who promptly burst into tears.

"Ouuuch," Emma said, glancing around. The whole room was covered in stacks of paper, piles of books. "Liv, mind the bandages."

"I can't believe you let those faeries whip you, oh, I hate them, I hate the Courts, I'll kill all of them—"

"'Let' is maybe not the word," Emma said. "Anyway, I'm all right. It was fine. It didn't even hurt that much."

"Ooh, you liar!" said Cristina, emerging from behind a stack of books with Diego beside her. *Interesting*, Emma thought. "It was very heroic, what you did, but also very stupid."

Diego looked at Emma with serious brown eyes. "If I had known what was to happen, I would have stayed and volunteered to be whipped myself. I am more muscular and larger than you, and I probably could have taken it better."

"I took it fine," said Emma, annoyed. "But thanks for the reminder that you're an enormous hulk. I might have forgotten otherwise."

"Argh! Stop it!" Cristina dissolved into a torrent of Spanish.

Emma held her hands up. "Cristina, slow *down*."

"Would it help?" said Diego. "Do you speak Spanish?"

"Not much," Emma said.

He gave a small smile. "Ah, well, in that case, she's complimenting us."

"I *know* those weren't compliments," Emma said, but then the door opened and it was Julian, and suddenly everyone was deputized to help carry books and line them up on the table and sort papers. Ty was sitting at the head of the table as if he were leading a board meeting. He didn't smile at Emma exactly, but gave her a sideways glance that Emma knew meant affection, and then looked back down at what he was doing.

Emma didn't look at Julian, no more than a glance, at least. She didn't think she could. She was aware of his presence as she crossed the room to the long table, though. He came and stood at Ty's left, looking down at his notes.

"Where are Tavvy and Dru?" she asked, lifting the top volume from a stack of books.

"Tavvy was getting stir-crazy. Dru took him down to the beach," said Livvy. "Ty thinks he might have figured something out."

"Who she was," Ty said. "Our Lady Midnight. Tavvy's book

reminded me of a story I read in one of the Blackthorn history books—"

"But we've looked through all the Blackthorn history books," Julian said.

Ty gave him a superior look. "We looked at everything going back a hundred years," he said. "But Tavvy's book said Lady Midnight was in love with someone she was forbidden to love."

"And so we thought, what's a forbidden love?" said Livvy eagerly. "I mean, people who are related, gross, and people who are way younger or older than each other, which is also gross, and people who are sworn enemies, which is not gross but is sort of sad . . ."

"People who like *Star Wars* and people who like *Star Trek*," said Emma. "Et cetera. Where are you going with this, Livs?"

"Or *parabatai*, like Silas Pangborn and Eloisa Ravenscar," Livvy went on, and Emma was instantly sorry she'd made a joke. She felt herself become very, very aware of where Julian was standing, how close he was to her, how much he had tensed. "But that doesn't seem likely. So then we thought—it was totally forbidden to fall in love with Downworlders before the Accords. It would have been a big scandal."

"So we dug into the earlier histories," said Ty. "And we found something. There was a family of Blackthorns who had a daughter who fell in love with a warlock. They were going to run off together, but her family caught them. She was sent to be an Iron Sister."

"'Her parents trapped her in an iron castle.'" Mark had caught up Tavvy's book. "That's what that means."

"You speak the language of fairy tales," said Diego. "Not surprising, I suppose."

"So then she died," said Emma. "What was her name?"

"Annabel," said Livvy. "Annabel Blackthorn."

Julian exhaled. "Where did all this happen?"

"In England," said Ty. "Two hundred years ago. Before 'Annabel Lee' was ever written."

"I found something as well," said Diego. From the inside pocket of his jacket, he produced a slightly wilted-looking stem with several leaves clustered on it. He laid it on the table. "Don't touch it," he said as Livvy reached out. She drew her hand back. "It's belladonna. Deadly nightshade. Only fatal if ingested or absorbed in the bloodstream, but still."

"From the convergence site?" said Mark. "I noticed it there."

"Yes," said Diego. "It is much deadlier than your average belladonna. I suspect it was what was smeared on the arrows that I bought at the Shadow Market." He frowned. "The odd thing is that it normally only grows in Cornwall."

"The girl who fell in love with the warlock," Ty said. "That was in Cornwall."

Everything in the room suddenly seemed very clear and bright and harsh, like a photograph brought into sudden focus. "Diego," Emma said. "Who did you buy the arrows from? In the Market?"

Diego frowned. "A human with the Sight. I think his name was Rook—"

"Johnny Rook," said Julian. His eyes, meeting Emma's, were dark with a sudden realization. "You think—"

She held out her hand. "Give me your phone."

She was aware of the others looking at her curiously as she took the phone from Julian and strode across the room, dialing as she went. The line rang several times before it picked up.

"Hello?"

"Rook," she said. "It's Emma Carstairs."

"I told you not to call me." His voice was cold. "After what your friend did to my son—"

"If you don't talk to me now, the next visit you get will be from the Silent Brothers," she snapped. There was rage in her voice, though little of it was actually about him. Anger was rising in her like a tide; anger, and the sense of betrayal. "Look, I know you sold my friend some arrows. They were poisoned. With a poison only the Guardian of the Followers would have access to." She was gambling now, but she could tell by the silence on the other end of the phone that her shot in the dark wasn't going wide. "You said you didn't know who he was. You lied."

"I didn't lie," Rook said after a pause. "I don't know who he is."

"Then how do you know it's a he?"

"Look, he always showed up in a robe and gloves and a hood, okay? Completely covered. He asked me to distill those leaves, make a compound he could use. I did it."

"So you could poison the arrows?"

She could hear the smirk in Rook's voice. "I had a little left over and thought I'd amuse myself. Centurions aren't too popular around the Shadow Market, and belladonna's illegal."

Emma wanted to scream at him, wanted to scream that one of the arrows he'd poisoned for fun had nearly killed Julian. She held herself back. "What else did you do for the Guardian?"

"I don't need to tell you anything, Carstairs. You don't have any proof I know the Guardian that well—"

"Really? Then how did you know that body was going to be dumped at the Sepulchre?" Rook was silent. "Do you know what the prisons in the Silent City are like? Do you really want to experience them firsthand?"

"No—"

"Then tell me what else you did for him. The Guardian. Did you use necromancy?"

"No! Nothing like that." Now Rook sounded a little panicked. "I did things for the Followers. Made luck charms for them, made sure they'd have some windfalls, access to parties, premieres, have people fall in love with them. Get their deals made. No big things.

Just enough to keep them happy and believing that it was worth it to stay. Believing the Guardian was taking care of them and they were going to get everything they wanted."

"And what did he do for you in return?"

"Money," Rook said flatly. "Protection. He warded my house against demons. He has some magical power, that guy."

"You worked for a guy who sacrificed people," Emma pointed out.

"It was a cult." Rook was practically snarling. "Those have always existed—they always will. People want money and power and they'll do anything to get them. That's not my fault."

"Yeah, people sure will do anything for money. You're proof of that." Emma tried to rein in her temper, but her heart was pounding. "Tell me anything else about this guy. You must have noticed his voice—they way he walked—anything weird about him—"

"Everything's weird about a guy who shows up completely wrapped in fabric. I couldn't even see his shoes, okay? He didn't sound like he was all there. He's the one who told me to tell you about the Selpulchre. He babbled a lot of nonsense, once he said he came to L.A. to bring back love—"

Emma hung up. She looked at the others with her heart slamming against her chest. "It's Malcolm," she said, her voice sounding distant and tinny in her ears. "Malcolm's the Guardian."

They looked at her with silent, stunned expressions.

"Malcolm's our friend," said Ty. "That doesn't— He wouldn't do that."

"Ty's right," said Livvy. "Just because Annabel Blackthorn was in love with a warlock—"

"She was in love with a warlock," Emma repeated. "In Cornwall. Magnus said Malcolm used to live in Cornwall. A plant from Cornwall is growing around the convergence. Malcolm's been helping us with the investigation, but he hasn't, really. He never translated a word of what we gave him. He told us this was a summoning spell—it's not, it's a necromantic spell." She started to pace up and down. "He has that ring with the red stone, and the earrings I found at the convergence site were rubies—okay, it's not exactly conclusive, but he'd have to have clothes for her, right? For Annabel? She couldn't go around in grave clothes when he brought her back. It makes more sense for the necromancer to keep clothes there for the person they were raising from the dead than it does for them to keep clothes for themselves." She whirled to find the others staring at her. "Malcolm only moved to L.A. about five months before the attack on the Institute. He says he was away when it happened, but what if he wasn't? He was High Warlock. He could have easily found out where my parents were that day. He could have killed them." She looked over at the others. Their expressions ran the gamut between shock and disbelief.

"I just don't think Malcolm would do that," Livvy said in a small voice.

"Rook told me that the Guardian he met with concealed his identity," Emma said. "But he also said the Guardian told him that he'd come to L.A. to bring back love. Remember what Malcolm said while we were watching movies? 'I came here to bring true love back from the dead.'" She gripped the phone so tightly it hurt. "What if he really meant it? Literally? He came here to bring his true love back from the dead. Annabel."

There was a long silence. It was Cristina, to Emma's surprise, who finally broke it. "I do not know Malcolm well, or love him as you do," she said in her soft voice. "So forgive me if what I say hurts. But I think Emma is right. One of these things could be a coincidence. But not all of them. Annabel Blackthorn fell in love with a warlock in Cornwall. Malcolm was a warlock in Cornwall. That itself is enough to raise suspicion high enough that it should be investigated." She looked around with earnest dark eyes. "I'm sorry. It is just that the next step for the Guardian is *Blackthorn blood*. And therefore we cannot wait."

"Don't be sorry, Cristina. You're right," Julian said. He looked at Emma, and she could see the unspoken words behind his eyes: *This is how Belinda knew about Arthur.*

"We need to find him," Diego said, his clear, practical voice cutting through the quiet. "We must move immediately—"

The library door burst open and Dru came rushing in. Her face was pink and her wavy brown hair had come out of its braids. She nearly collided directly with Diego, but jumped back with a squeak.

"Dru?" It was Mark who spoke. "Is everything all right?"

She nodded, bounding across the room toward Julian. "What did you need me for?"

Julian looked puzzled. "What do you mean?"

"I was down on the beach with Tavvy," she said, leaning against the edge of the table to catch her breath. "Then he came and said you had to talk to me. So I came running back—"

"What?" Julian echoed. "I didn't send anyone down to the beach for you, Dru."

"But he said . . ." Dru looked suddenly alarmed. "He said you needed to see me right away."

Julian rose to his feet. "Where's Tavvy?"

Her lip began to wobble. "But he said . . . He said if I ran back, he'd walk Tavvy home. He gave him a toy. He's watched Tavvy before, I don't understand, what's wrong—?"

"Dru," Julian said in a carefully controlled voice. "Who is 'he'? Who has Tavvy?"

Dru swallowed, her round face stricken with fright. "Malcolm," she said. "Malcolm has him."

# 24

## BY THE NAME
## OF ANNABEL LEE

"I don't understand," Dru said again. "What's happening?"

Livvy pulled Dru against her and put her arms around her younger sister. They were about the same height—you'd never have been able to tell Livvy was the elder unless you knew them—but Dru clung on gratefully.

Diego and Cristina stood silently. Ty, in his chair, had taken one of his hand toys from his pocket and was almost attacking it with shaking hands, tangling and untangling. His head was bent, his hair swinging into his face.

Julian—Julian looked as if his world had caved in.

"But why?" Dru whispered. "Why did Malcolm take Tavvy? And why are all of you so upset?"

"Dru, Malcolm's the one we've been looking for." It was Emma who spoke, her voice choked. "He's the Guardian. He's the murderer. And he took Tavvy—"

"For Blackthorn blood," said Julian. "The last sacrifice. Blackthorn blood to bring back a Blackthorn."

Dru fell against her sister's shoulder, sobbing. Mark was shaking—Cristina suddenly broke away from Diego and came over to him. She took his hand and held it. Emma gripped the edge of the table. She could no longer feel the pain in her back. She could no longer feel anything.

All she could see was Tavvy, little Tavvy, the smallest Blackthorn. Tavvy having nightmares, Tavvy in her arms as she carried him through the war-torn Institute five years ago. Tavvy covered in paint in Jules's studio. Tavvy, who alone among them had skin that could not hold a single protection rune. Tavvy, who would not understand what was happening to him or why.

"Wait," Dru said. "Malcolm gave me a note. He said to give it to you, Jules." She drew away from Livvy and fumbled in her pocket, retrieving some folded paper. "He said not to read it, that it was private."

Livvy, who had gone to stand near Ty, made a disgusted noise. Julian's face was stark white, his eyes blazing. "*Private?* He wants his *privacy* respected?" He snatched the paper from Dru's hand and almost ripped it open. Emma caught a glimpse of large block letters printed on the paper. Julian's expression turned to one of confusion.

"What does it say, Jules?" asked Mark.

Julian read the words aloud. "*I WILL RAISE YOU, ANNABEL LEE.*"

The room exploded.

A bolt of black light burst from the letter in Julian's hand. It shot toward the roof, smashing through the skylight with the force of a wrecking ball.

Emma covered her head as plaster and bits of glass rained down. Ty, who was directly beneath the hole in the roof, threw himself toward his sister, knocking her to the ground and covering her with his own body. The room seemed to rock back and forth; a shelf wobbled and fell, tipping toward Diego. Pulling away from Mark, Cristina shoved the shelf out of the way; it crashed to the side, missing Diego by inches. Dru shrieked, and Julian pulled her toward him, tucking her under his arm.

The black light was still shining upward. With his free hand, Julian flung the note onto the ground and slammed his foot down on it.

It crumbled into dust instantly. The black light vanished as if it had been switched off.

There was a silence. Livvy wriggled out from under her twin and stood up, reaching out to help him up after her. Livvy looked half-surprised, half-worried. "Ty, you didn't have to do that."

"You wanted to have someone to shield you from danger. That's what you said."

"I know," Livvy said. "But—"

Ty rose to his feet—and cried out. A jagged piece of glass was sticking out of the back of his calf. Blood had already started to soak the fabric around the cut.

Ty bent down and, before anyone else could move, yanked the glass out of his leg. He dropped it to the ground, where it shattered into clear, red-smeared pieces.

"Ty!" Julian started forward, but Ty shook his head. He was pulling himself into a chair, his face twisted with pain. Blood had started to pool around his sneakered foot.

"Let Livvy do it," he said. "It would be better—"

Livvy was already swooping down on her twin with an *iratze*. A bit of falling glass had cut her left cheek, and blood was visible against her pale skin. She wiped it away with her sleeve as she finished the healing rune.

"Let me see the cut," Julian said, kneeling down. Slowly, Livvy rolled up Ty's pant leg. The cut went across the side of his calf, raw and red but no longer open—it looked like a tear that had been sewn up. Still, his leg from the cut down was smeared with blood.

"Another *iratze* should fix it," said Diego. "And a blood-replacement rune."

Julian gritted his teeth. He had never seemed bothered by Diego the way Mark was, but Emma could tell that at the moment he was barely holding himself back. "Yes," he said. "We know. Thanks, Diego."

Ty looked up at his brother. "I don't know what happened." He looked dazed. "I wasn't expecting it—I should have been expecting it."

"Ty, no one could have expected that," Emma said. "I mean, Julian said some words, and boom, Hell's tractor beam."

"Is anyone else hurt?" Julian had efficiently slit Ty's pant leg open, and Livvy, her face the color of old newspaper, was applying healing and blood-replacement runes to her twin. Julian looked around the room, and Emma could see him doing his mental inventory of his family: *Mark all right, Livvy all right, Dru all right. . . .* She saw the moment he reached where Tavvy should be and blanched. His jaw tightened. "Malcolm must have enchanted the paper to set off that signal as soon as it was read."

"It *is* a signal," Mark said. The expression on his face was troubled. "I have felt this before, in the Unseelie Court, when black enchantments were brewing. That was dark magic."

"We should go straight to the Clave." Julian's face was bloodless. "Secrecy doesn't matter, punishments don't matter, not when Tavvy's life is at risk. I'll take the entire blame on myself."

"You will not take any blame," said Mark, "that I do not also take."

Julian didn't answer that, just held out his hand. "Emma, my phone."

She'd forgotten she still had it. She drew it out of her pocket slowly—and blinked.

The screen was blank. "Your phone. It's dead."

"That's strange," said Julian. "I just charged it this morning."

"You can use mine," Cristina said, and reached into her jacket. "Here it—" She blinked. "It's dead too."

Ty slid from his chair. He took a step forward and winced, but only slightly. "We'll check the computer and the landline phone."

He and Livvy hurried from the library. The room was quiet now, except for the sound of settling debris. The floor was covered in broken glass and bits of shattered wood. It seemed that the black light had blown out the glass oculus at the top of the room.

Drusilla gasped. "Look—there's someone at the skylight."

Emma glanced up. The oculus had become a ring of jagged glass, open to the night sky. She saw the flash of a pale face within the circle.

Mark darted past her and raced up the curving ramp. He threw himself at the oculus—there was a thrashing blur of movement—and he tumbled back onto the ramp, his hand gripping the collar of a lean figure with dark hair. Mark was shouting; there was broken glass around them as they struggled. They rolled together down the ramp, hitting out at each other, until they fetched up on the library floor.

The dark-haired figure was a slender boy in ragged, bloody clothes; he had gone limp. Mark knelt on top of him, and as he reached for a dagger and it flashed out gold, Emma realized that the intruder was Kieran.

Mark jammed his knife up against Kieran's throat. Kieran stiffened against the knife.

"I should kill you right here," Mark said through his teeth. "I should cut your throat."

Dru made a small sound. To Emma's surprise, it was Diego who reached out and laid a comforting hand on her shoulder. A small flicker of liking for him went through her.

Kieran bared his teeth—and then his throat, tipping his head back. "Go ahead," he said. "Kill me."

"Why are you here?" Mark's breath hitched. Julian took a step toward them, his hand at his hip, on the hilt of a throwing knife. Emma knew he could take Kieran out at this distance. And he would, if Mark seemed in danger.

Mark was gripping his knife; his hand was steady, but his face was anguished. "Why are you here?" he said again. "Why would you come to this place where you know that you're hated? Why do you want to *make me kill you?*"

"Mark," Kieran said. He reached up, clenched his hand in Mark's sleeve. His face was full of yearning; the hair that fell over his forehead was streaked with dark blue. "Mark, *please.*"

Mark shook his arm out of Kieran's grip. "I could forgive you if it was me you whipped," he said. "But you touched the ones I love; that I cannot forgive. You should bleed as Emma bled."

"Don't—Mark—" Emma was alarmed, not for Kieran—some part of her would have liked to see him bleed—but for Mark. For what hurting, even killing, Kieran would do to him.

"I came to help you," Kieran said.

Mark gave a hollow laugh. "Your *help* is not wanted here."

"I know about Malcolm Fade," Kieran gasped. "I know he took your brother."

Julian made a guttural noise. Mark's hand, on the knife, went bloodless. "Let him go, Mark," Julian said. "If he knows anything about Tavvy—we have to find out what it is. Let him go."

Mark hesitated.

"Mark," Cristina said softly, and with a violent gesture, Mark flung himself off Kieran and stood up, backing away until he was nearly beside Julian. Julian, whose grip on his own knife looked agonizingly tight.

Slowly, painfully, Kieran rose to his feet and faced the room.

He was a far cry from the arrogant gentry warrior Emma had first seen in the Sanctuary. His shirt and loose trousers were blood-stained and torn, his face bruised. He did not cower or look frightened, but that seemed less an act of bravery than almost one of hopelessness: Everything about him, from the way he was dressed to the way he stood to the way he looked at Mark, said that here was someone who did not care what became of him.

The door of the library burst open and Ty and Livvy spilled in. "Everything's knocked out," Livvy exclaimed. "All the phones, the computer, even the radios—"

She broke off, staring, as she took in the scene in front of her: Kieran facing the other occupants of the room.

Kieran gave a tiny bow. "I am Kieran of the Wild Hunt."

"One of the faerie convoy?" Livvy looked from Mark to Julian. "One of the ones who whipped Emma?"

Julian nodded.

Ty looked at Mark, and then the others. His face was pale and cold. "Why is he still alive?"

"He knows about Tavvy," said Drusilla. "Julian, make him tell us—"

Julian flung his dagger. It flew past Kieran's head, close enough to graze his hair, and embedded itself in the frame of the window behind him. "You will tell us now," he said in a deadly quiet voice, "everything you know about where Octavian is, what's going on, and how we can get him back. Or I will spill your blood on the floor of this library. I've spilled faerie blood before. Don't think I won't do it again."

Kieran didn't drop his eyes. "There is no need to threaten me," he said, "though if it pleases you, do it; it makes no difference to me. I came to tell you what you want to know. That is why I am here. The black light you just saw was faerie magic. It was meant to knock out all communication, so that you could not call for help from the Clave or Conclave. So that you could not seek help or save your brother."

"We could try to find a pay phone," Livvy said uncertainly, "or a restaurant phone, down on the highway—"

"You will discover that phone lines have been knocked out for several miles," said Kieran. There was urgency in his voice. "I beg you not to waste time. Fade has taken your brother, already, to the ley line convergence. It is the place where he performs his sacrifices. The place he plans to kill him. If you wish to rescue the boy, you must take up your weapons and go after him now."

Julian threw open the door of the weapons room. "Everyone, arm yourselves. If you're not in gear, get in gear. Diego, Cristina, there's gear hanging on the east wall. Take it, it'll be faster than going back to your rooms. Use any weapons you want. Kieran, you stay right there." He pointed toward the table in the middle of the room. "Where I can see you. Don't move or the next blade I throw at you won't miss."

Kieran gave him a look. A little of his visible despair seemed to have ebbed, and there was arrogance in his quick glance. "I believe it," he said, and moved toward the table as everyone scurried around arming themselves and buckling gear on over their clothes. Not patrol gear, which was lighter, but the heavy dark gear you wore when you thought you were going to fight.

When you *knew* you were going to fight.

There had been some discussion of whether all of them were going to go to the convergence, or whether Dru at least should stay back at the Institute. Dru had protested vociferously, and Julian hadn't fought it—the Institute didn't feel safe at the moment, with the oculus smashed open. Kieran had gotten in, and who knew what else could? He wanted his family where he could see them. And there wasn't much he could say to Dru about her age: He and Emma had fought and killed during the Dark War, and they'd been younger than she was now.

He had taken Ty aside, separately, and told him that if he wanted to stay behind from the fight because he was wounded, there was nothing shameful about that. He could lock himself in the car while they went into the convergence.

"Do you think I have nothing to contribute to a fight?" Ty had asked.

"No," Julian had said, and meant it. "But you're hurt, and I—"

"It's a fight. We might all get hurt." Ty had looked directly into Julian's eyes. He could tell that Ty was doing it for him, because he remembered that Julian had told him that people often looked directly into each other's eyes to show that they were telling the truth. "I want to go. I want to be there to help Tavvy, and I want you to let me. It's what I want, and that should matter."

Ty was in the weapons room with them now. It was a cavernous space with no windows. Every spare inch of the walls was hung with swords, axes, and maces. Gear, belts, and boots were stacked in piles. There was a ceramic tile bowl full of steles, and a table covered with a long cloth held seraph blades.

Julian could sense them all around him, his friends and family. He knew Mark was at his side, toeing off his shoes and kicking his feet into boots. He knew Emma was at the counter, lining up seraph blades that had already been named and prepared, sliding some into her belt and distributing the rest. His awareness of her swung as she moved around the room like the needle on a compass.

Above all, though, he was aware of Tavvy, out there somewhere, needing him. There was a cold terror in him that threatened to pull the determination out of his bones and sap his concentration. Pushing it away to focus on what was happening here and now was one of the hardest things he'd ever done. He bitterly wished that things were different, that they had the cooperation of the Clave, that they could have gotten to Magnus and asked for a Portal.

But it was no use wishing.

"Talk," he snapped at Kieran, pulling down a weapons belt from a shelf. "That black light, you said it was 'faerie magic.' Did you mean dark magic?"

Now that Mark was no longer looking directly at him, Kieran seemed bored and annoyed. He leaned against the central table, taking care not to come in contact with any of the weapons—not, his expression made clear, because they were sharp or frightening but because they were Nephilim weapons and therefore repellent.

"The question is whether it will show up on the Clave's map," said Ty, buckling on protective gauntlets. He was already in his gear, and the slight outline of the bandage on his calf was barely visible under the thick fabric. "The one Magnus uses to track dark magic use. Or is that blocked like the cell phones?"

"It was Unseelie magic, but not dark in nature," said Kieran. "It will not show itself on the map. They were very sure of that."

Julian frowned. "Who is *they*? In fact, how do you know so much about Malcolm?"

"Because of Iarlath," said Kieran.

Mark turned to stare. "Iarlath? What has he to do with this?"

"I thought you knew that at least," Kieran muttered. "Iarlath and Malcolm have been in this together since the attack on the Institute five years ago."

"They're allies?" Mark demanded. "How long have you known?"

"Only a short time," said Kieran. "I became suspicious when Iarlath so strongly refused to allow you to come back to Faerie. He wished you to stay here, so much so that he staged that charade of punishment with the whipping so that you would not return with us. After that I realized there was more to the plan of having you here at the Institute than finding the murderer who had taken faerie lives. It was about preventing anyone in your family from being able to go to the Clave until it was too late."

Emma had a seraph blade in each hand and Cortana on her back; she had paused, her face stiff with shock. "Iarlath said something to me when he was—when he was whipping me," she said. "That Shadowhunters don't know who to trust. He meant Malcolm, didn't he?"

"Most likely," said Kieran. "Malcolm's is the shadow hand that has guided the Followers, and Malcolm killed your parents five years ago."

"Why?" Emma was rigid. Julian wanted to go to her so badly it hurt. *"Why did he kill my parents?"*

"As I understand it?" Kieran said, and there was a tinge of pity to his voice. "It was an experiment. To see if the spell worked."

Emma stood speechless. Julian asked it for her, the question she couldn't voice. "What do you mean, an experiment?"

"Years ago, Iarlath was one of the Fair Folk who allied themselves with Sebastian Morgenstern," said Kieran. "He was also a friend to Malcolm. As you probably know, there are certain books warlocks are forbidden to own, but which can be found in some Shadowhunter libraries. Necromantic tomes and the like. One of those is the Black Volume of the Dead."

"The one that the poem talked about," said Dru. Though her face was still tearstained, she had put on her gear and was braiding her hair carefully back from her face. It hurt Julian's heart, to see her like that. "'Find the black book at any cost.'"

"There are many black books," said Kieran. "But this was one Malcolm specifically wanted. Once the Institute was cleared of Shadowhunters and Sebastian departed, Malcolm took the opportunity to slip in and steal the book from the library. After all, when else was the Institute going to be unguarded, the door open? He took it, and he found the spell he wanted, and he saw that it required the sacrifice of Shadowhunter life. That was when your parents returned to the Institute, Emma."

"So he killed them," Emma said. "For a spell." She gave a short, bitter laugh. "Did it at least work?"

"It didn't," said Kieran. "It failed, and so he left their bodies in the ocean, knowing that the murders would be taken to be Sebastian's work."

"Iarlath told you all this?" There was suspicion on Mark's face.

"I followed Iarlath to the Unseelie Court and listened to what he said there." Kieran tried to meet Mark's gaze. Mark looked away. "The rest is what I demanded he tell me at knifepoint. Malcolm was to misdirect and confuse you so that you would not realize what he was doing—he used Johnny Rook for some of that. He wanted you to engage yourself in an investigation that would prove fruitless. Mark's presence here would deter you from asking the Clave or the Silent Brothers to help you, thus protecting Malcolm's work with the Followers, his attempts to raise his old love from the dead. When Malcolm had done what he needed to do, he would take a Blackthorn, for the death of a Blackthorn would be the last key to the enchantment."

"But Iarlath hasn't got the power to authorize a faerie convoy to do something on this scale," said Mark. "He's just a courtier, not someone who can order Gwyn around. Who gave the permission for this to happen?"

Kieran shook his dark head. "I don't know. Iarlath did not say. It could have been the King, my father, or it could have been Gwyn—"

"Gwyn would not do that," said Mark. "Gwyn has honor, and he is not cruel."

"What about Malcolm?" Livvy demanded. "I thought he had honor. I thought he was our friend! He loves Tavvy—he's played with him for hours, brought him toys. He couldn't kill him. He couldn't."

"He's responsible for the killing of a dozen people, Livvy," said Julian. "Maybe more."

"People are more than one thing," said Mark, and his eyes brushed over Kieran as he spoke. "Warlocks too."

Emma stood with her hands still on the seraph blades. Julian could feel what she felt, as he always had, as if his own heart mirrored hers—the hot curl of anger rising over a choking sense of despair and loss. More than anything he wanted to reach out to her, but he didn't trust himself to do it in front of everyone else.

They'd be able to see right through him the moment he touched her, see his real feelings. And there was no way he could risk that now, not when his heart was being eaten alive with fear over his little brother, fear he couldn't show in case it demoralized the rest of his siblings.

"Everyone is more than one thing," said Kieran. "We are more than single actions we undertake, whether they be good or evil." His eyes gleamed, silver and black, as he looked at Mark. Even in this room full of Shadowhunter things, the wildness of the Hunt and Faerie clung to Kieran like the scent of rain or leaves. It was the wildness that Julian sometimes sensed in Mark, that had faded since he'd come back to them, but showed itself still in brief flares like gunfire seen from a distance. For a moment they seemed to him two feral things, incongruous in their surroundings.

"The poem that was written on the bodies," Cristina said. "The one that mentioned the black book. The story said it was given to Malcolm in the Unseelie Court."

"So goes the faerie story as well," said Kieran. "At first Malcolm was told that his love had become an Iron Sister. Later he found out that she had been murdered by her family. Walled up alive in a tomb. The knowledge drove him to seek out the King of the Unseelie Court and ask him if there was a way to raise the dead. The King gave him that rhyme. It was instructions—it is only that it took him almost a century to learn how to follow them, and to find the black book."

"That's why the library was destroyed in the attack," said Emma. "So no one would notice the book was missing, if they ever looked for it. So many books were lost."

"But why did Iarlath tell Malcolm that the Followers could kill faeries as well as humans?" said Emma. "If he was really in league with Malcolm—"

"That was something Iarlath wanted. He has many enemies in the Seelie Court. It was an expedient way for him to rid himself of some of them—Malcolm had his Followers slay them, and the murders could not be traced back to Iarlath. For a faerie to kill another of the gentry, that is a dark crime indeed."

"Where is Annabel's body?" asked Livvy. "Wouldn't she be buried in Cornwall? Wouldn't she have been walled up there—in a 'tomb by the sounding sea'?"

"Convergences are places out of space and time," said Kieran. "The convergence itself is neither here nor in Cornwall nor in any real space. It is a between place, like Faerie itself."

"It can probably be entered through Cornwall as well—that would be why those plants grow outside the entrance," said Mark.

"And what is the connection to the poem 'Annabel Lee'?" asked Ty. "The name Annabel, the similarities of the stories—it seems more than coincidence."

The dark-haired faerie prince only shook his head. "I only know what Iarlath told me, and what is part of faerie lore. I did not even know the name Annabel or the mundane poem."

Mark whirled on Kieran. "Where is Iarlath now?"

Kieran's eyes seemed to shimmer when he looked back. "We are wasting time here. We should be getting to the convergence."

"He isn't wrong." Diego was completely kitted out: gear, several swords, an ax, throwing knives at his belt. He wore a black cloak over his gear, pinned at the shoulder with the pin of the Centurions—it bore the pattern of a leafless stick, and the words *Primi Ordines*. He made Julian feel underdressed. "We must get to the ley line convergence and stop Fade—"

Julian looked around the room, at Emma and Mark, and then

at Ty and Livvy, and lastly at Dru. "I know that we have known Malcolm all our lives. But he is a murderer and liar. Warlocks are immortal, but not invulnerable. When you see him, put your blade in his heart."

There was a silence. Emma broke it. "He killed my parents," she said. "I'll be the one to cut out his heart."

Kieran's eyebrows went up, but he said nothing.

"Jules." It was Mark, having moved to stand at Julian's shoulder. His hair, that Cristina had cut, was tangled; there were shadows under his eyes. But there was strength in the hand he laid on Julian's shoulder. "Would you place a rune upon me, brother? For I fear that without them, I will be at a disadvantage in the battle."

Julian's hand went automatically to his stele. Then he paused. "Are you sure?"

Mark nodded. "It is time to let the nightmares go." He pulled the neck of his shirt aside and down, baring his shoulder. "Courage," he said, naming a rune. "And Agility."

The others were discussing the fastest way to get to the convergence, but Julian was aware of both Emma's and Kieran's eyes on him as he put one hand on Mark's back and used the other to draw two careful runes. At the first bite of the stele, Mark tensed, but relaxed immediately, letting out his breath in a soft exhale.

When Julian was done, he lowered his hands. Mark straightened up and turned to him. Though he had shed no tears, his two-colored eyes were brilliant. For a moment there was no one in the world but Julian and his brother.

"Why?" Julian said.

"For Tavvy," Mark said, and suddenly, in the set of his mouth, in the curve of the determined line of his jaw, Julian could see his own self. "And," Mark added, "because I am a Shadowhunter." He looked toward Kieran, who was gazing at them as if the stele had seared his own skin. Love and hate had their own secret languages,

Julian thought, and Mark and Kieran were speaking in them now. "Because I am a Shadowhunter," he said again, his eyes full of a private challenge. "Because *I am a Shadowhunter.*"

Kieran pushed himself away from the table almost violently. "I have told you everything I know," he said. "There are no other secrets."

"So I suppose you're leaving," Mark said. "Thank you for your aid, Kieran. If you are returning to the Hunt, tell Gwyn that I will not be coming back. Not ever, no matter what rules they decree. I swear that I—"

"*Don't* swear it," Kieran said. "You do not know how things will change."

"Enough." Mark began to turn away.

"I have brought my steed with me," said Kieran. He was speaking to Mark, but everyone else was listening. "A faerie steed of the Hunt can take to the air. Roads do not slow our travel. I will ride ahead and delay what is happening at the convergence until the rest of you arrive."

"I'll go with him," Mark said sharply.

Everyone looked at him in surprise. "Um," said Emma. "You can't knife him on the way, Mark. We may need him."

"Pleasant as that sounds, I wasn't planning to," said Mark. "Two warriors are better than one."

"Good thinking," said Cristina. She slid her two butterfly knives into her belt. Emma had finished fastening on the last of her seraph blades.

Julian felt the familiar chill of battle's expectation rising in his veins. "Let's go."

As they headed downstairs, Julian found himself beside Kieran. The hair on the back of his neck prickled. Kieran felt like strangeness, wild magic, the murderous abandonment of the Hunt. He couldn't imagine what Mark had found to love about him.

"Your brother was wrong about you," Kieran said as they descended the steps to the entryway.

Julian glanced around, but no one seemed to be listening to them. Emma was beside Cristina, the twins were together, and Dru was talking shyly to Diego.

"What do you mean?" he asked guardedly. He had learned well in the past to be wary of the Fair Folk, their verbal entrapments and their false implications.

"He said you were gentle," said Kieran. "The most gentle person he knew." He smiled, and there was a cold beauty to his face when he smiled, like the crystalline surface of frost. "You are not gentle. You have a ruthless heart."

For several long moments Julian was silent, hearing only the sounds of their steps on the stairs. At the last step he turned.

"Remember it," he said, and walked away.

*Because I am a Shadowhunter.*

Mark stood beside Kieran on the sweep of grass that led down to the bluff and then the sea. The Institute rose behind them, dark and lightless, though from here, at least, the hole in the roof was invisible.

Kieran put his fingers in his mouth and whistled, a sound achingly familiar to Mark. The sight of Kieran was still enough to make his heart ache, from the way he held himself, every line of his body speaking of his early Court training, to the way that his hair had grown too long since Mark had not been there to cut it, and the blue-dark strands fell into his eyes and tangled with his long eyelashes. Mark remembered being enchanted by the curve and sweep of those lashes. He remembered how they felt against his skin.

"Why?" Kieran said. He was standing facing a little away from Mark, his posture rigid, as if he expected to be slapped. "Why come with me?"

"Because you require watching," said Mark. "I could trust you once. I cannot trust you now."

"That is not the truth," said Kieran. "I know you, Mark. I know when you lie."

Mark spun on him. He had always felt a little afraid of Kieran, he realized: of the power of his rank, of his unassailable surety in himself. That fear was gone now, and he couldn't say if it was because of the Courage rune on his shoulder or because he no longer desperately needed Kieran to live. Wanted him, loved him—those were different questions. But he could survive, either way. He was a Shadowhunter.

"Fine," Mark said, and he knew he should have said "very well," but the language wasn't in him anymore, it didn't beat in his blood, the high speech of Faerie. "I'll tell you why I wanted to come with you—"

There was a flash of white. Windspear cleared a small rise and bounded up to them, answering the call of her master. She whinnied when she saw Mark and nosed at his shoulder.

He stroked her neck. A hundred times she had carried him and Kieran in the Hunt, a hundred times they had shared a single mount, and ridden together, and fought together, and as Kieran climbed up onto the horse's back the familiarity was like fishhooks under Mark's skin.

Kieran looked down at him, every inch the prince despite his bloodstained clothes. His eyes were half-lidded crescents of silver and black. "So tell me," he said.

Mark felt the Agility rune burn on his back as he swung himself up behind Kieran. His arms went around Kieran automatically, hands settling themselves where they had always settled, at Kieran's belt. He felt Kieran inhale sharply.

He wanted to drop his head to Kieran's shoulder. He wanted to put his hands over Kieran's and lace their fingers together. He wanted to feel what he had felt living among the Hunt, that with Kieran he was safe, with Kieran he had someone who would never leave him.

But there were worse things than being left.

"Because," Mark said, "I wished to ride with you in the Hunt one last time." He felt Kieran flinch. Then the faerie boy leaned forward, and Mark heard him say a few words to Windspear in the Fair Speech. As the horse began to run, Mark reached back to touch the place where Julian had put the runes. He had felt a rush of panic when the stele touched his skin, and then a calm that had flowed through him, surprising him.

Maybe the runes of Heaven truly did belong on his skin. Maybe he'd been born to them after all.

He held tight to Kieran as Windspear lifted up into the sky, hooves tearing the air, and the Institute spun away below them.

When Emma and the others reached the convergence, Mark and Kieran were already there. They cantered out of the shadows on the back of a gorgeous white stallion that made Emma think of all the times in her childhood that she had wanted a horse.

The Toyota came to a stop. The sky was bare of clouds, and the moonlight was sharp and silver as a knife. It outlined Mark and Kieran, turned them into the brilliantly illuminated outlines of faerie knights. Neither of them looked human.

The field that reached to the bluff lay deceptively peaceful under the moonlight. The wide space of sea grass and sage bushes moved with soft rustles. The granite hill rose above it all, the dark space in the wall seeming to beckon them closer.

"We killed many Mantids," said Mark. His eyes met Emma's. "Cleared the way."

Kieran sat glowering, his face half-hidden by dark hair. Mark had his hands on Kieran's belt, steadying himself. As if suddenly recollecting this, Mark let go and slid to the ground.

"We'd better go in," Mark said, tipping his face up to Kieran's. "You and Windspear stand guard."

"But I—" Kieran began.

"This is Blackthorn family business," said Mark in a tone that brooked no argument. Kieran looked toward Cristina and Diego, opened his mouth as if to voice a protest, and then closed it again.

"Weapons check, everyone," Julian said. "Then we head in."

Everyone, even Diego, obediently checked their belts and gear. Ty fished an extra seraph blade out of the car trunk. Mark looked over Dru's gear, reminded her again that her job was to stay behind them and to stick close to the others.

Emma unbuckled her arm guard and rolled up her sleeve. She held her arm out to Julian. He looked at her bare arm and then up at her face and nodded. "Which one?"

"Endurance," she said. She was already marked with runes for courage and accuracy, runes for precision and healing. The Angel had never really given the Shadowhunters runes for emotional pain, though—there were no runes to mend grief or a broken heart.

The idea that her parents' death had been a failed experiment, a pointless throwaway, hurt more than Emma could have imagined. She had thought all these years they had died for some reason, but it was no reason at all. They had simply been the only Shadowhunters available.

Julian took her arm gently, and she felt the familiar and welcome pressure of the stele against her skin. As the Mark emerged, it seemed to flow into her bloodstream, like a shaft of cool water.

*Endurance.* She would have to endure this, this knowledge, fight past and through it. Do it for Tavvy, she thought. For Julian. For all of them. And maybe at the end of it, she would have her revenge.

Julian lowered his hand. His eyes were wide. The Mark blazed against her skin, infused with a brightness she had never seen before, as if the edges of it were burning. She drew her sleeve down quickly, not wanting anyone else to notice.

At the edge of the bluff, Kieran's white horse reared up against the moon. The sea crashed in the distance. Emma turned and marched toward the opening in the rock.

# 25

## TOMB BY THE SOUNDING SEA

**Emma and Julian led the way into the cavern, and Mark** brought up the rear, sandwiching the others between them. As before, the tunnel was narrow at first, the ground tumbled with uneven pebbles. The rocks were disturbed now, many of them kicked aside. Even in the dimness—Emma had not dared illuminate her witchlight—she could see where the moss growing along the cave wall had been clawed at by human fingers.

"People came through here earlier," Emma murmured. "A lot of people."

"Followers?" Julian's voice was low.

Emma shook her head. She didn't know. She was cold, the good sort of cold, the battle cold that came from your stomach and spread outward. The cold that sharpened your eyes and seemed to slow time around you, so that you had infinite hours to correct the sweep of a seraph blade, the angle of a sword.

She could feel Cortana between her shoulder blades, heavy and golden, whispering to her in her mother's voice. *Steel and temper, daughter.*

They came out into the high-ceilinged cavern. Emma stopped dead, and the others crowded around her. No one said a word.

The cavern was not as Emma remembered it. It was dim, giving the impression of immense space spreading away into darkness. The portholes were gone. Etched into the stone of the cave near her were the words of the poem that had become so familiar to them all. Emma could see sentences here and there, flashing out at her.

I was a child and she was a child,
In this kingdom by the sea,
But we loved with a love that was more than love—
I and my Annabel Lee—
With a love that the wingèd seraphs of Heaven
Coveted her and me.

*The wingèd seraphs of Heaven.*
Shadowhunters.

Julian's witchlight flared up in his hand, illuminating the space, and Emma gasped.

In front of them was a stone table. It rose chest high, the surface rough and pitted. It looked as if it had been carved out of black lava. A wide circle of white chalk, sketched on the floor, surrounded the table.

On it lay Tavvy. He seemed to be sleeping, his small face soft and slack, his eyes closed. His feet were bare, and his wrists and ankles were locked into chains that were attached by loops of iron to the table's stone legs.

A metal bowl, splashed with ominous-looking stains, had been placed by his head. Beside it was a jagged-toothed copper knife.

The witchlight cut into the shadows that seemed to hang in the room like a living thing. Emma wondered how big the cave really was, and how much of it was a shifting illusion.

Livvy cried out her brother's name and lunged forward. Julian caught hold of her, hauling her back. She struggled incredulously against his grip. "We need to save him," she hissed. "We have to get to him—"

"There's a protection circle," Julian hissed back. "Drawn around him on the floor. If you step through it, it could kill you."

Someone was murmuring softly. Cristina, whispering a prayer.

Mark had stiffened. "Be quiet," he said. "Someone's coming."

They did their best to melt back into the shadows, even Livvy, who had not stopped struggling. Julian's witchlight winked out.

A figure had appeared out of the darkness. Someone in a long black robe, a hood hiding their face. A tall someone with hands sheathed in black gloves. *He always showed up in a robe and gloves and a hood, okay? Completely covered.*

Emma's heart began to pound.

The figure approached the table, and the protection circle opened like a lock, runes vanishing and fading until there was a gap to step through. Head down, the figure came closer to Tavvy.

And closer. Emma felt the Blackthorns all around her, their fear like a living thing. She could taste blood in her mouth; she was biting her lip, so badly did she want to throw herself forward, risk the circle, grab Tavvy and run.

Livvy broke away from Julian and burst into the cavern. "No!" she cried. "Step away from my brother, or I'll kill you, I'll kill you—"

The figure froze. Slowly, it raised its head. Its hood fell back, and long, curling black hair spilled out. A familiar koi tattoo glimmered against brown skin. "Livvy?"

"Diana?" Ty spoke, voicing his sister's disbelief. Livvy was stricken silent.

Diana jerked away from the table, staring. "By the Angel," she breathed. "How many of you are here?"

It was Julian who spoke. His voice was level, though Emma could feel the effort it took to keep it that way. Diego was leaning forward, his eyes narrow. *Jace Herondale and the Lightwoods were betrayed by their own tutor.* "All of us," Julian said.

"Even Dru? You don't understand how dangerous this is— Julian, you have to get everyone out of here."

"Not without Tavvy," Emma snapped. "Diana, what the hell are you doing? You told us you were in Thailand."

"If she was, no one at the Bangkok Institute knew about it," said Diego. "I checked."

"You lied to us," Emma said. She remembered Iarlath saying: *Foolish Shadowhunters, too naive to even know who you can trust.* Had he meant Malcolm or Diana? "And you've barely been here, this whole investigation, like you were hiding something from us—"

Diana recoiled. "Emma, no, it's not like that."

"Then what is it like? Because I can't imagine what possible reason you could have for being here—"

There was a noise. Approaching footsteps, from the shadows. Diana flung out a hand. "Get back—get away—"

Julian grabbed for Livvy, hauling his sister back into the shadows just as Malcolm appeared.

Malcolm.

He looked just as he always did. A bit scruffy in jeans and a white linen jacket that matched his hair. In his hand he carried a large black book, tied with a leather strap.

"It *is* you," Diana whispered.

Malcolm looked at her calmly.

"Diana Wrayburn," he said. "Now, now. I didn't expect to see you here. I rather thought you'd run away."

Diana faced him. "I don't run."

He seemed to look at her again, to see how close she was to Tavvy. He frowned. "Step away from the boy."

Diana didn't move.

"Do it," he said, tucking the Black Volume into his jacket.

"He's nothing to you, anyway. You're not a Blackthorn."

"I'm his tutor. He has grown up in my care."

"Oh, come now," said Malcolm. "If you'd cared about those children, you'd have taken the post as head of the Institute years ago. But I suppose we all know why you didn't do that."

Malcolm grinned. It transformed his whole face. If Emma had still held lingering doubts about his guilt, about the story Kieran had told, they vanished in that moment. His mobile, amusing features seemed to harden. There was cruelty in that smile, framed against a backdrop of echoing, depthless loss.

A flare went up from the table, a burst of fire. Diana cried out and stumbled back, out of the circle of protection. It sealed itself up behind her. She hurled herself to her feet and threw herself toward Tavvy, but this time the circle held fast; she bounced off it as if off a glass wall, the force sending her staggering back.

"No human thing can cross that barrier," said Malcolm. "I'm guessing you had a charm to get you through the first time, but it won't work again. You should have stayed away."

"You can't possibly hope for success, Malcolm," Diana gasped. She was clutching her left arm with her right; the skin looked burned. "If you kill a Shadowhunter, the Nephilim will hunt you for the rest of your days."

"They hunted me two hundred years ago. They killed *her*," said Malcolm, and the throb of emotion in his voice was something Emma had never heard before. "And we had done nothing. Nothing. I do not fear them, their unjust justice or unlawful laws."

"I understand your pain, Malcolm," Diana said carefully. "But—"

"Do you? Do you understand, Diana Wrayburn?" he snarled—then his voice softened. "Maybe you do. You have known the injustice and intolerance of the Clave. If only you hadn't come here—it's the Blackthorns I despise, not the Wrayburns. I always rather liked you."

"You liked me because you thought I was too frightened of the Clave to look closely at you," Diana said, turning away from him. "To suspect you." For a moment she faced Emma and the others. She mouthed *RUN* at them silently, before turning back to Malcolm.

Emma didn't budge, but she did hear a movement behind her. It was quiet; if she hadn't been wearing a rune that sharpened her hearing, it would have been inaudible. To her surprise, the movement was Julian, disappearing from her side. Mark was next to him. Silently they slipped back into the tunnel.

Emma wanted to call after Julian—what was he doing?—but she couldn't, not without alerting Malcolm. Malcolm was still moving toward Diana; in a moment he'd be where he could see them. She put a hand to the hilt of Cortana. Ty was gripping a knife, white-knuckled; Livvy held her saber, her face set and determined.

"Who told you?" Malcolm said. "Was it Rook? I didn't think he'd guessed." He tipped his head to the side. "No. You weren't sure when you got here. You suspected . . ." His mouth turned down at the corners. "It was Catarina, wasn't it?"

Diana stood with her feet apart, her head back. A warrior stance. "When the second line of the poem was deciphered and I heard the phrase 'Blackthorn blood,' I realized that we weren't searching for a killer of mundanes and faeries. That this was about the Blackthorn family. And there is no one more likely to know about a grudge that goes back years than Catarina. I went to her."

"And you couldn't tell the Blackthorns where you went because of the reason you know Catarina," said Malcolm. "She's a nurse—a nurse to mundanes. How do you think I found out—?"

"She didn't tell you about me, Malcolm," snapped Diana. "She keeps secrets. What she told me about you was simply what she knew—that you'd loved a Nephilim girl and that she'd become an Iron Sister. She'd never questioned the story because as far as she knew, you'd never questioned the story. But once she told me that,

I was able to check with the Iron Sisters. No Nephilim girl with that story had become one of them. And once I realized *that* was a lie, the rest began to come together. I remembered what Emma had told us about what she'd found here, the clothes, the candelabra. Catarina went to the Spiral Labyrinth and I came here—"

"So Catarina gave you the charm to get you through the protection circle," said Malcolm. "Unfortunate that you wasted it. Did you have a plan or did you just rush here in a panic?"

Diana said nothing. Her face looked carved out of stone.

"Always have a plan," said Malcolm. "I, for one, have been crafting my current plan for years. And now here you are, the proverbial fly in the ointment. I suppose there's nothing to do but kill you, though I hadn't planned to, and exposing you to the Clave would have been so much more fun—"

Something silver bloomed from Diana's hand. A sharp-pointed throwing star. It whipped toward Malcolm; one moment he was in its path, the next he was across the room. The throwing star hit the wall of the cave and tumbled to the ground, where it lay glimmering.

Malcolm made a hissing noise, like an angry cat. Sparks flew from his fingers. Diana was lifted up into the air and flung back against the wall, then to the floor, her arms clamping themselves to her sides. She rolled into a sitting position, but when she tried to stand, her knees crumpled under her. She thrashed at her invisible bonds.

"You won't be able to move," Malcolm said in a bored voice. "You're paralyzed. I could have killed you instantly, of course, but well, this is quite a trick I'm about to perform and every trick needs an audience." He smiled suddenly. "I suppose I shouldn't forget the audience I have. It's just that they aren't very lively."

Suddenly the cavern was alive with light. The thick shadows behind the stone table dissolved, and Emma could see that the cavern reached back and back—there were long rows of seats set up, like church pews, neat and orderly, and the seats were filled with people.

"Followers," Ty breathed. He had only seen them before out of the window of the Institute, Emma thought, and wondered what he thought of them up close. It was strange to know that Malcolm had led all these people, that he had had such power over them that they did anything for him—Malcolm, who they'd all thought of as a foolish figure, someone who tied his own shoelaces together.

The Followers sat very still, their eyes wide open, their hands in their laps, like rows of dolls. Emma recognized Belinda and some of the others who had come to retrieve Sterling. Their heads were tilted to the side—a gesture of interest, Emma thought, until she realized how awkward the angle was and knew that it wasn't fascination that kept them so still. It was that their necks were broken.

Someone pressed forward and put a hand on Emma's shoulder. It was Cristina. "Emma," she whispered. "We must attack. Diego thinks we can surround Malcolm, that enough of us could bring him down—"

Emma stood paralyzed. She wanted to run forward, to attack Malcolm. But she could feel something in the back of her mind, an insistent voice, telling her to wait. It wasn't fear. It wasn't her own hesitation. If she hadn't known better, if she didn't think it would mean she was going crazy, she would have said it was Julian's voice. *Emma, wait. Please wait.*

"Wait," she whispered.

"Wait?" Cristina's anxiety was palpable. "Emma, we need to—"

Malcolm strode into the circle. He was standing close to Tavvy's feet, which looked bare and vulnerable in the light. He reached out to the draped object standing at the foot of the table and twitched the cloth off it.

It was the candelabra Emma remembered, the brass one that

had been bare of candles. It had become a far more macabre thing. Onto each spiked point was jammed a severed hand, wrist down. Rigid, dead fingers reached for the ceiling.

One hand bore a ring with a flashy pink stone. Sterling's hand.

"Do you know what this is?" Malcolm asked, a gloating note in his voice. "Do you, Diana?"

Diana looked up. Her face was swollen and bloody. She spoke in a croaking whisper. "Hands of Glory."

Malcolm looked pleased. "It took me quite a long time to figure out that this was what I needed," he said. "This is why my attempt with the Carstairs family didn't work. The spell called for mandrake, and it was a long time before I realized that the word 'mandrake' was meant to stand in for *main de gloire*—a Hand of Glory." He smiled with keen pleasure. "The darkest of dark magic."

"Because of the way they're made," said Diana. "They're murderers' hands. The hands of killers. Only a hand that has taken a human life can become a Hand of Glory."

"Oh." The small gasp in the darkness was Ty, his eyes wide and startled. "I get it now. I get it."

Emma turned toward him. They were pressed against opposite walls of the tunnel, looking across at each other. Livvy was next to Ty, Diego on his other side. Dru and Cristina were beside Emma.

"Diego said it was weird," Ty continued in a low whisper, "that the murder victims were such a mix—humans, faeries. It's because the victims never mattered. Malcolm didn't want victims, he wanted murderers. It was why the Followers needed Sterling back—and why Belinda cut off his hands and left with them. And why Malcolm let her. He needed the murderer's hands, the hands they'd killed with—so he could do this. Belinda took both hands because she didn't know which one he'd killed with—and she couldn't ask."

*But why?* Emma wanted to demand. *Why the burning, the drown-*

ing, *the markings, the rituals? Why?* But she was afraid that if she opened her mouth, a scream of rage would come out.

"This is wrong, Malcolm." Diana's voice was choked but steady. "I've spent days talking to those who've known you for years. Catarina Loss. Magnus Bane. They said you were a good, likable man. That can't be all lies."

"Lies?" Malcolm's voice rose. "You want to talk about lies? They lied to me about Annabel. They said she had become an Iron Sister. All of them told me the same lie: Magnus, Catarina, Tessa. It was from a faerie I found out that they had lied. From a faerie I learned what had really happened to Annabel. By then she was long dead. The Blackthorns, murdering their own!"

"That was generations back. The boy you have chained to that table never knew Annabel. These are not the people who hurt you, Malcolm. These are not the people who took Annabel from you. They're innocent."

"No one is innocent!" Malcolm shouted. "She was a Blackthorn! Annabel Blackthorn! She loved me, and they took her—they took her and walled her up and she died there in the tomb. They did that to me and I do not forgive! I will never forgive!" He took a deep breath, clearly forcing himself to be calm. "Thirteen Hands of Glory," he said. "And Blackthorn blood. That will bring her back, and she will be with me again."

He turned away from Diana, toward Tavvy, and picked up the knife that lay on the table by Tavvy's head.

The tension in the tunnel was sudden and silent and explosive. Hands reached for weapons. Grips tightened on hilts. Diego raised his ax. Five pairs of eyes turned to Emma.

Diana struggled even more desperately as Malcolm raised the knife. Light sparked off it, strangely beautiful, illuminating the lines of the poem on the wall.

*But we loved with a love that was more than love—*

*Julian*, Emma thought. *Julian, I've got no choice. We can't wait for you.*

"*Go*," she whispered, and they exploded out of the tunnel: Ty and Livvy and Emma and Cristina, all of them, Diego rushing straight for Malcolm.

For a split second Malcolm looked surprised. He dropped the knife—it hit the floor and, made of soft copper, the blade bent. Malcolm stared down at it, then back up at the Blackthorns and their friends—and began laughing. He stood, laughing, in the center of the protection circle, as they rushed at him—and one by one were slammed backward by the force of the invisible protective wall. Diego swung his battle-ax. The ax glanced off the air as if it had struck steel and recoiled backward.

"Surround Malcolm!" Emma shouted. "He can't stay in the protected area forever! Circle him!"

They spread out, surrounding the protective runes on the floor. Emma found herself across from Ty, knife in hand; he was looking at Malcolm with a peculiar expression on his face: half incomprehension, half hatred.

Ty understood acting, pretending. But betrayal on the scale Malcolm had practiced it was something else again. Emma couldn't understand it herself and she'd had a clear view of just what kind of betrayal people were capable of when she'd watched the Clave exile Helen and abandon Mark.

"You'll have to come out of there eventually," Emma said. "And when you do—"

Malcolm bent and seized his damaged knife from the floor. When he straightened up, Emma saw that his eyes were the color of bruises. "When I do, you'll be dead," he spat, and whirled to reach out a hand toward the rows of the dead. "Rise!" he called. "My Followers, rise!"

There was a series of groans and creaks. Throughout the cave the dead Followers began to stand.

They moved neither unusually slowly nor unusually quickly, but they moved with steady determination. They did not seem to be armed, but as they neared the main chamber, Belinda—her eyes blank and empty, her head cocked to the side—flung herself at Cristina. Her fingers were bent into claws, and before Cristina could react, Belinda had torn bloody gashes down the side of her face.

With a cry of disgust, Cristina shoved the corpse away from her, slashing her butterfly knife across Belinda's throat.

It made no difference. Belinda stood up again, the wound in her throat bloodless and flapping, and swung toward Cristina. Before she could take more than a single step there was a flash of silver. Diego's ax sang out, whipping forward, severing Belinda's head from her neck. The headless body sank to the ground. The wound still wasn't bleeding; it looked cauterized.

"Behind you!" Cristina shouted.

Diego whirled. Behind him two other Followers were reaching to grab and claw at them. He spun in a swift arc, his ax taking both their heads with it.

There was a noise behind Emma. Instantly she calculated where the Follower behind her was; she leaped, spun, kicked, and knocked him back. It was the clarinetist with the curly hair. She stabbed downward with Cortana, severing his head from his body.

She thought of him winking at her in the Midnight Theater. *I never knew his name*, she thought, and then whirled back around.

The room was in chaos. Just as Malcolm must have wanted, the Shadowhunters had abandoned the perimeter of the protection circle to ward off the Followers.

Malcolm was ignoring everything that was going on around him. He had seized up the candelabra with the Hands of Glory on it and carried it to the head of the table. He set it down beside Tavvy, who slept on, a rosy flush on his cheeks.

Dru had run to Diana and was struggling to help her get to her feet. As a Follower approached them, Dru whipped around and ran the woman through with her blade. Emma saw her swallow as the body crumpled and realized it was the first time Dru had killed someone in battle—even if that someone was already dead.

Livvy was fighting gloriously, feinting and parrying with her saber, driving Followers toward Ty. He was carrying a seraph blade, one that blazed brightly in his grip. As a blond Follower lurched into him, he drove the blade into the back of the dead man's neck.

There was a searing, crackling noise as the seraph blade met flesh and the Follower began to burn. He staggered away, clawing at his burning flesh, before tumbling to the ground.

"Seraph blades!" Emma called. "Everyone! Use your seraph blades!"

Lights blazed up through the cavern and Emma heard the murmur of voices calling the names of angels. Jophiel, Remiel, Duma. Through the haze of light she saw Malcolm with the bent copper knife. He ran a hand along the blade and it sprang back under his fingers, as sharp as it had been originally. He placed the tip of it against Tavvy's throat and sliced downward, slitting open the little boy's Batman T-shirt. The worn cotton curled open, revealing his thin, vulnerable chest.

Emma's world seemed to drop away. In the chaos of the room, she was still fighting, her seraph blade flaming as she plunged it into one Follower, then two, then three. Their bodies crumpled all around her.

She tried to push through them, toward Tavvy, just as she heard Julian's voice. She whirled around but couldn't see him—and yet his voice had been clear in her ears, saying, *Emma, Emma, move aside, away from the tunnel.*

She jumped aside, skirting the body of a fallen Follower, just as she heard a new noise: the thunder of hooves. A sound pierced the room, something between a howl and the crash of an enormous bell. It bounced off the walls, a brutal echo, and even Malcolm looked up.

Windspear exploded from the mouth of the tunnel. Julian sat astride him, his hands buried in the horse's mane. Mark was behind him, gripping his brother's belt. They seemed to blur almost into one person as Windspear leaped.

Malcolm gaped as the horse hurtled through the air, smashing through the protective barrier. As Windspear sailed over the table, Julian flung himself from the horse's back, falling heavily onto the flat stone surface beside Tavvy. Emma felt the bone-jarring shock of his pain go through her own body.

Mark kept his seat as Windspear swept over the table and landed on the other side of the circle. The circle itself, now pierced, began to writhe like an illuminated serpent, the runes flaring up one by one and then going out.

Julian was pulling himself up onto his knees. Malcolm snarled and reached for Tavvy—just as a figure dropped from the ceiling and knocked him to the ground.

It was Kieran. His hair shimmered blue-green and he raised a blade that was the same sea color. It plunged down toward Malcolm's chest, but Malcolm threw his hands up. Dark purple light exploded from his palms, hurling Kieran back. Malcolm rose to his feet, his face twisted in a snarl of hate. He flung out a hand to crush Kieran into dust.

Windspear gave a scream. The horse whirled around, hooves raised, and punched them into Malcolm's back; somehow Mark kept his seat. The warlock went flying. The horse, red eyes wide, reared and snorted. Mark, grabbing a fistful of Windspear's mane, leaned down, his other hand outstretched toward Kieran.

"Take it," Emma heard him say. "Kieran, take my hand."

Kieran reached up, and Mark pulled him upright, hauling him onto Windspear's back. They swung around and charged at a knot of Followers, the horse scattering them, Mark and Kieran reaching down to finish off the living dead with strokes of their swords.

Malcolm was dragging himself to his feet. His once-white jacket was liberally stained now with dirt and blood. He began to move toward the table, where Julian was kneeling over Tavvy, tugging at the chains that bound him. The protection circle surrounding them was still sputtering. Emma took a deep breath and raced for the table, leaping into the air.

She felt a wavering snap of electricity as she passed through the broken circle, crouched, and flung herself upward. She landed on the table in a kneeling position, beside Julian.

"Move away!" was all she had time to gasp. "Julian, move!"

He rolled away from his brother, though she knew that letting go of Tavvy was the last thing he wanted to do. He slid to the edge of the table and rose to his knees, leaning back. Trusting Emma. Giving her space.

*A blade made by Wayland the Smith can cut anything.*

She swung down with Cortana, a few inches from Tavvy's wrist. The edge of the blade sliced through the chain and it fell away, rattling. She heard Malcolm scream, and a flash of violet fire split the room.

Emma slashed down again with Cortana, severing the other chains holding Tavvy to the table. "Go!" she shouted at Julian. "Get him out of here!"

Julian caught up his little brother in his arms. Octavian hung limp, his eyes rolled back. Julian leaped down from the table.

Emma didn't see him vanish into the tunnel; she had already whirled back around. Mark and Kieran were trapped at one end of the room by a group of Followers, Diego and Cristina at another. Malcolm was advancing on Ty and Livvy. He raised his hand again—and a small figure flew toward him, holding up a blazing seraph blade.

It was Dru.

"Stay away from them!" she shrieked, her blade shining between them. "Stay away from my brother and sister!"

Malcolm snarled, curling his finger toward her. A rope of purple light coiled around Dru's legs, jerking her off her feet. The seraph blade rolled away, sputtering against the stone. "I still need Blackthorn blood," Malcolm said, reaching down for her. "And yours will do as well as your little brother's would have. In fact, you look like you'd have a lot more of it—"

"Stop!" Emma shouted.

Malcolm looked up at her—and froze. Emma was standing upright on the stone table. One hand clutched Cortana. The other held the candelabra of Hands of Glory.

"It took you a long time to collect these, didn't it?" she said in a cold voice. "The hands of thirteen murderers. Not so easy."

Malcolm released Dru and she scuttled away toward the far side of the room, scrabbling at her belt for another weapon. Malcolm's face contorted. "Give it back."

"Call them off," Emma said. "Call off your Followers, and I'll give you back your Hands of Glory."

"Deprive me of my chance to regain Annabel, and you will pay with agony," he snarled.

"Can't be worse than the agony of hearing you talk," Emma said. "Call them off or I'll cut these disgusting things into tiny pieces." She tightened her grip on Cortana. "Let's see if you can do a magic spell with those."

Malcolm's gaze swept the room. The bodies of Followers littered the cavern, but some of them were still on their feet, pinning Diego and Cristina in the corner of the room. Mark and Kieran were astride Windspear, both laying about themselves with blades. The horse's hooves were stained red-brown with blood.

The warlock's hands clenched at his sides. He turned and spat a few words in Greek, and the remaining Followers began to fall, crumpling to the ground. Diego and Cristina dashed over to Dru; Kieran brought Windspear to a halt and the faerie steed stood still as the dead fell dead once again.

Malcolm charged toward the table. Emma ran the length of it, sprang off the end, and landed lightly on the floor. Then she kept running.

She ran toward the rows of chairs that had been set up for the Followers, down the aisle between them, and into the shadows. The faint glow of Cortana gave enough light that she could see a dark corridor between rocks, snaking away into the hill.

She plunged into it. Only the glowing moss on the walls gave any illumination. She thought she could see a glimmer in the distance and pressed on, though running with the heavy candelabra was making her arm ache.

The corridor forked. Hearing footsteps behind her, Emma plunged to the left. She had only been running for a few yards when a glass wall loomed up in front of her.

The porthole. It had grown larger, filling nearly a whole wall. The massive lever Emma remembered protruded from the stone beside it. The porthole glowed from within, like an enormous aquarium.

Behind the glass she could see the ocean—it was radiant, a deep blue-green. She could see fish and drifting seaweed and strange lights and colors beyond the glass.

"Oh, Emma, Emma," said Malcolm's voice behind her. "You took the wrong path, didn't you? But one could say that about so much of your life."

Emma spun and jabbed the candelabra toward Malcolm. "Get away from me."

"Do you have any idea how precious those hands are?" he demanded. "For the fullest potency, they had to be severed just after the murder was performed. Setting up the killings was a feat of skill and daring and timing. You can't believe how annoyed I was when you took Sterling from me before I could collect his hand. Belinda had to bring me both of them so I could discern which was the murdering instrument. And then Julian calling me for help—a stroke of luck, I have to say."

"It wasn't luck. We trusted you."

"And I trusted Shadowhunters once," said Malcolm. "We all make mistakes." *Keep him talking*, she thought. *The others will follow me.*

"Johnny Rook said you told him to tell me about the body dump at the Sepulchre," she said. "Why? Why set me on your trail?"

He moved a step forward. She jabbed the candelabra toward him. He held his hands up as if to placate her. "I needed you distracted. I needed you focused on the victims, not the murderers. Besides, you had to learn about the situation before the faerie convoy arrived on your doorstep."

"And asked us to investigate the murders you were committing? What did you get out of *that*?"

"I got the absolute promise that the Clave would stay out of it," said Malcolm. "Individual Shadowhunters don't frighten me, Emma. But the whole mess of them could be a mess indeed. I've known Iarlath a long time. I knew he had connections to the Wild Hunt and I knew the Wild Hunt had something that would make you move Heaven and earth to keep information from the Clave and the Silent Brothers. Nothing against the boy personally; at least his Blackthorn stock is diluted by some good, healthy Downworlder blood. But I know Julian. I knew what he'd prioritize, and it wasn't the Law or the Clave."

"You underestimated us," Emma said. "We figured it out. We realized it was you."

"I thought they might send a Centurion, but I never guessed

he'd be someone you knew. Trusted enough to take into your confidence despite Mark. When I saw the Rosales boy, I realized I didn't have much time. I knew I'd have to take Tavvy right away. Thankfully, I had Iarlath's help, which has been invaluable. Oh," he added. "I heard about the whipping. I'm very sorry about that. Iarlath has his own ways of having fun, and they aren't mine."

"You're sorry?" Emma stared in disbelief. "You killed my parents, and you're *apologizing*? I'd rather be whipped a thousand times and have my parents back."

"I know what you're thinking. You Shadowhunters all think alike. But I need you to *understand*—" Malcolm broke off, his face working. "If you understood," he said, "you wouldn't blame me."

"Then tell me what happened," Emma said. She could see the corridor behind him, over his shoulder, thought she could see shapes, shadows in the distance. If she could keep him distracted and the others could attack from behind . . . "You went to Faerie," she said. "When you found out that Annabel wasn't an Iron Sister. That she'd been murdered. Is that how you know Iarlath?"

"Despite not being born gentry, he was the right hand of the Unseelie King back then," said Malcolm. "When I went, I knew the King might have me murdered. They don't much like warlocks. But I didn't care. And when the King asked me a favor, I did it. In return, he gave me the rhyme. A spell custom made to raise my Annabel. Blackthorn blood. Blood for blood, that's what the King said."

"So why didn't you just raise her right then? Why wait?"

"Faerie magic and warlock magic are very different," said Malcolm. "It was like translating something from another language. It took me years to decipher the poem. Then I realized it was telling me to find a book. I almost went out of my mind. Years of translation and all I got was a riddle about a book—" His eyes bored into hers, as if he were willing her to understand. "It was just chance that it was your parents," he said. "They returned to the

Institute while I was there. But it didn't work. I did everything the spell book said, and Annabel didn't stir."

"My parents—"

"Your love for them wasn't greater than my love for Annabel," Malcolm said. "I was trying to make things *fair*. It was never about hurting *you*. I don't hate the Carstairs. Your parents were sacrifices."

"Malcolm—"

"They would have sacrificed themselves, wouldn't they?" he asked reasonably. "For the Clave? For you?"

A rage so great it was numbing washed through Emma. It was all she could do to stay still. "So you waited five years?" She choked out the question. "Why five years?"

"I waited until I thought I'd gotten the spell right," said Malcolm. "I used the time to learn. To build. I took Annabel's body from her tomb and moved it to the convergence. I created the Followers of the Guardian. Belinda was the first murderer. I followed the ritual—burned and soaked the body, carved the markings onto it—and I felt Annabel move." His eyes shone, an unholy blue-violet. "I knew I was bringing her back. After that nothing could have stopped me."

"But why those markings?" Emma pressed herself back against the wall. The candelabra was heavy; her arm was throbbing. "Why the Unseelie King's poem?"

"Because it was a message!" Malcolm cried. "Emma, for someone who's talked so much about revenge, who's lived it and breathed it, you don't seem to understand much about it. I needed the Shadowhunters to know. I needed the Blackthorns to know, when the youngest of them lay dead, whose hand had dealt them that blow. When someone has wronged you, it isn't enough that they suffer. They need to look at your face and know why they suffer. I needed the Clave to decipher that poem and learn exactly who would be their destruction."

"Destruction?" Emma couldn't help her incredulous echo. "You're insane. Killing Tavvy wouldn't destroy the Nephilim—and none of them who are alive even know about Annabel—"

"And how do you think that feels?" he shouted. "Her name forgotten? Her fate buried? The Shadowhunters turned her into a story. I think several of her kinsmen went mad—they couldn't bear what they'd done, couldn't bear the weight of the secret."

*Keep him talking,* Emma thought. "If it was such a secret, how did Poe know? The poem, 'Annabel Lee'—"

Something flashed across the backs of Malcolm's eyes, something secretive and dark. "When I heard it, I thought it was a sickening coincidence," he said. "But it obsessed me. I went to talk to the poet, but he had died. 'Annabel' was his last work." His voice was bleak with memory. "Years went by, and I believed her to be in the Adamant Citadel. It was all that comforted me. That she was alive somewhere. When I found out, I wanted to deny it, but it was the poem that proved the facts of it—Poe had learned the truth from Downworlders, learned it before I did—how Annabel and I had loved as children, how she would have left the Nephilim for me, but her family heard of it and decided death was preferable to life with a warlock. They'd walled her up in a tomb by the Cornwall sea, walled her up alive. Later, when I moved her body, I kept it near the ocean. She always loved the water."

His breath was coming in sobs now. Emma, unable to move, stared. His grief was as raw and real as if what he were talking about had happened yesterday.

"They told me she'd become an Iron Sister. All of them lied to me—Magnus, Catarina, Ragnor, Tessa—corrupted by Shadowhunters, drawn in by their lies! And I, oblivious, grieving for her, until finally I found out the truth—"

Sudden voices echoed in the hall; Emma heard the sound of running feet. Malcolm snapped his fingers. Violet light shimmered in the tunnel behind them, its iridescence fading as it grew dimmer and more opaque, solidifying into a wall.

The sound of voices and footsteps vanished. Emma stood inside a sealed cave with Malcolm.

She backed up, clutching the candelabra. "I'll destroy the hands," she warned, her heart pounding. "I'll do it."

Dark fire sparked at his fingertips. "I could let you go," he said. "Let you live. Swim away through the ocean like you did before. You could carry my message back for me. My message to the Clave."

"I don't need you to let me go." She was breathing hard. "I'd rather fight."

His smile was twisted, almost sorrowful. "You and your sword, no matter its history, are no match for a warlock, Emma."

"What do you want from me?" she demanded, her voice rising, echoing off the walls of the cave. "What do you want, Malcolm?"

"I want you to understand," he said through gritted teeth. "I want someone to tell the Clave what they're responsible for, I want them to know the blood on their hands, I want them to know *why*."

Emma stared at Malcolm, a thin, stretched figure in a stained white jacket, sparks dancing along the edges of his fingertips. He frightened her and made her sad, all at the same time.

"Your why doesn't matter," she said finally. "Maybe you did what you did in the name of love. But if you think that makes any difference, you're no better than the Clave."

He moved toward her—and Emma flung the candelabra at him. He ducked away and it missed, hitting the rock floor with a clang. The fingers of the severed hands seemed to curl in as if to protect themselves. Emma planted her feet apart, remembering Jace Herondale, years ago in Idris, showing her how to stand so you'd never be knocked down.

She gripped the hilt of Cortana in a two-fisted grip, and this time she remembered Clary Fairchild, and the words she'd said to

Emma in Idris, when Emma had been twelve years old. *Heroes aren't always the ones who win. They're the ones who lose, sometimes. But they keep fighting, they keep coming back. They don't give up. That's what makes them heroes.*

Emma sprang toward Malcolm, Cortana upraised. He reacted with a second's delay—flinging his hand toward her, light bursting from his fingers. It sizzled toward her, a streak of gold-and-violet light.

The delay gave her time to duck. She spun and raised Cortana over her head. Magic slid off the blade. She threw herself at Malcolm again and he ducked away, though not before she had slashed open his sleeve, just above the elbow. He barely seemed to notice.

"The death of your parents was necessary," he said. "I had to see if the book worked."

"No, you didn't," Emma snarled, brandishing Cortana. "You should know better than to try to raise the dead."

"Because if Julian died, you wouldn't try to bring him back?" said Malcolm with a delicate rise of his eyebrows, and Emma recoiled as if he'd slapped her. "You wouldn't bring your mother and father back? Oh, it's so easy for you, as it is for all Shadow-hunters, standing there, making your moral pronouncements, as if you're better than the rest of us—"

"I am better," Emma said. "I'm better than you. Because I'm not a murderer, Malcolm."

To Emma's shock, Malcolm recoiled—a true recoil of surprise, as if he hadn't imagined being called a murderer before. Emma lunged, Cortana outstretched. The sword drove into Malcolm's chest, splitting his blazer—and rammed to a stop, as if she'd stabbed it into a boulder.

She shrieked with pain as what felt like a bolt of electricity went up her arm. She heard Malcolm laugh, and a wave of energy shot from his outstretched fingers, slamming into her body. She was lifted and hurled backward, magic tearing through her like a bullet ripping a hole through a paper screen. She hit the uneven stone ground on her back, Cortana still gripped in her nerveless hand.

Red pain misted behind her eyelids. Through the fog, she saw Malcolm standing over her. "Oh, that was precious." He grinned. "That was amazing. That was the hand of God, Emma!" He yanked his blazer open, and Emma saw what Cortana had struck—the Black Volume, tucked into the inside pocket of his jacket.

Cortana dropped from her hand, the metal hitting stone. Wincing, Emma shoved herself up onto her elbows, just as Malcolm bent down and seized the dropped candelabra. He looked at it and then down at her, his grin still slashed across his face.

"Thank you," he said. "These Hands of Glory would have been very hard to replace. Now, Blackthorn blood, that'll be easy."

"Stay away from the Blackthorns," Emma said, and was horrified to hear the weakness of her own voice. What had the Black Volume done to her? Her chest felt as if something heavy had been rolled onto it, and her arm burned and ached.

"You don't know anything," Malcolm snarled. "You don't know the monsters they are."

"Have you," Emma said in a near whisper, "have you always hated them? Julian and the rest?"

"Always," he said. "Even when it seemed like I loved them."

Emma's arm was still burning, an agony that felt as if her skin was being lanced down to the bone. Her Endurance rune felt as if it were on fire. She tried not to let it show on her face. "That's horrible. It's not their fault. You can't blame them for their ancestors' sins."

"Blood is blood," Malcolm said. "We are all what we were born to be. I was born to love Annabel and that was taken from me. Now I live only for revenge. Just as you have, Emma. How many times have you told me that all you want in life is to kill the one who killed your parents? What would you give up for it? Would you give up the Blackthorns? Would you give up your precious *parabatai*? The one you're in love with?" His eyes glittered as she shook her head in denial. "Please. I *always* saw the way you looked at each other. And then Julian told me that your rune had healed him from Rook's poison. No normal Shadowhunter's rune should have been able to do that."

"Not—proof of anything—" Emma gasped.

"Proof? You want proof? I saw you, the two of you. On the beach, sleeping in each other's arms. I stood over you and watched you and thought how easy it would be to kill you. But then I realized that that would be a mercy, wouldn't it? Killing the two of you while you were in each other's arms? There's a reason you can't fall in love with your *parabatai*, Emma. And when you find out what it is, you will feel the cruelty of the Shadowhunters, just as I have."

"You're a liar," she said in her weakest voice, her words trailing off into a whisper. The pain in her arm had gone. She thought of people who bled nearly to death, how they talked about the fact that in the last moments, all the pain vanished.

Smiling, Malcolm knelt down beside her. He patted her left hand; her fingers twitched. "Let me tell you a truth before you die, Emma," he said. "It is a secret about the Nephilim. They hate love, human love, because they were born of angels. And while God charged his angels to take care of humans, the angels were made first, and they have always hated God's second creation. That is why Lucifer fell. He was an angel who would not bow to mankind, God's favored child. Love is the weakness of human beings, and the angels despise them for it, and the Clave despises it too, and therefore they punish it. Do you know what happens to *parabatai* who fall in love? Do you know why it's forbidden?"

She shook her head.

His mouth quirked into a smile. There was something about

that smile, so faint and yet so full of bone-deep hatred, that chilled her the way none of his grinning had. "Then you have no idea what your death will spare your beloved Julian," he said. "So think about that as the life leaves your body. In a way, your death is a mercy." He raised his hand, violet fire beginning to crackle between his fingers.

He hurled his magic at her. And Emma flung her arm up, the arm that Julian had carved the Endurance rune on, the arm that had been burning and aching and screaming at her to use it since she'd struck the Black Volume.

Fire slammed into her arm. She felt it like a hard blow, but nothing more. The Endurance rune was pulsing through her body with its power, and alongside that power rose her own rage.

Rage at knowing Malcolm had killed her parents, rage for the wasted years she'd searched for their killer when he'd been right in front of her. Rage for every time he'd smiled at Julian or picked up Tavvy when his heart was full of hate. Rage at one more thing that had been taken from the Blackthorns.

She seized Cortana and wrenched herself to her knees, her hair flying as she drove the sword into Malcolm's gut.

This time there was no Black Volume to block her thrust. She felt the blade go in, felt it tear through skin and rip past bone. Saw the tip of it burst out through his back, his white jacket soaked through with red blood.

She sprang to her feet, yanking the sword free. He made a choking noise. Blood was spilling onto the ground, running across the stone, spattering the Hands of Glory.

"This is for my parents," she said, and slammed his body as hard as she could against the glass wall.

She felt his ribs snap as the glass behind him fissured. Water began to pour through the cracks. She felt it splatter against her face, salty as tears.

"I'll tell you about the *parabatai* curse," he gasped. "The Clave will never let you know it—it's forbidden. Kill me and you'll never learn—"

With her left hand, Emma yanked down the lever.

She threw herself behind the glass door as it swung open, and the current exploded through. It moved like a living thing—like a hand, shaped out of water, formed by the sea. It surrounded Malcolm, and for a frozen moment Emma saw him there clearly, struggling with feeble motions, within a whirlpool of water, water that spilled across the floor, water that gripped him, encircling him like an unbreakable net.

It lifted Malcolm off his feet. He gave a cry of terror and the ocean took him, the current rushing back out, carrying him with it. The glass door slammed shut.

The silence the water left behind was deafening. Exhausted, Emma slumped against the glass of the porthole door. Through it she could see the ocean, the color of the night sky. Malcolm's body was a pale white star in the darkness, drifting among the weeds, and then a dark, spiky talon curled upward, through the ripples, and caught hold of Malcolm by the ankle. With a quick jerk, his body was yanked down and out of view.

There was a bright flicker. Emma turned to see that the violet wall of light in the corridor behind her had vanished—spells disappeared when the warlocks who cast them died.

"Emma!" There were pounding footsteps in the corridor. Out of the shadows, Julian appeared. She saw his stricken expression as he caught her to him, his hands knotting in her soaked, bloodstained gear. "Emma, God, I couldn't get to you through the wall, I knew you were there but I couldn't save you—"

"You saved me," she said hoarsely, wanting to show him the Endurance rune on her arm, but she was pressed too tightly against him to move. "You did. You don't know it, but you did."

And then she heard their voices. The others, coming toward them down the corridor. Mark. Cristina. Diego. Diana.

"Tavvy," she whispered. "Is he—"

"He's fine. He's outside with Ty and Livvy and Dru." He kissed her temple. "Emma." His lips brushed hers. She felt a shock of love and pain go through her.

"Let me go," she whispered. "You have to let me go, they can't see us like this. Julian, let me go."

His head came up, his eyes full of agony, and he moved away. She saw what it cost him, saw the tremor in his hands as he lowered them to his sides. Felt the space between them like the space of a wound torn into flesh.

She dragged her gaze from his and looked down at the ground. The floor was awash with seawater and blood, ankle-deep. Somewhere Malcolm's candelabra floated beneath the surface.

Emma was glad. The salt would dissolve Malcolm's gruesome monument to murder, dissolve it and pick it clean, and it would be white bones, settling as Malcolm's body settled to the floor of the ocean. And for the first time in a long time, Emma felt grateful to the sea.

# 26
## THE WINGED SERAPHS
## OF HEAVEN

*The parabatai curse. The Clave will never let you know it—it's forbidden—*

Malcolm's words rang in Emma's ears as she made her way back out into the night, following the others down the damp corridors of the convergence. Julian and Emma walked deliberately apart, keeping distance between them. Exhaustion and pain were slowing Emma down. Cortana was back in its sheath. She could feel the sword humming with energy; she wondered if it had absorbed magic from Malcolm.

But then, she didn't want to think about Malcolm, the red tendrils of his blood unfurling through the dark water like banners.

She didn't want to think about the things he'd said.

Emma was the last to step out of the cave, into the darkness of the outside world. Ty, Livvy, and Dru were sitting on the ground with Tavvy—the little boy was cradled in Livvy's arms, seeming sleepy but awake. Kieran stood a distance away, a scowl on his face that relaxed only somewhat when Mark emerged from the convergence.

"How is Tavvy? Is everything all right?" Julian approached his siblings. Dru jumped up and hugged him tightly—then gasped and pointed.

A loud grinding noise cracked through the air. The gap in the hill was closing up behind them like a wound healing. Diana darted toward it, as if she could hold the pathway open, but the stone sealed shut; she snatched her hand back just in time to keep it from being crushed.

"You cannot stop it," said Kieran. "The opening and the path inside were made by Malcolm. This hill does not naturally hold within it tunnels and caves. Now that he is dead, his enchantments are failing. There may perhaps be another entrance into this space, at some other ley line convergence. But this door will not open again."

"How did you know he was dead?" Emma said.

"Lights going on in the city below," said Kieran. "The—I don't know what your mundane word is for it—"

"Blackout," said Mark. "The blackout's over. And Malcolm cast the spell that was responsible for the blackout, so—yeah."

"Does that mean we can get a signal on our phones?" Ty wondered.

"I'll check," Julian said, and walked away to press his phone to his ear. Emma thought she heard him say Uncle Arthur's name, but she couldn't be sure, and he moved out of earshot before she could hear another word.

Diego and Cristina had joined Livvy, Ty, and Dru. Cristina was bending down over Tavvy, and Diego was reaching for something inside his gear jacket. Emma moved to join them; as she drew closer, she saw that Diego was holding a silver flask.

"Not giving him booze, are you?" Emma said. "He's a little young for it."

Diego rolled his eyes. "It's an energy draught. Made by the Silent Brothers. Might counteract whatever Malcolm gave him to make him sleepy."

Livvy took the flask from Diego and tasted the contents; with a nod, she tipped the fluid into her little brother's mouth. Tavvy drank gratefully as Emma knelt down and put her hand to his cheek.

"Hey, sweetheart," she said. "Are you all right?"

He smiled up at her, blinking. He looked like Julian when he and Emma were children. Before the world had changed him. *My best friend and my best love.*

She thought of Malcolm. *The* parabatai *curse.* Her heart aching, she kissed Tavvy's baby-soft cheek and rose to her feet to find Cristina behind her.

"Your left arm," Cristina said gently, and led her a few feet away. "Hold it out?"

Emma obeyed and saw that the skin of her hand and wrist was red and blistered, as if she'd been burned.

Cristina shook her head, drawing her stele from her jacket. "There were a few minutes there, when you were behind that wall Malcolm made, where I thought you weren't coming out."

Emma bumped her head against Cristina's shoulder. "Sorry."

"I know." Cristina turned brisk, pushing up Emma's sleeve. "You need healing runes."

Emma leaned into Cristina as the stele ran over her skin, taking comfort in the fact that she was there. "It was weird, being trapped in there with Malcolm," she said. "Mostly he just wanted to tell me about Annabel. And the thing is—I actually felt bad for him."

"It's not weird," said Cristina. "It's a terrible story. Neither he nor Annabel did anything wrong. To see someone you love so horribly punished and tortured—to think they'd abandoned you only to find out that you abandoned them—" She shuddered.

"I hadn't thought about it that way," Emma said. "You think he felt guilty?"

"I'm sure he did. Anyone would."

Emma thought of Annabel with a pang. She had been blameless, a victim. Hopefully she had never been aware of anything, never been aware of Malcolm's efforts to revive her. "I told him he was as bad as the Clave and he actually seemed surprised."

"No one is ever the villain of their own story." Cristina released Emma, pausing to examine her healing handiwork. Already the pain in Emma's arm was receding. She knew a rune from Julian would most likely have worked more quickly, but after what had happened with the Endurance rune, she didn't dare let him rune her in front of everyone else.

Julian. Past Cristina's shoulder, she could see him, near the car. He was holding his phone to his ear. As she watched, he tapped the screen and slid it back into his pocket.

"So are the signals working again?" Ty asked. "Who were you calling?"

"Pizza," Julian said.

They all stared at him. Like the rest of them, he was filthy, a long scratch along his cheek, his hair tangled. In the moonlight his eyes were the color of an underground river.

"Thought we might all be hungry," he said with that deceptive mildness that Emma now knew meant that whatever was happening on the surface didn't match what was going on in Julian's mind.

"We should go," he said. "The convergence's collapse means the Clave is going to be able to see the dark magic emanating from this place on their map. When we get back, I don't think we'll be alone."

They hurried to get everyone ready to go: Livvy carrying Octavian on her lap in the backseat of the Toyota, Diana taking Cristina and Diego in the truck, which she had hidden among some scrub brush. Kieran offered the use of Windspear again to Mark, but Mark declined.

"I wish to ride with my brothers and sisters," he said simply.

Julian turned to Kieran. The faerie's eyes were flat, unreflective. Julian wished he could see what his brother had loved: a Kieran who had been warm toward Mark or kind. He wished he could thank Kieran for not leaving Mark alone among the Hunt.

He wished he felt less hatred in his heart.

"You don't need to come back with us," Julian said. "We don't need your help anymore."

"I will not go until I know Mark is safe."

Julian shrugged. "Have it your way. When we get back, don't come into the Institute until we say so. We'd be in trouble just for fighting alongside you."

Kieran's mouth hardened. "Without me, you would have been defeated this night."

"Probably," said Julian. "I'll remember to be grateful every time I see the scars on Emma's back."

Kieran flinched. Julian turned and walked toward the car. Diana cut in front of him, holding up a hand. She was wrapped in a heavy shawl, and her face was speckled with blood like light freckles.

"The Clave may well be waiting for you," she said without preamble. "If you want, I'll take the blame for everything and throw myself on their mercy."

Julian looked at her for a long moment. He had lived by ironclad rules for so long. *Protect Tavvy, protect Livvy and Ty, protect Dru. Protect Emma.* Recently that had widened out slightly—he would protect Mark, because Mark had come back, and he would protect Cristina, because Emma loved her.

It was a sort of love few other people could understand. It was total and it was overwhelming and it could be cruel. He would destroy a whole city if he thought that city posed some threat to his family.

When you were twelve years old and you were all that stood between your family and annihilation, you didn't learn moderation.

He considered now, with all the detachment he could muster, what would happen if Diana tried to take the blame—he entertained the idea, turned it over in his head, and rejected it. "No," he said. "And I'm not being kind. I don't think it would work."

"Julian—"

"You hide things," he said. "The Angel knows there's something you're still hiding, some reason you couldn't take over the Institute. Something you won't tell, anyway. You're a good hider, but you're not a good liar. They won't believe you. But they will believe me."

"So you already have a story for them?" Diana asked, her dark eyes widening.

Julian didn't say anything.

She sighed, pulling the shawl tighter. "You're a piece of work, Julian Blackthorn."

"I'll take that as a compliment," he said, though he doubted she meant it as one.

"Did you know I'd be here tonight?" she asked. "Did you think I was in league with Malcolm?"

"I didn't think it was likely," Julian said. "But then, I don't entirely trust anyone."

"That's not true," Diana said, looking across to where Mark was helping Emma into the driver's side of the car. Her blond hair flew like sparks in the starlight. Diana glanced back at Julian. "You'd better get back. I'll make myself scarce until tomorrow."

"I'll tell them you didn't know anything. It isn't as if people don't deceive their tutors all the time. And you don't even live with us." He heard the Toyota start up. The others were waiting for him. "So you'll drop Diego and Cristina at the Institute and then head home?"

"I'll head somewhere," she said.

He started toward the car, then paused and turned to look back at her. "Do you ever regret it? Choosing to be our tutor? You didn't have to."

The wind blew her dark hair across her face. "No," she said. "I am who I am because I've been part of your family. Never forget, Jules. The choices we make, make us."

The drive back was silent and exhausted. Ty was quiet, looking out the window of the passenger seat. Dru was curled into a ball. Tavvy was awake but barely, his head against Livia's shoulder. Emma was slumped against a backseat window, holding Cortana, her damp blond hair straggling around her face, her eyes closed. Mark was squeezed in beside her.

Julian wanted to reach for Emma, slide his hand into hers, but he didn't dare, not in front of the others. He couldn't stop himself from reaching back from the driver's seat to touch Tavvy's arm, though, making sure that his little boy was still alive, still all right.

They were *all* still alive, and it was little short of a miracle. Julian felt as if every nerve in his body had been pulled out of his skin. He visualized the nerve endings exposed, each one like a Sensor, reacting to the presence of his family around him.

He thought of Diana, saying, *You're going to have to let go.*

And he knew it was true. Someday he would have to open his hands, let his brothers and sisters go freely into the world, a world that would cut them, bruise them, knock them down and not help them back up again. Someday he would have to do that.

But not yet. Not quite yet.

"Ty," Julian said. He spoke quietly, so that the passengers in the backseat wouldn't hear him.

"Yes?" Ty looked over. The shadows under his eyes were as gray as his irises.

"You were right," Julian said. "I was wrong."

"I was?" Ty sounded surprised. "About what?"

"You coming with us to the convergence," said Julian. "You fought well—amazingly, in fact. If you hadn't been there . . ." His throat closed up. It was a moment before he could speak again. "I'm grateful," he said. "And I'm also sorry. I should have listened. You were right about what you could do."

"Thanks," said Ty. "For apologizing." He fell silent, which Julian assumed meant the conversation was over, but after a few seconds Ty leaned over and touched his head lightly to Julian's shoulder—a friendly head butt, as if he were Church, seeking affection. Julian reached out to ruffle up his younger brother's hair and nearly smiled.

The nascent smile vanished quickly when they bumped to a stop in front of the Institute. It was lit up like a Christmas tree. It had been dark when they'd left, and as they piled out of the car, Julian caught the faintest of faint glimmers on the air.

He exchanged a look with Emma. Light in the air meant a Portal, and a Portal meant the Clave.

Diana's truck pulled up, and Diego and Cristina spilled out. They slammed the doors behind them and the truck sped away. The Blackthorns had all emerged as well: some of them blinking and barely awake (Dru, Mark), some looking quietly suspicious (Ty), and some nervous (Livvy, who was clutching Tavvy tightly). In the distance, Julian thought he could see the faint pale shape of Windspear.

They headed toward the Institute steps together. At the top of the stairs, Julian hesitated with his hand on the front door.

Anything could be waiting for him on the other side, from the massed array of the Council to a few dozen Clave warriors. Julian knew there was no more hiding Mark. He knew what his plans were. He knew they balanced, like a million angels, on the head of a pin. Chance, circumstance, and determination held them together.

He glanced over and saw Emma looking at him. Though her tired and grimy face didn't break into a smile, he saw her confidence and her trust in him in her eyes.

He'd missed one, he thought. Chance, circumstance, determination—and faith.

He opened the door.

The light in the entryway was blazingly bright. Both witchlight chandeliers were burning, and the upstairs gallery was illuminated by rows of torches that the family almost never used. Light glowed beneath the doors of the Sanctuary.

In the middle of the room stood Magnus Bane, resplendent in an elegant outfit: a brocade jacket and trousers, his fingers adorned with dozens of rings. Beside him was Clary Fairchild, her bright red hair tied up in a messy bun, wearing a delicate green dress. They both looked as if they had just come from a party.

As Julian and the rest flooded into the room, Magnus raised an eyebrow. "Well, well," he said. "Kill the fatted calf and all that. The prodigals have returned."

Clary's hand flew to her mouth. "Emma, Julian—" She whitened. "*Mark?* Mark Blackthorn?"

Mark said nothing. None of them did. Julian realized that unconsciously, they had grouped themselves around Mark, a loose circle protecting him. Even Diego, wincing and blood-spattered, was part of it.

Mark stood silent, his ragged pale-blond hair a halo around his head, his pointed ears and polychrome eyes clearly visible in the bright light.

Magnus looked hard at Mark before glancing up toward the second floor. "Jace!" he called. "Get down here!"

Clary made a move toward the Blackthorns, but Magnus pulled her back gently. She was frowning. "Are you all right?" she said, directing the question to Emma but clearly meaning it for all of them. "Are you hurt?"

Before anyone could speak, there was a commotion at the top of the steps, and a tall figure appeared there.

Jace.

The first time Julian had really met Jace Herondale, who was famous throughout the Shadowhunter world, Jace had been about seventeen and Julian had been twelve. Emma, who had also been twelve, had not been shy about letting the world know she thought Jace was the handsomest and most amazing person who had ever graced the planet with his presence.

Julian had not agreed, but then, no one had asked him.

Jace descended the stairs in a manner that made Julian wonder if Jace thought he had a magnificent train trailing behind him—slowly, deliberately, and as if he were aware that he was the focus of all eyes.

Or maybe he was just used to being stared at. Emma had stopped going on about Jace at some point, but the Shadowhunter world in general considered him out of the ordinary in terms of looks. His hair was shockingly gold and so were his eyes. Like Magnus and Clary he looked like he had come from a party: He wore a wine-red blazer and an air of casual elegance. Reaching the bottom step, he glanced toward Julian—covered in blood and dirt—and then toward the rest of them, just as ragged and stained.

"Well, either you've been out fighting the forces of evil or you've come from a much wilder party than we have," Jace said. "Hello, there, Blackthorns."

Livvy sighed. She was looking at Jace the way Emma had when she was twelve. Dru, loyal to her crush on Diego, just glared.

"Why are you here?" Julian asked, though he knew the answer. Still, it was better to build up the idea that you were surprised. People trusted your answers more when they thought they weren't rehearsed.

"Dark magic," said Magnus. "A huge flare of it on the map. At the convergence site." He slid his gaze toward Emma. "I thought you might do something with that bit of information I gave you.

Where ley lines are concerned, the convergence is always key."

"Why didn't you go there, then?" Emma asked. "To the convergence?"

"Magnus checked it out with a spell," Clary said. "There was nothing there but some wreckage, so we Portaled here."

"From my sister's engagement party, to be precise," said Jace. "There was an open bar."

"Oh!" A look of happiness flitted across Emma's face. "Isabelle's marrying Simon?"

As far as Julian was concerned, no girl had ever been born who could compare to Emma, but when Clary smiled, she was very pretty. Her whole face lit up. It was something she and Emma had in common, actually. "Yeah," Clary said. "He's really happy."

"Mazel tov to them," said Jace, leaning against the banister rail. "Anyway, we were at the party, and Magnus got this alert about necromantic magic near the L.A. Institute, and he tried to reach Malcolm, but no luck. So we snuck out, just the four of us. Which is a big loss to the party if you ask me, because I was going to give a toast and it was going to be glorious. Simon would never be able to show his face in public again."

"Not really the point of an engagement toast, Jace," Clary said. She was looking worriedly at Diego—he *was* awfully pale.

"Four of you?" Emma looked around the room. "Is Alec here?"

Magnus opened his mouth to answer, but at that moment the doors of the Sanctuary burst open, and a tall, stocky man with dark hair emerged: Robert Lightwood, the current Inquisitor, second in command to the Consul of Idris, and in charge of investigating Shadowhunters who had broken the Law.

Julian had met the Inquisitor exactly once before, when he'd been forced to stand up in front of the Council and give his account of Sebastian's attack on the Institute. He remembered holding the Mortal Sword in his hand. The feeling of the truth being dragged out of you with knives and hooks, of your internal organs tearing apart.

He had never lied when he was asked about the attack, had never wanted or planned to. But it hurt just the same. And bearing the Mortal Sword, even for such a short time, had forged an indelible bond in his mind between truth and pain.

The Inquisitor strode toward him. He was a little older than the Robert Lightwood Julian remembered, his hair more liberally streaked with gray. But the look in his dark blue eyes was the same: hard and cold.

"What's going on here?" he demanded. "There was a flare of necromantic magic traced to this Institute several hours ago and your uncle claims to know nothing about it. More troubling, he refused to tell us where *you* disappeared to." He spun around, his eyes raking their group—and landing on Mark. "Mark Blackthorn?"

"I already said that," said Clary. Julian had the feeling she wasn't overly fond of her prospective father-in-law—if he was that. He realized he didn't know if Jace and Clary had plans to get married.

"Yes," Mark said. He was standing upright as if facing a firing squad. He met Robert Lightwood's eyes, and Julian saw the Inquisitor flinch at the sight of Wild Hunt eyes in a Shadowhunter's face.

They were an accusation against the Clave, those eyes. They said, *You abandoned me. You did not protect me. I was alone.*

"I have come back," Mark said.

"The Wild Hunt would never have released you," said the Inquisitor. "You were far too valuable to them. And faeries don't give back what they take."

"Robert—" Magnus began.

"Tell me I'm wrong," Robert Lightwood said. "Magnus? Anyone?"

Magnus was silent, his unhappiness evident. Jace's gold eyes were unreadable.

Dru made a frightened, stifled sound. Clary whirled on Robert.

"It's not fair to interrogate them," she said. "They're just kids."

"Don't you think I remember the trouble you and Jace got into when you were 'just kids'?"

"He has a point." Jace smiled at Julian and Emma, and the smile was like gold melted over steel. You could see how the softness was a disguise, and how what lay under it had won Jace the title of best Shadowhunter of his generation.

"We didn't use any necromancy," said Julian. "We didn't need to. The thing about faeries—they're always willing to make a deal."

Two figures appeared in the doorway of the Sanctuary. Anselm Nightshade, his sharp, bony face wary. And beside him, Arthur, looking tired and carrying a glass of wine. Julian had left the full bottle in the Sanctuary earlier that night. It was a good vintage.

The protected space of the Sanctuary extended slightly past the doors. Anselm edged a toe over the line, winced, and quickly pulled it back.

"Arthur. You claimed you were discussing Sophocles with Anselm Nightshade all evening?" Robert Lightwood said.

"'If you try to cure evil with evil you will add more pain to your fate,'" said Arthur.

Robert raised an eyebrow.

"He's quoting *Antigone*," said Julian wearily. "He means yes."

"Come into the room, Arthur," said Robert. "Please do not give me the impression you're hiding in the Sanctuary."

"When you use that voice, *I* want to hide in the Sanctuary," said Magnus. He had begun wandering around the room, picking up objects and setting them down. His actions appeared idle, but Julian knew better. Magnus did little without premeditation.

Neither did Jace. Jace was sitting on the lowest step of the stairs, his sharp gaze unwavering. Julian felt the weight of it, like pressure against his chest. He cleared his throat.

"My younger brothers and sisters have nothing to do with this," he said. "And Tavvy is exhausted. He was almost killed tonight."

"What?" Clary said, alarm darkening her green eyes. "How did that happen?"

"I'll explain," Julian said. "Just let them go."

Robert hesitated for a moment before nodding curtly. "They can leave."

Relief washed through Julian as Ty, Livvy, and Dru headed up the steps, Livvy still carrying Octavian against her shoulder. At the top, Ty paused for a moment and looked down. He was looking at Mark, and the expression on his face was fearful.

"It is the disease of tyranny to trust no friends, Inquisitor," said Anselm Nightshade. "Aeschylus."

"I did not come here, from my daughter's engagement party, for a classics lesson," said Robert. "Nor is this Downworlder business. Please wait for us in the Sanctuary, Anselm."

Arthur passed his glass to Anselm, who raised it ironically but went, seeming relieved to get away from the demarcation line where hallowed ground began.

The moment he was gone, Robert rounded on Arthur. "What do you know about all this, Blackthorn?"

"A convoy came to us from Faerie," said Arthur. "They offered to return Mark to his family, and in exchange, we would help them discover who was killing faeries in Los Angeles."

"And you said nothing of this to the Clave?" said Robert. "Despite knowing you were breaking the Law, the Cold Peace—"

"I wanted my nephew back," said Arthur. "Wouldn't you have done the same, for your family?"

"You're a Shadowhunter," said Robert. "If you must choose between your family and the Law, you choose the Law!"

"*Lex malla, lex nulla,*" said Arthur. "You know our family motto."

"He did the right thing." For once there was no humor in Jace's voice. "I would have done the same. Any of us would."

Robert looked exasperated. "And did you discover it? Who was killing faeries?"

"We discovered it tonight," said Julian. "It was Malcolm Fade."

Magnus stiffened, his cat eyes flashing. *Malcolm?* He executed a quick about-face and marched toward Julian. "And why do you think it was a warlock? Because we know magic? Is all dark magic to be blamed on us, then?"

"Because he said he did it," said Julian.

Clary's mouth fell open. Jace remained seated, face unreadable as a cat's.

Robert's expression darkened. "Arthur. You're the head of the Institute. Talk. Or are you going to leave that to your nephew?"

"There are things," Julian said, "things we didn't tell Arthur. Things he doesn't know."

Arthur put his hand to his head, as if it pained him. "If I've been deceived," he said, "then let Julian explain it."

Robert's hard gaze swept over their group and fastened on Diego. "Centurion," he said. "Step forward."

Julian tensed. Diego. He hadn't factored him in, but Diego was a Centurion, and as such, sworn to tell the truth to the Clave. Of course Robert would want to talk to Diego instead of him.

He knew there was no real reason for Robert to want to talk to him at all. He didn't run the Institute. Arthur did. Never mind that he'd been answering Robert's letters for years and recognized Robert's way of doing things better than anyone else here; never mind that in official correspondence, at least, they knew each other well. He was just a teenage boy.

"Yes, Inquisitor?" Diego said.

"Speak to us of Malcolm Fade."

"Malcolm isn't who you think," Diego said. "He has been

responsible for countless deaths. He was responsible for the deaths of Emma's parents."

Robert shook his dark head. "How is that possible? The Carstairs were murdered by Sebastian Morgenstern."

At the sound of Sebastian's name, Clary went pale. She looked immediately over at Jace, who matched her glance—a look woven through with years of shared history. "No," Clary said. "They weren't. Sebastian was a murderer, but Emma has never believed that he was responsible for her parents' deaths, and neither have Jace or I." She turned to look at Emma. "You were right," she said. "I always thought you would be proved right someday. But I'm sorry it was Malcolm. He was your friend."

"And mine," said Magnus, his voice strained. Clary moved toward him, placing her hand on his arm.

"He was also the High Warlock," said Robert. "How did this happen? What do you mean he'd been murdering people?"

"A series of killings in Los Angeles," said Diego. "He was convincing mundanes to commit murder and then harvesting their bodies for parts he could use in necromancy."

"The Clave should have been called in." Robert sounded furious. "The Clave should have been called in the moment a faerie convoy approached you—"

"Inquisitor," said Diego. He sounded tired. The whole right shoulder of his gear was dark red with blood. "I am a Centurion. I answer directly to the Council. I didn't report what was happening either, because once things were in motion, reporting would have meant slowing things down." He didn't look at Cristina. "The Clave would have begun the investigation over again. There was no time, and the life of a child hung in the balance." He put his hand to his chest. "If you wish to strip me of my medallion, I would understand. But I will maintain to the end that the Blackthorns did what was right."

"I am not going to strip you of your medallion, Diego Rocio Rosales," said Robert. "We have few Centurions, and you are one of the best." He looked at Diego critically, at his bloody arm and exhausted face. "The Council will expect a report from you tomorrow, but for now, see to your wounds."

"I'll go with him," Cristina said.

She helped Diego up the stairs, him leaning on her slender frame. Mark looked up at them and then away as they disappeared past the witchlight, into the shadows.

"Robert," said Jace when they were gone. "When Julian was twelve he testified in front of the Council. It's been five years. Let him talk now."

Despite the look of clear reluctance on his face, Robert nodded. "Very well," he said. "Everyone wants to hear you speak, Julian Blackthorn. So speak."


Julian spoke. Calmly and without flourishes, he began to describe the investigation, from the first bodies found to their realization that evening of Malcolm's guilt.

Emma watched her *parabatai* as he spoke, and wondered how things would have turned out differently if Sebastian Morgenstern hadn't attacked the L.A. Institute five years ago.

In Emma's mind, for years now, there had been two Julians. Julian before the attack, who was like everyone else—loving his family but annoyed by them too; a brother among brothers and sisters with whom he squabbled and argued and teased and laughed.

And Julian after. Julian, still a child, teaching himself how to feed and change a baby, cooking four different meals for four younger siblings who liked and disliked different things; Julian hiding his uncle's sickness from a mass of adults who would have taken his children away from him; Julian waking up from screaming nightmares that something had happened to Ty or Livvy or Dru.

Emma had been there to hold him, but she had never quite understood—how could she have, when she didn't know about Arthur, didn't know how alone Julian truly was? She only knew that the nightmares had faded and a quiet strength had settled over Jules, a hard determination before which the softness of childhood gave way.

He hadn't been a boy in a long, long time. It had been that boy that Emma had thought could be her *parabatai*. She would never have fallen in love with that Julian. But she had fallen in love with this one, without knowing it, because how could you fall in love with someone you only half-guessed existed?

She wondered if Mark recognized the same dissonance in some way, if he saw the strangeness in how Julian stood and spoke to the Inquisitor now, as if they were two adults together. If he saw the care with which Julian told the story of what had happened: the key details he left out, the way he made it seem natural, inevitable, that they hadn't told the Clave what they were doing. The way he left out Kit and Johnny Rook. He wove a tale of a series of events that was nobody's fault, that no one could have foreseen or prevented, and he did it without a shred of guile ever showing on his face.

When he was done, Emma shivered inside. She loved Julian, she would always love Julian. But for just that moment, she was a little afraid of him too.

"Malcolm was creating *murderers*?" Robert echoed when Julian had stopped speaking.

"It makes sense," said Magnus. He stood with his chin cupped in his hand, one long finger tapping against his cheekbone. "One of the reasons necromancy is forbidden is that so many necessary ingredients are things like the hand of a murderer who killed in cold blood, or the eye of a hanged man which still holds the image of the last thing he saw. Obtaining those ingredients by orchestrating the situations that create them was ingenious." He seemed to notice Robert glaring at him. "Very evil, also," he added. "Very."

"Your nephew tells a convincing story, Arthur," said Robert. "But you are notably absent from it. How did you not notice all this was going on?"

Julian had woven his story to make Arthur's absence seem natural. But Robert was like a dog with a bone. Emma supposed that was why he had been elected to the position of Inquisitor.

Emma looked across the room and met Clary's green gaze with her own. She thought of Clary kneeling in front of her in Idris, holding her hands, complimenting Cortana. She thought of how the kindnesses that were shown to children were things they never forgot.

"Robert," Clary said. "There's no need for this. They made difficult decisions, but they weren't wrong decisions."

"Then let me ask Arthur this, Clary," said Robert. "What punishment would he choose for Nephilim, even young Nephilim, who break the Law?"

"Well, that would depend," Arthur said, "on whether they were punished already, five years ago, by losing their father and brother and sister."

Robert flushed darkly. "It was the Dark War that took their family—"

"It was the Clave that took Mark and Helen," said Magnus. "We expect betrayal from our enemies. Not from those who are supposed to care for us."

"We would have protected Mark," said Robert Lightwood. "There was no need to fear the Clave."

Arthur was pale, his eyes dilated. Yet Emma had never heard him speak so eloquently, or with such clarity. It was bizarre. "Would you have?" he demanded. "In that case, why is Helen still at Wrangel Island?"

"She's safer there," snapped Robert. "There are those—not myself—who still hate the faeries for the betrayal of the Dark War.

How do you think they would treat her if she were among other Shadowhunters?"

"So you couldn't have protected Mark," said Arthur. "You admit it."

Before Robert could speak, Julian said, "Uncle Arthur, you can tell him the truth."

Arthur looked puzzled; as clearheaded as he had seemed, he didn't seem to know what Julian meant. He was breathing quickly, too, as he had in the Sanctuary when his head pained him.

Julian turned to Robert. "Arthur wanted to go to the Council as soon as the Fair Folk brought Mark here," he said. "We begged him not to. We were afraid our brother would be taken away. We thought if we could just solve the murders, if Mark helped us do it, it might make him look better in the eyes of the Council. Help convince them to let him stay."

"But do you understand what you did?" the Inquisitor demanded. "Malcolm—if he was in pursuit of dark power—he could have posed a threat to all the Clave." Robert didn't sound convinced, though.

"He wasn't in pursuit of power," said Julian. "He wanted to raise someone he loved from the dead. It was evil, what he did. And he's died for it, as he should have. But it was his only goal and only plan. He never cared about the Clave or Shadowhunters. He only cared about her."

"Poor Malcolm," said Magnus quietly. "To lose the person he loved, that way. We all knew that he had loved a girl who had become an Iron Sister. We had no idea of the truth."

"Robert," Jace said. "These kids haven't done anything wrong."

"Perhaps not, but I'm the Inquisitor. I can hardly conceal this. With Malcolm Fade dead, having taken the Black Volume to the bottom of the ocean with him, and with all of this having happened without the head of the Institute having noticed—"

Julian stepped forward. "There's something Uncle Arthur isn't telling you," he said. "He wasn't just letting us run around wild while he did nothing. He's been tracking down a different source of dark magic."

Julian looked at Magnus as he spoke. Magnus, who had helped them in the past. He seemed to be willing Magnus to understand and believe him.

"It's no coincidence that Anselm Nightshade is in the Sanctuary," Julian went on in a hard voice. "Arthur brought him because he knew you were coming."

Robert raised an eyebrow. "Is that true? Arthur?"

"You'd better tell them," Julian said, looking hard at his uncle. "They're going to find out anyway."

"I—" Arthur was staring at Julian. There was a blankness on his face that made Emma's stomach knot up. Julian appeared to be almost willing Arthur to follow his lead. "I didn't want to mention it," Arthur said, "because it seemed to pale in comparison to what we learned about Malcolm."

"Mention what?"

"Nightshade's been using dark magic for profit," said Julian. His kept his expression calm, a touch regretful. "He's been making money hand over fist using addictive powders in the pizza he makes."

"That's—totally right!" said Emma, speaking over Arthur's stunned silence. "There are people all over the city so addicted that they would do anything for him just to get more."

"Pizza thralls?" said Jace. "This is without doubt, the *weirdest*—" He broke off as Clary stomped on his foot. "Seems serious," he said. "I mean, addictive demon powders and all."

Julian crossed the room to the hall closet and yanked it open. Several pizza boxes slid out.

"Magnus?" Julian said.

Magnus threw the end of his scarf over his shoulder and

approached Julian and the boxes. He lifted the lid of a pizza box with as much gravity as if he were opening a locked treasure chest.

He held his hand out over the box, turning it from left to right. Then he looked up.

"Arthur's right," he said. "Dark magic."

A cry echoed from inside the Sanctuary. "Betrayal!" Anselm shouted. "*Et tu, Brute?*"

"He can't get out," said Arthur, looking dazed. "The outside doors are locked."

Robert took off running into the Sanctuary. After a moment Jace and Clary followed, leaving only Magnus, hands in his pockets, remaining in the foyer.

Magnus regarded Julian with serious green-gold eyes. "Nicely done," he said. "I don't know quite how else to describe it, but— nicely done."

Julian looked over at Arthur, who was leaning back against the wall by the Sanctuary door, his eyes half-shut, pain etched on his face. "I'll burn in Hell for this," he muttered in a low voice.

"There is no shame in burning for your family," said Mark. "I will burn beside you, gladly."

Julian looked at him, surprise and gratitude written across his face.

"And so will I," said Emma. She looked at Magnus. "I'm sorry," she said. "I'm the one who killed Malcolm. I know he was your friend, and I wish—"

"He was my friend," said Magnus, his eyes darkening. "I knew he had loved someone who died. I didn't know the rest of the story. The Clave betrayed him, just like they betrayed you. I've lived a long time—I've seen many betrayals, and many broken hearts. There are those who let their grief devour them. Who forget that others also feel pain. If Alec died—" He looked down at his hands. "I have to think I wouldn't be like that."

"I'm just glad I finally know what happened to my parents," Emma said. "Finally, I know."

Before anyone could add anything, there was an explosion of noise at the entrance to the Sanctuary. Jace appeared suddenly, skidding backward, his fancy blazer ripped and his blond hair mussed. He turned a smile on the rest of them, so bright it seemed to light up the room.

"Clary's got Nightshade pinned in a corner," he said. "He's pretty nimble for such an old vampire. Thanks for the exercise, by the way—and to think I thought tonight was going to be boring!"

After everything had been sorted out with the Inquisitor, who had hauled off Anselm Nightshade (still vowing revenge), and most of the Institute's inhabitants had crawled off to bed, Mark went to the front door and looked out.

It was nearly dawn. Mark could see the sunrise, far in the distance, at the eastern edge of the beach's curve. A pearlescent lightening of the water, as if white paint were spilling into the world through a crack in the sky.

"Mark," said a voice at his shoulder.

He turned. It was Jace Herondale.

It was strange looking at Jace and Clary, strange in a way he doubted it was for his siblings. After all, the last time he'd seen them they'd been Julian's age. They'd been the last Shadowhunters he'd seen before he'd disappeared into the Hunt.

They were far from unrecognizable—they were probably only twenty-one or twenty-two. But up close Mark could see that Jace had acquired an indefinable aura of decisiveness and adulthood. Gone was the boy who had looked into Mark's eyes and said in a shaking voice, *The Wild Hunt. You're one of them now.*

"Mark Blackthorn," Jace said. "I'd be polite and say you've changed, but you haven't."

"I have," Mark said. "Just not in a way you can see."

Jace seemed to take this with good grace; he nodded and looked out toward the ocean. "A scientist said once that if the ocean were as clear as the sky, if we could see everything in it, no one would ever go into the sea. It's that horrifying, what lives in the water, five miles down."

"There speaks one who does not know the terrors of the sky," said Mark.

"Maybe not," Jace said. "Do you still have the witchlight I gave you?"

Mark nodded. "I kept it with me through Faerie."

"I've only ever given witchlight rune-stones to two people in my life," said Jace. "Clary and you." He cocked his head to the side. "There was something about you, when we found you in the tunnels. You were frightened, but you weren't going to give up. I never had the slightest doubt I'd see you again."

"Really?" Mark looked at him skeptically.

"Really." Jace smiled his easy, charming smile. "Just remember that the New York Institute is on your side," he said. "Remind Julian if you're ever in trouble again. It's not simple running an Institute. I ought to know."

Mark began to protest, but Jace had already turned and gone back inside to rejoin Clary. Mark somehow doubted Jace would have paid any attention to his protest if he'd made it. He'd clearly seen the situation for what it was, but wasn't planning on doing anything to upset the balance.

Mark scanned the horizon again. Dawn was spreading. The road and the highway, the desert trees, all were thrown into sharp relief by the increasing light. And there by the edge of the road stood Kieran, looking out toward the sea. Mark could see him only as a shadow, but even as a shadow Kieran could never have been anyone else.

He went down the steps and over to where Kieran was standing. He had not changed his clothes, and the blade of his sword, which hung by his side, was stained with gore.

"Kieran," Mark said.

"You will stay?" Kieran asked, and then caught himself with a rueful look. "Of course, you will stay."

"If you're asking if I'm going to remain with my family or go back to the Wild Hunt, then yes, you have your answer," said Mark. "The investigation is over. The murderer and his Followers are gone."

"That was not the letter of the bargain," said Kieran. "The Shadowhunters were to release the murderer into the custody of Faerie, for us to mete out justice."

"Given that Malcolm is dead, and the magnitude of Iarlath's betrayal, I expect your folk to look with leniency upon my choice," said Mark.

"*My* folk?" Kieran echoed. "You know they are not lenient. They have not been lenient with me." Mark thought of the first time he had seen Kieran's black eyes staring out defiantly from the tangle of his dark hair. He thought of the glee of the other Hunters at having a prince to torment and mock. How Kieran had borne it, with an arrogant curl to his lip and a lift of his chin. How he had borne the fact that his father had thrown him to the Hunt the way a man might throw a bone to a dog. Kieran had not had a brother who loved him and fought to get him back. He had not had Julian. "But I will fight for you," he said, meeting Mark's gaze. "I will tell them it is your right to stay." He hesitated. "Will we—see each other again?"

"I don't think so, Kieran," said Mark, as gently as he could. "Not after all that has happened."

A brief ripple of pain, quickly hidden, passed across Kieran's face. The color of his hair had faded to a silvery-blue, not unlike the shade of the ocean in the morning. "I did not expect a different answer," he said. "I hoped, though. It is hard to kill hope. But I suppose I lost you a long time ago."

"Not that long," said Mark. "You lost me when you came here with Gwyn and Iarlath and you let them whip my brother. I could forgive you for any pain incurred by me. But I will never forgive you for what Julian and Emma suffered."

"Emma?" said Kieran, his brows drawing together. "I thought it was the other girl who had drawn your fancy. Your princess."

Mark gave a choked laugh. "By the Angel," he said, and saw Kieran blanch at the Shadowhunter words. "Your imagination is limited by your jealousy. Kieran . . . everyone who lives under this roof, whether they are bound by blood or not, we are tied together by an invisible net of love and duty and loyalty and honor. That is what it means to be a Shadowhunter. Family—"

"What would I know of family? My father sold me to the Wild Hunt. I do not know my mother. I have three dozen brothers, all of whom would gladly see me dead. Mark, you are all I have."

"Kieran—"

"And I love you," Kieran said. "You are all that exists on the earth and under the sky that I do love."

Mark looked into Kieran's eyes, the silver and the black, and he saw in them, as he always had, the night sky. And he felt that treacherous pull under his rib cage, the one that said that the clouds could be his road. That he need never worry about human concerns: money and shelter and rules and laws. He could ride through the skies over glaciers, through the treetops of forests no human being knew existed. He could sleep in the ruins of cities lost for centuries. His shelter could be a single blanket. He could lie in Kieran's arms and count the stars.

But he had always given the stars his brothers' and sisters' names. There was beauty in the idea of freedom, but it was an illusion. Every human heart was chained by love.

Mark drew his elf-bolt necklace up over his head. He reached out and took Kieran's hand, turning it over so it was palm up, and dropped the necklace into it.

"I will draw no more bows for the Wild Hunt," he said. "Keep this and perhaps remember me."

Kieran's hand tightened on the arrowhead, his knuckles whitening. "The stars will go out before I forget you, Mark Blackthorn."

Lightly, Mark touched Kieran's cheek. The faerie prince's eyes were wide and tearless. But in them Mark could see a great wilderness of loneliness. A thousand dark nights spent riding with no home to arrive at. "I do not forgive you," he said. "But you came to help us, at the end. I do not know what would have happened if you hadn't. So if you need me—if it is a true need—send for me and I will come."

Kieran half-closed his eyes. "Mark—"

But Mark had already turned away. Kieran stood and watched him go, and though he did not move or speak, at the edge of the bluff Windspear reared up and cried out, his hooves pawing at the sky.

Julian's window looked out over the desert. At any point during the past five years he could have switched out for Mark's room, which had a view of the ocean, but it would have felt like giving up on the idea that Mark would ever come back. And besides, his was the only room with a window seat, lined with now slightly threadbare cushions. He and Emma had spent hours there together, reading and drawing, the sun through the glass turning her pale hair to fire.

He was sitting there now, the window cranked open to carry away the scents that still seemed to hang over him, even after a shower: blood and wet stone, seawater and dark magic.

Everything ended eventually, he thought. Even the strangest

night of his life. Clary had taken him and Emma aside after Anselm had been captured, hugged them, reminded them that they could always call. He knew Clary was, in her quiet way, trying to tell him, tell both of them, that it was all right to lay their burdens on her.

He knew he never would.

His phone trilled. He glanced down at the screen: It was Emma. She'd sent him a photo. No words, just the picture of her closet: the door open, the photographs and maps and string and notes spilling out.

He threw on jeans and a T-shirt and headed down the hall. The Insitute was dead silent, wrapped in sleep, the only sound the desert wind outside, soughing against glass and stone.

Emma was in her room, sitting up against the footboard of her bed, her phone on the floor beside her. She was wearing a nightgown, long with thin straps, pale white in the fading moonlight.

"Julian," she said, knowing he was there without looking up. "You were awake, right? I had a feeling you were awake."

She stood up, still looking at her closet.

"I don't know what to do with it," she said. "I spent such a long time collecting everything that seemed like evidence, making guesses, thinking about this and nothing but this. This was my big secret, the heart of everything I did." She looked toward him. "Now it's just a closet full of junk."

"I can't tell you what you should do with all that," he said. "But I can tell you, you don't need to think about it now."

Her hair was down, like spun light around her shoulders, tickling her face with the ends of curls, and he dug his fingers into his palms to keep himself from pulling her against him so he could bury his face and hands in it.

He looked instead at the healing cuts on her arms and hands, the fading red of her burned wrist, the evidence that tonight had not been easy.

Nothing they did ever was.

"Mark's staying," she said. "Right? There's nothing the Clave can do to take him away now?"

*Mark. Her first thought is about Mark.* Julian pushed the thought down, away: It was unworthy, ridiculous. They weren't twelve anymore.

"Nothing," Julian said. "He was never exiled. The rule was only that we couldn't look for him. We didn't. He found his way home and they can't change that. And I think, after the help he gave us with Malcolm, it would be a very unpopular move if they tried."

She flashed a faint smile at him before clambering up onto the bed, sliding her long bare legs under the coverlet. "I went to check on Diego and Cristina," she said. "He was passed out in her bed and she was asleep in the chair next to him. I'm going to make so much fun of her tomorrow."

"Is Cristina in love with him? Diego, I mean," Julian asked, sitting down on the side of Emma's bed.

"Not sure." Emma wiggled her fingers. "They have, you know. Stuff."

"No, I don't know." He copied her gesture. "What's that?"

"Unfinished romantic business," Emma said, pulling the blanket up.

"Finger wiggling means unfinished business? I'll have to keep that in mind." Julian felt a smile tug the corners of his mouth. Only Emma could make him smile after a night like the one they'd had.

She turned back a corner of the blanket. "Stay?"

There was nothing he wanted more than to crawl in beside her, to trace the shape of her face with his fingers: wide cheekbones, pointed chin, half-lidded eyes, eyelashes like lace against his fingertips. His body and mind were beyond exhausted, too worn out for desire, but the yearning for closeness and companionship remained. The touch of her hands, her skin, was a comfort nothing else could reproduce.

He remembered the beach, lying awake for hours, trying to memorize what it was like to hold Emma. They'd slept beside each other so many times, but he'd never realized how different it was when you could encompass the shape of someone else in your arms. Fit your breathing to their breathing.

He crawled into bed beside her, clothes still on, and slid under the covers. She was on her side, her head propped on her hand. Her expression was serious, intent. "The way you orchestrated everything tonight, Julian. You scared me a little."

He touched the edge of her hair, briefly, before dropping his hand. A slow ache was spreading through his body, a deep ache that seemed to come from the marrow of his bones.

"You should never be scared of me," he said. "Never. You're one of the people I would never hurt."

She reached out a hand and put her palm against his heart. The fabric of his T-shirt separated her hand and his chest, but he felt the touch as if it were on his bare skin. "Tell me what happened when we got back, with Arthur and Anselm," she said. "Because I don't think even I understand it."

So he told her. Told her about how for months he'd been emptying the dregs of the vials Malcolm gave him for Arthur into a bottle of wine, just in case. How he'd left the wine containing this super-dosage in the Sanctuary. How he'd realized at the convergence that they would need Arthur to be clearheaded when they returned, to be functioning. The way he'd called Arthur, telling him he needed to offer the wine to Anselm and drink some himself, knowing it would affect only his uncle. How he knew he'd done a terrible thing, dosing his uncle without his knowledge. How he'd planted the pizza boxes in the foyer the first time they'd ordered it, just in case; how he knew he'd done a terrible thing to Anselm, who did not deserve the punishment he was likely to get. How he didn't know who he was sometimes, how he was capable of doing the things he did, and yet how he couldn't not do them.

When he was done, she leaned in, touching his cheek gently. She smelled faintly of rosewater soap. "I know who you are," she said. "You're my *parabatai*. You're the boy who does what has to be done because no one else will."

*Parabatai.* He had never thought of the word with bitterness before, even feeling what he felt and knowing what he knew. And yet now, he thought of the years and years ahead of them in which there would be no time in which they felt fully safe together, no way to touch or kiss or reassure each other without fear of discovery, and a sudden emotion surged through him, uncontrollable.

"What if we ran away?" he said.

"Ran away?" she echoed. "And went where?"

"Somewhere they wouldn't find us. I could do it. I could find a place."

He saw the sympathy in her eyes. "They'd figure out why. We wouldn't be able to come back."

"They forgave us for breaking the Cold Peace," he said, and he knew he sounded desperate. He knew his words were tripping over themselves. But they were words he had wanted to say, not dared to say, for years: They were words that belonged to a part of himself that had been locked up so long he had wondered if it were even still living. "They need Shadowhunters. There aren't enough of us. They might forgive us for this, too."

"Julian—you wouldn't be able to live with yourself if you left the kids. And Mark, and Helen. I mean, you just got Mark back. There's no way."

He held back thought of them, of his brothers and sisters, as if he were Poseidon holding back the tide. "Are you saying this because you don't want to go away with me? Because if you don't want it—"

In the distance, down the hall, a thin cry rose: Tavvy.

Julian was out of the bed in seconds, the floor cold against his bare feet. "I'd better go."

Emma pushed herself up on her elbows. Her face was serious, dominated by her wide dark eyes. "I'll go with you."

They hurried down the hall to Tavvy's room. The door was propped open, a dim witchlight burning inside. Tavvy was curled up half in and half out of his tent, tossing and turning in his sleep.

Emma was on her knees next to him in moments, stroking his disarrayed brown hair. "Baby," she murmured. "Poor baby, by the Angel, what a night for you."

She lay down on her side, facing Tavvy, and Julian lay down on the little boy's other side. Tavvy gave a cry and curled back into Julian, his breath softening as he relaxed into sleep.

Julian looked across his little brother's curly head at Emma. "Do you remember?" he said.

He could see in her eyes that she did remember. The years they'd taken care of the others, the nights they stayed up with Tavvy or with Dru, with Ty and Livvy. He wondered if she'd spun fantasies, as he had, that they were married and these their children.

"I remember," she said. "That's why I said you couldn't ever leave them. You couldn't stand it." She propped her head on her hand, the scar on her forearm a white line in the dimness. "I don't want you to do something you'll spend your life regretting."

"I've already done something I'm going to spend my life regretting," he said, thinking of the circles of fire in the Silent City, the rune on his collarbone. "Now I'm trying to fix it."

She lowered her head gently to the floor beside Tavvy, her pale hair making a pillow. "Like you said about my closet," she said. "Let's talk about it tomorrow. Okay?"

He nodded, watching as she closed her eyes, as her breaths evened out into sleep. He'd waited this long, after all. He could wait another day.

\* \* \*

After the dawn, Emma woke from a nightmare, crying the names of her parents—and of Malcolm—aloud. Julian picked her up in his arms and carried her down the hallway to her own bedroom.

# 27

## SEVER MY SOUL

**The last time Kit Rook ever saw his father, it was an ordinary** day and they were sitting in their living room. Kit was sprawled on the floor reading a book on cons and scams. According to Johnny Rook, it was time to "learn the classics"—which for most people would have meant Hemingway and Shakespeare, but for Kit meant memorizing things like the Spanish Prisoner and the Melon Drop.

Johnny was in his favorite chair, in his usual thinking pose—fingers templed under his chin, legs crossed. It was times like this, when the sun slanted through the window and lit up the fine, sharp bones of his father's face, that Kit wondered about all the things he didn't know: who his mother had been, if it was true, as was whispered in the Market, that Johnny's family was English aristocracy who'd tossed him out when he manifested his Sight. It wasn't that Kit yearned to be aristocracy so much as he wondered what it would be like to be in a family that had more than two people in it.

The ground suddenly seized up under him. Kit's book went flying and he slid several feet across the floor before slamming into the coffee table. He sat up, heart speeding, and saw his father already at the window.

Kit got to his feet. "Earthquake?" he said. When you lived in Southern California you got used to small shiftings of the fault lines in the earth, waking up in the night with the glasses rattling in the kitchen cupboards.

Johnny turned away from the window, his face deathly pale. "Something's happened to the Guardian," Johnny said. "The protection spells on the house have faded."

"What?" Kit was bewildered. Their house had been warded for as long as he could remember. His father had always spoken of the wards as if they were the roof or the foundation: essential, necessary, built into the fabric of their home.

He remembered, then, last year, his father saying something about demon protection spells, more powerful ones—

Johnny swore, a fluent string of curses, and whirled toward the bookcase. He seized a worn spell book. "Get downstairs, Kit," he said, moving to kick aside the rug in the middle of the room, revealing the protection circle there.

"But—"

"I said get downstairs!" Johnny took a step toward his son, as if he meant to reach out to him, to touch his shoulder perhaps. Then he dropped his arm. "Stay in the cellar and don't come out, no matter what happens," he barked, and turned back to the circle.

Kit began to back toward the stairs. He stumbled down one step, and then another, before pausing.

Johnny's phone was on a low shelf of the bookcase, reachable from the steps. Kit grabbed it up, looking for the name, her name. *But if you change your mind, you have my number in your phone. Under Carstairs.*

He barely had time to type out a message when the floor of the living room exploded upward. *Things* spilled up from the space below. They looked like massive praying mantises, their bodies the bitter green of poison. They had small triangular heads with wide mouths filled with jagged teeth, long bodies that gleamed with slime, and jagged, razored forelegs.

Kit's father stood frozen in the middle of his circle. A demon flung itself toward him, and bounced off the spell that surrounded him. Another followed, equally unsuccessful. The demons set up a loud chittering.

Kit couldn't move. He knew about demons, of course. He'd seen pictures, even smelled the scent of demonic magic. But this was different. He caught his father's eye: Johnny was glaring at him in a mixture of panic and fury. *Get downstairs.*

Kit tried to make his feet move, to carry him. They wouldn't. Panic made him freeze.

The largest demon seemed to catch the scent of him and buzzed in excitement. It began to scuttle toward him.

Kit looked at his father. But Johnny didn't move. He stayed in his circle, his eyes bulging. The demon lunged for Kit, razored forelegs extended.

And Kit jumped. He had no idea how he did it, or how his body knew what to do. He pushed off from the stairs and hurtled over the banister, landing in a crouch in the living room. The demon, which had been reaching for him, gave a loud screech as it lost its balance and toppled downstairs, smashing into the wall of the landing.

Kit whirled back around. For a moment he caught his father's eye. There was something in Johnny's expression that was almost sorrowful—a look Kit had never seen before—and then another chunk of the floor collapsed, taking a section of the protection circle with it.

Kit flung himself backward. He flipped into the air and came down balanced on the arms of a chair, just in time to see two of the demons seize his father and rip him in half.

★ ★ ★

Emma was in the middle of a very confusing dream about Magnus Bane and a troupe of clowns when she was awoken by a hand on her shoulder. She muttered and dug herself deeper into the bedclothes, but the hand was insistent. It stroked down her arm, which was actually very pleasant. A warm mouth brushed the edge of her lips.

"Emma?" Julian said.

Vague memories of him carrying her down the hall to her bedroom and then collapsing beside her drifted through the tired fog in her brain. *Hmm*, she thought. There really seemed to be no reason to get up at all, not when Julian was being affectionate. She feigned sleep as he kissed her cheek, and then along her jaw, and then—

She sat bolt upright, sputtering. "You stuck your tongue in my ear!"

"Yup." He grinned. "It did get you moving, didn't it?"

"Eugh!" She threw an I LOVE CALI pillow at him, which he nimbly ducked. He was wearing jeans and a gray T-shirt that made his eyes look lapis blue. He was clearly just awake and tousle-haired and so adorable that she could only keep herself from attacking him by putting her hands behind her back.

"Why are you putting your hands behind your back?" he asked.

"No reason." She wrinkled up her nose. "That ear thing was weird. Don't do it again."

"How about this?" he suggested, and leaned in to kiss the base of her throat.

Sensation spiraled out from the places his lips touched—her collarbone first, then her neck, then the side of her mouth.

She drew her hands out from behind her back and reached for him. His skin was sunshine-warm.

Their faces were so close that she could see the small starbursts of color inside his eyes: pale gold, paler blue. He wasn't smiling. His expression was too intent for that. There was a wanting in his eyes that made her feel like she was breaking apart.

Their legs tangled in the blankets as they came together, mouths seeking. He still wasn't an expert kisser, but she liked that. She liked being reminded that he hadn't been with anyone but her. That she was his first. She liked that something as simple as a kiss was still a source of amazement for him. She used her tongue to trace the corners of his mouth, the seam of his lips, until he sank back on the bed, pulling her on top of him. His body shuddered, arching up toward hers, his hands sliding down to grip her hips.

"Emma?" There was a knock on the door. They jerked away from each other, Julian rolling off the bed, Emma sitting upright, her heart pounding. "Emma, it's Dru. Have you seen Jules?"

"No," Emma croaked. "I haven't."

The door started to open.

"Don't," Emma called. "I'm—I'm getting dressed."

"Whatever," Dru said dismissively, but the door didn't open further. Resolutely, Emma didn't look toward Julian. *Everything's fine,* she told herself. *Calm, be calm.* "Well, if you see him, can you tell him Tavvy and everyone need lunch? Livvy and Ty are making a mess in the kitchen, too."

Her voice held the satisfied tone of a sibling tattling on another sibling.

"Sure," said Emma. "Did you check the studio? He might be there."

There was a rustle. "No, I didn't. Good idea. See you later!"

"Bye," Emma said, faintly. Dru's footsteps were already receding down the hall.

Finally Emma let herself look at Julian. He was leaning against the wall, his chest rising and falling fast, his eyes half-lidded, teeth digging into his lip.

He exhaled. "Raziel," he whispered. "That was close."

Emma got to her feet, her nightgown swishing around her knees. She was shaking. "We can't," she started. "We can't—we'll get caught—"

Julian was already across the room, taking her in his arms. She could feel his heart slamming against his rib cage, but his voice was steady. "It's a stupid Law," he said. "It's a bad Law, Em."

*There is a reason you can't fall in love with your* parabatai, *Emma. And when you find out what it is, you will feel the cruelty of the Shadowhunters just as I have.*

Malcolm's voice, unwelcome and unavoidable, pushed its way into Emma's brain. She'd done all she could to forget it, forget what he'd said. He'd been lying—he'd lied about everything else. This had to be a lie, too.

And yet. She'd put it off, but she knew she had to tell Julian. He had the right to know.

"We have to talk," she said.

She felt his heart skip. "Don't say that. I know it's not good." He pulled her tighter against him. "Don't get scared, Emma," he whispered. "Don't let us go because you're frightened."

"I am frightened. Not for me, for you. Everything you've done, all the hiding and pretending, to keep the kids together—the situation hasn't changed, Julian. If I hurt any of you—"

He kissed her, stemming the tide of words. Despite everything, she felt the kiss all through her body. "I used to read Law books," he said, drawing away from her. "The parts about *parabatai*. I read them a million times. There's never been a case of a pair of *parabatai* who fell in love and got caught and were forgiven. Only horror stories. And I can't lose my family. You were right. It would kill me. But the horror stories are about the ones who got caught." He breathed in deep, holding her gaze. "If we're careful, we won't be."

She wondered if Julian had pushed himself past some point the night before, a point where the responsibilities that bowed him under seemed insurmountable. It was absolutely unlike Julian to want to break the rules, and though she wanted what he wanted, it unnerved her nonetheless.

"We'd have to set rules," he said. "Strict ones. When we could see each other. We'd have to be careful. Much more careful than we have been. No more beach, no more studio. We have to be absolutely sure, every time, that we were somewhere we wouldn't be walked in on."

She nodded. "In fact, no talking about it either," she said. "Not in the Institute. Not where someone might hear us."

Julian nodded. His pupils were slightly dilated, his eyes the color of an oncoming storm over the ocean.

"You're right," he said. "We can't talk here. I'll throw some lunch together for the kids, so they don't keep looking for me. Then meet me down on the beach, okay? You know where."

*Where I pulled you out of the water. Where this all started.*

"Okay," she said, after a slight hesitation. "You go first and I'll meet you there. But I still have something I need to tell you."

"The important thing is that we stay together, Emma. That's what matters—"

She raised herself up on her tiptoes and kissed him. A long, slow, intoxicating kiss that made him groan low in his throat.

When she drew away, he was staring at her. "How do people handle these feelings?" He seemed honestly bewildered. "How are they not all over each other all the time if they're, you know, in love?"

Emma swallowed against the sudden urge to cry. *In love.* He hadn't said it before.

*I love you, Julian Blackthorn,* she thought, looking at him there in her room, as he had been a million times before and yet it was completely different now. How could anything be so safe and familiar and yet so terrifying and all-encompassing and new at the same time?

She could see the faint pencil scratch markings on the door-frame behind him where they had once recorded their heights each year. They'd stopped doing it when he'd gotten taller than her, and the highest of the marks, now, was far below Julian's head.

"I'll see you on the beach," she whispered.

He hesitated for a moment, then nodded and walked out of the room. There was a strange feeling of foreboding in her chest as she watched him go—how would he react to what Malcolm had told her? Even if he dismissed it as lies, how could you plan a life of hiding and sneaking around as if it were a happy thing? She'd never really understood the point of engagement parties and the like before (though she was happy for Isabelle and Simon) but she got it now: When you were in love you wanted to *tell people about it*, and that was exactly what they couldn't do.

At least she could reassure him, though, that she loved him. That she always would. That no one could take his place.

Her thoughts were interrupted by a loud buzzing. Her phone. She padded over to the bureau to pick it up, using her thumb to open the home screen.

A text message was displayed there, in bold red letters.

EMERGENCY

PLEASE COME NOW

PLEASE

KIT ROOK

"Cristina?"

Cristina uncurled herself slowly. Her back and legs ached; she'd fallen asleep in the chair beside her bed. She could, she supposed, have curled up on the floor, but it would have been more difficult to keep an eye on Diego that way.

The wound to his shoulder had been much worse than she'd thought: a deep cut surrounded by the red blister-burn of dark magic that made healing runes nearly ineffective. She'd cut his bloody gear off him and the shirt under it as well, soaked through with sweat and blood.

She'd brought towels and padded the bed under him with them, wetted some of them down to sponge the blood from his face and neck. She'd given him painkilling rune after painkilling rune, healing rune after healing rune. Still, he'd tossed and turned much of the night, his storm-black hair tangled against the pillows.

Not since she'd left Mexico had she so clearly and painfully remembered what they had been to each other when they were younger. How much she had loved him. Her heart had felt torn to pieces when he cried out for his brother, pleading with him. *Jaime, Jaime, ayúdame. Help me.* And then he had cried out for her, and that was worse. *Cristina, no me dejes. Regresa.*

*Cristina, don't leave me. Come back.*

*I'm here,* she'd told him. *Estoy aquí,* but he hadn't woken up, and his fingers had clawed at the sheets until he'd fallen into an uneasy slumber.

She didn't remember how long after that she'd fallen asleep herself. She'd been able to hear the sound of voices from downstairs, and then footsteps in the hall. Emma had ducked in to check on her and Diego, had hugged her and gone to sleep when Cristina had assured her that everything was all right.

But there was light streaming through the window now, and Diego was looking at her with eyes clear of pain and fever.

"*¿Estás bien?*" she whispered, her throat dry.

He sat up, and the sheet fell away from him. It was, Cristina thought, rather a sudden reminder that he wasn't wearing a shirt. She focused on the fact that there was a mark on his chest where Malcolm's magic had struck him. It was over his heart, like a marriage rune would be, and it was a more intense violet than a bruise. It was almost the color of Malcolm's eyes.

"Yes, I am," he said, sounding a little surprised. "I am all right. Were you with—" He looked down, and for a moment he was very much the little boy Cristina remembered, trailing in Jaime's disastrous wake, weathering trouble and scoldings in quiet silence. "I dreamed you stayed with me."

"I did stay with you." She resisted the urge to lean forward and push his hair back.

"And everything's all right?" he asked. "I don't remember much after we returned."

She nodded. "It worked out surprisingly well."

"This is your room?" Diego said, glancing around. His gaze lit on something past her left ear and he smiled. "I remember that."

Cristina turned to look. Perched on a shelf by the bed was an *árbol de vida*, a tree of life—a delicate pottery framework hung all over with ceramic flowers, moons, suns, lions, mermaids, and arrows. The angel Gabriel rested at the bottom, his back against the tree, his shield across his knee. It was one of the few reminders of home she'd brought with her when she left.

"You made it," she said. "For my birthday. I was thirteen."

He leaned forward, hands on his knees. "Do you miss home, Cristina?" he asked. "Even a little bit?"

"Of course I miss it," she said. The line of his back was smooth, unbroken. She remembered digging her nails into his shoulder blades when they kissed. "I miss my family. I miss even the traffic in the D.F.—not that it's much better here. I miss the food, you wouldn't believe what they call Mexican food here. I miss eating *jicaletas* in the park with you." She remembered lime and chile powder on her hands, a little bit sour and a little bit hot.

"I miss you," he said. "Every day I miss you."

"Diego . . ." She slid from the chair onto the bed and reached for his right hand. It was broad and warm in hers, and she felt the pressure of his family ring against her hand—both of them wore the ring of the Rosales family, but hers had the pattern of the Mendozas on the inside, and his the Rocios. "You saved my life," she said. "I regret that I was so unforgiving. I should have known better. Should have known you better."

"Cristina . . ." His free hand found her hair, her cheek. His fingertips brushed her skin lightly. He leaned toward her, giving her ample time to back away. She didn't. When his mouth found hers, she tipped her head up for the kiss, her heart expanding with the strange feeling that she was moving toward both her future and her past at the same time.

Somewhere, Mark thought. It was somewhere in the house. Julian had told him that he'd boxed up everything in Mark's room and put it into the eastern storage area. It was past time for him to reclaim his old belongings and make his room look like someone lived in it. Which meant he had to find the storage space.

Mark would have just asked Julian where it was, but he hadn't been able to find him. Maybe he was hiding himself somewhere, scribbling away on Institute business. It seemed more than strange to Mark that things were going to go back to the way they had been, with Julian running the Institute and the Clave never knowing.

Surely there must be some way to help take the burden off his brother. Certainly now that he and Emma knew, it would be easier on Jules. The time had probably come to tell the younger ones too. Silently, Mark vowed he would stand by his brother through that. It was easier to live in truth than a lie, Kieran had always said.

Mark flinched at the thought of Kieran and yanked a door open. A music room. Clearly not one that anyone used much—there was a dusty piano, a series of stringed instruments hung on the wall, and a violin case. The violin case, at least, looked polished. Emma's father had played the violin, Mark recalled. The faerie Courts' obsession with those who could play music had kept Mark far away from any interest in melody.

"Mark?"

He jumped and turned. Ty was behind him, barefoot in a black sweater and dark jeans. The dark colors made him look even thinner.

"Hello, Tiberius." Mark liked the long version of his little brother's name. It seemed to suit him and his solemn demeanor. "Were you looking for something?"

"I was looking for you," said Ty in his direct way. "I tried last night, but I couldn't find you, and then I fell asleep."

"I was saying good-bye to Kieran," said Mark.

"Good-bye?" Ty hunched his shoulders up. "Does that mean you're staying here definitely?"

Mark couldn't help a smile. "I am. I'm staying here."

Ty exhaled a long sigh; it sounded like half relief, half nervousness. "Good," he said. "That's good."

"I thought so."

"It is," Ty said, as if Mark was being a bit slow, "because you can take over from Julian."

"Take over?" Mark stared in puzzlement.

"Julian isn't technically the oldest," said Ty. "And even though they'd never put you in charge officially because you're half-faerie, you could still do what Julian does. Look after us, tell us what to do. It doesn't have to be him. It could be you."

Mark braced himself against the doorway. Ty was wearing a completely open expression, and there was hope in the back of his pale gray eyes, and Mark felt a wash of panic that nearly made him sick. "Have you said anything about this to Julian?" he demanded. "Have you told him that you were planning on asking me this?"

Ty, not catching the half-furious note in Mark's voice, drew his delicate dark brows together. "I think I mentioned it to him."

"*Ty,*" Mark said. "You can't just arrange other people's lives like that. What would make you think that this was a good idea?"

Ty's eyes darted around the room, resting everywhere but on Mark. "I didn't mean to make you angry. I thought you had a good time that night, in the kitchen, when Julian left you in charge—"

"I had a good time. We all had a good time. I also set fire to the stove and covered your little brother in sugar. That's not how things are supposed to be all the time. That's not how—" Mark broke off, leaned back against the wall. He was shaking. "What on earth would make you think I was qualified to be Tavvy's guardian? Or Dru's? You and Livvy, you're older, but that doesn't mean you don't need a *parent.* Julian's your parent."

"Julian's my brother," Ty said, but the words came out strained. "And so are you. You're like me," he added. "We're like each other."

"No," Mark said sharply. "We're not. I'm a mess, Ty. I barely know how to live in this world. You're capable. I'm not. You're a whole person—you were raised by someone who loved you, loved you more than his own life, and that's not anything to be grateful for, that's what parents *do,* but for years, I haven't had that. By the Angel, I barely know how to take care of myself. I certainly can't take care of the rest of you."

Ty's lips had gone white. He took a step back, then bolted out into the hallway, his running steps fading.

*God,* Mark thought. *What a disaster. What a total disaster.* He was already starting to panic. What had he said to Ty? Had he made him feel like a burden? Had he wrecked things with his little brother, hurt Ty in some unfixable way?

He was a coward, he thought, cringing from the responsibility that Julian had carried for so many years, panicked at the thought of what could happen to his family in his thoughtless, inexperienced hands.

He desperately needed to talk to someone. Not Julian; it would be another burden on him. And Emma couldn't keep a secret from Julian. Livvy would murder him; the others were too young. . . .

Cristina. Cristina always gave him good advice; Cristina's sweet smile calmed his heart. He hurried toward her room.

He should have knocked, of course. That was what normal people did. But Mark, who had lived in a world without doors for so many years, put his hand to Cristina's and pushed it open without a thought.

Sunlight was streaming through her window. She was sitting up on her bed, propped against the pillows, and Diego, kneeling in front of her, was kissing her. He was holding her head in his hands as if it was something precious, and her black hair was spilling out between his fingers.

Neither of them noticed Mark as he froze in the doorway or as he pulled the door shut as silently as he could. He leaned against the wall, shame burning through him.

*I've misunderstood everything,* he thought, *wrecked everything.* His feelings for Cristina were muddled and strange, but seeing her kiss Diego hurt more than he would have thought. Some of the pain was jealousy. Some was the realization that he had been away from mortal people so long that he no longer understood them. Perhaps he never would.

*I should have stayed with the Hunt.* He slid to the floor, burying his face in his hands.

A cloud of dust and wood and plaster rose from the place where the Rooks' floor had been destroyed. Now a fine spray of blood joined it. Kit slid from the chair he'd been standing on and stood stunned. His face was splattered with blood and he could smell it in the room, the hot iron stench of it.

*My father's blood.*

The demons were gathered in a circle, tearing at something on the floor. The body of Kit's father. The sound of ripping flesh filled the room. Sickened, Kit felt his stomach lurch—just as the demon who had tumbled down the stairs came screeching back up them.

Its eyes, milky bulbs in its spongy head, seemed fixed on Kit. It advanced on him, and he seized up the chair beside him and held it out like a shield. In the back of his mind he was conscious that it probably shouldn't be possible for an untrained fifteen-year-old boy to swing around a heavy piece of oak furniture like it was a toy.

But Kit didn't care; he was half-insane with panic and horror. As the demon reared up in front of him, he swung the chair at it, knocking it backward. It surged up and lunged again. Kit feinted but this time a razored foreleg came down, slicing the chair in half. The demon sprang toward him with its teeth bared, and Kit held up the remains of the chair, which shattered in his hands. He was flung backward against the wall.

His head hit, hard, and dizziness flooded through him. He saw, through a haze, the praying mantis monster rearing up over him. *Make it quick*, he thought. *For God's sake let me die fast.*

It descended toward him, mouth open, showing row upon row of teeth and a black gullet that seemed to fill his vision. He raised a hand to ward it off—it was closer, closer—and then it seemed to burst apart. Its head went one way, its body another. Green-black demon blood spattered onto him.

He stared upward and through the haze he saw two people standing over him. One was the blond Shadowhunter girl from the Institute, Emma Carstairs. She was brandishing a golden sword, stained with ichor. Beside her was another woman who looked a few years older. She was tall and slender, with long, curling brown hair. Vaguely, he knew he had seen her before—in the Shadow Market? He wasn't sure.

"You deal with Kit," said Emma. "I'll take care of the other Mantids."

Emma disappeared from the narrow field of Kit's vision. He could see only the other woman. She had a sweet and gentle face, and she looked at him with surprising affection. "I'm Tessa Gray," she said. "Get up, Christopher."

Kit blinked. No one ever called him Christopher. No one but his father, when his father was angry. The thought of Johnny stabbed through him, and he stared over at the place where his father's body lay crumpled.

To his surprise, there were two people there. A tall man with dark hair, wielding a sword-headed cane, had joined Emma, and the two of them were laying about themselves, slicing the demons to ribbons. Green ichor sprayed into the air like a geyser.

"My father," Kit said, licking his dry lips and tasting blood. "He . . ."

"You must grieve later. Right now you are in great danger. More of those things may come, and worse things as well."

He looked at her through the haze. His mouth tasted bitter. "Are you a Shadowhunter?"

"I am not," Tessa Gray said with a surprising firmness. "But you are." She reached her hand down toward him. "Come now," she said. "On your feet, Christopher Herondale. We've been looking for you a long time."

"Say something," Emma said. "Please."

But the boy in the passenger seat next to her didn't speak. He was looking out the window toward the ocean; they had made it all the way to the coast highway without Kit saying a word.

"It's all right," Tessa said from the backseat of the car. Her voice was gentle, but then, her voice was always gentle. "You don't need to speak, Christopher."

"No one calls me that," said Kit.

Emma jumped a little. Kit spoke in a monotone, staring out the window. She knew he was a little younger than she was, but more from his demeanor than anything else. He was quite tall, and his moves back at his house, fighting the Mantid demons, had been impressive.

He wore bloody jeans and a blood-soaked T-shirt that had probably once been blue. The ends of his pale blond hair were sticky with ichor and blood.

Emma had known there was trouble the moment she'd arrived at Johnny Rook's. Though the house looked the same, though the door was closed and the windows shuttered and quiet, she'd felt a lack of the magical energy that had been apparent when they'd been there before. She'd glanced back down at the text message on her phone and drawn Cortana.

The inside of the house looked as if a bomb had gone off. It was clear the Mantids had come from the ground under the house—demons often traveled beneath the earth to avoid daylight. They had burst up through the floorboards; ichor and blood and sawdust were everywhere.

And Mantids. They looked far more grotesque in Johnny Rook's living room than they had on the cliff tops of the Santa Monica Mountains. More insectile, more monstrous. Their razored arms sheered through wood walls, slashed apart furniture and books.

Emma swung Cortana. She sliced one Mantid apart; it disappeared with a screech, leaving her view of the room unobstructed. Several of the other Mantids were splashed with red, human blood. They circled the remains of what had been Johnny Rook, in pieces on the floor.

*Kit.* Emma looked around wildly, saw the boy crouching by the stairs. He was unharmed. She started toward him—just as he seized up a chair and smashed it down over a Mantid demon's head.

Only training kept Emma from stopping in her tracks. Human

children didn't *do* that. They didn't know how to fend off demons. They didn't have the instinct—

The door behind her blew open, and again only her training kept her from halting in surprise. She managed to sever the head of another Mantid demon, slicking Cortana's blade with ichor, even as Jem Carstairs raced into the room, followed by Tessa.

They had plunged into the battle without a word to each other or to Emma, but Emma had exchanged a glance with Jem as they fought, and knew that he wasn't surprised to see her. He looked older than he had in Idris—now closer to twenty-six, more a man than a boy, though Tessa looked just the same.

She had the same sweet expression Emma remembered, and the same kind voice. She had looked at Kit with love and sadness when she had gone over to him and held out her hand.

*Christopher Herondale.*

"But Kit is short for Christopher, is it not?" Tessa asked now, still gently. Kit said nothing. "Christopher Jonathan Herondale is your true name. And your father was Jonathan, too, right?"

*Johnny. Jonathan.*

There were a thousand Shadowhunters named Jonathan. Jonathan Shadowhunter had founded the whole race of Nephilim. It was Jace's name as well.

Emma had heard Tessa back at the house, of course, but she still couldn't quite believe it. Not just a Shadowhunter in hiding, but a Herondale. Clary and Jace would need to be told. They would likely come running. "He's a Herondale? Like Jace?"

"Jace Herondale," Kit muttered. "My father said he was one of the worst."

"One of the worst what?" Jem asked.

"Shadowhunters." Kit spat the word. "And I'm not one, by the way. I'd know."

"Would you?" Jem's voice was mild. "How?"

"None of your business," Kit said. "I know what you're doing. My dad told me you'd kidnap anyone under nineteen with the Sight. Anyone you thought you could make into a Shadowhunter. There's barely any of you left after the Dark War."

Emma opened her mouth to mount an indignant protest, but Tessa was already speaking. "Your father said many things that weren't true," she said. "Not to speak ill of the dead, Christopher, but I doubt I am telling you anything you don't already know. And it is one thing to have the Sight. It is another thing to fight off a Mantid demon with no training."

"You said you've been looking for him?" Emma asked, as the run-down Topanga Canyon Motel flashed by, its smeared windows dull brown in the sunshine. "Why?"

"Because he is a Herondale," said Jem. "And the Carstairs owe the Herondales."

A faint shudder went through Emma. Her father had spoken the same words to her, many times.

"Years ago, Tobias Herondale was convicted of desertion," said Jem. "He was sentenced to death, but he could not be found, so the sentence was carried out on his wife instead. She was pregnant. A warlock, Catarina Loss, smuggled the baby to safety in the New World."

"The sentence was carried out on his pregnant wife?" Kit said. "What is wrong with you people?"

"That is screwed up," Emma said, for once in agreement with Kit. "So Kit here is descended from Tobias Herondale?"

Tessa nodded. "There is no defense for the Clave's actions. As you know, I was Tessa Herondale once—I knew of Tobias; his story was a legend of horror. But only a few years ago was I told by Catarina of the survival of the child. Jem and I decided to find what had become of the Herondale line. Much searching led us to your father, Kit."

"My father's last name was Rook," Kit muttered.

"Legally, your family has had several names," said Tessa. "It made it quite hard to find you. I assume your father knew of his Shadowhunter blood and was hiding you from us. Certainly posing out in the open as a mundane with the Sight was clever. He was able to make connections, ward his house, bury his identity. Bury you."

Kit spoke in a dull voice. "He used to say I was his biggest secret."

Emma turned onto the road to the Institute.

"Christopher," said Tessa. "We are not Shadowhunters, Jem and I. We are not the Clave, bent on making you something you do not want to be. But your father had many enemies. Now that he is dead and cannot protect you, they will come after you. You will be safest in the Institute."

Kit grunted. He looked neither impressed nor trusting.

It was odd, Emma thought, as they pulled up at the end of the road. The only things Kit had in common with his father, looks-wise, were his height and slenderness. As he stepped out of the car, hunching over his bloody shirt, his eyes were a clear blue. His hair, pale gold waves—that was pure Herondale. And his face, too, the fine bones of it, the gracefulness. He was too bloody and scratched and miserable-looking to tell now, but he'd be devastating someday.

Kit looked at the Institute, all glass and wood and shining in the afternoon light, with loathing. "Aren't Institutes like jails?"

Emma snorted. "They're like big houses. Shadowhunters from all over the world can stay there. They have a million bedrooms. I live in this one."

"Whatever." Kit sounded sullen. "I don't want to go in."

"You could run away," Tessa said, and for the first time Emma heard the hardness under the gentle tone of her voice. It was a reminder that she and Jace shared some of the same blood. "But you would most likely be eaten by a Mantid demon as soon as the sun set."

"I'm not a Shadowhunter," Kit said, getting out of the car. "Stop acting like I am."

"Well, there's a quick test for it," said Jem. "Only a Shadowhunter can open the door of the Institute."

"The door?" Kit stared at it. He was holding one arm close against his body. Emma's gaze sharpened. With Julian as a *parabatai*, she had become familiar with the way boys handled themselves when they were trying to conceal an injury. Maybe some of that blood was his.

"Kit—" she began.

"Let me get this straight," he interrupted. "If I try to open that door and I can't, you'll let me go?"

Tessa nodded. Before Emma could say anything else, Kit limped up the stairs. She dashed after him, Tessa and Jem behind her. Kit put his shoulder to the door. He shoved.

The door flew open and he half-fell inside, nearly knocking over Tiberius, who had been crossing the entryway. Ty stumbled back and stared at the boy on the floor.

Kit was kneeling, his hand clearly cradling his left arm. He was breathing hard as he looked around, taking in the entryway—the marble floor, carved with runes. The swords hanging on the walls. The mural of the Angel and the Mortal Instruments. "It's impossible," he said. "I can't be."

Ty's look of astonishment faded. "Are you all right?"

"You," Kit said, staring up at Ty. "You pointed a knife at me."

Ty looked uncomfortable. He reached up to tug on a lock of his dark hair. "It was just work. Not personal."

Kit started to laugh. Still laughing, he sank back onto the floor. Tessa knelt down next to him, putting her hands on his shoulders. Emma couldn't help seeing herself, during the Dark

War, breaking down when she realized her parents were dead.

Kit looked up at her. His expression was blurry. It was the expression of someone who was using every bit of his willpower not to cry. "A million bedrooms," he said.

"What?" Emma said.

"You said there were a million bedrooms here," he said, rising to his feet. "I'm going to find an empty one. And then I'm going to lock myself into it. And if anyone tries to break the door down, I'll kill them."

"Do you think he'll be all right?" Emma asked. "Kit, I mean?"

She was standing on the front steps with Jem, who was cradling Church in his arms. The cat had come running up a few moments after Jem had arrived, and practically launched his small furry body into Jem's arms. Jem was petting him now, rubbing absent-mindedly under his chin and around his ears. The cat had gone limp under his ministrations, like a washcloth.

The ocean rose and fell at the horizon. Tessa had stepped away from the Institute to make a phone call. Emma could hear her voice in the distance, though not the individual words.

"You can help him," said Jem. "You lost your own parents. You know what it's like."

"But I don't think—" Emma was alarmed. "If he stays, I don't know—" She thought of Julian, of Uncle Arthur, of Diana, of the secrets they were all hiding. "Can't *you* stay?" she said, and was surprised at the wistfulness in her voice.

Jem smiled at her over Church's head. That smile she remembered from the first time she'd really seen Jem's face, the smile that reminded her, in a way she couldn't have described, of her father. Of the Carstairs blood that they shared. "I would like to stay," he said. "Since we met in Idris, I have missed you, and thought of you often. I would like to visit with you. Spend time with my old violin.

But Tessa and I, we must go. We must find Malcolm's body, and the Black Volume, for even leagues underwater a book like that can still cause us trouble."

"Do you remember when we met at my *parabatai* ceremony? You told me you wished you could be watching over me, but there was something you and Tessa had to find. Was that something Kit?"

"Yes." Jem set Church down, and the cat wobbled off, purring, in search of a shady spot. Smiling, Jem looked so young, it was impossible for Emma to think of him as an ancestor—even an uncle. "We've been searching for him for years. We narrowed the search to this area, and then finally to the Shadow Market. But Johnny Rook was an expert at hiding." He sighed. "I wish he hadn't been. If he'd trusted us, he might be alive now." He pushed a hand distractedly through his dark hair. A lock of it was silver, the color of aluminum. He was looking over at Tessa, and Emma could see the expression in his eyes when he looked at her. The love that had never dimmed over a century.

*Love is the weakness of human beings, and the angels despise them for it, and the Clave despises it too, and therefore they punish it. Do you know what happens to* parabatai *who fall in love? Do you know why it's forbidden?*

"Malcolm—" she began.

Jem turned back toward her, the light of sympathy in his dark eyes. "We heard everything from Magnus. He told us that you were the one who killed Malcolm," he said. "That must have been hard. You knew him. It's not like killing demons."

"I knew him," Emma said. "At least, I thought I did."

"We knew him too. Tessa was heartbroken to hear that Malcolm believed that we all lied to him. Concealed from him that Annabel was not an Iron Sister, but was dead, murdered by her family. We believed the story, but he died thinking we all knew the truth. What a betrayal that must have felt like."

"It's strange to think he was your friend. Though I guess he was our friend too."

"People are more than one thing. Warlocks, no less. I would not even hesitate to say that Malcolm once did much good, before he did evil. It is one of the great lessons of growing up, learning that people can do both."

"His story—the one about Annabel—such terrible things happened to both of them, just because they fell in love. Malcolm said something—and I wondered if it was true. It just seemed so strange."

Jem looked puzzled. "What was it?"

"That the Clave despises love because love is something human beings feel. That that's why they make all those Laws, about people not falling in love with Downworlders or with their *parabatai*. . . . And the Laws don't make sense. . . ." Emma watched Jem out of the corner of her eye. Was she being too obvious?

"The Clave can be awful," he said. "Hidebound and cruel. But some of the things they do are rooted in history. The *parabatai* Law, for instance."

Emma felt as if her body temperature had dropped several degrees. "What do you mean?"

"I don't know if I should tell you," said Jem, looking off toward the ocean, and his expression was so somber that Emma felt her heart freeze inside her chest. "That's a secret—a secret even from *parabatai* themselves—only a few know: the Silent Brothers, the Consul . . . I took a vow."

"But you're not a Shadowhunter anymore," Emma said. "The vow doesn't hold." When he said nothing, she pressed on: "You owe me, you know. For not being around."

The corner of his mouth flicked up into a smile. "You drive a hard bargain, Emma Carstairs." He drew in a breath. Emma could hear Tessa's voice, faint on the wind. She was saying Jace's name. "The ritual of *parabatai* was created so that two Shadowhunters could be stronger together than they were apart. It has always been one of our most powerful weapons. Not everyone has a *parabatai*, but the fact that they exist is part of what makes Nephilim what they are. Without them, we would be infinitely weaker, in ways it is forbidden for me even to explain. Ideally, the ceremony increases each *parabatai*'s power—runes given to each other are stronger—and the closer the personal bond, the greater the power."

Emma thought of the healing runes she'd drawn on Julian after the arrow poisoning. The way they'd glowed. The Endurance rune he'd given her. How it had behaved like no Endurance rune she'd ever known.

"It was not long after the ritual had been in use for some generations," Jem said, lowering his voice, "that it was discovered that if the bond was *too* close, if it tipped into romantic love—then it would begin to warp and change the kind of power that was generated by the spell. One-sided love, a crush even, all that seems to pass by the rule—but real, requited, romantic love? It had a terrible cost."

"They'd lose their power?" Emma guessed. "As Shadowhunters?"

"Their power would grow," Jem corrected. "The runes they created would be unlike any others. They would begin to wield magic as warlocks do. But Nephilim are not meant to be magicians. Eventually the power would make them mad, until they became as monsters. They would destroy their families, the others they loved. Death would surround them until eventually they died themselves."

Emma felt as if she were choking. "Why don't they tell us that? Why not warn Nephilim, so they know?"

"It's *power*, Emma," said Jem. "Some would have wisely avoided the bond, but many others would have rushed to take advantage of it for the wrong reasons. Power will always attract the greedy and the weak."

"I wouldn't want it," Emma said softly. "Not that kind of power."

"There is also human nature to take into account," Jem said, and smiled down at Tessa, who was off the phone and coming up the path toward them. "Being told that love is forbidden does not kill love. It strengthens it."

"What are you two talking about?" Tessa smiled up at them from the foot of the steps.

"Love," Jem said. "How to end it, I suppose."

"Oh, if we could end love just by willing it, life would be very different!" Tessa laughed. "It's easier to end someone else's love for you than kill your love for them. Convince them that you don't love them, or that you are someone they cannot respect—ideally both." Her eyes were wide and gray and youthful; it was hard to believe she was older than nineteen. "To change your own heart, that's nearly impossible."

There was a shimmer in the air. A Portal suddenly appeared, glowing like a ghost door, just above the ground. It opened, and Emma could see as if she were looking through a keyhole: Magnus Bane stood on the other side of the Portal, and beside him was Alec Lightwood, tall and dark-haired and holding a little boy in a white shirt, with navy-blue skin. Alec looked messy and happy, and the way he held Max reminded Emma of the way Julian used to hold Tavvy.

In the middle of raising a hand to greet Emma, Alec paused and turned his head, and said something that sounded like "Raphael." Odd, Emma thought. Alec handed Max over to Magnus and disappeared back into the shadows.

"Tessa Gray!" Magnus shouted, leaning out of the Portal as if he were leaning over a balcony. Max cooed and waved. "Jem Carstairs! Time to go!"

Someone was walking up the road from the beach. Emma could see only a silhouette. But she knew it was Julian. Julian, coming back from the beach where he had waited for her. She would always know it was Julian.

With the courtliness of a generation many years past, Jem bent over her hand in a gentle bow.

"If you need me, tell Church," he said, straightening up. "As you've seen, he can always find me. He'll make sure I come to you."

Then he turned and strode away toward the Portal. Tessa took his hand and smiled up at him, and a moment later they had stepped through the glowing door. It disappeared with a flash of pale gold light, and Emma, blinking, looked down to where Julian stood staring up at her from the foot of the steps.

"Emma?" Julian bounded up the stairs, reaching for her. "Emma, what happened? I waited on the beach—"

She drew away from his touch. A flicker of hurt crossed his face, then he glanced around, as if realizing where they were, and nodded.

"Come with me," he said in a low voice. Emma followed him, half in a daze, as they circled the Institute to the parking lot. He ducked out past the statues and the small garden, Emma behind him, until they were screened from the building by rows of scrub trees and cactus.

He turned so that they stood face-to-face. She could see the worry in his eyes. He reached to cup her cheek in his hand, and she felt her heart thrash against her rib cage.

"You can tell me," he said. "Why didn't you come?"

In a leaden voice, Emma told him about the panicked message from Kit, how she'd bolted immediately for the car. How after everything that the Institute had been through the day before, she hadn't been able to bear dragging anyone else along with her to Rook's. How Rook felt like her responsibility. How she'd tried to call Julian to tell him where she'd gone, but he hadn't picked up. About the Mantids at Rook's house, Jem and Tessa's arrival, the truth about Kit. Everything but what Jem had said to her about *parabatai*.

"I'm glad you're all right," he said, when she was done. His thumb brushed her cheekbone. "Though I guess if you'd been hurt—I would have known."

Emma didn't raise her hands to touch him. They were clenched into fists at her sides. She had done hard things in her life, she thought. Her years of training. Surviving her parents' deaths. Killing Malcolm.

But the look on Julian's face—open and trusting—told her that this would be the hardest thing she'd ever done.

She reached up and covered his hand with hers. Slowly she intertwined their fingers. Even more slowly, she drew his hand away from her face, trying to quiet the voice inside her head that said, *This is the last time he'll ever touch you like this, the last.*

They were still holding hands, but hers lay stiffly in his, a dead thing. Julian looked puzzled. "Emma—?"

"We can't do this," she said, her voice flat and uninflected. "That was what I wanted to tell you, earlier. We can't be together. Not like this."

He drew his hand out of hers. "I don't understand. What are you saying?"

*I'm saying it's too late,* she wanted to tell him. *I'm saying the Endurance rune you gave me saved my life when Malcolm attacked me. And as grateful as I am, it shouldn't have been able to do that. I'm saying that we're already becoming what Jem was warning me about. I'm saying it isn't a matter of stopping the clock, but of making it run backward.*

*And for that, the clock will need to be broken.*

"No kissing, no touching, no being in love, no dating. Is that clear enough for you?"

Julian did not look as if she had hit him. He was a warrior: He could take any blow, and be ready to strike back twice as hard.

It was much worse than that.

Emma wanted desperately to take back what she'd said, to tell him the truth, but Jem's words echoed in her mind.

*Being told that it is forbidden does not kill love. It strengthens it.*

"I don't want to have this kind of relationship," she said. "Hiding, lying, sneaking around. Don't you see? It would poison everything we have. It would kill all the good parts of being *parabatai* until we weren't even friends anymore."

"That doesn't have to be true." He looked sick but determined. "We only have to hide for a little while—only as long as the kids are young enough to need me—"

"Tavvy's going to need you for *eight more years*," said Emma, as coldly as she could. "We can't sneak around for that long."

"We could put it on hold—put *us* on hold—"

"I'm not going to wait." She could feel him watching her, feel the weight of his pain. She was glad she could feel it. She *deserved* to feel it.

"I don't believe you."

"Why would I say it if it wasn't true? It doesn't exactly paint me in the best light, Jules."

"Jules?" He choked on the word. "You're calling me that again? Like we are kids? We're not children, Emma!"

"Of course not," she said. "But we're young. We make mistakes. This thing between us, it was a mistake. The risk is too high." The words tasted bitter in her mouth. "The Law—"

"There's nothing more important than love," Julian said, in an odd, distant voice, as if he were remembering something he'd been told. "And no Law higher."

"That's easy enough to say," Emma said. "It's just that if we're going to take that kind of risk, it should be for a real, lifelong love. And I do care about you, Jules, obviously I do. I even love you. I've loved you my whole life." At least that part was true. "But I don't love you enough. It's not enough."

*It's easier to end someone else's love for you than kill your love for them. Convince them that you don't love them, or that you are someone they cannot respect.*

Julian was breathing hard. But his eyes, locked on hers, were steady. "I know you," he said. "I know you, Emma, and you're lying. You're trying to do what you think is right. Trying to push me away to protect me."

*No*, she thought desperately. *Don't give me the benefit of the doubt, Julian. This has to work. It has to.*

"Please don't," she said. "You were right—you and I don't make sense—Mark and I would make sense—"

Hurt bloomed across his face like a wound. *Mark*, she thought. Mark's name was like the sly elf-bolt he wore, able to pierce Julian's armor.

*Close*, she thought. *I'm so close. He almost believes.*

But Julian was an expert liar. And expert liars could see lies when other people told them.

"You're trying to protect the kids, too," he said. "Do you understand, Emma? I know what you're doing, and I love you for it. *I love you.*"

"Oh, Jules," she said, in despair. "Don't you see? You're talking about us being together by running away, and I just came from Rook's. I saw Kit and what it means to live in hiding, the cost of it, not just for us, but what if we had kids someday? And we'd have to give up being what we are. I'd have to give up being a Shadowhunter. And it would kill me, Jules. It would just rip me apart."

"Then we'll figure out something else," he said. His voice sounded like sandpaper. "Something where we'll still be Shadowhunters. We'll figure it out together."

"We won't," she whispered. But his eyes were wide, imploring her to change her mind, to change her words, to put what was breaking back together.

"Emma," he said, reaching for her hand. "I will never, *never* give up on you."

It was a strange irony, she thought, a terrible irony that because she loved him so much and knew him so well, she knew exactly what she had to do to destroy everything he felt for her, in a single blow.

She pulled away from him and started back toward the house. "Yes," she said. "You will."

Emma didn't know quite how long she'd been sitting on her bed. The house was full of noises—she'd heard Arthur shouting something when she first came back inside, and then quiet. Kit had been put in one of the spare rooms, as he'd asked, and Ty was sitting outside of it, reading a book. She'd asked him what he was doing—guarding Kit? Guarding the Institute *from* Kit?—but he'd just shrugged.

Livvy was in the training room with Dru. Emma could hear their muffled voices through the floor.

She wanted Cristina. She wanted the one other person who knew how she felt about Julian, so she could cry in Cristina's arms and Cristina could tell her things were going to be all right, and that she was doing the right thing.

Though whether Cristina would ever really think that what she was doing was right, Emma wasn't sure.

But she knew in her heart it was necessary.

She heard the click of the doorknob turning and closed her eyes. She couldn't stop seeing Julian's face as she'd turned away from him.

*Jules,* she thought. *If only you didn't believe in me, this wouldn't be necessary.*

"Emma?" Mark's voice. He hovered in the doorway, very human-looking in a white henley shirt and jeans. "I just got your message. You wanted to talk?"

Emma stood up and smoothed down the dress she'd changed into. A pretty one, with yellow flowers on a brown background. "I need a favor."

His pale eyebrows went up. "Favors are no light thing to faeries."

"They are no light thing to Shadowhunters, either." She squared her shoulders. "You said you owed me. For taking care of Julian. For saving his life. You said you would do anything."

Mark crossed his arms over his chest. She could see black runes on his skin again: at his collar, at his wrists. His skin was already browner than it had been, and there was more muscle on him, now that he was eating. Shadowhunters put it on fast.

"Please continue, then," he said. "And if it is a favor in my power to grant, I will grant it."

"If Julian asks—" She steadied her voice. "No. Whether he asks or not. I need you to pretend with me that we're dating. That we're falling in love."

Mark's arms fell to his sides. "What?"

"You heard me," she said. She wished she could read Mark's face. If he protested, she knew that she had no way of forcing him. She could never bring herself to do that. She lacked, ironically, Julian's ruthlessness.

"I know it seems strange," she began.

"It seems very strange," said Mark. "If you want Julian to think you have a boyfriend, why not ask Cameron Ashdown?"

*If you and Mark ever . . . I don't think I could come back from that.*

"It has to be you," she said.

"Anyone would be your boyfriend. You're a beautiful girl. You don't need someone to lie."

"This isn't for my ego," Emma snapped. "And I don't want a boyfriend. I want the lie."

"You want me to lie just to Julian, or to everyone?" Mark said. His hand was at his throat, tapping against the pulse there. Looking, perhaps, for his elf-bolt necklace, which Emma only now realized was missing.

"I suppose everyone will have to believe it," Emma said reluctantly. "We can't ask them all to lie to Julian."

"No," Mark said, and his mouth twitched up at the corner. "That would be impractical."

"If you're not going to do it, tell me," Emma said. "Or tell me what I can say to convince you. This isn't for me, Mark, this is for Julian. This could well save his life. I can't tell you more than that. I have to ask you to trust me. I've protected him all these years. This—this is part of that."

The sun was setting. The room was suffused with a reddish light. It cast a rosy glow over Mark's hair and skin. Emma remembered her twelve-year-old self, how she'd thought Mark was handsome. It hadn't gone so far as a crush, but she could see another past for herself, one where Mark wasn't taken from them. One where he'd been there, and so she'd fallen in love with him and not his brother. One where she'd been Julian's *parabatai* and married to his brother, and they'd been in each other's lives, bound permanently in every way people could be bound, and it would have been everything they should have wanted.

"You want me to tell him, tell everyone, that we are falling in love," he said. "Not that we are in love already?"

She flushed. "It needs to be believable."

"There is much that you are not telling me." His eyes were bright. He was looking less human and more faerie now, she thought, sizing up the situation, positioning himself within the careful dance of deception. "I assume you will want everyone to know we have kissed. Perhaps done more."

She nodded. She could definitely feel her cheeks burning.

"I swear to you, I'll explain as much as I can," she said, "if you agree. And I swear it could save Julian's life. I hate to ask you to lie, but—"

"But for the ones you love, you'd do anything," he said, and she had no answer to that. He was definitely smiling now, his mouth curved in amusement. She couldn't quite tell if it was human amusement or the amusement of Faerie, which thrived on chaos. "I can see why you chose me. I am here, and close, and it would have been easy for us to begin a relationship. We are neither of us attached to someone else. And you are, as I said, a beautiful girl, and hopefully you don't find me hideous."

"No," Emma said. Relief and a thousand other emotions sang through her veins. "Not hideous."

"So I suppose I only have one more question," Mark said. "But first—" He turned around, and very deliberately closed her door.

When he faced her again, he had never looked to her so much like one of the Fair Folk. His eyes were full of a feral amusement, a carelessness that spoke of a world where there was no human Law. He seemed to bring the wildness of Faerie into the room with him: a cold, sweet magic that was nevertheless bitter at the roots.

*The storm calls you as it calls me, does it not?*

He held out a hand to her, half-beckoning, half-offering.

"Why lie?" he said.

# Epilogue

*Annabel*

**For years her coffin had been dry. Now seawater dripped in** through the fine, porous holes in the wood and stone, and with the seawater, blood.

It fell onto parched bones and dry sinew, and soaked her winding shroud. It moistened her withered lips. It brought with it the magic of the ocean, and with it the blood of the one who had loved her, a stranger magic still.

In her tomb by the sounding sea, Annabel's eyes opened.

# Notes on the Text

"Water washes, and tall ships founder, and deep death waits" is from Swinburne's "Hymn to Proserpine."

"Your heart is a weapon the size of your fist" is real graffiti, made famous by being written first on a wall in Palestine. Now you can find it everywhere.

"All the blood that's shed on earth runs through the springs of that country" is from the ballad "Tam Lin."

All chapter titles are taken from the poem "Annabel Lee."

Many of the places Emma goes are real or based on real places in Los Angeles, but some are imaginary. Canter's Deli exists, but the Midnight Theater doesn't. Poseidon's Trident is based on the seafood shack Neptune's Net, but the Net doesn't have showers out back. Malcolm's house and Wells's are based on real houses. I grew up in Los Angeles, so in many ways this is the L.A. I always imagined as a child, full of magic.

# Acknowledgments

It takes a village to keep a book from falling apart. Sarah Rees Brennan, Holly Black, Leigh Bardugo, Gwenda Bond and Christopher Rowe, Stephanie Perkins, Morgan Matson, Kelly Link, and Jon Skovron all helped and advised. Maureen Johnson, Tessa Gratton, Natalie Parker, Ally Carter, Sarah Cross, Elka Cloke, Holly and Jeffrey Rowland, and Marie Lu all cheered from the sidelines. Viviene Hebel did my Spanish translations, for which I will always be grateful. I may have grown up in L.A., but my Spanish, like Emma's, is terrible. I owe Emily Houk, Cassandra Piedra, Catrin Langer, and Andrea Davenport an inestimable debt.

My always-gratitude to my agent, Russell Galen; my editor, Karen Wojtyla, and the team at Simon & Schuster for making it all happen. And lastly, my thanks to Josh, the true MVP.

*Lady Midnight* was written in Los Angeles, California; San Miguel de Allende, Mexico; and Menton, France.

Turn the page to read

# A Long Conversation,

A NEW STORY FEATURING

CLARY AND THE CHARACTERS FROM

THE MORTAL INSTRUMENTS.

———◆———

# A LONG CONVERSATION

**Clary looked around the Institute's music room with a tired but** gratified smile. It was a hot New York summer night, the windows were flung open, and Magnus had magicked up icicles that sparkled down from the ceiling and cooled the space. The room was filled with people Clary loved and cared about, and in her personal opinion it looked pretty good, considering she'd had to race to find somewhere in the Institute they could hold a party on about twenty-four hours' notice.

There was really no reason *not* to smile.

Two days previously, Simon had showed up at the Institute, breathless and wild-eyed. Jace and Clary had been in the training room, checking in on the new Institute tutor, Beatriz Mendoza, and some of the Conclave students.

"Simon!" Clary had exclaimed. "I didn't know you were in town."

Simon was a graduate of Shadowhunter Academy, Clary's *parabatai*, and a Recruiter, a job created by the Consul to help replenish the diminished ranks of Shadowhunters. When likely candidates for Ascension were found, Simon would talk to them about what it meant to become a Shadowhunter after a mundane life. It was a job that often took him away from New York, which was its downside;

in the plus column, Simon seemed to truly enjoy helping scared mundanes with the Sight feel like they weren't alone.

Not that Simon looked like a dependable voice of reassurance at the moment. He looked like a tornado had hit him.

"I just proposed to Isabelle," he announced.

Beatriz screamed with excitement. Some of the students, fearing a demon attack, also screamed. One of them fell off a rafter and thumped to the ground on a training mat. Clary burst into happy tears and threw her arms around Simon.

Jace lay down on the floor, arms thrown wide. "We're going to be family," he said glumly. "You and me, Simon, we're going to be brothers. People will think we're *related*."

"No one will think that," Simon said, his voice muffled against Clary's hair.

"I'm so delighted for you, Simon," Clary said. "You and Izzy will be so, so happy." She turned and glared at Jace. "As for you, get up and congratulate Simon or I'll pour all your expensive shampoo down the drain."

Jace bounced up, and he and Simon pounded each other on the back in a manly way, which Clary was pleased to feel she had engineered. Jace and Simon had been friends for years now, but Jace still seemed to think he needed excuses to show his affection. Clary was happy to provide them.

"Did the proposal go well? Was it romantic? Did you surprise her? I can't believe you didn't tell me you were going to do it." Clary smacked Simon on the arm. "Did you have roses? Izzy loves roses."

"It was on impulse," Simon said. "An impulse proposal. We were on the Brooklyn Bridge. Izzy had just snipped the head off a Shax demon."

"Covered in ichor, she had never appeared to you more luminous?" said Jace.

"Something like that," said Simon.

"That's the most Shadowhunterish thing I've ever heard," said Clary. "So, details? Did you get down on one knee?"

"Shadowhunters don't do that," said Jace.

"That's a pity," said Clary. "I love that part in movies."

"So why are you looking so wild-eyed?" Jace asked. "She said yes, didn't she?"

Simon raked his fingers through his hair. "She wants an engagement party."

"Open bar," said Jace, who had developed an interest in mixology that Clary found amusing. "Definitely open bar."

"No, you don't get it," said Simon. "She wants it in two days."

"Um," Clary said. "I can see why she'd be excited to share this with her friends and family but surely it can wait a little longer . . . ?"

When Jace spoke, his voice was flat. "She wants to do it on Max's birthday."

"Oh," Clary said softly. Max, the smallest, the sweetest Lightwood, Izzy and Alec's little brother. He would be fourteen now, almost the same age as Tiberius and Livvy Blackthorn. She could understand entirely why Isabelle would want to have her engagement party at a time when it would feel most genuinely to her that Max was there. "Well, did you think of asking Magnus?"

"Of course I did," said Simon. "And he said he'd help if he could, but they have the whole situation with Rafael . . ."

"Right," Clary said. "So you want our help?"

"I was hoping we could have it here," Simon said. "In the Institute. And you could help me with a few things I don't really understand?"

Clary felt a growing sense of dread. The Institute had undergone major renovations recently; some were still ongoing. The ballroom that was hardly ever used was being turned into a second training room, and several floors were full of stacks of tiles and lumber. There was the music room, which was enormous, but packed with old cellos, pianos, and even an organ. "What kind of things?"

Simon looked at her with big brown puppy eyes. "Flowers, catering, decorations . . ."

Clary groaned. Jace ruffled her hair. "You can do it," he said, and she could tell just from the tone of his voice that he was grinning. "Come on, you saved the world once, remember? I believe in you."

And that was how Clary had come to be standing in the Institute's music room, with Magnus's sparkling icicles dripping down onto her green dress. Every once in a while Magnus would change it up a little, and illusory rose petals would blow through the room. Some of Maia's werewolf pack had helped move the harp, the organ, and a smatter of other instruments into the adjoining empty room. (Its door was closed firmly now, half-obscured by a glamoured waterfall of tumbling butterflies.)

It reminded Clary a little of the Court of the Seelie Queen, which had been different each time she had visited it years ago: sparkling ice at some times, plush scarlet velvet at others. She felt a small pang, not for the Queen herself, who had been cruel and traitorous, but for the magic of the fey. Since the Cold Peace had been put into practice, she had not visited the Courts of Faerie again. Central Park was no longer filled with dancing on nights when the moon was full. You could no longer see pixies and mermaids in the waters of the Hudson. Sometimes, late at night, she would hear the high lonely sound of the Wild Hunt's horn as they pounded through the sky, and think of Mark Blackthorn, and grieve. But Gwyn and his people had never been subject to any laws, and the sound of the Hunt was no replacement for the music of faerie revels that had once drifted from Hart Island.

She had talked to Jace about it, and he had agreed with her, both in his capacity as her boyfriend and also as second head of the Institute: the Shadowhunter world, without the Fair Folk, was unbalanced. Shadowhunters needed Downworlders. They always had. Trying to pretend the Fair Folk didn't exist would only lead to disaster. But they weren't the Council—they were only the very young leaders of a single Institute. So they waited, and tried to be prepared.

Certainly, Clary thought, there was no other Institute she could think of that would be likely to host a party quite like this one. Beatriz's students were standing in as waiters, carrying platters of canapés around the room—the canapés had been provided by Simon's sister, who worked at a restaurant in Brooklyn, and the platters and cutlery were pewter, not silver, out of deference to werewolves present.

Speaking of Downworlders, Maia was laughing in a corner of the room with her hand in Bat's. She wore a floating orange dress, her curls piled on her head and her Praetor Lupus medallion gleaming at her brown throat.

She was talking with Clary's stepfather, Luke, whose glasses were pushed up onto his head. There was a bit more gray in Luke's hair these days, but his eyes were as bright as ever. Jocelyn had gone off to one of the offices to have a long chat with Maryse Lightwood, Simon's prospective mother-in-law. Clary couldn't help but wonder if she was delivering the maternal speech about how the Lightwoods were lucky to have Simon in their family and they'd better not forget it.

Julie Beauvale, Beatriz's *parabatai*, passed by them, carrying a platter of tiny puff pastries. As Clary watched, Lily, the head of the New York vampire clan, snagged a pastry off the platter, winked at Bat and Maia, and sashayed over to the piano, passing by Simon—who was making conversation with Isabelle's father, Robert Lightwood—on her way. Simon wore a charcoal-gray suit and looked nervous enough to jump out of his skin.

Jace was playing, his velvet blazer tossed over the back of his chair, his slim hands dancing over the piano keys. Clary couldn't help but remember the first time she'd seen him in the Institute, playing the piano, his back to her. *Alec?* he'd said. *Is that you?*

Jace's expression was focused and intent, the way it was only when he was doing something he considered worthy of his entire focus—fighting, or playing music, or kissing. He glanced up as if he could feel Clary's gaze on him, and smiled at her. Even after all this time, he still gave her shivers down her spine.

She was amazingly proud of him. They had been as surprised as anyone when the Conclave had voted them in as the new heads of the Institute when Maryse had left. They'd been only nineteen years old, and she supposed they'd assumed Alec or Isabelle would take over, but neither of them wanted it. Isabelle wanted to travel, and Alec was involved with the Downworlder-Shadowhunter Alliance he was building.

They could always turn it down, Clary had said to Jace at the time. No one could force someone to head up an Institute, and they'd planned to go around the world together, while Clary painted and Jace fought demons in unusual locations. But he'd wanted to do it. She knew that in his heart he felt it was a way of paying back for the people they'd lost in the war, the people they hadn't been able to save. For the good fortune they'd had in coming through it all with most of the people they loved unscathed. For the fact that the universe had given him Alec, and Isabelle, and Clary, when once he'd thought that he would never have a best friend, or a sister, and that he would never fall in love.

Running the Institute was hard work. It required all Jace's ability to charm, and Clary's instinct to keep peace and build alliances. Alone, neither one of them could have done it, but together, Clary's determination balanced his ambition, her knowledge of the mundane world and its practicalities, his ancient Shadowhunter blood and training. Jace had always been the natural leader of their small group, a proven strategist, excellent at being able to judge who would be best at what. Clary was the one who could reassure the frightened, as well as the one who finally got a forbidden computer installed in the strategy room.

Lily said something in Jace's ear, probably a song request—she'd died in the twenties and was always demanding ragtime—before twirling on her red heels and heading off toward a blanket that had been spread in one corner of the room. Magnus was seated on it, his son Max, a three-year-old warlock with navy-blue skin, curled up against his side. Also on the blanket was a five-year-old boy, this one a Shadowhunter, with tangled black hair, who reached for a book Magnus held out to him and gave the warlock a shy smile.

Beatriz was suddenly at Clary's side. "Where's Isabelle?" she whispered.

"She wants to make an entrance," Clary whispered back. "She was waiting for everyone to get here. Why?"

Beatriz gave her a meaningful look and cocked her head toward the door. A few seconds later, Clary was following her down the hall, the skirt of her dress hoisted up so she wouldn't trip on the hem. She could see herself in the mirror along the corridor wall, her green dress the color of a flower stem.

Jace liked her in green, and it matched her eyes, but there had been a time when the color had troubled her. She had been unable to look at it without thinking of her brother, Jonathan, whose eyes had turned green when he died.

When he had been Sebastian, his eyes had been black. But that had been years ago.

Beatriz led her into the dining room, which was full of flowers. Dutch tulips, Clary was pretty sure. They were piled on the chairs, on the table, on the sideboard.

"These just got delivered," Beatriz said in a dire tone, as if they were a dead body and not some local flora.

"Okay, so what's the problem?" Clary said.

"Isabelle's allergic to tulips," said a voice from the shadows. Clary jumped. Alec Lightwood was seated in a chair at the far end of the table, wearing an untucked white shirt over black suit pants and holding a yellow tulip in one hand. He was busy plucking off the petals with his long fingers. "Beatriz, can I talk to Clary for a second?"

Beatriz nodded, looking relieved to have the problem handed off to someone else, and slipped from the room.

"What's wrong, Alec?" Clary asked, taking a step toward him. "Why are you in here and not with the rest of the party?"

"My mother told me the Consul might drop by," he said darkly.

Clary stared. "And?" she said. It wasn't as if Alec was a wanted criminal.

"You know about Rafe, right?" he said. "I mean, all the details."

Clary hesitated. A few months previously, Alec had been sent to Buenos Aires to follow up on a set of vampire attacks. While there, he had come across a five-year-old Shadowhunter boy, a survivor of the decimation of the Buenos Aires Institute during the Dark War. He and Magnus had Portaled back and forth from Argentina over and over, telling no one what they were doing, until one day they appeared in New York with a skinny, wide-eyed little boy and announced that they were adopting him. He would be their son, and Max's brother.

They named him Rafael Santiago Lightwood.

"When I found Rafe, he was living on the street, starving," Alec said. "Stealing food from mundanes, having nightmares because he had the Sight and could see monsters." He bit his lip. "The thing is, they let us adopt Max because Max is a Downworlder. Nobody wanted him. Nobody cared. But Rafe is a Shadowhunter and Magnus—isn't. I don't know how the Council will feel about a Downworlder parenting a Nephilim kid, especially when they're desperate for new Shadowhunters."

"Alec," Clary said firmly. "They won't take Rafe away from you. We won't let them."

"I won't let them," said Alec. "I'd kill them all first. But that would be awkward and ruin the party."

Clary had a brief but vivid mental image of Alec shooting at the party guests with his bow and arrow while Magnus took them out with magical fire. She sighed. "Do you have any reason to think they'll take Rafe? Has there been any sign, any complaint from the Council?"

Alec shook his head. "No. It's just—you know this Council. The Cold Peace means they're edgy all the time. And even though there are Downworlders on the Council now, they don't trust them. Sometimes I think they're worse than they were before the Dark War."

"I'm not going to say you're wrong," Clary said. "But can I suggest something?"

"Is it poisoning the punch?" Alec asked with worrisome eagerness.

"No," Clary said. "I was just going to say that you might be displacing your anxiety."

Alec looked puzzled. Mundane psychological terms were fairly hit or miss with Shadowhunters.

"You're really worried because having a kid is a big deal, and this was sudden," said Clary. "But Max was sudden too. And you and Magnus are terrific parents. You love each other so much, and that just makes for more love that you have to give. You should never worry that you don't have plenty of love for as many kids as you would ever want to have."

Alec's eyes glittered for a moment, bright blue under coal-black lashes. He stood up and came over to where Clary was standing by the door. "Wise girl," he said.

"You didn't always think I was wise."

"No, I thought you were a pest, but I know better now." He dropped a kiss on top of her head and went out the door, still carrying his tulip.

"Throw that out before you get back to the music room!" Clary called after him, imagining Isabelle laid out on the floor with hives.

She sighed and stared at the tulips. She supposed they could have a party without flowers. Still—

There was a knock on the door. A girl in a patchwork silk dress with long brown braids peeked around it. Rebecca, Simon's sister. "Can I come in?" she asked, swinging the door open. "Whoa, tulips!"

"Isabelle's allergic to tulips," said Clary grimly. "Apparently."

"Bummer," said Rebecca. "Can you talk for a second?"

Clary nodded. "Sure, why not?"

Rebecca came in and perched herself on the corner of the table. "I wanted to thank you," she said.

"For what?"

"For everything." Rebecca looked around the room, taking in the portraits of Shadowhunter ancestors, the motifs of angels and crossed swords. "I still don't know all that much about this Shadowhunter business. Simon can only tell me a little bit without tripping off some kind of alarm. I don't really know what his job is—"

"He's a Recruiter," said Clary, knowing that this would mean nothing to Rebecca, but she was proud of Simon. Everything that had happened to him that was hard, that was painful, that was a challenge—being a vampire, losing his memories, becoming a Shadowhunter, losing George—he had turned into a way to help people. "We lost a lot of Shadowhunters in the war five years ago.

And since then we've been trying to make new ones. The best candidates are mundanes who have some Shadowhunter blood, which often means they don't know they're Shadowhunters but they do have the Sight. They can see vampires, werewolves, magic—things that might make you think you were going crazy. Simon talks to them, tells them about becoming a Shadowhunter, why it's hard—and why it matters."

Clary knew she probably shouldn't be saying any of this to a mundane. On the other hand, she probably shouldn't have let Rebecca into the Institute at all, much less hired her to provide catering. But when Clary and Jace had taken over running the Institute, they had sworn to each other that they would be a new kind of guardian.

After all, Clary and Simon had both once been mundanes who weren't supposed to be in the Institute too.

Rebecca was shaking her head. "Okay, I don't understand any of this. But my little brother is a big deal, right?"

Clary smiled. "He's always been a big deal to me."

"He's really happy," Rebecca said. "With his life, with Isabelle. And that's all thanks to you." She leaned forward and spoke in a conspiratorial whisper. "When you and Simon first got to be friends and he brought you home from school, my mom said to me: 'That girl is going to bring magic into his life.' And you did."

"Literally," Clary said. Rebecca looked blank. Oh, dear. Jace would have laughed. "I mean, that's lovely, and I'm so glad—you know I love Simon like a brother—"

"Clary!" Clary looked up in alarm, fearing that it was Isabelle, but it wasn't. It was Lily Chen, with Maia Roberts. The heads of the New York vampire clan and the New York werewolf clan, together.

Not that it was that unusual to see them together: They were friends. But they were also political allies who occasionally found themselves on the opposite sides of an argument.

"Hi, Rebecca," Maia said. She waved, and the plain bronze band on her finger glittered. She and Bat had exchanged promise rings some time ago, but nothing was official. Maia was head of the werewolf pack of Manhattan, in charge of rebuilding the Praetor Lupus, and pursuing a BA in business management. She was terrifyingly competent.

Lily looked at Rebecca without interest. "Clary, we must speak to you," she said. "I tried to talk to Jace, but he is playing the piano, and Magnus and Alec are busy with those small creatures."

"Children," Clary said. "They're children."

"I *informed* Alec we needed assistance, but he told me to ask you," said Lily, sounding put out. She was fond of Alec, in her way. He'd been the first Shadowhunter to truly buckle down and work with Maia and Lily, fusing his Shadowhunter knowledge with their Downworlder skills. When Jace and Clary had taken over the Institute, they'd taken on the odd alliance as well, and Isabelle and Simon joined in when they could. Clary had put together a strategy room for them, full of maps and plans and important contacts in case of emergency.

And there were plenty of emergencies. The Cold Peace meant that the parts of Manhattan that had belonged to the Fair Folk had been ripped away from them, and other Downworlders scuffled and battled over the scraps. Many were the nights that Clary and Jace, with Alec and Lily and Maia, had sat up trying to hammer out some detail of the vampire/lycanthrope truce or stop a revenge plan before it could begin. Magnus had even woven special spells so that Lily could come into the Institute despite the fact that it was hallowed ground, something that Jace said, as far as he knew, had never been done for another vampire.

"It's about the High Line," said Maia. The High Line was a public park built atop a disused elevated train line on the West Side, recently opened to the public.

"The *High Line*?" Clary said. "What, you're suddenly interested in urban development projects?"

Rebecca waved at Lily. "Hi, I'm Rebecca. Your eyeliner is incredible."

Lily ignored this. "Because of its elevation, it is a new piece of land in Manhattan," she said, "and therefore it does not belong to either the vampires or the lycanthropes. Both clans have been trying to claim it for their own."

"Do we really have to talk about this now?" Clary said. "It's Isabelle and Simon's engagement party."

"Oh God!" Rebecca leaped up. "I forgot! The slideshow!"

She bolted from the room, leaving Clary staring after her. "The slideshow?"

"I understand that at functions such as this, it is a tradition to humiliate the future bride and groom with pictures from their childhoods," said Lily. Clary and Maia both stared at her. She shrugged. "What? I watch television."

"Look, I know it's a bad time to be bothering you," said Maia, "but the thing is, apparently there's a group of werewolves and a group of vamps facing off there right now. We need an assist from the Institute."

Clary frowned. "How do you know this is going on?"

Maia held up her phone. "I just talked to them," she said.

"Give it to me," Clary said grimly. "All right, who am I talking to?"

"Leila Haryana," said Maia. "She's one of my pack."

Clary took the phone, hit the redial button, and waited until a girl's voice picked up on the other end. "Leila," she said. "This is Clarissa Fairchild at the Institute." She paused. "Yes, the head of the Institute. That's me. Look, I know you're on the High Line. I know you're about to fight a clan of vampires. I need you to stop."

Indignant yelling followed. Clary sighed.

"The Accords are still the Accords," she said. "And this breaks them. According to, um, section seven, paragraph forty-two, you're required to bring a territorial dispute to the nearest Institute for settling before you start a fight."

More subdued arguing.

Clary cut it off. "Tell the vampires what I said. And be here tomorrow at the Sanctuary, early." She thought of the champagne in the music room. "Maybe not that early. Get here at eleven, two vamps and two lycanthropes, and we'll hash this out. If not, you'll be considered enemies of the Institute."

Grumbled agreement.

Clary paused. "Okay," she said. "Good-bye, then. Have a nice day." She hung up.

"Have a nice day?" Lily said, raising her eyebrows.

Clary groaned, handing Maia back her phone. "I suck at a good sign-off."

"What's section seven, paragraph forty-two?" Maia asked.

"I have no idea," Clary said. "I made it up."

"Not bad," admitted Lily. "Now, I am going to go back to the music room and tell Alec that next time we need him, he had better hop to it or I might nibble one of those children of his."

She flounced off in a swirl of skirts.

"I'm going to go prevent that disaster from happening," Maia said hastily. "See you later, Clary!"

She departed, leaving Clary to lean back against the massive table in the middle of the room and take deep, calming breaths. She tried to envision herself in a soothing place, maybe at the beach, but that just made her think of the Los Angeles Institute.

She and Jace had gone there in the year after the Dark War to help put the place back together—it had been the most badly hit of the Institutes Sebastian had attacked. Emma Carstairs had helped them in Idris, and Clary felt protective of the small blond girl.

They'd spent a day sorting books in the new library, and then Clary had taken Emma down to the beach, to look for shells and sea glass. Emma had refused to go in the water, though, or even really look at it for very long.

Clary had asked her if she was all right.

"It's not me I worry about," Emma had said. "It's Jules. I would do anything, if only Jules would be all right."

Clary had given her a long look then, but Emma, gazing out at the flaring red-orange sunset, hadn't seen it.

"Clary!" The door burst open again. It was finally Isabelle, looking radiant in a lilac silk dress with sparkling sandals. The moment she stepped into the room, she started to sneeze.

Clary bolted upright. "By the Angel—" The Shadowhunter epithet came to her now without a thought, when once it had seemed an odd saying. "Come on."

"*Tulips,*" Isabelle said in a choked voice as Clary steered her out into the hallway.

"I know," Clary said, fanning the other girl and wondering if a healing rune would help allergies. Isabelle sneezed again, her eyes watering. "I'm *so* sorry—"

"Ib not your foot," Isabelle said, which Clary translated as allergic-speak for *it's not your fault.*

"It is, though!"

"Pffbt," Isabelle said inelegantly, and waved a hand. "Doan worry. It'll be better in a second."

"I ordered roses," Clary said. "I swear I did. I don't know what happened. I'll go down to the florist and kill them tomorrow. Or maybe Alec might do it. He seems murderous tonight."

"Nothing's ruined," Isabelle said in a more normal voice. "And no one needs to be killed. Clary, I'm getting married! To Simon! I'm *happy!*" She beamed. "I used to think there was something weak about giving your heart to someone. That they might break it.

But I know better now. And it's thanks to Simon, but also thanks to you."

"What do you mean, thanks to me?"

Isabelle shrugged a little shyly. "It's just that you love so much. So hard. You give so much. And it's always made you stronger."

Clary realized she was tearing up. "You know, you marrying Simon means we're going to be sisters, basically, right? Isn't the person married to your *parabatai* like your sister?"

Isabelle threw her arms around her. For a moment, they clung to each other in the shadowy hallway. Clary couldn't help but remember the first friendly overtures she and Isabelle had really made toward each other, so long ago now, here in the hallways of the Institute. *I wasn't just worried about Alec, I was worried about you, too.*

"Speaking of love and love-related things," Isabelle said with a mischievous smile, drawing away from Clary, "what about a double wedding? You and Jace—"

Clary's heart skipped a beat. She'd never been someone who was good at hiding her expressions or feelings. Isabelle looked at her, puzzled, about to ask something—probably if there was anything wrong—when the door to the music room opened and light and music poured into the hallway. Isabelle's mother, Maryse, leaned out.

She was smiling, clearly happy. Clary was pleased to see it. Maryse and Robert had finalized their divorce after the Dark War. Robert had moved to the Inquisitor's house in Idris. Maryse had remained in New York to run the Institute, but she had handed it over gladly to Clary and Jace a few years later. She had stayed in New York, nominally to help them in case they were ever in over their heads, but Clary suspected it was to be closer to her children—and to her grandson Max. There was more white in her hair now than Clary remembered her having when they'd met, but her back was straight, her stance still a Shadowhunter's. "Isabelle!" she called. "Everyone's waiting."

"Good," Isabelle said, "then I can make an entrance," and she linked her arm with Clary's before starting down the hallway. The flaring lights of the music room were in front of them suddenly, the room full of people turning, smiling to see them in the doorway.

Clary saw Jace, as she always did: his was always the first face she saw when she walked into a room. He was still playing, a light, unobtrusive melody, but he looked over when she came into the room and winked.

The Herondale ring on his finger sparked in the illumination from the dozens of star-shaped globes of light that were drifting around the room—doubtless Magnus's work. Clary thought of Tessa, who had given her that ring to give to Jace, and wished she were there. She always loved to see Jace play the piano.

A cheer had gone up when Isabelle came into the room. She looked around, glowing, clearly in her element. She blew a kiss toward Magnus and Alec where they sat snuggled up with Max and Rafe, who was watching with dark-eyed puzzlement. Maia and Bat whistled, Lily raised her glass, Luke and Rebecca beamed, and Maryse and Robert watched proudly as Isabelle stepped forward and took Simon's hand.

Simon's face blazed with happiness. On the wall behind him, the slideshow Rebecca had mentioned was still going on. A framed quote flashed up against the wall: *Marriage is like a long conversation that always ends too soon.*

Ack, Clary thought. Morbid. She saw Magnus put his hand over Alec's. Alec was watching the slideshow, Rafael on his lap. Pictures of Simon—and much fewer of Isabelle; Shadowhunters weren't big on photographs—flickered, appearing and disappearing on the blank wall behind the harpsichord.

There was Simon as a baby, in his mother's arms—Clary wished she could have been here, but Elaine's knowledge of Shadowhunters was nil. As far as she knew, Isabelle was a nice girl who worked in a tattoo parlor. And Simon when he was six, grinning with two teeth missing. Simon as a teenager with his guitar. Simon and Clary, ten years old, in the park, under a shower of falling autumn leaves.

Simon glanced at the picture and smiled at Clary, his eyes crinkling around the corners. Clary touched her fingers to her right forearm, where her *parabatai* mark was. She hoped he could see in her eyes all that she felt: that he was her anchor, the bedrock of her childhood and the guidepost of her adult life.

Through a blur of tears she realized the music had stopped. Jace was across the room, whispering to Alec, their dark and light heads bent together. Alec's hand was on Jace's shoulder and he was nodding.

For so long she had looked at Jace and Alec and seen best friends. She'd known how much Jace loved Alec, known since the first time she'd seen Alec injured and Jace—whose self-possession was near terrifying—had come apart. She'd seen the way he'd looked at anyone who said a bad word about Alec, his eyes narrowed, deadly gold. And she'd thought she understood, thought *best friends*, the way she and Simon were.

Now that Simon was her *parabatai*, she understood so much more. The way you were stronger when your *parabatai* was there. The way they were like a mirror that showed you your best self. She couldn't imagine losing your *parabatai*, couldn't imagine what hell it would be.

*Keep him safe, Isabelle Lightwood,* she thought, looking at Isabelle and Simon, hand in hand. *Please keep him safe.*

"Clary." She'd been so lost in thought she hadn't seen Jace move away from Alec and come toward her. He was behind her now; she could smell the cologne she'd given him for Christmas, the faint scent of his soap and shampoo, felt the softness of his blazer as he brushed his arm against hers. "Let's go—"

"We can't duck out, it's our party—"

"Just for a second," he said, in that low voice of his that made bad ideas seem like good ones. She felt him step backward and followed; they were near the door to the strategy room, and they slipped through it unnoticed.

Well, nearly unnoticed. Alec was watching them go, and as Jace shut—and locked—the door behind him, he flashed Jace a thumbs-up gesture. Which puzzled Clary a great deal, but she didn't dwell on it, mostly because Jace strode toward her with a determined look on his face, took her in his arms, and kissed her.

Her whole body sang, the way it always did when they kissed. She'd never grown bored or tired of it or used to it, any more than she imagined that you could get tired of beautiful sunsets or perfect music or your favorite book in the world.

She didn't think Jace had gotten tired of it either. At least not from the way he held her, as if each time could be the last time. It was often the way, with him. She knew he'd had a childhood that had left him uncertain of love, and fragile as glass in some ways, and she tried to be mindful of that. She was worried about the party and the guests outside, but she let herself relax into the kiss, her hand lingering against his cheek, until they finally drew apart to breathe.

"Wow," she said, running her finger around the inside edge of his collar. "I guess all that romance and flower petals falling from the sky did a number on you, huh?"

"Shh." He grinned. His blond hair was tousled, his eyes sleepy. "Let me be in the moment."

"What moment is that?" She glanced around, amused. The room was dim, most of its light coming from the windows and the band of illumination beneath the door. She could see the shapes of musical instruments, pale ghosts covered in white sheets. A baby grand piano was wedged up against the wall behind them. "The moment of hiding in a closet while our friends' engagement party happens?"

Jace didn't answer. Instead he took her by the waist and lifted her up, sitting her down on the closed lid of the baby grand. Their faces were on a level; Clary looked at him, surprised. His expression was serious. He leaned in to kiss her, hands on her waist, fingers knotting in the material of her dress.

"Jace," she whispered. Her heart was pounding. His body leaned into hers, pressing her back against the piano. The sounds of laughter and music from outside were blurring; she could hear Jace's quick breathing, remembered the boy he had been, in the grass with her in front of the Wayland Manor in Idris, when they had kissed and kissed and she had realized that love could cut you like the edge of a blade.

She could feel his pulse. His hand slid up, caressed the strap of her dress. His lowered eyes glittered in the dark. "'Green to mend our broken hearts,'" he quoted. It was part of a Nephilim children's rhyme, one Clary knew well. His eyelashes brushed her cheek; his voice was warm in her ear. "You mended my heart," he whispered. "You picked up the pieces of a broken, angry boy and you made him into a happy man, Clary."

"No," she said in a shaking voice. "You did that. I just—cheered you on from the sidelines."

"I wouldn't be here without you," he said, soft as music against her lips. "Not just you—Alec, Isabelle, even Simon—but you're my heart."

"And you're mine," she said. "You know that."

He raised his eyes to hers. His were stark gold, hard and beautiful. She loved him so much her rib cage hurt when she breathed.

"So will you?" he said.

"Will I what?"

"Marry me," he said. "Marry me, Clary."

The ground seemed to sweep out from under her. She hesitated, only for a second, but it felt like an eon; she could have sworn a fist was squeezing her heart. She saw the beginning of puzzlement cross his face, and then there was an explosion and the door of the room blew open in a shower of splinters.

Magnus strode in, looking hectic, his black hair sticking up and his clothes rumpled.

Jace leaned away from Clary, but only slightly. His eyes were narrowed. "I would say 'Don't you knock?' but it seems evident you don't," he said. "We are, however, busy."

Magnus waved a dismissive hand. "I've walked in on your ancestors doing worse," he said. "Besides, it's an emergency."

"Magnus," said Clary, "this better not be about the flowers. Or the cake."

Magnus scoffed. "I said an emergency. This is an engagement party, not the Battle of Normandy."

"The battle of what?" said Jace, who was not up on his mundane history.

"The alarm connected to the map went off," said Magnus. "The one that charts necromantic magic. There was a blast of it in Los Angeles just now."

"But I was going to give a toast," said Jace. "Can't the apocalypse wait?"

Magnus gave him a dark look. "The map's not that exact, but the blast was close to the Institute."

Clary straightened up, alarmed. "*Emma*," she said. "And Julian. The kids—"

"Remember, last time this happened, it was nothing," said Magnus. "But there are a couple things that worry me." He hesitated. "There's a big convergence of ley lines not far from them. I checked it out, and it looked like something had happened there. The area was wrecked."

"Have you tried to reach Malcolm Fade?" Jace asked.

Magnus nodded grimly. "No answer."

Clary slid off the piano. "Have you told anyone?" she asked Magnus. "Besides us, I mean."

"I didn't want to ruin the party for a false alarm," Magnus said. "So I only told—"

A tall shadow appeared in the doorway. Robert Lightwood, a

bag looped over his shoulder; Clary could see the hilts of several seraph blades protruding from the top. He stopped short as he caught sight of Clary and Jace's disheveled attire and flushed faces.

"—him," Magnus finished.

"Excuse me," said Robert.

Jace looked awkward. Robert looked awkward. Magnus looked impatient. Clary knew he wasn't enormously fond of Robert, though their relationship had improved since Alec and Magnus had adopted Max. Robert was a good grandfather in the way he had never been a good father: willing to get down on the ground and roll around with Max, and now Rafe as well.

"Can we stop being weird about Jace and Clary's sex life and get going?" Magnus asked.

"That's kind of up to you," Clary said. "I can't make the Portal—I didn't see the map. You're the one who knows where we're going."

"I hate it when you're right, biscuit," Magnus said in a resigned tone, and spread his fingers wide. Blue sparks illuminated the room like targeted fireflies, a strangely beautiful effect that opened out into a wide rectangle, a shimmering Portal through which Clary could see the outline of the Los Angeles Institute, the long stretch of distant mountains, the surge and roll of the sea.

She could smell salt water and sage. Jace moved up beside her, taking her hand in his. She felt the light pressure of his fingers.

*Marry me, Clary.*

When they returned, she would have to give him her answer. She dreaded it. But for now, they were Shadowhunters first. Back straight, head high, Clary stepped through the Portal.

Turn the page for
Cassandra Clare's
guide to Emma's Los Angeles.

# CASSANDRA CLARE TAKES US THROUGH EMMA'S LOS ANGELES

**I was born in Tehran, Iran, but I grew up in Los Angeles—went** to high school there, learned to drive there, first fell in love there. When I became a writer, even as I penned books set in New York City and London, I knew I'd eventually be returning to my home turf, and now, with *Lady Midnight*, I've finally gotten the chance.

Los Angeles is a much-maligned and much-misunderstood city. I often hear people dismiss it as a snarl of freeways, traffic, and smog, but that's never been how I thought of it. Los Angeles grows like a beautiful, poisonous flower out of the place where the desert crashes into the ocean. It's a place of unpredictable fires, mudslides, and massive crashing waves. As a teenager I loved the beach, and I nearly drowned several times trying to learn how to surf, so I relate to Emma's fascination with and fear of the ocean.

Though I've lived all over the world now, nothing sinks into your bones like the place you grew up in as a child. And nothing makes you think of the supernatural so much as a city you've seen in its off hours and secret times. Griffith Park empty in the dead of night. Miles of deserted, moonlit beaches, and eerie caves tunneling into the Santa Monica Mountains. The Sunset Strip with nobody on it. The wind howling through Topanga Canyon at night.

I wanted to capture and celebrate that essence of a Los Angeles most people don't see. There were adventures I had long imagined taking place there, scenes that had been dancing around in the back of my mind for years. As I worked on other projects, those ideas germinated, and *Lady Midnight* grew out of them. I took those places and the adventures I'd had and imagined having there, and gave them to Emma, to Cristina, to Mark and Julian and Ty and the others.

Los Angeles is a city of contradictions: grit and glamour, desert and ocean, shimmering lights and seedy underbelly, extravagant dreams and hopes destroyed. While some landmarks exist in the places I mention them, I have also taken liberties with geography for the sake of the story. The Los Angeles Institute itself does not exist, but it is partly inspired by the Serra Retreat, a Catholic retreat center in the Santa Monica Mountains. The site of the convergence isn't in a specific place, but it's based on some of the scenery in Point Mugu State Park. The Midnight Theater is intended as an homage to the many haunted theaters of Los Angeles. Grauman's Chinese Theatre, the Pantages Theatre, the Vogue Theatre . . . You could do a whole tour of haunted theaters!

Canter's Deli is real and is located on Fairfax Avenue, just like in the book. They're open twenty-four hours, perfect for Shadowhunters. Hidden Treasures Vintage, where Emma and Cristina shop for semiformal attire, exists in Topanga Canyon. Leo Carrillo State Park is home to the sea caves that play an important role in *Lady Midnight*. It's a beautiful place to visit, and I highly recommend it.

The Shadow Market is either completely made up, or very well hidden from mundanes.